MAXIM JAKUBOWSKI is a London-based novelist and editor. He was born in the UK and educated in France. Following a career in book publishing, he opened the world-famous Murder One bookshop in London in 1988 and has since combined running it with his writing and editing career. He has edited a series of 15 bestselling erotic anthologies and two books of erotic photography, as well as many acclaimed crime collections. His novels include *It's You That I Want To Kiss*, *Because She Thought She Loved Me* and *On Tenderness Express*, all three recently collected and reprinted in the USA as *Skin In Darkness*. Other books include *Life In The World of Women*, *The State of Montana*, *Kiss Me Sadly* and *Confessions Of A Romantic Pornographer*. In 2006 he published *American Casanova*, a major erotic novel which he edited and on which 15 of the top erotic writers in the world have collaborated, and his collected erotic short stories as *Fools For Lust*. He compiles two annual acclaimed series for the Mammoth list: *Best New Erotica* and *Best British Crime*. He is a winner of the Anthony and the Karel Awards, a frequent TV and radio broadcaster, crime columnist for the *Guardian* newspaper and Literary Director of London's Crime Scene Festival.

D1589205

THE MAMMOTH BOOK OF
Best British Crime

Edited and with an Introduction
by Maxim Jakubowski

RUNNING PRESS
PHILADELPHIA · LONDON

Constable & Robinson Ltd
3 The Lanchesters
162 Fulham Palace Road
London W6 9ER
www.constablerobinson.com

First published in the UK by Robinson,
an imprint of Constable & Robinson, 2009

A copy of the British Library Cataloguing in Publication
Data is available from the British Library

UK ISBN 978-1-84529-925-5

1 3 5 7 9 10 8 6 4 2

First published in the United States in 2009 by Running Press Book Publishers

9 8 7 6 5 4 3 2 1
Digit on the right indicates the number of this printing

US Library of Congress number: 2008942198
US ISBN 978-0-7624-3630-9

Running Press Book Publishers
2300 Chestnut Street
Philadelphia, PA 19103-4371

Visit us on the web!
www.runningpress.com

Printed and bound in the EU

CONTENTS

ACKNOWLEDGMENTS

RUMPOLE'S SLIMMED-DOWN CHRISTMAS by John Mortimer, © 2007 by John Mortimer. First appeared in THE STRAND MAGAZINE. Reprinted by permission of the author's agent United Agents.

MONEY SHOT by Ray Banks, © 2007 by Ray Banks. First appeared in EXPLETIVE DELETED, edited by Jennifer Jordan. Reprinted by permission of the author.

WHERE THERE'S A WILL by Amy Myers, © 2007 by Amy Myers. First appeared in ELLERY QUEEN MYSTERY MAGAZINE. Reprinted by permission of the author and the author's agent The Dorian Literary Agency.

THE STOLEN CHILD by Brian McGilloway, © 2007 by Brian McGilloway. First broadcast on BBC Radio 4. Reprinted by permission of the author.

THE PEOPLE IN THE FLAT ACROSS THE ROAD by Natasha Cooper, © 2007 by Natasha Cooper. First appeared in ELLERY QUEEN MYSTERY MAGAZINE. Reprinted by permission of the author and the author's agent Gregory & Co.

MANDELBROT'S PATTERNS by Keith McCarthy, © 2007 by Keith McCarthy. First appeared in ALFRED HITCHCOCK MYSTERY MAGAZINE. Reprinted by permission of the author.

NO PLACE TO PARK by Alexander McCall Smith, © 2007 by Alexander McCall Smith. First appeared in THE STRAND MAGAZINE. Reprinted by permission of the author's agent David Higham Associates Limited.

GIRL'S BEST FRIEND by Judith Cutler, © 2007 by Judith Cutler. First appeared in ELLERY QUEEN MYSTERY MAGAZINE. Reprinted by permission of the author.

THE PREACHER by Kevin Wignall, © 2007 by Kevin Wignall. First appeared in EXPLETIVE DELETED, edited by Jennifer Jordan. Reprinted by permission of the author.

THE ANGEL OF MANTON WORTHY by Kate Ellis, © 2007 by Kate Ellis. First appeared in ELLERY QUEEN MYSTERY MAGAZINE. Reprinted by permission of the author.

GOING BACK by Ann Cleeves, © 2007 by Ann Cleeves. First appeared in ELLERY QUEEN MYSTERY MAGAZINE. Reprinted by permission of the author.

THE FIERY DEVIL by Peter Tremayne, © 2007 by Peter Tremayne. First appeared in THE MAMMOTH BOOK OF DICKENSIAN WHODUNNITS, edited by Mike Ashley. Reprinted by permission of the author and the author's agent A.M. Heath & Co Limited.

UN BON REPAS DOIT COMMENCER PAR LA FAIM . . . by Stella Duffy, © 2007 by Stella Duffy. First appeared in PARIS NOIR, edited by Maxim Jakubowski. Reprinted by permission of the author.

ROOM FOR IMPROVEMENT by Marilyn Todd, © 2007 by Marilyn Todd. First appeared in ELLERY QUEEN MYSTERY MAGAZINE. Reprinted by permission of the author.

MAKEOVER by Bill James, © 2007 by Bill James. First appeared in ELLERY QUEEN MYSTERY MAGAZINE. Reprinted by permission of the author.

TRAIN, NIGHT by Nicholas Royle, © 2007 by Nicholas Royle. First appeared in 3:AM. Reprinted by permission of the author.

THE PRINTS OF THE BEAST by Michael Pearce, © 2007 by Michael Pearce. First appeared in THE MAMMOTH BOOK OF DICKENSIAN WHODUNNITS, edited by Mike Ashley. Reprinted by permission of the author.

GLAZED by Danuta Reah, © 2007 by Danuta Reah. First appeared in GETTING EVEN, edited by Mitzi Szereto. Reprinted by permission of the author.

TWENTY DOLLAR FUTURE by John Rickards, © 2007 by John Rickards. First appeared in EXPLETIVE DELETED, edited by Jennifer Jordan. Reprinted by permission of the author.

SERVED COLD by Zoe Sharp, © 2007 by Zoe Sharp. First appeared in A HELL OF A WOMAN, edited by Megan Abbott. Reprinted by permission of the author and the author's agent Gregory and Co.

THE MYSTERY OF CANUTE VILLA by Martin Edwards, © 2007 by Martin Edwards. First appeared in THE MAMMOTH BOOK OF DICKENSIAN WHODUNNITS, edited by Mike Ashley. Reprinted by permission of the author.

ROSEHIP SUMMER by Roz Southey, © 2007 by Roz Southey. First appeared on the website of the Literary and Philosophical Society of Newcastle upon Tyne. Reprinted by permission of the author.

ENTANGLEMENT by H.P. Tinker, © 2007 by H.P. Tinker. First appeared in EXPLETIVE DELETED, edited by Jennifer Jordan. Reprinted by permission of the author.

THE MUMMY by Peter Turnbull, © 2007 by Peter Turnbull. First appeared in ELLERY QUEEN MYSTERY MAGAZINE. Reprinted by permission of the author.

NORA B. by Ken Bruen, © 2007 by Ken Bruen. First appeared in A HELL OF A WOMAN, edited by Megan Abbott. Reprinted by permission of the author.

THE END OF LITTLE NELL by Robert Barnard, © 2007 by Robert Barnard. First appeared in THE MAMMOTH BOOK OF DICKENSIAN WHODUNNITS, edited by Mike Ashley. Reprinted by permission of the author's agent Gregory and Co.

JOHNNY SEVEN by David Bowker, © 2007 by David Bowker. First appeared in EXPLETIVE DELETED, edited by Jennifer Jordan. Reprinted by permission of the author.

BUMPING UGLIES by Donna Moore, © 2007 by Donna Moore. First appeared in A HELL OF A WOMAN, edited by Megan Abbott. Reprinted by permission of the author.

EPIPHANY by Margaret Murphy, © 2007 by Margaret Murphy. First appeared in ELLERY QUEEN MYSTERY MAGAZINE. Reprinted by permission of the author.

CALL ME, I'M DYING by Allan Guthrie, © 2007 by Allan Guthrie. First appeared in A HELL OF A WOMAN, edited by Megan Abbott. Reprinted by permission of the author.

HEROES by Anne Perry, © 2007 by Anne Perry. First appeared in a different version from Barrington Stokes. Reprinted by permission of the author's agent MBA Literary Agents Limited.

MOTHER'S MILK by Chris Simms, © 2007 by Chris Simms. First appeared in ELLERY QUEEN MYSTERY MAGAZINE. Reprinted by permission of the author's agent Gregory and Co.

THE SHAKESPEARE EXPRESS by Edward Marston, © 2007 by Edward Marston. First appeared in ELLERY QUEEN MYSTERY MAGAZINE. Reprinted by permission of the author.

THE OTHER HALF by Colin Dexter, © 2007 by Colin Dexter. First appeared in THE STRAND MAGAZINE. Reprinted by permission of the author.

THREAT MANAGEMENT by Martyn Waites, © 2007 by Martyn Waites. First appeared in SUCCOUR. Reprinted by permission of the author and the author's agent Gregory and Co.

FINGERS TO THE BONE by Andrew Taylor, © 2007 by Andrew Taylor. First appeared in ELLERY QUEEN MYSTERY MAGAZINE. Reprinted by permission of the author and the author's agent Sheil Land Associates Limited.

THE PRICE CONFEDERATE by Andrew Martin, © 2007 by Andrew Martin. First appeared in THE STRAND MAGAZINE. Reprinted by permission of the author.

POPPING ROUND TO THE POST by Peter Lovesey, © 2007 by Peter Lovesey. First appeared in ELLERY QUEEN MYSTERY MAGAZINE. Reprinted by permission of the author.

THE UNINVITED by Christopher Fowler, © 2007 by Christopher Fowler. First appeared in INFERNO, edited by Ellen Datlow. Reprinted by permission of the author.

INTRODUCTION

Maxim Jakubowski

Welcome to this attempt to gather the best crime and mystery stories written by British authors during the course of the preceding calendar year.

Look up either the British or the American bestseller lists on any given week, and you are guaranteed to find them in majority occupied by crime, mystery and thriller titles. The genre continues to be wonderfully popular all over the world, and will ever continue to thrive. I will not bore you here with a discourse about the reasons why crime writing enjoys such a worldwide appeal, but suffice it to say that it invariably presents us with stories that go from A to B, strong characters, puzzles, action and a rainbow of strong emotions.

Crime short stories are for me a perfect gift, encapsulating as they do all the ingredients to be found in novels, but in a miniature format that retains all the pluses and none of the possible negatives of novels. Commentators often complain about the relative lack of publishing outlets for short stories, but I am pleased to say this is not the case when it comes to crime and mystery. The tales I have harvested this year come from established and newer magazines, thematic anthologies and widely diverse sources both in print and on radio and the internet. It's just a matter of knowing where to look.

Since I completed this year's selection, one of the stories (by Marilyn Todd) has been shortlisted for an American award. The previous year's volume resulted in a Crime Writers' Association award for Martin Edwards' short story; the year before that it was, similarly, Peter Lovesey. In fact, all but two volumes so far in the series have resulted in a Crime Writers' Association award for best short story of the year.

Both Martin and Peter are on board again this year, as is Danuta Reah, winner some years back, but I am also proud to introduce many new names to the series on this occasion. New that is, of course to us, but naturally already well-known outside of the series for their previous books and stories. I am hopeful not only thousands of readers will enjoy the tales in these pages, but maybe also certain judges, so we can make it three prize-winning years in a row!

Popular series characters like Rumpole and Charlie Fox are here to entertain you, and Colin Dexter, now having forsaken Inspector Morse, is still with us, as are many fabulous writers from all the generations past and present of British crime writing.

Savour these stories (but do not try any of the criminal acts scattered across the pages of this volume at home . . .)

Maxim Jakubowski

RUMPOLE'S SLIMMED-DOWN CHRISTMAS

John Mortimer

Christmas comes but once a year, and it is usually preceded by Christmas cards kept in the prison officers' cubby holes round the Old Bailey and "Away In A Manger" bleating through Boots, where I purchase for my wife Hilda (known to me as She Who Must Be Obeyed) her ritual bottle of lavender water, which she puts away for later use, while she gives me another tie which I add to my collection of seldom worn articles of clothing. After the turkey, plum pudding and a bottle or two of Pommeroy's Chateau Thames Embankment, I struggle to keep my eyes open during the Queen's Speech.

Nothing like this happened over the Christmas I am about to describe.

Hilda broke the news to me halfway through December. "I have booked us in for four days over Christmas, Rumpole, at Minchingham Hall."

What, I wondered, was she talking about? Did She Who Must have relatives at this impressive sounding address? I said, "I thought we'd spend this Christmas at home, as usual."

"Don't be ridiculous, Rumpole. Don't you ever think about your health?"

"Not really. I seem to function quite satisfactorily."

"You really think so?"

"Certainly. I can get up on my hind legs in court when the occasion demands. I can stand and cross-examine, or make a speech lasting an hour or two. I've never been too ill to do a good murder trial. Of course, I keep myself fortified by a wedge of veal and ham pie and a glass or two of Pommeroy's Very Ordinary during the lunch time adjournment."

"Slices of pie and red wine, Rumpole. How do you think that makes you feel?"

"Completely satisfied. Until tea time, of course."

"Tea time?"

"I might slip in to the Tastee-Bite on Fleet Street for a cup of tea and a slice of Dundee cake."

"All that does is make you fat, Rumpole."

"You're telling me I'm fat?" The thought hadn't really occurred to me, but on the whole it was a fair enough description.

"You're on the way to becoming obese." She added.

"Is that a more serious way of saying I'm fat?"

"It's a very serious way of saying it. Why, the buttons fly off your waistcoat like bullets. And I don't believe you could run to catch a bus."

"Not necessary. I go by Tube to the Temple Station."

"Let's face it, Rumpole, you're fat and you're going to do something about it. Minchingham Hall is the place for you." She said, sounding more and more like an advert. "So restful, you'll leave feeling marvellous. And now that you've finished the long fraud case . . ."

"You mean," I thought I was beginning to see the light, "this Minchingham place is a hotel?"

"A sort of hotel, yes."

Again I should have asked for further particulars, but it was time for the news so I merely said, "Well, I suppose it means you won't have to cook at Christmas."

"No, I certainly won't have to do that!" Here She Who Must gave a small laugh, that I can only describe as merciless, and added, "Minchingham Hall is a health farm, Rumpole. They'll make sure there's less of you by the time you leave. I've still got a little of the money Auntie Dot left me in her will and I'm going to give you the best and the healthiest Christmas you've ever had."

"But I don't need a healthy Christmas. I don't feel ill."

"It's not only your health, Rumpole. I was reading about it in a magazine at the hairdresser's. Minchingham Hall specializes in spiritual healing. It can put you in touch with yourself."

"But I've met myself already."

"Your *true* self, Rumpole. That's who you might find in 'the restful tranquillity of Minchingham Hall'," She quoted from the magazine.

I wondered about my true self. Had I ever met him? What would he turn out to be like? An ageing barrister who bored on about his old cases? I hoped not, and if that was all he was I'd rather not meet him. And as for going to the health farm, "I'll think it over," I told Hilda.

"Don't bother yourself, Rumpole," She said. "I've already thought."

"Tell me quite honestly, Mizz Probert," I said in the corridor in front of Number 6 court at the Old Bailey, "would you call me fat?"

Mizz Liz, a young barrister and my pupil, was defending Colin Timson who, in a pub fight with a rival gang, the Molloys, was alleged to have broken a bottle and wounded Brian Molloy in the arm.

"No, I wouldn't call you that."

"Wouldn't you?" I gave her a grateful smile.

"Not to your face, I wouldn't. I wouldn't be so rude," Mizz Liz Probert replied.

"But behind my back?"

"Oh, I might say it then."

"That I'm fat?"

"Well, yes."

"But you've nothing against fat men?"

"Well, nothing much, I suppose. But I wouldn't want a fat boyfriend."

"You know what Julius Caesar said?"

"I've no idea."

"Let me have men about me that are fat;/ sleek headed men and such that sleep o'nights."

Mizz Probert looked slightly mystified, and as the prosecuting counsel, "Soapy" Sam Ballard QC, the head of our chambers approached, I went on paraphrasing Julius Caesar. "Yond Ballard has a lean and hungry look; he thinks too much. Such men are dangerous."

As Ballard came up I approached him. "Look here, Bollard, I've been meaning to talk to you about the Timson case" I said. "We all know the bottle broke and Brian Molloy fell on to it by accident. If we plead guilty to affray will you drop the grievous bodily harm?"

"Certainly not."

"But surely, Bollard, you could be generous. In the spirit of Christmas?"

"The spirit of Christmas has got nothing to do with your client fighting with a broken bottle."

"Good will and mercy to all men except Colin Timson. Is that it?"

"I'm afraid it is."

"You should go away somewhere to have your spiritual aura cleansed, Bollard. Spend Christmas somewhere like a health farm."

The result of all this was that the young Timson went to prison and I went to the health farm.

On Christmas Eve we took a train to Norwich and then a taxi across flat and draughty countryside (the wind, I thought, blew directly from the Russian Steppes, unbroken by any intervening mountains).

Minchingham, when we got there, appeared to be a village scattered round a grey walled building that reminded me, irresistibly, of Reading Gaol. This was Minchingham Hall, the scene of this year's upcoming Christmas jubilations.

The woman at the reception desk was all grey – grey hair, grey face and a grey cardigan pulled down over her knuckles to keep her hands warm.

She told us that Oriana was giving someone a "treatment" and would be down soon to give us a formal welcome and to hug us.

"Did you say 'hug' . . .?" I couldn't believe my ears.

"Certainly, Mr Rumpole. People travel here from all over England to be hugged by Oriana Mandeville. She'll suffuse you with 'good energy'. It's all part of the healing process. Do take a seat and make yourselves comfortable."

We made ourselves uncomfortable on a hard bench beside the cavernous fireplace and, in a probably far too loud whisper, I asked Hilda if she knew the time of the next train back to London.

"Please, Rumpole!" she whispered urgently. "You promised to go through with this. You'll see how much good it's going to do you. I'm sure Oriana will be with us in a minute."

Oriana was with us in about half an hour. A tall woman with a pale beautiful face and a mass of curling dark hair, she was dressed in a scarlet shirt and trousers. This gave her a military appearance – like a female member of some revolutionary army. On her way towards us she glanced at our entry in the visitors' book on the desk and then swooped on us with her arms outstretched.

"The dear Rumbelows!" Her voice was high and enthusiastically shrill. "Helena and Humphrey. Welcome to the companionship of Minchingham Hall! I can sense that you're both going to respond well to the treatments we have on offer. Let me hug you both. You first, Helena."

"Actually it's Hilda." Her face was now forcibly buried in the scarlet shirt of the taller Oriana. Having released my wife her gaze now focused on me.

"And now you, Humphrey . . ."

"My first name's Horace," I corrected her. "You can call me Rumpole."

"I'm sorry. We're so busy here that we sometimes miss the details. Why are you so stiff and tense, Horace?" Oriana threw her arms around me in a grip which caused me to stiffen in something like panic. For a moment my nose seemed to be in her hair, but then she threw back her head, looked me straight in the eye and said, "Now we've got you here we're really going to teach you to relax, Horace."

We unpacked in a bedroom suite as luxurious as that in any other country hotel. In due course, Oriana rang us to invite us on a tour of the other, less comfortable attractions of Minchingham Hall.

There were a number of changing rooms where the visitors, or patients, stripped down to their underpants or knickers and, equipped with regulation dressing gowns and slippers, set out for their massages or other treatments. Each of these rooms, so Oriana told us, was inhabited by a "trained and experienced therapist" who did the pummelling.

The old building was centred round the Great Hall where, below the soaring arches, there was no sign of mediaeval revelry. There was a "spa bath" – a sort of interior whirlpool, and many mechanical exercise machines. Soft music played perpetually and the lights changed from cold blue to warm purple. A helpful blonde girl in white trousers and a string of beads came up to us.

"This is Shelagh," Oriana told us. "She was a conventional nurse before she came over to us and she'll be giving you most of your treatments. Look after Mr and Mrs Rumbelow, Shelagh. Show them our steam room. I've got to greet some new arrivals."

So Oriana went off, presumably to hug other customers, and Shelagh introduced us to a contraption that looked like a small moving walkway which you could stride down but which travelled in the opposite direction, and a bicycle that you could exhaust yourself on without getting anywhere.

These delights, Hilda told me, would while away the rest of my afternoon whilst she was going to opt for the relaxing massage and sun-ray therapy. I began to wonder, without much hope, if there were anywhere in Minchingham Hall where I could find something that would be thoroughly bad for me.

The steam room turned out to be a building – almost a small house – constructed in a corner of the Great Hall. Beside the door were various dials and switches, which, Shelagh told us, regulated the steam inside the room.

"I'll give you a glimpse inside," Shelagh said, and she swung the door open. We were immediately enveloped in a surge of heat which might have sprung from an equatorial jungle. Through the cloud we could see the back of a tall, perspiring man wearing nothing but a towel round his waist.

"Mr Airlie!" Shelagh called into the jungle. "This is Mr and Mrs Rumpole. They'll be beginning their treatments tomorrow."

"Mr Rumpole. Hi!" The man turned and lifted a hand. "Join me in here tomorrow. You'll find it's heaven. Absolute heaven! Shut the door, Shelagh, it's getting draughty."

Shelagh shut the door on the equatorial rain forest and returned us to a grey Norfolk afternoon. I went back to my room and read Wordsworth before dinner. There may have been a lot wrong with the English countryside he loved so much – there was no wireless, no telephone, no central heating and no reliable bus service. But at least at that time they had managed to live without health farms.

Before dinner all the guests were asked to assemble in the Great Hall for Oriana to give us a greeting. If I had met myself at Minchingham Hall I also met the other visitors. The majority of them were middle aged and spreading, as middle aged people do, but there were also some younger, more beautiful women who seemed particularly excited by the strange environment and a few younger men.

Oriana stood, looking, I thought, even more beautiful than ever as she addressed us. "Welcome to you all on this Eve of Christmas and welcome especially to our new friends. When you leave you are going, I hope, to be more healthy than when you arrived. But there is something even more important than physical health. There is the purification of our selves so that we can look inward and find peace and tranquility. Here at Minchingham we call that 'bliss'. Let us now enjoy a short period of meditation and then hug our neighbours."

I meditated for what seemed an eternity on the strange surroundings, the state of my bank balance and whether there was a chance of a decent criminal defence brief in the New Year. My reverie was broken by Oriana's command to hug. The middle aged, fairly thin, balding man next to me took me in his arms.

"Welcome to Minchingham, Rumpole. Graham Banks. You may remember I instructed you long ago in a dangerous driving case."

It was the first time in my life that I'd been hugged by a solicitor. As it was happening, Oriana started to hum and the whole company joined in, making a noise like a swarm of bees. There may have been some sort of signal, but I didn't see it, and we processed as one in what I hoped was the direction of the dining room. I was relieved to find that I was right. Perhaps things were looking up.

The dining room at Minchingham Hall was nowhere near the size of the Great Hall but it was still imposing. There was a minstrels' gallery where portraits hung of male and female members of the Minchingham family, who had inhabited the Hall, it seemed, for generations before the place had been given over to the treatment industry.

Before the meal I was introduced to the present Lord Minchingham, a tall, softly spoken man in a tweed suit who might have been in his late fifties. His long nose, heavy eyelids and cynical expression were echoed in the portraits on the walls.

"All my ancestors – the past inhabitants of Minchingham Hall," he explained and seemed to be dismissing them with a wave of his hand. Then he pointed to a bronze angel with its wings spread over a map of the world as it was known in the seventeenth century. "This is a small item that might amuse you, Mr Rumpole. You see, my ancestors were great travellers and they used this to plan in which direction they would take their next journey," and he showed me how the angel could be swivelled round over the map. "At the moment I've got her pointing upwards as they may well be in heaven. At least some of them."

When we sat down to dinner Hilda and I found ourselves at a table with Graham Banks (the solicitor who had taken me in his arms earlier) and his wife. Banks told us that he was Oriana's solicitor and he was at pains to let me know that he now had little to do with the criminal law.

"Don't you find it very sordid, Rumpole?" he asked me.

"As sordid and sometimes as surprising as life itself," I told him, but he didn't seem impressed.

Lord Minchingham also came to sit at our table, together with the corpulent man I had last seen sweating in the steam room, who gave us his name as Fred Airlie.

Dinner was hardly a gastronomic treat. The aperitif consisted of a strange, pale yellowish drink, known as "yak's milk". We were told it is very popular with the mountain tribes of Tibet. It may have tasted fine there, but it didn't, as they say of some of the finest wines, travel well. In fact it tasted so horrible that as I drank it I closed my eyes and dreamt of Pommeroy's Very Ordinary.

The main course, indeed the only course, was a small portion of steamed spinach and a little diced carrot, enough, perhaps, to satisfy a small rodent but quite inadequate for a human.

It was while I was trying to turn this dish, in my imagination, into a decent helping of steak and kidney pie with all the trimmings that I was hailed by a hearty voice from across the table.

"How are you getting on, Rumpole? Your first time here I take it?" Fred Airlie asked me.

I wanted to say "the first and I hope the last" but I restrained myself. "I'm not quite sure I need treatments," was what I said.

"The treatments are what we all come here for," Airlie boomed at me. "As I always say to Oriana, your treatments are our treats!"

"But fortunately I'm not ill."

"What's that got to do with it?"

"Well, I mean it's bad enough being treated when you're ill. But to be treated when you're not ill . . ."

"It's fun, Rumpole. This place'll give you the greatest time in the world. Anyway, you look as though you could lose half a stone. I've lost almost that much."

"Ah! Is that so?" I tried to feign interest.

"You've come at a fortuitous moment," Airlie said. "Oriana is going to give us a special Christmas dinner."

"You mean turkey?"

"Turkey meat is quite low in calories," Airlie assured me.

"And bread sauce? Sprouts? Roast potatoes?"

"I think she'd allow a sprout. So cheer up, Rumpole."

"And Christmas pud?"

"She's found a special low calorie one. She's very pleased about that."

"Wine?" I sipped my glass of water hopefully.

"Of course not. You can't get low calorie wine."

"So the traditional Christmas cheer is 'Bah Humbug'."

"Excuse me?" Airlie looked puzzled.

"A touch of the Scrooge about the health farm manageress, is there?" It was no doubt rude of me to say it, and I wouldn't, probably, have uttered such a sacrilegious thought in those sanctified precincts if Oriana had been near.

For a moment or two Airlie sat back in his chair, regarding me with something like horror, but another voice came to my support.

"Looking round at my ancestors on these walls," Lord Minchingham murmured, as though he was talking to himself, "it occurs to me that they won several wars, indulged in complicated love affairs and ruled distant territories without ever counting the calories they consumed."

"But that was long ago," Airlie protested.

"It was indeed. Very, very long ago."

"You can't say Oriana lacks the Christmas spirit. She's decorated the dining room."

There were indeed, both in the dining room and the Great Hall, odd streamers placed here and there and some sprigs of holly under some of the pictures. These signs had given me some hopes for a Christmas dinner, hopes that had been somewhat dashed by my talk with Airlie.

"In my great-grandfather's day," Minchingham's voice was quiet but persistent, "a whole ox was roasted on a spit in the Great Hall. The whole village was invited."

"I think we've rather grown out of the spit-roasting period, haven't we?" Airlie was smiling tolerantly. "And we take a more enlightened view of what we put in our mouths. Whatever you say about it, I think Oriana's done a wonderful job here. Quite honestly, I look on this place as my home. I haven't had much of a family life, not since I parted company with the third Mrs Airlie. This has become my home and Oriana and all her helpers are my family. So, Mr Rumpole, you're welcome to join us." Airlie raised his glass and took a swig of yak's milk, which seemed to give him the same good cheer and feeling of being at one with the world as I got from a bottle of Chateau Thames Embankment.

"And let me tell you this." He leant forward and lowered his voice to a conspiratorial whisper. "When I go all I've got will go to Oriana, so she can build the Remedial Wing she's so keen on. I've told her that."

"That's very good of you." Minchingham seemed genuinely impressed. "My old father was very impressed with Oriana when he did the deal with her. But he wasn't as generous as you."

"I'm not generous at all. It's just a fair reward for all the good this place has done me."

He sat back with an extremely satisfied smile. I've always found people who talk about their wills in public deeply embarrassing, as though they were admitting to inappropriate love affairs or strange sexual behaviour. And then I thought of his lost half stone and decided it must have had enormous value to bring such a rich reward to the health farm.

Thomas Minchingham left us early. When he had gone, Airlie told us, "Tom Minchingham rates Oriana as highly as we all do. And, as he told us, his father did before him."

Whether it was hunger or being in a strange and, to me, curiously alien environment, I felt tired and went to bed early. My wife Hilda opted for a discussion in the Great Hall on the "art of repose", led by two young men who had become Buddhist monks. I had fallen asleep some hours before she got back and, as a consequence, I woke up early.

I lay awake for a while as a dim morning light seeped through the curtains. My need for food became imperative and I thought I might venture downstairs to see if breakfast was still a custom at Minchingham Hall.

When I turned on the lights the dining room had been cleared and was empty. I thought I could hear sounds from the kitchen but I was stopped by a single cry, a cry of panic or a call for help. I couldn't tell which. I only knew that it was coming from the Great Hall.

When I got there, I saw the nurse Shelagh, already dressed, standing by the door to the steam room. The door was open and hot steam was billowing around. Looking into the room I saw Fred Airlie lying face down; a pool of blood had formed under his forehead.

Shelagh came towards me out of the mist. "Is he hurt badly?" I asked her.

"Is he hurt?" she repeated. "I'm afraid he's dead. He couldn't get out, you see."

"Why couldn't he? The door opens . . ."

Shelagh bent down and picked up a piece of wood, about a foot long; it could have been part of a sawn-off chair leg. As she held it out to me she said, "Someone jammed the door handle with this on the outside. That's how I found it when I came down."

She showed me how the wood had been jammed into the oval circle of the door handle. Fred Airlie had been effectively locked into a steam filled tomb and left there to die.

"I think you'd better call someone, don't you?" I asked Shelagh. She agreed and went at once to the small closet that held the telephone. I waited for her to come back and, once she arrived, told her that I was going to my room and would make myself available if needed.

It was Christmas morning. The bells of the village church rang out the usual peals of celebration. The sun rose cheerfully, flecking the empty branches of the trees with an unusually golden light. In our bedroom Hilda and I exchanged presents. I received my tie and socks with appropriate gasps of surprise and delight and she greeted her lavender water in the same way. It was difficult to remember that, in the apparently peaceful health farm, a man had been done horribly to death while we were asleep.

"I don't know what it is about you, Rumpole," She Who Must Be Obeyed told me, "but you do seem to attract crime wherever you go. You often say you're waiting for some good murder case to come along."

"Do I say that?" I felt ashamed.

"Very often."

"I suppose that's different," I tried to excuse myself. "I get my work long after the event. Served up cold in a brief. There are names, photographs of people you've never met. It's all laid out for a legal argument. But we had dinner with Fred Airlie. He seemed so happy," I remembered.

"Full of himself." He had clearly failed to charm She Who Must Be Obeyed. "When you go downstairs, Rumpole, just you try to keep out of it. We're on holiday, remember, and it's got absolutely nothing to do with you."

When I got downstairs again there was a strange and unusual quietness about the Great Hall and the dining room. The steam room door was closed and there was a note pinned to it that said it was out of order. A doctor had been sent for and had gone away after pronouncing Airlie dead. An ambulance had called and removed the body.

Oriana was going round her patients and visitors, doing her best to spread calm. As I sat down to breakfast (fruit, which I ate, and special low calorie muesli, which I avoided) Graham Banks, the solicitor, came and sat down beside me. He seemed, I thought, curiously enlivened by the night's events. However he began by accusing me of a personal interest.

"I suppose this is just up your street, isn't it, Rumpole?"

"Not really. I wouldn't want that to happen to anyone." I told him.

Banks thought this over and poured himself a cup of herbal tea (the only beverage on offer). "You know that they're saying someone jammed the door so Airlie couldn't escape?"

"Shelagh told me that."

"They must have done it after midnight when everyone else was asleep."

"I imagine so."

"Airlie often couldn't sleep so he took a late night steam bath. He told me that, so he must have told someone else. Who, I wonder?"

"Yes. I wonder too."

"So someone must have been about, very early in the morning."

"That would seem to follow."

There was a pause then, whilst Banks seemed to think all this over. Then he said, "Rumpole, if they find anyone they think is to blame for this . . ."

"By 'they' you mean the police?"

"They'll have to be informed, won't they?" Banks seemed to be filled with gloom at the prospect.

"Certainly they will. And as the company's solicitor, I think you're the man to do it," I told him.

"If they suspect someone, will you defend them, whoever it is?"

"If I'm asked to, yes."

"Even if they're guilty?"

"They won't be guilty until twelve honest citizens come back from the jury room and pronounce them so. In this country we're still hanging on to the presumption of innocence, if only by the skin of our teeth."

There was a silence for a while as Banks got on with his breakfast. Then he asked me, "Will I have to tell them what Airlie said about leaving his money to Oriana?"

"If you think it might be relevant."

The solicitor thought this over quietly whilst he chewed his spoonful of low calorie cereal. Then he said, "The truth of the matter is that Minchingham Hall's been going through a bit of a bad patch. We've spent out on a lot of new equipment and the amount of business has been, well, all I can say is disappointing. We're not really full up this Christmas. Of course, Oriana's a wonderful leader, but not enough people seem to really care about their health."

"You mean they cling to their old habits, like indulging in turkey with bread sauce and a few glasses of wine?" I couldn't resist the jab.

He ignored me. "The fact is, this organization is in desperate need of money."

I let this information hang in the air and we sat in silence for a minute or two, until Graham Banks said, "I was hungry during the night."

"I know exactly what you mean." I began to feel a certain sympathy for the solicitor.

"My wife was fast asleep so I thought I'd go down to the kitchen and see if they'd left anything out. A slice of cheese or something. What are you smiling at?"

"Nothing much. It's just so strange that well-off citizens like you will pay good money to be reduced to the hardships of the poor."

"I don't know about that. I only know I fancied a decent slice of cheese. I found some in the kitchen, and a bit of cake."

"Did you really? Does that mean that the kitchen staff are allowed to become obese?"

"I only know that when I started back up the stairs I met Oriana coming down." He was silent then, as if he was already afraid that he'd said too much.

"What sort of time was that?" I asked him.

"I suppose it was around one in the morning."

"Had she been to bed?"

"I think so. She was in a dressing gown."

"Did she say anything?"

"She said she'd heard some sort of a noise and was going down to see if everything was all right."

"Did you help her look?"

"I'm afraid not. I went straight on up to bed. I suddenly felt tired."

"It must have been the unexpected calories."

"I suppose so."

Banks fell silent again. I waited to see if there was going to be more. "Is that it?" I asked.

"What?"

"Is that all you want to tell me?"

"Isn't it enough?" He looked up at me, I thought pleadingly. "I need your advice, Rumpole. Should I tell the police all that? After all, I'm a friend of Oriana. I've known her and been her friend for years. I suppose I'll have to tell them?"

I thought that with friends like that Oriana hardly needed enemies. I knew that the solicitor wouldn't be able to keep his story to himself. So I told him to tell the police what he thought was relevant and see what they would make of it. I was afraid I knew what their answer would be.

Someone, I wasn't sure who at the time, had been in touch with the police and two officers were to come at two thirty to interview all the guests. Meanwhile two constables were sent to guard us. Hilda and I wanted to get out of what had now become a Hall of Doom and I asked for, and got permission to walk down to the village. The young officer in charge seemed to be under the mistaken impression that barristers don't commit murder.

Minchingham village was only half a mile away but it seemed light years from the starvation, the mechanical exercises and the sudden deathtrap at the Hall. The windows of the cottages were filled with Christmas decorations and children were running out of doors to display their presents. We went into the Lamb and Flag and made our way past a Christmas tree, into the bar. There was something here that had been totally absent at Minchingham Hall – the smell of cooking.

Hilda seemed pleased to be bought a large gin and tonic. Knowing that the wine on offer might be even worse than Pommeroy's, I treated myself to a pint of stout.

"We don't have to be back there till two thirty," I told her.

"I wish we never had to be back."

I felt for She Who Must in her disappointment. The visit to Minchingham Hall, designed to produce a new slim and slender Rumpole, had ended in disaster. I saw one positive advantage to the situation.

"While we're here anyway," I said, "we might as well have lunch."

"All right," Hilda sighed in a resigned sort of way. "If you don't *mind* being fat, Rumpole."

"I suppose I could put up with it," I hoped she realized I was facing the prospect heroically, "for another few years. Now, looking at what's chalked up on the blackboard, I see that they're offering steak pie, but you might go for the pizza."

It was while we were finishing our lunch that Thomas Minchingham came into the pub. He had some business with the landlord and then he came over to our table, clearly shaken by the turn of events.

"Terrible business," he said. "It seems that the police are going to take statements from us."

"Quite right," I told him. "We're on our way back now."

"You know, I never really took to Airlie, but poor fellow, what a ghastly way to die. Shelagh rang and told me the door was jammed from the outside."

"That's right. Somebody did it."

"I suppose it might be done quite easily. There's all that wood lying around in the workshop. Anyone could find a bit of old chair leg . . . I say, would you mind if I joined you? It's all come as the most appalling shock."

"Of course not."

So his lordship sat and consumed the large brandy he'd ordered. Then he asked, "Have they any idea who did it?"

"Not yet. They haven't started to take statements. But when they find who will benefit from Airlie's will they might have their suspicions."

"You don't mean Oriana?" he asked.

"They may think that."

"But Oriana? No! That's impossible."

"Nothing's impossible," I said. "It seems she was up in the night. About the time Airlie took his late night steaming. Her solicitor, Graham Banks, was very keen to point out all the evidence against her."

Minchingham looked shocked, thought it over and said "But *you* don't believe it, do you, Mr Rumpole?"

"I don't really believe anything until twelve honest citizens come back from the jury room and tell me that it's true." I gave him my usual answer.

The Metropolitan Police call their country comrades "turnips", on the assumption that they are not very bright and so incapable of the occasional acts of corruption that are said to demonstrate the superior ingenuity of the "townees".

I suppose they might have called Detective Inspector Britwell a turnip. He was large and stolid with a trace of that country accent that had almost disappeared in the area round Minchingham. He took down statements slowly and methodically, licking his thumb as he turned the pages in his notebook. I imagined he came from a long line of Britwells who were more used to the plough and the axe than the notebook and pencil. His side-kick, Detective Sergeant Watkins, was altogether more lively, the product, I imagined, of a local sixth form college and perhaps a university. He would comment on his superior's interviews with small sighs and tolerant smiles and he occasionally contributed useful questions.

They set up their headquarters in the Great Hall, far from the treatment area, and we waited outside for our turns.

Graham Banks was called first and I wondered if he would volunteer to be the principal accuser. When he came out he avoided Oriana, who was waiting with the rest of us, and went upstairs to join his wife.

Thomas Minchingham was called in briefly and I imagined that he was treated with considerable respect by the turnips. Then Shelagh went in to give the full account of her discovery of Airlie and the steam room door.

Whilst we were waiting Oriana came up to me. She seemed, in the circumstances, almost unnaturally calm, as though Airlie's murder was nothing but a minor hitch in the smooth running of Minchingham Hall. "Mr Rumpole," she began. "I'm sorry I got your name wrong. Graham has told me you are a famous barrister. He says you are something of a legend round the courts of justice."

"I'm glad to say that I have acquired that distinction," I told her modestly, "since the day, many years ago, when I won the Penge Bungalow murder case alone and without a leader."

There was a moment's pause as she thought it over. I looked at her, a tall, rather beautiful woman, dedicated to the healing life, who was, perhaps, a murderess.

"I'm entitled to have a lawyer present, when I'm answering their questions?"

"Certainly."

"Can I ask you to be my lawyer, Mr Rumpole?"

"I would have to be instructed by a solicitor."

"I've already spoken to Graham. He has no objections."

"Very well then. You're sure you don't want Graham to be present as well?"

"Would you, Mr Rumpole," she gave a small, I thought rather bitter, smile, "in all the circumstances?"

"Very well," I agreed. "But in any trial I might be a possible witness. After all, I did hear what Airlie said. I might have to ask the judge's permission . . ."

"Don't let's talk about any trial yet." She put a slim hand on mine and her smile became sweeter. "I would like to think you were on my side."

I was called next into the dining room and the turnip in charge looked hard at me and said, without a smile, "I suppose you'll be ready to defend whoever did this horrible crime, Mr Rumpole."

"In any trial," I told him, "I try to see that justice is done." I'm afraid I sounded rather pompous and my remark didn't go down too well with the Detective Inspector.

"You barristers are there to get a lot of murderers off. That's been our experience down here in what you'd call 'the sticks'."

"We are there to make an adversarial system work," I told him, "and as for Minchingham, I certainly wouldn't call it the sticks. A most delightful village, with a decent pub to its credit."

When I had gone through what I remembered of the dinner time conversation, the DI said they would see Oriana next.

"She has asked me to stay here with her," I told the DI, "as her legal representative."

There was a silence as he looked at me, and he finally said, "We thought as much."

Oriana gave her statement clearly and well. The trouble was that it did little to diminish or contradict the evidence against her. Yes, the Minchingham Hall health farm was in financial difficulties. Yes, Airlie had told her he was leaving her all his money, and she didn't improve matters by adding that he had told her that his estate, after many years as a successful stock-broker, amounted to a considerable fortune. Yes, she got up at about one in the morning because she thought she heard a noise downstairs, but, no, she didn't find anything wrong or see anybody. She passed the steam room and didn't think it odd that it was in use as Airlie would often go into it when he couldn't sleep at night. No, she saw nothing jamming the door and she herself did nothing to prevent the door being opened from the inside.

At this point the Detective Sergeant produced the chair leg, which was now carefully wrapped in cellophane to preserve it as the prosecution's Exhibit A. The DI asked the question.

"This was found stuck through the handle of the door to the steam room. As you know, the door opens inwards so this chair leg would have jammed the door and Mr Airlie could not have got out. And the steam dial was pushed up as far as it would go. Did you do that?"

Oriana's answer was a simple "No."

"Do you have any idea who did?"

"No idea at all."

It was at that point that she was asked if she would agree to have her fingerprints taken. I was prepared to make an objection, but Oriana insisted that she was quite happy to do so. The deed was done. I told the officers that I had seen the chair leg for a moment when the nurse showed it to me, but I hadn't held it in my hand, so as not to leave my own prints on it.

At this DI Britwell made what I suppose he thought was a joke. "That shows what a cunning criminal you'd make, Mr Rumpole," he said, "if you ever decided to go on to the wrong side of the law."

The DI and the DS laughed at this and once more Oriana gave a faintly amused smile. The turnips told us that they planned to be back again at six p.m. and that until then the witnesses would be carefully guarded and would not be allowed to leave the Hall.

"And that includes you this time, Mr Rumpole," Detective Inspector Britwell was pleased to tell me.

Oriana made a request. A school choir with their music master were coming to sing carols at four o'clock. Would they be allowed in? Rather to my surprise DI Britwell agreed, no doubt infected by the spirit of Christmas.

As I left the dining room I noticed that the little baroque angel had been swivelled round. She was no longer pointing vaguely upward, and her direction now was England, perhaps somewhere in the area of Minchingham Hall.

The spirit of Christmas seemed to descend on Minchingham more clearly during that afternoon than at any other time during our visit. The Great Hall was softly lit, the Christmas decorations appeared brighter, the objects of exercise were pushed into the shadows, the choir had filed in and the children's voices rose appealingly.

"Silent Night," they sang, "Holy Night, All is calm, All is bright. Round yon Virgin, Mother and Child, Holy Infant so tender and mild, Sleep in heavenly peace."

I sat next to Shelagh the nurse, who was recording the children's voices on a small machine. "Just for the record," she said. "I like to keep a record of all that goes on in the Hall."

A wonderful improvement, I thought, on her last recorded event. And then, because the children were there, we were served Christmas tea, and a cake and sandwiches were produced. It was a golden moment when Minchingham Hall forgot the calories!

When it was nearly six o'clock Detective Inspector Britwell arrived. He asked me to bring Oriana into the dining hall and I went with her to hear the result of any further action he might have taken. It came, shortly and quickly.

"Oriana Mandeville," he said. "I am arresting you for the willful murder of Frederick Alexander Airlie. Anything you say may be taken down and used in evidence at your trial."

I awoke very early on Boxing Day, when only the palest light was seeping through a gap in the curtains. The silent night and Holy night was over. It was time for people all over the country to clear up the wrapping paper, put away the presents, finish up the cold turkey and put out tips for the postman. Boxing Day is a time to face up to our responsibilities.

My wife, in the other twin bed, lay sleeping peacefully. Hilda's responsibilities didn't include the impossible defence of a client charged with murder when all the relevant evidence seemed to be dead against her. I remember her despairing, appealing look as Detective Inspector Britwell made her public arrest. "You'll get me out of this, won't you?" was what the look was saying, and at that moment I felt I couldn't make any promises.

I bathed, shaved and dressed quietly. By the time I went downstairs it had become a subdued, dank morning, with black, leafless trees standing against a grey and unsympathetic sky.

There seemed to be no one about. It was as if all the guests, overawed by the tragedy that had taken place, were keeping to their rooms in order to avoid anything else that might occur.

I went into the echoing Great Hall and mounted a stationary bike and I started pedaling on my journey to nowhere at all. I was trying to think of any possible way of helping Oriana at her trial. Would I have to listen to the prosecution witnesses and then plead guilty in the faint hope of getting the judge to give my client the least possible number of years before she might be a candidate for parole? Was that all either she or I could look forward to?

I had just decided that it was when I heard again in that empty hall, the sound of the children's voices singing "Once In Royal David's City". I got off the bike and went to one of the treatment rooms. Nurse Shelagh was alone there, sitting on a bed and listening to her small tape recorder.

When she saw me she looked up and wiped the tears from her eyes with the knuckles of her hands. She said, "Forgive me, Mr Rumpole. I'm being silly." And she switched off the music.

"Not at all," I told her. "You've got plenty to cry about."

"She told me you're a famous defender. You'll do all you can for her, won't you, Mr Rumpole?"

"All I can. But it might not be very much."

"Oriana wouldn't hurt anyone. I'm sure of that."

"She's a powerful woman. People like her are continually surprising."

"But you will do your best, won't you?"

I looked at Shelagh, sadly unable to say much to cheer her up. "Could you turn me into a slim, slender barrister in a couple of days?" I asked her.

"Probably not."

"There, you see. We're both playing against impossible odds. Is that what you used to record the children?" I picked up the small recording machine. It was about as thick as a cigarette packet but a few inches longer.

"Yes. Isn't it ridiculous? It's the dictaphone we use in the office. It's high time we got some decent equipment."

"Don't worry," I said, as I gave it back to her. "Everything that can be done for Oriana will be done."

The dining hall was almost empty at breakfast time, but I heard a call of "Rumpole! Come and join us." So I reluctantly went to sit down with Graham Banks, the solicitor, and his wife. I abolished all thoughts of bacon and eggs and tucked into a low-calorie papaya biscuit. I rejected the yak's milk on this occasion in favour of a pale and milkless tea.

"She wants you to represent her," Banks began.

"That's what she told me."

"So I'll be sending you a brief, Rumpole. But of course she's in a hopeless situation."

I might have said, "She wouldn't be in such a hopeless situation if you hadn't handed over quite so much evidence to help the police in their conviction of your client's guilt," but I restrained myself and only said, "You feel sure that's what she did?"

"Of course. She was due to inherit all Airlie's money. Who else had a motive?"

"I can't think of anyone at the moment."

"If she's found guilty of murdering Airlie she won't be able to inherit the money anyway. That's the law, isn't it?"

"Certainly."

"I'll have to tell her that. Then there'd be no hope of the health farm getting the money either. Tom Minchingham's father made the contract with her personally."

"Then you've got a bundle of good news for her." I dug into what was left of my papaya biscuit.

"There is another matter." Banks looked stern. "I'll also have to tell her that the prosecution will probably oppose bail because of the seriousness of the offence."

"More good news," I said, but this time the solicitor ignored me and continued to look determinedly grave and hopeless. At this point Mrs Banks announced that they were going straight back to London. "This place is now too horrible to stay in for a moment longer."

"Are you going back to London this morning, Rumpole?" Banks asked me.

"Not this morning. I might stay a little while longer. I might have a chat with some of the other people who were with us at the table with Airlie."

"Whatever for?"

"Oh, they might have heard something helpful."

"Can you imagine what?"

"Not at the moment."

"Anyway." Graham Banks gave me a look of the utmost severity. "It's the solicitor's job to go round collecting the evidence. You won't find any other barrister doing it!"

"Oh yes, I know." I did my best to say this politely. "But then I'm not any other barrister, am I?"

It turned out that She Who Must Be Obeyed was of one mind with Mrs Banks. "I want to get out of here as quickly as possible," she said. "The whole Christmas has been a complete disaster. I shall never forget the way that horrible woman killed that poor man."

"So you're giving up on health farms?"

"As soon as possible."

"So I can keep on being fat?"

"You may be fat, Rumpole, but you're alive! At least that can be said for you."

* * *

I asked Hilda for her recollection of the dinner table conversation, which differed only slightly from my own memory and that of Banks and his wife. There was another, slim, young couple at our table, Jeremy and Anna, who were so engrossed in each other that they had little recall of what else had been going on. The only other person present was Tom Minchingham.

I obtained his number from Shelagh and I rang him. I told him what I wanted and suggested we discuss it over a bottle of wine in the dining hall.

"Wine? Where do you think you're going to find that at the health farm?"

"I took the precaution of placing a bottle in my hand luggage. It's vintage Chateau Thames Embankment. I feel sure you'd like it."

He told me that it would have to be in the afternoon, so I said that would suit me well.

After lunch was over and the table had been cleared I set out the bottle and two glasses. I also moved a large and well covered potted plant nearer to where we were going to sit.

Then I made a brief call to Shelagh and received a satisfactory answer to the question I should have asked earlier. I felt a strange buzz of excitement at the almost too late understanding of a piece of the evidence in Oriana's case which should have been obvious to me. Then I uncorked the bottle and waited as calmly as I could for the arrival of the present Lord Minchingham.

He arrived, not more than twenty minutes late, in a politely smiling mood. "I'm delighted to have a farewell drink, with you, Rumpole," he said. "But I'm afraid I can't help you with this ghastly affair."

"Yes," I said. "It's very ghastly."

"It's terrible to think of such a beautiful woman facing trial for murder."

"It's terrible to think of anyone facing a trial for murder."

"You know, something about Oriana has the distinct look of my ancestor Henrietta Ballantyne, as she was before she became Countess Minchingham. There she is, over the fireplace."

I turned to see the portrait of a tall, beautiful woman dressed in grey silk, with a small spaniel at her feet. She had none of Oriana's features except for a look of undisputed authority.

"She married the fourth Earl in the reign of James the Second. It was well known that she took lovers, and they all died in mysterious circumstances. One poisoned, another stabbed in the dark on his way home from a ball. Another drowned in a mill stream."

"What was the evidence against her?"

"Everyone was sure she was guilty."

"Perhaps her husband did it."

"He was certainly capable of it. He is said to have strangled a stable lad with his bare hands because his favourite mare went lame. But the Countess certainly planned the deaths of her lovers. You're not going to defend her as well, are you, Rumpole? It's a little late in the day to prove my dangerous ancestor innocent?"

"What happened to her?"

"She lived to the age of cighty. An extraordinary attainment in those days. Her last three years were spent as a nun."

"As you say, a considerable attainment," I agreed. "Shall we drink to her memory?"

I filled our glasses with the Chateau Thames Embankment that I had thoughtfully included in my packing. His Lordship drank and pulled a face. "I say, this is a pretty poor vintage, isn't it?"

"Terrible," I told him. "There is some impoverished area of France, a vineyard perhaps, situated between the pissoir and the barren mountain slopes, where the Chateau Thames Embankment grape struggles for existence. Its advantages are that it is cheap and it can reconcile you to the troubles of life and even, in desperate times, make you moderately drunk. Can I give you a refill?"

In spite of his denigration of the vintage Lord Minchingham took another glass. "Are you well known for taking on hopeless cases, Rumpole?" he asked me, when his glass was empty.

"Some people might say that of me."

"And I should think they may be damned right. First of all you want to defend my ancestor, who's dead, and now I hear you've taken on the beautiful Oriana, who is clearly guilty."

"You think that, do you?"

"Well, isn't it obvious?"

I poured myself another glass and changed the subject. "You're devoted to this house, aren't you?"

"Well, it does mean a lot to me. It's the home of my ancestors. Their portraits are on the walls around us. If they could speak to us, God knows what they would say about the present occupants."

"You don't think that the health farm should be here?"

"You want me to be honest, Rumpole?"

"Yes," I said. "I'd like you to be that."

"This house has been in my family since Queen Elizabeth made one of her young courtiers the first Earl of Minchingham, probably because she rather fancied him. I don't say that my ancestors had any particular virtues, Rumpole, but they have been part of British history. We fought for the King in the Civil War. We led a regiment at Waterloo. We went out and ruled bits of the British Empire. One was a young Brigadier killed on the Somme. I suppose most of them would have fancied Oriana, but not as a marriage proposition. But as for the rest of the people here, I don't think there's a chance that any one of them would have received an invitation to dinner."

"Do you think they would have invited me to dinner?"

There was a pause and then he said, "If you want me to be completely honest, Rumpole, no."

"Didn't they need lawyers?"

"Oh yes. They needed them in the way they needed game-keepers and carpenters and butlers and cooks. But they didn't invite them to dinner."

I considered this and refilled our glasses. "I suppose you think your old father did the wrong thing, then?"

"Of course he did. I suppose he became obsessed with Oriana."

"Did you argue with him about it?"

"I was away in the Army at the time. He sent me a letter, after the event. I just couldn't believe what he'd done."

"How did he meet Oriana?"

"Oh, she had some sort of health club in London. A friend recommended it to him. I think she cured his arthritis. It couldn't have been very bad arthritis, could it?"

I couldn't help him about his father's arthritis, so I said nothing.

"I imagine he fell in love with her. So he gave her this – all our history."

"But she must have been paying for it. In rent."

"Peanuts. He must have been too besotted when he signed the contract."

We had got to a stage in the conversation where I wanted to light a small cigar, Lord Minchingham told me that I was breaking all the rules.

"I feel the heart has been taken out of the health farm," I told him.

"Good for you. I hope it has."

"I can understand how you must feel. Where do you live now?"

My father also sold the Dower House. He did that years ago, when my grandmother died. I live in one of the cottages in the village. It's perfectly all right but it's not Minchingham Hall."

"I can see what you mean."

"Can you? Can you really, Rumpole?" He seemed grateful for my understanding. "I'm afraid I haven't been much help to you."

"Don't worry. You've been an enormous help."

"We all heard what Airlie said at dinner. That he was leaving his fortune to Oriana."

"Yes," I agreed. "We all heard that."

"So I suppose that's why she did it."

"That's the generally held opinion," I told him. "The only problem is, of course, that she didn't do it."

"Is that what she's going to say in court?"

"Yes."

"No one will believe her."

"On the contrary. Everyone will believe she didn't do it."

"Why?" Lord Minchingham laughed, a small, mirthless laugh, mocking me.

"Shelagh told me what she found. The steam turned up from the outside and a chair leg stuck through the door handle to stop it opening from the inside."

"So that's how Oriana did the murder."

"Do you really think that if she'd been the murderer she'd have left the chair leg stuck in the handle? Do you think she'd have left the steam turned up? Oriana may have her faults but she's not stupid. If she'd done it she'd have removed the chair leg and turned down the steam. That would have made it look like an accident. The person who did it wanted it to look like a murder."

"Aren't you forgetting something?"

"What am I forgetting?"

"No one else would want to kill Airlie."

"Oh, Airlie wasn't considered important by whoever did this. Airlie was just a tool, like the chair leg in the door handle and the steam switch on the outside. If you want to know which victim this murderer was after, it wasn't Airlie, it was Oriana."

"Then who could it possibly be?"

"Someone who wanted Oriana to be arrested, and tried for murder. Someone who would be delighted if she got a life sentence. Someone who thought the health farm wouldn't exist without her. I haven't seen the contract she signed with your father. Did his lawyer put in some clause forbidding indecent or illegal conduct on the premises? In fact, Lord Minchingham, someone who desperately wanted his family home back."

The effect of this was extraordinary. As he sat at the table in front of me Tom Minchingham was no longer a cheerful, half-amused aristocrat. His hand gripped his glass and his face was contorted with rage. He seemed to have turned, before my eyes, into his ancestor who had strangled a stable lad with his bare hands.

"She deserved it," he said. "She had it coming! She cheated my father and stole my house from me!"

"I knew it was you," I told him, "when we met in the pub. You talked about the chair leg in the door handle. When Shelagh rang you she never said anything about a chair leg. She told me that. I suppose you've still got a key to the house. Anyway, you got in after everyone had gone to bed. Airlie told us at dinner about his late night steam baths. You found him in there, enjoying the steam. Then you jammed the door and left him to die. Now Oriana's in an overnight police cell, I suppose you think your plan has been an uncommon success."

In the silence that followed Tom Minchingham relaxed. The murderous ancestor disappeared, the smiling aristocrat returned. "You can't prove any of it," he said.

"Don't be so sure."

"You can invent all the most ridiculous defences in the world, Mr Rumpole. I'm sure you're very good at that. But they won't save Oriana because you won't be able to prove anything. You're wasting my time and yours. I have to go now. I won't thank you for the indifferent claret and I don't suppose we will ever meet again."

He left then. When he had gone I retrieved, from the foliage of the potted plant on the table, the small dictaphone I had borrowed from Shelagh. I felt as I always did when I sat down after a successful cross-examination.

Going home on the train Hilda said, "You look remarkably pleased with yourself, Rumpole."

"I am," I said, a little cheered.

"And yet you haven't lost an ounce."

"I may not have lost an ounce but I've gained a defence brief. I think, in the case of the Queen versus Oriana, we might be able to defeat the dear old Queen."

MONEY SHOT

Ray Banks

I'd thought about it.

Jesus forgive me, but I'd actually thought about it.

Mel Gibson in *Lethal Weapon*. Muzzle to the forehead, the temple, wedged between teeth. He'd lost his wife, same as me. Unlike Mel, though, my wife was still alive. At least I thought so. The flickering image of her on my telly kept her alive. That moan she'd make, hot breath in my ear as I beat myself into submission, the tears coming five seconds after I did.

Then I wanted to bite down on the barrel of a gun. Because there was no beauty left in the world once the semen started to dry.

My nights were spent like this. Too many to count, far too many to admit. I had a flatmate but I waited until he'd gone to bed. Daryl spent his days watching *Trisha* and old movies, smoking his weight in tack. Sometimes I'd join him for the movies, the old black and whites. Burt Lancaster shaking in his boots because *The Killers* were after him.

Daryl: "They don't make 'em like they used to."

And then he'd stick *Lethal Weapon* in the video. A lot of people forget, he told me, that Mel Gibson *is* the lethal weapon of the title. He's the nutcase. He's crazy. Look at him jump off that building; watch him try and get the stubbly guy to shoot him. He's fucking bat-shit. Look at him in his trailer with that gun. The hollow point bullet so he'd be sure to take the back of his skull clean off.

"You know why I don't do it? The job. Doing the job . . ."

Daryl: "Franco Zeffirelli offered him Hamlet because of that scene."

(Daryl was the one who got me the gun.)

Daryl: "You're not gonna do this."

Me: "You don't know that."

Daryl: "I know it. I know *you*. You're not that fucking mental. You're trying to draw a psycho pension."

Like a movie. He even pointed. I even turned away. The light from the telly cast dark shadows over my eyes, I'm sure. I lit a cigarette while he puffed on the joint.

I heard someone say: "God hates me. That's what it is."

And I said: "Hate him right back. Works for me."

Daryl said: "You talking to the telly again, mate?"

But I was already out the door.

I'd shaved my head. Did it as a ritual, like a monk. Had a Bernard Herrman accompaniment as I did it, watching the hair fall to the floor, my skull prominent in the stained mirror. I took a Bic to the rest, made sure I was clean by the time I'd finished. She wouldn't recognize me; nobody would. I'd spent most of my life with curtains in front of my face; now I had nothing to hide behind. I ran a hand over my head. It felt weird. And cold.

Most cities in the world, they have a porn district. There was a hooker pub up on City Road before they turned it into a media watering hole, but there was no real porn district. We didn't have pornographers in Newcastle. Something about the Geordie accent that put people off their wanking stride.

I caught the Metro into town, sat near the back. Fat girls on a night out further up the carriage, singing a song I'd never heard of. Not that I would've recognized it, anyway. There was the clink of WKD and Breezer bottles, the high-pitched squeals after a dirty joke. There were plenty of dirty jokes. I pretended not to notice them, but I was watching them all the same. Thinking all of them naked and gagged and going down on each other. Thinking if they refused, there really was a gun in my pocket and I wasn't just pleased to see them. Screaming and lapping and shuddering all at the same time.

Fuck them.

I said we didn't have pornographers in Newcastle. That wasn't right. We did. They called themselves something different. They toted the monikers of "indie film producer", "adult entertainment CEO" and "erotica entrepreneurs". Like a turd covered in gold leaf.

I got headaches. Bad ones. Like when you have too much ice cream or milk and you have to close one eye if you're going to get any relief. We all have bloody thoughts. Morality's like some twisted fucking thing you never get to understand because no matter what you do, there's always someone waving a pamphlet, denouncing you as an animal. There was always someone, thought they knew better than you, lived more than you, understood the ways of the world more than you. What did they understand? They understood fuck all, just meshed their experience into some kind of bullshit ethos. The parents who despised corporations, booking their kids into a McDonalds party because they were too fucking weak to say no, had no way of explaining it. Fighting for multi-culturalism and crossing the street when they saw a gang of pakis coming.

I loved curry. Loved the pakis. Hated what they did to me.

This bloke I was going to see, he was a paki. I think. He looked like a paki, dressed like a paki, but he could've been Turkish, Somalian, whatever the fuck refugees we were letting into the country this fucking week without the proper papers. That's why they bombed us, I thought. They bombed us because they could. It was the same reason the big smiling clown kept poisoning the kids, making them fat and useless. Because we were too scared to stop them.

Sometimes fear only gets you so far. Then you crawl out the other side angry as fuck.

And then you get a weapon.

Didn't take too much persuading. Daryl got off on the idea of playing a Leo Getz ("You get it? Leo . . . *gets!*") or Morgan Freeman in *Shawshank*, the kind of bloke, you want something, *anything*, he's the bloke to go to. He'll hunt it down, he'll be your finder.

I mumbled: "This is a real badge, I'm a real cop, and this is a real fucking gun."

And it was a weight against my rib cage, that recommissioned replica. Daryl knew this guy on the Leam Lane who sold them for a tonne apiece. I thought it was a bit steep at the time, but feeling the heft of the gun, I knew I'd spent wisely.

Daryl: "You want a proper pistol, you pay proper money. You want something to scare the fucker with, then you're better off with a replica."

Me: "I don't want a fucking replica. I want a real one."

Got off the Metro at Monument. I had to walk through the Saturday night orgies on the streets. Orca girls in tight tops that didn't cover a thing. Screaming, screeching in the shadows, like a feeding frenzy. The low humping noise of a dozen blokes in that same check-shirt-gold-chain combo coming up the street. Red faced, stinking of alcohol, itching to slap some cunt because he's looking at them fuckin' funny, like he's a fuckin' poof or a fuckin' nonce or something.

I kept my head down as I walked. Started towards the Bigg Market and the crowds got heavy, packed together. A sudden yell at my left and I saw this young lad get dragged out of a club across the ground. He was shirtless. The bouncer dragging him made sure he went over a pile of broken glass. Planted a fist in the lad's throat.

"I TELT YEH NOT TO FUCKIN' COME BACK, YA CUNT!"

Put my head down again, cradled the gun in my coat. The heavy throb of bass underfoot, I ducked into an alley, passed by All Saint's Church, lit up. Fucking incongruous to have a church here. I crossed myself, pushed down to the Quayside. There was a God. He was away on business, but he'd come back.

What was it? The meek shall inherit. Aye. The meek and the armed.

Up towards City Road now, where the office buildings jostled for attention with the council flats. Building new student accommodation up here, another push to get the undesirables out. Ship 'em off to the West End. Let 'em breed like the fucking pigs they were, then shut 'em in and drop the pellets.

A ratty woman with knock knees under a street light. She had a mobile pressed against her ear.

"I telt yeh yeh had to pick us up, didn't I telt yeh . . . ya fuckin' cunt, divven't . . . divven't LIE to us . . . yez're a fuckin' LIAR . . . a FUCKIN' LIAR CUNT . . . how, me fuckin' battery's gannin', it's gannin' . . . pick us up . . . yer not

at yer mam's, I fuckin' knaa yer not at yer mam's . . . CUZ I
PHONED YER FUCKIN' MAM THAT'S HOW I FUCK-
IN' KNAA . . . Aye . . . Aye . . . pick us up . . . pick us up . . .
fuckin' . . . howeh, pick us up, ya cunt . . . me fuckin' battery
. . . PICK-US-UP."

She pulled the phone from her ear and threw it against a
partly-built wall. It smashed. She let out a noise like she'd been
punched, started with: "Ahhhh, nooooo."

I passed her and she spun my way.

Her: "How, yeh gorra tab, mate?"

I shook my head.

Her: "Howeh, yeh got any spare change, like?"

She got in my way.

I smiled at her, showed her all my teeth. Nodded like I was
going to give her something, like I was reaching for my wallet.
Should've seen her eyes light up at that. Like, fuckin' hell, he's
gonna givvus fuckin' NOTES.

I showed her the gun.

Took her a moment to realize what it was, still matching my
smile.

When I clicked the barrel against her rotting teeth, her eyes
took on the sheen of the newly-weeping. And I opened my
mouth wide in a silent scream, felt my jaw click with the
effort.

Hers wasn't silent.

But I let her run. It was funny. A heel snapped off and she
almost went pocked arse over sagging tit. I laughed.

Just another cracked skeleton in this fucked up town, dis-
appearing into the night.

And then I walked some more, made sure to replace the gun
under my armpit. I knew I could draw easily now. Something
that'd bugged me up till now. Because I needed to be swift when
the time came.

God, my wife. Why was she my wife?

Hair: Blonde.

Eyes: Blue.

Same as an angel. Same as an angel was *supposed* to look.

Stood about five foot eight in heels. Had a walk to her that
made the trousers tight.

She was my wife. I was bound to think that. But everyone thought that. Could turn a bender straight, make a dyke out of a cocklover. But she was an angel, too. You couldn't look at her and not see that. She wasn't about the fucking sex. That wasn't her. She was about love. Beauty.

And look what he did to her. Look what he made her into.

I found the place easily enough. Been by here enough times to know this was his office. I'd phoned ahead to make sure he was in, too. When I pressed the buzzer on the intercom, a gruff voice answered:

"What?"

"Here to see Harry Grace."

"He expecting you?"

"I phoned."

"Right."

The buzzer sounded again. I went in. Couldn't see much in the corridor. Might've been the giant with the square head blocking out the strip light. Looked like a huge clone of Tor Johnson.

Big Tor: "Go upstairs."

Me: "Right."

I went upstairs. Knocked on the door to his office. It smelled bad in here, like aftershave from the seventies.

A voice from inside: "Come in."

I did.

Set the scene, make it plausible. A huge office, like the entire top floor of the building. Like someone took an entire safari park and buckshot the fucking lot across the walls. Leopard print, tiger stripes, that dull yellow fur of the lion, the black and white zebra. The lot. Scatter cushions and a fucking glitter ball hanging from the ceiling. Along the walls posters of straight-to-video releases: *Airtight Bitch; Hot Fudge Sunday; Lesbos Lactation*. Bean bags. Somewhere a stereo plays classical music, throwing my synapses out of whack.

Silvia Saint sitting on a bean bag in a yellow bikini. Except it wasn't Silvia Saint. It was an older version of Silvia Saint. Covered in downy blonde fluff. Looked closer and her fingernails were filed to points. Something wrong with her eyes, and they were cat contact lenses. Blonde hair scooped back to reveal two pointed ears and when she opened her kewpie mouth to hiss at me, she had fangs.

"Easy, Kitty."

Coming from the end of the office, waaay down there. A massive desk, shining. Covered in leather. The man liked his animals. Loved skinning them, making them into decorations. Flash on Ed Gein and understand the whole fucking room.

"You come to audition?"

Every inch the erotic entrepreneur. Cypriot, I thought. Something not English, anyway, but he had a plummy accent that sounded like he'd learned the language from Charles Hawtrey. Had a belly on him, straining at his dress shirt. A Nehru jacket hanging on a stand behind him. Big cuffs, bigger cuff links catching the light and throwing it in my face.

Me: "No, I've not come to audition."

Him: "You sure? You look like the type."

"What's the type?"

"You."

Kitty hissed some more. Heard the rustle of the bean bag. Wanted to put that gun in her fucking face and pull the trigger. Wound up? Aye. Wound up like a fucking spring.

Me, squinting, my best Clint: "I've come about Liz Fairbride."

Him: "Who the fuck's Liz Fairbride? And what you packing there, son?"

"You what?"

"What you got? You able to rise on cue?"

"I'm not auditioning. Liz Fairbride."

"I don't know her."

"You know her."

"I don't."

Kitty growled.

Me: "Put a leash on your pussy."

Him: "Kitty. Stay put, love."

Harold Grace, all fifty-seven years of him, pulled himself around his desk and knocked on a cabinet. As he opened the top, music played and his face illuminated. He pulled out a crystal decanter filled with something yellow. "You want a drink?"

I shook my head.

"Amber Raines."

He poured himself a drink and turned. Said: "What?"

"Amber Raines. You made her change her name."

"Amber Raines." He sipped his drink. His lip retreated up his gums as he swallowed. "I know Amber Raines. She's the pisser."

I started unzipping my jacket.

"She was a good little actress. You sure you don't want to audition?"

"Getting comfortable. Go on."

"She was a good actress. Wasn't pretty enough to be a star, but she had talent in the watersports. Give as well as receive. She got off on it."

"No, she didn't."

"Nice tits. Nipples like tent pegs."

Kitty growled some more, ended it with a loud hiss.

Grace: "You like Kitty?"

Me: "No."

Another drink, another show of teeth. "Kitty's a star. *Feral Pink*. Big market for it. Kinkier the better. Some men . . . Some men like their women *hirsute*. That's all real, all that hair on her. She grows it herself. I don't go for the fake stuff. Like my movies, they're all real tits. None of the silicone shite. Can't stand it. So you're a fan of Amber Raines?"

I shook my head.

"I didn't know her real name was Liz, like."

Keep talking.

He kept talking.

"Blast from the past, Amber Raines. Christ, what is she now? Like forty or something? But she was fucking good and a good fuck, know what I mean? What, you like the vintage shite? I got plenty of classic stuff for you. Thinking about—"

– *thinking about pulling the gun now*—

"– a line of retro-movies. You got all this coverage of *Deep Throat* and *Debbie Does Dallas*, people get these movies thinking they're gonna be real—"

– *DEAD real DEAD*—

"– hardcore stuff and it's all tits and arse, know what I mean?"

YOU KILLED HER
Me, softly: "You killed her."

Harold Grace stood there with his glass halfway up to his lips. A pause, then he drank. More teeth, this time bared like a wild animal.

Him: "Who are you?"

Wanting him to know.

Telling him now.

Me: "I'm her husband."

He spluttered. Laughed. HA HA HA. You're joking, mate. You're out of your mind. I didn't know Amber had a fucking HUSBAND. She got a husband, Kitty? You hear that? And Kitty made a noise like a cat laughing, a weird *choo-choo-huff* sound. And you're her husband. What are you, fucking twenty or something? And you're her hus—

First shot cracked like a bullwhip, like Indy Jones' whip, WAP.

Caught Grace in the whisky glass, smashed it, stuck him in that round belly. Blood in the hand that held the glass, blood flowering thick and fast on his dress shirt. Him wondering what the fuck just happened.

Second shot in the eye, right from across the room. WAP.

Didn't snap his head back like I thought it would. Harold Grace standing there, mouth hanging open, tongue rested on his bottom set of capped teeth.

Then he dropped.

And Kitty went wild. The rustle from the bean bag gave her away, but I didn't turn too quick – still wanted to marvel in that one dead eye looking at me – and she sank those filed teeth into my leg. Pain shook me back to the present, stench of piss in the air. The warm feeling of blood on my ankle. I looked down. There was Kitty. Screeching. I pressed the gun to her scalp and pulled the trigger. More warmth against my leg, but it wasn't my blood this time.

I kicked her crumbled head away, hobbled to the door as Tor Johnson threw it open and filled up the doorway. His eyes wide and bulbous, I stuck the gun in his nose and pulled the trigger. Muffled, but still loud.

Tor's head *did* snap back.

Fucking glorious. Finally.

I climbed over his body and took the stairs two at a time, both hands on the walls to throw myself down. Landed heavily at the bottom. On the bad ankle. Yelled. Partly out of pain, partly out of release.

Lunged my way down to the Quayside, hugging my open jacket around the gun. There was blood on me and I couldn't run, but I saw a cab and pushed a slapper out of the way to get to it. Her face turned in on itself and she grew a forked tongue, but I made the driver pull away before she could slam on the side of the cab.

Pulling away in a big car with lots of windows. Hearing the sounds of the night. Looking out of the side window like it was *Jurassic Park*.

"The point is . . . you're alive when they start to eat you . . ."

"You what, mate?"

"Nothing."

You're not her husband. How old are you?

Doesn't matter. I'm her husband.

She must be forty by now.

Well out of it. She's dead.

You killed her, Grace. You made her into this fucking beast.

And you made me into the same kind.

Just fucking shut up.

I paid the cab with some notes and some change that I managed to scrape out of my jacket. He saw the gun, I'm sure. I didn't care. He dropped me three streets away from my flat. I limped the rest of the way. Rain started to fall. It felt cold and good against my shaved head. Cleansing.

I got into the flat, bumped into Daryl.

Daryl: "You did it?"

Me: "Aye."

Daryl: "You're not trying to draw a psycho pension. You really are crazy."

I nodded and limped through to the living room. Daryl said he was going to bed. I didn't answer him.

Just went over to the video and put on a movie. One of Liz Fairbride's early works. My wife. That blonde angel, moaning just for me. And I wasn't old enough to be her husband, but maybe back then I would've been. I put the gun on the floor, sat cross-legged. Something white against the black blood.

Kitty's tooth.

I pulled out the canine and turned it in my fingers as my wife breathed. The slap of flesh against flesh, getting quicker now.

Then I flicked the tooth to one side, unzipped my combat trousers and wept silently as both me and my wife came together.

That was love. That was beauty even after the semen dried.

WHERE THERE'S A WILL . . .

Amy Myers

I'm a wicked old man, so all my dearly beloved relations fondly tell me. They don't know the half of it. They've got a shock coming their way when I'm finally hauled kicking and screaming into the afterworld. Not yet awhile. I'm a hundred years old today, and in full possession of all my faculties. Silas Carter at your service. Just like that creepy old bore Humphrey Bone claims he's at mine. Who needs lawyers? Death and divorce is all they're good at. Just as well – he's got a shock heading his way too.

Look at that marquee out there. No need for it at all. A little bit of rain never hurt anyone. Anyway, it's always sunny on my birthday; that's what darling niece Mary coos at me, bending over me with all her cleavage showing – as though there were anything to look at. Thank the Lord I never had kids of my own. I'm at liberty to see my relations as clear as God made them, and an ugly sight they make. She with her holier than thou simper, Don with his knobbly knees, shorts and binoculars, always twittering on about birds (the feathered kind, alas), and "young" Nigel, Mr Arty Crafty himself, and more of the craft than art if you ask me. A long-haired skinny white wiggling grub, he is. Never see any of them except when they're crawling here on pilgrimage to my bank account.

Now they've had the nerve to stay in my house, without so much as a by-your-leave to me. We've fixed it all with William, Mary beams, as though they expect me to leap up in my wheelchair and cry out Oh Whoopee because my servants and family have saved me the trouble of organizing my own birthday. Leap? That I should be so lucky. It's no fun being old, being wheeled everywhere. You have to work hard to make your own fun when you're a hundred years old.

So, believe me, I have.

"It's high time you updated your will," Mr Humphrey Bore Bone snuffled to me some weeks ago.

"You're right, Humphrey," sighed I, pretending to be all tired and weary, though only ninety-nine at the time.

I'm not only wicked, you see. I'm also very rich. Perhaps that's the reason for it. Never had a wife, well, not for the last seventy years, so I can please myself what I do with my money. Oh the pleasure of freedom. I've only mentioned these particular relations, but I've a vast family out there. All the Christmas cards check in dutifully once a year, but now they're all screaming down on me like vultures licking their lips in person at the thought of a slice of my golden pie when I hop it.

"How about charities?" Humphrey said dolefully to encourage me on my will updating.

"How about them?" I said rudely.

"Have you no favourite causes?"

"Only one. Mine," I snapped. Then I relented. Humpity-Humph is a boring old stick but he means well. Perhaps. "Tell you what, Humphrey, you find me a charity that looks after blind atheist stamp collectors with moles on their cheeks or aged aunts who run homes for stray elephants and I'll support them."

He couldn't of course, so when he sent his bill in I didn't pay him – don't believe in encouraging failure. And, I informed him, I'd be writing my own will, and sending it to him in due course.

Humphrey's eyes had glinted, the first sign of life I'd seen for a long time. He told me that one day my jokes would take me too far. Maybe he's right. Jolly good. Nothing like living dangerously when you're a hundred – in your mind, at least. Fat chance I've got of fighting off sharks or climbing Everest from this chair.

The vultures have landed. I can see them all outside in the garden, gathering for the big feast at my expense. Why should I have to pay for my own birthday party? You'd think if they all loved me so much they'd be queuing up to treat me. No way. I reckon that everyone in that mob below flatters himself he's

entitled to walk in and help himself to my money the minute I'm
dead. Well, I've scotched that little plan. I've outlived my
brothers and sisters – told them all I would, and I did – so
it's the next generation and the one after that I have to watch.
Mary's in the former category, Nigel and Don in the latter.
They march together in the vanguard of the "why don't you
leave it all to me?" brigade. The Three Gargoyles I call them;
always goggling at me with their ugly faces and nothing but
water running down their veins.

They'd no sooner arrived yesterday than they bounded up to
me to ask if I'd like a trip to my old home next month. Bah.
Humbug. I grew up in a two-up two-down terrace house in
Huddersfield. No, I'll stay here in my Surrey mansion, thanks
very much, where Woeful William answers my every whim.
Most of these are to press Venus boobs. I've got a bar behind
the library books; one touch on the carved lady's tender parts on
the panelling underneath and out floats nectar – or whisky if you
prefer its real name. And that's one thing the Three Gargoyles
don't know about. Let 'em stick to water. They're welcome to
it. If any showed up in my veins they'd burst with shock.

Here come the Gargoyles now, I can see them marching
purposefully from the marquee towards the house, and – oh
goodie – Humphrey Bone the Bore is with them. Only William
to collect on the way and we're off. Mary's at the front of course,
mutton dressed as lamb, or as I like to think of it, soggy
shepherd's pie with a white topping. Don's on one side –
trousers today, I see! Even a sporty blazer. I *am* honoured. I
can do without the sight of his knees on my birthday. And I can
glimpse darling Nigel's supercilious nose poking out on Mary's
other side, as he struts along in his arty pale cream suit. No
artist starving in a garret, he. Nothing but the best for him –
especially if it comes courtesy of my bank account. Any one of
them would see me dead tomorrow if it wasn't for the fact they
can't be *certain* who's in my will because I might change it. If
only I could see their faces when they find out . . .

Ah well, time for my big appearance. I've been smothered with
cards and presents today. Even the Queen sent a card via a
minion. She's the only unselfish one amongst them, and she's
not getting a slice of anything. Her blinking government will get

their paws on anything coming her way in the way of tax. Perhaps I'll send her a lump of stale birthday cake in compensation.

"Well, Uncle Silas, are we all ready?" Mary beamed.

Of course I am, you silly old cow, I wanted to reply, but I could see Humphrey looking at me in that way of his, so I decided to behave. "Hello, Mary," I quavered. "Think I'd be late for my one glass of champagne?" Not on your life, I thought. Or more pertinently, on mine, which is a great deal more valuable to me.

"Happy birthday, Uncle," Don said heartily, peering at me as though I was a wounded goldfinch.

"Sorry. I'm still alive," I said tartly, and seeing Humphrey's compressed lips, added, "Just my little joke, darling boy." Boy? He looks like an antiquated frog. No frogs are too lively for our Humph. Toad's more like it. Sits on its bottom and blinks – waiting for the fees to roll in.

Nigel must have been nervous for once. "Many happy returns," he bleated, pumping my hand up and down.

"As a ghost?" I retorted politely, but seeing my grin the party took this as a witticism in which everyone could join. Even Woeful Willie, looming over me with first aid kit in hand in case I pass out with pleasure at their company, giggled, although Toad Humphrey remained solemn-faced.

So here we go. Off to my hundredth birthday party. As I was wheeled into the tent the crowds parted like the Red Sea for Moses. Quite right too. I could see the place was packed, with all those Christmas cards having sprung to life and put their happy happy faces on, while they waited for the champagne. I decided to make them all listen to me for an hour at least before they got their reward.

At the end of the first half hour of my speech, I beamed at their now flagging faces. I was wiping their smiles away splendidly.

"And now, my dears," I announced, "I'm going to tell you something very important."

The whole assembled company leaned forward very hopefully. But it wasn't going to be about my will. Oh no. That's going to be a sweet surprise. I didn't talk about money at all. I lectured them on the importance of happiness in families, how nice it was to see them all together getting on so well. Poppycock. My brothers and sisters used to quarrel like a pack of hyenas, and their offspring followed suit. Even Mary, Don and Nigel couldn't stand the sight of each other normally. They are only united today by a common hope that they alone will be my sole heir. I have, I admit, been teasing each of them separately that he or she is the person to whom I've left all my money. And it's the truth – in a way.

I do like teasing people.

I'm even teasing you, whoever reads this. You're all expecting me to drink my glass of champagne, gag, clasp my throat and fall gasping for air, poisoned by one of my dearest and nearest kinfolk, unable to wait a minute longer for my millions.

Well, I've news for you. The party's over, and I'm still alive.

"Good morning, Mr Bone." William opened the door of the Manor to me, and led me into the late Mr Silas Carter's library cum living room. Once it was a dark and sombre place, but no longer. The blinds were up and sunlight streamed in, as if glad to reach the previously forbidden places. I approved. I had always dreaded coming here, but it made my unwelcome task of this morning much easier if the sun were fighting on my side. Silas Carter was, I regret to say, a wicked old man, with a sharp, if lively, tongue. He was no judge of character however. Assuming the role of boring old lawyer is a useful device for me (and never more so than with Silas Carter) and would be so again in the meeting about to take place.

"My condolences, William," I said formally. Might as well stick to being Humphrey the Bore for the moment. "What will you do once everything is cleared up?" It had obviously been sensible for me as executor – at least as *apparent* executor – to ask his carer to stay on while the disastrous mess of the estate was being sorted out.

"I daresay I'll find something. I've always dreamed of a cottage of my own, but it won't be the same." William looked sad. "I've been here over twenty years now."

I could see his point. Being ill-treated in a palace might be more palatable than loneliness in a cottage, and William must be over fifty now. Not an age to go searching for new Silas Carters to tend.

"I've prepared coffee for you all, Mr Bone. I'll be in the kitchen if you want me. Just ring."

He'd be used to that all right, I thought as he left me. Everything in its place, cups, saucers, coffee keeping warm. If only my life had been as simple over the estate of Silas Carter: instead it had presented me with The Great Muddle. Not a word that lawyers take kindly too. We prefer words – and wills – that are cut and dried, not muddled. Especially where the family of the deceased are concerned. I was ready to implement my plan, and I was only awaiting the three most vocal over their demands to know how matters stood over the will. I fear – no, that is not the word I should be using – in this case of these three, I am *delighted* to tell them. Indeed I shall relish it. As the old rhyme has it, I do not like thee, Dr Fell, the reason why I cannot tell. For Dr Fell, read Mary Simpkins, Donald Paxton and Nigel Carter. I never have liked them on the rare occasions we have met, but since the events of Silas's hundredth birthday, I have added deep suspicion to my dislike.

These three had stayed in the house the night before and the night of Silas's birthday; the latter was also the night of his death. Accidental death, the coroner had concluded, and for someone not personally acquainted with Silas that would be the obvious conclusion. However, I *did* know the old skinflint well. The doctor had been sufficiently imbued with the notion that Mr Carter would live for ever, to notify the coroner at his unexpected death. Poor Silas had proved to be stuffed full of his sleeping pills, with only his fingerprints on the bottle and water beaker. Natural enough, the coroner must have thought, for him to be overcome with the excitement of his birthday party and the glass or two of champagne he had drunk there, and not realize the number of pills he was taking.

That old boozer? I knew better. Silas Carter was far too well accustomed to alcohol to be thrown off his usual careful habits by a mere five or six glasses of champagne – I lost count of the number I saw him drink. If ever I saw a man heading for being pickled for posterity by the whisky inside him, it was Silas Carter.

No, it's far more probable that one of the gruesome three-some helpfully crushed his pills up for him and saw them safely down his throat. Which though? One of them? All three? Did I care? I most certainly did. Someone might have cheated Silas out of years of life. I began to look forward to this meeting with some eagerness.

The three hopefuls were on time, indeed some minutes early, and I decided I would play doddering lawyer as well as a boring one, while I fumbled with serving coffee and biscuits and fussed about sugar and milk. By the time I'd finished, they were all twitchy. Ever since I'd seen early Hollywood films with lawyers solemnly reading out wills to the assembled company, I'd wished we had the same tradition here in England, and now I was to get my opportunity – at least to some of those most concerned in this mess. Those who, as Silas had kindly explained in the letter he sent to me with "the will" and which was to be opened after his death, had had expectations. Expectations, as opposed to hope, I suppose. Every Carter in Christendom must be eagerly searching their family tree on the news of Silas Carter's death.

I wouldn't be reading out the will today, but at least I could enjoy my position of temporary power. Not that Silas had demanded to be buried in Siberia or anything like that. Oh no, he was too cunning.

The trio sat on the huge sofa opposite me like the three monkeys, Hear No Evil, See No Evil, Speak No Evil. And I, when I wish, can be very evil.

"It seems to be taking a remarkably long time to clear up dear Uncle Silas's estate," Mary began jovially. I notice she'd worn a smart(ish) black suit perhaps hoping to clearly hoping to impress me how businesslike she could be. She needn't have worried; most people get very businesslike when it comes to inheriting money. Donald was more cunning; he had decided on a simple country-man's approach, anorak, casual trousers and sports shirt. As if to pretend he wasn't interested in sordid lucre. Nigel plainly didn't care. He was playing man about town, with long hair and linen suit, and sunglasses. I rather wished the blinds *had* been down. It would have punctured his ego to have to take them off.

"And will take longer," I said gravely, looking at them over the top of my glasses. Instant panic.

"Why?" Nigel ceased to be mysterious, and became very focussed. "It's a simple will, I'm sure. Everything was left to me. He told me so."

Mary looked reproachful. "You misunderstood. It was to me, Nigel. Uncle told me so."

A polite cough from Donald, as though he wished to impress me that he was the reasonable one of the three. He might be right. "To me actually."

A pause while they summed each other up. "He wanted the family name to continue," Nigel snapped, a trifle more uncertainly now. "So it must be me. You two come through the female line."

Time for the boring lawyer to put a word in. "Might I enquire *when* he told you this?"

"Several times. The last occasion was the evening he died," Mary looked triumphantly as if she'd played an ace. "I went to his room to say goodnight, and he told me I was a good girl and could look forward to a happy rich retirement."

"What time?" Nigel demanded

"About eight o'clock," Mary replied with dignity.

Nigel chuckled. "He clearly changed his mind after you left. I went at eight-thirty, and he told me the same."

"That you were a good girl?" Donald sneered. "In fact, you're both barking up the wrong tree, because I went about nine-fifteen, and he told me I was the sole heir. So, if, Aunt Mary, you are telling the truth, or even you, Nigel, Great-Uncle Silas was clearly planning to change his mind and write a new will."

They fell to squabbling then, until I put in my boring Humphrey cough. "Mr Silas Carter's confusion that evening could have been induced by the sleeping pills. Was he already feeling sleepy, perhaps, and so didn't know what he was saying?"

"No!" The word was spat out unanimously – hardly surprisingly.

"It's obvious," Mary appealed to me, "he was clear-headed when he spoke to me, and that he either took, or was helped to take," she said meaningfully, "the pills later."

"Are you implying, *Auntie* Mary –" Nigel emphasized the word, probably to help me get the message that she was ancient and therefore out of her tiny mind – "that either Donald or myself administered a fatal dose of sleeping pills to uncle?"

"If the cap fits . . ." Mary said belligerently.

"Did any of you notice the pills on his bedside table?" I asked firmly. I needed control here.

A pause, while they all thought about their own best interests. "I saw his water beaker and a flagon of water. I didn't notice the pills. Did you, Donald?" Mary asked stiffly.

Nigel instantly chimed in to say he hadn't either, and Donald claimed the moral high ground. "I did, as a matter of fact. I noticed the bottle was nearly empty. Thought I should mention it to William in case Great-Uncle Silas needed a new prescription."

Mary retorted with a stage gasp. A hand flew to her throat. (Nice one, I thought.) "And you didn't think dear uncle might have taken too many?"

"I didn't know how many pills dear uncle had left from the night before," Donald snapped back. Perhaps his birds never gave him this trouble. "And might I point out, Aunt Mary, that if he had already taken all those pills he wouldn't have been compos mentis enough to talk to any of us."

"Unless one of you is lying," Mary said brightly. "As I was the first there, it's clearly not me."

Nigel retaliated. "How do we know you went at seven thirty, not nine thirty?"

"Because I say so." Mary stood up angrily, then must have realized this was hardly going to help, so she sat down again.

Divide and rule, I thought. An excellent maxim. I had them all on the run now. Or did I?"

"Just a minute, Mr Bone." From the look on his face Donald was trying to metamorphose into Hercule Poirot. "Why on earth should any of us want to bump dear old Great-Uncle Silas off, even if we did each of us think we were his sole legatee? Not to put too fine a point on it, we'd be getting our money pretty soon anyway in the natural course of events. Moreover, even if he'd left his money between the three of us we'd get a fair amount each."

The other two rapidly appreciated his point and nodded solemnly. "Quite a few million each, I imagine," Nigel remarked hopefully.

He was right. More than a few in fact. The three of them smiled at me.

Time for me to puncture their little balloon. I too can be a wicked old man. I sighed heavily. "Do you know how many times Mr Carter has either changed his will or threatened to?"

There was instant silence.

"I see you do," I continued. "Your point is answered. Need I say more?"

Apparently not.

"All right then," Nigel said at last, not nearly so belligerently, "what did the blasted will say? Which of us did he leave it to?"

My big moment. Hollywood, here I come. I remembered the delightful letter Silas had written to me with the will. "You're blasted well going to work for your money, Humphrey, since I shan't be here to see you squander my money." And then he'd told me why.

Uproar had broken out again as they each debated the merits of their own case for sole inheritance.

I cleared my throat, then: "Silence," I roared.

Startled, the three of them instantly obeyed.

"I am sorry to say," I continued blandly, "that none of you is the sole beneficiary."

A silence of a different sort. "You mean we have to share it?" Donald asked warily.

"In a way."

"What the devil does this will say then?" Nigel was getting very edgy. What a shame, poor lad.

"It's a question of which will," I answered.

"What the hell do you mean?" Nigel roared. "You mean he wrote more than one? That's no problem. The relevant one is the one with the later date. When did—"

"Please!" I held up my hand, looking very grave indeed.

"Which will?" Nigel's voice went satisfactorily out of control. No pretensions to being arty crafty now. "Were there three of them?"

"No."

"How many then?" Mary squeaked impatiently.

"Seventeen."

Puzzlement at first, then:

"*Seventeen?* You mean drafts?" Donald asked weakly.

"No, Mr Paxton. Seventeen wills all fully signed and witnessed and in order. All different in content."

Nigel broke the stunned silence. "The latest is the valid one, you fool. Which is it?" I was delighted to tell him. "All seventeen wills are dated the same day. All posted that day too."

"But there must be a way of telling which was signed last. Weren't you present? What the hell were you playing at?" Donald was growing squeaky, Nigel and Mary gaping like goldfish.

"I was not present. All the signatures are valid; all of them, Mr Carter informed me, were witnessed together by the same two people, a postman and the gardener. Just the signatures; they weren't told what the documents were, I gather." You bet they weren't. They might have spoiled his fun.

"But who are the beneficiaries?" Nigel yelped.

"Each will leaves everything to a different person."

A nice moan from Mary now, but Nigel's brain was meeting the challenge admirably. "You mean there are seventeen people all thinking they're sole legatees?" A short laugh. "Of course the old chap was out of his mind. We can overthrow this easily if—" a glance at the other two – "we stick together."

Good. Another excellent line coming up for me to deliver. "Certainly, Mr Carter. Provided of course—"

Instant attention now. "Provided what?" he snarled.

"You have no objection to risking your inheritance. The will asserts that Mr Silas Carter is writing this in full possession of his faculties—"

"So what? That means nothing—"

"And," I continued happily, "that – to translate into lay terms – if anyone disputes this and tries to upset the will, they lose their inheritance."

"So what the hell happens now? It goes to court? They'll see it's nonsense . . ." Nigel suddenly saw the problem.

"Indeed. Which will be the valid will out of the seventeen?" I took up the reins again. "In such cases, it is usually far more effective to present the court of probate with a way out of the dilemma."

"Which would be?" Mary asked eagerly.

"All seventeen of you have to meet to agree a solution, the most obvious of which is that the net estate be divided between all of you."

"But even we three never agree on anything," Donald wailed.

"Perhaps that is what Silas had in mind," I murmured, although at a rough guess a million or so after tax would provide quite a few feathers to adorn their nests.

The gruesome three looked at each other. "All right," Nigel obviously spoke for all of them. We'll have to go along with it I suppose. Who are the other fourteen lucky devils?"

I paused. Now for my best line, which I flatter myself I then delivered with elegance and simplicity:

"I don't know."

They didn't quite follow me at first. Then reality struck. "What do you mean you don't know?" Donald yelled, in a tone he would never have used within a mile of one of his feathered friends.

"Just that," I replied. "All Mr Carter sent me was a letter telling me the situation, and just one will. He did not tell me who the other beneficiaries were or where the relevant wills might be found."

A terrible silence now.

"Then how do we know there were any more?" Mary was excelling herself. "It could be an elaborate joke. Dear uncle was so fond of teasing people. He obviously just wrote the one will – to *me*. Of course."

Nigel glanced at Donald. "Who was the legatee in the will you hold, Bone?"

Now I don't like being addressed as Bone, and it was therefore with particular pleasure that I put on my best boring lawyer look of reproof. "I regret I am unable to say. It would be unethical until I have either gathered in the other wills, or established whether this is indeed a practical joke."

Donald's lip was trembling. "Then we don't know –" he warbled.

"Precisely." I could not help it. I beamed. "None of you know whether you have inherited a single bean. It could all, as you yourselves have pointed out, be Mr Carter's little joke."

⋆　　⋆　　⋆

After speaking to the family, it did not take long for me to realize how Silas Carter had met his end. At first I had remained inclined to the view that the gruesome threesome had conspired to bring about his end, but discarded this notion. Those three couldn't agree on anything much less to keep mum about murder. For I had no doubt at all that's what it was. I decided to have one last look at the scene of this crime, and having visited Silas Carter's bedroom with William at my heels, we then repaired to the living room.

"Only those three know about their presumed inheritance, of course," I said casually. "He'd told them, but none of the others." I paused. "Certainly not you, William."

He flushed. "He didn't leave me one, the rotten skinflint."

"So that's why you murdered him, didn't you?"

He went very white, and I quickly pressed Venus's left breast for the whisky. The estate had been paying to keep the supply going. "Me?" he squeaked.

"He told you he wasn't leaving you a penny, and you knew he meant it, didn't you? When you found out about those new wills, you saw your opportunity to get your revenge. If by bad luck the death was queried, there would be plenty of more likely suspects than yourself in the frame."

"How could I have known about those wills?"

"Easily, William. He could get all those wills signed without you, but he couldn't *post* them without you. You wheeled his chair, you saw them go into the box even if you didn't put them in yourself. You probably stamped them too. Envelopes with wills inside are a distinctive shape, and each one was addressed to a firm of lawyers. So after that you asked him what he was going to do for you, who'd looked after him so faithfully for all those years."

"That don't mean I murdered him."

"Someone did, and it could only be you. The others all assumed pills were in the water, and only you knew Silas never drank water at night, only whisky. You crushed them up in the whisky glass, removed it in the morning, and put traces of crushed pill in the water beaker."

"There's no proof." William watched me carefully. "You can't go to the rozzers."

"No proof, but I could stir the waters, so to speak. With a murder investigation, probate on those wills could be held up for a long time."

"So what? Nothing coming to me." He looked at me uncertainly when I did not comment. "What are you going to do then?" he asked.

"I'll tell you what I'm going to do, William." And I did.

Now here we sat two years later, enjoying our last glass of whisky together at Silas's expense. My fees had added up nicely. It had taken nearly all this time before we had finally sorted out the truth, and then we had to hold the meeting for those of the seventeen who wished to attend, and negotiate the agreed division with those who didn't. Two had died in the meantime, leaving further complications with their estates; three preferred not to attend the meeting, but the other twelve met at a most interesting and lively gathering. The Court of Probate duly agreed the resulting settlement, and at last I was free of my obligations to Mr Carter.

William is a rich man – and so am I – for William was a beneficiary of Silas's will. Indirectly, that is. In fact through me.

There never was a seventeenth will, not a genuine one anyway. Silas only wrote sixteen. With so many other wills before them, all with the same text and signatures, save for the legatee's name, how likely was the court to notice that one was forged? Or that, faced with such overwhelming evidence of the letter's truth, the signature to that too was forged. Silas's original letter had stated only sixteen wills. I myself added the seventeenth.

I developed many useful skills during that period of work. I could hardly make the forged will out to myself, but in William I had seen the opportunity I was waiting for. We have gone fifty-fifty on the proceeds. Can I trust him to hand over my share? Of course. He isn't going to risk his inheritance going up in smoke if the will is declared a forgery. Can he trust me not to blackmail him for more? Of course, he can . . . I'm a lawyer.

I told you I was a wicked old man.

THE STOLEN CHILD

Brian McGilloway

The cry, when it came, was not what she had expected. For five months she had sat, night after night, her legs gathered beneath her on the sofa, the baby monitor resting on the arm of her chair, waiting, hoping to hear a cry. But, what she heard was not so much a cry as a ghost of a cry, like an echo without a source, its presence confirmed more by the flickering of the lights on the monitor than the tinny sound it produced. It was enough, certainly, to make her shiver involuntarily, to rub the goose-bumped skin of her arm with her palm. The second cry, though, was stronger, building in intensity then cutting short with a strangled yelp.

Thoughts tumbling, Karen stumbled to the foot of our stairs, staring up at the nursery door, willing herself to go up. Gripping the banister rail with whitened knuckles, she attempted to lift her foot onto the first step, but her legs weakened and she staggered. The floor seemed to shift beneath her and she had to grab the other banister rail in order to lower herself onto the step. It was there that she was sitting, her face bleary with tears when I got in from work later.

"What's wrong?" I asked.

"I heard a baby crying. In the monitor. Will you check?" she urged. "I can't go up; it might be Michael."

I took the stairs two at a time, opened the nursery door and flicked on the light, but the room was quiet. A teddy bear had fallen off the dresser and lay on the floor, face down. I picked it up, smelt the newness of its fur.

"Is everything ok?" she called up, her mouth a tight white line.

"Fine," I muttered, closing the door behind me.

She looked at me quizzically. "You don't believe me, do you?" she said. "I did hear it. He cried so hard. Why would he cry so hard?"

I stared at her, but could think of nothing adequate to say.

"There *was* a cry," she said, one week later. "I know you don't believe me but I did hear a child. And I don't think it was Michael."

"I know it wasn't Michael," I replied.

"Where did it come from?" She looked at me pleadingly.

"There must be a simple reason for it," I suggested. "I'll find out."

I dug out the box for the baby monitor on which was a help line number.

"Can I help you?" The voice was female, English, young.

"We have your monitor system," I explained. "My wife heard a baby cry in it."

A pause. "Is that not what the monitor is meant to do?"

"Yes. Sorry. I understand," I said, a little flustered. "It wasn't our baby. She heard someone else's baby crying through our monitor."

"Are you sure it wasn't your own child?"

"Certain."

"It could be that someone else in your street has the same monitor as you. If they are operating on the same frequency, you'll hear *their* baby and they'll hear *yours*."

"I see," I said.

"Can I help you with anything else today, sir?" English asked.

"I'm afraid not."

One week later, Karen was sobbing when I came home, her arms gathered around her, her left hand at her mouth, her small teeth worrying her thumbnail.

"He's been crying all night," she whispered. "It's Michael. He needs me."

As I opened my mouth to speak, the monitor crackled with static. The lights registered the sound briefly, and subsided.

But, when the crying started, there could be no doubt. It developed from a raw scream into coughing sobs, as if the child was tiring. But no one responded to its cries.

Karen, initially elated with vindication, began to cry. "Make it stop," she said balling her fists against the side of her head. "Do *something*."

I followed the curve of our street, pausing outside each house, straining to hear a child crying. At the second-last house, I believed that I did. I rang the doorbell. Through the door's frosted glass I could see a figure move into the hallway, then retreat back into the room from which he had come. I heard something slam. Heard a cry seconds later.

But the cry was from the wrong direction. Karen was out of our house.

"I heard it," she shrieked. "I heard it being killed."

"What?"

"The baby was crying. I heard a smack and it stopped," she screamed. "You let it be killed." She pulled back from me. "You let him be killed," she repeated, then spat in my face.

The police officer squeezed into our armchair. "Devlin," he'd said, by way of introduction.

"And it couldn't have been your own child?" Devlin asked after listening to Karen's story.

"No," she said.

"Where is your child?" he said, glancing around the room.

"He's Michael," Karen answered.

"Can I see him, please?" he asked, putting down his notebook.

"No," Karen said.

"I'd like to see your child, Ma'am."

"You can't, Inspector," I replied, moving to my wife. "You see we . . . we don't . . . we don't actually have a child."

Devlin returned a few moments later, having walked down to the house where I had heard the baby crying. I stood out on our pathway as we spoke, out of earshot of Karen, my hands in my pockets.

"Anything?" I asked him.

He shook his head.

"Did you check?"

He hesitated, glancing towards our doorway to check that Karen wasn't listening. "I can't check someone's house on the word of your wife. I mean no disrespect, but she needs help."

"She getting all the help she needs," I said, defensively.

"It's not working," he replied. He stared at me a moment, as if deciding something. "What happened to her?"

So I told him about Michael. I told him about how he died at birth. I told him about Karen's therapy, how she had set up the nursery as if Michael was alive, how she sat with the baby monitor we'd bought, hoping some night to hear her son. I told him everything because he was the first person in five months to ask. Because it's the woman who's affected in these things. Not the father. But then, I'm *not* a father.

Devlin considered all I said. "Do you know your neighbour up there?" he asked finally.

I shook my head.

"I do," Devlin said. "Trevor Conlon. Collects old clothes for charities." He fished in his jacket pocket and handed me a folded green flier. "Funnily enough," he continued, "he also runs a second-hand retro clothes shop. He has no children." He paused. "None of his own, anyway."

The phantom child slept in our bed, with us, alongside our dead son, Michael, whose presence was never more physical than that night, when he filled the space between us.

At dawn I sat in the kitchen, staring out at the grey pall of rain that hung over the city, misting the windows, clinging to the red brick of the houses opposite. I read the charity flier Devlin had given me. *Clothes Wanted. Will collect. No donation too small.* What had the policeman said? "He has no children." Yet I had heard the child crying; it wasn't just Karen's imagination. There was a child in that house, looking for someone. Looking to be found.

I phoned the number on the flier just after nine o'clock. The man who answered sounded groggy. I told him I had a donation to make; suggested he call after eight that evening, gave an address far enough away to keep him out of his house for a good half hour. Long enough for me to search his house myself.

I watched his van leave at seven forty five, then went down the alley behind our houses, and climbed over his back wall. His house was like my own. A sash window at the back, the clasp so loose a bank card could flick it open. I slid the window up, the blistered paint flaking off on my hands. I stepped down into his sitting room. Black bags lined one wall. The settee was covered with clothes, labelled and priced.

To my right, the kitchen, dishes piled on the white work top, beer cans, bent doubled on the floor.

I crept out into the hallway and listened. The house sounded empty.

The staircase seemed to creak louder the more carefully I trod. The bathroom faced me at the top of the stairs, a toilet roll tube lying on the floor. There were no toys in the bath, no small tooth brushes in the scum-stained glass on the sink.

The other two rooms were likewise empty – no children, no toys, or clothes. One room was being used as a store. The other was the main bedroom. A duvet lay gathered on the floor, beside it an ashtray spilt butts onto the carpet.

The next set of stairs led to the attic room, filled with junk. The curtains were drawn, but the windows so dirty, the light from the street lamps made little difference. I scanned the room quickly. It was only when I turned to leave that I heard the soft thumping. It seemed to be coming from the cupboard. My stomach flipped as I approached the door, hand out. Hesitated. Opened the door.

The child had black hair. His blue eyes were wide, his mouth covered with brown parcel tape, a slit cut in the middle to allow him to breath. He looked up at me in terror. He kicked his foot against the bottom of the cardboard box in which he had been placed. It thumped softly against the inside of the wardrobe. He was the length of my forearm, maybe four or five months old. He reached out his arms to me, his small fists balled as I lifted him.

At that moment the door downstairs slammed shut, the

window in the attic room shuddering with the force. I heard Conlon swearing as his footsteps thudded on the stairs. I tried to crouch down, hide behind the piles of lumber, but the child in my arms was squirming now, kicking to be free. He cried lightly; the sounds stopped below and I heard Conlon come to the stairs leading up to us.

"Who's up there?" he shouted. I imagined his foot on the step. I heard thudding and it took me a moment to realize it was someone banging on the front door.

Conlon didn't move for a second. More banging at the door, insistent. Finally I heard his footfalls as they retreated down the hallway.

I listened to the muffled conversation beneath us. Momentarily I heard someone mount the stairs.

"Just to keep you happy, Trevor," a voice I recognized said. The policeman – Devlin. His bulk appeared in the doorway for a second.

"All empty," he called without looking in.

Several minutes later I heard them leaving the house.

Weeks later we were at Sunday Mass. Afterwards, Karen stopped to light a candle for Michael, our stolen child. In the porchway I met Devlin again. He was waiting for us, a plastic bag in his hand.

"I saw you in there," he said. "Thought you might be interested. We got a tip off a week or two ago. Saw someone breaking into your neighbour Conlon's house. When we arrived, we arrested him labelling clothes from charity bags for his shop. He claimed there was someone in his house. When we went back later, we found birth certificates for a number of children. Turns out Trevor's been smuggling children into Ireland for illegal adoption."

Karen and I looked at him. He paused, as if waiting for us to speak, before continuing. "He brought in five children in all. We've traced four. One seems to have vanished."

I had to swallow several times, before speaking. "What happened to him?"

"Well, I hope whoever has *him* will look after him a hell of a lot better than Conlon did. Or than the state would. Maybe he'll be lucky."

Karen placed her hand on my arm. "We need to go."

Devlin nodded. "I understand." He turned to leave, then faced us again. "I almost forgot," he said, taking a small teddy bear from the plastic bag he was carrying. "I picked up this for your wee boy. Michael's his name, isn't that right?"

I could not respond. Karen, however, replied in a clear voice. "No. Paul's his name. After his father."

"Of course," Devlin said, leaning into the pram. He placed the toy beside the sleeping child, rubbed his index finger against the child's cheek. "You be sure to spoil him, now." He straightened up, smiled mildly, scrunched the empty plastic bag into a ball which he stuffed into his coat pocket and walked away from us. He did not look back.

As Karen fixed Paul's blanket, I dipped my finger into the water font and said a prayer to Michael. I prayed he would not mind our taking our second chance. I prayed he would not resent Paul's place with us. I promised him that he still owned a piece of my heart that would never stop being his.

Then I stepped out into the sunlight with the rest of my family.

THE PEOPLE IN THE FLAT ACROSS THE ROAD

Natasha Cooper

It had been a ghastly day. I'd decided to work at home so I could finish the proposal for our biggest client's new campaign. The copy was urgent, you see, because they'd pulled back the meeting by three days. My boss and I were due to make the presentation at ten next morning, and the designers were waiting in the office to pretty up my text and sort out all the PowerPoint stuff for us.

The trouble was, I hadn't expected the interruptions: far more at home than in any office; and worse because of having no receptionists or secretaries to fend them off.

First it was the postman. Not my usual bloke but a temp who couldn't tell the difference between 16 Holly Road, where I live, and 16 Oak Court, Holly Road, which is a flat just opposite. Even so, I shouldn't have shouted. It wasn't *his* fault he couldn't read much; or speak English, either.

And he wasn't to know how many hours I've wasted over the past year redirecting all the mail I get that obviously isn't meant for me. Letters and packages with all sorts of names. I never pay much attention to the names once I've seen they're not mine, so I couldn't tell you what they were now.

I opened one parcel by mistake, not having read the label before I ripped off the brown packing tape. Wondering why someone was sending me a whole bunch of phone adaptors and wires and stuff, I turned the package over and saw it was meant for the flat. That was when I crossed the road and made my third attempt to introduce myself and sort it out. The funny thing was, you see, that in all the months I'd been dealing with their mail I'd never actually seen any of them. Once or twice, there'd been a hand coming through the net curtains to open or shut a window, but that was all.

As usual, I got no answer, even though all the lights were on and there was a radio or TV blaring. I thought I heard their footsteps this time too, and voices, but I suppose it could have been imagination.

Anyway, I was so cross they couldn't be bothered to do their neighbourly bit that I stopped bothering to take their mail across the road. I didn't even correct the wrongly addressed stuff (some of the senders missed out the Oak Court bit too; it wasn't only the postmen who got it wrong). Instead I'd scrawl "Not Known Here" or "No one of this name at this address" on the packages and envelopes before stuffing them back into the postbox on my way to work. If the packages were too big, which happened occasionally, I'd stomp round to the post office on Saturday mornings and dump them at the end of the counter. It took much longer than carting them across the road and leaving them on the flat's doorstep, but it was way more satisfying.

Which maybe explains – though of course it doesn't excuse – the way I shouted at the poor stand-in postie this time round. He took three steps backwards and muttered some kind of apology, so of course I had to join in and explain I hadn't meant to yell.

Anyway, he was only the first. When it wasn't people collecting for charity – decent, kind, clean, well-spoken people, who didn't deserve to be glared at and sent away empty-handed – it was miserable, hopeless-looking young men trying to sell me ludicrously expensive low-grade dusters I didn't want. Or Jehovah's Witnesses. How was I supposed to flog my brain into producing light-hearted, witty sales copy with all this going on? I was ripe for murder, I can tell you.

And then there was the small man in decorator's overalls who had the cheek to ring my bell and tell me my neighbours had been complaining about my overhanging hedge. He offered to cut it back and take away the debris for some even more ludicrous sum. He got all the insults I'd been choking down all morning, and no apology, and I still think I was justified. Almost. At least I didn't lay a hand on him.

When I'd slammed the door in his face, I went back to my copy and re-read the pathetically little I'd managed to write. I had to delete the whole lot. You can imagine how I felt. I bolted some yogurt for lunch and spilled most of it down my T-shirt, so I had to change that and fling it in the washing machine, which wasted yet more time.

Then it was the end of the school day and there were shrieks from all the little darlings who'd been pent up in their class-rooms for too long, and the exasperating heavy *slap-slap* of a football being kicked up and down the road. And chat from the little darlings' attending adults, who all seemed to want to stand right outside my front windows, either talking to each other or jabbering into their mobiles.

When they'd all gone and the street was blessedly quiet once more, the doorbell went again. I shrieked out some filthy word or other (actually, I know quite well what it was, but I don't want to shock you) and ran to the door, wrenching it open and snarling, only to see my ten-year-old godson, looking absolutely terrified.

I apologised again, of course, and discovered he'd only come to return the tin in which I'd delivered his birthday cake. He's great, and on normal days I enjoy his company. He has an interesting, offbeat take on the world, and his talk of school and sports and music often gives me ideas I can use for work when we're pushing children's products. So I had to ask him in and offer him some Diet Coke, which was the only suitable thing I had in the house. Still looking scared, he shook his head and scuttled away like Hansel escaping from the wicked witch's gingerbread house.

I managed a quiet hour after that, and I had about twenty-five per cent of the copy written when the early evening crowd started: the meter readers, more charity-collectors, and then the party canvassers. Apparently we were going to have a by-election the next week. I eventually got down to real work at about eight, which was the time I'd have got back from the office on an ordinary day. I was spitting.

Still, I got the copy finished in the end – and it had just the right edgy but funny tone for the product. I was pretty sure the clients would like it. But when I saw it was half eleven, I knew the poor designers weren't going to be happy. I'd kept them hanging on for hours. I hoped they wouldn't be so angry they screwed up. We needed the presentation to *look* brilliant as well as sound it.

So I e-mailed my text to them with a genuine apology, and asked them to get it back to me by eight the next morning with all the pix and whatever stylish tarting-up they could manage. Then I copied everything to my boss, with an e-mail to say I'd meet him at the clients' at nine forty-five. That would give me plenty of time to have the crucial six hours' sleep and get my hair sorted and pick the best clothes to say it all: cool; monied; efficient; sexy.

As you can imagine, I was pretty hyper by this time, so I took a couple of sleeping pills. Only over-the-counter herbal stuff. I think they're mainly lettuce, and the label on the packet always makes me laugh: "Warning: May Cause Drowsiness."

I was calming down a bit. I chased the pills with a glass of wine and a bit of bread and cream cheese with a smear of mango chutney, which reminds me of the sandwiches my mother used to make me when I was ill as a child.

So, fed, wined, and drugged to the eyeballs with lettuce, I took myself to bed. Just to be sure, I opened *The Unbearable Lightness of Being*, which hardly ever fails to send me to sleep. It did its stuff pretty soon. I ripped off my specs and turned out the light, to find myself in that state where you fall hundreds of feet through the air, while still being plastered to the mattress. Heaven, really.

Through the lovely muzzy feeling, I thought I heard the phone ring once or twice. I ignored it and it stopped long before the answering machine could've cut in.

The next thing I knew I was floating on twinkling turquoise waves in warm sunlight with dolphins leaping in the distance and a raucous London voice yelling, "Go, Go, Go." I'd barely got my eyes open when there was this almighty crash downstairs and thundering feet and cracking wood as my bedroom door burst open, spraying splinters and bits of the lock all over the place. I got chips of wood in my hair and all over my face.

I'd always been a coward. But I'd never been afraid before. Not like this.

I couldn't breathe. It was as if I'd been hit in the throat. My heart was banging like a pneumatic drill. And I thought I'd throw up any minute. Or pee in my bed.

The worst of it was I couldn't see anything much. There seemed to be dozens of sturdy thighs in jeans at eye level and stubby black things that looked like gun barrels.

It seemed mad. But it's what they looked like. All I could hear was panting: heavy, angry panting. Whatever they were going to do, I knew I had to be able to see, so I reached for the specs on my bedside table. A voice yelled at me to f – ing stay where I was and not move. I couldn't. I mean, my arm was way too heavy. It crashed down on the table and knocked the specs to the floor with the lamp and my book. It made them jam one of the black things nearer my face and yell at me to stay still.

It really was a gun.

Then a hand came and grabbed the edge of the duvet. I hadn't got anything on under it, but that didn't strike me until they ripped the duvet off me and let the cold air in. I twitched. I couldn't help it, in spite of the guns. But nothing happened. Except that one of them swore. I don't know what he thought he'd see under my duvet except me.

"*What?*" said one of the others. He moved his head a bit. At least, I think it was his head. All I could see was a kind of furry pink mass where his face must be. He raised his voice: "What've *you* got?"

"Nothing," called another man from further away. "There's no one else. Only a kind of study, with a computer and filing cabinets and magazines and things."

"Magazines? What magazines?"

"Women's stuff. *Cosmo. Vogue.* Things like that."

He came closer and bent right down into my face. That's when I saw he had a dark-blue peaked cap with a chequered headband and POLICE in neat white letters.

I began to breathe again.

"God, you scared me," I said, and my voice was all high and quavery. I tried to toughen it. "Can I have my glasses, please? And a dressing gown?"

"Don't move." Three gun barrels came even closer to my face. And I heard the scrunch of glass. I don't suppose they did it deliberately, but one of them mashed my new Armani specs under his heavy great feet.

That was enough to make me more cross than scared. Or maybe it was reaction. Shock or something. Anyway, whatever it was, I forgot their guns and not having any clothes on and I just yelled at them, in a voice even my grandmother would have admired. And no one was grander than my grandmother.

"Stop being so damned silly. You've got the wrong sodding address, like the sodding postman. You want the people in the flat across the road. Now let me get up and get my dressing gown. And stop playing silly buggers with those *idiotic* guns."

The nearest man took a step back and I knew I'd won. After a bit, another of them handed me my dressing gown, smiling and nodding in a sloppy apologetic kind of way, like a bashful terrier. A minute ago he'd been holding a gun to my face; now he wanted to be friends? Mad.

MANDELBROT'S PATTERNS

Keith McCarthy

The phone's call was magnified by the dark of the night, a demanding intrusion that was not going to be ignored.

First there was a sigh, then a hand reached out for the phone and a deep, almost husky male voice asked, "Yes?" There was a pause. "Yes, that's right . . . Where?" Another of the same. "Who?" This with some interest. "You're sure? . . . Okay." Once more, nothing was said, before, "No, don't worry. I'll contact her. I think she's visiting her mother."

The phone was placed back on its stand and there was silence again, as if the room were empty.

Then softly . . .

"Trouble?" This voice was female.

"Dead woman. Found in the bath. Apparently her wrists were slit."

"Suicide? What's it got to do with us?"

"It's Kate Reed, the wife of Dr Phil Reed."

For the first time, there was a sense of interest in the room.

"Reed? The forensic pathologist?"

"The same. He was actually the one who phoned in with the call."

After a moment, "I still don't see why they have to phone a detective sergeant in the middle of the night."

"They were after his detective inspector."

"So they found her, although they don't know that. I still don't see why they were after either of us."

An unearthly yowling sounded in the distance as fox called

to fox between the dustbins, and with a sigh, the answer was given.

"Apparently he sat there and watched her do it."

They spent the remaining hours of darkness at a very plush five-bedroom detached house in the suburbs, feelings of deja vu fighting with feelings of boredom. They had seen the body naked in the bath, the rose-pink water almost completely hiding her embarrassment, a pallid face showing a degree of relaxation that no living human could ever hope to assume. There was no evidence of a fight, nothing even to suggest an argument, a row, or even a small tiff. Their examination of the house had revealed no money problems, no evidence of extra-marital affairs, nothing that suggested anything other than an ordinary marriage.

"I still don't believe it."

"Believe it, Hannah. Believe it."

"Phil Reed is not a murderer."

Sam had learned to have great respect for Hannah Angelman's abilities in the seven months he had known her, but this time he thought that she was wrong.

"But when she was found, he was sitting in the bathroom just looking at her corpse, as if it were the most normal thing in the world. The scalpel was on the side of the bath. He'd been drinking wine – had a couple of glasses. There was even a half-empty glass of wine on the side of the bath by the body, as if to make out that she'd joined in."

"But has he admitted to murder?"

"He hasn't said anything much. He wants to talk to you."

She leaned back in her chair, looking toward Sam as he stood in front of her desk, yet not seeing him.

"Are we sure the house was secure?"

"Completely."

"So there was no possibility of third-party involvement?"

"None whatsoever."

Another possibility excluded, she reflected that the options were running out for Dr Philip Reed.

Outside the window of her office some seagulls, ranging far from their usual home around the Gloucester docks, called raucously as they hovered in the swirling spring air. As if called by them, she rose from her chair and went to stare out of the window at the constant traffic of Lansdowne Road; the morning rush into Cheltenham was just beginning.

"It's an odd way to murder someone . . . maybe it *is* suicide."

"With him watching? Anyway, his fingerprints are all over the handle of the scalpel, which is clear evidence that he took an active part in things. I don't know what else you need. Accept it, Hannah. He killed her."

"Other than the cuts to her wrists, was there any evidence of trauma to the body?"

"The pathologist says the only thing he can find are two tiny puncture marks, one by each of the cuts."

"Nothing else? No ligature marks? No head injury?"

"No."

"That would suggest that she allowed him to do it."

"Unless she was drugged. Perhaps that's what the puncture marks mean; or perhaps he put something in her wine. We'll only know for sure when we get the toxicology back in a day or two."

Hannah turned back to him. "No, she was complicit. At worst this was assisted suicide."

Sam snorted. "Assisted and spectated, then. She was naked in the bath, Hannah. He must have sat there and watched her die."

"Poor sod."

He couldn't believe what he had heard. "Why do you say that? After what he's just done, I don't think he deserves any sympathy."

"There's a lot of history in that marriage, Sam."

"I think he drugged her while she was in the bath – hence her glass of wine – then slit both her wrists and sat and watched her while she bled to death. That's horrible, that's unforgivable. No amount of history comes anywhere near to excusing that."

"It might explain it, though."

"I don't see how."

She turned abruptly around. "Why don't we go and find out? Where is he?"

"Room three. Fisher's with him."

*   *   *

As they walked down the stairs to the interview rooms, Sam said, "He had everything. Large house, big car, beautiful wife, and now he's thrown it all down the drain. What drives a man to do that? Surely it can't just have been a row."

"Which is why I'm having a problem with this. Something tells me that there's more to this than is at present apparent."

It was when they had nearly reached the interview room that Sam asked, "What did you mean by 'history'?"

"They had a child, but it died after a few weeks. Internal abnormalities or something. It was a blessing, really."

"Oh."

"They never had any more luck. Phil and his wife had many good things in their lives, but I don't think they ever considered them adequate compensation. I look at Phil and I see a lovely man who's as crippled as effectively as if he were paraplegic."

It was the tone as much as the words that impressed Sam. He asked with a slight smile that hid concern, "Have you got a thing for him, Hannah?"

She laughed. "There's no need for jealousy, Sam."

For Sam's liking, this was altogether too public a place for such sentiments. "Not so loud. I thought we were being discreet. You know what this place is like. There's always someone listening."

"Oh, of course." She lowered her voice to a stage whisper. "Mustn't have a DI sleeping with her sergeant. The world might end."

"It might . . . for us."

She stopped quite abruptly so that he had to turn slightly to face her. She asked, "Would that bother you?"

"Of course it would."

"I'm not just another conquest?"

He looked around, as if the painted stone walls might hide camouflaged eavesdroppers. "Of course not!"

She examined him for a brief moment, twitched a smile, then sighed. "Good."

He stepped toward her and said in a low tone, "I mean it, Hannah."

A nod, but one that was not as certain as it might have been. "Good."

She began walking again and he fell into step. "So why are you so convinced about Phil Reed's innocence?" he asked.

She had to think about that one. Eventually, all she could produce was: "I've just known him a long time. He's not a killer."

"Wasn't maybe. He is now."

"Is that steak okay? It certainly looks good."

Her mouth full, Kate nodded at once. "Mmm . . . delicious."

He thought, You're beautiful. Even a blind man would be able to tell that.

"And the wine? You like the wine?"

"I certainly do."

Reed smiled. "So I should hope, considering the price."

He hadn't really been able to afford the restaurant – if truth be told, he felt out of place in it – but he had things to say tonight.

"Well it's very good . . . mmm . . . very good indeed."

"*I* thought so."

The couple at the table next to them were in their late sixties and would not have looked out of place at an imperial ball; he suspected that they were looking secretly askance at the whipper-snappers so uncomfortably close to them, perhaps unable to believe that they had let people in who were not related to the Lord Lieutenant of the County.

"So what's the excuse for such extravagance?"

"Do I need an excuse?"

"Well . . . it's hardly in character."

He pretended outrage. "How dare you! I'll have you know, I've been known to spend three pounds on a bottle of wine."

"And the rest!" Her smile gilded a lily and somehow improved it.

"Anyone would think I'm a cheapskate."

She leaned forward conspiratorially. "Wouldn't they just?"

"Oh! So that's what you think, is it?" He turned his face away, corners of his mouth turned downward. If he hoped for sympathy, it was a hope that was doomed from the off.

"Me and a few thousand others . . ."

There was no background music in the restaurant, no violins. As he let the silence between them grow, the chattering around them intruded.

His timing was good, though.

"So you wouldn't want to marry me?" The tone – hurt innocence – was also good.

"What?"

Feigned surprise. "You wouldn't want to marry me. What with me being a cheapskate."

As she realized what he had said, her face erupted with bright delight. "Oh . . . Oh, God . . ."

"Fair enough," he went on, apparently oblivious of her reaction. "I'll strike you off the list and then move on . . ."

"You mean it?"

He shrugged. "It was only an idea. It doesn't matter."

She reached out, grasped his hand, as if to make him realize that she had something to say. "Of course I do! My God! Of course I do. I thought you'd never ask."

He continued in the same slightly distracted tone, "Only, now that I've got a consultant's job . . ."

"You what?" Her voice rose appreciably, and Lord and Lady Muck next door did not like it.

"Didn't I tell you? I've been appointed as consultant pathologist at Saint Benjamin's. I start in three months."

"That's fantastic!"

"Is that a 'yes' to marriage, then?"

"Of course it is!"

He shook his head. "You just want to marry a doctor. You're a gold digger."

At last he smiled, and after a moment's pause, she sighed huge relief.

"You bet," she said.

"Interview commencing at eight twenty a.m., Friday, the seventh of June 2006. Present are Dr Philip Reed, Detective Sergeant Sam Rich, and Detective Inspector Hannah Angelman. Dr Reed has been cautioned but has declined to take up his right to have a solicitor present."

Hannah smiled at the man across the desk. "Hello, Phil."

He bowed his head. His demeanor was one of exhaustion, but his smile was genuine. "Hannah."

"You know Sam?"

"I think we've met a couple of times."

She relaxed back in her chair as if she were in a coffee shop, as if this were a meeting between old mates from university. "I must say, I never expected to find us in this position."

His head bobbed from side to side. "A life without surprise would be a poor life indeed. It might, though, be marginally better than one that contains too many of them."

"Or ones that are too big."

He acknowledged this graciously. "Indeed."

"How long have we known each other, Phil?"

"Oh, I suppose it must be seven, maybe eight years."

She nodded. "I thought I knew you."

"No human being ever truly knows another."

"But I think I can usually tell the killers. God knows I've known a few."

Reed closed his eyes. Sam thought that he looked ready to sleep for a thousand years. His jacket was creased and looked tired, his shirt collar grimed. He said slowly, didactically, "Killing and killers aren't a specific type, Hannah. Even I know that, and I'm only the meat man, the poor blood infantry, the pathologist. I'm only the one who has to come face to face with whatever atrocity someone has brought upon another."

"So what happened last night?"

He explained with brutal simplicity, "My wife died."

"That we know. It's what we don't know that I need you to tell me, and you're the only one who can."

Sam thought for several seconds that he was showing no emotion at all, but then he realized his mistake. Reed's eyes were aqueous, sparkling despite the gloom of the surroundings. "No one on the outside knows what goes on between four walls."

"But you were on the inside."

He sighed, and with perfect timing a single tear tracked down his right cheek. "Yes."

"So tell me what happened."

Now he drew in breath, a ragged, almost juddering sound. "I thought it would all be straightforward. I thought that it would be an ending."

"And isn't it?"

"No."

Sam said in a low tone, "It was for your wife."

Reed seemed surprised that anyone else was in the room. "Yes," he agreed.

Hannah asked, "How do you feel about that, Phil?"

"How do you expect me to feel? My wife's dead."

"Who's fault is that?"

He even managed to smile. "On the face of it, mine."

"Is that a confession?"

At which he was given pause. "Ah, thereby is suspended a very interesting tale."

"Did you kill Kate?"

His reply might have been to a question about the answer to number twenty-one down. "I've been thinking long and hard about that. I suppose, taking everything into account, I would have to admit that I bear some responsibility for her death, yes . . . Yet, no. There was a degree of inevitability about the events that culminated in Kate's death."

"So you admit that you slit her wrists?"

He took this, considered it, then admitted, "Yes, she asked me to."

Sam was incredulous. "She asked you to? She asked you to grab hold of her hands and slice through her wrists?"

"Something like that."

"And then you sat there? You're asking us to believe that she was quite happy for you to watch her die?"

Reed protested. "We talked. We remembered the good times that we'd had together."

Sam had heard stories on *Jackanory* that were more believable. "You're asking us to believe that you just sat there while she sat in a bath of water, completely naked, and bled to death?"

"She *was* my wife. I had seen her *sans culottes* before."

"You know what I'm saying."

"Yes, Detective Sergeant, and I am asking you to believe what I'm saying. I loved Kate. I wouldn't murder her."

"Yet you admit that you slit her wrists."

"That's right."

"What reason would she have for suicide? An attractive woman, a happy marriage . . . it *was* a happy marriage, wasn't it?"

Reed smiled. "Are any truly happy?"

"We're talking about yours."

Reed looked up at him, tears still bright in his eyes. "Well, since you ask, no it wasn't . . . But that wasn't because we didn't love each other. Far from it."

Sam thought that he was onto something. "Why was it unhappy? Was it money? Or was she having an affair? Were you, perhaps?"

"No, nothing like that."

"Then why did you kill her?"

"I . . ."

Sam wasn't interested in his protestations. "Come on, Doctor. There's no point in refusing to tell us. You're going to be convicted of murder whether you say anything or not. The only difference is whether you get parole sooner rather than later. The Parole Board don't like people who refuse to accept guilt."

Reed turned to Sam's boss. "I didn't murder Kate, Hannah. I loved her."

Hannah raised her eyebrows. "So you what? Put her out of her misery?"

Reed might have been about to protest, but instead he paused, then said, "That would be a fair description."

"But why? What misery did Kate have to be put out of?"

Reed had begun to weep again. For protracted seconds he said nothing, his head bowed low, then he said sadly, "Death."

"That went well, I think."

Reed, who was tired, raised a smile as he brought a tray of dirty crockery out to the kitchen. "It was superb. The desserts were brilliant."

"Thank you. I thought so."

"Mind you, it was obvious that Will and Ruth preferred my main." He decided this with perfect seriousness, apparently after considered study.

Kate was outraged. "You think? You really think?"

Careful not to smile. "I know."

She shook her head. "You sad man."

He had put down the tray and was helping his wife unload the dishwasher. "Where does this go?"

"Don't you know?"

"Obviously not."

"You should be ashamed of yourself. It just goes to show how little you do around here."

"Thank you for that. I'll tell you what, I'll give up the day job – and the money it brings in – and become a house husband. You can support us."

She straightened up. She was wearing a figure-hugging bright blue, almost iridescent evening dress. "I may only be a humble publisher," she pointed out, "but I think you'd notice it if I packed it in tomorrow."

"I seriously doubt it."

And, abruptly, her demeanor changed and became almost fearful. "You really think so?"

"What does that mean?"

A slight hesitation now came upon her. "It's still supposed to be a secret, but Ruth's just found out that she's pregnant. She told me this evening."

"Really?"

"She's thrilled."

For a moment, he was blind to her thinking. "I'm not surprised . . ." It was at this point that he came to realization. "Oh . . ."

"Wouldn't it be wonderful? To have a baby?" Something joyous had come into her face, something that frightened him.

"Well . . . I suppose so."

"Maybe twins," she rushed on. "At any rate, we could eventually have two, or maybe three."

He held up his hands. "Whoa. Hang on there. We've haven't decided on having one yet. We've only been married three years."

"But you want children, don't you? You've always said that you did."

He felt buffeted by her passion, wanted to swim to shore. "Yes . . ."

"Well, then."

He gestured with his hands that she should slow down. He was fully aware that if he just refused she would be upset, there might even be a row, and he didn't want that. At the same time, he wanted her to calm down, think rationally, where now he was sure that she was driven by instinct. "I just wasn't expecting things to change quite so quickly. We've got a good life together."

"And we'll have an even better one when we're parents. You'll see."

"This is all a bit sudden, Kate."

She couldn't see it. "After three years?"

"I hope we're going to be married a long time."

Despite his wish to avoid confrontation, she was plainly becoming angry at his intransigence. "But what's the point of marriage without children?"

"For Christ's sake, marriage is more than just a means of making babies, Kate."

"But it's also more than just two people enjoying themselves." Her voice was rising, a frown beginning to form on her face. "It's more than just dinner parties, holidays, and good sex." She stopped. Her next sentences were dug out of a very deep pit of emotion. "I want a child, Phil. I want a baby."

And before such depth of passion he found too late that he had nowhere to swim to, no safe haven to find. Before it, he was powerless. "Oh, God . . . Come here, Kate."

As they held each other, she said through tears against his shoulder, "I didn't realize before how much I wanted children, but I've been unable to get the idea of babies out of my head. And then when Ruth told me . . ."

Even then, he knew not only that she would have her way, but also that her way would be costly.

"About five months ago, Kate was diagnosed with glioblastome multiforme."

"And what's that?"

Reed smiled sadly. "It's a lovely name, isn't it? Sounds properly scientific, suitably imposing. Much more impressive than words like *cancer*, or *brain tumour*."

"Is that what it is? Cancer?"

He sighed. "Oh yes. It's a brain tumour, but it's a brain tumour and a half . . . a supercharged brain tumour. A really nasty, aggressive one. Down the microscope, it looks beautiful, but then all the really vicious diseases look like that. It's one of

God's little jokes." He paused, then with intense sourness he added, "Full of jokes, is God. Full of them. A right comedian."

Hannah glanced at Sam, then asked Reed, "But she was being treated . . .?"

"She was being *palliated*."

"What does that mean?"

"It's a euphemism. Have you noticed how we live in a euphemistic society? Everything has to be disguised, hidden, pushed away. Call it by another name and then all will be better. The trouble is, deep down they're still the same. The unpleasant is still unpleasant, the vicious is still vicious, the untreatable is still untreatable."

"She was going to die?"

"Oh yes. She was going to die, and how. Maybe in three months, maybe in six."

Sam thought that he understood. "So you killed her."

"So I did as she asked," Reed said with justifiable pedantry.

Sam, though, seemed less impressed by Reed's aspiration to mercy. "Why like that? Why naked in a bath? Why not tablets? You must have access to any number of tablets."

"I know about death, Sergeant. It's my job, God help me. You have to be careful with tablets. They can make you sick, they can make you fit, they can give you unendurable stomach pains. Whereas lying in a warm bath, your lifeblood slowly draining away . . . there is no pain or vomiting or convulsion. Just slow, lazy unconsciousness from which you never wake up."

"You say you slit her wrists and that she was quite happy for you to do it. I can't believe that. It must have hurt like hell. No one would willingly allow someone else – no matter how much they love them – to put a blade through their flesh."

Reed's demeanour suggested that he was in front of a particularly dense medical student. "You're right, of course . . . unless you use local anaesthetic first."

Hannah understood. "The puncture marks on her wrists."

Despite everything, Reed seemed impressed by this piece of professionalism. "They were noticed? Good. Who's your pathologist?"

"Colin Browne."

He nodded, then said gently, "Tell him to treat her with dignity."

"I'm sure he will."

Sam remained untainted by sentimentalism and intruded on the moment. "Forgive me for being dense, but you're asking us to believe that you sat there and watched her die? Isn't that a bit ghoulish?"

"What was I supposed to do? Go and make a cup of tea? Perhaps watch *Countdown* on the telly?"

"But just to sit there? To watch your own wife, who you claim to love, dying?"

Reed was distracted, the last hours of his wife still playing in his mind. "She didn't want to die alone. Who does?"

"Is that the only reason?"

"Yes. Why shouldn't it be?"

"Because I think you enjoyed sitting there while she died."

He shook his head. "It's a funny thing. I know all about death. I'm totally familiar with what it does in all its forms; so much so I can work back from the traces that it leaves on the corpse to deduce what form it took when it visited. That's my skill." He paused, then said, "Yet I know nothing about *dying*. That's as alien to me as the surface of Jupiter."

Sam thought he understood. "So you treated your own wife's death as some sort of peep show?"

"No, Sergeant. I did not enjoy the experience one bit."

"I think you're sick, Dr. Reed. I think you drugged your wife, slit her wrists, and then sat there drinking wine and enjoying her death."

At which Reed gave up on his student. "I don't really care what you think, Sergeant Rich."

"It's bad enough that you were willing to cut your wife's flesh yourself, but then to watch her bleed to death . . ."

Reed's head was bowed, as if penitent. "I didn't want to do it, but when the time came, she couldn't do it herself." In a slightly louder voice he asked, "You don't think I enjoyed doing it, do you?"

"You were fascinated, weren't you? A little experiment: Slit the wrists and then sit back and watch. Did you make notes? Did you get off on it? Was it worth—"

"Shut up!" Reed suddenly looked up at Sam and rose slightly

from his chair, so that they were face to face in a posture of animal aggression.

Hannah said mildly, "Well, perhaps we've got as far as we're going to get for now. Come on, Sam." They stood up, then to Reed she said, "We're going to have to charge you, I'm afraid."

"Of course."

"I'll need to discuss with the superintendent whether it's manslaughter or murder."

"Perhaps—"

She failed to notice that Reed had something more to say. "And of course, when we get the toxicology and the full autopsy reports back, they may change matters."

"No doubt, but—"

"Even if you were acting from the best of motives, I'm afraid that what you did was illegal. Manslaughter is the very best you can hope for."

Reed smiled. "You think so? I would have said that the best would be redemption."

"Redemption for what, Phil? You claim that what you did was some sort of act of kindness, don't you?"

"I suppose so."

"Well, then . . ." She shrugged. "I think you can switch the tape off now, Sam."

But at this, Reed said suddenly, "No!"

"No? Why not?"

He took a deep breath. "I want to tell you something more."

She looked at him, then sat back down slowly. "Really? We don't often get such voluble people in here."

"It's your lucky day, then."

"What do you want to tell us about, Phil?"

"The swirling patterns."

This non sequitur found her lost. "I'm sorry?"

Slowly he repeated the phrase. "The swirling patterns." His tone was dreamy, almost awe filled. "As I cut Kate's wrists, the blood dripped into the bath water and made swirling pink patterns that faded as they curled around and around . . ."

She looked again at Sam, saw that he was as intrigued as she. "What about them?"

But Reed, it seemed, was in a circumlocutory mood. "It

wasn't a happy marriage – hadn't been for some time – but we still loved each other, and as we sat together while she died, we both realized just how much." His voice trailed away for a moment, before, "Of course, happy marriages are made, not born, and ours was made unhappy by only one thing."

"Which was?"

"Children. When they're born, they keep you awake at night, they scream and they puke and they dribble. The lie in their own excrement, and they live entirely for themselves. They suck you dry and then come back for more. They drive you beyond the limits that you thought you could endure, and with a heartlessness that not even the most evil dictator in the world would ever show, they come back for more of you." And with surprise they saw that there were tears in his eyes, and more than that, for he was crying almost uncontrollably. His last words were almost lost in this flood of sorrow, were uttered in a soft moan. "And we could not have them."

Over the sound of a late-night news programme on the radio, Reed heard what might have been the sound of weeping coming from the en suite shower room. He sat forward in bed. "Kate? Are you all right?"

There was no response. "Kate? What's wrong?"

The door opened. Kate, dressed only in a long nightdress, came out. Her eyes were red, her manner combative. "What do you think is wrong? The usual, of course. Another bloody period."

"Oh." He relaxed back into the pillows. As she climbed in beside him he said gently, "Don't worry, Kate. It doesn't matter . . ."

Which was precisely the wrong thing to say. "Of course it matters! It matters to me anyway."

"And to me."

She was on the edge of tears again, but these were not just the tears of sadness and frustration, these were also of anger and suspicion. "Really?"

"Yes, of course."

She stared at him, examined him as if she had caught a pickpocket. "You've never been keen on having a baby." This had been an unspoken accusation for some months now, the elephant in the corner that was, until now, ignored by both of them.

"Yes, I am." He protested his innocence as vehemently as he could, but the effect was spoiled when he went on, "It's just that I'm a bit scared. It's a big step. And there's a lot going on at work . . . I'm under a lot of stress at the moment."

Kate pounced. "Oh, that again." In a caricature of his voice she said, "*I'm tired, Kate. I've had a stressful day.*"

"That's not fair."

She grabbed hold of the duvet, clenched it as if she could squeeze from it life, life that could be poured into a child. "I want a baby, Phil. I *need* one."

He reached across to her, held her. "And we'll have one, Kate. We just need to be patient."

She remained stiff in his arms. "We've been patient for two years now."

"Well . . . sometimes it takes that long."

His words had no effect. "I'm running out of time, Phil."

"Nonsense. You're only thirty-five."

But she was implacable – or rather, the idea that had been growing inside her was implacable.

"I want to see someone."

"What?" Despite asking the question, he knew exactly what she meant. He drew back from her.

"I want to see someone. See if there's a problem."

"Of course there isn't a problem."

"How do we know that?"

"I told you, it's just a question of time and patience."

"But it won't be long before we run out of time." She changed subtly from an accuser to a supplicant. "We have to make sure that everything's all right now."

"Oh, Kate."

"Please?"

Every instinct told him that this was a mistake, that he was heading for consequences that he would regret.

But he loved her. Loved her more and more as the anguish within her grew.

After a long while, he said, "Okay, okay. You win. We'll see someone . . . make sure everything's all right."

"So we went to a specialist. Professor Carter. Nice chap. Bumbling and hearty. Should have been an oncologist – no one would have minded the bad news hearing it from him. I certainly didn't."

Hannah asked, "What was the bad news?"

"Kate's ovaries were misfiring badly. She wasn't producing many eggs, and even if by some chance she managed to throw one down her Fallopian tubes, it was extremely unlikely it would do any good. You see, I'm not up to scratch. I can stand to attention when required, but my little chaps, my storm troopers, are not of the best. A sick and weedy bunch, not at all the kind of recruits who held the British Empire together for so long. I am, to use Professor Carter's oh-so-charming expression, *subfertile*."

"So?"

"So we couldn't have children, not without help."

Sam asked tentatively, "But I thought—"

"That we had a child?" Reed's question was sour enough to scald.

"Yes."

"We live in a modern society, Sergeant. There are always ways and means, if you have enough money."

"IVF."

Reed nodded just once. "In vitro fertilization." He laughed, this time shaking his head. "Do you know what that entails, Hannah?"

"Tell me."

"Pots and pots of money, for a start. And pain – mustn't forget the pain. Injections, examinations, operations. Then there's the humiliation. Oh, there's a great big, excruciating, toe-curling dollop of that; it doesn't stop, either. You think you're over the worst, and then they find some other way to make you feel like a laboratory rat, like the useless excuse for a man that you really are."

"But you were successful," she pointed out.

Reed, though, wasn't listening. "And even that's not really the worst."

"What was the worst?" she asked, although she might just as well have not bothered.

"Five times we went through it. For two long years we counted out our lives with injections and blood samples and disappointments, soaring to the summit of expectation, then plunging into the deepest and darkest of despairs. *That* was the worst. The continual disappointments."

"Eventually it worked, though."

"Yes." He paused, then sighed. "Eventually we had a child."

Reed only remembered to ring at the last moment. He had his overcoat on as he waited for her to answer.

"Kate? Listen . . ."

But Kate had news of her own. "No, Phil. Listen to me. I've got—"

"Kate? I'm sorry. I haven't got much time. I'm afraid I won't be home until late tonight. They've found a body in Nettleton Woods. A teenage boy, and he's naked."

Reed's growing reputation as a forensic pathologist meant that occasions like this were becoming increasingly common. He was aware that it was impinging on Kate, hoped that she understood.

"But—"

"I'm on my way there now, and the police want the autopsy done tonight, so I'll be lucky if I'm home much before two tomorrow morning."

He was sure that she understood. The income was not inconsiderable, after all.

"Oh, but—"

"I know, I know. I'm sorry, but it can't be helped. I really am going to have to go now. Bye, love."

"But I've got some news, Phil—"

Reed, though, was already out of the office, the line already dead. Slowly, Kate pulled the phone away from her ear, then looked at it. In a low voice she said sadly, "Wonderful news . . . I'm pregnant."

"We rowed the next day. No, we *battled*. Nuclear warfare broke out. I was tired – knackered – and Kate, not surprisingly, was crushed. She had planned a big celebration, which I had ruined. Yet how was I to know that she had bought champagne, that for her she had achieved the ultimate, that her sole ambition had been realized? I tried to explain, and then I tried to apologize, but I couldn't get the tone in my voice right; no matter how hard I tried, it always sounded petulant, defensive, even to my ears. Eventually, of course, my reserves of compassion ran out, and I entered combat. I said that she was being pathetic, that it didn't matter which day we celebrated. And, in turn, she questioned my commitment to parenthood, said that I had never really wanted a child.

"We sank deeper and deeper into the fray, rummaging into the far corners of our arsenals for older and older weapons to use, ancient slights and mistakes real and imagined resurrected." He paused for a moment, then as if he had been drinking in a well of memory, he went on, "It lasted all day, and I think that that was the point at which our marriage started to perish, a fruit that had lost its bloom, that had gone beyond the point of maximum sweetness, had slipped into sourness . . . And you know the worst of it?"

"Tell me."

"She was right. The news that she was pregnant made me realize that I *didn't* want a child. I had enough responsibility in my life, without the worry that a newborn would bring. It had always been Kate's desire, not mine, and I had deceived myself into thinking that it was a wish that we shared because I loved her, because I wanted to please her."

"That's only natural."

"Maybe, but it's not enough. I appreciated consciously then for the first time that a baby would only widen the crack that had been gradually appearing between us. I think it was at that moment that I realized how bleak our future was together."

Sam asked, "So you killed her?"

Reed was tired of Sam's hostility. "Is one of us being stupid? I told you – she had an incurable brain tumour. That's why I helped her to die."

With unmistakable sarcasm, Sam said, "Oh yes. I forgot."

Hannah asked, "Did you ever come to blows?"

"Never."

"But the marriage broke down."

He gave this deep consideration. "No, not really. It just *changed*. The reality hit me. If I wanted Kate, I would have to accept a baby as well. Without a baby, there would be no Kate."

"Did that upset you?" This from Sam.

"You keep trying to suggest that Kate and I lived in some sort of conflict, but we didn't. I had no hatred for Kate, never did have." He turned to Sam's superior. "I *loved* her, Hannah. Surely you understand that?"

Sam pointed out, "Most people who love someone don't help them to die."

"There *is* no greater love. I gave away that which I prized above all else."

"Which is a jolly useful excuse for a killer."

Reed made a disgusted noise at the back of his throat, refusing to respond. It was Hannah who asked, "What happened when you realized that things had changed?"

"For the next six months a kind of truce prevailed; no written terms, but in the back of our minds, I think, was the fear that another such skirmish and we might go too far for redemption. For my part, at least I knew that I still loved Kate with just as much conviction as before, and after last night, I know that she still felt the same about me. It was just that we had different needs, wanted different things from our relationship.

"Then her water broke just before Christmas. She was only twenty-five weeks. Until then we had dared to hope that everything was going to be all right, that we would at least be spared a difficult pregnancy."

"But you weren't," guessed Hannah.

"Fat chance." He took a long breath. "She had to be induced, for fear of infection. What came out was a girl, not obviously deformed . . ."

"But?"

"Alice was a weak and pathetic thing, which made it worse. The intensity of Kate's love for her was difficult to witness . . ."

"Why difficult?" Sam's question interrupted his intense reverie.

"Have you ever been in love, Sergeant?"

"Well . . ."

"Of course you have, and you should appreciate this terrible thing called jealousy. Jealousy, not envy, although perhaps there was some of that as well."

"What's the difference?"

"Envy is the desire to possess. Jealousy is the fear of losing something precious. When I looked at Kate, at how she became completely encased by her relationship with Alice, I saw no room for me, saw that I had lost her. In turn, I envied the love that Alice received, wanted a share, thought that I was entitled to one."

"Yet you've stayed with Kate, even after Alice died."

"Oh yes. You see, jealousy is born of love; the stronger the love, the greater the jealousy. When Alice died, only the jealousy was gone." He paused to reconsider. "But not, I see now, the guilt."

"Guilt?"

But Reed did not hear. "It soon turned out that Alice had terrible internal abnormalities. Her lungs failed to develop as they should, and she was functionally blind, probably also deaf although they could never be sure. She had cardiac abnormalities too. She could breathe, but only on near-pure oxygen. She had one kidney, and most probably malformation of her genital tract . . . In the six weeks that she lived, she had *five* bouts of pneumonia."

"Is that what killed her?"

Once more, Reed failed to hear, or at least react. "I knew the neonatologist in charge of her care – have done since medical school. I could see that when he took me to one side, sat me down in his office, he was having a hard time. His voice trembled slightly as he told me that he doubted Alice would live much more than another four weeks, that even if God granted us a miracle, Alice's quality of life would be intolerable . . ." Reed seemed to become lost in the past. Certainly he seemed to be disoriented because his next remark was disjointed. "It was the swirling patterns, I remember best . . ."

Sam breathed. "Swirling patterns again."

Hannah silenced him angrily, but it didn't matter because Reed wasn't listening. "I know the reason for them. It's because you're mixing two liquids of different densities and one flows through the other for a short while before they become totally and perfectly mixed. But it's the beauty of the patterns that I can't get over. Benoit Mandelbrot described it mathematically, talked about partial dimensions, fractals, making it sound like science fiction, as if there were creatures from another place doing something to make them."

"What about the swirls, Phil?"

But Reed was a long way back in his past.

The music of critical care, symphonic variations on life and death, on dying and surviving, on fading into and coming out of a coma. He'd never felt comfortable in an intensive therapy unit, even one decked out with tinsel and with a Christmas tree in the corner. As a pathologist he was of the opinion that what the medical staff did was too far removed from normal medical and nursing practice. Here, it wasn't patients that were treated, but measurements; they worried about the central venous pressure, the blood gas levels, blood biochemistry. The patients were often deliberately sedated, the victims of multiple puncture wounds where tubes entered wounds in the neck and the feet and even in the groins. The patients became not human, but manufactured entities, biomedical organisms, human fused with machine. In a neonatal intensive care unit, however, the victims fought back. Despite being almost overwhelmed by the enormity of the medical intervention to which they were subjected, their humanity was, if anything, magnified. They evoked even greater compassion because they were so small, so apparently incapable of overcoming this adversity.

Alice was intubated again because of the pneumonia, her breathing dictated by a machine. She was still so small, still so sickly, so *raw*. The nurse and doctors were at a hand-over session, their attention as usual on readouts and test results.

Reed stopped in front of the incubator, a small bag of saline dripped slowly into a tube extending from his dying daughter's right ankle. It was nearly nine o'clock at night, and as far as Kate was concerned, Reed was working late, another bloody postmortem.

He looked around. No one was paying attention to him – they were used to one of them (usually Kate) hanging around, getting in the way, unwanted but unassailable, given their part in the drama – and it was all over in ten seconds.

"What was over?" Hannah could sense something terrible and needed to break through Reed's cage of recollection.

"I was planning to turn, walk out at once . . . certainly not hang around . . ."

"What was over?"

"They caught my eye. They were so beautiful, I had to stop and watch them . . ."

"What was over, Phil?"

"It's obvious when you know. Two liquids of different densities . . ."

"What did you do?" She remained patient, though God knew that it was difficult.

"So beautiful, yet so deadly." His voice had taken on a singsong quality.

"Was it the bag of saline? Did you do something to that bag of saline?"

He came to, saw her again. "She was going to die, Hannah, and her death would not have been good. She had nothing to look forward to, no memories to comfort her. She was in limbo . . ."

"What did you put in the bag?"

But Mandelbrot's patterns had caught him again. "The patterns were translucent, like liquid crystals, precious jewels that were slowly dissolving as they moved, dissipating, becoming another small part of the whole."

"I know why, Phil. I need to know *how*."

"And having done it, I walked away. I went to the desk, told them how grateful I was, told them to ring if anything happened, then walked out, past Alice's incubator, past the bag of saline, now looking as clean and pure as it had before . . . I hated myself for that, for the hypocrisy and the lies that I had to tell those doctors and nurses, for pretending not to know what I knew." He paused for breath, then, "The phone call came an hour later, and all hell broke out . . ."

Hannah would have kept asking the question until doomsday. "What was it? What did you put in the bag of saline?"

He looked at her, challenged her almost. "Potassium chloride. Just a 20 ml ampoule, but quite enough . . ." He frowned. "We need potassium, but not too much. A dangerous thing to play with. Too much and the heart stops. No PM will find it, not given those clinical circumstances, and there was no puncture mark, at least none that the medical staff hadn't made."

She asked her next question with studied calm. "You know what you're saying, Phil? You're admitting to the murder of your baby."

"I admit that I gave peace to Alice, Hannah, but I didn't murder her. To murder, you have to take life and Alice never had any. No power on Earth was ever going give her that."

Sam said sarcastically, "Another doctor playing God."

"Another father having to do something terrible for the greater good."

"Who's good? Yours?"

"No," contradicted Reed. "Kate's."

"You're kidding! You did it for yourself. You've admitted to being jealous of your own child."

"You don't understand, Sergeant, and perhaps you never will. Just pray tonight that you're never in a similar position."

"I know that I won't commit murder, and I know that I won't destroy my wife's life."

"Do you think that I enjoyed what I did? That I took some sort of pleasure in seeing Kate's distress? Yet all the while I knew also that what I had done hadn't *caused* it; what I had done had only brought it forward, and at the same time I had ended Alice's awful life."

"You needn't have told us, you know."

"All these years I have wanted to confess to Kate, but never dared. What would have been the point? As she lay there and died, I nearly said something maybe half a dozen times, but held back. I wanted her last hours on Earth to be as happy as possible." He suddenly straightened up in his chair, assumed some dignity. "And I think that I would have continued the silence had I not seen the blood drop into the water, had I not seen it swirl down into nothingness. Dr. Mandelbrot has a lot to answer for, you know."

Hannah sounded almost depressed as she said, "We'll almost certainly have to charge you with murder."

"You think I care about that? You think I care about anything anymore?"

She shook her head. Sam just stared at Reed, who in turn had his head bowed. She said in a formal tone, "Interview terminated at ten thirty-six."

Then she stood up, Sam following her lead. "I'll pray for you, Phil, but they'll roast you alive. They'll chew you up, spit you out, and then smear you into the pavement."

And all Reed said was, "Do me a favour, Hannah."

"What's that?"

"Don't pray for me. Pray that there's no afterlife, that after death, there's nothing."

"Why?"

"Because if there is something that follows life, if by the slightest of chances there is a heaven or hell or something like that, then Kate's there now. She's there even as we speak, and she knows." He suddenly shivered, as if a cold wind had blown past him, as perhaps it had. "She knows, Hannah. She *knows* what I did. I can't cope with that thought."

"Don't count on me in that quarter, Phil. I'm sorry."

She walked to the door, then turned. "We'll be back shortly."

As they walked back to Hannah's office, Sam said quietly, "He deserves everything he's going to get."

"Probably."

He was surprised by the doubt in her voice. "Probably?"

They were on the stairs before she spoke again. "Do you love me as much as that?"

"What do you mean?"

"Do you love me enough to do what he did?"

He couldn't see what she was talking about. "He murdered two people. You want me to copy him?"

She halted, turned to him. "Sam, he threw away his soul – and not just his soul, his whole earthly being, as well – for the woman he loved. Would you do that for me?"

"Don't be stupid, Hannah. He just did what he did for himself."

"You think so?"

"How else can you explain it? You surely don't believe that crap he fed us about loving her."

"Hatred's not the only reason for killing . . . in fact, it's quite a rare one. Love's a far commoner motive."

"I'd never kill for love."

She looked at him long and hard, then continued walking up the stairs. There was a small smile on her face.

"No," she said. "I can see that you wouldn't."

NO PLACE TO PARK

Alexander McCall Smith

1.

It started as a challenge, the unforeseen outcome of an absurd conversation at a writers' festival in Western Australia. There was the usual panel on stage, and an audience made up of the sort of people who frequent the crime panels – predominantly women, but with a sprinkling of men; highly educated, highly literate, and highly imaginative. And they shared another characteristic of the reader of mysteries: they were fascinated by the gory details of behaviour in which they would themselves never engage. These people would never commit a murder, not in their wildest dreams. Nor would they mix with people who did such things, no matter how fascinating they might find their company – on the page. But they loved to read about murder, about the sudden, violent termination of human life, and of how it was done.

The panel was discussing realism in crime fiction. Two practitioners of the art, writers of well-received *policiers* were pitted against the literary critic of a local paper. The critic, who read some, but not very much, of such fiction expressed the view that there was a surfeit of realistic gore in the contemporary mystery.

"Look at the average crime novel these days," he pointed out, stabbing at the air with an accusing finger. "Look at the body count. Look at the compulsory autopsy scenes, some of which actually start the novel, would you believe it! The autopsy room, so familiar, so comforting!. Organs are extracted and weighed. Wounds examined for angle-of-entry, and it's all so, well . . . it's all so *graphic*." He paused. From the audience there came a brief outbreak of laughter. It could not be graphic enough for these people.

He warmed to his theme. "But there are crimes other than murder, aren't there? There's fraud and theft and extortion. There's tax evasion, for heaven's sake! And yet all we read about in books in this genre is murder. Murder, murder, murder." He paused, and looked accusingly at the two authors beside him. "Why not write about more mundane offences? Why not write about things that actually happen? Murder's very rare, you know. Not that one would think so to read your books."

One of the author's grinned at the audience. "Weak stomach," he said, gesturing to the critic. "Can't take it."

The audience laughed. They had no difficulty taking it.

"Seriously, though," said the critic. "How about it? How about a realistic crime novel dealing with something day-to-day – some low level offence that really happens."

"Such as?" asked one of the authors.

The critic waved a hand in the air. "Oh anything," he said lightly. "Parking violations, perhaps. Those happen all the time. They're real."

Everybody joined in the laughter, even the critic. "Go on," he said to the authors. "Why doesn't one of you people do something like that. Give up murder. Get real. Start a new genre."

One of the authors, George Harris, a successful crime writer from Perth, stared at him. He had been laughing, but now he looked thoughtful.

2.

George shared a small bungalow with a girlfriend, Frizzie, who ran a tie-and-dye tee-shirt store in Fremantle. They had lived together for five years now, always in the same, narrow house near Cottesloe Beach. George liked to surf, and Cottesloe was a good place to do it, as the Indian Ocean broke directly on the broad expanse of sand, unhindered by anything more than the tiny sliver of Rottnest Island. He still surfed, although the thought of what was in the water beneath him was always in his mind, a nagging fear, repressed, but still there, somewhere below the surface. Eight months earlier somebody whom he knew, although only vaguely, had been taken by a great white within a stone's throw of the edge of the beach. It had not only brought it home to him that surfing in Australia had its perils – one was in *their* habitat, after all – but it gave him an idea for the plot of his next book. There would be rivalry amongst surfers, something to do with a lover or a motorbike, and one surfer would plan to dispose of another. What better way than to fake a shark attack, which would be administered, from below, by a large knife which he had specially made in his garage. This knife would have a number of serrations along the edge, each carefully honed to the shape of a shark's tooth, and it would leave just the right wounds for the inevitable conclusion (in the autopsy room) – death by shark attack. It would be carried out at a time when nobody else was about and certainly nobody would see the diver down below, with his knife glinting in the water like a silver fish. It was a good plot, even if it would not make comfortable reading for surfers. And it was not comfortable writing, George reflected, for a crime novelist who happened to be a surfer.

He had barely started this new novel, this surfing story, and was tempted to give it up. He had once before persisted with a book his heart was not in, and he had wasted eight months in the gestation of something that did not work and that had to be abandoned. He was determined not to make the same mistake again, and so when he started to think about this parking story he was ready for a new project. The suggestion that a crime novel should concern itself with something so minor as illegal parking had been made in jest, of course, but, when one thought about it, why not? It was such an outrageously silly idea that it could well end up making its mark in a genre of fiction that was becoming increasingly crowded. This was different, and people wanted something different. There were so many police procedurals, all dealing with hard-bitten homicide squads on their mean streets. Now here was something that was at the completely opposite end of the spectrum, and it would register with people. They needed a smile, and he would give it to them. It would be gentle, whimsical stuff, devoid of violence and mayhem. He could set it on his own doorstep, in Western Australia, and it could be full of local colour.

He warmed to the idea, and began to imagine a plot. There would be tension within the parking department. There would be rivalry as to who could give motorists the most tickets. There would be a budding love affair between two parking officers, and this would be frowned upon by the police superintendent. They would have to meet in secret, at the busy end of the street, perhaps, where motorists were always parking in the wrong place and getting ticketed . . .

George smiled at the thought of it. But there was a serious matter to consider: he would have to get the world of parking officers right. He would have to go to the traffic department at his local police headquarters and get permission to tag along for a day or two with one of the officers. There should be no difficulty about this: the Perth police had always co-operated with him and he, in turn, had painted a flattering picture of them. In George's books, the Perth police always outsmarted visiting detectives from Sydney or Melbourne. They liked that.

He told his Frizzie about the next plot. She was the only person in whom he confided about his books before they were published. She was a surfer, like him, and they would sometimes lie on their boards, out beyond the waves, talking about the ins and outs of whatever book he was working on. As they chatted, the water lapping against their boards, George hoped that there was nothing down below, listening – so to speak.

3.

It was arranged for him to go out with a parking officer on a Friday. It was a good day, they explained to him, as farmers often came into town then and parked illegally.

"They forget that they're in a city," joked the officer. "They think they're out in the bush still and they can park anywhere! We sort them out for sure!"

George noted the vindictive edge to this remark. Farmers deserved sympathy, he thought, with their struggle against drought and pests and low agricultural prices. But he did not say anything; he just filed the comment away for future use. He looked at the officer. He was a small man, with a rather defeated look about him. Obviously parking duty was not for the high-flier. High-fliers went to homicide, he imagined.

They spent the morning going up and down a busy shopping street. There were several violations noticed, each of which was explained to him in great detail by the officer.

"This driver is a serious offender," the officer said, pointing to a battered Holden. "Tax disc is out-of-date. He hasn't even bothered to put money in the machine, and . . ." the and was stressed, as the final word in a litany of sins might be given extra weight. "*And* he's way over the line. Look at that! Creating a hazard for other drivers. Shameless!"

"What are you going to do?" asked George, staring at the offending car. It was a homely vehicle, much-loved, he suspected, and on the back seat was a child's toy, a teddy bear.

"I'm going to book him for the lot," said the officer, taking out his notebook and beginning to write down the list of violations.

After that encounter they moved off, on foot, down a side-street. It was a narrow access lane and there were prominently-displayed signs stating that parking was forbidden. Yet there was a car parked halfway down the street.

"Look at that," said the officer. "Blatant. And they're sitting in the vehicle too. Bold as brass."

The two men in the car, deep in what appeared to be heated conversation, had not seen them and they gave a start of surprise when the officer tapped smartly on the half-lowered window on the driver's side.

"Do you realize that you're illegally parked, Sir?" said the officer firmly. "Would you show me your driver's licence please."

The driver opened his mouth to say something, but no sound came. He looked shocked.

"Come on, Sir," said the officer. "Don't hold me up."

After that it all happened rather quickly. The driver reached forward, started the engine and thrust the car into gear. Then, with a roar, it pulled away. George reeled back in surprise, while the officer fumbled for his radio.

It was then that that they saw the body under the car, lying with arms stretched out, an ugly red-black stain on the front of his shirt. It was a body of the sort which crime writers like to describe in graphic detail. Eyes open but unseeing. Fingers clenched. Hair tousled. Feet at an odd angle. And so on.

4.

The fact that the officer managed to get the registration number of the car meant that a rapid arrest was made. The driver and his companion, it emerged, were well-known members of the Perth criminal underworld, such as it was. One of them, the passenger, was in fact the brother of somebody whom George knew in surfing circles and who sometimes helped Frizzie take her board off the car if George was not around. He had also seen him exchange a few casual words with Frizzie on the beach. Perth was like that; it was a friendly city, intimate; people could get to know one another.

George was called as a witness in the murder trial. There was not much that he could say, of course, other than that he had seen the two men at the scene of the crime. But it was enough to worry the surfing brother, who came to George and asked him whether he would be kind enough not to give evidence.

"But I have to," said George. "It's my civic duty. I have to give evidence. Sorry it's your brother."

"In that case, mate," said the surfer. "Watch your back. Something unpleasant could happen to you, you know, if you dob my brother in. Just remember that."

George contemplated going to the police to report this rather unsubtle attempt at intimidation, but decided against it. It would be difficult to prove that a threat had been made, as there were no witnesses to the occurrence. He knew all about that problem, as he had used it once in a novel. It was strange, he thought, how truth emulated fiction – eventually.

Frizzie was uncomfortable. She urged him not to give evidence, or to be a bit vague about the identification.

He said to her: "Anyone would think that you wanted that guy to get off. Just because his brother helps you with your surf board. What am I to think? That you're having an affair with him or something?"

"Don't be ridiculous," she said.

5.

Two weeks before the trial was due to take place, he went surfing. It was early morning, the time he liked best, when there was virtually nobody around at Cottesloe Beach, other than the occasional dog-owner taking a dog for a run along the sand. Such beauty, he thought; the sky so wide, the sea, the sand. Such beauty in this country. All around one.

He paddled out and rode one or two waves in. The surf was quite high and the water was warmer than usual. There was somebody else, another surfer, some way away, and then he seemed to go away again; it was very quiet. George paddled his board back out. He looked up at the sky and wondered.

He looked down. There was something in the water and his heart gave a lurch. He peered down. It was easy to confuse shadows or a frond of seaweed for something they were not; one had to control the imagination. He searched the water. A flash of metal, from down below it seemed. Impossible, he thought. Impossible. I told nobody.

And he thought, as he slipped into the water, how life was not like this, that it was absurd that parking of all things should have this result. Absurd and unlikely. But now there was only water, and regret.

GIRL'S BEST FRIEND

Judith Cutler

When a guy presents you with an engagement ring, a socking great oval ruby surrounded by diamonds, it might seem a tad ungrateful to subject it to scrutiny with a jeweller's eyepiece.

Griff, my adoptive grandfather, business partner, and antique-dealer extraordinaire, wouldn't ever soil his lips with expressions like *looking a gift-horse in the mouth*. But he did ask, as he prepared supper that evening, "Surely that breaches all rules of etiquette, my darling Lina?"

I slipped the ornate jewel back on to my ring finger, which I wiggled so that it picked up the candlelight. Griff always made meals an occasion, even worrying about the niceties of what cutlery to use when serving Thai stir-fry in an Elizabethan cottage at the heart of a Kentish village. "I think I was a bit bowled over," I conceded slowly. "All that bended-knee stuff and the promise of a round-the-world cruise for our honeymoon. For me, Lina Townend!"

"And there I thought chivalry had died out in your generation," he said.

"Apparently not," I said coolly. But how could I snub my dearest friend? "Griff, what was I doing? This is Piers Hamlyn, for goodness' sake!"

"Piers Hamlyn, who, despite his predilection for cords and body-warmers, is a most dashing piece of manhood," Griff burbled. "Those shoulders! That neat bum!"

"Those cornflower-blue eyes, perfect complexion, and honey-coloured hair," I added.

"And second cousin once removed of your own father, Lord Elham," Griff reflected, with distinctly less enthusiasm.

"Which doesn't say much for him, does it?" I asked quietly.

"Just because Lord Elham – how strange that neither of us ever refers to him as anything more intimate – is not the purest diamond in the tiara doesn't mean his cousin is flawed. Though I must admit," he continued, allowing a tiny quaver to creep into his voice, and sinking into his frail-old-man mode, "it has been what we used to call a whirlwind romance."

It had. And considering that women of my generation tended not to demand courtship and rings and weddings before – as Griff gracelessly put it – hopping into bed, it was a very romantic romance. Flowers; candlelit dinners; the question popped within two weeks of our first meeting at a big and classy antiques fair at a vast country pile – it belonged to another of his cousins – and no attempt to go beyond a not terribly passionate snog.

What on earth had I been doing? The ring said, in a very snide voice, "Doing pretty well for yourself, considering."

I whipped it off and peered closely at it again.

"Oh, Griff, why didn't I tell Piers to ask you for my hand? You could have asked him about his prospects and how he meant to maintain me!" Which would have given me time to think.

"I take it you wouldn't want me to go so far as to reject him as a suitor?"

"Yes. No. I wish I knew." I gave the ring another squint. What was wrong with me? Or rather, what was wrong with it? What had got all my divvy's antennae a-twitch?

Its provenance, for one thing. Every dealer likes to know where an item's been before it comes to him. You might think it's enough to know the maker, but forging manufacturer's marks is easy-peasy to a master, as is copying a painter's signature on a faked masterpiece. So you want to know who bought it and from whom, all through its life. In the case of a picture, the number of times it's been exhibited and where. As for a ring like this, it's tricky and hardly worth bothering, so long as you can see the hallmark on the band, in this case one declaring it was made in Birmingham, that City of a Thousand Trades, way back in 1879. So it was the right age to have a silver mount for the stones, as opposed to the stronger platinum claws used later.

Everything was right about it.

Or not.

"I'd love you to take a look at it," I said. "After all, it's not exactly my area, is it?"

"At our level, dear heart, we have to be Jacks and Jills of all trades. I know you can beat most people hollow when it comes to Victorian china, but that doesn't mean you shouldn't turn your hand to other things. I know, I know. You were spot-on with the date – but then," he added, "I'd have been disappointed if you hadn't been. You worked hard to learn the assay marks." He smiled, and tucked a lock of my hair in place. "There's a good brain between those ears of yours, my child. For all you worry about having no paper qualifications, you're a very bright young woman."

I didn't argue. But school and I had been relative strangers to each other, thanks to my life in care after my mother's death. You'd have expected my father to take me in, maybe. But not my father, Lord Elham, of Bossingham Court. Lord Elham, old rogue that he was, had taken no more notice of me than he'd taken of my other thirty siblings. But then, he claimed he'd never known about any of us, not in any detail. And indeed, it was me who'd found him, not the other way round. ("*I* who'd found him, dear heart," Griff would have told me gently.) And he hadn't been especially keen on me, at least not until I'd dug him out of a particularly nasty hole and managed to cast him in the light not of a greedy criminal but of a public benefactor. My father called himself a gentleman – but since I'd always believed in the adage *gentleman is as gentleman does*, I'd yet to see him deserve the term. Or the title Noble Lord. Lord Elham. And no, that didn't make me Lady anything, since I was born on what Griff would call the wrong side of the blanket. Well, with all those brothers and sisters in the picture, you'd probably worked that out for yourself. He'd taken the huff when I'd refused to leave Griff and go and live at Bossingham Hall, but that's another story.

"Now, do I look at this bauble as if admiring your betrothed's taste, or as if valuing it for auction?"

"As my dearest friend," I said humbly. "And under a very strong lamp."

"Tomorrow morning, then."

Before I washed up I hung the ring on a little Edwardian ring-tree that for as long as I could remember Griff had kept beside the kettle. That was Griff for you. Forward planning. Or, more likely, seeing a charming little item going cheap and giving it a good home. Most of the stuff we bought we had to sell, of course – that's how dealers make a living. But Griff made it a rule that we only bought what we ourselves liked. Usually.

"If you like something, you find out about it," he'd told me when he'd first employed me. "And the more you know about something the more people regard you as an expert and come to trust you. Trust is like virtue – it's its own reward."

"And it doesn't damage your prices."

He'd chuckled. "Clearly, dear heart, you are a dealer in the bud."

Over the next two or three years, I'd blossomed a bit. What I was best at was restoring damaged Victorian china, and *not* passing it as perfect. Unlike some I could name. So people trusted me when I said something was good, you see. And my prices rose accordingly. Occasionally other dealers would come to me when they found something hard to shift. If it was pukka, and only then, I'd pop it on our stall and sell it at the usual commission. Not that I would be selling Piers's ring on my stall, for goodness' sake!

"What worries me," Griff said as he wiped up, "is that despite his lineage Piers works at the lowest end of the market. Collectibles, indeed! Junk, in other words."

"There's room for all sorts – and we're not exactly at the top end ourselves."

I wished the words back: What Griff was really afraid of was that I'd abandon him.

If only I could have talked Piers over with a woman. But I hadn't many women friends my own age, thanks to my miserable upbringing, and Griff, though he was dearer to me than anyone seemed able to imagine, was hardly a role model for someone as young and romantic as me (or should that be *I?*): He'd been in a settled if semi-detached relationship for more years than he cared to remember.

Washing-up done, I dried my hands and slapped on some cream. As beauty routines went, it didn't go far, and Griff tended to nag when I didn't use sunblock or moisturiser. I had to admit that the ring looked better on well-tended mitts than it would have done on my pre-Griff paws. Or did it look too good? Despite Griff's offer, I took it and the eyeglass up to my workroom and switched on the strong spotlight I need for the most delicate restoration work. And then I called Griff.

"You've got better eyes than I have," he said, somewhat grudgingly since I'd hauled him from his favourite television programme, a docudrama about civilians being tested to SAS standards. "But you're right. Those two stones aren't exactly the same as the others. Pretty close. But a ring that age is bound to have been repaired."

"Cleaned and repaired?"

"Why not? The young man wants to impress his beloved."

"Piers didn't say anything about a repair. He said it came straight from a sale – he'd only cleaned it up a bit to see what he'd got."

"He's cleaned it very well indeed. To professional standards," Griff mused. "So why didn't he come clean – as clean as this ring, in fact – and simply tell you it had come with two stones missing and he'd had them replaced?"

"Why indeed?"

Next time we met, this time in a church hall in the Cotswolds so cold that Griff's knuckles turned bluey-white, the rest of his fingers purple, Piers presented me with another ring.

"I'm not asking you to choose between them," he said pettishly as I slipped it admiringly onto my right hand: It was a sapphire version of my ruby, with a lovely Sri Lankan stone, much lighter than you get these days, that put it back into the Victorian period.

I bit my lip: I'd better not tell him I preferred it.

"I'm asking you to sell it. It's too good for my stall: It'll just disappear amongst all the collectibles. But you've got nice, classy stuff. Everything guaranteed antique, with nothing less than a hundred years old."

I nodded. We were totally out of place at this fair, as Griff bitterly acknowledged, to which we'd only come because Griff had a Thespian friend in the area and because I could meet up with Piers.

"China, glass, and treen," I said. "No jewellery."

"Then it'll stand out all the better, especially with a spotlight trained on it. And your hand to model it." He kissed it with enough passion to tempt me.

"I'll have to ask Griff," I said.

"He lets you fly solo with your restored china," he pointed out. "I can't see how he could object if you want to branch out into jewellery, particularly stuff as nice as this."

"I'll ask," I said coldly, "because I value his opinion." He should have known by now never to argue about anything concerning Griff.

"Do I recollect that you come of age shortly, my child?"

"You know I do. And we agreed to have no fuss." Largely because Griff was increasingly terrified by his own birthdays, and in any case celebrating being twenty-one was a bit old-fashioned these days.

"It occurs to me that you are so attracted to that sapphire ring that it would make an ideal gift."

I looked him in the eye. "Not so much attracted as suspicious, Griff. You look." I passed the lovely thing to him.

"The sapphire's exquisite," he sighed. Then he stopped. "How many dodgy stones do you make it?"

"Three this time. I shall have to mark it sold as seen."

"And the price? If you do that it'll never reach what he's asking. And I have an idea you were relying on the commission to buy your wedding dress."

"Wedding, shmedding." I took the ruby ring off as well. The two big stones blinked enticingly at me. The diamonds surrounding them didn't.

"Shame," Piers greeted my confession that we'd not been able to sell the ring. "But why don't you keep trying? And I was hoping you'd shift these earrings for me." He produced an elaborate case, fine leather and watered silk, containing a dazzling pair with free-hanging emeralds and diamonds on tiny springs.

"Victorian again." They were so fine I'd have expected to see them at Christie's.

"Got this aunt who's fallen on hard times. Doesn't want anyone to know." He tapped the side of his nose. "Noblesse oblige, and all that."

My eyes widened at the price he wanted. "That's well above our usual range – but still not enough for such a lovely set." I braced myself. "Are you sure these aren't off the back of some lorry, Piers?"

"From the collection of Lady Olivia Spedding." He looked coldly down at me, rather like the Duke of Wellington, now I came to think of it, holding out his hand for the earrings.

I returned them, shrugging. "No skin off my nose," I informed him, my voice at its most common, all accent and attitude.

I wasn't so much surprised as taken aback when, as we packed up at the end of a not especially profitable day, Piers sidled up, dropping the familiar jeweller's box on our stall. "Usual commission," he said, and disappeared.

It was Griff who got first look at them with the eyeglass this time. "Continental," he said. "And all good stones."

"You mean—?"

"What do you think?"

I peered. "Beautifully clean. Everything hunky-dory for the period. Feel the weight – they wouldn't half stretch the old earlobes. Lovely quality stones – all of them. I'd be honoured to sell these."

I thought I heard Griff mutter something about sprats catching mackerel, but perhaps I was mistaken.

A couple of weeks later I handed over the cash for the earrings in the traditional brown envelope. It was hardly out of my hand when another slightly battered jewel case appeared, purple leather outside, purple silk in, showing off a diamond pendant and matching earrings to perfection. Victorian, again, and perhaps a bit fussy for modern tastes.

It was all so low-key we might have been business partners,

not engaged to become life partners. Theoretically engaged. Anyone who could palm off a piece with stones I could feel in my bones were false was no longer my fiance. I said nothing yet. Grassing someone up was something not to be done lightly. But in a trade that totally depended on trust, what else could I do?

Griff removed the eyepiece and rubbed his face. "And what four-letter word, first letter S, last letter M, springs to your suspicious mind?"

"Scam," I said flatly.

"A profitable one, too. You buy a couple of these so-called man-made diamonds for a song, remove two decent-sized but not particularly noticeable stones from pieces where no one will immediately notice the exchange, replace them with the fakes, and pocket the difference. If you got brave enough to replace a one-carat diamond, say, with a fake one, you could profit by four or five thousand pounds."

I nodded. "To get away with it, you really need someone totally reliable like us. If by any chance people found they'd bought a wrong 'un they'd hotfoot it back to us and complain. And we could only say we'd had them from someone else and terribly sorry and here's your money back."

"And you complain to Piers, who laughs in your face. Or says his great-aunt or whatever must have replaced them to raise cash for her gambling habit. Or his aunt's dead, and he reminds us it's *caveat emptor*."

There weren't many Latin phrases I knew but that was one of them. "To my mind it's more a case of *caveating* Trading Standards or even the police."

"Oh, dear one, you can't use *caveat* like that," he sighed. "But you're right about the legal implications. To my mind, the only question is how much Piers knows about it."

"If his genes are anything like Lord Elham's, a lot. But we need proof: You and I know there's something wrong, but neither of us could stand up in a court of law and say what these stones actually are. And surely, Griff, in that thick Filofax of yours, you've got the number of a – whatsit – a jewel expert."

"Gemologist, angel heart. Yes, I'm sure I have. One, more-

over, I can trust implicitly. Now, that chicken should be cooked
to perfection."

Over supper we debated long and loud what we should do
next. My initial impulse was to pack up the pendant and
earrings and send them straight back to Piers. With both
gorgeous rings. But if we did, he'd certainly try to palm them
off on someone else less canny than us.

"Equally, of course, Piers might be an innocent dupe of
someone to whom he'd innocently taken old items to be
cleaned," Griff observed resignedly. "And it's the cleaner
who's at fault."

I pulled a face. But it was of course true. "So how do we find
out – any of this?"

I might have known who would do the dirty work. Yours truly,
of course. Well, not for anything would I have put Griff at risk.
His arthritis was better since he'd cut down the drink and was
downing measures of an evil-looking liquid prescribed by an
alternative therapist, but he tended more and more these days to
let me go to sales while he stayed at home and ran the shop.
That way he had more energy to go to the very taxing antiques
fairs we set up our stall at. So there was no argument. Especially
as I didn't tell him what I was planning.

He and Lord Elham had disliked each other at sight. Lord
Elham loathed Griff's campiness, Griff Lord Elham's dishonesty. At bottom, I suspect Lord Elham wanted to wrest me from
Griff's care, for no better reason than that he needed a skivvy.
Griff wanted to keep me with him because he loved me. There
was no point in forcing them into each other's company: I'd
sussed out that getting to know each other would only make
matters worse. The main reason why I'd spend occasional days
at Bossingham Hall was because Lord Elham had rooms full of
the most amazing junk, some of it extremely saleable. Since his
favourite tipple – indeed, his only tipple – was champagne, my
skill in sorting out items I could sell for him was called for quite
often. This time, on the principle of setting a thief to catch a
thief, I popped round at a time when daytime TV was at its
nadir, taking with me a couple of homemade casseroles he could
warm up in his new microwave. He looked worse than ever:

Though he was ten years younger than Griff, his complexion was purply-grey and very dry looking. At least since I'd come on the scene his hair looked better: He'd seen some terribly expensive product in a TV advert and I now bought some whenever I shopped for his champagne. If only I could get him to exercise something other than his zapper thumb and drinking elbow.

"Piers Hamlyn!" he exploded. "Going to marry Piers Hamlyn! And why didn't the young bastard seek my permission?"

I ignored the term "bastard," quite restrained of me in the circumstances. "I don't think young men do, these days." It was one thing wishing I'd asked Griff to vet my choice, quite another letting Lord Elham in on the act. "In any case, I said I was engaged to him, not that I was going to marry him." I explained about the dodgy diamonds.

He slammed his fist on the Sheraton occasional table beside his chair. I winced. "Any young man who puts fake diamonds on my daughter's hand will not marry her."

All that champagne was making him a bit slow. Or it might have been his diet, mostly Pot Noodles, with the odd frozen ready-meal thrown in.

"He doesn't know I know they're fake," I said, taxing his limited abilities.

"If you say they are, they are," he declared loyally, topping up my 1860 cut-crystal flute.

"I need to prove it. And I want to know if it's his scam, or if he's a victim, like me. He's brought a few things for me to sell – from the collection of Lady Olivia Spedding, he says."

"Olivia Spedding! Good God! I didn't know she was still alive."

"Fallen on hard times; having to sell bits and pieces. Would she have had a few stones replaced here and there?"

"More likely to have the whole lot exchanged for paste," he mused. "You sure she's still alive?"

"He ought to know: He's her nephew. Great-nephew."

"Is he indeed? That must mean I'm related to her. Are you sure?" He peered at me, then, more hopefully, at the bottom of his glass.

"It's what he says. Anyway, what shall I do?"

A familiar expression of piggy greed settled on his puffy features. "Sell that sauceboat for me and I'll make a few enquiries."

It may have looked like a sauceboat, but it was in fact an eighteenth-century ladies' urinal – a vessel for ladies to wee into during long sermons or ceremonies. But that made it more, rather than less, valuable. I hoped that the women in the family had more sense of hygiene than my parent, or I couldn't have sworn that anyone had washed it before it had come to its present use.

Even with my ten per cent commission, I was able to return a week or so later with four cases of champagne.

"That Piers Hamlyn chappie still sniffing after you?" he greeted me, though his eyes were on the cardboard boxes in the back of our van.

"He's in Ireland," I said. "Doing a few sales." Which was unlikely, come to think of it, given his stock in trade, which last time I saw him included a couple of Ty Beanie Bears. If he'd taken me, with my divvy skills, I'd have made us a mint. But for some reason he'd never suggested it, and I was too sure I didn't want to marry him to ask. And then I cursed myself for being so damned moral – maybe Ireland was where he got his dodgy gems.

Lord Elham sniffed. "Not good enough for you, my girl. Not good enough."

Not good enough for the illegitimate daughter of a drunken old lecher like him? Griff referred to him fastidiously as a reprobate, which sounded nicely eighteenth-century.

"The man's a fraud. At least that tosh about Olivia Spedding is. Popped her clogs years ago: no stamina, those Speddings. So wherever he's getting it from it's not Olivia. In any case, she spent all her dosh on the gee-gees: never wore a diamond in her life. You sure you got the name right?"

I didn't see how I could have misheard a name like that, but until I got all that booze into his domain and a glass of it in his hand, I'd get no more sense out of him.

When he was settled at last, I asked, "Has Piers any other relations who might have asked him to sell the jewellery?"

"That was the respectable branch of the family. Have you met Hamlyn's family yet?"

I shook my head. I had an idea it was because he was afraid I wouldn't pass muster, and would start dropping aitches and eating my peas with a knife. Or was it only the middle classes like Griff who worried about such niceties?

"Or his friends?"

Another shake of the head.

"Are you sure he's kosher?"

I looked him straight in the eye. "That's what I'm hoping you'd tell me."

He took the sort of pull on his champagne that I can only manage on water, and then it gives me hiccups. "Tell you what, you sell those plates for me and get me some more bubbly, and I'll see what I can do."

I nodded. I knew of old that the plates were a pretty tatty collection, mostly more Piers's sort of price range than mine, but for the information he might come up with I'd buy him a case of fizz myself.

In the event, I didn't have to. I found a red anchor mark Chelsea plate at the bottom.

"Ireland!" Griff repeated, when I reported back our conversation as word for word as I could make it. "Why didn't you tell me the little rat had gone to Ireland?"

"Because I know you don't like me talking about him, and I thought you'd think I was upset not to be invited."

He frowned as he worked out what I meant. That was the trouble with not finding words easy: Sometimes they shuffled themselves into clumsy lumps. "And you weren't upset?"

"Glad not to be. I wouldn't want to sleep with him under false pretences."

"God knows where you got your moral principles from – not Lord Elham."

"Mostly from you!"

I could see he was pleased. But he added, quite seriously, "On the other hand, think of the stuff you could have picked up over there. Anyway, Ireland. And Dublin in particular. Diamond merchant."

"Not Amsterdam? Or Hatton Garden?"

"We're not talking about real diamonds, are we, petal? Not according to my contact." He touched his nose.

"They are fakes?"

"As true as a six-pound note. As we always suspected."

"But that doesn't get us any further forward with Piers. For my own satisfaction, Griff, I need to know if he's running the show or if he's a dupe. I may suspect . . . but I need to know."

"For that, my love, unless you wish to involve the police, you may have to rely on Lord Elham."

"Set a thief to catch a thief, you mean."

"Not in your trade vehicle!" Lord Elham insisted.

"I'm not going to turn up advertising it's me, am I? We'll do what Griff and I always do if we want to go to London. We catch the train, and after that take a cab. There's nothing more incognito than a cab, surely."

"And you're happy to lurk outside the establishment – in that cab, for prcfcrcncc – while I Do the Deed?"

I wasn't, but I didn't see my getting admitted into what called itself a massage parlour but sounded more like a high-class brothel, except as an employee. And I'd always drawn the line at that even when I was at my lowest, before Griff came to my rescue.

So when the day came, and Lord Elham had had the nod and the wink he'd hoped for, I collected him in my Fiesta and drove us to Ashford International Station.

"Travel first class? Dear me, I can't afford that!" was his reaction to my offer, but I could tell he was sacrificing himself. However, he perked up considerably when he saw even the second-class areas were comfortable and our seats even had a little table on which to place our champagne, which I was determined to ration. To my amazement, he showed me how to tackle Sudoku, rattling through *The Times*' fiendish puzzle as if he were a child with an abacus. The journey passed surprisingly quickly.

"Now," I prompted him, "you remember how that little tape recorder works? And you won't have more than one bottle?"

"Shampoo at six hundred pounds a pop? You jest!"

*   *   *

All three faces were serious as we sat around Griff's dining table. He'd made a huge effort, not to impress Lord Elham, but to show me how generous-spirited he was, entertaining a man he still saw as his rival under his own roof. To be honest, the delicate soup, tender guinea fowl, and exploding meringues were wasted on my father. But he too was on his best behaviour, praising as judiciously as if we didn't know that Spicy Beef Pot Noodles were his real preference, and gossiping about the famous faces he'd seen at the brothel. I'd spotted, from the depths of my cab, a further couple he'd missed. One face we'd both seen was Piers Hamlyn's.

At last Lord Elham extended a spatulate finger and pressed the Play button. We could hear Piers's voice quite clearly, against the chink of glasses and the raucous voices of the rich. He was boasting about his fence, how it was like taking candy from a baby.

And then we heard Lord Elham's voice: "Young man, it happens to be my baby from whom you are taking the confectionary. My little girl Lina. She will not be marrying you, of course. And, unless you want an expose that would shock even your family to the roots, I suggest you listen very carefully to what I say . . ."

"The Falklands!"

"I do wish, my love, you wouldn't squeak," Lord Elham reproached me, just as if he were Griff. "Yes, the Falklands. I believe he will find his niche out there: sheep or mineral rights, whichever interests him more. Not forever. Just long enough for you to mop up all the fake gems he's scattered about the country." He laid a wad of notes on the table. "That should suffice. You will keep any change." He looked at my ringless finger. "You should find enough there to purchase genuine stones for the two rings in your keeping." He sat back, belched, and looked as his watch. "Now, I always watch *Big Brother* at this time. And then, my child, you can run me home."

THE PREACHER

Kevin Wignall

Hector could see that one apology wasn't going to be enough. Either that or the old man hadn't really believed his first apology, which was understandable because it hadn't been genuine. But then, Hector had only been flippant because he'd thought the old man had to be joking. Because who took offence over stuff like that in this day and age? Hector's grandmother was nearly ninety and she could probably teach this old guy some new words. Even so . . .

"Hey look, I really am sorry, man, I didn't realize. I'll be more careful." He didn't get a response so he looked across at him.

"Just keep your eyes on the road."

Hector faced forward and made a show of looking out at the night-time streets.

Sidney, the old man, had the feeling he and the young punk wouldn't become friends. It wasn't just the cursing and the profanity, it was an air the punk had about him, like no standard was too low. And he just didn't shut up, either – he just never ran out of things to say.

Of course, Mr Costello had asked Sidney to take him under his wing, felt he just needed a little guidance, that he'd come on with the right role model, so here they were, driving out to Nolan's house to sort out a little company business. And because Mr Costello had asked him to take the punk along, he was taking the punk along, that's the guy he was.

He could tell the punk was thinking about something now, that he was itching to speak yet again.

Hector had kept turning the word over in his mind, the word that had upset the old man. Having said that, the old man was such a stickler, he probably got upset if someone pronounced "oregano" in the wrong way. But the word that had actually upset him also upset a lot of people, and the more he thought about it, that hardly seemed fair, because it was a good word.

"You know," said Hector, "that word I just used, you know, the word you didn't like, I mean, the F word . . ."

"I know which word you mean," snapped Sidney.

"Yeah, well that one. I mean, why is it a bad word? I don't mean, why is it like a curse word, I mean, why do people use it to talk about bad things, because it's a good thing. You know, to fu . . . What I'm saying is, to do that thing is a good thing, enjoyable, so why do people use the word to describe bad things?"

It was a twenty minute drive to Nolan's place, forty minutes there and back, and Sidney wasn't convinced he'd be able to do the whole trip without shooting the punk just to shut him up. He wouldn't mind if he said anything that made the slightest bit of sense, but it was all this rambling stream-of-consciousness weirdness.

"Are you on drugs? I mean, are you high right now?"

Hector laughed and said, "I'm serious, man. You know it's like . . . well, let's call it the C word, you know, to describe a woman's er . . ."

"I *know* which word you mean."

"I would hope so," said Hector with a knowing smile that made Sidney want to slap his face. If the punk hadn't been driving he'd have done just that. "It's a bad word, the worst word, but it describes one of the greatest things ever. Haven't you ever wondered, why that is?"

"No, Hector, I haven't, just like your parents probably never wondered why you didn't get into Harvard." Sidney thought he'd try to change the subject and said, "How d'you end up with a name like Hector, anyway?"

"My dad was half Spanish."

"Which half?"

"On his mother's side, obviously." He glanced across at the old man and said, "My name's Murphy." The old man nodded his understanding and pointed forward, telling him to keep his eyes on the road.

The old man was senile, that was clearly the problem. Or else he'd done loads of coke or something back in the day. He acted all prim and proper, but these guys were all young in the '70s and he'd seen *Casino*, he'd seen *Scarface* – they were all the biggest cokeheads.

"Oh, man, this friend of mine had a cousin called Tamara and she'd get wasted at parties when she was, like, sixteen, and let us play Tamara's Ti . . . Well, I won't say the word, I know you don't like words like that, but I'm referring to her, you know, her bre . . ." Hector wasn't sure if even breasts would be out of bounds. "Her chest things, packets, whatever."

Sidney was staring at him, dumbstruck. It was bad enough when his nonsense was actually related to the here and now, but this new story had apparently been plucked out of the ether.

"I know the word you're looking for, but that still doesn't make it any clearer. What on God's good earth are you talking about?"

"Give me a minute, man. This game. See, she'd strip naked to the waist and lay on a table and let all us guys snort coke right off her . . . you know, the things we were just talking about." He was overcome briefly by the memory of the last such party, the summer before last. "And she was loaded up top, if you know what I'm saying. She was *nice*."

"Why would you tell me that story?" Sidney was wondering if this kid had frazzled something in his brain and had lost any sense of discernment or understanding of what might be an appropriate story for the company he was in. "Seriously, what is it about me that made you think I might want to hear that story? Better than that, tell me what suddenly inspired you to share it with me! I'm curious, Hector, I really would like to know . . . Actually, forget that, I don't want to know what's going on in your mind, but I'd like to know why you thought that was an appropriate story to tell on this occasion."

Hector had changed his mind. Clearly, the old man hadn't done enough drugs back in the day. If he had, he wouldn't be quite so uptight now. And man, was he uptight.

"It's just a story, you know. Just something I thought of. I mean, isn't that what we're supposed to do? Like, we're two buddies on a job together, talking about stuff, swapping stories."

"You hear me telling any stories?"

"I bet you could tell some stories, things you did back in the day." He was about to give the old man a playful punch on the arm but didn't, thinking he probably wouldn't go in for that kind of thing, either. Besides, he was old, really old, and a playful punch on the arm could be bad news – it could cause a blood clot or something serious like that.

"Back in the day! You don't know what you're talking about. And we're not buddies, and we're not on a job together – you're tagging along to watch me, to learn some people skills. That'll actually involve you watching and keeping your mouth shut."

"I'm all eyes and ears, no mouth, trust me." With an afterthought, he said, "Does that mean no stories at all?"

Sidney had to hand it to him, the kid was persistent. "It means no stories like that one. I have a daughter who's sixteen."

"Is her name Tamara?"

"If her name was Tamara I'd be chopping you into pieces in a dumpster right now."

"Hey man, I was only joking." Though clearly, it was completely wasted because the old man's sense of humor had been sucked out of his nose by aliens or something – they probably had it in a jar on their home planet right now, realizing they'd stolen the wrong one. "I knew Tamara wasn't your daughter. For one, she's eighteen now, not sixteen, and she's my friend's cousin, you know."

"I was joking too," said Sidney, realizing that even the broadest brush strokes of humor were wasted on the punk. "I haven't chopped anyone up in a dumpster in nearly twenty years."

Now they were getting somewhere. "You really did that!"

"No, I'm still joking." He remembered what Mr Costello had said about showing him the ropes, giving him the right moral guidelines. "Hector, you have to understand that we're in a serious business, and you don't run a serious business on threats and violence. Sure, sometimes threats and violence are necessary, just to make people understand how serious you are about your business ethic, but it is always the option of last resort."

Hector waited a couple of beats, wondering if the old man was finished. For someone who didn't like talking, he was good at churning out the boring speeches. God help them all when his daughter got married. On the good side, he guessed the old man was talking about the job, Nolan – the option of last resort.

"Can I do him?"

It was pointless, thought Sidney. He didn't know if there was such a thing as a clinical moron, but this kid Hector was about as close as anyone was ever likely to get.

"Can you do who?"

"Nolan. The option of last resort."

"Kid, you don't know what you're talking about. You just leave everything to me when we get to Nolan's place. You just watch and learn, remember?"

"Sure, I remember," said Hector. It was pretty frustrating though, knowing he'd have to watch this fossil blow Nolan's brains out when he was itching to do it himself. That was how people learned, by picking up the gun and pulling the trigger.

"I had someone pull a gun on me once. Threatened to shoot me in the . . . well, you know, he threatened to shoot me so I wouldn't ever have kids, in the groin-type area."

The guy with the gun had clearly been a generation too late, but Sidney decided to play this one straight, giving the punk the benefit of the doubt, offering him the opportunity to give a little background. "So he wasn't a friend?"

"He's not a friend anymore," said Hector. "He was my best friend until he pulled a gun on me. Never seen him since, and if I saw him again, I'd pop a cap in his . . . well, I'd hurt him. He was a motherfu . . . He wasn't nice, if you know what I'm saying."

"What did you do?"

This guy was just like his parents. Hector couldn't believe it. Old people were always just too quick to jump on top of them. What did you do? You must have done something. There's always two sides to every story. Always the same thing.

"I didn't do anything. Why would you assume I'd done something?"

"Hector, I'm not a cop, I'm just asking what happened. If it helps, why did your friend pull a gun on you?"

"It was nothing. I was doing his girlfriend, that's all."

"You were *doing* his girlfriend?"

"Yeah, you know, I was . . . that word, the word I apologized for, I was . . ."

"Hector, I know what you mean. I was just questioning how that constitutes nothing at all." The kid looked baffled and Sidney wondered if he was just so completely out of step, that morals had disappeared completely. He hated to think any of his own children would end up like this. "Do you consider it normal to date your friend's girl?"

"I wasn't dating her, I was . . ."

"Hector, I know!"

"Well, yeah." The old man obviously thought he'd been around the block a couple of times, but Hector could clearly teach him a thing or two. "Let me tell you, this had always been my policy and I've had more girls in more ways than you could imagine. See, for one thing, you don't have any of the responsibility – no taking them out, no buying them stuff. For another, it's easier, you know, because there's only one other guy. With a single girl, you're up against all the other guys in the world. So ask yourself, why be in competition with every guy when you can just be in competition with just one?"

The punk looked pleased with himself, like he was only one step away from being awarded the Nobel Prize in some newly created category. Sidney waited, thinking he'd own up to it being another not very funny joke, but he kept looking smug and in the end, Sidney said, "What about loyalty and honour, doesn't that mean anything to you?"

"Of course! I'm the most honourable and loyal guy you'll ever meet." Hector didn't know where the old man was getting off – what was he doing trying to connect girls and stuff with loyalty and honour. It just didn't make any sense.

Sidney thought of his wife and daughter and how much he'd rather be with them right now, not heading out to Nolan's place with this deranged punk. Still, he'd be back with them soon enough, and he knew one thing, if either one of them ever had to deal with someone like Hector, he wouldn't be responsible for his actions.

He could see Nolan's house on the tree-lined street up ahead of them so he said quickly, "That joke I made about the dumpster. It wasn't a joke, it was 1983, and if you're ever so much as in the same room as my daughter, I won't even hesitate."

"You're pretty scary," said Hector, flattering the old man, because in truth, he reckoned it was all front, like a lot of these guys from the past.

"I know," said Sidney, but he wondered if Hector had the slightest idea how scary he'd been and could still be. "It's that house on the left. Pull over."

"Nice place," said Hector as he parked, looking across the lawn at the double-fronted house with ivy growing all the way to the roof.

"Remember . . ."

"I know, listen and learn."

They got out of the car and walked up the path, then up the three steps to the front door. Hector was faster up the steps and rang the bell, then cursed under his breath because he knew the old man would get all precious about it. Sidney let it go, the punk was just eager, but he couldn't see him ever coming to anything.

Nolan opened the door. He was in his shirt sleeves and was either wearing contacts or just didn't bother with his glasses in the house. He stared at Hector first, but then fixed on Sidney with the shock of recognition and said fearfully, "You're the preacher."

Hector looked at the old man. He'd heard a couple of people talk about a guy called the preacher, but he'd never realized they were talking about him. The old man had just nodded in response and now Nolan looked like he was about to cry and wet himself all at the same time.

"Please, I'll do anything, I'm begging you please." He put his hand up, changing his plea, as he said, "Okay, but look not here, not in front of my family."

This was cool, thought Hector, the old man was the preacher and this guy Nolan was about to be dog food.

"Mr Nolan, you don't understand," said Sidney, reaching inside his jacket.

Nolan started sobbing, his words almost inaudible, but something about mercy. What was it with people nowadays, thought Sidney, that they never listened? He held the envelope, fat and pleasing in the hand, out towards Nolan, who looked at it like Sidney had just offered him a pineapple.

"What's this?"

"Mr Nolan, if you'd let me finish, Mr Costello wanted me to tell you that there had been a misunderstanding and that he's very sorry for any distress this might have caused to you or your family. He's been completely happy with your legal work on his behalf, he completely understands if you won't want to work with him in the future, and this is just a small compensation. We're really very sorry."

Sidney might as well have let Hector do the talking because Nolan was staring at him like he'd explained the visit in Swahili. He took the envelope in slow motion and opened it to look at the bundle of notes inside. He looked up again, and stared in confusion at Sidney.

He laughed then, and said, "I thought, I mean . . ."

"I know," said Sidney, sympathetically. He heard someone coming down the stairs behind Nolan then, and said quietly, "Dry your eyes, Mr Nolan."

Nolan took a handkerchief and dried his eyes and blew his nose, and looked grateful to Sidney for thinking about how he'd look in front of his family.

Hector was struggling to connect here, like the aliens had been and sucked something out of *his* brain and suddenly nothing made sense. He'd just heard the old man named as the preacher, one of the most fearsome men ever talked about, and they'd come all the way out here to apologize to someone! What next, helping old ladies across the road?

Then he got distracted. The old man and Nolan were saying something to each other when the most beautiful girl appeared on the stairs in the hallway, dressed in one of those skinny-rib T-shirts – they did it for him every time, and she didn't have much going on up there, but she was *nice*.

Sidney saw the girl and heard Hector's tongue hit the floor, even though she had to be fourteen at most. He really was a sick puppy. "Okay, Mr Nolan, we have to be going. Once again, sorry for the distress."

"Thank you. Thank you very much."

"Let's go, Hector."

The door closed quickly and the two of them headed back to the car. Hector wasn't happy. Not only had they not killed anyone, or even given anyone a beating, just as things had been getting interesting, the old man had called it a day.

"That was one beautiful piece of . . ."

"Don't say it, Hector."

Sidney took his gun out and gave Hector a sharp little crack across the top of the head.

"Fu . . . Fiddle! What did you do that for!"

"You're a degenerate. I'm trying to knock some decency into that thick skull of yours."

Hector got into the car, rubbing his head, but couldn't help laughing. "My grandfather used to do that. Not with a gun obviously, but he used to crack me on the head and say he'd knock some sense into me."

He pulled away and Sidney said, "I'm guessing he either hit you too hard, or not hard enough."

Hector laughed. It was all on a pretty weird wavelength but the old man was actually pretty funny, even if it was a pain in the posterior that he couldn't curse or use profanity around him, or talk about sex or drugs. Had he just *thought* the word posterior? That was something – he was even censoring his thoughts around the old man.

"Say, anyway, why do they call you the preacher?"

Sidney looked at him and said, "Take a wild guess," and the punk started to laugh. Sidney laughed too. He wasn't sure they were both laughing at the same joke, but they were both laughing at the same time, and he guessed that was a start. Maybe he'd show him the ropes yet.

THE ANGEL OF MANTON WORTHY

Kate Ellis

I felt his tight grip on my arm as I slumped into the passenger seat and when my hand went up to the blindfold he ordered me not to touch it. I did as I was told and clung to the soft leather of the seat, trying to work out where we were heading.

We travelled for hours on a fast, straight road and I guessed that we must be well out of London. When the roads started to wind I sensed that we were out in the country somewhere and we seemed to drive for miles before I felt the car swing sharply to the left. I heard the crunch of gravel beneath the tyres as though we were on some sort of driveway, and when we stopped he told me to take the blindfold off. I could see my surprise at last.

I untied the blindfold and sat there blinking as my eyes got used to the light. I'm sure I swore when I realized where I was. But then I saw the excitement on Paul's face – like a little boy at Christmas – and I forced my mouth into a smile until the muscles began to ache. I think I managed to say what he wanted to hear. I could hardly have let him know the truth.

I managed to keep the smile in place when he told me the house was called the Old Rectory, and I rushed up to the front door, forcing out enthusiastic oohs and aahs as he pointed out each new desirable feature. He expected excitement and that's what he got. He had the Merc, the million-pound apartment in London, and now he had the place in the country he'd been promising himself for years. To have poured cold water on his triumph would have been like snatching away a kid's birthday present . . . and I couldn't have done that to him. Not when I saw how thrilled he was.

He was twenty years older than me and too many business lunches meant that what he'd lost in hair he'd gained in weight. But I was fond of him – I suppose I might even have said I loved him if I believed in love, which I don't. We stayed in a hotel in Exeter that evening and he ordered a bottle of champagne to toast our new country life. After the bubbles had booted some of my inhibitions out of the window I asked him if he realized what life was really like in a place like Manton Worthy. But he just laughed and said he'd bought the best house in the village so the peasants could kiss his arse. People in the restaurant looked round and I felt myself blushing. Paul never worried about what people thought . . . unless he was doing business with them.

Looking back, I couldn't complain about the house itself. It was like an oversized doll's house to look at . . . symmetrical with long, square-paned windows painted in gleaming white. Paul said it was Georgian and it had a long gravel drive and a shiny black front door you could see your face in, with bright brass fittings. It had belonged to a TV executive from London who had spent a fortune on the place and only used it on weekends. Inside, the previous owners had kitted it out with gold and silk drapes and thick cream carpets. It hadn't always been like that, of course – once it had been a draughty, rambling place where the old vicar lived; where the parish bigwigs held their long, boring meetings and where the vicar's skinny wife organised her fetes and good works. But times change.

Paul had lived in London all his life and what he knew about the country came from watching old episodes of Miss Marple and reading the colour supplements. He said I should get to know the area, perhaps chat up a few locals . . . there was no harm in cultivating useful contacts. But I said no, thanks, I had better things to do, and began to paint my nails. There was no way I was going out there. Not in Manton Worthy.

I had an uncomfortable feeling that it wouldn't be long before things began to go wrong . . . and it turned out I was right. The cockerel next door started it: cock-a-doodle-bloody-doo over and over again at five o'clock every morning. I knew Paul would take it badly . . . he needed his sleep, and by the third day he was threatening to throttle the bird with his bare hands. I told him that crowing is what cockerels do . . . that it was all part of the country experience. But there was no reasoning with Paul when something annoyed him.

He dealt with it, of course . . . like he dealt with everything. He stormed round to see the farmer, who was called Carter – "an inbred lump in a flat cap and waxed jacket," according to Paul. As soon as I heard Carter's name I knew I had to take care not to get caught up in Paul's little feud.

When the cockerel carried on I tried to convince Paul that you couldn't stop the forces of nature. But he said he'd have a bloody good try if they kept him awake at night. I suggested moving into one of the bedrooms at the back of the house and to my relief he agreed. I started to hint about spending more time at the London apartment, but Paul said that no inbred yokel was going to drive him out of the home he'd worked his backside off for. He always had a stubborn streak.

So there we were, stuck in the middle of nowhere, and as I stared out of our old bedroom window across the rolling green landscape, the sight of Carter's farmhouse squatting there in the field nearby made me shudder. I should have got out then . . . I know that now with hindsight. But how could I have hurt Paul?

Another thing that spoiled the rural peace Paul thought he'd bought was the noise of the church bells. They rang on Tuesday evenings and woke us up every Sunday morning. One Tuesday Paul fetched a pair of shears from the garden shed and I feared the worst. But I thought quickly and said that I loved the sound of the bells and how glad I was that we lived so near to the church. Paul looked at me as though I were mad, but the shears were returned to the shed.

When the bells stopped that evening, I walked to the bottom of the garden and hid myself behind the hedge to watch the ringers leave the church. I saw Carter, leading them down the church path – probably to the pub – and my body started to shake at the sight of him. He had hardly changed. He still had the slicked-down hair I remembered so well – although it was grey now rather than black – and he'd put on weight. I watched him until he disappeared round the corner, then I hurried back into the house, taking deep breaths, trying to still my trembling hands. I made for the downstairs cloakroom, where I threw up, scared that Paul would hear me . . . but he didn't. I told him that I had been outside putting something in the bin and he seemed to believe me. I hated lying to him, but I had no choice.

From then on I made sure we stayed indoors on Tuesday evenings and the change of bedroom had dealt with the cockerel problem. After a couple of weeks I was becoming more confident that I could manage the situation. But being in Manton Worthy still made me nervous, and I woke up each morning dreading what the day ahead would bring. And yet I put on a smile for Paul's sake.

Paul had decided to spend less time in London and run the business from the Old Rectory. I offered to act as his PA – after all, we'd met when I'd started work as his secretary . . . just as he was becoming bored with his first wife. And doing my bit for the business gave me the perfect excuse not to go out.

But I suppose it was inevitable that I would meet someone from the village sooner or later, and one Monday morning, as I was getting dressed, the doorbell rang. I let Paul answer it while I stood hidden at the top of the stairs, peering down into the hallway to see if the caller's face and voice were familiar. Once I was sure that I had never seen the visitor before in my life, I walked down the stairs, smiling graciously, and invited her in. She introduced herself as Mandy Pettifer and she seemed nice enough in her way, although she wasn't really our type . . . all floral dress and flat sandals. But I knew that a contact on the outside might be useful.

I took her through into the lounge – or the drawing room, as Paul insisted on calling it – and offered her a coffee. This was my chance to discover the lie of the land. Who was who now and what was what in Manton Worthy.

Mandy was the chatty type. In fact, once you started her on the subject of the locals it was hard to shut her up. She'd lived in Manton Worthy for ten years and she was married to an IT consultant who worked abroad a lot. She taught part-time at a primary school in the nearby town of Ashburn, the local school having closed down years ago, and I guessed that she had come visiting because she was at a loose end in the school holidays. She was one of those people who'll tell you her life story before you can get a word in edgeways.

"I expect most people in the village have lived here for years," I said when she paused to take a sip of coffee.

She looked disappointed, as though she wanted me to reveal as much about myself as she had . . . but I wasn't playing that game.

"Actually the nice thing about Manton Worthy is that most of the people are newcomers like you and me." She leaned forward, as if she was about to tell some great secret. "To tell you the truth, I don't think most of the locals can afford the house prices. I know the people who used to have our cottage live in Ashburn now. In fact, I only know of one person who's lived here all her life, apart from some of the local farmers, of course."

"Who's that?" I asked, trying to sound casual.

"Miss Downey: She lives next door to me. She's in her seventies now but she used to teach in the village school when there was one."

"Nobody else?"

Mandy shook her head.

"What about the bell ringers?"

Mandy looked surprised, as though she'd never considered that human beings rang the church bells. "I've no idea. Perhaps they come in from Ashburn. Most of the cottages were owned by a local estate and when they were sold off the tenants couldn't afford to buy at the prices they were asking. Most of them moved to the estate in Ashburn."

"And the cottages?"

"Bought as second homes or by people like us."

"So there's nobody apart from Miss Downey?"

Mandy laughed . . . a tinkling, irritating sound. "You'll have to meet her; she knows a lot about local history and all that. If you ever want to know what's gone on in Manton Worthy in the past, she's the person to ask."

I smiled but didn't answer. That afternoon I went for a walk through the village. It nestled in rolling, patchwork fields; chocolate-box pretty with its thatched cob cottages and ancient stone church next-door to the pub – everyone's ideal English village. Perhaps I had been wrong to be afraid. Perhaps everything would be okay . . . as long as I avoided Carter.

Over the next weeks I became bolder. I walked through the village – well away from Carter's land – and I even took Mandy up on her invitation to call round anytime for a coffee. Perhaps I needed to see someone other than Paul. Or perhaps I just felt I needed to know what was going on in the outside world.

One afternoon I found myself sitting in Mandy's front room overlooking the main village street. She had done it up nicely, I'll give her that. There was an old-fashioned inglenook fireplace and she'd taken up the carpet to reveal the original stone floor which she had promptly covered up again with a large abstract rug in shades of grey. There was a whiff of minimalism in the air, which surprised me as Mandy hadn't seemed the type for that sort of thing. She talked at length about interior design . . . and I listened. She had gone for a fusion of old rustic and modern, she said. I nodded and let her rabbit on. But I had more important things to worry about.

She mentioned the murder just as I had bitten into a Danish pastry. I felt myself choking and grabbed at the mug of coffee. By the time Mandy had fetched me a glass of water from her new beech kitchen with its slate-tiled floor, I had composed myself, although my heart was still pounding against my ribs. Who could have thought that the mere mention of it would bring back all the old terrors? But Mandy can't have noticed anything was wrong because she kept on talking, telling me how the girl had been found up by the woods, on the site of the old gallows. She'd been strangled, Mandy told me, enjoying every detail of the story. Strangled with a bell rope from the church. The police knew who'd done it, of course, but they could never prove anything. The boy had had learning difficulties and his mother had given him an alibi.

I asked her where she'd heard all this and she tapped the side of her nose. "A woman I work with used to live here. She told me."

"Did she mention Mr Carter who has the farm next-door to us?" I regretted the question as soon as I'd asked it. But Carter was on my mind. In fact, if Paul knew how scared I was of Carter, he'd have done something about it, so I kept quiet. Trouble was the last thing I wanted in Manton Worthy.

Mandy looked puzzled. "No, I don't think she did. I can ask her about him if you like." She leaned forward, eager to please. She reminded me of a dog we had once owned, a stupid animal who was all enthusiasm and no sense. It had been put down and we'd buried it in the back garden.

"No. It's okay. It's not important." I hoped she couldn't sense the fear in my voice.

We got through three cups of coffee before I looked at my watch and realised how late it was getting. Paul would start to worry if I wasn't home soon. Perhaps it was the age gap between us that made him treat me like a child sometimes. Mandy tried to persuade me to stay – she was probably lonely there in that cottage, that cage of rustic minimalist chic, with her husband away so much – but I had to get away. She was beginning to get on my nerves.

Now that I knew the village was full of incomers like myself I felt more comfortable walking back. But as I hurried back down the main street towards the Old Rectory I heard a voice behind me.

"Karen? It is Karen, isn't it?"

I stood there frozen to the spot for a few seconds before I took a deep, calming breath and turned round. I tried to smile but I felt my mouth forming into an expression more of pain than pleasure.

The woman was small, bent with age. Her hair was snowy white and her flesh looked like thin parchment stretched over the bones. But her sharp eyes hinted at an agile brain behind that mask of age. I heard myself saying, "Sorry, you've made a mistake. My name's Petra."

But the woman's bright grey eyes were focussed on mine like searchlights. She hesitated, a knowing smile playing on her lips. "I'm so sorry, my dear, you just reminded me of one of my old pupils. I'm Edith Downey. I live in Beech Cottage . . . just over there." She waved a gnarled finger in the vague direction of a row of thatched, pastel-painted cottages straight off a picture postcard. I shuffled my feet, anxious to get away. "So you've moved here recently?"

"Yes." She looked at me expectantly. She wanted more. "We've moved into the Old Rectory . . . me and my husband

. . . Paul. We've come from London." I tried to smile but I
don't think I quite managed it.

Miss Downey took a step closer. Her eyes were still on mine,
as though she were reading my thoughts. "It's all new people
now . . . apart from the Carters and myself. I taught at the
village school . . . when there was a village school."

"Really." I tried to sound interested but I felt the adrenalin
pumping around my body as I prepared for flight.

"Have you been to the church yet?"

I shook my head.

"It's worth seeing. It has a medieval screen with some fine
angel carvings. Some of the people who used to live here still
come for Sunday service . . . most of them live in Ashburn now
but they still feel they have ties here."

There was a hint of recrimination in her voice; a subtle
criticism, as though she was hinting that I was personally
responsible for driving up the village house prices and evicting
people from their homes. But I said nothing. I wanted the
encounter to be over. I wanted to get back to Paul.

I remember running back to the Old Rectory as though the
hounds of hell were after me. I sank three large gin and tonics
before I began the supper. Paul was busy in his office so I don't
think he noticed.

It was a while before I summoned up the courage to walk
through the village again. I made excuses to myself: I had to use
my new Range Rover because I wanted to do some shopping in
Exeter or visit a supermarket ten miles away . . . I didn't dare
risk the one at Ashburn. I was making any excuse not to walk
past Miss Downey's cottage. But how could I avoid the woman
forever?

Somehow I had to persuade Paul that moving to Manton
Worthy had been a mistake. But as I wondered how to go about
it, I carried on day after day, driving through the village in the
Range Rover wearing my dark glasses. The days passed, and
before I knew it the lanes were filled with farm vehicles and the
fields hummed day and night with the noise of combine har-
vesters. When Paul complained, as I knew he would, I took my
chance and said that farms were noisy places and we might be
better off somewhere else. But he was determined to stay put.

Once Paul had made a decision, he would never admit he was wrong.

Soon after that a leaflet came through the door. It was an invitation to the church's harvest festival, followed by a hot-pot supper in the church hall. Naturally I threw it straight in the bin and I had the shock of my life when Paul found it there and said he wanted to go. He said he'd decided it was about time we became part of the community. My mouth went dry and my hands began to shake. This was the last thing I wanted.

I was thinking how to talk Paul out of it when I went out into the hall and found the note lying on the doormat.

"Miss Downey was knocked down and killed on Wednesday night . . . hit-and-run driver." Mandy leaned forward, anxious to share this juicy piece of gossip.

"That's awful," I said. "Have the police any idea who . . .?"

"Well, I've heard that an old Land Rover was seen speeding around the village earlier that evening. Someone said the police have questioned Mr Carter, who has the farm next-door to you . . . it's said he often takes his Land Rover to the Wagon and Horses. These country people sometimes think they're above the law where drunk driving is concerned, you know."

"So they think it was Carter?"

Mandy shrugged. After virtually accusing the man, she couldn't bring herself to deliver the final verdict. She leaned forward confidentially. "Remember I told you about that murder . . . the girl who was found strangled? Well, I asked about it and apparently she was Carter's daughter . . . and he was questioned about it at the time."

"Was he?" I felt my hands shaking.

"There were rumours going round that he was abusing her, but the police never found any evidence . . . that's what I was told anyway. Don't repeat it, will you?"

"No." I could hear my heart beating. "Of course I won't." I hesitated. "What happened to the boy the police suspected?"

"I think his family left the area. Why?"

"No reason," I said, as casually as I could manage. "Just curious."

I stood up. I wanted Mandy to go. I wasn't in the mood for company. I was wondering how to stop Paul from going to the harvest supper . . . how I was going to keep him away from Carter. But then I realized that I didn't have to go with him. I could develop a strategic headache. As long as I didn't come face-to-face with Carter and the nightmares of my childhood, I'd be all right.

"You're shaking. What's the matter?" Mandy's voice was all concern.

"Nothing." I tried to smile.

It was half an hour before she left and as she was leaving she asked me if I was going to Miss Downey's funeral. I said no. After all, I didn't know the woman.

As soon as she'd gone I rushed upstairs and opened my underwear drawer. I felt underneath the layers of flimsy lace for the note, and when I found it I took it out and read it.

Dear Karen,
 I've been thinking about our meeting the week before last and I've been wondering what to do for the best. I do understand your feelings but I think it would be helpful to talk. Perhaps you would call on me one day for tea.
                                        Yours sincerely,
                                        Edith Downey

I tore it into tiny pieces and put it down the waste disposal unit in the kitchen. I was stupid to have kept it, but I vowed not to make any more mistakes. That evening I told Paul that I wanted to go back to London but his response was that it was still early days . . . and the harvest supper was just what I needed to get to know people.

The next day I heard from Mandy that Carter had been released without charge.

I lived in a strange state of limbo for a week, pretending to Paul that I was looking forward to the harvest supper . . . and all the time making plans to avoid it at all costs. The most worrying thing was that Paul seemed to have reached some understanding with Carter. He had taken to visiting the Wagon and Horses some evenings and one night when he returned, he said that he had been talking to Carter and he seemed all right, really: You couldn't always judge by first impressions.

The change in Paul shocked me: He claimed that the slow pace of country life was lowering his blood pressure and making him feel calmer. Why run around like a headless chicken in London when you could enjoy the simple pleasures of a small community and open spaces? Paul seemed hooked and, like converts the world over, he began to enter into his new enthusiasm with a gusto lacking in the born-and-bred countryman. He talked of learning to ride, maybe joining the local hunt. To my horror, he even suggested inviting Carter round for lunch one Sunday as he was on his own, an idea which sent me straight to the bathroom to throw up.

Paul was going native and with every new development I became more and more certain that I had to get back to the city . . . any city . . . anywhere away from Manton Worthy. I had to get out before it was too late.

On the night of the harvest supper I developed a headache as planned and told Paul to go on his own. He looked disappointed, like a kicked puppy, but I had no choice. After some persuasion he went, and once I was alone I locked all the doors and settled down to an evening by the telly with some interior design magazines – I wanted to do something with the en suite bathroom so I found myself a pair of scissors to cut out any pictures that might provide me with some inspiration. I opened a bottle of Chardonnay, too – I needed something to steady my nerves.

At half-past nine it was pitch dark outside. Darkness in the countryside is nothing like darkness in the city and I could see nothing outside the windows, as though someone had hung black velvet drapes on the other side of the glass. But with the curtains drawn and the telly on I felt cosy and safe. Until I heard the noise of our polished brass doorknocker being raised and lowered three times.

I froze. The telly still babbled on, oblivious to the crisis, as three more knocks came. Then another three. I went through all the possibilities in my mind. Could Paul have forgotten his key? Could Mandy be calling to see how I was? I crept along the hall in the darkness, making for the front door. There were no windows in the door but the TV executive had installed a spyhole and security lights. I stood on tiptoe to look through the spyhole, but although the front step was flooded with halogen light, there seemed to be nobody there.

I was about to return to the safe warmth of the lounge when the knocking began again. My body started to shake and I tried to peer out of the spyhole but again there seemed to be nobody there.

I know now that I shouldn't have opened the door, but it was an automatic reaction – and I suppose I assumed that I could just close it against any danger if the worst happened. But things are rarely that straightforward. As soon as I had turned the latch, the door burst open and I fell backwards. I think I screamed. I think I tried to lash out. But it was useless. It was dark in the hallway and I could see very little, but I felt strong arms dragging me towards the lounge. I tried to kick, but it was as though I was caught in a web like a fly . . . at the mercy of some monstrous, unseen spider. I screamed again, but then I realized that this was the countryside. There was nobody there to hear me.

We were in the lounge now and Carter was bundling me onto the sofa. I could smell his waxed jacket as he held me . . . the same smell I remembered from all those years ago. And I could see his face . . . full of hatred.

"I saw you." He spat the words like venom. "I saw you run her over."

I tried to wriggle free, but he held me tight.

"But you were too late. She'd told me already that you were back."

"I don't know what you're talking about." The words came out as a squeak, unconvincing even to myself.

"Miss Downey, that's what I'm talking about. I got talking to that husband of yours. Funny how you didn't tell him much about yourself. He's no idea, has he?"

I felt his breath on my face and I tried to push him away. But it was no use. He was stronger than me.

"Why, Karen?" he hissed, putting his face close to mine. "Just tell me why. What had she ever done to you?"

"I don't know what you mean."

"My Jenny . . . why?"

"Luke Fisher killed Jenny. Everyone knew that."

His hands began to tighten around my neck. "Once you'd gone, Luke told the police what he saw. They didn't believe him — just because he wasn't all there they thought he was making it up. But I knew he was telling the truth. You were always a sly little bitch . . . a bully. You made my Jenny's life a misery. No wonder your mam and dad moved away so bloody quick after she died. Did they know, eh? Always looked so bloody innocent, didn't you . . . face like one of them angels in the church. Did they know what you were really like? Did they know what you'd done?"

With an almighty effort I pushed him off and sprang up. I don't remember much about what happened next. Only that there was a lot of blood and I felt that same strange detachment I'd felt after I had killed Jenny Carter . . . when I looked down and saw her dead, bulging eyes staring up at me.

The memory returned like a tidal wave, everything that had happened that day all those years ago. The bell ropes in the church had been replaced and the old ones had been left lying in the back pew, perfect for the game I'd made up . . . the game of dare. I dared Jenny Carter to go to the old gallows and put the rope around her neck. Luke followed us: He was hard to get rid of . . . older than us, big and soft and too simple to know when he wasn't wanted. But I hadn't known he was watching when I tightened the rope around Jenny's neck, just to see what it would be like to kill somebody . . . to have the power of life and death. Once I'd started pulling on that rope I couldn't stop. I'd watched, fascinated, as her face began to contort and her eyes started to bulge. I was all-powerful, the angel of death; just like the angels on the screen in the church . . . only different. As I stood over the body of Jenny's father, I felt the same elation . . . the same thrill. But when I heard a voice calling in the hall the feeling disappeared and my brain began to work quickly.

I began to sob and I sank to the floor. The scissors I'd grabbed from the coffee table were in my hand and I threw them to one side. I was shaking and crying hysterically by the time Paul entered the room. And when he took me in his arms I slumped against him in a dead faint.

I pretended to be unconscious when the doctor and the police arrived. I thought it was best. And when I came round, in my own good time, I told my story in a weak voice. Carter had arrived and pushed his way in, then he had tried to . . . I hesitated at this point for maximum effect, but the policewoman with the sympathetic eyes knew just what I meant. Women alone in the countryside were so vulnerable and hard-drinking men like Carter, sensing weakness, knowing a woman would be alone . . . She was the sort of woman who believes all men are potential rapists and she believed every word I said. I was the victim, she said, and I mustn't feel guilty. I never liked to tell her that I didn't.

We left Manton Worthy soon after, of course, and made a tidy profit on the Old Rectory, which we sold to a city broker who wanted it for a weekend retreat. I told Paul that I couldn't bear to stay there after what had happened and he was very sympathetic: He even blamed himself for getting too pally with Carter. The day before we left I wandered into the church and I looked at the angel on the screen, the one with the sword, and I couldn't help smiling. I was Manton Worthy's angel of death . . . and nobody would ever know.

Once we were back in London I resumed my old life. I was Petra, Paul's wife; a lady who lunched and did very little else. Karen was dead.

It was six months later when Paul was found dead at the foot of the stairs in his office. He'd been working late and I'd been at the gym, working out with Karl, my personal trainer. Of course, when I say working out, I use the term loosely: What we were doing had very little to do with exercise bikes and weights. Karl had a girlfriend, but I wasn't worried about that: He was just a bit of fun, a way of passing the time . . . and Paul would never get to know.

The policeman who came to tell me about Paul's death wasn't very sympathetic. He questioned me for hours about where I'd been and about my relationship with Paul. I said nothing about Karl, of course. And when he asked me how much I stood to inherit on Paul's death, I told him the truth. Five and a half million, give or take a few quid. Of course I'd assumed that Paul's death was an accident, cut and dried. But it just shows you how wrong you can be.

The police said that Paul hadn't fallen; there were signs of a struggle and fibres from my coat were found under one of his fingernails. I told the police that he'd caught his nail on my coat that morning. And I told them he had some pretty dodgy business associates . . . he'd even moved to Devon once to get away from them. But they wouldn't listen, and when they charged me with Paul's murder even Karl turned his back on me and refused to give me an alibi because he was scared of his cow of a girlfriend.

I was convinced it would never come to trial. After all, I hadn't done anything. But every time I tried to convince the police of my innocence, they wouldn't listen. My defence barrister told the court how six months ago I'd been the victim of an attempted rape, but even that didn't seem to earn me much sympathy. The jury was full of brain-dead idiots who found me guilty by a majority of ten to two, and as the police bundled me past the crowds waiting outside the Old Bailey, someone flung a coat over my head and pushed me into a van that smelled of unwashed bodies and urine.

Even when they took the coat off my head the windows in the van were too high to see out of and I couldn't tell where we were or what direction we were driving in. We seemed to drive for hours on a fast, straight road, then we slowed down and the roads started to wind.

I asked the sour-faced woman I was handcuffed to where we were going and she turned to me and smiled, as though she was enjoying some private joke.

"Oh, you're going to Gampton Prison. You'll like it there. It's in the country . . . right in the middle of nowhere."

When she started to laugh I screamed and banged on the side of the prison van until my hands were sore.

GOING BACK

Ann Cleeves

Susan had thought she would recognize the place immediately. The pictures in her head were solid and precise. She revisited them regularly, saw them like photos. The grey line of houses surrounded by grey hills. The school playground only separated from fields by a low stone wall, so the wind blowing across it chapped their lips and turned their fingers blue. The tubular steel climbing frame, where she'd hung from her knees, her skirt falling over her upper body and the three girls in the corner of the yard, sniggering and pointing, shouting at the boys to look. *We can see your knickers! We can see your knickers!* The chimney-shaped stove in the junior classroom, which the caretaker filled with coke and which belched out sulphur-tasting fumes. Her mother's mouth crimped in disapproval.

But everything was different. The village had become a fashionable place to live, within easy commuting distance of Leeds. You could tell that rich people lived here. The school had been converted into a picture from a glossy magazine. Through plate glass windows you could see a pale wood mezzanine floor and exposed beams. Susan wondered if there was any chance of seeing inside, of smelling the wood and touching the heavy fabric of the curtains. Changes to the School House, where she'd lived, were more modest, but the lines of the severe square box had been softened by a conservatory and hanging baskets. In her memory she saw the house through drizzle and fog. Her mother's resentment at being forced to live there had imposed its own micro-climate. Today there was the pale, lemon sunshine of early spring.

And she was back. A fiftieth birthday present to herself. What did they call it? Exorcizing ghosts.

So she stood for a moment trying to find her bearings. She sensed Tom's impatience, but this was her time. Let him wait. She stared fiercely down the road, then closed her eyes and laid the pattern of houses over the landscape of her memory.

"They've widened the lane," she said. "The verge was deeper then."

He kept quiet. He knew it was important not to say the wrong thing.

When they'd moved here from Leeds, her mother had called it a cultural desert. It had been her father's first headship and he'd had no real choice in the matter. He hadn't fitted in at his previous school and had been told by the director of education to apply. He had no vocation for teaching. In the war he'd been happy, had hoped the fighting would go on forever. Afterwards, what could he do? The government needed teachers and would pay him to train.

Her mother had met him when he was a mature student and had rather liked the idea of marrying a teacher. It was a respectable profession. Perhaps she pictured him in a gown taking assembly in an oak-panelled hall. Susan thought she couldn't have been aware then of the reality – the poor pay, the grubby children who wet their pants and carried nits. Her father didn't have the academic qualification to teach in a grammar school. He was reduced to drilling the four times table into the heads of bored seven-year-olds, to supervizing the half-dressed prancing to Music and Movement on the wireless. It was no job, he said, for a grown man.

And this, he had to admit, was no real headship. There were only thirty children, fifteen infants and fifteen juniors. He took the juniors in one classroom and Miss Pritchard took the infants in the other. Susan's mother never liked Miss Pritchard, who was plump, comfortable and vacuous. She liked nothing about the village at all. All she could think of was moving back to the city.

The house was always cold. Even in summer the damp in the walls and the floor seeped into your bones. The wind blew over the Pennines and under the doors. Susan remembered the building in black and white, like the fuzzy pictures on the television in the corner of the front room. Her parents sat every evening in silence watching television, surrounded by their utility furniture, the few good pieces of china her mother had inherited from a well-off aunt, an inscribed tankard which had been given to her father when he left his last school. And always, sometimes even drowning out the voices on the TV, there was the sound of the sheep on the hill. Like a baby crying in the distance.

Susan had escaped outside, to ride her bike down the lane and play on the climbing frame in the school yard. Always on her own. Nobody wanted to be friends with the teacher's lass. They were frightened she'd tell on them. She saw them sometimes, the other girls, Heather and Diane and Marilyn sitting on the pavement outside the council houses down the hill, their heads together over some game. She never went to join them. She knew she wouldn't be welcome and besides, her mother didn't like her mixing. But she watched them. She always knew what they were up to.

She had been so strong then, so easy in her body. She'd walked miles across the hills. There'd been handstands against the wall, reckless slides across ice on the playground, cartwheels. Her mother hadn't approved. If she saw her daughter on the climbing frame she'd rap on the kitchen window to call her into the house.

"What's the matter?" Susan knew how to play the innocent. She'd had to learn.

"Behaving like that. Showing your underwear to that boy." The boy was Eddie Black, a slow, gentle fifteen-year-old who lived in the cottage next to the school. He spent much of his time in the garden, in a wire mesh aviary, caring for his birds.

Susan wondered why that was so wrong. Why was that different from doing Music and Movement in front of her father? Or his coming into her bedroom when she was dressing. But she said nothing. She knew it was impossible to argue with her mother when her mouth was stretched in that thin-lipped way. When the sherry bottle was uncorked on the kitchen table and the first glass was already empty.

One evening stuck in her memory. It had been just before Easter and her mother had gone into Leeds to a concert. The

Messiah. She'd driven herself in the black Morris Minor. An adventure, but an ordeal. She'd never enjoyed driving. When she returned she was a different woman. Susan thought, if she'd bumped into her in the street, she wouldn't have recognized her, the colour in her cheeks, the way she stood. It was like coming back to the village and not recognizing that. Susan had sat on the stairs wrapped up in the candlewick dressing gown listening to her mother's voice.

"Let's move, Philip. Please can we move back? A fresh start."

She hadn't heard her father's answer, but the next day nothing had changed and the move was never mentioned again. She couldn't tell if anything was different between them.

And me? Susan wondered. What was I feeling in this house I don't know anymore? Nothing. I crept around on the edge of their lives, frozen and silent, trying above all not to make things worse. In school it was the same. Making myself invisible so they wouldn't poke and pinch and jeer. I only felt alive when I was outside, when I was running or climbing. Or watching.

"Well?" Tom asked, breaking into her memories.

"The gate into the field's in the same place."

It could even be the same gate. It was green with lichen and sagging on its hinges. The same sound of wind and sheep. The quarry had finished working even before her day. Now only a tractor would go through occasionally. This was rough grazing and took little work.

"We used to have Sports Day in that field, the flat bit near the gate. The quarry's up the hill."

She said *used to* but as far as she could remember it had only happened once. Her father must have made some arrangement with the farmer. They'd all trooped out through the open gate. No uniform sports kit. It wasn't that sort of school. She was the only one with an airtex shirt and navy blue shorts. Heather Mather wore a cotton dress, very short. The fashion. She was in her last year of juniors and already had breasts, which bounced as she ran. Not that she'd put much effort into the running. It had been a simpering show. She'd looked around her making sure they were all watching. But Susan had won the race. She'd crossed the line even before the boys. *That'll show them*, she'd thought. Flying across the field, she'd felt triumphant. This small world was hers. Let the other girls say what they liked. And of course they'd had plenty to say. Real girls didn't run. Not like that.

Now, middle-aged, she felt the first twinges of arthritis in her shoulders and her knees. She was overweight and unfit. All her movements were tentative. She'd never have that freedom again. The confidence to balance, arms outstretched on the top bar of the farm gate. That sense of running over the uneven grass. She caught her breath to prevent a wail of loss and regret.

Soon after Sports Day, Heather Mather had gone missing. At first everyone thought she'd run away, hitched a lift into Leeds or sneaked on to the secondary modern bus. She was a flighty thing. "Too old for her years," said Mrs Tillotson, the widow who took the Sunday school and played the out of tune organ in the church. A policeman came to the school and talked to them all in turn, looking very big and clumsy sitting on one of the children's chairs, his bum hanging over each side. They hadn't laughed at him. They knew he was trying to be friendly. Her father had stood at the front of the class, watching and frowning. Even if Susan had wanted to tell the policeman what she knew about Heather Mather and where she was, it would be quite impossible with her father listening in.

Then, when Heather didn't return, the word in the village was that Eddie Black had taken her. Eddie lived with his mother and though he'd left school, he didn't work. Susan knew Eddie hadn't taken Heather. He wouldn't know how to hurt her. He was painfully careful when he held his birds, and once when Susan had tripped and fallen, grazing her knee so it bled, he had cried. But everyone in the village said he'd taken her. One night someone threw a rock through Mrs Black's bedroom window. The next morning Eddie woke up to find that two of his birds were dead. Their necks had been twisted. He stood in his garden and looked round him, bewildered, his mouth slightly open, as if couldn't really understand what had happened.

Heather never turned up and her body was never found. The police wanted to charge Eddie with her murder, but decided that they had insufficient evidence. Even in those days, more was needed than neighbourhood gossip and a gut feeling that the boy was odd. They needed a body.

Beside her, Tom coughed. He didn't want this to last all day. He wanted to be home in Durham before it got dark. He knew it was important, but he was a great one for routine. He liked to get his dinner on time. Susan untied the frayed baler twine which attached the gate to the post, lifted it on its hinges over the long grass and they walked through.

"This way," she said. "Mind though, it's a bit of a walk."

Heather Mather had boyfriends nobody knew anything about. Not a real boyfriend. Not a lad her own age to have a giggle with, holding hands on the way down from the hill. Games of doctors and nurses in the shed at the bottom of the garden, brief forbidden kisses and flushed red faces. The other girls played games like that, but not Heather. She *was* too old for her years, as Mrs Tillotson had said, and when she thought no one was looking she had a watchful, wary look. Sometimes Susan thought, if she hadn't been the teacher's daughter, they might have been friends. Heather's boyfriends were older. They were men, not boys. She got into their cars and drove off with them and when she got back she lied about where she'd been. Even to Marilyn and Diane.

Uncle Alec took me to the pictures in town.

And Uncle Alec lied about it too.

It were a good film, weren't it, love?

His arm around her, protective, as they stood on the short strip of pavement, the only pavement in the village, outside her house. Alec Mather, her Dad's brother, who worked as gamekeeper on the big estate, who was tall and strong and carried a gun. Who had a dog which would do anything Alec told it, which would go through fire for him, everyone said, but which snarled and bared its teeth at anyone else. Susan tried for a moment to remember the name of the dog. Why wouldn't it come to her, when everything else was so clear? Soon she gave up. She had other, more disturbing memories.

It hadn't been Alec's car Heather had climbed into, her skirt riding up, so she nearly showed *her* knickers, the first time Susan had watched her. It could have been one of Alec's friends who was driving. He was about the same age, dark hair, greased back, a tattoo on the back of his hand. And later, when he dropped Heather back in the lane down to the church, Alec was there to meet them. When Heather wasn't looking (though Susan was, hiding at the top of a high stone wall, which surrounded the churchyard) the stranger handed him a five pound note. Alec slipped it quickly into the pocket of his jacket. The wall was nearly three feet thick, covered with ivy and overhung with branches. Susan could remember the smell of the ivy even now, as they walked across the field, up the hill towards the quarry. This was the first of several encounters she witnessed over the months. Sometimes the men were strangers and sometimes she recognized them. Money usually changed hands.

Would she have described this to the friendly policeman when he came to the classroom to ask about Heather, if her father hadn't been there, listening in? Perhaps she would. Then everything would have been different. Her whole life. She wouldn't be here, walking up the hill with Tom on an April afternoon.

After that day she watched Heather more closely. She listened to the women talking after church. Heather's father had gone away to work. He'd got a job as a cook in the merchant navy. Alec spent a lot of time with the family to keep an eye on things. It only made sense.

And one afternoon Susan watched Heather climb into her father's car, the teacher's car. It was soon after Sports Day, at the start of the school holidays, one of those rare hot, still days. In the house there had still been a chill caused by the rotting walls and her parents' antagonism. Her father said he had an NUT meeting in Leeds and her mother wanted a lift into town. He'd told her it wasn't possible. He'd promised a lift to colleagues from the villages on the way. There wouldn't be room in the Morris for Sylvia too. She'd sulked, fetched the sherry from the sideboard, which she only did at lunchtime when she was severely provoked. Outside it was airless. Susan felt the sun burning her bare arms and legs, beating up from the tarmac of the playground. She went to her nest on the churchyard wall not to watch, but to find some shade.

She saw Heather first. She was on her own. No Alec. No Marilyn and Diane. She walked slowly down the lane, her head

bent, looking down at her sandals. In September she'd move on
to the big school and already Susan could sense that gulf
between them. It was very quiet. There was a wood pigeon
calling from the trees behind the church and the distant,
inevitable sheep. Then a car engine and the Morris Minor,
squat and shiny as a beetle, drove solely past. It stopped just
beyond Heather. She didn't change her pace or look up, but
when she reached the passenger door, she opened it and got in.
Despite the sun reflected from the car's bonnet, which made her
screw up her eyes, Susan was frozen. She wanted to shout out.
Hello. Heather. Look at me. Come and play. Anything to stop her
climbing into the car. But the words wouldn't come. The car
pulled slowly away, backed into the church entrance to turn,
then drove off.

Alec was there when it returned. He was leaning against the
wall, turning his face to the sun, so close to Susan that she could
almost have reached out and touched his hair. The dog was with
him, lying on the road, its tongue out, panting. Her father was
alone in the car. The window was open and she could see his
face, very red. He was furious.

"You cheated me," he said. It was a hiss not a whisper. Alec
hadn't moved from the wall and if her father had spoken more
softly he wouldn't have been heard. Susan thought he sounded
a bit like one of the little boys in the infants' class, complaining
about a stolen toy. *It's not fair.* That was what her father meant,
even if he didn't say it.

"She came with you, didn't she?" Still Alec leaned against
the wall, his arms folded against his chest, that smile on his face.

"But she wouldn't even let me . . ."

"That were down to you, weren't it? She's only a slip of a
thing."

"For Christ's sake, man."

"Anyway, that were the deal. Ten pounds. No going back
now. Any road, it's already spent. Where is she?"

"Up on the hill. Near the quarry. We went for a walk. I
thought . . ." He didn't finish the sentence.

"Aye well, I reckon she'll come down in her own time. I'll
have a word. Make her see sense. You can fix up to take her out
later, if you like."

Her father didn't reply. He didn't mention the money again, though money was always tight in their house. It was one of the things her parents fought about. He wound up the window and drove off. She wondered where he went. Not to the union meeting. He wouldn't have had time to get to Leeds and back. Later though, when it was dark outside and they were watching the television, he talked about the resolutions they'd discussed at the meeting and the men he'd met. Susan would have been entirely taken in if she hadn't known he was lying. She wondered how many times he'd lied to them before. It was as if everything was a game and nothing was real any more.

Heather didn't go home that night. That was the day she disappeared.

Susan thought she couldn't have been the only person in the village to know about Heather's men friends and how Alec organized it all. They must have seen the strangers' cars, realized there were nights when the gamekeeper had cash to spend in the pub. But nobody spoke. When the police asked questions the villagers talked about shy Eddie Black. Otherwise they kept their mouths firmly shut. Alec's dog had a mad eye and Alec had a fierce temper, even when he was smiling. They didn't want to know what had really happened to Heather.

Susan knew. When her father had driven off and Alec had sauntered back to the village, towards the house he shared with Heather's mum, she'd scrambled down from the wall, pulling away the ivy in her haste. Despite the heat she'd gone to the hill, running all the way. She hadn't opened the gate into the quarry field that day, she'd climbed it. Then, she'd been young and strong. From halfway up the hill, she'd seen Heather lying flat on her back at the edge of the old workings. At first she'd thought she was asleep, but as she approached, scattering the sheep in her path, she'd realized that the girl's eyes were open and there were tears on her cheeks.

Heather heard her coming. She must have done. By then Susan was out of breath, panting, and there'd be the sound of her footsteps and the sheep loping off. But she didn't sit up until the very last minute.

"Oh," she said. "It's you."

"Who were you expecting?" Susan demanded. "Alec? My Dad?"

"Your father? He's pathetic."

That was what they always called *her*. It was the jeer that followed her around the playground. *You're pathetic, you are.* Shouted in turn by Marilyn, Diane and Heather. It was the word that made her fight back.

"Not as pathetic as your Dad. Moving out and letting Alec take up with your Mam. Not as pathetic as you, going off with all those men, just because he tells you."

She was shocked by her own courage. She'd never stood up to one of them before. Heather was stunned too. She got to her feet but didn't say anything. Susan thought she might run down the hill and home. But she didn't. She just stared.

At last Heather spoke. "If you say anything at school, I'll tell them about your father. I'll tell them he made me go off with him."

"I wouldn't tell them!" Susan moved forward. "I never would." In her head she had a picture of the two of them, sitting on the pavement outside the council houses, friends brought together by the shared secret. Besides, who would she tell?

Heather must have seen the step towards her as a threat. She backed away, lost her footing, slipped. Susan might have been able to save her. She was strong. And there was a moment when she almost did it. When she almost reached out and grabbed the girl's arm. If she saved Heather's life, wouldn't she have to be her friend? But she decided not to. She wanted to see what it would look like. What Heather would look like rolling down the steep bank until she reached the overhang and fell into nothing. What sound she would make when she hit the stones below. It was as if all the watching had been leading up to this moment. And it was all very satisfactory, very satisfying. There was the expression of panic when Heather scrabbled to save herself and realized it was useless, the moment of flight, the dull thud. And then her undignified resting place amongst the rubble of quarry waste, her skirt around her waist, her legs spread out. Susan would have liked to leave her there for everyone to see.

But that wouldn't do. Someone might have seen Susan get over the gate into the field. Then there'd be questions she didn't want to answer. And Susan wanted to get closer to the body. She was curious now to see what it looked like. She peered down over the lip of the cliff to the face of the quarry where the stone had been hacked away. It was a difficult climb, but not impossible for her, not so very different from scrambling down from the churchyard wall. Only in scale. At the bottom she took a minute to catch her breath. She stood over Heather, who didn't really look like Heather at all now. Then she rolled her close into the cliff face and piled her body with the loose rocks which lined the quarry bottom. That was more exhausting than the climb back. When she reached the top the sun was very low. She took one last look down the cliff. Because of the angle it was hard to see where Heather was lying and even if you could see the place it would look as if there'd been a small rock fall.

When she got in her mother told her off for being so filthy. *When are you going to start acting like a girl?* Her father talked about the union meeting. They watched television. There was shepherd's pie for tea.

The policeman came into school to ask his questions and later she wished she'd told him what had happened. She could have explained that it was an accident. She could have said she'd panicked. They'd have had to accept that. They'd have given her help. But perhaps by then it was already too late. The trouble was she'd enjoyed it. The moment when Heather fell had been so exciting. It had the thrill and the power of running across the field in sports day, of crossing the line first. It had caused sparks in her brain. She'd wanted to recreate that buzzing sensation. She'd thought of nothing else. That was why she'd killed Eddie's birds. But birds aren't like people. It wasn't the same.

Tom wasn't much more fit than she was and it took them longer than she'd expected to walk up the hill to the disused quarry. Since her time they'd put up a fence and a couple of notices saying it was unsafe. It wasn't as deep as she'd remembered.

"That's where she is," she said. "Under that pile of rubble at the bottom of the cliff. That's where you'll find Heather Mather."

"So," he said. "The scene of your first crime."

"Oh no," she was offended. "Heather was an accident. Not like the others."

She liked Tom. He was her named officer at the prison. She'd refused to speak to the detectives and the psychiatrists who'd tried to persuade her to tell them where Heather Mather was. Her first victim, as they called her. The first of four before she was caught. All pretty girls, who simpered and pouted and made up to older men.

Tom spoke into his radio and she could already see the police officers who'd been waiting in the van coming through the gate. She let him take her arm and steer her down the hill. He'd be ready for his dinner.

THE FIERY DEVIL

Peter Tremayne

A curse upon the fiery devil, thundering along so smoothly
. . . He loitered about the station, waiting until one should
stay to call there; and when one did, and was detached for
water, he stood parallel with it, watching its huge wheels
and brazen front and thinking what a cruel power and
might it held. Ugh! To see the great wheels slowly turning
and to think of being run down and crushed!
          Chapter 55, *Dombey and Son*, Charles Dickens, 1848

"Captain Ryder?"

Mr Josiah Plankton peered myopically at the business card
that the young man had offered and glanced up with a quick
bird-like motion of his head. Then he adjusted his gold-rimmed
pince-nez and turned his gaze back to the card.

"Captain Ryder of the Detective Department of the Metropolitan Police?" There was a slight inflection of incredulity in
his tone.

"Exactly so, sir," nodded the young man who stood before
him with a pleasant smile on his tanned features.

"You'll excuse my momentary consternation, sir," Mr
Plankton said as he motioned his visitor to a seat in front of
the large ornate desk he occupied. "I was unaware that the
members of the Detective Department of the London Metropolitan Police held military rank."

The young man appeared unabashed as he seated himself in
the chair.

"My captaincy was in the 16th Lancers, sir. I was . . ." He
shifted his weight slightly to adjust his position to one of greater

comfort. "I was wounded last year at the Battle of Mudki during the Sutlej Campaign and thus, being unable to serve the colours further, I was persuaded by Colonel Rowan to join the Metropolitan force in the newly established Detective Department. The colonel considered that I had a talent in that direction."

Mr Plankton laid the young man's card on the ink blotter before him and glanced quizzically at the detective.

"Commissioner Sir Charles Rowan, eh? I have had the pleasure of his acquaintance, for he helped some years ago with the framing of the Solicitors' Act in Parliament. I then represented the Incorporated Law Society of England and Wales. So, do I presume that you are here in an official capacity on behalf of the Commissioner?"

"Your presumption is correct, sir, in that I am here representing the Metropolitan Police."

"Then how may the firm of Scratch, Nellbody and Plankton assist you?"

"I am given to understand that you are solicitors acting for Dombey and Son, the shipping company?"

Mr Plankton gave a sad smile. "I am not sure that such a state of affairs will last many days longer. You have doubtless heard the news from Threadneedle Street?"

Captain Ryder made a faint motion of his hand.

"Then there is truth in the story that the company may soon go into liquidation? Or at least Mister Paul Dombey is to be declared a bankrupt?"

Mr Plankton was serious.

"In any other circumstances, Captain Ryder, I would have replied to you that I am bound by my client's confidence, but the news is all about the town. Dombey and Son will soon cease to trade. Mister Dombey may well be able to call on some reserves but if the firm lasts out a twelve-month, I will be surprised."

"As Dombey and Son are a considerable trading company that, surely – and if I may be so bold to say so – will impinge on the business connection with your own firm, sir?"

Mr Plankton smiled wryly and gestured to his office with an encompassing sweep of his hand. Captain Ryder became aware of several boxes and cases in various stages of being packed. Even some pictures had been taken off their wall hanging in preparation to be crated.

"I am about to retire. The few remaining accounts that exist are being placed elsewhere by my chief clerk, who is also moving to another practice."

"But Messrs Scratch and Nellbody . . .?"

"Have been deceased these last ten years, sir. I am sole partner and now it is time for me to have some peaceful retirement. My intention is to move to France. I think the sun and wine of Provence will be conducive to my constitution after the smog of the City. London is no place for retirement."

"I see, sir," nodded the young man. He paused and then cleared his throat. "I am, sir, placed in a delicate position for my duty persuades me that I need to trespass into what you may deem as the confidential matters of your client."

Mr Plankton replied with a thin smile.

"In which case, sir, I shall decline to answer your questions. However, if you place those questions before me, I will be better able to judge to what extent you may trespass or not."

Captain Ryder gave an apologetic grimace.

"Speaking for the Metropolitan force, our jurisdiction scarcely reaches to Woolwich. We have only recently been requested to extend our policing to that area of the Arsenal. Therefore it is as a special matter of government intervention that we have been asked to pursue some inquiries pursuant to an incident that took place further abroad."

Mr Plankton looked bewildered.

"Government intervention, sir? I am not sure that I am following you."

"We have been asked to intercede in a matter following a request by no less a person than Mister Cudworth of South Eastern Railways who has the ear of . . . of certain government officials."

Mr Plankton spread his hands, still mystified.

"I am at a loss sir. South Eastern Railways? I know of no business dealings between Dombey and Son and South Eastern Railways and . . ."

The solicitor suddenly paused and looked thoughtful.

"Just so, sir," the young man smiled briefly, noting the change of expression. "Two weeks ago today there was an incident at the railway station of Paddock Wood. It used to be called Maidstone Road Halt until a few years ago. It is, as you doubtless know, a station on the main railway line running from London Bridge to Dover. A man was killed at that station. South Eastern Railways, of course, own that line."

A look of understanding began to form on Mr Plankton's features.

"Your client, Mister Paul Dombey, was a witness to this incident," added Captain Ryder as if to clarify matters.

"The incident being when a former employee of Mister Dombey fell in front of the express train from Dover to London," sighed Mr Plankton, shaking his head as though it was distasteful to be reminded of the unpleasantness.

"You are correct in that particular, sir. Except that this was no mere employee but a certain James Carker who had been manager of Dombey and Son and who had recently run away with Mrs Edith Dombey, the wife of his employer."

Mr Plankton made a disapproving sound by clicking his tongue against the roof of his mouth.

"I am aware of these unhappy circumstances, sir, but I hardly see the relevance of any inquiry . . ."

"Furthermore," went on Captain Ryder, interrupting, "certain charges had been laid against James Carker as a suspect in embezzling large sums of money from the company. It is that embezzlement that, in my understanding, has brought the company to the verge of ruin."

"I fail to see in what capacity Mr Cudworth of South Eastern Railways has asked for the inter . . . the intervention of the Detective Department of the Metropolitan force in this matter? Surely the local coroner has dealt with the matter?"

Captain Ryder shook his head in admonishment.

"The inquest is delayed, sir. The running over and killing of a man at a railway station by an express train is not a matter to be dismissed without consequence, sir. South Eastern Railways can be charged with felonious homicide. Naturally, they wish to clear the name of their company and employees. There are many matters to consider. There are those who would like to see

South Eastern Railways suffer misfortune. Considerable wealth has changed hands with that company now attracting a near monopoly on the transportation of goods. Until the line opened four years ago, shipping companies had sent goods by barge along the Medway. Those who invested in such waterway transport would like nothing better than to see this railway forced to close. So this is why we must ask, did the man stumble accidentally under the wheels? Was his death as a result of some negligence by an employee of the railway? Or . . .?" The young man shrugged and left the question hanging in the air. "I have already made initial enquiries and certain sinister facts emerge."

Mr Plankton looked startled, his body more erect in the chair. "Pray, what manner of sinister facts?" he demanded.

"That the late James Carker was a former manager of Dombey and Son, that he had apparently been accused of embezzlement from the firm for not inconsiderable sums, and that he had run away with Mrs Edith Dombey, the wife of his employer." Captain Ryder ticked the points off on the fingers of his right hand. "These facts lend a certain – shall we say? – interest to his sudden demise. What lends the sinister element is the fact that no less a person than Mr Paul Dombey himself was on the railway platform at the time. The coincidence is singular, to say the least. And there was another, as yet unidentified, person there with him at the precise moment that Carker fell to his death."

"Are you implying that Mister Dombey . . .?"

"It is not my task to imply, sir. I merely state the facts."

"Yet from the facts you seem to speculate . . ."

"Speculation, sir, is a fruitless task. Facts must breed more facts, sir. And it is facts that I come in search of."

"I will say nothing that may harm my client," replied Mr Plankton firmly, folding his hands on the desk before him. "Mister Paul Dombey is a worthy gentleman and already faced with shame and ruin by the deeds of this man Carker and, may God forgive me, but I must say that it is a just recompense for his evil deeds that he has departed life in this manner."

"It is not in the brief of my official capacity to indulge myself in moral judgements," murmured Captain Ryder, "but simply to gather the facts for presentation to be assessed by judge and jury."

Mr Plankton shook his head.

"What I meant . . ." He paused.

"Precisely what did you mean?"

"Simply, that in the demise of James Carker, the world has no cause to grieve. However, his death is little compensation for the financial and emotional loss that Mister Dombey has suffered."

"Again, you express a moral judgement, sir, which I am not at liberty to comment on."

There was an uncomfortable pause.

"What is it that you want from me?" asked the solicitor, finally breaking the silence.

"I believe that you knew James Carker?"

"He was, as you have correctly stated, the manager of Dombey and Son and so we knew each other in a business capacity."

"And in a social capacity?"

"Certainly not," snapped Mr Plankton. "He was sharp of tooth, sly of manner with a watchful eye, soft of foot and oily of tongue. He was, to sum up, sir, a most disagreeable creature. A thorough-going scoundrel. I did not trust him, sir, and certainly would not include him among my social acquaintances."

"Did you ever mention your views to Mister Dombey?"

"It was not my place to question Mister Dombey's judgment of the men that he employed. Mr Dombey was a man not to be trifled with so far as his business dealings were concerned."

"Yet you were his legal adviser?"

"And legal advice I gave him when he requested it."

"Did you also know Mrs Dombey?" the young man asked so abruptly that Mr Plankton blinked.

"I have, on occasion, met her." The reply was more guarded.

"I am given to understand that she was formerly the widow of a Colonel Granger before she became Paul Dombey's second wife. Were you aware of that?"

"I was. Mister Dombey's first wife had died in childbirth when his son was born. The son was a weak child and eventually died, leaving Mister Dombey a widower with a daughter who he neglected. He decided to marry again and, as you say, Mrs Granger was thought a suitable match. Again, should you seek a personal opinion, I did not share that view. I once represented her mother, the late Mrs Cleopatra Skewton, over a matter of a small land purchase some years ago. It was not an experience that provided me with esteem for her or her daughter."

"So you knew Mrs Granger before she married Mister Dombey?"

"Briefly, sir, briefly. Never more than a nod, an exchange of polite pleasantry."

"She eloped, if I might apply the word to this matter, with James Carker and they both fled to France?"

"That is so. The facts are not unknown to me as well as to several others in the City. Alas, sir, such scandals are never kept secret for long."

"Indeed. The facts are given in a statement made by Mister Dombey taken down by the superintendent of police at Maidstone. The parish constable at Paddock Wood felt he needed more expert guidance after the incident when the basic facts were known."

Mr Plankton coughed delicately.

"As I say, the facts are not unknown to me. You will have seen from the statement that I was attending on Mister Dombey at the time that he gave his statement to the superintendent. I acted in the capacity of his legal adviser, of course."

"Of course, sir. Which begs the question. How was it that you were on hand when the statement was made? The accident happened at four o'clock in the morning when the Dover to London Express was passing through Paddock Wood station. The same day at precisely noon, you were with Mister Dombey at Paddock Wood. Mister Dombey had passed the night at the Forester's Arms, the inn there, indeed, as had the victim of the accident, James Carker. How were you alerted to the incident and able to travel down to Kent so quickly? The accident prevented any train running on that line until midday. You'll forgive me, sir, but I do so dislike a question unresolved."

Mister Plankton smiled thinly, an almost habitual expression before answering a question.

"Then pray do not trouble yourself, for the resolution is simple. I was already staying at Maidstone where I had proceeded to settle some legal business with an old client preparatory to my retirement."

"Indeed?" Captain Ryder sighed reflectively. "That places you within eight miles of Paddock Wood. How did you . . .?"

"I had booked into the hotel in King Street on the afternoon before the accident. On the morning . . . I left the hotel for a walk, it being my custom to take a stroll every morning. As you may know, sir, the Maidstone police station is also situated in King Street, and at that time I encountered the superintendent of police, with whom I had a passing acquaintance. He told me that a James Carker had fallen under a train at Paddock Wood and the local parish constable was troubled by the circumstances. He had sent to the superintendent to interview a Mister Dombey who had witnessed the incident. I was astonished and felt obliged to point out my connection with Mister Paul Dombey. The superintendent suggested that I should accompany him in his horse and fly to Paddock Wood."

The young detective sat nodding slowly.

Then he said quickly: "So, we have Mister Paul Dombey and James Carker, both having stayed at the Forester's Arms in Paddock Wood. How did they come there on that precise night? Both had just returned from France and separately, with Mister Dombey a few hours behind James Carker."

Mister Plankton sat back, toying for a moment with a silver letter opener that he had picked up from his desk.

"You make it sound extremely sinister, sir. Do you imply that Mister Dombey was following Carker?"

The young man shook his head as if suddenly bewildered.

"Mister Dombey admits to travelling to Dijon in France to confront his wife and Carker after they had eloped together. He had discovered where they were staying on the intelligence of a Mrs Brown. Mister Dombey admits that a confrontation took place but that he left Carker and his wife unharmed and returned via Paris. The fact is that Mister Dombey did board a ferry sailing from Calais only a few hours after the ferry on which Carker had sailed. That both men wound up at the same railway halt to which they were strangers when both might have logically proceeded directly to London is rather singular, is it not? What conclusion would you draw from these facts?"

Mr Plankton's brows drew together.

"Implications do lead to speculation, sir, and I thought that you denied the habit?" he observed dryly.

When Captain Ryder did not respond, the solicitor added defensively: "I have said that I will not say anything which impugns the good name of Mister Dombey."

"You do not have to, sir. However, Mister Dombey admitted during my subsequent inquiry that these were the facts. Therefore I was able to ask my colleague Monsieur Caissidiere, at the Prefecture de Police in Paris, to contact a police officer in Dijon to take a statement from Mrs Dombey. She confirms the essentials; that she had run off with Carker on a whim to spite her husband whom she thought little of. But she thought even less of Carker. Dombey came to see them in the apartment she had taken in Dijon. There was an altercation but not of a violent kind. Verbal blows were all that were struck. Dombey then left to return to England, leaving his wife to her chosen path. Mrs Dombey then told Carker what she really thought of him and he, in a rage, also took his baggage and left. She further alleged that, while doing so, he had muttered something about settling with someone in London with whom he had business. His parting taunt to her was that she would be sorry, for he was a rich man."

There was a silence while Mr Plankton studied the face of the young officer before offering a comment.

"You will have read Mister Dombey's statement that he spent a day or two in Paris and so we must conclude that it was purely by chance that he arrived at Dover soon after Carker had landed."

"And a further coincidence that Mister Dombey took a local train and decided to alight at Paddock Wood, the very place where Carker had also alighted," responded the young man sceptically. "Another coincidence that both men stayed the night at the Forester's Arms? Come, sir, one coincidence might be acceptable but surely . . .?"

Mr Plankton shrugged.

"I represent to you the facts as told to me by Mister Dombey and which he placed in his statement. I do not comment on them. All I say is that I have never known Mister Dombey to add dishonesty to the fault of poor judgment of character."

Captain Ryder smiled a trifle sadly.

"If that is so, sir, then we must believe there is a logical explanation for these coincidences. Let us proceed with what we know. I can add that my friend Monsieur Caissidiere was thorough on my behalf. He checked Mister Dombey's movements in Paris and found that he had paid a visit to the Agence Havas."

Mr Plankton raised an eyebrow slightly.

Captain Ryder leaned forward in his chair.

"Ah, sir, are you acquainted with the Agence Havas?"

The solicitor shook his head at once.

"The Agence Havas is known even in London, Captain. It is what is called a news agency; a place for the dissemination of news. Monsieur Havas formed it some ten years ago. He has what are called correspondents in each capital who send news items to him in Paris; items from the newspapers that are translated and passed on by the Agence Havas. By use of carrier pigeons they are able to get stories from London morning newspapers so that they can be published in the Paris afternoon editions. It is, indeed, amazing how small the world is growing."

"Exactly so."

"The fact is interesting, sir. But I fail to see . . .?"

"But what would Mister Dombey have to do with a news agency?" smiled Captain Ryder. "Did he not mention his visit to you?"

"Not at all."

"Strange that he did not. Do you know Monsieur Solliec, the Agence Havas correspondent in London?"

Mr Plankton frowned.

"I do not, sir. Oh, I have met him a few times in the coffee house I frequent at luncheon but I cannot say I know him."

"Then have you had any business dealings with a Mister Morfin?"

There was a moment's hesitation before Mr Plankton replied.

"Naturally. Mister Morfin was the assistant manager of Dombey and Son and, since Mister Carker went to France,

Mister Morfin has acted as manager. A worthy young man, but he shares the fault with Mister Dombey of not being the best judge of character."

"Perhaps you could elucidate?" Captain Ryder raised an eyebrow.

"He is enamoured of Miss Harriette Carker."

"Ah, you speak of James Carker's sister?"

"Just so, sir. Just so. There is bad blood in that family, sir. Bad blood."

The young man looked thoughtfully at the solicitor.

"I presume that you refer not only to James but to his older brother, John Carker, who also is employed by Mister Dombey?"

"You have carried out a thorough investigation, sir," Mr Plankton observed, nodding quickly. "Do you know of the background of John Carker?"

"I know from my inquiries that he admitted to embezzling money from the firm when he was a young man but claims he immediately reformed and paid it back. However, his younger brother, the late James Carker, never let him forget the matter and mistreated him badly."

Mister Plankton sniffed.

"Reforms do occur, sir. Paul on the road to Damascus and all that. Personally, I place no faith in reformed characters nor in reformers."

"Did you know that Mister Morfin sent John Carker to Dover to meet Mister Dombey from the boat?"

Mr Plankton frowned.

"How did he know when Mister Dombey was arriving?"

"As I have said, Mister Dombey called in at the Agence Havas in Paris. He paid a clerk there to send one of the carrier pigeons that the agency uses to keep in touch with its correspondents in each of the European capitals to Monsieur Solliec in London. The intelligence was that Mister Dombey aimed to arrive in Dover at a particular time. Monsieur Solliec was acquainted with Mister Morfin and was able to pass this on. John Carker was therefore despatched to Dover to meet Mister Dombey. This step was taken because Mister Morfin wanted to give news of the extent of the embezzlement, which had then been fully uncovered. Now, sir, here we have another mystery. There is no mention of John Carker in the statement given by Mister Dombey and which you were witness to."

Mr Plankton was looking astonished.

"I, also, had no knowledge of him at the scene," he replied quietly. "Mister Dombey did not mention him."

"Yet John Carker met Paul Dombey at Dover and they both caught a local train to Paddock Wood, there being no direct trains to London. Unable to further their journey, they stayed at the Forester's Arms, presumably with the intention of remaining there until the first London train the next morning. Now, sir, it seems a coincidence that they both stayed in the same inn as James Carker."

"How do you learn that John Carker was actually with Mister Dombey at the inn, sir?"

"The landlord, naturally."

"But when I went to Paddock Wood . . ."

"Yes, sir? Tell me what transpired?"

"The superintendent from Maidstone and I found Mister Dombey in the inn, fortified by the solicitations of the landlord with some whisky, but was very shaken and horrified by the incident."

"And there was no sign of John Carker?"

"None at all, sir."

"And Mister Dombey's account?"

"As I said, he did not mention John Carker to me. It could be the shock had momentarily caused a lapse in memory. As he put in his statement, he had left the inn to await the arrival of the London train. The express train came through first. It was, of course, dark and he could see little. He was aware of someone entering the station after him and moving to one end of the platform. He took no further notice. The express came through and it was only when he heard a terrifying scream and the train came to a stop a little further along the line that he was aware of the tragedy. It was only some while later that the station master and parish constable identified the person who had been killed, a name recognized by Mister Dombey who fainted in shock. But, surely, Captain Ryder, all this you have already read in Mister Dombey's statement, which I witnessed?"

"I have, indeed, sir. It is the things that are not in the statement that concern me. We know from Mister Morfin that John Carker was sent to meet Mister Dombey at Dover and we know from the innkeeper that two men alighted at Paddock Wood from the Dover train to await the London connection the next morning. Why did they alight there and go to the inn where James Carker was? How is it, sir, that John Carker seems to have disappeared from an account of these events?"

Mister Plankton sat back and his fingers drummed a tattoo on his desk top.

"I should think, sir, that even I – who am not a detective – might postulate a probability."

"Which is?" pressed the young man.

"I have already said, there is bad blood in the Carker family. Both brothers have embezzled. But James Carker has embezzled such sums as will bring the firm of Dombey and Son into bankruptcy and liquidation. Consider this, sir . . . who are the beneficiaries from Carker's demise?"

Captain Ryder examined him carefully.

"John and Harriette Carker?"

"Exactly so, sir."

The young man nodded.

"Indeed, indeed. They stand to inherit whatever funds stood to the credit of their brother at his death. But we have already examined his accounts and, do you know the strangest thing? James Carker certainly left a small sum of money but nowhere near the sums that Mister Morfin and the firm's accountants show that he embezzled during his period as manager."

Mr Plankton thought for a moment and then he smiled grimly.

"I have already mentioned that Mr Morfin is devotedly attached to Miss Harriette Carker. Have you checked his accounts? Perhaps . . .?"

Captain Ryder sighed.

"You suggest a conspiracy, sir."

Mr Plankton bent forward intently.

"Have you questioned Mister Dombey about John Carker?"

"We would be poor detectives had we not tried to do so. He claimed he did not think it of pertinence at the time and that he was, in any case, in a state of agitation. But he tells a story that brings forward other questions."

"I do not follow."

"Mister Dombey confirms that John Carker met him at Dover. John Carker then revealed the extent of his brother's embezzlement. Furthermore, he told Dombey that before he had left his lodgings in London a boy delivered a note from Mr Morfin informing him that he should break his return journey at Maidstone, where he should repair to a certain warehouse. There, the note said, John Carker would find goods and materials that were the property of Dombey and Son. He was to ensure their safe transportation to the London ware-house. Dombey himself was unaware of such matters but agreed that the two men should travel from Dover to Paddock Wood, where, a few years prior, the branch line to Maidstone had been opened. However, on arrival, there were no trains continuing to Maidstone until a local train at a quarter to four o'clock the next day. Seeing no reason to spend a further lengthy period at Maidstone, Mister Dombey decided to await the London train at Paddock Wood while his companion, John Carker, went on to Maidstone to deal with the business matters. John Carker left Paddock Wood at a quarter to four, leaving Dombey to await the London slow train at a quarter past the hour. In the intervening time, at precisely four o'clock, came the express, at which time James Carker emerged on the platform and met his death."

Mr Plankton was shaking his head.

"An amazing coincidence of circumstance, sir."

"Even more amazing in a singular manner was the fact that when John Carker reached the warehouse to which he had been directed, no one had heard of any goods or materials for Dombey and Son. Nor did Mister Morfin later admit to sending any such note to John Carker."

"A curious convenience, sir," commented Mr Plankton dryly.

"Convenient, indeed. Leaving Mister Dombey alone on the railway platform with James Carker."

"I refuse to believe the implication. I would presume there is now a warrant out for John Carker? It is clear that there was some base deception here of which Mister Dombey is wholly innocent. As I suggested, the Carkers are a bad lot and I would remind you that Mister Morfin wishes to marry into that family. Conspiracy, sir. It smacks of conspiracy."

Captain Ryder grimaced.

"We have now recovered the note sent to John Carker." He touched his breast pocket lightly. "Which brings me to other matters that worry me. From the start, the facts that have brought me to conclusions of a sinister nature seemed to point to the fact that James Carker's life was taken in unnatural fashion. The evidence now confirms it. His death was brought about by contrivance and terrifying premeditation. He was pushed under the express train but not for reasons of revenge but for gain. You, yourself, have suggested the motive. He had embezzled such a large sum from Dombey and Son that would be an attractive enough proposition. The person who committed the heinous crime of pushing James Carker in front of the express train was clearly a confederate . . . a partner in crime. He was the banker, if you like, of the monies embezzled over the years."

Mr Plankton pulled a face expressing his scepticism.

"But there are several problems with this story. Firstly, you have explained how it was known when Dombey was arriving at Dover. But how did the murderer know James Carker was returning to London and that the arrivals would be close together? If not coincidence, then by wizardry. How did the murderer know James Carker would be at Paddock Wood? It would be an impossible crime without such knowledge."

Captain Ryder sat back, nodding slowly.

"In fact, the murderer knew the movement of James Carker a few days before he knew those of Paul Dombey. The entire set of events was manipulated from the first. The murderer knew both Dombey and Carker would be at Paddock Wood at the same time and his plot was to involve them in his gruesome plan."

Mr Plankton sniffed.

"I don't see how . . . unless we return to suspecting Mister Dombey himself."

"Perhaps we don't have to go that far. The mail system between Dijon and here is remarkably good. We tend to think of

France as back in the days of the *poste aux chevaux* but such is not the case. Indeed, sir, they are in advance of us. It is known that three years ago the French introduced a designated wagon on their trains from city to city in which the mail is sorted after it is collected. It saves an entire day in transportation. Mail is collected and delivered every second day in every municipality in France. Before he left Dijon, James Carker wrote a short letter to his confederate telling him that he was *en route* to London. He told him when he was expected to arrive and that he would call on his confederate for his share of the money."

Mr Plankton leaned back with a frown. "Do you say so, sir? Do you have the note?"

"I do say so," confirmed Captain Ryder without responding to the second question. "The confederate did not want to share the riches he had hidden in his accounts with Carker. What is more, the confederate in London wrote care of the harbour master at Dover asking that the note be delivered into the hands of Carker when he arrived. That note suggested that Carker break his journey at the Forester's Arms where he would be met and the matter sorted. Paddock Wood was a quiet spot outside of London and suitable for such a transaction as the murderer had in mind. James Carker obeyed without suspicion."

Captain Ryder paused for a moment before continuing.

"Then came the news from Paris by carrier pigeon as to when Paul Dombey was arriving and – this is the only coincidence – it was to be that same night as James Carker. It so happened that the correspondent of the Agence Havas, Monsieur Solliec, met the murderer, whom he knew by means of the fact that they sometimes frequented the same coffee house. Having discovered that John Carker was being sent to Dover, it was then easy to send a messenger with a note purporting to be from Mister Morfin to John Carker's lodging before he left, a message knowing that it would bring him and Paul Dombey to the inn at Paddock Wood."

"As a solicitor, I see several problems with the story," declared Mr Plankton.

"Let me continue, first. James Carker did not find his confederate at the inn. The landlord said Carker drank a lot of wine with his dinner and displayed various signs of impatience. He then went to his room and fell asleep, having asked to be roused in time to get the early morning train to London, due at four fifteen in the morning. A short time after, Dombey and John Carker arrived. The murderer had arrived in the darkness of the night and was awaiting his opportunity. We know how the opportunity came about. By the way, the note making the rendez-vous was found on the bloody remains of James Carker."

"Amazing, sir. Simply, amazing. By whom was the note signed?"

Captain Ryder shook his head.

"Alas, the hand that penned the note added no signature. One thing, however, was apparent – it was the same hand that penned the note to John Carker instructing him to break the journey at Paddock Wood."

Mr Plankton raised his eyebrows. "By my soul, sir. What a fascinating story you tell. So it was all a plot. A plot to incriminate John Carker in the murder of his brother?"

"It would seem so, sir. A very ingenious plot, if I may say so."

"No one could deny you saying so, sir. Yet I still see some questions that need resolution, sir. If the murderer's plot was to meet with James Carker in the inn and kill him, why wait hidden away until early morning, when John Carker had left for Maidstone on the milk train, and when he had to follow James Carker to the station and hope there were no witnesses to watch him being pushed under the train? It seems a messy plot to me, sir."

"An improvised plot is sometimes a messy one, Mister Plankton."

"Improvised?"

"But the murderer had neglected the fact that an early train would leave Paddock Wood for Maidstone bearing John Carker away from the scene. However, it left Mister Dombey on the platform both as suspect and witness."

"Mister Dombey? Indeed, there is only one person in this tale that would then be the culprit other than John Carker . . . no, no . . . I cannot believe it. It means that it could only be Paul Dombey himself who pushed James Carker to his death."

Captain Ryder leant back with narrowed eyes.

"On the contrary, sir. There was one other person who had the opportunity. Who arranged this entire charade, who actually helped James Carker embezzle and bank the money, using his business connection with Dombey and Son? Indeed, that person's connection with Monsieur Solliec, the correspondent of Agence Havas, allowed him to pick up the intelligence as to the fact that John Carker was meeting the boat at Dover. There was only one person here in London who had access to the information and who James Carker had mailed that he was coming to settle with him and this person was able to stage the meeting at Paddock Wood. I do not have to tell you who that person is, sir."

Mr Josiah Plankton was sitting back with a dreamy look on his face, nodding slightly. He was smiling but there was an expression of vindictive passion on his features.

"You had gone to Maidstone because, for obvious reasons, you did not want to be identified at Paddock Wood," went on Captain Ryder grimly. "You probably waited until well after midnight and perhaps walked or more likely rode the ten miles to the Forester's Arms. You had not realized that John Carker would take the first morning train to Maidstone, a local milk delivery train. And when you reached the inn, you observed some movement. There was Paul Dombey on the station platform. Then came James Carker. You took your opportunity and after the deed was done you vanished into the darkness. You return to Maidstone and arriving there in time for breakfast as if out for an early morning walk. And when you emerged from the hotel . . . that was then you fell in with the superintendent of police. Perhaps that had not been part of your plan, to be forced to go as Paul Dombey's lawyer to the scene of your crime. Yet it was all quite clever. Too clever. But there were too many coincidences to make it believable."

Mr Josiah Plankton did not answer.

In his mind's eye he saw the onrushing black engine with its red warning lights, the shriek of its whistle and pounding roar of its wheels; saw the figure in front of him, soundlessly shrieking against the noise of the great engine, as, like some rag doll, the body was caught up, whirled away upon a jagged mill, struck limb from limb and cast into mutilated fragments in the air. He smiled as he remembered the blood soaked ashes spread across the tracks. How he hated the idea of having to share the wealth with a man like James Carker. But now he was rich. Now he did not have to share those riches with anyone.

He was still smiling absently when Captain Ryder rose, moved to the door and beckoned in the two uniform constables who had been waiting patiently outside.

UN BON REPAS DOIT COMMENCER PAR LA FAIM . . .

Stella Duffy

The journey from London to Paris is easy. Too easy. I need
more time, to think, prepare, get ready. Security, supposed
to be so important now, these days, ways, places, is lax to the
point of ease. I love it, welcome the apparent ease. I believe
in fate, in those big red buses lined up to knock us over, in
your number being up, the calling in of one's very own
pleasure boat. I do not believe that taking off our shoes at
airports will save us. I show my ticket and my passport, walk
through to the train, and get off at the Gare du Nord. Too
easy. Too fast.

Less than three hours after leaving London I walk straight
into a picket line. It seems the French staff are less fond of the
lax security than I. Or perhaps they just don't like the non-
essential immigrants they say Eurostar is employing. I accept
the badly copied leaflet thrust into my hand and put it in my
pocket. *Bienvenue en France.*

I can't face the Metro. Not yet, this early, it is not yet mid-
morning. In real life I would choose to be asleep, safe in bed –
not always achieved, but it would be my choice. I like my Metro
in the afternoon and evening, a warm ride that promises a drink
at the other end, a meal maybe, lights. In the morning it is too
full of workers and students, those interminable French students, segueing from *lycée* to university with no change of
clothes between. Ten years of the same manners, same behaviour day in day out, week after week of congregating in loud
groups on footpaths where they smoke and laugh, and then

suddenly they're in the world and somehow those ugly duckling student girls are born again as impossibly elegant Parisiennes, fine and tidy and so very boring in their classic outfits. French and Italian women, groomed to identical perfection and not an original outfit among them. So much more interesting naked. Round the picket line, out into the street. Road works, illegal taxi drivers offering their insane prices to American tourists doing London (theatre), Paris (art), Rome (Pope). The Grand Tour as dictated by the History Channel.

I cross the street in front of the station, head down, heading down towards the river. There is something about traversing a map from north to south that feels like going downhill, even without the gentle slope from here to the water. Where I'm headed it certainly feels like going downhill. I don't want to look at this city, not now. I see gutters running with water, Paris prides itself on clean streets, on washing every morning, a whore's lick of running cold to sluice out the detritus. Two young women with their hands held out sit at the edge of businessmen's feet, rattling coins in McDonalds cups. I try to pass but their insistence holds me, I say I don't speak French, they beg again in English. I insist I don't speak that either, they offer German, Italian and Spanish. I have no more words in which to plead either ignorance or parsimony, I scavenge in three pockets before giving them a dollar. It's my only defence against their European polyglossary.

Still too early. Still too soon.

Paris is small. The centre of Paris I mean. Like every other city with a stage-set centre, there are all those very many suburbs, the ones Gigi never saw, where cars burn and mothers weep and it is not heaven accepting gratitude for little girls. It is not heaven I am thanking now. I continue my walking meditation, past innumerable Vietnamese restaurants, and countless small patisseries where *pain au chocolat* and croissants dry slowly on the plates of high glass counters, and bars serve beers to Antipodean travellers who really cannot believe this city and call home to tell loved ones readying for bed about the pleasures of a beer in a cafe at ten in the morning. That glass pyramid can wait, this is art, this is the life.

It is a life. Another one.

There are no secrets. This isn't that kind of story. Nothing to work out. I can explain everything, will explain everything. But not yet. There are things to do and it must be done in order and the thing is, the thing is, we always had lunch first. She and I. She said it was proper, correct. That French thing, their reverence for food, an attitude the rest of the world outwardly respects and secretly despises. It's just food for God's sake, why must they make such a fuss? The linen the glass the crockery the menu the waiters with their insistence on pouring and placing and setting and getting it all right. Pattern, form, nothing deviating, nothing turning away, nothing new. Like the groomed women and the elegant men and the clean, clipped lapdogs. Nothing to surprise. So perhaps more than a reverence for just food, a reverence for reverence, reverence for form. Female form, polite form, good form, true to form. Formidable. Hah. Polyglot that.

(So strange. I can walk down the street, give money to a beggar, I can make a play on word form. I am able to buy a train ticket, sit in a bar, order wine and slowly drink the glass as if nothing has happened, as if life just goes on. Even when I know how very abruptly it can stop.)

So. Lunch. Dinner. From the Old French disner, original meaning: breakfast, then lunch, now dinner. Because any attempt to dine, at whatever time of day, will of course break the fast that has gone before, whatever time period that fast encapsulated, night, morning or afternoon. Whenever I broke my fast with her, for her, she insisted we dine first.

Some time ago I spent a weekend with friends in London. At their apartment, their flat, my London friends talk about words. The English are very good at discussing words, it lessens their power, words as landmines, easily triggered, makes them readable, understandable. Stable. My friends discussed lunch or dinner, dinner or tea. If the difference were a north/south divide or a class construct. In London they talk about north and south of the river, here it is left and right. The faux-bohemian sinister and the smooth, the neat, the adroit. I prefer north and south, it's harder to get lost. Apparently they've found her. Marie-Claude. Found her body. It's why I'm here.

When I tear my eyes from the gutters and the beggars and the street corners designed to frame a new picture with every stone edge, I look to high chimneys. I am not keen to see shop doors and windows, avenues and vistas, not yet. There is something I need to see first. One thing. I can manage right up and far down, to the far sides, I have the opposite of tunnel vision. There is graffiti, very high, on tall chimneys and cracked walls where one building has been leaning too long on another. This is not what they mean when they talk about a proper view, a scene in every Parisian glance, but it's diverting enough. I am eager to be diverted. I take a left turn and a right one and another left, still closer to the river, nearer the water, but a narrow road uphill now, heading east, there are more people on the street, or less space for them to walk, they touch me sometimes, their clothes, coats, swinging arms. I do not want to be touched, not like this anyway, not dressed, covered, hidden. It will all be open soon.

These side streets, those to the left and the right, east and west, are not so pretty as the views the tourists adore. She and I sat together once, in the restaurant, and listened to an old Australian couple discuss the difference between London and Paris. The woman said Paris was so much prettier, the French had done very well not to put the ugly modern beside the old beautiful. Her husband agreed. And then he said, in a tone calculated to reach the walls of stone, that the French had capitulated during the war. That is why their city was not bombed, why Paris was prettier than London. Though he agreed, the weather was better too, which helped no end. The afternoon progressed, the Australian man drank more wine, and he went on to eat every course the waiters placed before him. I cannot begin to think how much of the waiters' saliva he must also have enjoyed.

The street I find myself in now is not that pretty. It is poor and messy. Here they sell kebabs and Turkish slippers and cigarettes, and the bread in these shops was not freshly baked on the premises first thing this morning, and the fruit has not been raised lovingly in a farmer's field with only sunshine and rain to help it on its way, there are no artisans here. But this is Paris too, regardless of how few tourists see these sights. Marie-Claude showed me these streets, brought me here to explain that there were worlds where no one cared if the Pyramid was appropriate or not, that the walls around Rodin's garden were too high for locals to climb, that even one euro for a good, fresh, warm croissant is too much for too many. She insisted she knew these streets well and they knew her and that what I read as amused tolerance in the faces of the half-strangers she greeted was friendship and acceptance to her. It may well have been. She is not here now for me to compare the look in her eyes against theirs and I do not have the courage to lock eyes with these men. These shopkeepers are all men. I have thought about this many times. Where are the women shopkeepers? Can they really all be at home with so many children and so much housework and such a lot to do that they do not want to run their own family business, stand alongside their loved one, work hand in hand? Or perhaps they do not have the skill to sell all this stuff? These lighters and batteries that will die in a day. These shoes made by God knows how many small children in how many village factories. Perhaps it is simply that women are better with fruit and vegetables, the items that were once, more recently, living. Maybe this is why the women run market stalls while their husbands and sons and fathers run shops. Or perhaps the women are afraid of bricks and mortar, always ready to pick up their goods and run.

She did not like to run, Marie-Claude, said it made her too hot, sticky. Sticky was not good. Cool and calm and smooth and tidy and groomed and perfect. These things were good, right, correct. To be that way, held in, neat, arranged, arrayed, that was appropriate, proper. *Propre*. Which is clean. And it is also own, as in one's own. Thing, possession, person. One word, two meanings. So many ambiguous words. Yes. No. The things that can be read into any phrase. And accent makes a difference of course, culture, upbringing. We often fail to understand those we grew up with, our brothers and sisters, mistaking their yes for no, truth for lies, despair for hope. How much harder to understand total strangers, when they stand at shop doors, form a picket line, love you, leave you, cheat, lie, misbehave.

It was the drugs of course. It always is. She simply couldn't say no, *non, nyet, nein, ne*. That's what I hate about all those heroin chic films – one of the many things I hate about all those heroin chic films – how they always make the users look so dirty. Messy. Unkempt. She, as I have explained, was the opposite.

Our media, those stupid cop shows and the angry young men films made by angrier (but so much duller, and often older than they admit) young men, has convinced us that the drugs make you ugly, your hair lank, eyes glazed, skin grey. Which could not be further from the truth in her case, her metabolism loved it, thrived on it. Yes, she might not have been able to keep going at this rate for more than another decade, she'd have had to slow down eventually, but careful, planned use, clean equipment and good veins, hungry lungs, open mouth, eager nose – her body loved it all. Loved all her body. I did. He did. They did. She did. We did. Maybe you did. I don't know, it doesn't matter, this is my side of the story. Yes. Yes. In my own time, taking your time to explain. I apologise, I know you value your time . . .

I do not mean explain as in excuse. I mean as in reason. There are always reasons.

There was the habit of course, the way ex-smokers regret the loss of a packet to open, cellophane to rip off, mouth to hold, match to strike. I know she liked the accoutrements, the little bit of this and little bit of that, the choice of vein, the pick of needles – in her job she had the pick of needles – the choice of drug too of course. For up or down or round and round.

Here it is. He was her husband, is her husband, and I her lover. Then he found out, talked to me, told me some of her other truths, and now she is dead. That's why I'm here, to help with the confirmation. She is drowned, was drowned, has been drowned. Which makes sense. She adored her bath, Marie-Claude, sadistic marquise in soothing warm. The bathroom was her shrine. It was the right place to do it, to stop, in the shrine to herself and her form and her desire. Always her desire. Not for her the current vogue for minimalist white, cool and plain. She chose the palest pale apricots and soft barely-there peaches and tiniest hints of warm flesh to tint her warm room, the warmer shades coloured her own skin tones better. Only very tiny babies look good in white, she once said, it suits their newborn blue, the veins that are not yet filled out with warm blood, blue and white and the clean absence of colour suit only a learner heart, lungs in practice. The rest of us need warmth on our skin, colour in our light. Cold winter mornings were her hardest time. Although that must have been hard too, the night last week, a warm evening and her face held under the water, nose and grasping mouth under the water, until her lungs exploded and she breathed a mermaid's breath just once.

There is a plan here. I have followed it to the letter. His letter.

I go to her restaurant, our restaurant, their restaurant. I ask for her table. The waiter, clearly a part-timer, one I have not seen before, raises an eyebrow, the maitre d', just turning from seating a couple of regulars, sees me, hurries over. Pushes the foolish young man aside, takes both my hands in his, takes my jacket, takes my arm, takes me. He is so very sorry. I must be tired. Here, here is my seat, here is her table, there are tears in his eyes. They will feed me he says, it will be their pleasure, they are so sorry. I expect they are. She was here almost every day. Not always with me. Of course the staff here are sorry.

I eat my meal. Three courses. I do not need to order, the patron himself tells the waiter to say that this is his recommendation, I agree. The patron does not come to speak with me, not yet, not now. He has work to do, and so do I. And anyway, he and I should not be seen together, not yet. Wine. Water. Coffee. Armagnac. She thought it was very foreign of me to ask for a liqueur with my coffee. The kind of thing only tourists or old ladies might do. Apparently it was inelegant, childish. I did it despite her disapproval. I do it to spite her now, despite her now.

A classic French meal, in a classic Paris restaurant. Sun shining through the mottled glass windows, lead light yellow and green and red. A businessman dines alone across from me. He too has three courses and wine and coffee, and will go to the office after his three-hour break and work steadily until dark. A wealthy tourist couple argue over the menu, which is entirely in French, it makes no concession to their cash, demands they rack their misspent youth for lost words. To my right a young couple, run from their work for half an hour here and an hour in bed, then back to run the world. To my left a middle-aged gay couple and their sleeping dog. This is civilized Paris, the dog is as welcome as the homosexuals. Everyone should eat well, taste is all. I could sit here all afternoon and stare around me. I could never go to my next appointment. I have no choice.

It is fortunate that the young man who places the burning plate in front of me with a low "attention Madame" annoys me, draws me back to this place, this time, to what happens next. He annoys me in two ways. One, as he too clearly stated, I am Madame, not Mademoiselle. He could have been kinder, generosity is always welcome. Two, I didn't think it was just the plate he was suggesting needed care. This I understand as well. Those that fed her knew her. There are many things of which I must be careful.

They are well-trained though, these young men. Young men only of course, no waitresses, the food too precious to be tainted by women's hands. These are the best. There is the waiter who, hearing a lighter fail to strike three times across the room, arrives with another lighter, working correctly. The customer wishes to light his own cigar and the waiter leaves it beside him. Two minutes later, cigar lit and smoking, the customer continues to strike again and again at his own lighter, striking against hope, the failure of his own tool still a problem despite the waiter's speedy solution to the immediate problem. And where any normal person might laugh at the man, or think him a bloated fool, too occupied in his missing flame to pay attention to his charming dinner companion, she who sits bored and irritated by his attention to pointless detail, the waiter senses the man's distress as well as the woman's slow fury, takes away the offending lighter, there is fuel in the kitchen he says, and returns just moments later, the fresh flame a bright torch to lead him on.

I love these windows, in summer they slide back to tables on the street, in winter they hold back, with their coloured glass, the worst of the grey. Today they keep me in warmth, for now. Cheese. Time is passing. Time is near. I feel it, waiting, demanding. I wonder if she felt it, if she knew her time was near. I doubt it. She had such an exquisite sense for food, for wine, for sex, for fabric – a perfect cut, an ideal line. But very little awareness at all of the kind of day-to-day passing of time that most of us understand once we have left youth behind, once we are Madame not Mademoiselle. One of the perfectly trained young men takes a short stout knife and digs me out a crumbling chunk of Roquefort. It is not what I asked for. I did not ask. In his wisdom he decided this was the correct coda to my meal. It is perfect, both creamy and crystalline, aggressive in my mouth. I also requested goat's cheese. His disdain is too well trained to show a customer of my long standing. In contrast to the Roquefort it is a smooth bland paste. The young man is right, it is no doubt wrong to eat the two together, yet, in my mouth, where they belong, the blend is perfect. The one all flavour and bite, the other a queen of texture, of touch. Marie-Claude and I were no doubt wrong together, actually perfect. No doubt perfect, actually wrong.

Through the hatch at the back of the room, I watch the only black man in the building. Daoud has spent the past hour washing dishes, will give hours yet. Sweat falls in a constant drip from his face to the scalding greasy water, his bare hands plunge repetitively, constant action, disregarded heat, all movement, all moment. I am fond of Daoud, my French is poor, his English non-existent, we have smiled to each other through his hatch, during a hundred or more lunches. I have always thanked him too, for his work. Marie-Claude said that in Algeria he had his own restaurant. She dismissed it though, said the food could not be of any standard. I am not especially fond of North African food myself, often find it cloying, heavy. But Daoud is a generous man and, much as I suspect he found her non-recognition easier to bear than my typical foreign civility to all, he did not repel my need to patronise, to charm. Today he has not once looked towards me. He must know I am here, but he has not offered me a glance. In the time-honoured tradition of silent servants and slaves everywhere, I assume he knows what was done. Or maybe he's just pissed off I haven't been here for so long. I doubt many of the customers here feel enough white liberal guilt to specifically insist that some of the tip must be shared with the dishwasher. I wonder which annoys him more? My need to expiate the colonialist's guilt with ten-euro notes or my part in the death of his boss's wife? Fortunately I do not speak his languages. He will never be able to tell me.

Near the end of the service the man himself comes out from the kitchen, the patron. A big man, with the hair-cut he fell in love with at the age of eighteen and hasn't cared to change for forty years, his broad body held into the black shirt and trousers beneath the stained apron, not a traditionally good-looking man by any means, but his food is beautiful. His staff must have told him I was here the moment I entered the building, but he has waited until after the meal, as always, to come and be among his guests. He walks the room, greeting customers and friends as if they were all alike. He does not come to my table, to me at her table. I understand. This is a public place, he must be careful. We must be careful.

I drain the last of my armagnac, an oil slick of golden liquid clinging to the side of the glass. I am tempted to run my finger in the residue, lick it up. I don't. I pay my bill, leave the room, I have an appointment near the river.

I leave the restaurant in the quiet street with no river view, full of food and wine and apprehension. I enjoyed the meal, it was always good to eat there, but as so often, on leaving, I wonder if a meal in an elegant room with subdued lighting and quiet conversation can ever be as ripe or delicious as the proverbial chunk of bread and lump of cheese in the fresh air with a river view? Certainly it is not that much more expensive, the river view comes at such a cost these days, every modern city in the world having finally realized the pleasure of water and priced their dirty old riverside or waterfront or sea wall or boardwalk accordingly. In the old days, when rivers were full of filth and traffic and we could not control their tides, the choice for those who could afford it was to look away from the water, to turn the backs of their buildings to it. In time though, roads became our dirty passageways and now the water is the view of choice. It is the place where people stand, gazing out and down, demanding explanation from a flow that has existed long before us and will, global warming notwithstanding, continue. The river will always continue, no matter what gets in its way. Which is how I come, at the appointed time, in the correct place, with due formality and careful ceremony, to be staring down at the bloated body of my lover.

The Seine was not made for death, there has been the occasional broken princess at its side, but by and large Parisians have done well to keep their bloodied and often headless corpses firmly in the squares, on dry land – not easy when the square is an island – but they've done pretty well. The polite man in a white coat is telling me they pulled her from the river just over a day ago, then brought her here. She had no bag, no wallet, no phone, no identifying tags. She had my name and number, written small, folded smaller, in the discreet gold charm on her discreet gold bracelet. My French is schoolgirl French at the best of times, good for menus and directions and, once, for flirting with young soldiers in New Caledonia, drunken conversations with Spanish relations where French is our only common language – confronted with Marie-Claude's bloated body and seaweed hair, the best I could do was stutter no, *non, encore non*, and eventually *oui, c'est elle* – Marie-Claude.

After that came a long time of asking questions, her home, her details, her family. I suggested they call her husband, he'd know these answers. I gave them her home number, a junior was sent to call, returned saying there was no reply. Well, no, he was probably still at work. Why did she carry my number on her? I didn't know. I didn't know she did. Were we good friends? Yes we are. Were. Were we lovers? Yes. We had been. A long time ago. When did I last see her? It has been a month, I was due to visit next week. We both have lives of our own, we did not see each other all that often. Just enough. They said they would probably have more questions for me later, there were certain things they didn't understand. I expect one of them was that the water in her lungs was not the same as the water in the river. I didn't suggest this though, if they hadn't figured it out yet, they would in time. They asked me for my passport and requested I didn't leave the city. I told them I understood. I would be as helpful as I possibly could. I cried. Both in truth and for effect. I was – am – sad for her. They were very grateful for my help. And I think they believed me, it's always hard to be sure of the truth in translation.

More than four hours had passed by the time I left. I assumed they'd have someone follow me, if only to make sure I didn't jump in the river as well. She didn't jump, they must know that. I walked a long time by the water and it was cold and damp, but that felt right. I had expected her to look bad, to look dead. I hadn't thought about her being ugly, dirty, unsuited to the place. Marie-Claude could never have been suited to that place.

The light was far too white. Eventually, when I had walked far enough and long enough I found a bar and began to drink. I drank to my good health and her bad death. I drank to a night in Paris when I came here with a girlfriend and left with a drunken Glaswegian squaddie. I drank to the birthday lunch I ate once in a half-broken mausoleum in Pere-Lachaise, wet and alone and angry. I drank to the day I showed my mother Paris, she who never thought she'd visit the city of light and found it pretty, but wanting. She could not abide tourists, and I did not know what else to show her, not then. I did not know Paris so well then, did not have Marie-Claude's desire to guide me. I drank to him, the husband, how good he had been, how useful, how loving, how lovely. What a good husband and what a good lover. And I drank to her and to me.

Late that night, very late, I have no idea exactly how late, I was not looking at watches or clocks, paying attention to opening hours or closing, I took a taxi to a hotel I remembered from many years ago, a hotel that had nothing to do with her or with me. I leaned against the door and rang the bell until a furious night porter let me in and I bribed him with a fifty-euro note to give me a bed for the night. The young woman who had been shadowing me since I left the mortuary waited on the other side of the road until I was shown to a room, drunkenly closed my curtains and, half an hour later, turned off my light. She waited an extra fifteen minutes to be sure, and then trod wearily home. I expect she thought police work might be more fun.

And now I am sober. I am no actress, I admit that, but it is easy to persuade a young woman watching at a distance of twenty feet that grief is drunkenness, lust is love, despair merely an absence of hope.

I arrange my bag, collect my things. I was in this hotel last week, left a case with the friendly night porter. He is a better actor than his work record would show, I thought he really was angry when he answered the door. Or perhaps it was just a way for him to demand the fifty I gave him instead of the twenty we had agreed. Either way, he has done as requested. It is all here. The case with my new clothes and the wig, glasses and keys. The keys to her apartment, our apartment, the home in which I loved Marie-Claude. Our Paris home. I had thought it special and separate, I did not know there were two other keys she also kept as well as the one home she shared with her husband, other apartments she maintained. She was very good at it, the hiding, the lies. Me too. I get changed as quickly as I can, leave the front door looking like a different woman. Even if the watcher has stayed longer than I believe she has, she will not see me now.

Those people complaining at the Gare du Nord are right, it is easy to get in and out of the country. It is easy not to have your passport checked on leaving Britain when you journey to Bilbao in a friend of a friend's yacht. When you arrive in a tiny seaside village early in the morning where no one cares where you've come from, as long as you are prepared to spend money. It is simple to take one train to Barcelona and then another through to Toulouse and buy a car and drive to Paris to meet your lover's furious husband. I don't suppose, however, that entirely white group of protestors at the Gare du Nord were complaining about the travel plans of someone like me. A woman growing older becomes more and more anonymous. A wig with more grey than brunette, make-up carelessly applied, dull clothes that don't quite fit, plain and low-heeled shoes – the mask of a middle-aged mother is not a difficult disguise and the vanity pangs when passing a mirrored shop front are a price well worth paying for the gift of near-invisibility in the eyes of the young men who man the passport and customs desks.

I hurry away. To a place he has told me of. We meet there in secret, in case he too is being watched. We burn her diaries. I do this as myself, wig and false clothes removed. The light of the small fire keeps me warm, as does his skin. We are careful. It is too good to spoil, this being together. When the work is done, her words burned, he turns to the little case he brought with him, takes out a picnic of bread and cheese and wine, and we toast each other. Our very good fortune to have found each other. And we thank her, for the introduction. In an hour it will be time for me to hurry back to the hotel, hide this other me, he will need to get to the markets, to carry on, as a good widower, and a better restaurateur, in dependable grief.

It began six months ago. He called and asked me to come. So I did. He made the travel arrangements, explained what he had decided needed to happen. We met at the restaurant, late, when only Daoud was still there, hosing down the floor, sluicing away bread and blood and grease so the kitchen would be clean for the morning. Daoud was surprised to see me and, I quickly understood, disappointed. His boss shouted at him for staying so late, taking so long, told him to fuck off, there were plenty of other illegal immigrants hungry for work. I said I did not know that Daoud was illegal, the patron did not either, not for sure, but the way his employee ran from the building suggested he had made the right guess.

We had a drink. One then another. He explained how he found out, the confrontation, the confession. First she told him about us and then, horrible and painful, for me to listen to, and – so he said – for him to explain, about the other lover. And the other. Her one husband and her three lovers. A third drink. There is a peculiar sadness in finding yourself one of many, we are human, we search for the tiny spark of difference. I was the only woman in her selection of lovers, for that I was grateful, a little.

Her latest conquest was a young man, totally besotted, telling all and sundry apparently, not aware of the rules of engagement, the tradition that his attitude ought to have been quiet and careful. The husband was worried for his wife. Worried that other people would realize what she'd been doing, uncover her lies. That they too would see her for the beautiful whore she was. I said I did not think her a whore, he said we were the ones who paid for her charms. In kind, in love, in our constant waiting for her to return. It was not a financial transaction, but a debt paid was still a debt paid. I began to see his point of view.

I had known about her drug habits, had thought them part of her charm really, a hint of access to a world I had never understood, touching the glamour of oblivion when I touched her. He told me it was worse than that, the new young man fed her habits, enjoyed them with her. He said it was becoming a problem, she only saw me once a month, she was able to make her use look as tidy as I believed it was, but in truth, she was further gone than I realized. Further away than I realized.

He fed me that first night. After all the talking and the tears, took me out to the kitchen and fed me. A mouthful of this, half a slice of that. A little more wine, another bite, a sip again, bread, cheese, water, wine, meat, bread, wine, wine, wine, him. Fed me himself. I think now I must have known that would happen. I must have walked into the meeting that night and seen him and known we would fuck. Perhaps I had always known, right back when she first took me to the restaurant and ordered my meal for me and made my choices and fed me his food and paraded me in front of his staff. I was complicit in their married games from the beginning and maybe it was inevitable I would switch sides. Certainly it did not feel as if I made a choice that night. He fed me well, I fucked him well, we were both sick with jealousy and love for her. He was a good lover though, as was she. I am not a French woman, either classic or modern. I do not take an absurdly inflated interest in grooming or diet or accessories – she did, we were her accessories – I am, though, inordinately interested in passion. Food and passion. He was skilled in both. Both take careful preparation, he was well planned.

He became my lover, she continued as my lover. She continued with her other lovers. She became increasingly indiscreet as the fervour for her young man increased. As I explained, she did not look like the classic televisual drug addict, the more she played with the young man though, the more he enjoyed her illicit largesse, the wider her mouth, spilling secrets. Eventually her husband decided the time had come. *Aux grands maux les grands remèdes.* Cliche is so French.

I would come to visit her, tell her I knew about her young lover. We would arrange to meet him. There would be a scene, somewhere public. I would force from her confession of their desire. Then I would reveal I also knew of the other lover. Daoud, the washer of filthy dishes in her husband's kitchen. She would deny, fight, shout, and finally, worn down by my heartbreak, agree. Admit. Admit in front of the young man, who would not be sober or clean, who would vow to do something about it. And when her body was found, a day or a week later, the mark of suspicion would be ready on his brow.

It was complicated, uncertain, not at all possible to guarantee what would happen. And yet, in the hotel room bed, in his wide arms, with his food in my belly and his kiss in my mouth, I was persuaded it could all work out. If not exactly as planned, then at least go some of the way towards making the potential true. All we really needed was for her to admit and for him to become angry.

I suppose I could have said no. At any time really, I could have taken my jealousy and fury home with me, travelled away from that city and never seen her again, left them to their desire and bitterness and passion. But I agreed with him, it wasn't fair, she wasn't fair. One understands the role of spouse, or of mistress, either of these makes sense. And a spouse knows there is the chance to be cuckolded, a mistress understands she is not first. But a third lover? A fourth? He was right. She was taking the piss. And besides, after just a short while, I quite liked the idea of having him to myself. He was – is – a very attractive man. If not conventionally so. But then I am not, unlike so many French women, a lover of convention.

And it appears the plans of her husband, my lover-chef, have worked. I dressed in the disguise he chose for me, travelled as another woman, hid in this city and drowned another woman. Now she is dead and she is not beautiful, the drowned are not beautiful. I have been here a week. First the police came to speak to Daoud, but he had an alibi, he was washing dishes. Plenty of people saw him doing so. The husband had an alibi – he was working, in the kitchen, talking to his customers, creating art from raw ingredients, feeding the discerning masses. The young man did not have an alibi. He was sitting at home that night, alone, shooting up with the heroin substitute she brought him from her office, using the syringe she brought him from her office. Her husband told the police about her lovers, her drug habits, her hidden life. He did not tell the police how we parcelled her up in restaurant waste bags and carried her to his van, more often used for transporting sides of beef and mutton, and we took her to the river and we let her fall. So much is hidden under cover of darkness. And London has more CCTV cameras than any other city in Europe. But not Paris, those ugly cameras spoil the view. I told the police about our relationship. They were surprisingly ready to believe a respected medical professional could behave in such a manner, for them, the addition of lust to substance multiplied readily into disaster. It made it simple too, for them to understand the jealousy of her young lover, his head swimming, his hands holding her beneath the water. Crime passionnel is no longer a defence of course, but I trust his time in prison may help him with his addiction problems. *Tout est bien qui finit bien.*

I did not have an alibi. But then I was not in France. My passport proves it, the strong security both our countries now pride themselves on proves it. There may have been a middle-aged woman in a grey wig and ill-fitting clothes at some point. She may have been in France, in Paris, but she was not noticed.

I miss her, of course, though not too much, I suspect we were nearing the end of our time anyway, everything has its time. And I have my new lover now, he who feeds me so well. Too well almost. It is lucky my own husband and children demand so much energy at home, keeping me busy, I might get fat otherwise. Family is so important, isn't it?

ROOM FOR IMPROVEMENT

Marilyn Todd

I looked at the couple hovering in the doorway, him in Savile Row, her all blue Chanel and pearls, and thought: so rich, so wholesome. So unhappy.

"Mr and Mrs Cuthbertson," he said by way of introduction, and there were enough plums in his mouth that I could have made jam, were I that way inclined. "We . . ." he cast a sideways glance at his wife, who had found a sudden need to check that the buttons on her jacket were in line. "We have an appointment with Mr Hepburn."

"Please come in."

I made a point of glancing at the diary on my desk, then smiling at the clock on the wall in a way that commended their promptness. They were on the dot. And had no idea how the rough end of the law worked.

"I'm afraid Mr Hepburn's been summoned to an urgent court appearance," I lied, shaking Mrs Cuthbertson's limp white calfskin glove. "But he briefed me on your situation before he left, and asked me to run through the details with you."

This is the point where I bring out my most reassuring smile, proof that all those lengthy visits to the dentist do pay off.

"I'm his daughter, Lois." Ouch. Mr Cuthbertson's handshake wasn't only solid, though. I detected a distinct Freemason squeeze. "I guarantee you the same level of confidence and discretion that my father would give you."

They glanced at each other, still a little uneasy. But they hadn't travelled all this way just to take the next train home.

"That's perfectly all right," Mrs Cuthbertson said, and whatever her other faults, she was a terrible liar.

"Yes, indeed." Her husband, now, he scored a little higher, but only a fraction, I'm afraid. "Y'see, Miss Hepburn, we would like this . . . business organized as quickly as possible."

And that indeed was the truth.

"Absolutely." I ushered the pair into my fictitious father's office before taking a seat behind my fictitious father's desk. After all, the year might be 1959 and Brighton might be Britain's most sophisticated town outside of London, but the world still wasn't ready for single female private investigators. To be honest, I'm not sure I was, either.

"My solicitor informs me that you can help speed up our divorce," Mrs Cuthbertson said, in a manner that made it sound as though Stratton, Hall and Stratton might yet be playing a practical joke.

"I can." This time I didn't smile, but steepled my fingers. "Though you need to understand what's involved."

Mr Cuthbertson was the shuffling-in-his-chair kind. His wife was the avoid-direct-eye-contact type. I really did feel for them both.

"On the contrary, Mr Stratton was specific," she said, toying with the clasp on her matching Chanel handbag. "Indeed, he went to some pains to explain how one of the very few grounds for a rapid divorce is adultery, and that providing proof can be given that one party has been indiscreet . . ." Her voice trailed off, and I noticed two bright red patches had sprung up to mar her immaculately rouged cheeks.

"Then there is a certain acceleration in the severance of the marriage that cuts years off the waiting time, yes," I finished for her. "But this isn't Reno, Mrs Cuthbertson." Someone needed to point this out, and trust me, it was never going to be some posh, pin-striped solicitor. "One of you—" (usually the man, gentlemanly conduct and all that) "– needs to be photographed in what the courts like to describe as a compromising position."

"But you do the . . . uh . . . groundwork?" her husband asked.

"If you mean by booking a hotel room and hiring a co-respondent, then yes, Mr Cuthbertson. This agency takes care of that."

As succinctly as possible, I ran through the procedure. The time for details was later, but this young couple needed to know here and now that evidence of not just a one-night stand but a long-standing, ongoing affair needed to be established. In practice, this was simply a matter of the man changing his tie for each of the photographs. The girls carried a change of clothing as a matter of course. I'd make lunch appointments every half-hour at different restaurants, dinner appointments in the evening, so there'd be wadges of photographs to lay before the court. The lovebirds holding hands between courses. The naughty couple toasting each other, whispering sweet nothings across the salt cellar, swanning in and out of hotels, that sort of thing.

"I will provide a back-dated contract that shows Mrs Cuthbertson approached this agency three months ago, asking us to investigate her husband's infidelity," I said, "but all this proves is that her husband has been meeting another woman over a period of time."

To grant her a divorce, the courts need meat on their bones.

"At a prearranged time, one of our agents –" I truly hoped I'd made it sound as though there was more than one of me – "goes to the hotel room, and because the courts require the corroboration of an independent witness, persuades the housekeeper to unlock the door." I paused. "Then we snap the client in as compromising a position as they can muster."

The men were uniformly reserved, but the girls had no such qualms. At the required moment, they threw caution and their brassieres to the wind. No wonder the husbands looked so startled in the photos.

"Jolly good." Mr Cuthbertson was relieved that his input to the arrangements would be minimal.

Mrs Cuthbertson didn't even try to hide her joy at being left out of it completely. "That is excellent, Miss Hepburn," she gushed, and I swear that little feather in her hat perked up. "Really excellent."

I wasn't convinced excellent was the word.

"Are you quite sure this is what you want?" This time I spoke to Mr Cuthbertson directly. "There's no going back," I told him. "You'll be publicly branded an adulterer, your name will be blazoned across the newspapers—"

"Miss Hepburn," his wife interrupted gently, "my husband and I married in haste, we have already repented. We have no desire to add to the leisure."

I wondered whether they always did their arguing in such civilized terms, or whether they'd simply passed beyond that stage.

"The thing is, Miss Hepburn, both Margaret and I have met someone else," Mr. Cuthbertson said. "We just want this marriage ended as quickly as possible, so we are free to marry again."

It all seemed so gracious and polite that I imagined the four of them round the Cuthbertson's elegant dining table, discussing it over a bottle of Margaux and a nice fillet steak. I thought it was about time someone added the mustard. "You *are* aware of the costs involved?"

"My family's in tractors and my husband is in baby foods," Mrs Cuthbertson said, carelessly rubbing her diamonds, "Money is no object, Miss Hepburn."

"Then you're also aware of why this fast-track divorce ploy is so expensive?" I leaned across the desk and looked her husband squarely in the eye. "If anything goes wrong, it's not just you," I told him. "We could both end up in jail."

They glanced at each other, gulped, then nodded. Of the two, the wife's nod was the least grim, I decided.

But then she wasn't the one looking at porridge.

I want to make it very clear that what I do has no connection whatsoever with prostitution. Quite the opposite, in fact, because the girls I hire are usually married themselves and lead otherwise normal, respectable lives. It's just that, like me, they need the money – and for this kind of money, people take risks. Wouldn't you?

And it's because there's so much at stake, fixing up fake adultery cases, that I (a) charge exorbitant fees and (b) plan to the very last detail – then go over it time and again. That way, should anything go belly up, at least I have the satisfaction of having some money behind me to take care of Susan, plus I can wile away my stretch in the sure and certain knowledge that I did the best I could, which is all anyone can ask. Even crooked female private eyes.

So my confidence was pretty high as I took the elevator to the Belle Vue's second floor. Of course, that had as much to do with the hired mink as my meticulous forward planning, because even though I'd never earn enough to buy one for myself, you really do feel a million dollars wrapped inside real fur. And a girl certainly needs the right clothes in a hotel like the Belle Vue. For one thing, it's the best hotel by a mile, and that's where several of my competitors tripped up. They'd tried to cut costs, and realized too late that judges, especially divorce-court judges, aren't lemons. No man who has his shirts handmade in Jermyn Street books into a cheap hotel with an even cheaper floozy. So that's the first rule. Horses for courses, and since you only get the one chance in a place like the Belle Vue, you need to convince the housekeeper with a single glance that you're a bona fide guest who's foolishly left her key behind.

"Here we are, madam. Two-two-three."

The housekeeper made to knock, but I pointed to the "Do Not Disturb" sign hanging dutifully on the doorknob, and you'd be surprised how far a five-pound note still goes in the middle of an afternoon in 1959. While she jiggled the master key in the lock, I whipped my camera out of a vanity case designed for rather more feminine and undoubtedly more trivial activities, then checked the corridor for the billionth time. Still deserted, but on these carpets, you wouldn't hear a herd of wildebeest charging down on you. The lift whirred gently in the background.

"Say cheese," I breezed, as the housekeeper flung open the door.

"Jeez," the housekeeper said.

So used to all this, I'd taken the photo before I even realized. It was a man on the bed, all right, but he wasn't undressed and there was no sign of Mavis or her hired fox fur. (For the same reasons, I can't have Mavis wandering round the Belle Vue without looking the part, either). But to be honest, I wasn't surprised she'd done a bunk. His head lay at a horribly unnatural angle.

My first thought was for Mrs Cuthbertson.

My second was to get the hell out of there.

"This situation needs to be handled with the utmost discretion," I told the housekeeper, backing carefully out of the room. "You fetch the manager. I'll wait here, to make sure no one goes in."

The trouble was, I couldn't hear myself speak, there was this terrible din in the background. Not what one expects from the Belle Vue, I thought idly. What on earth was the place coming to? Then I turned round.

So much for keeping it quiet, I realized, and so much for slipping away.

That din was the housekeeper's scream.

With no quick or easy way out, it was now a case of damage control. At the first screech, the lift boy, two chambermaids, some straight-backed, po-faced security manager, and a fat room-service waiter appeared out of nowhere, while there I was, camera in hand, pretending to be Mrs Two-two-three. My gut instinct said play up the distraught widow thing, who's to say what grief will do, why *shouldn't* the poor wife run off, the girl's in shock? But it only goes to show. In the past, on the very few occasions I'd ever ordered room service, the waiters proved aloof and snooty specimens. Trust me to pick the breed's only bleeding heart. And then there was the Belle Vue's director.

"Drink this," he insisted, pushing a cognac into my hand, having personally escorted me down to his office.

"How kind," I sniffed, thinking, good, I can sneak away now, but compassion, it seems, has no bounds at plush hotels. He left a desk clerk as a deposit, and you wouldn't believe how fast the police can move, either. When they try.

So there I was, surrounded on all sides by red velvet and gilt while the piano in the foyer tinkled Gershwin, computing a multitude of likely stories. I pictured Mrs Cuthbertson, fiddling with her handbag, fiddling with her pearls, and realized that I couldn't maintain the pretence of being her. Her marriage might be failing, but her husband had been willing to put his upper-crust reputation on the line for her, and in any case, a murder investigation would quickly reveal that I wasn't the genuine article. No, I'd have to be someone else who'd gone out without her damn room key. I warmed the cognac in my hand and sipped. Ultra smooth, but what else would one expect of the Belle Vue. And the more I thought about it, the better this scenario played out. If I was a woman who was stupid enough to forget her room key, I was certainly stupid enough to get the numbers muddled up. I finished off the brandy and pasted on my coy-but-nonetheless-ravishing smile for the benefit of the desk clerk. After all, who *better* to probe about the current guest list?

Within ten minutes, I was Mrs Henry Martin, newlywed bride, because if honeymoons don't make a girl jittery, what the hell does? Not the sex. The fact that she's committing to a lifetime with someone, bearing his children, washing his socks. That would scare the pants off me, I can tell you. So. Providing the police didn't interrogate me in the presence of the desk clerk (300–1), there was no way of being caught out on my story, especially since the Martins had gone sightseeing in Eastbourne and would not be back before supper (7:30 onwards, dinner jackets only). Yes, indeed. Between the mink and the cognac, my confidence was restored and while the desk clerk answered the director's phone, I whipped the film from my camera and stuffed it behind my suspender.

"Inspector Sullivan is on his way down to see you," he announced, but even before he'd finished, the door had opened and the entire gap was filled by a man with a mop of unruly dark hair and a face that looked like it had come second in a fight with a brick wall.

I stood up, though if I wasn't to be at a height disadvantage, I'd really need to stand on a chair. Still, I was ready, and I ran through the key points in my head. Mrs Martin. Just married. Nervous. Excited. Definitely light-headed. Then—

"Don't I know you?" Inspector Sullivan asked, and his voice was rough from too many cigarettes, too little sleep. "Mrs Hepburn, right?" I *hate* conscientious policemen.

"Miss."

"You run Hepburn Investigations?"

No point in stalling. I brought out my card. "Clients with confidence," I said with none.

"Hm." He chewed his lip, rubbed his jaw, ran his hand through his hair. And all the time his eyes were fixed on my camera.

My thoughts were of Susan. Growing up with her aunt. Visiting her mother in jail. Rapidly becoming estranged . . .

"If I didn't know better," Sullivan said at length, "I'd say you were fixing up one of those phoney divorce cases."

I said nothing for the simple reason that the next person I intended talking to was my lawyer.

"Only the problem there," he said, "is that Mr Hall wasn't married."

Mr Who? Then the penny dropped. I may have *booked* room two-twenty-three for Mr Cuthbertson and the lovely Mavis, but now I started to think about something other than covering my own backside, I realized that Mr Cuthbertson wouldn't have been seen dead (pardon the pun) in a pale blue check suit. Relief made my knees tremble.

"So do you mind telling me why you burst in on an unmarried commercial traveller to take his photograph, Miss Hepburn?"

In fact I was so overcome with relief that I nearly blurted out the truth.

"That new road-safety officer came to the school again today."

Susan was sitting on my lap braiding my hair, and although she's a little too old and (dare I say it) a little too heavy, such moments are rare. For this reason alone, they are precious.

"He's a scream," she gushed. "Ever so funny."

I really, really didn't want to talk about policemen right then, but children can be immeasurably cruel.

"Do you know what happens if you don't look right?" she persisted, using my spiky, mismatched plaits as handlebars. I shook my head as best I could. "You go *wrong*," she squealed.

Maybe I would also have found this excruciatingly funny if I'd been nine years old. Somehow I doubted it.

"Do you have a crush on this teacher of yours?" Because suddenly there was me just turned seventeen, Mr Rolands my old maths master, and the only good thing to come out of that affair weighed seven and a half pounds and has his beautiful, soft golden hair.

"Oh, Mum!" Susan rolled her eyes. "The road-safety man's not a teacher, and anyway he's *old*."

What constitutes old to a nine-year-old? Mr Rolands turned out to be thirty-six, and even now, I still wonder how I fell for that old I'll-leave-my-wife line.

"So's Rock Hudson," I pointed out, "but his face is plastered all over your bedroom wall."

"That's different, he's a film star." She stopped braiding and sighed. "If I had a daddy, I'd like him to be like the road-safety man. He's *ever* so handsome."

If I had a daddy . . .? Next she'd be pulling out my fingernails with pliers.

"More handsome than Elvis?" I asked, because all good mothers know how to change the subject, and within no time we were jiving round the living room to "Jailhouse Rock", "Blue Suede Shoes", and generally getting "All Shook Up".

It was only later, with Susan tucked up in bed and me patiently untangling the knots in my hair, that the enormity of what I'd risked today hit me. I could have lost everything, and I do mean everything, on the turn of a door key. I needed to think seriously about the future. When the next solicitor telephoned, asking could I help out, would I? *Would I risk it?* I let Elvis run through "Don't Be Cruel" and thought, damn right I would. My daughter is not going to end up an unmarried mother at the age of seventeen. Susan's a bright kid, on course for the grammar school, and what's more, she's desperate to go. But. I reached for as wide a toothed comb as I could find. Grammar schools are expensive. There's the uniforms, the tennis racquets, the hockey sticks, the music lessons, not forgetting innumerable bus trips and a million other extra hidden costs. Truly, though, I do not care. My daughter will never be forced to earn her living grubbing through dustbins, following faithless husbands down lover's lanes, or tracing children who've run away because their home life's so damned wretched. Never. I will do whatever it takes to keep Susan from violent men and abusive women, and she will never need to take covert shots of homosexuals or men with prostitutes simply to pay the rent. Maybe, once she starts attending the grammar school, she'll be ashamed of me. Of what I do and what I am. I hope not, I really, really do. But that's another risk I am prepared to take.

All the same, I don't sleep well. I worry.

*   *   *

"Miss Hepburn."

I recognized that distinctive gravel without needing to look up. "Inspector."

He lumbered into the inner office where I was typing up a perfectly legitimate infidelity assignment, but did not sit down. I wished to God I'd locked the filing cabinets, or even closed that open drawer, but Sullivan didn't glance at them. To be honest, I would have rifled through every last one, had I been in his shoes.

"Room two-two-three," he said, leaning with his back against the wall and folding his arms over his chest. "Rented one night to Stanley Hall, aged twenty-six, commercial rep in motor oil."

I didn't know Stanley Hall, had never heard of Stanley Hall, could swear on a stack of Bibles that I was not involved with anything connected to Stanley Hall, and with great enthusiasm, I imparted this knowledge. "I know sod all about motor oil, too," I added with gusto.

"Hm." Sullivan scratched his cheek and stared at the sparrows pecking at the crumbs along the windowsill. "What about a Mr and Mrs Cuthbertson?" he asked, still not bothering to look at me. "Know anything about them?"

At times like this there's nothing else a girl can do but drop her file on the floor. "Name doesn't ring a bell," I said, although my voice was a tad muffled, seeing as how my head was stuck under the desk.

"No?" His suddenly appeared on the other side, and for large hands, they were surprisingly deft at picking up foolscap. "Only Mrs Cuthbertson made a reservation yesterday morning, specifically asking for that particular room."

I like that room, I wanted to say. It faces the sea front, and from the bandstand you can, if you stand on the furthestmost bench to the right, get a half-decent snap of anyone in the bay window. The courts liked that sort of thing, especially when they were presented with photos of the clients closing the curtains. Furtive always goes down well with a judge.

"Really?" I scrabbled for an imaginary paper clip.

"It probably doesn't mean anything," he said, actually finding one. "Maybe they'd stayed there on their honeymoon, maybe she just liked the view."

"Maybe," I said and, still on my knees, pretended to arrange the scattered papers, even though I knew I'd never find anything in this damned file again.

"Who knows?" If he wasn't craggy when he smiled, how come the wolf in Little Red Riding Hood suddenly sprang to mind? "But it seems they were so disappointed that the guest in two-twenty-three hadn't booked out as expected that when the Cuthbertsons were given three-one-seven, they hardly stayed more than a couple of hours."

"Oh?" I murmured, rubbing the bump where I'd brought up my head sharply.

"I expect it's a class thing," he said, straightening up and brushing the dust off his trousers. "All the same, though." He paused. "Don't you think it's strange they didn't check in until two-thirty-five, yet were gone by the time I went to question them at half-past four?"

Was that squeak as noncommittal a squeak as I'd hoped? Because here's the thing. I'd agreed to supply the Cuthbertsons with evidence for a quick divorce. Their deposit was already earning interest in Susan's trust fund. So the minute Sullivan had finished questioning me the day before, I'd flown upstairs to three-one-seven, stuffed a new film in the camera, and grabbed the nearest chambermaid.

At this point, I want to tell you about Mavis. She's nowhere near as common as her name suggests, and very pretty with it, in a busty sort of way. But her husband left her for a bus conductress last September and . . . well, to cut a long story short, Mavis gets what I suppose you'd call lonely. I guess Mr Cuthbertson got bored waiting for my knock.

I think it's safe to say that this was one set of evidence the divorce courts would not be querying.

"Can I go to the park with Lynn and Josie, Mum?"

"Yes, of course." I know the park warden. The girls will be fine. He beat that last flasher to a pulp.

"There's a bag of bread for the ducks," I said, nodding towards the table. "But take a scarf, love, it's cold."

"Mum!" She dragged it into two syllables. "It's summer."

"It's the second of October. Take a scarf."

I couldn't help but smile, hearing her belt out "Hound Dog" at the top of her little off-key voice while she skipped upstairs to fetch it. You keep that crush on Elvis, I thought happily. You dream about Rock Hudson, girl.

> "You look over your shoulder,
> Before you stick your right arm out.
> When it's clear, then you manoeuvre . . ."

"*That's* not Elvis."

"It's what the road-safety officer taught us. He says that if you sing it to your favourite song, *then you ain't gonna get mown down . . .*"

As I stuffed sage and onion into a chicken, I consoled myself with the fact that the RSO was "old", and that if she did have a crush on him, she'd soon grow out of it. Lightning surely can't strike twice?

"And you wrap it round your neck," I insisted.

My daughter knows when she is beaten. She might have stuck her tongue out, but that scarf went round twice.

"Mummy, what's a bastard?"

Four pounds of poultry slid straight through my fingers. Nine years I'd been waiting for this moment. Every single day for nine years I'd braced myself. And I *still* wasn't ready.

"It's . . . someone whose parents aren't married, darling." I have a feeling my voice was rather quaky as I explained the intricacies of illegitimacy, the fact that there was still a stigma attached to such children, though there shouldn't be because it certainly wasn't their fault, and that anyone who called children by that name ought to be shot.

"So when Peter Bailey called Jimmy Tate a little bastard, he was being horrid?" she asked, tipping her head on one side.

"P-Peter Bailey?"

"In the playground yesterday. Jimmy took his penknife and dropped it down the drain, so Peter called him a dirty little—"

"Hey! That's enough bad language out of you, my girl!"

Relief rushed through me like water down a flood drain, and my knees were still imitating aspens as the door banged behind her, so much so, I didn't even yell at her for slamming. But as she wheeled her bike adroitly through the gate then pedalled down the road, it wasn't really Susan I was seeing. It was maths teachers. It was schoolgirl crushes, sleepless nights, schoolgirls growing into typists, then bumping into her old teacher one summer's day.

Why, Mr Rolands! Those same old palpitations.

Please. It's Stephen, now.

I should have stuck with "Mr", because images of stolen kisses, secret meetings, declarations of true love flashed through at breakneck speed, and no doubt it was the pain of that damned chicken landing on my toe, but my eyes were watering like crazy. All I could think of were promises and reassurances that were as empty as his heart.

And over the kitchen chair draped casually, as if by chance, hung Susan's scarf.

"Are you busy, Lois?"

Lois. He calls me Lois now. "I'm always busy, Sullivan. It's how I pay the rent."

I shoved the incriminating photographs of Mr Cuthbertson back in the envelope, and thought, *Really, Mavis! That's no way to treat a hired fox fur!* And that's when you realize that, civilized or not in the way rich people handle things, the cracks in that marriage were very wide indeed.

"I know how you pay the rent," Sullivan rumbled, and there seemed twice as much gravel in his mouth this time. "That's why I want to talk about the camera you were waving round room two-two-three." He made himself comfortable perching on the edge of the desk and I thanked God it was solid oak. "You're sure there was no film in it?"

"I showed you. It was empty." I can do innocent. You just bulge your big brown eyes. "I even let you go through my handbag and pockets at the time."

"Women have a surprising number of storage facilities," he said in a way that suggested the species was foreign to him. "Tell me you're not holding back on me, Lois."

"But I explained."

"Yes." He nodded patiently. "You were visiting an old school friend, a Mrs Martin, on her honeymoon, in your hired mink, of course—"

"Who says it's hired?" I asked indignantly.

"Lois, you rent a ground-floor flat on Albert Street, which is not a prime location, where you live with your daughter and no husband, and you also pay the rent on these offices, which are in a prime location but which are far too large for you, in order to sustain the fiction that this is a much bigger business than it is. Does a woman in that position really splash out on furs?"

"I wanted to impress my friend." It sounded weak, even to me.

"I'm sure bursting in unannounced with a blank camera would have been very impressive indeed. Had Mrs Martin ever heard of you. Had you not asked the housekeeper to open room two-two-three with her master key. Had—"

"All right, that was a lie." What else could I do, but admit it? "But I'm going to claim client confidentiality here, Sullivan, and you'll just have to take my word that it has nothing to do with Stanley Hall's murder."

That grunt sounded unconvinced, but he didn't follow up.

"As for the film," I said, "There were a dozen witnesses who can swear I never touched that camera, including the Belle Vue's director, his security manager, and that stuffy little desk clerk."

"I know." There it was again. That wolf-from-Little-Red-Riding-Hood smile. "Which is why I'm asking you directly."

"Then trust me." I'm also very good at lying directly. "There was no film in the camera and no photograph of Mr Hall sprawled with his neck at right angles on that bed."

"Right angles, eh." He looked at his watch. Looked at the clock on my wall. Checked with the church clock over the street. They all read eight minutes to one. "Get your coat, Lois."

My heart sank. This meant police stations, formal questioning, warrants to search my offices and home and, even as he held the door open for me, I was frantically working on ways to weasel out of the lie.

"I don't know why you women wear high heels, if walking in them makes you limp," he said, in the street.

"It's not the shoes. I dropped a chicken on my foot."

"Hm," he said, and I'm not sure at what point he linked my arm through his, but the support certainly made walking easier. "Right, then. Here we go."

I thought he meant the car, although I wouldn't normally have associated beige sports models with police cars. Instead, he meant the restaurant, decked out in red, white and green stripes.

"Surprised?"

"You could say that." Italian, too. "You struck me as the sort who only eats at the police canteen."

"You struck me as the sort who doesn't eat at all," he said, looking me up and down as if I were a racehorse, and I must admit I do lose track of time when I'm working, but was I honestly that bony? I looked at my wrists and thought, damn.

"How did you get into the PI business?" he asked, over antipasti of sardines and tomatoes.

It seemed an innocuous enough question, so I explained how I'd been temping as a shorthand typist in a solicitor's (no one offers unmarried mothers permanent employment), and how, during the course of my assignment, I was privy to various telephone conversations between the partners and firms of private eyes. It didn't need Einstein to calculate the difference between shorthand typing and the amount of money that could be made from divorce. Strangely, it took me right through the saltimbocca and halfway into my tiramisu to explain all this, though I omitted to mention that this was the first time I'd ever told anyone my history.

"You never wanted to get married?"

"To the father of my child? Of course I did!" What kind of strumpet did he take me for? "Unfortunately, he never had any intention of leaving his wife and at the first sniff of the word pregnancy, he dropped me like a brick."

No offer of child support. In fact, no support of any kind. And he knew I was far too sweet to go blabbing to his wife.

"Dammit, Sullivan, he even denied the baby was his!"

"I, er, meant afterwards. The last few years."

Oh. "Too busy," I said, and then, in another burst of unaccustomed frankness (I blame the Chianti), I admitted that no one had ever asked me. "Men aren't exactly tripping over themselves to put a ring on an unmarried mother's finger."

Instead they think of us as easy, which is why I took up judo and why I make Susan go to classes every Tuesday.

"What about you?" I asked, calming down over the coffee. "Are you married?"

"Nope." He shrugged. "Engaged once, but she didn't like the hours I kept and married a nine-to-five accountant. Then again." He grinned. "It might have been because I'm so damned ugly."

Not handsome, that's for sure. Craggy/rugged/lived-in, call it what you will, that face was never going to end up on an advertising poster. But ugly . . .?

"We'd better go," he said. "The restaurant is closing."

Was it? I hadn't realized we'd been sitting there so long, and though I can't remember how we ended up going from trattoria to cinema, I have vague recollections of someone saying something about Cary Grant, which led to the fact that *North by Northwest* was playing at the Odeon, which in turn led to there being just enough time to catch the matinee before I met my daughter after tap class.

I knew full well what Sullivan was playing at. Softening me up, winning me over, drawing me into his confidence. It wouldn't work, I didn't care. It was the first time I'd been to the pictures in a decade. I'd forgotten what popcorn tasted like. It tasted bloody good.

October turned to November. Sunshine turned to rain. The nights began to draw in really fast. From time to time, like twice a week, Sullivan would drop by my office to discuss the Belle Vue murder – or at least vent his frustration at the lack of leads and progress – and invariably we'd end up having lunch or taking in a film. *Ben-Hur. Rio Bravo. Some Like It Hot* with Jack Lemmon and Marilyn Monroe.

"I just wish I could find a motive," he would say, spiking his fingers through that dark, unruly mop. "The door was locked, there was no key on the inside, and commercial reps in motor oil can't break their own necks, that's for sure."

"Not and lock the door afterwards," I'd agree, and trust me, I did feel sympathy. Needless to say, had I believed that holding back that photograph prevented him from bringing the perpetrator to justice, I'd have mailed it to him – anonymously, of course. Okay, he'd know it was me (even though I'd have denied it with my dying breath), but there was still the possibility, however remote, that someone else had snapped the dead man in that hotel bedroom. But I'd studied that picture over and over. It was just a dead man in a hotel bedroom, end of story.

"He'd stayed at the Belle Vue several times, that's the silly part."

The first time Sullivan kissed me was during the chariot race in *Ben-Hur*, and if anyone ever tells you that's exciting, believe you me, it was nothing compared to the thrill of that kiss. I decided there and then that I liked being softened up, won over, drawn into a policeman's confidence. Torture me all you like, Officer, I still won't tell.

"I guess he made enemies in Brighton –"

"Motor oil is a dangerous business," I grinned.

"But legitimate," he said. "I checked, and he had genuine appointments in Brighton on every occasion that he stayed at the Belle Vue, even though the company he worked for didn't spring for their uncompromising rates."

That was odd, I thought. Usually reps stayed at fleapits and charged the higher allowance to make a bob or two, not the other way around. I was about to point this out, even though I'm sure Sullivan was way ahead of me, but then he leaned over the table and kissed me full on the mouth and in public, and it went straight out of my head. I had other things to worry about.

"My daughter has a crush on her road-safety officer," I said. Lately we'd taken to having lunch on Saturdays, when Susan went to Josie's. "She thinks he's handsome, clever, funny, a real scream—"

"That doesn't sound like a crush." The gravel in his throat churned up in laughter. "It sounds to me like she's found a friend, but in any case, where's the harm? She's nine."

"Hero worship? Nothing." I downed half a glass of wine in a single swallow. "Providing she grows out of it."

And there it was again, too much damned Chianti, because suddenly I was blurting out my own stupidity at falling in love with an older, married man—

"Whoa." His hand covered mine and half the table. "Why do you keep blaming yourself? The bastard knew exactly what he was doing, Lois. He's the one who preyed on your youth and innocence. He's the one who led you on, lied to you, and cheated. And Lois, he's the one who bailed when you got pregnant."

I'd never really thought of it like that, any more than I'd imagined Stephen Rolands as a child molester, who ought to be locked up and the damn key thrown away for good. If Sullivan ever got his hands on him, so help him, he said, Rolands would need a bloody plastic surgeon. What odds the bastard was still doing it today?

"Is he still teaching?"

"Long Road Secondary Modern, but—"

"But nothing. You said yourself, you'd only just turned seventeen, but times have changed in ten years, Lois. Rock and roll has taken over, Teddy boys are in, girls are wearing make-up, looking older. I'll bet you a pound to a penny Rolands is targeting fifteen-year-olds or younger."

I wanted to do something, say something, be really grown up about this business of scales dropping from the eyes. Instead I burst into tears.

"Don't worry, we'll stop him," Sullivan said softly. "He won't ruin any more lives, you have my word."

"It's not that," I blubbed. In fact, it wasn't even the thought of Susan's father rotting in jail – nothing half so noble.

The thing is, right up till that moment, I'd genuinely believed that I was special.

It's surprising how businesslike you become when there are no illusions left. How detached you feel snapping adulterous husbands with mistresses/call girls/rent boys and in places most decent people couldn't imagine, or how disconnected you become furnishing cast-iron proof of wives with gambling addictions, drug addictions, lovers, or just a love affair with the bottle. After all, who was I to judge what constitutes an unfit mother? I only needed to take one look in the mirror.

As a result, shades of grey no longer figured in my life. My job was to secure Susan's future, and whereas before, when it came to runaway children, my heart was torn between finding them and reporting their whereabouts to their parents, I simply reminded myself that if I hadn't intended to return them, I shouldn't have taken the job in the first place. Black and white worked well. With the cheque from Mrs Cuthbertson's solicitor, for instance, I could send Susan on a foreign-exchange visit, maybe two. Her life would never be like mine.

So Guy Fawkes Night came and went. We roasted potatoes in the bonfire, let off rockets from a milk bottle, tied Catherine wheels to the next-door neighbour's shed, and frightened his dog with our jumping jacks. Susan took up ice skating and fell in love with horses, and since cases didn't come in any faster, I found myself with more time on my hands than I'd ever known.

That's what comes from being too efficient.

Which is why I was sitting at my desk one Wednesday afternoon, poring over the photograph of Stanley Hall's dead body.

Someone broke his neck with one clean snap, Sullivan told me, shortly after the results of the postmortem had come through. That, to me, suggested someone who'd been in the army. You can't kill that cleanly and that swiftly without training and (I'm sad to say) without practice. Then there was the trunk. Commercial representatives in motor oil don't lug around huge amounts of samples. There are no demonstration models to tuck away in cases. For one night's stay, he wouldn't need much in the way of change of clothing, and as a lowly rep aged twenty-six from a council house in London's notorious East End, he was unlikely to be sporting a tuxedo.

I made myself a cup of tea and dunked a ginger nut. Why the Belle Vue, either? I'd never met Stanley Hall and maybe it was unfair to judge, but somehow I wasn't getting the impression that this was his own special personal treat. That blue check suit was more at home on a bookie's runner than at Brighton's top hotel. If Hall was pampering himself on the sly, subsidizing the room rate out of his own pocket, surely he'd have treated himself to more apposite attire? Or at least, like me, rented something suitable? Questions, questions, questions. I could see why Sullivan was so frustrated. The difference was, he had a dozen other cases to work on, while I had nothing to distract me except a bit of filing and maybe window cleaning. (It's Christmas that widens the gulf in marriages to the point of irrevocability. Not the run-up).

More tea. More ginger nuts. And I guess it's all that osso bucco and fettuccine, but I noticed the other day that my hips have got some shape at last, and those poached eggs on my chest no longer need so much cotton wool inside their bra. And I thought of Stanley Hall. His body still not released for burial. What his poor mother must be going through—

"Sullivan, it's me. Well, no, it's not *me*, of course, it's the security manager. That's who killed Stanley Hall."

"Lois, slow down. You're running all your words into one."

"Then listen faster, Sullivan. Why didn't Stanley Hall check out on time?"

"Because he was dead, darling."

"Yes, but why didn't someone go and check? He was supposed to have vacated the room by 9:30 in the morning, yet the "Do Not Disturb" sign was still hanging on the doorknob after lunch. Someone either told Housekeeping that this was fine—"

"She says cleaning two-twenty-three wasn't on her list."

"Exactly. Or, if you'd only let me get a word in edgeways, someone deleted that room number from her roster. And the only other person who has access to the housekeeper's room is the manager of security!"

After eight years in the PI business, I know hotels inside out.

"The very first thing that struck me about him was his military bearing," I continued firmly, before he could interrupt again. "I can't be sure, but you check his army records and if he didn't serve in Korea and have experience of one-to-one combat, I'll eat my brand-new pedal pushers."

"Please don't, you look unendurably sexy in them." I could hear his pencil scratching down the line. "So assuming you're right, that's taken care of means and opportunity. How about a motive?"

"Don't CID ever talk to ordinary people?"

All it needed was a few discreet enquiries of the staff at the Belle Vue – and okay, I admit it, a few discreet ten-pound notes as well – to drag out the fact that three or four times in the past year, some of their clients had been robbed.

"The desk clerk confirmed – incidentally, I'm expecting Her Majesty's police force to reimburse me for these expenses – but anyway, he confirmed that these robberies coincided with every one of Stanley Hall's visits."

That's why that loud check suit didn't matter. He never intended leaving the room. It was the security manager who had both keys and access. He who stole money, jewels, various other valuables.

"Just a few bits here and there, and never enough to justify the Belle Vue's guests calling the police, but enough to launch an in-house investigation."

In which their upright, vetted, army veteran was hardly going to investigate himself!

"Stanley Hall was the fence?"

"If you've ever been to the East End, Sullivan . . ."

I didn't tell him this was where I was born, or that, council house or not, my family still disowned me, not just for being an unmarried mother, but for being a PI to boot. The shame is just too much to bear.

"That's why he needed such a large trunk, and I'll bet that's why he was killed."

"He started to get greedy?"

It would have been the perfect murder, had it not been for me and the Cuthbertsons' divorce. Because having calmly hung the "Do Not Disturb" sign on the door he'd locked behind him, the security manager was waiting until the mid-afternoon lull before removing his accomplice's body, and in the victim's own trunk, too. No wonder he'd arrived so quickly on the murder scene. No wonder he'd looked so bloody grim. But equally . . . I stared into the telephone. If it hadn't been for me hanging on to evidence, he could have got away with it. I tried to console myself with the fact that at least now Mrs Hall could bury her son in time for Christmas. Tried is the operative word.

"By the way, Sullivan, one other thing."

"What's that?"

"Did you just call me darling?"

Susan was wheeling her bike down the hall on her way to Josie's when I heard her call out, "Hello, Mr Sullivan."

I blinked. I hadn't associated him with either ice skating or pony rides.

"Hello, Susan." He tapped her on the head with a rolled-up page of foolscap. "Still practising what I taught you?"

She laughed, in a happy, friendly, offhandedly familiar sort of way before bursting into song in the front doorway.

"*You look over your shoulder*
Before you stick your right arm out.
When it's clear, then you manoeuvre . . ."

She was still Hound-Dogging away as the door slammed in her wake, and if she leaves that scarf behind one more time, I'll throttle her with the bloody thing.

"*You're* the road-safety officer?"

It was the first time he'd come to the flat, and I'd reckoned on Susan being gone by eleven-thirty. She's usually pretty prompt. Else I dock her pocket money.

"That's me. Handsome, funny, clever . . . and what was that other thing again?"

"Old," I snapped. "And you could at least have the decency to look sheepish."

"Why? Susan and I hit it off straightaway, it's how I knew who you were, remember? You're all she talks about, you know."

"Really?" It takes pathetically little to make a mother's heart swell.

"Uh-huh." His nose wrinkled. "Until Rusty the pony came along, anyway."

It's only a small flat and he seemed to fill up most of it. "Here," he said, handing me the sheet. "I thought you'd like a copy of the security manager's confession." He glanced at me from the corner of his eye as he made us both a cup of coffee. "Are you sure you didn't write it for him? It's almost word for word what you told me."

I was so busy reading that it took me a few minutes to realize how quickly he'd made himself at home. Or how right it felt.

"Female intuition," I said glibly.

"And a good memory," he said, concentrating surprisingly hard on stirring coffee that contained neither milk nor sugar. "The size of that trunk? The colour and design of his suit? Neck at right angles to the body? One might almost say photographic."

In a book, I'd have had the grace to blush. In real life, I stared him out.

"A word of advice, though, Lois." When he leaned back in the chair, I heard it creak. Then again, it could have been a low chuckle in the back of his throat. "Next time, either tuck the roll into the inside of your stocking or wear a less figure-hugging skirt. By the way, happy birthday," he said, tossing a box across the table.

No point in asking who had told him. "What is it?"

"What does it look like?"

It looked like a diamond solitaire. "A reward from the Belle Vue?"

"Are you kidding? Those people won't even give their fleas away." His craggy face grew serious. "Lois, please say you're not going to make me go down on one knee."

I dropped the box. We banged heads picking it up.

"You're asking me to *marry* you?"

"Why not?" He ran his hand over his jaw. "I get free housing through my job, which would save you rent on this place, for a start. Then it's not like Susan and I don't get on." *If I had a daddy, I'd like him to be like the road-safety man.* "And . . . well . . ."

"Well what?" This time I was determined he would do it.

"And I love you."

I loved him too, but I was holding that one up my sleeve. "I won't change what I do, Sullivan. I'll still be Hepburn Investigations with seedy divorces and even seedier clients."

"It never occurred to me that you would change, Lois, and I don't want you to. Not ever."

"I still bank my cheques in Susan's trust fund?"

"Absolutely."

I told him I supposed it was a deal, only on this occasion we didn't seal it with a handshake. Afterwards, and once you could wipe the grin off my face, because that's something else I hadn't done in a decade, I have to admit that committing to a lifetime with someone didn't seem half so scary.

Slowly, the world turned back to a million shades of grey.

MAKEOVER

Bill James

Of course, the murmur went around the Monty club in Shield Terrace more or less immediately and – also, of course – reached its owner, Ralph Ember. Versions did vary in detail, but all said a club member, Cordell Maximillian Misk, known mostly as Articulate Max, somehow wangled himself into the team who did the copycat bank raid on International Corporate Diverse Securities, and came away with a very delightful, individual share in untraceables. So, when Articulate turned up with his mother and great aunt Edna at the club, asking to see Ralph personally, he had an idea what they wanted, even before any conversation began. Ralph was in his upstairs office at the time testing the mechanisms of a couple of Heckler and Koch automatics. A barman called on the intercom to tell Ember they would like a conference.

It was the Press, not Ember, who gave the International Corporate Diverse Securities raid this "copycat" title, because it seemed so accurately modelled on that huge suction job done at the Northern Bank in Belfast, maybe by the IRA, in December 2004. Although the takings from ICDS in Kelita Street, Holborn, London, were not up to the Belfast haul of £26 million, the methodology looked similar: basically, get among the bank executives' families and keep them hostage until the managers opened up the vaults and let the money go. Ralph thought the idea might have come from an American novel and film, *The Friends of Eddie Coyle*.

The ICDS product, as Ralph heard it, varied from £21 million to £12 million. Even the larger amount did fall short of Belfast, but both these lesser figures were clearly satisfactory millions, all the same, and so were the eight between – that is, 13, 14, 15, 16, 17, 18, 19 and 20. Ralph and most other people familiar with Misk would have considered this sortie beyond his class, even in a dogsbody role. Some accounts said he'd been lookout, others that he ran the phone link at one of the hostage homes. But the rumours putting him on the operation in some sort of job persisted. And, as soon as Ralph came down to meet the three, he did notice a new jauntiness in Articulate. That was how Ralph would describe it, "jauntiness". In his view, jauntiness in an established Monty member such as Max often meant a whack of recently obtained safe loot, "safe" indicating two factors: (a) it had been lifted from someone's *safe*, for example a Holborn, London, bank's, and (b) the notes were old and, therefore, reasonably *safe* to spend.

Usually, Ralph saw in Articulate the standard, niggly, comical, defeated self-obsession of a small time crook who believed unwaveringly that next week he'd be big-time, and who'd believed unwaveringly for an age he'd be big-time next week, these next weeks having slipped long ago into the past. Max's nickname came the satirical way some blubber lump weighing 300lb might be called "Slim". More than any other quality, Articulate lacked articulateness, so, joke of jokes, label him with it. People mocked his taste for sullen silence. And, until now, in Ember's opinion, Misk had been the feeble sort who put up with mockery, possibly even expected it, not someone formidable and esteemed enough to get asked on to an enterprise like the ICDS, all expenses paid, retrospectively.

One major point about Ralph Ember was that he wanted to hoist the Monty to a much higher social level very soon, and people like Articulate and his relations would obviously be the first to get permanently kicked out. Ralph hoped to polish up the Monty to something like the prestige glow of big London clubs, such as the Athenaeum or the Garrick, with their memberships of powerful and distinguished people – bishops, editors, high civil servants, TV faces, company chairmen. Articulate did not really suit. In fact, most of the present Monty membership did not really suit. Ralph would have bet the Athenaeum rarely staged celebration parties for jail releases,

turf war victories, suspended sentences, parole and bail suc-
cesses. These happened regularly at his club.

Just the same, while Articulate and folk like him remained on
the Monty's books, Ralph regarded it as a prime duty to treat
them with all politeness and decency, and, yes, friendliness, as if
they truly counted for something. Membership of the Monty
was membership of the Monty and entailed absolute recognition from its proprietor. Articulate and the two women called in
the afternoon, when the club was quiet, so he could allow them
some of his time. Ralph came to the Monty at these off-peak
periods more often than previously, because he liked to do a
thorough, undisturbed daily check on club security. Ralph
naturally had enemies, and lately they had begun to look and
sound a few troublesome degrees more focused. Anyone who
collected £600,000 a year untaxed from drugs commerce, besides profits from the Monty and some entrepreneurial com-
missions, was sure to have envious enemies, well-focused
envious enemies. Hence the H and Ks. Hence, also, the shield
fixed on one of the internal pillars and intended to give Ralph
protection from gunfire when he sat behind the bar at a little
shelf-desk checking on stock and sales. He'd had the shield
covered with a collage of illustrations from *The Marriage of
Heaven and Hell*, a work by the poet William Blake, so that it
would look like part of the decor and, in fact, add some class.
But it was thick steel. In Shield Terrace he needed a shield. For
instance, a lad called Luke Apsley Beynon had begun to get very
bothersome. Something terminal might have to be done there
before too long.

Mrs Misk said as soon as Ralph joined them in the bar now:
"Considerable legacies have recently come to us – to Edna, Max
and me – from my side of the family, Ralph."

"Always I'm confused in such cases about whether to offer
congratulations or commiserations, since a legacy clearly implies a death, perhaps of a greatly loved one," Ember replied.
He gave this ample solemnity, but not too much, in case the
legacies mattered more to them than the loved one, who might
have been hardly loved at all, just loaded. That is, supposing
there had *been* a loved one to confer the legacies, and not simply
the emptied Holborn bank. "I reconcile such opposites by

thinking that the departed, although much missed, would wish his/her bequests to affect positively the future lives of those so favoured. This would be his/her motive, surely, in selecting them as beneficiaries." Before coming down from the office, Ralph had put the guns away and washed the cordite smell from his hands. These H and Ks were necessary because of people like Beynon, but Ember hated any association of firearms with the club. Almost certainly no Athenaeum member carried a piece on the premises, unless, possibly, the head of MI5 belonged.

Articulate, his mother and great aunt would probably want to use Ralph and some of Ralph's connections to launder Misk's gains, now charmingly fictionalized as three legacies. Ralph could increase the Monty booze and cigarette orders, using their money to cover the additions. They would then re-sell the goods to clubs, pubs, clubs, off-licences. Plainly, they'd take an account book loss, because Ralph required a commission, and the people they sold to would want good profit possibilities. But that was the standard way the market worked for difficult money, even untraceables. Also, as the currency for such trading had been stolen, it became crazy to speak of a loss. This amounted to a loss on treasure Articulate should never have had. Crucially, the wealth must not be spent in a style that drew attention or people would start asking how he and his family grew so rich so fast. Such people might be police people, such as Iles or Harpur. Dangerous. Or they might be villain people who'd decide that if Articulate had a lot they'd get some of it, at least some of it. Dangerous.

But drink and tobacco rated only as marginal elements in this type of business plan. Where there was real, lavish money, the lucky holders might, for instance, think about investing in properties, maybe for occupying themselves, or for renting out, or because, even in tricky economic times, most buildings kept their value or moved up. However, if Articulate and his mother and great aunt Edna approached a normal estate agent and tried to buy four de luxe, five-bed, heated pool, Doric pillared, golf-village houses in the Algarve, Portugal, at 750,000 Euros each, offering payment in cash, there would be some surprised, sharp intakes of professional breath and, afterwards, some sharp outgoings of professional breath in gossip about these potential customers who could cough approaching two million pounds sterling in suitcased notes. *Potential* customers might be as far as it went. Many – most? – normal estate agents would refuse to handle that kind of deal, despite longing for it and their cut, because they'd fear the wealth came from where it did come from, a bust, and that the culprits might one day be identified and their spending projects identified also. These potential customers could make *them* potential accessories, and possibly destroy the firm's reputation as upholders of that venerable, wise, holy code of behaviour laid down for estate agents.

But it was fairly generally recognized among Monty members that Ralph Ember knew certain professional people – solicitors, food inspectors, planning officials, and, especially, estate agents – who would find a way around venerable, wise, holy codes of behaviour if those codes seemed malevolently and perversely to be operating against the interests of buoyant trading in special markets. Such services were costly, yes, and so were middleman skills like Ralph's. Folk who collected heavy legacies could afford the best, though, and should expect to pay for it.

"These legacies we wish to be used positively," Mrs Misk said.

"If I may say, this is what I would expect of your family," Ralph answered. "Positivism."

"Not frittered," she said.

This did sound to Ralph like property. Purchase of sizeable villas in Portugal could not in any fashion be termed frittering.

"Or to put it briefly, Ralph, we want to share in your vision," Edna said. Fervour touched her voice.

"In which respect?" Ralph replied. So, *not* property. He thought he could guess what she might mean instead, but prayed he had this wrong.

"Yes, to be a part of it," Mrs Misk said.

"In which respect?" Ralph replied.

Articulate had always seemed a bit passive as well as tongue-tied. His mother, and especially great aunt Edna, handled family policy. Mrs Rose Misk would be over sixty and Edna well over seventy. Their combined life experience left Articulate trailing. Even now, although Articulate somehow gave off the impression of a new confidence and bounce, he did not speak very much. The women dominated, maybe domineered. Edna almost always wore flashy red or green leather – trousers and tasselled jacket – including to major, formal Monty events such as celebrations of a christening or acquittal on a technicality. Today, red. She said: "We know you have wonderful ambitions for the Monty, Ralph – makeover ambitions."

"These inspire us," Rose Misk said.

"Yes," Articulate said. "Oh, definitely."

"This is why, as Rose remarked, we wish to be part of it, Ralph," Edna said.

Hell, he'd been right.

"The money – the legacies, that is – could be *so* vital here," Rose Misk said.

"Definitely," Articulate replied.

"Your plan, your brilliant plan, will cost you a bit, Ralph," Edna said. "I hope you won't regard this as presumptuous, but we could help bankroll the transformation – would be proud to help bankroll the transformation."

"Exactly what I meant by not frittering," Rose said. "A worthwhile and, in our view – Edna's, Max's and mine – a magnificently promising commitment."

"Definitely," Articulate replied.

Edna said: "Without, I hope, being cruel, Ralph, we look at the club as it is now – the type of member, the need for a bullet proof slab up there to guard you – we look at all this and cannot believe the Monty today satisfies someone of your taste and refinement."

"No, no, not a shield," Ember said, with a fair show of amusement. "It's a board to maximize ventilation by helping control air currents. But please don't ask me how!"

"All right, all right, we can understand why you don't want the Monty thought of as a pot-shot range," Rose said.

"We're talking of an infusion to the Monty development funds of at least hundreds of thousands, Ralph," Edna said. "As starters."

"That's it," Articulate replied. New self-belief still brightened his features, but a kind of misery clothed these words.

"Your first move has to be expulsion of nearly all the present Monty membership, hasn't it, Ralph?" Edna said. "You won't draw the type of people you want while the club still looks like Low Life Inc. Initially you'll have to take some mighty losses – ending of membership fees and, obviously, a collapse of bar profits. This could be where our funds became useful."

Edna's survey of the problems was spot-on, and Ralph vastly resented it. To him there seemed something fucking indelicate about describing his cull plans with such disgusting accuracy. This was exactly the kind of crude approach to sensitive things that ensured Edna in her damn gear would be an early victim of a Monty clear-out, along with Articulate and his mother. Did Edna, this pushy, leathery and leather-garbed old intruder imagine she and the other two were "the type of people" he wanted? Did she think they could buy their way into not just assured membership of the new Monty with their bank loot, but perhaps take a share of the ownership and the profits through the size of their investment? She had her scheming eye on a partnership. Ralph regarded that as farcical, but it infuriated him.

He said with a happy lilt to his tone: "Many people come to me with ideas of development of the Monty, and I'm heartily grateful to them. And I'm heartily grateful to you now, Edna. These approaches – so positive and well-meant – show how fondly some members regard the club."

"The Monty's underachieving on its possibilities, Ralph," Rose Misk said.

And did they imagine he hadn't realized this? Did they think they could advise him about his own cherished club, cherished even in its present rough-house state? "To all these proposals I listen with full interest and, as I say, gratitude," he replied. "It is encouraging to know there's a groundswell of creative ideas among the Monty's faithful. I ponder all these ideas, let me assure you, and at some stage ahead I might act on one of them, or perhaps a mixture of several. But at present those ideas have to remain as such – ideas only." He gave a small, regretful, but determined smile.

"This is the moment for it, Ralph," Edna said.

They were sitting at a table near the snooker alcove and Ralph had brought a bottle of Kressmann Armagnac and glasses. He did some refilling. The club remained fairly quiet. A small group talked at the bar. Nobody played snooker.

Ember stood. "I have to get to my chores now," he said. "I'll leave the bottle. You chat on, by all means."

"But we haven't really got anywhere," Rose said.

"I certainly would not say that," Ralph said. "I've filed away in my head the very promising suggestions you've given me tonight. In due course, or even sooner, I will bring that file out and consider it properly in context."

"What does that mean?" Edna said.

"What?"

" 'In context,' " Edna said.

"Yes, true, Edna. That has to be the way of it – in context," Ember replied.

"Part of the context now, Ralph, is that we have the funds entirely available and entirely ready," Edna said. "This might not be so 'in due course'. We wish to apply these legacies in forward-looking, rewarding fashion as an immediate priority, not 'in due course'. There are other openings for investment. We chose to put you and the Monty first on our schedule. If this does not attract an instant response, we might feel it right to turn elsewhere."

"I've come to learn that in this kind of business, the context, a review of all options, is vital," Ralph said. He left them and did an inspection of the snooker tables baize to make sure there were no snags or rips. He felt proud of his management of the meeting with those three. At no point had he allowed his rage at their gross cheek and clumsiness show itself. Snarls had ganged up inside him ready for use, but he suppressed them.

He went home to his manor house, Low Pastures, for a sleep and stroll around the paddocks, and, as was routine, returned to the club just after 1 a.m. to supervise close-down for the night at two o'clock, unless extra merry-making broke out. He sat at his shelf-desk behind the bar with another glass of Kressmann's, admiring the wild-looking William Blake pictures on the metal screen. Articulate Max, alone now, and in a fine, made-to-measure pin stripe suit and wide silver and yellow tie, came and took a high stool opposite him on the other side of the bar. He had a glass of what might be Kressmann's in his right hand.

Perhaps he thought this a way to acceptance and fellow-feeling from Ember.

"They won't give up, Ralph."

"Who?"

"Great aunt Edna and my mother."

"They're real Monty fans, I'll say that for them," Ember replied with an admiring chuckle.

"Such out-and-out bollocks," Articulate replied.

"What?"

"That idea – to put money into the club."

"I appreciated their affection for the Monty," Ember replied.

"Idiotic."

"Oh?"

"Like throwing money down an old coal pit."

"Oh?"

"You know, I know, and so does everyone else with any trace of a brain that the Monty is never going to change, Ralph. Not change as they meant, anyway. I suppose the police might shut it down onc day because of your drugs link."

Ember thought about hitting this twat. He could stand and lean forward quickly and reach him across the bar. Ralph had never heard him put so many words together before, and now, when he did grow verbal, it was to insult Ralph and the Monty. "I wouldn't say your great aunt Edna or your mother lacked brain, Articulate," he replied.

"The money has shoved them off-balance."

"The legacies?"

"That's it, the legacies. Yes, the legacies," Articulate said. "As if they feel they have to compensate for something."

"Compensate for what – for receiving a legacy?"

"That's it, Ralph. For receiving a legacy."

"A sort of guilt?"

"Yes, like guilt."

"Guilt because they and you have profited from a death? This does happen to legatees sometimes, I know. Guilt over where the money comes from."

"Yes, over where it comes from. So, to rid themselves of this shame, they want to find some noble project where they can put the lucre – and get a return. Some noble, mad project."

"I don't see it like that," Ember replied.

"No, I shouldn't think you do. Why I had to come tonight for a chinwag, on our own."

Ember found the Kressmann bottle and topped both of them up.

"Look, you're getting aggro, aren't you, Ralph?"

"Aggro?" Ember said, giving a real, puzzled smile.

"You wouldn't have stuck the *Marriage of Heaven and Hell* up there otherwise, would you?"

"Much misunderstood," Ember replied. "That baffle board is to—"

"As I hear it, you've been on the end of very forceful invitations to take out a protection policy for the club, an invitation from Luke Apsley Beynon and his firm. That's the buzz."

And, as so often, the buzz had things wonderfully correct. The shield might help against Luke and his cohort. The H and K automatics might help against Luke and his cohort. The increased security visits by Ralph to the Monty might help against Luke and his cohort. Or none of them might help against Luke and his cohort. "Luke is getting to fancy himself a bit, I gather," Ember said with no tremor at all.

"Obviously someone of your calibre, Ralph, is not going to cave in to protection threats from an apprentice lout like Luke."

"Hardly. That is, if there'd been any threats."

"You'll turn down his invitations. And, that being so, there could be some grim events at the Monty to prove that you actually *need* the protection of Luke and his firm. Events such as gunfire or incendiarizing or bad affrays and blood in the bar. Well, I don't need to describe it. You know how club protection works."

Ralph said: "It's kind of you to look in, Max, but I don't really think someone like Luke Beynon could—"

"Here's the bargain, then, Ralph," Articulate replied. "I'll get rid of Beynon if you promise you won't ever pick up on that offer from my mother and great aunt Edna." He became intense. "Listen, Ralph, all due respect to you and the Monty, but I'm not going to have my money squandered like that by two old dames suddenly gone ga-ga. You said you'd file their notion away for another consideration some time. I want you to keep it filed away, or, even better, ditch it."

"*Your* money? It wouldn't all be yours, would it? I thought there were *three* legacies."

"Yes, well let's not play about any longer, all right? *My* money. *My* earned money. Mine but . . . Ralph, I've always let my mother and great aunt Edna organize the big things in my life, you know."

"That so?"

"Look at me, Ralph."

"Yes?"

"I'll tell you what you see, shall I?"

"What I see is—"

"You see a bloke of thirty-two in a suit that cost over two grand, physically sound, and suddenly very successful."

"Successful. You mean getting the legacy?"

"Right, getting the legacy."

The description Articulate gave of himself was not bad, although it didn't deal with the wide shoulders on a thin body and his longish, deadpan face, as if purposefully manufactured to defeat interrogation. He had a large but unmirthful mouth, skimpy fair eyebrows and bleak blue eyes.

"I respect mum and great aunt Edna, naturally. That will never alter. But I can't be run by them any more. I'm grown up, Ralph."

The bank raid had transformed him. This was not just a matter of what Ralph thought of at first as "jauntiness". That could come and go. Max had climbed a little late into maturity and would stay there. He could spiel. He fancied himself as a warrior now – a warrior who could still show gallant deference to his mother and great auntie Edna, but who also knew that a true warrior's main and perhaps only real role was to fight and kill. He'd had a makeover.

Ember said: "There's a phrase for this – 'rites of passage'."

"Great. I could get fond of phrases." Articulate put an arm across the bar, skirting the Kressmann bottle with its striking black label. "A handshake will do for us, I think, Ralph," he said. It was clipped, matey, foursquare. "You keep turning down my mother's and great aunt Edna's loony scheme for my funds and I see to Luke Apsley Beynon."

Ralph took his hand with wholehearted firmness. Sure. This agreement could be only a bonus. He would never have given great aunt Edna, Mrs Misk and Articulate the least fucking financial footing in the Monty, anyway, and, yes, Luke Beynon *was* beginning to look more and more like severe peril.

And, because Beynon looked more and more like severe peril, Ralph went again to the Monty during the afternoon next day to do his security checks. He was touring the Monty yard to satisfy himself no mysterious packages had been left against club doors, when an unmarked Volvo drove in and parked. Assistant Chief Constable Desmond Iles and Detective Chief Superintendent Colin Harpur left the car and walked towards him, Iles looking as jolly as napalm. These two often arrived at the Monty, on the face of it to see all licensing conditions were observed, but actually, in Ralph's view, to terrorize the members and enjoy a few free drinks. "Hunting firebombs, Ralphy?" Iles said.

Ember took them to the bar and mixed a gin and cider in a half-pint glass for Harpur and a port and lemonade for Iles, "the old whore's quaff", as he described it. Today, although it was only afternoon, the club had twenty or so members in, mostly at the bar or playing snooker and pool. Iles did his usual arrogant glare about, as if he couldn't believe how some of these people were out of jail, or any of them.

They sat at a table, Ember again on the armagnac. Harpur said: "I gather Articulate was here last night for quite a dialogue. Had he suddenly turned *really* articulate? He'd emerged somehow?"

"I see such one-to-one conversations with long-time members as a very worthwhile and, indeed, pleasurable experience," Ralph replied, "and an essential factor in one's job as host."

"How true," Iles replied.

"Handshaking, also," Harpur said.

"We're civilized, you know, Mr Harpur. All the usual courtesies are practised at the Monty," Ember replied. It always hurt him to think the club had members who watched things here and straight off reported to the police, for some measly fee, most likely.

"And then Articulate and his mother and great aunt Edna in earlier," Harpur said. He was big and thuggish looking, some said like a fair-haired Rocky Marciano, the one-time heavy-weight champion of the world. Alongside him, Iles looked dainty, but in fact lacked all daintiness.

"This sounds like real activity," Harpur said.

"What does?" Ember said.

"These visits," Harpur said.

"This is a club. People drop in," Ember replied.

Iles said: "We wondered, Colin and I, whether you could recall the gist of your talk with Articulate, or even with Articulate and his mother and great aunt Edna."

"I talk to many members over any twenty-four hours, you know," Ralph said.

"They're lucky to have you, Iles said. Everyone realizes that. But don't piss Col and me about, Ralph, there's a chum. Just give us what Max said, what you said, what the women said, would you? Something agreed at the afternoon meeting and then Articulate comes in late to confirm? Or cancel?"

"Casual conviviality, that's all. You make it all sound very purposeful and businesslike, Mr Iles," Ralph said, "whereas—"

"Yes, purposeful and businesslike," Iles said. "That's our impression."

"Your impression via a fink," Ember said, "as through a grass darkly."

"Wow, Ralph!" Iles said.

"It's the later conversation that really interests us," Harpur said.

"Generalities, I should think," Ember said. He did a frown to indicate he meant to try to help them and recollect. "Weather. Holidays. Cricket. The usual small talk. We try to avoid politics – too controversial. I bump into so many people in the club and have a few unimportant yet, I trust, comradely words. These little pow-wows seem to merge into one pleasant and not very significant encounter. I don't know whether Max would recall things better than I. It might be in your interests to talk to him, if you feel something significant might have come up."

"The thing about Articulate is he's dead," Iles replied.

"My God," Ralph said. The shock was real.

"Which is why what he talked about with you might be to the point," Harpur said.

"Generalities," Ralph said.

"Shot," Harpur replied.

"My God," Ralph said.

"Our impression is that he meant to bop Luke Apsley Beynon, but got bopped himself," Harpur said.

"As most of us would have forecast," Iles said. "I mean, was Articulate Max anywhere near capable as executioner?"

"The whisper's around, isn't it, that he was in on the ICDS robbery with some sort of stooge function?" Harpur said. "Did that make him feel suddenly big and mature and competent – and free up his voicebox?"

"Poor deluded prat," Iles said. "He gave himself a mission on your behalf? Luke Apsley Beynon's been breathing untender words to you, hasn't he, Ralph? This is our information."

"Luke Benyon?" Ember replied.

"Did Articulate, with his new gloss, offer to knock him over for you?" Iles said. "Suddenly he thinks he's one of Nature's hit men? Were you and he talking some kind of deal? You'll see why we're concerned about his appearances here, especially the second one, without his minders, the women. Did he need to say something they shouldn't hear?"

"Deal?" Ember said.

"*Quid pro quo*ism of some sort," Iles said.

"Generalities," Ralph replied.

"We're charging Luke," Harpur said. "He'll go down. His firm will break up without him."

"So you don't come out of this at all too badly, Ralph, do you?" Iles said. "You won't have to cower behind the collage any more."

Ember replenished their drinks and took more armagnac himself. "I think about his mother and great aunt Edna," he said.

"Those two are provided for, we believe," Iles said.

"I mean their grief," Ralph said.

"You were always one for tenderness to prized club members, Ralphy," Iles replied.

TRAIN, NIGHT

Nicholas Royle

Alex, I never said it *was* you. I never said the man on the Tube *was* you. I said he *looked like* you. So much like you it was like we were back together again. And since I couldn't be with *you* any more, I could be with this *version* of you. That's what I was saying. That's what I said.

I never said he was you. I made it perfectly clear that he couldn't be you and that I understood that. His head was shaved. You would never do that. You're too proud of your hair. You wouldn't deny yourself the pleasure of wearing it long. He was also younger, ten, maybe fifteen years younger. But his bone structure was the same, his eyes were identical. You know what, I'm coming round to the idea that he was you, after all. Nor was it on the Central line that I saw him. It was the Hammersmith & City line. That's what I said and that's what it was. I got on at Shepherd's Bush, you got that bit right. I got on at Shepherd's Bush and he was already on, having boarded at Hammersmith or Goldhawk Road. There he was, in my carriage, and there was a seat right opposite him, so I took it. Because it was the Hammersmith & City line, I saw him in natural light, and natural light leaves no room for doubt. The Central line is underground at Shepherd's Bush and while I'll admit the Central line does have a peculiarly attractive light, it's not the same. I might not have been so certain. Plus, if it had been the Central line, how would I have followed him off the train at King's Cross?

I didn't say I followed him into an abandoned building either. I followed him into an art gallery, that place on Wharf Road, that big one with the exposed brick walls. I said it *looked like* an abandoned building. Just as the man on the train *looked like* you. Geddit?

Anyway, I found out who he is. OK? Maybe this will make you happy, because it should demonstrate to you once and for all that I don't think he's you. I know he's someone else. He's an actor. I know because I saw him in something on TV. I was watching this crime drama, alone in the flat, because, you know – I live alone these days, with my unwashed towels and chipped cereal bowls dusted white with crushed paracetamol. That's another thing about your email. You contradict yourself. One minute you say I walked out on you, then you're saying *you* left *me*. Make your mind up. You can't have it both ways. So I'm watching this thing. It was ITV but it was quite good. You wouldn't have given it a chance, of course. That was how I knew you wouldn't be watching it, because it was on ITV. I presume you don't watch ITV with Fareda, either. I presume you're as judgmental as you ever were. See, I don't mind writing her name, now I know what it is. I don't bear her any ill will. As a matter of fact I feel sorry for her. Are you going to do to her what you did to me? Poor girl.

There he was, in the background in one scene. Little more than an extra but he did have a line of dialogue. It was him, I was certain of it, and he looked as much like you on TV as he had on the train. His name was in the credits. Let's call him Anthony.

I discovered something else. That film you showed me shortly after we first started seeing each other – *Un soir, un train* – that black and white Belgian film from the 1960s. You said I looked like Anouk Aimée. Looking back, maybe you wanted me to infer that you looked like Yves Montand. I watched it again the other day. As you know, when I say the other day, I generally mean the other week. You used to find this charming. The way the film pans out is a bit like what happened to us. That village where Mathias and his two companions end up, where they can't understand a word the villagers are saying, that's a bit like us at the end. It was like we were speaking different languages, and not just different languages from the same group, like two romance languages, but two *completely* different languages from different origins entirely. Arabic and Hungarian, Inuit and Welsh. Although, of course, only one of us had changed the language they were speaking.

It's scary, a bit creepy, that film. Maybe you shouldn't give a copy to Fareda. Maybe you shouldn't take her dancing, either. That's when I fell in love with you, you know. When we were dancing at that party in Shepherd's Bush and every five minutes a train went by on the elevated line above the market. You grabbed me and made me watch as one went past.

"Look at them watching us," you shouted into my ear.

"They think we look good together."

I watched the figures silhouetted by the yellowish light inside the carriage, while you held me around the waist.

How I wish now I could have been one of those passengers inside the train looking out at the people dancing. You would have been no more than a frame-grab to me and I would have got off at Hammersmith and carried on with my life. A different life.

A couple of days after the party, we watched *Un soir, un train* for the first time.

I guess you thought the two of them – Mathias and Anne, Yves Montand and Anouk Aimee – were supposed to represent the two of us. If so, then the flashback in London is probably when they are happiest. The way they sit in the back of Michael Gough's car when he takes them on a drive through Rother-hithe, both of them in the back so they can be together, leaving the front passenger seat empty, like it was a taxi. The way they hold hands, later when they're out of the car. The look Michael Gough gives them when he sees them holding hands. I think he's envious of them because they're so happy together. Like we used to be.

The tape was recorded off Japanese TV. Do you remember that? A friend of yours had taped it for you because it was so rarely screened. So it was in French with Japanese subtitles. We had to watch it six or seven times before we knew what was going on and we laughed when we realized that Mathias and his companions couldn't understand what the people in the village were saying either.

I started looking out for Anthony on the Hammersmith & City line. After all, I'd seen him twice, so there was a good chance he worked or lived somewhere along the line. A good chance I'd see him again. I didn't carry my DV camera. I wasn't going to film him this time.

The reason the footage I sent you was so uneven and featured other people as well as him, especially the stuff I shot in the gallery, was because I was having to do it on the sly. It's not easy filming from inside a half-fastened coat.

I tried boarding the same carriage as the last time I'd seen him. Then I tried varying which carriage I got in. I still didn't see him.

I was looking out for him on TV, too, and in *Time Out* and online, but it seemed like he wasn't doing anything that was listed anywhere.

I watched *Un soir, un train* yet again, rewinding the tape endlessly to study the scenes shot in Rotherhithe. Both locations were previously unknown to me, yet notable enough to appear in *The London Encyclopaedia*, which you may remember buying me. I hung around the gallery on Wharf Road, but I didn't see Anthony there either.

Then one morning I got on the train and there he was again. Sitting more or less in the same place. Looking every bit as much like you as he had done before. I didn't stop to think. If I had done, I might have got tongue-tied and everything might have played out very differently. I contrived a conversation. It was easy. He was reading a script. I asked him if he was an actor and he smiled and said he was. It was so easy. Because his bone structure is the same as yours, his smile is the same as yours too. His teeth are slightly whiter, but that's OK. It really did feel like I was sitting there and talking to you. Except it felt like talking to you at the beginning, not the end. And not now. Talking to you now – writing to you now – feels very different. We talked until King's Cross, where he said he had to get off. I said I was getting off there too. I wondered if he was going to Wharf Road again, but I didn't ask him that. I said, "Where are you going?" He said he was going to a rehearsal. He had a part in a play and they were using the director's flat on Gray's Inn Road as a rehearsal space. I said that sounded exciting.

He asked me what I did. It wasn't like he'd only just thought to ask. I'd just not given him the chance.

"I'm a film-maker," I told him, as we were about to part on the street.

"Really?" he said. "Now *that's* exciting."

The way he said it, I could tell he meant it. I guessed he preferred film to the stage.

"Do you have a card?" he asked me. A card! Me!

"I've run out," I said, and as I scribbled my number on an old receipt, my sleeve rode up and I realized he'd be able to see the marks on my forearm.

"Well, I never had any," he said carefully, then wrote his own number in small, precise figures on an empty page of a little notebook that he produced from his shoulder bag. He tore the page out along its perforation and added: "I should probably get some." We said goodbye and I set off in the opposite direction to his, but then turned to watch him go, weaving through the commuters. He's even a similar height to you.

I waited for him to call me and when he did I said there was a location in Rotherhithe I needed to have another look at and would he like to meet there for a drink? Before leaving the house I slotted the tape into the VCR again. The thing I discovered about *Un soir, un train* is that it's not actually a black and white film, after all. I looked it up to check something, and every source that lists it, from *Time Out* to the IMDb, has it down as colour. Maybe some incompatibility between Japanese TV and the UK standard. I couldn't – and still can't – figure out why you gave it me so close to the end. What was it – a week, two at the most, before things fell apart? Were you trying to convince yourself we still had a future? Was your butterfly mind already selecting a new film to show to Fareda?

I picked up the remote and had a last look at those London scenes. In the back of the car. Michael Gough telling Mathias and Anne how Rotherhithe is "notorious". His dialogue, of course, is in English. Their arrival at Bermondsey Wall East, walking on to Cherry Garden Pier, then the visit to the Angel pub. Some kind of balcony, sitting down, holding hands, Michael Gough remaining standing, but that's when he notices their clasped hands.

I also opened a file on my laptop and brought it up to date. When I've finished with it, I'll print it out and close the machine down.

I'll take the tube to London Bridge and walk down impossibly narrow streets between fantastically tall buildings. Converted wharves. Exclusive flats, apartments. Portered, gated. The kind of place we could have ended up sharing in another universe. I'll skirt the Design Museum, cross a bridge of wire and stainless steel. The river a constant presence on my left, tide creeping in.

Bermondsey Wall West, cut inland, along a bit.

Derelict wharves and warehouses. Gaps in the gentrification. Back towards the river. Bermondsey Wall East, Cherry Garden Pier, the first of the two static locations. I can't walk on to the pier as they did in the film. It's owned by a private company now. City Cruises plc. I'll walk up the ramp towards a blue door with a no-entry sign on it, barbed wire coiled above. A security light will flick on, blinding me.

A hundred yards further downstream, the Angel. Lights burning at the windows will turn the blue air a half-shade darker. The light won't last much longer. In the film, Mathias and Michael Gough enter the pub while Anne remains outside. Next shot, the two men are on a balcony, where Anne joins them.

I'll push open the door and go inside. The first thing I'll notice, like the last time I was there, will be the Sam Smith's logo on all the taps and bottles and I'll think to myself, as I did before, that you wouldn't have liked that. This pub has been there since the fifteenth century, and the moment you come along, you find out it's a Sam Smith's joint. Beer's just beer to me, as you know. But I remember how Sam Smith's used to provoke extreme reactions in you. I'll look around. There'll be a handful of locals in. Sam Smith's or no, it's a decent-looking old-fashioned boozer, lots of wood and brass, comfortable seats. I'll move through into the back bar and my eye will be drawn to the picture window. On the other side of the window a balcony, and out on the balcony I'll see Anthony's shaved head shining under the artificial lights. As if sensing my arrival, he will turn round.

Anthony will already have a drink. He won't be bothered by it being a Sam Smith's pub. He'll be trying their own-label wheat beer, which is OK, he'll say. I'll get him another as I buy myself one. We'll sit on the balcony overlooking the river. I'll make sure he's sitting on my right, like in the film. I'll imagine Michael Gough leaning on the handrail looking alternately out at the river traffic and back at the two of us. Anthony will ask me about "my work". I'll take out my DV camera and tell him I'm in the middle of making a short film. I'll say I'd be grateful for his help and he'll say he'd be glad to provide it.

"Samuel Pepys used to drink here," I'll tell him, "and Judge Jeffreys, the Hanging Judge, so called for obvious reasons."

"A strict disciplinarian, I presume?" he'll say.

"He would sit here and watch pirates being hanged on the other side of the river at Execution Dock," I'll tell him.

"Execution Dock?" he'll ask.

I'll point across the river to Wapping Old Stairs.

"They used to bring convicted pirates from Marshalsea Prison. The rope they used to hang them only had a short drop, which wasn't enough to break their necks, so they'd do 'the Marshal's dance' as they slowly suffocated."

"And people call us uncivilized today," Anthony will say.

"They'd be left there until three tides had washed over them," I'll say as I balance my camera on the hand rail to get a shot of us sitting side by side, me and the man who looks like you. This is the shot from Michael Gough's POV. I'll ask Anthony if we can hold hands for a moment. He'll agree. He's a professional.

I might hold his hand for slightly longer than I need to for the shot. Then I'll explain that the next shot is more complicated and that his role will be to act as cameraman. I'll tell him I'm going to disappear for a bit. I'll walk to the tube at Rotherhithe, which is only a couple of minutes from the pub. Take the East London line one stop under the river to Wapping, then walk to Wapping Old Stairs. I'll ask him to stay on the balcony and watch out for me coming down the steps on to the foreshore and then film me, zooming in for a close-up.

"Won't it be very grainy?" he'll ask. "The river's wide here."

"That doesn't matter," I'll say.

I'll produce a stamped padded envelope with your name and address on it and ask him, when the shot is complete, whatever he thinks of it, to stick the tape in the envelope and post it. He'll nod, but look puzzled.

"You'll be coming back, right? Or do you want me to come round there?" he'll ask me.

"Neither," I'll say.

Still he'll look confused.

"I want you to hang on to the camera for me. Post the tape and hang on to the camera." If he remains silent and just sort of frowns at me, I will go on: "You've heard of Dogme? Lars Von Trier? His set of rules for film-makers?"

"It's something like that?" he'll say, brightening up.

"Why didn't you say?"

"Great," I'll say. "But I want you to promise me you'll keep filming, even if it looks a bit weird. A bit extreme. Just keep filming. There's only about ten minutes' space left, in any case."

"And then I post it to this –" he'll look at the label—

"Alex guy? What's he, your editor? Your collaborator?"

"Something like that. Promise?"

He'll promise.

"OK, I'm going to go now," I'll say to him. "Thanks for your help. Thanks for everything."

I might kiss him, or I might make do with having held his hand.

When I've gone, he'll sit and wait for a bit, then start to get impatient as he watches the stairs across the river. It is a long way, almost 300 metres. He may experiment with the zoom on the camera, see if that gives him a better view. What he gains in image size he'll lose in definition. He keeps checking, both with the camera and the naked eye. He'll pick up the padded envelope and perhaps feel the outline of something already inside it. I think he'll take a look, see it's a sealed envelope bearing the same name as on the label, and quickly put it back. He'll check his watch, see it's been fifteen minutes already. How long can it take to go one stop? He'll think about having another drink, but will decide he's too nervous and mustn't risk missing me.

Eventually, just when he's about to try my mobile number, he'll see a vague shape coming down the steep slippery steps of Wapping Old Stairs. He won't be able to recognize me, but he won't question that it's me for a moment. Why should he? In a slight panic, although he'll have had almost half an hour to prepare, he'll fiddle with the camera, trying to frame the best shot. He'll press the red button before I'm quite ready, but that won't matter. He'll squint at the tiny screen, trying to work out what I'm doing. He'll wonder if I'm waving or semaphoring or doing something weird with a rope. At that distance, he won't be able to tell, not even on full zoom. He might be able to see my feet leave the ground. He'll need to rest the camera on the hand rail to keep it steady, while on the screen he'll watch a grainy, degraded image of me dancing.

THE PRINTS OF THE BEAST

Michael Pearce

It was the best of times, it was the worst of times, for such a thing to happen. Christmas Eve! When for the first time since, after the collapse of all my expectations and I had joined Herbert in the Counting House in Cairo, we had managed to take a break together, intending for once to celebrate Christmas in the traditional English style. And now this! The bottle was nothing. Even the mysterious footprints in the sand could surely be explained. But the dead man in the barn—

"Handel, old fellow," said Herbert, calling me by that pet name he had always used, "something must be done!"

It certainly must. Someone in the village must be told, no doubt the Pasha's men would have to be informed. In no time the house would be crawling with people.

But.

This was Christmas Eve. *Our* Christmas Eve, the one we had been planning for so many months. Enough had gone wrong already. And was it now all, at the last moment, to be spoiled?

"Herbert—" I said.

"Yes, old chap?"

"Would it make so very, very much of a difference if the body was not found for a day or two longer?"

"It is certainly very unfortunate that we should come across it just now," said Herbert, "at the very start of our holiday."

We both knew enough of the ways of Egypt to recognize that once the body was declared that would be the end of the holiday we had hoped for. Even though the body was, strictly speaking, nothing to do with us, the fact that it had been found on our property, if only our temporary property, meant that in the eyes

of the villagers we would, so to speak, own it. At the very least
we would have to tell our story, even if we had no story to tell.
And we would have to tell it over and over again. The omda
would have to hear it. It was too much to hope that he would
only have to hear it once. The whole village would have to hear
it. Several times. Officials from the nearest town would need to
write it down. The Pasha's men would inevitably become
involved and who knows what that could lead to? In their
capricious way they might even incarcerate us in some
scorpion-infected, plague-ridden hell hole while they made
up their minds.

Herbert's mind was clearly running on similar lines to mine.

"We have responsibilities back in Cairo," he said.

"Clara!" I said. "The children!"

"The House," he said, looking grave.

"It would only be a question of postponing," I said. "We
would not really be interfering with the course of justice."

"In the end it would make no difference."

"It might even help," I said, "if we were not there."

"How so, old chap?"

"It would mean that they were not distracted by unnecessary
complications."

"Complications?"

"The bottle," I said. "Would they understand it? Abstinence
is enjoined on them by their religion."

"True, true," said Herbert. "Let us say nothing about the
bottle."

"Nor about the footprints."

"Nor about the footprints," agreed Herbert. "They might
not believe us."

"It might lead them astray again. For who knows how
speculation or superstition might work on their weak minds?"

"It would only be for a short time," Herbert remarked, as we
moved the body.

After some deliberation we moved it into one of the out-houses.
It was a long low building dug out of the ground and lined with
bricks and had once, I think, been an ice-house. It had obviously not been used for some time and sand had drifted in and

now filled half the space. Yet, situated below ground as it was, and with the roof so well lined, it was still cool enough to arrest the body's deterioration, which would mean, as I pointed out to Herbert, that the investigation would not be affected.

"True," said Herbert. "True."

He seemed, however, a little uneasy.

"It does mean, of course," he said, "that it will not be possible to bury the poor fellow the same day."

It was the practice in Egypt to bury the dead on the day that they departed; a sensible, hygienic practice in the heat.

"But, then," I pointed out, "that could not have happened anyway. They will have to send for the mamur from Toukh and by the time he gets here and has heard all the depositions it will be Tuesday and by then we will have returned to Cairo."

He still seemed a little troubled, however.

"It is, perhaps, as well, after all, that Clara couldn't come," he said suddenly.

At the very last moment, even as the carriages were being loaded, one of the children had developed a stomach-ache.

"It's just excitement," Herbert had said. But Clara, a connoisseur in her children's illnesses, had shaken her head.

"It's more than that," she had said. She had suspected that it might be the onset of malaria.

"If you think that, my dear," said Herbert, "then we shouldn't go!"

"It seems a pity, though," said Clara, "when you and Pip have been so looking forward to it."

And indeed we had. We had been slaving away in the Counting House for nearly two years without a break.

"No, you must go," she said now with decision. "You go and I will stay here with the children."

Of course, we dissented vehemently.

"No," she said firmly, "you must go. I have been thinking for some time that you are both beginning to look rather peaky. And, besides," she had said, with a smile, and putting her hand on my arm, "you will enjoy recapturing the intimacy of those old bachelor days in London!"

"Just as well that she couldn't," I said now to Herbert, and we returned to the house.

Running along the front of the house was a broad verandah, on which there was a table and some cane chairs with cushions. After the sand storm of the previous day the cushions were covered with sand which had drifted in. Herbert raised the cushions to give them a shake and in doing so uncovered a pair of scorpions.

"How very annoying!" said Herbert, brushing them away. "The headman swore that the house had been cleaned!"

It had, indeed, been flooded, as was the usual custom when a house was about to be reoccupied, to rid it of any infestation.

"I suppose their attention did not extend to outside the house," I said.

"Yes, but—"

I laid my finger on my lips.

"Now, Herbert," I said, "did we not swear before we left that we would pay no attention to trifles? That we would put aside all care for the proper discharge of duties in others? Put the Counting House entirely behind us?"

"We did, old chap, we did. And we will!"

He plumped up the cushion and sat down, and I went into the kitchen to find a bottle to replace the one that had disappeared. The sand which had blown in the day before, just after we had arrived, was still there on the floor of the sitting room, and still there were the huge, bestial footprints.

I took the bottle out on to the verandah and poured out two glasses.

"Your health, dear Herbert! And a very good Christmas!"

"And to you, too, my very dear Handel!"

He put the glass down.

"If a strange one."

"You are thinking of your family," I said gently.

"I acknowledge it. Of the children especially. The Christmas stockings, you know."

"We can go back at once, if you wish."

"No, no. Clara would not forgive me."

He toyed with his glass.

"And, besides," he said, "are there not things to be done here?"

"You are still disquieted about the body, Herbert?"

"I am, I must confess. For suppose the body is not to be separated from the strange things that happened last night? If we conceal those things from them, how are they to proceed?"

"You mean, we should disclose –? But I thought we had discussed that, Herbert."

"Yes, yes. And you rightly convinced me that the strangeness of the happenings here might prey upon their weak minds. But you see where that leads to, Handel?"

"That we should tell—"

"No, no. Not at all. That we should investigate the matter for ourselves and present our findings to them when we have all the answers."

The house we had secured was in a remote village, about fifty miles from Cairo in the Damiatta direction. It had once been a farm house and was surrounded by plantations of orange trees and fields of dourah, which is the corn they have thereabouts, and cotton. Being closer to the sea, the air was fresher than it was inland and the temperature slightly lower, a mere ninety degrees in the shade and 120 in the sun. At night the temperature fell sharply and we deliberated whether to sleep outside on the verandah or to retreat indoors where it would be warmer. In the end we decided for indoors.

That night, as I lay in my bed, I could hear through the open window as well as the singing of grasshoppers and frogs the distant cry of wolves, answered occasionally by the cries of jackals and hyaenas. Later, there appeared to be a pack of wild desert dogs circling the house. It was, as Herbert had said, a strange place to spend Christmas.

Clara had entrusted me with a veritable mound of presents, among which I was surprised to find a not inconsiderable number for myself. We opened them over coffee on the verandah. I could see that they turned Herbert's thoughts to home so after a while I crept away leaving him there to muse. He was still sitting there an hour later, when I thought the time had come to direct his mind to other things.

"My dear Herbert—" I said.

He sat up with a start.

"You are right, my dear Handel," he said. "It is time to begin."

The facts, such as they were, were that we had arrived the previous afternoon, just as the sun was setting in a red ball of fire above the desert. Even as we looked, it seemed to darken over.

"Is that a sandstorm?" said Herbert. "How untimely!"

We went round the house closing all the shutters. By the time we had finished, the wind was rising and fine particles of sand were beginning to seep through the slats of the shutters. We knew from long experience that there was nothing now to be done but sit it out. We gave ourselves a hasty supper and cleared the plates away before the full force of the storm hit us – there is nothing worse than sand in your food, in your wine, in your mouth. Then we sat down opposite each other and put blankets over our heads and a bottle of wine on the table in front of us. From time to time one of us would put out a hand and refill the glasses, putting a table mat over the glass as soon as it was filled, to keep out the sand. Then we would retreat beneath our blankets.

And then, I suppose, we went to sleep, for the next thing I was aware of was an exclamation from Herbert.

"The bottle, Handel! What have you done with the bottle?"

"On the table."

"No, it is not!"

I emerged from under my blanket.

"I am sure I restored it to the table. In any case, was it not you who helped last?"

There was a little silence.

"On reflection, Handel, it was. But, then, where the deuce could I have put it?"

"On the ground, perhaps."

Herbert stood up and looked around. I heard him give a startled gasp.

"My dear Handel! Look! Look!"

I stood up beside him. The floor was covered with a thin film of sand. And in the sand were some enormous footprints.

*   *   *

They were of bare feet. They entered from the door, made straight across the room, passed the table and then went out through the door which led on to the verandah.

"He . . . she . . . it took the bottle," said Herbert, in a stunned voice.

It could have been any of the three. The foot was large for a man, very large for a woman. Which made one think . . .

Some ape-like creature? But what ape-like creature existed in the wastes of Egyptian desert? A jackal? Of that size? Preposterous! A hyaena? Ridiculous! It was not to be thought of.

A man, then. That was most likely. The bottle argued for that, too. But, then, would any man round here have a taste for the best Cypriot wine? Would not wine have been against his religious principles? Unless, of course – But the bare feet argued against the presumption that he was an Englishman or a European.

We followed the tracks out on to the verandah. The storm had died down a little now although a thin wind put grit into our mouths and stung our faces. The footprints led to the edge of the verandah and then down and across the yard. In the darkness we had no inclination to follow them.

But the next morning they were still there on the verandah. Out in the yard, however, where the sand had blown more freely, we quickly lost them. There was a new, thick layer of sand which covered everything. Whatever footprints there had been had disappeared.

Around the farm, enclosing the buildings and the yard, was a six-foot-high wall, a barrier against the wild dogs and other unwelcome creatures. Part of the wall was sheltered by one of the outhouses and on that part we found traces of intrusion. The man, or creature, had obviously placed its hands on top of the wall – we could see the marks, although they were less clear than the footprints. The sand on top of the wall was disturbed, as if someone had clambered over. And, down on the other side, where the out-house still gave shelter against the wind and the sand, just for a few yards, were the footprints again. Only not going away from the house but coming towards it.

* * *

So much we had seen on that first exploration. But that was not all. For, as we returned to the house, going round the side of one of the out-houses, back in the yard, we came across the body of a man lying face down in the sand. The sandstorm had blown over him and left a layer of sand all over the body. From its undisturbed thickness and from the stillness of the body we had known that the man was dead.

And had been content to leave it so. In Egypt the sight of a dead body is not uncommon: a beggar expired in the street, an infant baby dead in childbirth or abandoned shortly after birth by its mother. After a while you become hardened. You do not normally enquire too closely.

But perhaps Herbert was right. The circumstances were so strange in this instance that inquiry into them could not responsibly be left to others.

"My dear Herbert—"

It was time, yes, to begin.

The first thing to be done was to identify the dead man and the manner of his death.

"Need we?" But Herbert answered himself. "Of course, Handel. You are right."

Which meant revisiting the ice-house. We pulled the body out into the sun and examined it. It was that of a middle-aged man, a fellah – that is to say, a peasant – from his clothes and general appearance, possibly from the village nearby.

"Where else, out here, could he be from?" asked Herbert.

But that, in my view, raised once more the question of informing the villagers, who, if, indeed, he came from the village, would be able to identify him at once.

There was, however, a powerful argument against this. Examination revealed a savage wound in the neck. The flesh was so badly torn that it was impossible to tell how it had been inflicted. A knife, perhaps? But used with an astonishing degree of violence. What, however, could not be ruled out was . . .

"I am afraid so, my dear Handel."

A bite.

And if so, a bite perhaps from that strange creature – if

creature it was and not a man, which would have been stranger still – that had invaded our privacy two nights before.

But what effect might this have if it were revealed to the village? Would it not cause alarm and despondency? Terror, even? Might it not lead to acts of despair in a people lacking Christian philosophy?

"No, Herbert. Better to remain mute until we can present them with the answer as well as the question."

But how to advance beyond the question in the first place?

Herbert bent over the body.

"Handel."

"Herbert?"

"Do you smell what I smell?"

I forced myself to stoop closer.

"He had been imbibing."

From his lips, where now the flies buzzed incessantly, came a faint smell of alcohol.

"And consider the fingers, Handel."

"The fingers?"

They were abraded, as if he had been scrabbling at something.

"The wall?"

We went back to the wall, to the place we had found. What we saw now, inspecting it more closely were faint smears of mud, dried out, of course, but still perfectly clear.

"Handel."

"Herbert?"

"The fingers, again. Did you see the nails? They were packed with mud."

"And the knees," I said. "And the feet. Muddy also."

"A potter, perhaps?"

"Or someone working on the canal?"

The fields around the village were irrigated by a system of canals which drew water off the Nile and fed it over the surrounding land. The system worked well and to it was due the astonishing abundance of the fields. But the abundance came at a price. The canals had to be maintained as they quickly became choked with sand. Every year, in the dry season, after the Inundation, gangs of labourers descended on the system and worked to make it good again, digging out the sand, repairing the sides, and re-piling the earth on the raised banks which protected it against the wind and the sand.

The work was heavy and was not done voluntarily. A corvee had been introduced by means of which villagers were compelled to give their labour. Although the work was in their interest, the villagers saw the benefit as going largely to the Pasha, and it was bitterly resented.

We walked down to the village, passing women hoeing in the fields. One of them, an unusually tall black lady, straightened her back and looked at us. The others continued their labour indifferently.

The canal was on the other side of the village. What we had hoped to see, I do not know. What we saw were men up to their chests in water digging out sand and throwing it up on the sides while others went along moving the sand back and forming banks. Behind them, patrolling steadily, was a man with a long whip, the overseer, usually the Pasha's man, exercising the whip whenever he thought fit.

We went back to the village. It was a small one, just a few houses clustered around an open space which served as a square, one or two tebaldi trees and beneath them a well. Women were dipping a bucket into the well and filling their pitchers, and, not far away, a group of men were sitting, the village elders.

One of them rose as we went past. It was the village omda, the headman, whom we had met when we arrived. He asked us if the house was to our liking. We said it was; only the sand had blown in during the storm. He said he would send a woman up to clean through the house again. She had done it earlier, he said apologetically, only at this time of year, when there were frequent sandstorms, it was hard to keep it like that.

I said that to us, after Cairo, the village seemed very peaceful. He said that all the men were away working on the canal. He hoped they would not be away for too much longer as there would soon be a need for them in the fields.

We asked him if he found it difficult supplying the necessary labour for the corvee. He shrugged.

"They know it has to be," he said.

I asked if any of the villagers tried to evade it. He said that if they did it would fall upon the family and on the village, so on the whole people didn't.

Herbert asked if anyone at work ever tried to slip away. Seldom, said the omda, for then the whole gang was flogged. He seemed about to add something, then stopped; then burst out that in fact it had happened only a few days before. A man had disappeared. "The wound is still fresh in our minds," he said. He pointed to a woman filling her pitchers alone by the well. The other women had departed.

"That is his wife," he said. From now on, he said, or at least until he gave himself up, his wife would have to fill her pitchers alone.

"And what if he never comes back?" Herbert asked.

The headman did not answer directly. He said only that the Pasha's reach was wide.

We walked back up to the house in silence.

"We know now, at any rate, the identity of our man," Herbert said, throwing himself into one of the chairs on the verandah.

And yet the mystery had only deepened. We now knew who the poor fellow was. But how had he met his end? And for what reason?

We could now understand, we thought, the explanation for his presence in the farm. He had fled from the gang working on the canal and, seeking refuge, climbed over the wall, believing the farm-house to be still deserted. There, at least, he would be safe from the wild beasts outside.

Was it not possible, however, that in doing so he had come face to face with a creature wilder than any of those he feared?

There were other questions. Had he been pursued to the farm? Or had he come there and inadvertently stirred an inhabitant who, or which, had turned on him perhaps in panic and killed him?

All this seemed possible and likely. What did not seem possible or likely was the tale told by the footprints: that some one or thing should enter the room while we were actually in it, our heads covered, it is true, but nevertheless there, pick up the bottle and then walk calmly out with it and disappear into the sandstorm.

Later in the afternoon, after we had enjoyed the splendid Christmas lunch that Clara had prepared for us, the woman that the omda had promised came up to clean the house again. It was the woman we had seen on her own beside the well. Perhaps the omda had sent her up in pity, knowing that without her husband she would be in need of any recompense that we might offer.

She was a sturdy peasant women in her thirties, bare-legged and bare-footed, though without her face covered, as it would perhaps have been in the town. While we were enjoying our coffee and brandy, she set to work in the kitchen and soon had swept it clean. Then she came into the dining room with her brush. She saw the footprints, there, still in the sand that covered the floor, and stopped.

Then, without a word, she swept the floor clean and afterwards moved on to the bedrooms.

"There goes our chance," said Herbert quietly, "of keeping this from the village."

When she had finished she went home. Herbert and I sat out on the verandah wondering what we should do. If she revealed what she had seen, the whole village would be up here. They would rout around and almost certainly come across the body in the ice-house. And then, as Herbert pointed out, it would not look good for us. We decided that in the circumstances we would have to revise our plans. We would go to the omda first thing in the morning and disclose the presence of the body.

That night I found it hard to get to sleep. Inside the house it was insufferably hot so I moved my bed things out on to the verandah; but there the bright moon light made it almost as clear as day. I lay awake, listening to the cries of the jackals and the wild dogs, and the distant cry of a hyaena.

In the end I could stand it no more and got up. I did not wish to disturb Herbert but walked out into the yard. In my mind were strange memories – the memory of someone else who had once been fleeing from bondage and in his flight had come across a small boy. From that boy he had received a helping hand and that helping hand had stayed with him for the rest of his life. It had transformed his life, made it different not just from what it was but from what it might have been. It had put a light into the darkness of his mind, an *ignis fatuus*, perhaps, a false light, like those marsh gases or corpse lights that dance in graveyards, but nevertheless a light, and, on reflection, I would not have had it otherwise.

Now my mind was turning over uneasily another poor creature who had fled from bondage: for was it not bondage, where work was enforced with the whip?

Flight, flight: did we not all flee from pain? And hadn't I, too, eleven years before fled from pain by leaving England? But was not that flight a false light, too? I had thought to distance myself from a cruel but broken woman. But can one ever distance oneself from one's own heart? I knew now that if I had my chance again I would not distance myself but try, in whatever way I could, to mend what was broken. But chances, I have learned, do not come twice.

Thus musing, I turned on my heel, and, as I did so, I caught what seemed to be a movement in one of the out-houses. For a moment my blood froze. Could it be that our visitant of the first night had returned?

I roused Herbert and together we went over to the barn the noise had come from. There it was again! Something was definitely moving inside.

There were two doors. Herbert went round to the one at the rear while I stood by the main entrance. Something was coming towards it. It came very quietly, a soft padding of bare feet. It came through the door. I seized it and called for Herbert's aid.

It was not as I had expected. Smaller, softer. Weaker. It struggled in my grasp. Herbert came running. I shifted my hands to get a better grip.

And then I nearly let go! The form beneath my hands was unmistakeably that of a woman.

I pulled her out into the moonlight. Herbert came rushing round the corner of the barn, saw her and stopped.

It was the woman who had been cleaning the house for us earlier.

"What are you doing here?" he said sternly.

She spat at him.

I dragged her towards the house. She resisted for a moment and then suddenly submitted.

On the verandah she sat silently and at first would say nothing.

Then she burst out:

"Where is he?"

Herbert and I looked at each other. Could we tell her?

"Who?" I said, temporizing.

"My man."

"Your husband?" said Herbert.

She nodded impatiently.

Herbert and I looked at each other again.

"He is gone," said Herbert.

She sat there still for a moment. Then—

"So he is gone," she said. Her whole body seemed to slump. "So he is gone," she said again. She shrugged. "I knew it," she said bitterly, "I knew it when I saw—"

She stopped.

"He was not a good man," she went on, after a moment. "He used to beat me. Especially when he had been drinking. He went with other women. I complained to the omda and the omda told him he would have to leave the village if he couldn't mend his ways. But still he drank, and still he went with them. One especially. I told him I would denounce her to the omda and he would have her stoned. He begged me not to. He swore he would put her aside and be a good husband to me in future. He cried. He always cried after he had been drinking. And he said he would mend his ways. He had said it before, but this time I believed him.

"And I was right to, for he did try to put her away. And she was angry and taunted me, saying I was no good to a man, that I would never bear him children. And then she taunted him, saying that he was not a proper man. Still he would not go with her; but he went back to drink. He could not do his work properly. The Pasha's man berated him and whipped him, and one day he could stand it no longer and ran away.

"He came home to me and I said: 'If you stay here, they will find you. Hide yourself in the old farm-house and I will bring you food.' But then I heard that you had moved in, so I dared not. But when I came up this afternoon I brought food for him. But I could not find him. I thought perhaps he had fallen asleep somewhere, so tonight I came again. But again I could not find him. And now you tell me he is gone."

"Handel, old chap—" began Herbert.

I knew what he was thinking. We could not continue with our deception. It was cruel to this unfortunate woman. Let the consequences be what they would, we would go to the omda in the morning and declare all.

The first thing in the morning we went down to the village and asked to see the omda. The villagers had sensed that something was toward and had begun to gather. The omda came out of his house and sat down on a bench in front of it. He had chairs brought for Herbert and myself. As the crowd grew deeper I grew more and more concerned about what we had to say.

But then something surprising happened. The cleaning lady stood up first.

"Omda, I have come to declare a fault," she said.

"Speak on."

"I helped my man when he fled in fear from the Pasha's man."

"So?" said the Pasha's man, who was standing at the back of the crowd, fondling his whip.

"He came to me at our house and I said: 'If you stay here, they will take you. Go to the old farm-house and hide there.' I meant to take him food."

"And did you, Amina?"

"No. At least, I did: but I could not find him. Because by then he had fled."

"Fled, Amina?"

"Yes, omda. With this woman."

She was pointing at a woman in the crowd, the big, dark woman we had noticed among the hoers.

"I?" said the woman. "I?"

"Yes, you, Khabradji."

"But I am here!"

"And he is not. But you know where he is, Khabradji."

She looked at the omda.

"That is what I have come to declare, omda," she said, and sat down.

Hands pushed Khabradji forward.

"She lies, omda. It is not so!"

Amina rose again.

"You were in the house with him."

"Not so!"

"It was so. I saw your footprints."

"What!" said Herbert and I simultaneously.

"They will confirm it," said Amina, turning to us.

I stood up.

"Certainly, we saw footprints in the sand," I said. "But whose they were—?"

"We thought they might be of some strange beast!" said Herbert excitedly.

"Strange beast?" said the omda, raising an eyebrow.

"They were large and—"

"Large, certainly," said the omda, looking at Khabradji. Everyone laughed. She looked self-conscious. Evidently her size was a by-word in the village.

"– but no strange beast!" said the omda.

The crowd laughed again.

Herbert stood up.

"It was a mistake," he said. "And yet in that mistake truth lies. Khabradji, you were certainly in the house. We saw your footprints. You came right into the room where we were sitting. And now, Khabradji, I have a question for you: did you take the bottle?"

"Bottle?" said the omda.

"Bottle?" said Amina.

Herbert turned to her—

"I know, alas, that you are familiar with bottles, Amina.

Because of your husband. But was not Khabradji, too? So let me
ask my question again: did you take the bottle that was on the
table?"

"I – I –" stuttered Khabradji.

"I think you did, Khabradji."

"Well, what if I did?"

"What did you do with it?"

"Do with it? I – I drank it."

There was an amazed laugh from the crowd.

"No, you didn't. You took it out and gave it to Amina's
husband."

"What if I did?" muttered Khabradji. "What if I did?"

"Where is he, Khabradji? cried Amina suddenly. "Give him
back to me!"

Khabradji seemed to shake herself.

"Give him back?" she said. "That I cannot."

She sat down, as if she had said all she was going to.

I rose from my place.

"But, Khabradji," I said, "that is not all, is it? You gave him
the drink, yes; and then what?"

"I do not know," muttered Khabradji.

"I do. When he had drunk and was stupefied, you killed him."

"Killed him!"

There was a gasp of horror from the crowd.

"Killed him?" cried Amina, and made to throw herself at her
rival. Hands held her back.

Khabradji now rose in her turn.

"Yes," she said, calmly. "I killed him. With my hoe. While
he lay dulled and sleeping." She looked at Amina. "I was not
going to let you take him back. While I was in the field, I saw
him running and guessed where he was going. That night I
went to the farm-house myself and found him. I pleaded with
him to come back to me. But he would not and spoke bad words.
I was angry and rushed from him. But then I looked into the
house and saw the bottle and the evil thought came to me: why
should not I be revenged? So I took the bottle to him and let
him drink; and then I killed him."

*   *   *

As we were leaving, I heard one villager say to another:
    "What was all that about a beast?"
    "There wasn't one."
    "Odd that they should think there was. Strange minds these Englishmen have!"
    "Superstition," said the other villager. "That's the problem."

All in all it was an odd Christmas indeed. But it had one effect that was lasting. It had taken my mind back to another time when my life had become strangely bound up with that of a poor fugitive. Indeed, it was that which had ultimately led to my flight to Egypt. Reflecting on that, I realized that I had left unfinished business behind me. It occurred to me that the time had come to return to England and address it. Perhaps, too – I confess it – it was the children's Christmas stockings, bringing home to me that there was more to life than work in a Counting House. Anyway, I went back to England, expecting not great things now but very little: finding, however, when I got there more than I had ever dared to expect.

GLAZED

Danuta Reah

Anthony Richardson woke up in the spare bedroom, aware that the mattress was not the well-sprung one he was accustomed to. His back was aching. He climbed out of bed and opened the curtains, looking out on to the grey November day.

He pulled on his dressing gown and tiptoed barefoot to the marital bedroom. He pushed the door open silently. Molly was asleep, her face hidden, her red hair spilling across the pillow. Her hair had lost its brightness over the years, and her face, though it still had its delicate prettiness, was creased from sleep. At one time, seeing her like that would have been a powerful incentive for him to climb back into the bed they had shared for over twenty years, but not any more.

Quietly, he collected his clothes from the wardrobe. He would shower in the other bathroom rather than risk waking her. He'd stayed too late the night before with Olivia, falling asleep next to her perfumed softness. "You see," she'd whispered as he climbed reluctantly out of her bed, "It's time to let Molly know. It's for the best, darling. *I* wouldn't want to keep you in a dead marriage if it was me."

He sighed. He still cared for Molly. Of course he did. But . . . The image of Olivia, fair-haired, beautiful, and most of all *young* rose up in front of him.

Anthony Richardson had met Molly when she was twenty-one. He was handsome, in his thirties, sophisticated and successful with his own chain of exclusive designer stores. She was a graduate from St Martin's College, with a degree in ceramics and a talent for design that was yet to be fully recognized. She was beautiful, of course. She had to be. Anything less than beautiful would have done. And she wasn't just beautiful, she was one of the most talented ceramicists he had ever met. Her designs had a quality he had never seen before, designs that her current employer had dismissed because people who want cups with feet on them and smiling teapots tend to be limited in their appreciation of style. It was an added advantage that she was very young and not very confident.

It was serendipity. Molly needed a Svengali. Anthony needed her talent. His business, though successful, had reached a plateau. He worked by finding good designs and importing them, but a lot of other people were doing the same thing and there was nothing to distinguish his company, Richardson Design, from the mass. The continuing success of his shops depended on his having something new, something distinctive, something that no one else had. And in Molly, he had found it.

Molly Norman Ceramics became the cornerstone of his company, Richardson Design. RD, the discreet silver logo that marked his company, became a byword for the best in fine china.

Anthony was a good husband. He kept the business running well and provided a comfortable, even luxurious, home for her. And though any man has a need for variety that even a young, talented and beautiful wife can't entirely fulfil, he kept his infidelities low key and away from home.

The marriage was a success. Except that they didn't have children. Not really. Molly had got pregnant a few years into their marriage but the child was born defective – Down's Syndrome, the doctors said. A Mongol. Anthony believed in calling a spade a spade. He had made sure that there were no more children. He wanted no more defectives in his family.

Molly made a reasonable job of raising the boy who was now fourteen, a lumbering presence in the house. She insisted on private schooling, which was an irony Anthony found hard to bear. A real son would have gone to Eton of course, but Dominic . . . "He's a lot more able that you give him credit for," Molly had said sharply. "I want him to be able to earn some kind of a living." In fact, the youth would be a drain on his resources forever.

And then, just a week ago, Olivia had hit him with the bombshell of her pregnancy. "Don't worry, darling," she'd said briskly. "I can deal with it. I know you've got problems with . . ." Her eyes, dark-lashed, flickered sideways to the photo of Molly that stood where it always did, on his desk.

And he realized what the dissatisfaction with his life was. He had achieved the material success he craved. Now he needed the personal fulfilment of knowing there was someone to carry on that success. He wanted a son, a proper son, not one with a lolling tongue and an incoherent voice, one that only a mother could love. He wanted a son he could be proud of. He finally understood why men of his age took up with younger wives. They achieved success with their first wives and raised a family with their second and it was an unfortunate trick of nature that prevented women from doing the same.

"You were late last night." Molly came into the room, tying the cord on her dressing gown. Her hair was untidy and she looked pale.

"Yes." He didn't elaborate.

One thing that had been holding him back from the final decision was that once he'd asked her for a divorce, the company would lose Molly's talents and – at a time when he was planning a major expansion – he would have to give a large part of his wealth to her. He had discussed this with Olivia who happened to be a lawyer specializing in the divorces of the wealthy and powerful. The company, she suggested, was his. Molly was an employee, not a joint owner and she had earned a good income through the years. As for her leaving, well, the company was more than the Molly Norman range of ceramics and anyway, Richardson's had the copyright on the Molly Norman name and all the designs she'd done for the company over the years.

He could find and promote another designer. Molly was probably getting a little passe now, a little past her prime creatively as well as physically.

He'd have to get his lawyers on to it. He didn't want a prolonged fight.

He realized he hadn't heard what she was saying. ". . . start training Tim as an assistant today. He's really very . . ."

"What?"

"Tim. He's been with us for six months now. He loves the pottery – he knows the work – he's helped me often enough and . . ."

A few months ago, she'd taken on a youth from some charity she was involved with that looked after people with so-called "learning difficulties". The young man was another Dominic, another flat faced defective with a protruding tongue that stumbled and spluttered over the few words he could manage. The pottery needed a general dogsbody – someone to make the tea and sweep up, the kind of work he was fit for and there were grants available for companies who took these people on, so Anthony hadn't argued.

But now Molly was planning to spend good money training this man, this Tim, as an assistant in the pottery, letting him load the kiln, even let him switch it on and keep an eye on the firing. "No," he said.

He saw Molly's puzzled frown. "I told you last week. I've already promised . . ."

He vaguely remembered her mentioning something. It was typical of Molly to drop something important into her general chat. She probably did it, knowing he wasn't paying attention. "Then you'll have to un-promise." He saw her open her mouth to argue – she could be stubborn sometimes – and said, "I'll see you later."

He left the house, intending to go straight to the office. Instead, he drove to Olivia's. It was time they made some decisions.

Tim Sergeant was cleaning up in the workshop. Every morning when he came in, he mopped the floor to clear up any dust that had settled in the night. At the end of each day he cleaned up all the dropped clay, all the spatters of glaze, all the wood ash and bone meal for the colours that Mrs Richardson used on her pots, leaving everything clean and scrubbed for the next day. Then in the morning, he came in early and mopped everything again so that the decks would be cleared (Mum) and ready for the beautiful things that Mrs Richardson made.

He liked the pottery in the early morning. It was quiet with no one to distract or confuse him. He liked the wheel with the seat where you could sit and make it spin with a treadle. He did that now, pretending he was throwing a pot and making it grow under his fingers like Mrs Richardson did. When he'd first started, he'd been afraid of the kilns, especially the big gas one. The first time he'd seen flames come shooting out of the little hole in the door, he'd gone away and hidden, but Mrs Richardson had explained the kiln was supposed to do that.

There were rows of pots on the table waiting to be glazed. At first, Tim hadn't understood about the glaze. Mrs Richardson had shown him a bowl of pale sludge, and she'd dipped the beautiful, fragile bowl into it, then she'd swirled her brush along the side. It didn't look like anything special to Tim. Just sludge.

But then it had gone in the kiln with all the other pots, and when it came out, it had been the most beautiful yellow, bright as the sun. "It's like Mum's canary," he had breathed. "It's magic."

Mrs Richardson had laughed, but not in a mean way. She'd been pleased. "Yes, like canary feathers. You're right." After that, she'd let him help with the glazes. She'd taught him how to use the ball mill to grind up the materials, and he helped to mix the glazes she wanted to use, carefully adding the wood ash, the flint, the felspar, the bone meal, making something ugly that somehow, miraculously became beautiful in the fire.

And today was a special day. For weeks now, he'd watched her as she'd packed the kiln and closed the heavy door, sealing it shut by turning the wheel on the outside. He'd been allowed to turn on the gas tap as she wielded the flaming wand that made the gas ignite with a *whoof*. And she'd taught him how to keep checking the temperature gauge hour after hour as the heat crept up and up. "Red hot" she'd say, then 'White hot," as it reached the magic number: 1300. And the last time they had done this together, she had nodded to Tim and, not able to keep the grin off his face, he had turned off the gas. Then the kiln would have to be left for a day and a night to cool down. "I think you're ready," she'd said to him, the last time they'd fired the kiln together.

Today, she was going to let him pack it by himself. She would be there in case he needed help, but she was going to let him do it, and she was going to let him use the wand to light the gas and then she was going to let him watch by himself until the time came to turn off the gas. He wouldn't be the cleaner any more. He would be Mrs Richardson's assistant. He would be a potter.

He watched from the window as Mrs Richardson's car pulled into the car park and went to make her a cup of tea in one of the teapots she designed. His hand hovered over the yellow one, but then he decided to use the one with the deep red glaze that was so fine and delicate that you could almost see the tea as you poured in the boiling water. He put a cup and saucer on the tray, and some biscuits carefully arranged on a plate.

He carried the tray through, keeping his eyes fixed on it so that it stayed level, and put it carefully down on the table in Mrs Richardson's room as she came through the door. "Tea," she said. "Just what I wanted. Thank you, Tim." But there was something in her voice that worried him. She was frowning as she poured the tea as if she was thinking about something else. She needed to be left alone to work.

"I'll go and finish sweeping," he said.

Molly watched Tim leave, cursing herself for being a coward. She should have told him that the days of working as her assistant were over. Anthony wouldn't tolerate it. When he looked at Tim, he saw Dominic and he couldn't forgive the boy for being less than the perfect son he had envisaged. She used to fool herself, tell herself that his distance from the child was self-protection, that he didn't want to be too close to a child whose health was giving them concern. But she couldn't do that any more.

She had stayed because, for a long time, she had loved him. Later, she had stayed because Dominic needed the long term security that money could buy. He wasn't like Tim who was able to earn money and have some independence. Dominic's handicap was much more severe and he would need caring for all his life. She dreaded what would happen to him if she died, if she hadn't managed to make provision for him. She had to make certain that his future was secure.

She put on her overalls and went into the pottery to finish the designs on the new Molly Norman range. Her mind focused on her work and her worries faded into the background.

It was late morning before Anthony arrived. She was just putting the finishing touches to a special commission, something that would bring a great deal of business into the firm, if it went right. She was making a set of long-stemmed cups, fragile and beautiful that she was glazing to try and capture some essence of the fire that would create them. She could see the colour in her mind – a clear, translucent glow. She hadn't quite managed to get that in her various experimental firings, but this time – maybe this time she'd got it right.

"What's this?" Anthony's voice broke into her thoughts.

"It's the De Clancy commission."

"Haven't you got that done yet?"

"It's got to be right." She swivelled her chair to face him. "Anthony, about Tim . . ."

He interrupted her. "Olivia's pregnant," he said.

She felt as though something had kicked her in the stomach. "Pregnant . . ."

"I want a child," he said.

She could feel the anger growing inside her. "You have a child."

His jaw set. "I meant a proper child. You can't give me one. Olivia can. I want a divorce."

She could only think of Olivia pregnant, about the children she hadn't been able to have because there was only her to look after Dominic. Deep down she had always known that Anthony would be no father to his son.

He was still speaking. "You'll want to leave the firm, of course. You'll get a generous pay off, I'll make sure of that." A generous payout. That wouldn't be enough to keep Dominic, not for the rest of his life.

"I'll fight," she said.

"Then I'll fight back and we'll all lose."

Molly watched him leave and felt a black wave of despair wash over her.

Tim felt a jump of excitement as Mrs Richardson came out of her office. He'd been getting more and more worried. It took twelve hours to fire the kiln. He'd told Mum it was one of the nights he would be late, but the day went on, and Mrs

Richardson stayed in her workshop, painting the pretty cups
she'd been working on for days.

When he saw her, his heart sank. She had changed out of her
overalls and was carrying her bag. She was going home. She'd
forgotten. "Come and sit down in the kitchen," she said. "I
want to talk to you."

Slowly, he put down his brush and followed her. "Tim,
you've been an excellent worker. I'm very pleased with you,
you know that, don't do?"

"Yes, Mrs Richardson." He looked at her, willing her to tell
him he was still her assistant, waiting for her to smile at him, but
she didn't.

"I'm very sorry," she said, "but you can't be my assistant any
more. Not just now. You'll still do your other work, of course
you will. But Mr Richardson doesn't think you're ready. And
. . . Tim, listen. Things are changing round here. I might be
leaving." Her voice was odd and far away, and he got the
impression she wasn't really seeing him at all.

"But . . ." He couldn't imagine the pottery without Mrs
Richardson. He wanted to protest but the words wouldn't
come. His tongue felt big and unwieldy in his mouth.

"I'm so sorry, Tim. You go home now. Take the rest of the
day off and enjoy the weekend." She smiled then. "Don't forget
to lock up."

She still trusted him to do that, but Tim's bubble of happiness had burst. He watched her as she left the pottery. He saw
her walk across the car park to her car and get in. He dropped
his mop onto the floor and sat down. He could feel the
disappointment inside him like a knife. He'd told Mum that
he'd be late tonight because he was working overtime. "I'm
promoted," he'd told her.

"Promoted!" she'd said. "I'm proud of you, Tim." And now
he'd have to go back and tell her, and she'd think that he'd got it
wrong because he wasn't clever and he did make mistakes.

The pottery was quiet. Everyone had gone home. It was a
long weekend and they wanted to get away for their holidays.
There was only Tim, sitting there in the gloom, and he wasn't
crying, not really, because he was grown-up now, and grown-
ups didn't cry, but something was making his face wet. He

sniffed and wiped his hand across his nose. He might as well go home.

Instead, he went into the room where the big gas kiln stood, its door open, waiting for the pots that Tim would no longer be loading in there. He'd set everything ready, the supports that would keep the shelves secure, the shelves on which each layer of pots would stand and he'd planned exactly where each pot would go.

And then he had his idea. When it popped into his mind, he couldn't believe he was thinking it, and it made him so frightened that he found it hard to breathe. He hid his face and waited for it to go away. But his mind wouldn't let it go and the more he thought about it, the less scared he became.

All the pots were ready. There was no reason why they shouldn't be fired. The weekend – the long weekend with a holiday – would be wasted otherwise. He would stack the kiln. Mrs Richardson wouldn't be there to watch him, but he would do it as slowly and as carefully as he could. Then he would light the kiln – when he thought about the flames of the gas wand, he had to hide his face again for a while – but he would switch on the gas, light the gas wand, and listen to the *whoof* as the burners in the kiln ignited. After that, he just had to wait. Then Mr Richardson would know that he was good enough to be the assistant.

When he went into the work room, he saw the pots for the firing were on the table, all carefully glazed, all covered with the dull, dry film that the magic of the fire would turn into glorious colours like canaries' feathers and butterflies' wings. And there, on Mrs Richardson's own work table were the long-stemmed cups that she had been working on that day, using the new glaze that Tim had ground and mixed and ground and mixed again as she tried to get it right. When they were fired, they were going to be more beautiful than anything, and Tim couldn't wait.

But if he didn't get today's firing right, then he wouldn't be allowed to assist Mrs Richardson again. He turned away from her table, and began to load the pots onto the trolley.

"What the hell do you think you're doing!"

The voice came from behind him. Tim jumped and dropped the pot he was holding, a tall jug with a delicate handle. It shattered on the floor and Tim wanted to weep. He'd never broken anything before.

Mr Richardson was standing behind him. "Where's my wife?"

"She's gone home," Tim tried to say. He could feel his legs shaking and he wanted the toilet.

Mr Richardson turned on his heel and went into the kiln room. When he came back, his face was dark with fury. "Were you going to load that kiln?"

Tim nodded.

"Does my wife know what you're doing?"

Tim always told the truth. He shook his head. He couldn't speak.

Mr Richardson's lip curled. "You're fired. Get out before I kick you out!"

Tim felt his nose clog up as his eyes filled with tears. He'd done it wrong. Mum had been so proud of him being an assistant, and now Mr Richardson had fired him.

As he stood there, Mr Richardson started shouting. "Well? Did you hear me? Are you too stupid?" He grabbed Tim's arm and started pushing him towards the door. They were near Mrs Richardson's table and he was going to knock into it and make the beautiful long-stemmed cups fall over and shatter. He panicked. He pushed Mr Richardson away, hard. The grip on his arm loosened and he waited with his eyes screwed tight shut, waiting for Mr Richardson to start shouting at him again.

Nothing happened, and cautiously, Tim opened his eyes.

Mr Richardson was lying on the floor. There was blood on the corner of the stone table, and blood on the floor coming out of Mr Richardson's head and ears. Tim felt sick. Mr Richardson would tell the police that Tim had attacked him. He was going to go to prison. He watched, frozen, and then as he saw Mr Richardson's face turn blue and bubbles come out of his mouth, he realized he was in even more trouble than he thought.

Mr Richardson wasn't going to get up at all.

Tim sank down to the floor and forgot about being a grown-up. He cried.

*   *   *

After a long time, he mopped his eyes. It was no good crying over spilled milk (Mum). He screwed up his face, trying to think. That was the trouble with not being clever. It took him a long time to know what to do. Usually, he asked Mum, but this time, he couldn't. And eventually, he worked it out.

It was a good job he had the trolley. Mr Richardson was heavy. He wheeled him into the kiln room, and, grunting slightly with the effort, he slid Mr Richardson into the kiln. A leg flopped out, and then another. Tim stood there, perplexed. He bent Mr Richardson's leg and then the other, and wedged it against the kiln wall. He had to try several times before Mr Richardson was safely folded in.

But now, there was no room for the pots. They were all big, heavy ones. "We'll start you off on the basic stuff," Mrs Richardson had said.

Tim screwed his face up as he thought. When the idea came, it scared him as much as when he'd thought about doing the firing on his own. He wished, now, that he'd just gone home, but it was too late for that. Look before you leap (Mum). But he didn't have time to hide his face and wait for the idea to go away.

There was just space in the kiln for one shelf of small pots. Very carefully, he set the supports. Bits of Mr Richardson kept getting in the way, and he had to remember that Mr Richardson wouldn't be there all the time to prop up the shelf. It was an hour before he'd got it right and he was confident that shelf would stay in position by itself. Then, his tongue clamped between his teeth, he picked up the long-stemmed cups, one at a time, and placed them on the shelf. He felt as though he hadn't breathed in all the time he was doing it, and when the last one was in place, he had to sit down for a while.

Then he swung the heavy door of the kiln shut, and turned the wheel to seal it. Everything was ready. He turned on the gas, lit the gas wand – he wasn't even a bit scared of it now – and slipped it into the ports where the burners were waiting to be lit. *Whoof!* The kiln ignited.

He went into Mrs Richardson's office to phone Mum. He was going to be out all night and he didn't want her to worry. "Will you get a lift back?" Mum asked.

"Yes." Tim didn't like telling lies, but he knew the early bus would get him home safely. All he needed to do now was wait. He sat on the floor watching the temperature gauge. It was going to take a long time. After a while, the smell of something cooking began to fill the room and Tim realized he was hungry. He went to his locker to find the sandwiches that Mum had made for him that morning.

Anthony didn't come home all weekend. Molly hadn't expected him to. When she went into work on Tuesday morning, she expected to find him there with the details of the divorce all worked out. She was going to fight him. She wanted every penny that he owed to her to secure a future for their son, and she wanted what he owed her for other children, the ones he would never agree to and now she would never have.

His car was in the car park when she arrived, but there was no sign of him.

Puzzled, she went into the pottery. Tim was already there, down on his hands and knees scrubbing the work room floor. "There's no need to do that," she said. "Just mopping it is fine." He muttered something, and she realized that he was rigid with tension. She looked round the room and saw at once that a jug was shattered on the floor.

"Don't worry if you've . . ." and then she saw that the long-stemmed cups were missing.

Her eyes went back to Tim's. He dropped his gaze.

"Tim," she said. "What have you done?"

He didn't answer, but the way his eyes moved towards the kiln room told her all she needed to know. She ran through, hoping that she was wrong, but when she got there, she saw the kiln door closed. She touched it. It was still warm. "Oh, my God, Tim!" Anger fought with guilt. She should never have let him think he could do this. She should never have left him alone in the pottery. She'd have to start from scratch, the commission would be delayed . . .

She checked the temperature than spun the handle and dragged open the door of the kiln.

And what she saw silenced her.

She was aware of Tim, a silent presence in the entrance behind her, but all she could see were the cups. She'd never seen such a quality in a glaze. The colour had the deep translucence she had been dreaming of. Scarcely breathing, she lifted one out and held it to the light as she turned it in her hands. They were the best things she had ever done.

"Tim," she said. "What did you do?" For there had to have been something in the firing that gave it this extra quality, a quality she had never planned because she didn't know it existed.

Then she noticed that there was ash in the bottom of the kiln. She leaned forward and studied it. It wasn't just ash. There were lumps of charred . . .

"What's this?" she said, straightening up.

His face flooded red. "Just . . . stuff."

There was a pool of metal on the floor, something melted beyond recognition, something about the size of a man's watch . . . Her eyes met Tim's. His face was wretched with guilt. She remembered him scrubbing the workroom floor, his face tense with effort.

She looked at the pots again and found herself wondering what the effect would have been of very high levels of carbon in the kiln during the firing, carbon from—

"Fine," she said slowly. "I'll get rid of it."

No one ever found out what had happened to Anthony Richardson. The investigation into his disappearance went on for several weeks. His car was found in the car park at his office. His secretary said that he had left shortly after six. As far as she knew, he was going home.

His wife told them that her husband had been having an affair and that they were planning to divorce. His mistress told them the same thing, but both women had alibis for the evening he had last been seen.

No one really asked Tim any questions at all. No one knew that Mr Richardson had visited the pottery before he went home, no one knew Tim had stayed late, apart from his mother, and no one asked her. Tim was pleased about that. He didn't like telling lies. He knew the best lies were the ones you never had to tell because nobody ever asked you the question.

And the long-stemmed cups that he'd fired were the best things that the pottery had ever produced. But Mrs Richardson decided to keep them. "These are special," she said. "I'm going to give them to the people I think should have them." To Tim's surprise, she gave one to Mr Richardson's lawyer, Olivia. "For drinking a toast when the baby's born."

And she picked out one for herself and one for him.

"Let's celebrate you becoming my assistant," she said. "Champagne, Tim?"

TWENTY DOLLAR FUTURE

John Rickards

It is night when the ghosts come for Abdi. He stands, as he has taken to doing, on the low pile of rubble behind their house. From the top of the mound of stones he can see the stars above mirrored by the waves on the distant sea, as if the edge of town is the edge of the world and there is nothing beyond it but the void. He stands there when the ghosts come so that he will not wake his sisters. So that if they do wake, they will not see him cry.

His mother, reaching out to him as she calls his name. Sometimes in her soft voice, a voice he only knows from dreams he was so young the last time he heard it for real. Sometimes she calls to him in the dying screams she let out giving birth to little Aisha, his youngest sister.

Yusuf and his parents, all burnt and broken. Black, staring holes where Yusuf's eyes were. Everything pinched and cracked just as it was when they found them. Yusuf's father was a big man, but this had not mattered to the militia.

Abdi's own father, blood soaking his shirt around the bullet wounds. Wordlessly mouthing something he cannot understand, some word forever frozen on his lips.

Other faces, people he never knew. Never had the time to know. Seen briefly through windshields or walking in the street. No names, but accusing faces. Blood, bullet wounds. Rape and murder. People say it is the way of things, but these ghosts ask Abdi why they died, why they suffered. They plead with him and paw at him, afraid and confused.

His father again, this time as he was before it all went so wrong. Standing tall and wise as he always did, working to provide for their family. He stands at the base of the rubble and holds out the twenty-dollar bill for Abdi to take.

Abdi knows all too well what the money means. He cannot forget the first time his father gave it to him.

"Take this to Jama," he said, pressing it into Abdi's hand. "He will know what it is for." The money would have taken his father almost two weeks to earn. He must have arranged something very important with Jama, a trader, and Abdi was thrilled to be entrusted in this way at twelve years of age, even if all he had to do was take the money across the town. He took it and wedged it deep into one pocket.

"Good boy," his father said and patted him on the head. Abdi trotted out of the door, into the dusty African sunshine.

His good feeling lasted until he ran into the militia. Half a dozen of them, lounging by a burned-out building with walls pock-marked by gunfire. He didn't recognize them, men of another clan, and he felt fear clench his throat and his heart pounded in his ears.

"Hey, boy," one of them said as Abdi tried to pass by on the far side of the street. "This is a checkpoint. You think you can walk through here without permission? There is a tax for walking this street. Security costs money. Keeping the streets safe costs money."

"Of course," Abdi said. This was the same militia bullshit he had heard so many times. "But I do not have any. I'm sorry. I am just going to take a message to Jama in the market. I have no money."

The militia man scowled, and his friends gathered around Abdi. "You are not willing to pay for security and safety? Who would not pay for this? Maybe you are a thief or a criminal. Maybe we should arrest you. Maybe you do not want the people here to be safe and secure."

"No, no. I'm just poor. Please."

"Let's check this 'poor' boy. I don't believe him and I don't like him." The man leaned in close and stared hard at Abdi. His breath reeked.

Abdi struggled, but the militia held him pinned while their leader checked through his pockets. The man yelled in triumph when he found the twenty dollars and waved it in Abdi's face.

"You filthy liar! You try to keep this from us? The rich boy does not want to pay his taxes?"

The blow came out of nowhere. The man slammed the butt of his Kalashnikov into Abdi's chin. Pain seared through his head and he could taste blood and dust as he dropped to the floor. The kicks the man followed up with hammered into his ribcage, but he could hardly feel them. His head swam with agony and he could do nothing more than lie there until the man picked him up and threw him across the street.

As he crawled away, trying to wheeze as quietly as possible, all he could think about was that his father's money was gone. He had failed his family, and perhaps now they would face hunger and hardship.

"Their militia are nothing but pigs," Hassan said. He was a friend of Abdi's, at thirteen, a year older than him. Two years before, his father and three other members of his family had died in a fire at a refugee centre. "They should be taught that they cannot act that way."

It was Hassan's idea to take the money back. They would steal the money back from another trader, one from the same clan as the militia, and then everything would be equal. Hassan's older brother, Osman, who had been a member of their own militia, would help them. Bring them guns and knives even though Hassan thought they could do it without any fighting, so long as they were quiet.

Osman looked up from flicking stones into the dust and nodded. "This is right," he said, with a voice like flat rock. "We don't make a sound, and we can take what we want. And if they do find us, we will be able to fight them."

And Abdi again agreed, because he couldn't face going home to his father and admitting that he'd failed him.

Hassan laughed and patted him on the shoulder. "That is good! Maybe we will even find something for ourselves there."

Abdi knew then that some people value children as fighters for their ferocity and bravery. But he also knows, now, that children do not think like men or plan like men.

When the three of them reached the trader's home and climbed in through a window, they were thinking many things. Imagining what might lie within. Worried, perhaps, that the trader would be less rich than they thought. Abdi certainly was. This could all be for nothing. But none of them expected to find his guards in the building.

Osman had not even reached the stairs when a burst of AK-47 fire cut him to pieces, the bullets shredding his body like paper. As he fell, he turned towards Abdi with a look, it seemed, of surprise and shock. He said nothing. Made no sound at all. His brother Hassan, though, screamed with horror and anguish. The guards fired again and bullets crashed into the walls around the two boys.

They chased Hassan and Abdi into a small room at the back of the building. Hassan, sobbing the whole time, turned and fired wildly through the doorway behind them. Abdi heard someone scream in pain, and someone else yell for them to cover the back. He scrambled through the narrow window.

"Hassan! Come on!" he hissed. But he did not wait for him. Instead, he ran away into the bushes before the guards could come around the outside of the building. Only once he was safe, out of sight in the dry scrub, did he hunker down and turn to look for his friend.

Hassan was still half in, half out of the opening when they caught him. Abdi heard them shouting and silently willed his brother to move faster, to break free, to run. Then he heard the gunshots and he buried his face in the dirt. When he looked back, Hassan was hanging limp, his blood washing the stones.

He stayed, staring wide-eyed at the scene, for a moment. Then he ran from the house. There were tears in his eyes and his heart was wedged like a stone in his throat.

Abdi still didn't know if the guards saw him running and recognized him. Or if Hassan was only wounded when they shot him and they hurt him so he would give up their names. It didn't matter in the end, not really.

His father was dead by the time he returned home.

He found him executed, shot three times in the doorway to their home, punished for what they had done. Abdi's world ended at that moment. He felt as though everything he had or loved or dreamed was suddenly gone, and he was empty. His sisters were hiding in a closet. The men who did it arrived in a car, they said. Abdi's father would not let them into the house, even though they had guns and he did not. So they killed him where he stood.

Little Aisha clutched his hand. "Is father hurt?" she said. "When will he be better?"

Abdi could do nothing but stare at the man lying dead on the floor. His father. The man who had raised him for so many years on his own. All gone.

"Abdi?" Aisha said, voice choking. "Why won't he stand up?"

His other sisters, Hamdi and Habiba, led her away as the tears began.

The next morning, the leader of their militia, Osman's former commander, came to the house. He told Abdi that he would need to earn money to support his family, but that the clan would not fail them, so long as he did not fail the clan. He would join the men on the road-blocks. He would carry a Kalashnikov and protect their people. He would shoot their enemies and the rewards would be shared by all.

Or he and his sisters would starve.

They are all there now. Abdi's father. Hassan. Osman. And, at the back, another man. One he knows he will never see in this life. A kind, tall man, standing with his arms around his wife and three children, all healthy and strong. That they are all smiling is no comfort to Abdi, for he knows that the man is himself in a future he can no longer have. That his actions have destroyed everything he might have been as well as everything he was.

So Abdi stands there in the night, the ghosts all around him. And he does not fight them and he does not run from them. He stands there, a twelve-year-old man, a soldier and a killer, wishing that his father would speak to him and tell him that this is not his fault. That he does not blame him. That his life will change and he will never have to touch a gun again. That he could somehow give his father back that twenty dollars and stop any of this happening.

Then, he stands there, crying in the dark.

SERVED COLD

Zoë Sharp

Layla's curse, as she saw it, was that she had an utterly fabulous body attached to an instantly forgettable face. It wasn't that she was ugly. Ugliness in itself stuck in the mind. It was simply that, from the neck upwards, she was plain. A bland plainness that encouraged male and female eyes alike to slide on past without pausing. Most failed to recall her easily at a second meeting.

From the neck down, though, that was a different story, and had been right from when she'd begun to blossom in eighth grade. Things had started burgeoning over the winter, when nobody noticed the unexpected explosion of curves. But when summer came, with its bathing suits and skinny tops and tight skirts, Layla suddenly became the most whispered-about girl in her class.

A pack of the kind of boys her mother was usually too drunk to warn her about took to following her when she walked home from school. At first, Layla was flattered. But one simmering afternoon, under the banyan and the Spanish moss, she learned a brutal lesson about the kind of attention her new body attracted.

And when her mother's latest boyfriend started looking at her with those same hot lustful eyes, Layla cut and run. One way or another, she'd been running ever since.

At least the work came easy. Depending on how much she covered up, she could get anything from selling lingerie or perfume in a high-class department store, to exotic dancing. She soon learned to slip on different personae the same way she slipped on a low-cut top or a demure blouse.

Tonight she was wearing a tailored white dress shirt with frills down the front and a dinky little clip-on bow tie. Classy joint. The last time she'd worn a bow-tie to wait tables, she'd worn no top at all.

The fat guy in charge of the wait staff was called Steve and had hands to match his roving eye. That he'd seen beyond Layla's homely face was mainly because he rarely looked at his female employees above the neck. Layla had noted the way his eyes glazed and his mouth went slack and the sweat beaded at his receding hairline, and she wondered if this was another gig she was going to have to try out for on her back.

She didn't, in the end, but only, she realized, because Steve thought of himself as sophisticated. The proposition would no doubt come after. Still, Steve only let his pants rule his head so far. Enough to let Layla – and the rest of the girls – know that he'd be taking half their tips tonight. Anyone who tried to hold anything back would be out on her ass.

Layla didn't care about the tips. That wasn't why she was here, anyhow.

Now, she stood meekly with the others while Steve walked the line, checking everybody over.

"Got to look sharp out there tonight, girls," he said. "Mr Dyer, he's a big man around here. Can't afford to let him down."

He seemed to have a thing for the name badges each girl wore pinned above her left breast. Hated it if they were crooked, and liked to straighten them out personally and take his time getting it just so. The girl next to Layla, whose name was Tammy, rolled her eyes while Steve pawed at her. Layla rolled her eyes right back.

Steve paused in front of her, frowning. "Where's your badge, honey? This one here says your name is Cindy and I *know* that ain't right." And he made sure to nudge the offending item with clammy fingers.

Layla shrugged, surprised he picked up on the deliberate swap. Her face might not stick in the mind, but she couldn't take the chance that her name might ring a bell.

"Oh, I guess it musta gotten lost," she said, all breathless and innocent. "I figured seeing as Cindy called in sick and ain't here

– and none of the fancy folk out there is gonna remember my name anyhow – it don't matter."

Steve continued to frown and finger the badge for a moment, then met Layla's brazen stare and realized he'd lingered too long, even for him. With a shifty little sideways glance, he let go and stepped back. "No, it don't matter," he muttered, moving on. Alongside her, Tammy rolled her eyes again.

Layla had the contents of her canape tray hurriedly explained to her by one of the harassed chefs and then ducked out of the service door, along the short drab corridor, and into the main ballroom.

The glitter and the glamour set her heart racing, as it always did. For a few years, she'd dreamed of moving in these circles without a white cloth over her arm and an open bottle in her hand. And, for a time, she'd almost believed that it might be so.

Not any more.

Not since Bobby.

She reached the first cluster of dinner jackets and long dresses that probably cost more than she made in a year – just for the fabric, never mind the stitching – and waited to catch their attention. It took a while.

"Sir? Ma'am? Would you care for a canape? Those darlin' little round ones are smoked salmon and caviar, and the square ones are Kobe beef and ginger."

She smiled, but their eyes were on the food, or they didn't think it was worth it to smile back. Just stuffed their mouths and continued braying to each other like the stuck-up donkeys they were.

Layla had done this kind of gig many times before. She knew the right pace and frequency to circulate, how often to approach the same guests before attentive turned to irritating, how to slip through the crowd without getting jostled. How to keep her mouth shut and her ears open. Steve might hint that she had to put out to get signed on again, but Layla knew she was good and he was lucky to have her.

Well, after tonight, Stevie-boy, you might just change your mind about that.

She smiled and offered the caviar and the beef, reciting the same words over and over like someone kept pulling a string at the back of her neck. She didn't need to think about it, so she thought about Bobby instead.

Bobby had been the bouncer in a roadhouse near Tallahassee. A huge guy with a lot of old scar tissue across his knuckles and around his eyes. Tale was he'd been a boxer, had a shot until he'd taken one punch too many in the ring. Then everything had gone into slow motion for Bobby and never speeded up again.

He wore a permanent scowl like he'd rip your head off and spit down your neck, as soon as look at you, but Layla quickly realized that was merely puzzlement. Bobby was slightly over-matched by the pace of life and couldn't quite work out why. Still plenty fast enough to throw out drunks in a cheap joint, though. And once Bobby had laid his fists on you, you didn't rush to get up again.

One night in the parking lot, Layla was jumped by a couple of guys who'd fallen foul of the "no touching" rule earlier in the evening and caught the rough side of Bobby's iron-hard hands. They waited, tanking up on cheap whisky, until closing time. Waited for the lights to go out and the girls to straggle, yawning, from the back door. They grabbed Layla before she had a chance to scream, and were touching all they wanted when Bobby waded in out of nowhere. Layla had never been happier to hear the crack of skulls.

She'd been angry more than shocked and frightened – angry enough to stamp them a few times with those lethal heels once they were on the ground. Angry enough to take their over-flowing billfolds, too. But it didn't last. When Bobby got her back to her rented double-wide, she shook and cried as she clung to him and begged him to help her forget. That night she discovered that Bobby was big and slow in other ways, too. And sometimes that was a real good thing.

For a while, at least.

"Ma'am? Would you care for a canape? Smoked salmon and caviar on that side, and this right here's Kobe beef. No, thank *you*, ma'am."

Layla worked the room in a pattern she'd laid out inside her head, weaving through the crowd with the nearest thing a person could get to invisibility. It was a big fancy do, that was for sure. Some charity she'd never heard of and would never benefit from. The crowd was circulating like hot dense air through a fan, edging their way up towards the host and hostess at the far end.

The Dyers were old money and gracious with it, but firmly distant towards the staff. They knew their place and made sure the little people, like Layla, were aware of theirs. Layla didn't mind. She was used to being a nobody.

Mr Dyer was indeed a big man, as Steve had said. A mover and shaker. He didn't need to mingle, he could just stand there, like royalty, with a glass in one hand and the other around the waist of his tall, elegant wife, looking relaxed and casual.

Well, maybe not so relaxed. Every now and again Layla noticed Dyer throw a little sideways look at their guest of honour and frown, as though he still wasn't quite sure what the guy was doing there.

Guy called Venable. Another big guy. Another mover and shaker. The difference was that Venable had clawed his way up out of the gutter and had never forgotten it. He stood close to the Dyers in his perfectly tailored tux with a kind of secret smile on his face, like he knew they didn't want him there but also knew they couldn't afford to get rid of him. But, just in case anyone thought about trying, he'd surrounded himself with four bodyguards.

Layla eyed them surreptitiously, with some concern. They were huge – bigger than Bobby, even when he'd been still standing – each wearing a bulky suit and one of those little curly wires leading up from their collar to their ear, like they was guarding the president himself. But Venable was no statesman, Layla knew for a fact.

She hadn't expected him to be invited to the Dyers' annual charity ball, and had worked hard to get herself on the staff list when she'd found out he was. A lot of planning had gone into this, one way or another.

By contrast, the Dyers had no protection. Well, unless you counted that bossy secretary of Mrs Dyer's. Mrs Dyer was society through and through. The type who wouldn't remember to get out of bed in the morning without a social secretary to remind her. The type whose only job is looking good and saying the right thing and being seen in the right places. There must be some kind of a college for women like that.

Mrs Dyer had made a big show of inspecting the arrangements, though. She'd walked through the kitchen earlier that day, nodding serenely, just so her husband could toast her publicly tonight for her part in overseeing the organization of the event, and she could look all modest about it and it not quite be a lie.

She'd had the secretary with her then, a slim woman with cool eyes who'd frozen Steve off the first time he'd tried laying a proprietary hand on her shoulder. Layla and the rest of the girls hid their smiles behind bland faces when she'd done that. Even so, Steve took it out on Tammy – had her on her back in the storeroom almost before they were out the door.

The secretary was here tonight, Layla saw. Fussing around her employer, but it was Mr Dyer whose shoulder she stayed close to. Too close, Layla decided, for their relationship to be merely professional. An affair perhaps? She wouldn't put it past any man to lose his sense and his pants when it came to an attractive woman. Still, she didn't think the secretary looked the type. Maybe he liked 'em cool. Maybe she was hoping he'd leave his wife.

At the moment, the secretary's eyes were on their guest. Venable had been free with his hosts' champagne all evening and his appetites were not concerned only with the food. Layla watched the way his body language grew predatory when he was introduced to the gauche teenage daughter of one of the guests, and she stepped in with her tray, ignoring the ominous looming of the bodyguards.

"Sir, can I interest you in a canape? Smoked salmon and caviar or Kobe beef and ginger?"

Venable's greed got the better of him and he let go of the girl's hand, which he'd been grasping far too long. She snatched it back, red-faced, and fled. The secretary gave Layla a knowing, grateful smile.

Layla moved away quickly afterwards, a frown on her face, cursing inwardly and knowing he was watching her. She was here for a purpose. One that was too important to allow stupid mistakes like that to risk bringing her unwanted attention. And after she'd tried so hard to blend in.

To calm herself, to negate those shivers of doubt, she thought of Bobby again. They'd moved in together, found a little apartment. Not much, but the first place Layla had lived in years that didn't need the wheels taken off before you could call it home.

He'd been always gentle with Layla, but then one night he'd hit a guy who was hassling the girls too hard, hurt him real bad, and the management had to let Bobby go. Word got out and he couldn't get another job. Layla had walked out, too, but she went through a dry spell as far as work was concerned, and now there were two of them to feed and care for.

Eventually, she was forced to go lower than she'd had to go before, taking her clothes off to bad music in a cheap dive that didn't even bother to have a guy like Bobby to protect the girls. As long as the customers put their money down before they left, the management didn't care.

Layla soon discovered that some of the girls took to supplementing their income by inviting the occasional guy out into the alley at the back of the club. When the landlord came by twice in the same week threatening to evict her and Bobby, she'd swallowed her pride. By the end of that first night, that wasn't all she'd had to swallow.

Even Bobby, slow though he might be, soon realized what she was doing. How could he not question where the extra money was coming from when he'd been in the business long enough to know how much the girls made in tips – and what they had to do to earn them? At first, when she'd explained it to him, Layla thought he was cool with it. Until the next night when she was out in the alley between sets, her back hard up against the rough stucco wall with some guy from out of town huffing sweat and beer into her unremarkable face.

One minute she was standing with her eyes tight shut, wondering how much longer the guy was going to last, and the next he was yanked away and she heard that dreadful crack of skulls.

Bobby hadn't meant to kill him, she was sure of that. He just didn't know his own strength, was all. Then it was his turn to panic and tremble, but Layla stayed ice cool. They wrapped the body in plastic and put it into the trunk of a borrowed car before driving it down to the Everglades. Bobby carried it out to a pool where the 'gators gathered, and left it there for them to hide. Layla even went back a week later, just to check, but there was nothing left to find.

They stripped the guy before they dumped him, and struck lucky. He had a decent watch and a bulging wallet. It was a month before Layla had to put out against the stucco in the alley again.

How were they supposed to know he was connected to Venable? That the watch Bobby had pawned would lead Venable's bone-breakers straight to them?

A month after the killing, Venable's boys picked Bobby and Layla up from the bar and drove them out to some place by the docks. Bobby swore that Layla wasn't in on it, that they should leave her alone, let her go. Swore blind that it was so. And eventually, they blinded him, just to make sure.

Layla thought she'd never get the sound of Bobby's scream-ing out of her head as they'd tortured him into a confession of sorts. But even when they'd snapped his spine, left him broken and bleeding on that filthy concrete floor, Bobby had not said a word against Layla. And she, to her eternal shame, had been too terrified to confess her part in it all, as though that would make mockery of everything he'd gone through.

So, they'd left her. She was a waitress, a dancer, a hooker. A no-account nobody. Not worth the effort of a beating. Not worth the cost of a bullet.

Helpless as a baby, damaged beyond repair, Bobby went into some institution just north of Tampa and Layla took the bus up to see him every week for the first couple of months. But, gradually, getting on that bus got harder to do. It broke her heart to see him like that, to force the cheerful note into her voice.

Eventually, the bus left the terminal one morning and Layla wasn't on it.

She'd cried for days. When she'd gotten word that Bobby had snuck a knife out of the dining hall, waited until it was quiet then slit his wrists under the blankets and quietly bled out into his mattress during the night, there had been no more tears left to fall.

Layla's heart hardened to a shell. She'd let Bobby down while he was alive, but she could seek justice for him after he was dead. She heard things. That was one of the beauties of being invisible. People talked while she served them drinks, like she wasn't there. Once Layla had longed to be noticeable, to be accepted. Now she made it her business simply to listen.

Of course, she knew she couldn't go after Venable alone, so Layla had found another bruiser with no qualms about burying the bodies. And, once he'd had a taste of that spectacular body, he was hers.

Thad was younger than Bobby, sharper, neater, and when it came to killing he had the strike and the morals of a rattlesnake. Layla knew he'd do anything for her, right up until the time she tried to move on, and then he was likely to do anything *to* her instead.

Well, after tonight, she wouldn't care.

She slipped out of the ballroom but instead of turning into the kitchen, this time she took the extra few strides to the French windows at the end of the corridor, furtively opened them a crack, then closed them again carefully so they didn't latch.

By the time Layla returned to the ballroom, the canapes were not all she was holding. She'd detoured via the little cloakroom the girls had been given to change and store their bags. What she'd collected from hers she was holding flat in her right hand, hidden by the tray. A Beretta nine millimeter, hot most likely. As long as it worked, Layla didn't care.

A few moments later someone stopped by her elbow and leaned close to examine the contents of the tray.

"Well hello, *Cindy*." A man's voice, a smile curving the sound of it. "And just what you got there, little lady?"

Thad, looking pretty nifty in the tux she'd made him rent. He bent over her tray while she explained the contents, making a big play over choosing between the caviar or the beef. And underneath, his other hand touched hers, and she slipped the Beretta into it.

"Well, thank you, sugar," he said, taking a canape with a flourish and slipping the gun inside his jacket with his other hand, like a magician. When the hand came out again, it was holding a snowy handkerchief, which he used to wipe his fingers and dab his mouth.

Layla had made him practise the move until it seemed so natural. Shame this was a one-time show. He would have made such a partner, someone she might just have been able to live her dreams with. If only he hadn't had that cruel streak. If only he'd touched her heart the way Bobby had.

Poor crippled, blinded Bobby. Poor *dead* Bobby . . .

Ah well. Too late for regrets. Too late for much of anything, now.

Layla caught Thad's eye as she made another round and he nodded, almost imperceptibly. She nodded back, the slightest inclination of her head, and turned away. As she did so she bumped deliberately into the arm of a man who'd been recounting some fishing tale and spread his hands broadly to lie about the size of his catch. He caught Layla's tray and sent it flipping upwards. Layla caught it with the fast reflexes that came from years of waiting crowded tables amid careless diners. She managed to stop the contents crashing to the floor, but most of it ended up down the front of her blouse instead.

"Oh, I am *so* sorry, sir," she said immediately, clutching the tray to her chest to prevent further spillage.

"No problem," the man said, annoyed at having his story interrupted and oblivious to the fact it had been entirely his fault. He checked his own clothing. "No harm done."

Layla managed to raise a smile and hurried out. Steve caught her halfway.

"What happened, honey?" he demanded. "Not like you to be so clumsy."

Layla shrugged as best she could, still trying not to shed debris.

"Sorry, boss," she said. "I've got a spare blouse in my bag. I'll go change."

"Okay, sweetheart, but make it snappy." He let her move away a few strides, then called after her, "And if that's caviar you're wearing, it'll come out of your pay, y'hear?"

Layla threw him a chastised glance over her shoulder that didn't go deep enough to change her eyes, and hurried back to the little cloakroom.

She scraped the gunge off the front of her chest into the nearest trash, took off the blouse and threw that away, too, then rummaged through her bag for a clean one. This one was calculatedly lower cut and more revealing, but she didn't think Steve would object too hard, even if he caught her wearing it.

She pulled out another skirt, too, even though there was nothing wrong with her old one. This was shorter than the last, showing several inches of long smooth thigh below the hem and, without undue vanity, she knew it would drag male eyes downwards, even as her newly exposed cleavage would drag them up again. With any luck, they'd go cross-eyed trying to look both places at once.

She swapped her false name badge over and took the cheap Makarov nine millimeter and a roll of duct tape out of her bag. She lifted one remarkable leg up onto the wooden bench and ran the duct tape around the top of her thigh, twice, to hold the nine in position, just out of sight. The pistol grip pointed downwards and she knew from hours in front of the mirror that she could yank the gun loose in a second.

She'd bought both pistols from a crooked military surplus dealer down near Miramar. Thad insisted on coming with her for the Beretta, had made a big thing about checking the gun over like he knew what he was doing, sighting along the barrel with one eye closed.

Layla had gone back later for the Makarov. She didn't have enough money for the two, but she'd been dressed to thrill and she and the dealer had come to an arrangement that hadn't cost Layla anything at all. Only pride, and she'd been way over-drawn on that account for years.

Now, Layla checked in the cracked mirror that the gun didn't show beneath her skirt. Her face was even more bland in its pallor and, just for once, she wished she'd been born pretty. Not beautiful, just pretty enough to have been cherished.

The way she'd cherished Bobby. The way he'd cherished her.

She left the locker room and collected a fresh tray from the kitchen. The chefs were under pressure, the activity frantic, but when she walked in on those long dancer's legs there was a moment of silence that was almost reverent.

"You changed your clothes," one of the chefs said, mesmerized.

She smiled at him, saw the fog lift a little as the disappointment of her face cut through the haze of lust created by her body.

"I spilled," she said, collecting a fresh tray. She felt every eye on her as she walked out, smiled when she heard the collective sigh as the door swung closed behind her.

It was a short-lived smile.

Back in the ballroom, it was all she could do not to go marching straight up to Venable, but she knew she had to play it cool. The four bodyguards were too experienced not to spot her sudden surge of guilt and anger. They'd pick her out of the crowd the way a shark cuts out a weakling seal pup. And she couldn't afford that. Not yet.

Instead, she forced herself to think bland thoughts as she circled the room towards him. Saw out of the corner of her eye Thad casually moving up on the other side. The relief flooded her, sending her limbs almost lax with it. For a second, she'd been afraid he wouldn't go through with it. That he'd realize what her real plan was, and back out at the last minute.

For the moment, though, Thad must think it was all going according to plan. She stepped up to the Dyers, offered them something from her tray. The secretary still hadn't left his side, she saw. The girl must be desperate.

Layla took another step, sideways towards Venable, ducking around the cordon of bodyguards. Offered him something from her tray. And this time, as he leaned forwards, so did she, pressing her arms together to accentuate what nature had so generously given her.

She watched Venable's eyes go glassy, saw the way the eyes of the nearest two bodyguards bulged the same way. There was another just behind her, she knew, and she bent a little further from the waist, knowing she was giving him a prime view of her ass and the back of her newly-exposed thighs. She could almost feel that hot little gaze slavering up the backs of her knees.

Come on, Thad . . .

He came pushing through the crowd nearest to Venable, moving too fast. If he'd been slower, he might have made it. As it was, he was the only guy for twenty feet in any direction who didn't have his eyes full of Layla's divine body. Venable's eyes snapped round at the last moment, jerky, panicking as he realized the rapidly approaching threat. He flailed, sending Layla's tray crashing to the ground, showering canapes.

The bodyguards were slower off the mark. Thad already had the gun out before two of them grabbed him. Not so much grabbed as piled in on top of him, driving him off his legs and down, using fists and feet to keep him there.

Thad was no easy meat, though. He kept in shape and had come up from the streets, where unfair fights were part of the game. Even on the floor, he lashed out, aiming for knees and shins, hitting more than he was missing. A third bodyguard joined in to keep him down, a leather sap appearing like magic in his hand.

There was that familiar crack of skulls. *Just like Bobby* . . .

Layla winced, but she couldn't let that distract her now. Her mind strangely cool and calm, Layla stepped in, ignored. The fourth bodyguard had stayed at his post, but Layla was shielded from his view by his own principal, and everyone's attention was on the fight. Carefully, she reached under her skirt and yanked the Makarov free, unaware of the brief burn as the tape ripped from her thigh.

The safety was already off, the hammer back. The Army surplus guy down in Miramar had thrown in a little instruction as well. Gave him more of a chance to stand up real close behind her as he demonstrated how to hold the unfamiliar gun, how to aim and fire.

She brought the nine up the way he'd shown her, both hands clasped round the pistol grip, starting to take up the pressure on the trigger, she bent her knees and crouched a little, so the recoil wouldn't send the barrel rising, just in case she had to take a second shot. But, this close, she knew she wouldn't need one, even if she got the chance.

One thing Layla hadn't been ready for was the noise. The report was monstrously loud in the high-ceilinged ballroom. And though she thought she'd been prepared, she staggered back and to the side. And the pain. The pain was a gigantic fist around her heart, squeezing until she couldn't breathe.

She looked up, vision starting to shimmer, and saw Venable was still standing, shocked but apparently unharmed. How had she missed? The bodyguard had come out of his lethargy to throw himself on top of his employer, but there was still an open window. There was still time . . .

Layla tried to lift the gun but her arms were leaden. Something hit her, hard, in the centre of her voluptuous chest, but she didn't see what it was, or who threw it. She frowned, took a step back and her legs folded, and suddenly she was staring up at the chandeliers on the ceiling and she had to hold on to the polished wooden dance floor beneath her hands to stay there. Her vision was starting to blacken at the edges, like burning paper, the sound blurring down.

The last thing she saw was the slim woman she'd taken for a secretary, leaning over her with a wisp of smoke rising from the muzzle of the nine millimeter she was holding.

Then the bright lights, and the glitter, all faded to black.

The woman Layla had mistaken for a secretary placed two fingers against the pulse point in the waitress's throat and felt nothing. She knew better than to touch the body more than she had to now, even to close the dead woman's eyes.

Cindy, the name tag read, even under the trickle of the blood. She doubted that would match the woman's driver's licence.

She rose, sliding the SIG semi-automatic back into the concealed-carry rig on her belt. Two of Venable's meaty goons wrestled the woman's accomplice, bellowing, out of the room. She turned to her employer.

"I don't think you were the target, Mr Dyer, but I couldn't take the chance," she said calmly. She jerked her head towards the bodyguards. "If this lot had been halfway capable, I wouldn't have had to get involved. As it was . . ."

Dyer nodded. He still had his arms wrapped round his wife, who was sobbing, and his eyes were sad and tired.

"Thank you," he said quietly.

The woman shrugged. "It's my job," she said.

"Who the hell are you?" It was Venable himself who spoke, elbowing his way out from the protective shield that his remaining bodyguards had belatedly thrown around him.

"This is Charlie Fox," Dyer answered for her, the faintest smile in his voice. "She's *my* personal protection. A little more subtle than your own choice. She's good, isn't she?"

Venable stared at him blankly, then at the dead woman, lying crumpled on the polished planks. At the unfired gun that had fallen from her hand.

"You saved my life," he murmured, his face pale.

Charlie stared back at him. "Yes," she said, sounding almost regretful. "Whether it was worth saving is quite another point. What had you done to her that she was prepared to kill you for it?"

Venable seemed not to hear. He couldn't take his eyes off Layla's body. Something about her was familiar, but he just couldn't remember her face.

"I don't know – nothing," he said, cleared his throat of its hoarseness and tried again. "She's a nobody. Just a waitress." He took another look, just to be sure. "Just a woman."

"Oh, I don't know," Dyer said, and his eyes were on Charlie Fox. "From where I'm standing, she's a hell of a woman, wouldn't you say?"

THE MYSTERY OF CANUTE VILLA

Martin Edwards

"Why should an innocent and respectable lady of good family and in her late middle years, never touched by a breath of scandal, be haunted by a mysterious stranger whose name is entirely unknown to her?"

The woman in the railway carriage nodded. "You have expressed the problem in a nutshell."

Her companion tugged at his beard. "It is a tantalizing puzzle, I grant you, my dear Mrs Gaskell."

As the train rattled round a bend, she said, "I only hope that I have not called you up to Cheshire on a wild goose chase."

He gave a little bow. "Your summons was so intriguingly phrased, how could any man fail to hasten to your side?"

"Of course," she said, "I am profoundly grateful to you for having agreed to spare me a little of your precious time. I realize that there are many calls upon it."

More than you know, dear lady. Charles Dickens suppressed a sigh. It had been his intention to evaporate – as he liked to describe it – from London to spend a few pleasant days with Ellen Ternan. However, as no doubt she had calculated, Mrs Gaskell's telegram had fascinated him. Within an hour of its receipt, he was on the train heading north to Manchester. He had an additional motive for racing to her side, being determined to seize an opportunity to improve relations between them. Once they had been on first class terms, but ever since their wrangles over the serialization of *North and South*, she had displayed a stubbornness unbecoming (if not, sadly, uncommon) in any woman, let alone the wife of a provincial clergyman.

He smiled. "Do you remember why I used to call you Scheherezade?"

She blushed. Not, he was sure, because her memory had failed, but rather from that becoming modesty that had entranced him in the early days of their acquaintance.

"You must recall my saying I was sure your powers of narrative can never be exhausted in a single night, but must be good for at least a thousand nights and one. Besides, your message was so teasing that no man with an ounce of curiosity in his blood could possibly resist."

She permitted herself a smile. "You have not lost your gift for flattery, my dear Mr Dickens."

"Charles, please." He gave an impish grin. "Scheherezade."

As if to cover her embarrassment, she looked out of the window at the fields and copses flying by. "We have reached Mobberley. Soon we shall be arriving."

He clapped his hands. "I eagerly await my first sight of Cranford! Tell me, meanwhile, more about your friend Mrs Pettigrew."

"Ah, dear Clarissa. It is difficult for me to think of her by the Major's name. To me, she will always be Clarissa Woodward or, at a pinch, Mrs Clarissa Drinkwater."

"You have met her second husband, Major Pettigrew?"

"Only once, at the wedding."

"You do not care for the Major or his habit of bragging about his service in India?"

"I did not say that."

"And I did not ask if it were true," he said briskly. "I asserted it as a fact, inferred from your manner whenever you have mentioned the fellow's name."

Elizabeth cast her eyes to the heavens, but managed to suppress a sigh of irritation. "I suppose I can hardly complain if, having been enticed here by the invitation to conduct yourself as a detective, you start to play the part at every conceivable opportunity."

He laughed. "We have that fascination for the work of a detective in common, do we not? I recall that splendid little piece you wrote for me on disappearances. *Let me say, I am thankful I live in the days of the Detective Police. If I am murdered, or commit bigamy, at any rate my friends will have the comfort of knowing all about it.*"

"Your memory is remarkable."

"So is my inquisitiveness. Why have you not seen fit to inform the local constabulary of Mrs Pettigrew's distress?"

"For no other reason than that, in her letter, she pleaded with me not to do so."

"And why, pray, do you think she was so reluctant for the matter not to be investigated?"

"I suspect that her husband would not approve. She appears to be reluctant to do anything without his permission."

Dickens peered out of the window. "The station approaches!"

His companion gazed out of the window. "The coming of the railway has made such a difference to Knutsford. The embankment divides our old chapel from the rest of the town."

"The march of progress, my dear Scheherezade!"

They were to be conveyed to the Royal George Hotel, where Elizabeth had booked quarters at the rear overlooking the Assembly Rooms. The journey was short but, with his characteristic zest for exploration, Dickens insisted that they be taken the long way round, by way of Princess Street and the Heath, so that he could imbibe the air of a town he had known hitherto only from the pages of his companion's novel.

"That is Clarissa's home," Elizabeth said, pointing towards a grey and forbidding double-fronted house standing in grounds that overlooked a large tract of open land. "Canute Villa takes its name from the ancient king who is supposed to have forded a river here. It is one of the finest houses in Knutsford."

"A splendid situation. She and the Major can have scant need to practise the elegant economy which I associate with Cranford."

"I prayed that she would be happy." She spoke with such soft sadness that Dickens needed to strain to hear over the clatter of hooves on the cobbles. "But when she wrote to me, her terror was evident. I was appalled. Clarissa has known her share of tragedy, but her spirit has always been strong enough to enable her to face the vagaries of Fortune."

Dickens nodded. "Merely to read the letter is to recognize the fear instilled in its author by the events she describes. You have known her since childhood?"

"She is seven years older than myself, but our families, the Woodwards and the Stevensons, lived a few doors apart from each other and were always on good terms. My brother John was friendly with her twin brother Edgar."

Dickens knew a little of John. His death had been one of the tragedies of Elizabeth Gaskell's life. He was a seaman who had sailed the Seven Seas but been lost when his sister was seventeen; some said he was drowned, some that he had been set upon by brigands in the sub-continent, and there was even a picturesque story that he had been killed by pirates. Elizabeth had drawn on her grief when writing; disappearances haunted much of her finest work.

"She married a man called Drinkwater, you say?"

"Thomas was a solicitor, a man fifteen years Clarissa's senior. He was thought to be a confirmed bachelor, but on meeting my friend at a party, he was quite swept off his feet. Clarissa could have had taken her pick of men, but she saw in Thomas a steadfastness that she found admirable."

"To say nothing of a handsome income?"

Her eyes blazed. "Charles, that is a scurrilous thing to say! Thomas was a thoroughly decent man. I know that you entertain a certain scepticism about members of the legal profession, but I really . . ."

"Please forgive me, Scheherezade," he said quickly, and with unaccustomed humility. "I did not mean to cast aspersions on your friend's integrity."

"I should hope not indeed! The fact is that the marriage was one of the happiest I have known. When he died of apoplexy three years ago, she was heartbroken."

"There were no children?"

"No, to the dismay of both Clarissa and Thomas."

"And what of brother Edgar?"

"He died ten years ago. Poor fellow, his heart was always weak. He was the last of the male Woodwards."

"Thus she was left not only alone but also very wealthy?"

As the carriage pulled up before the stables in George Yard, Elizabeth Gaskell slowly inclined her head.

Over afternoon tea in the comfortable public room of the hostelry, Dickens summarized the essentials of the conundrum that Clarissa Pettigrew had posed.

"Since her second marriage, your friend has become a virtual recluse. By nature she is charming and convivial, popular because she has always been not only attractive in appearance but generous and thoughtful. Nowadays, however, she and the Major shun neighbours, friends and even relatives. Your opinion is that this is at his insistence."

"I refuse to believe otherwise."

"Very well. According to your observation, the Major is not only considerably younger than Clarissa, but also appears to lack independent means."

"He is a fine figure of a man, but at the wedding, there was gossip that he had not a penny to his name until he took her for his wife. Some folk said he'd run into trouble while he was serving in India and that if he hadn't left the army, he would have been disgraced."

Naturally there would be gossip; this was Cranford. However, Dickens kept the thought to himself. He drained his cup of tea and helped himself to a slice of gateau.

"The effect of the marriage is, as you will appreciate, to transfer into the Major's name your friend's inheritance. The house, her first husband's investments, everything. A scandalous state of affairs, in my opinion. Nevertheless, that is the law."

"Indeed." Elizabeth's face was a mask.

"Still, although the two of you had enjoyed only limited contact by way of correspondence since the wedding, you had no reason to believe that anything was amiss until you received the letter."

"Friends in the town had informed me of their sorrow, that Clarissa and the Major appeared to be cutting them off. Nobody could believe that was Clarissa's wish. Everyone blamed her new husband. Rumour had it he once blacked her eye when in a drunken rage. But who would dare to come between man and wife? I felt helpless until she wrote and asked for my aid."

"Did you know that she had been unwell?"

"Not at all. You may imagine my dismay when she told me that for several weeks illness had confined her to the house."

"She speaks of a malady affecting her nerves."

"Which is quite unlike Clarissa. As a girl, I rather idolized her. She was blessed not only with a delightful personality but a robust constitution and ready wit. Very far removed, if you will forgive me, from a Dora Copperfield."

"According to Clarissa, on Monday last she spied a stranger lurking outside Canute Villa. An unkempt tramp in a battered hat and coat, hiding amongst the trees at the far side of the Heath. At first she paid him scant attention, but on the following day she noticed him again. He appeared to keep watch on the comings and goings of the household."

Elizabeth eyed him sharply. "You say *according to* Clarissa. Do you imply scepticism concerning her veracity?"

"We cannot rule out anything."

She flushed. "Well, I can! Clarissa would never dream . . ."

"If we are to stand in the shoes of members of the detective police," Dickens interrupted, "we must refuse to be swayed by personal loyalties or affections. Without logic, Elizabeth, a detective is lost!"

"Please proceed," she said, struggling for an icy calm.

Dickens cleared his throat and launched into the story, with as much gusto as if reciting *Mrs Gamp* or *Sikes and Nancy*.

"In ordinary circumstances, she would have approached the man and shooed him off. However, when she ventured from the door at the side of the house, he vanished. Later that night, however, when noting that the housemaid had drawn the curtains imperfectly and left a gap between them, she caught a glimpse in the moonlight of a dark figure loitering on the edge of the Heath and subjecting Canute Villa to intensive scrutiny. She could not see him clearly, but he was wearing a low-brimmed hat and she was sure that the tramp had returned. Fearing burglary, she informed her husband, but although he went out to inspect the grounds of their home, he could find nothing.

"On his return, he accused Clarissa of succumbing to flights of fancy and went so far as to question her state of mind. She came close to believing that she had indeed imagined the whole episode, but the following day, through the window she caught sight once more of the mysterious stranger. When he saw her looking at him, he disappeared from view. The Major was out of the house at the time and when he returned and she told him what had happened, he consulted the housemaid, a girl by the name of Alice. She denied having seen the apparition and the Major lost his temper – not, I gather, an unusual occurrence – and said that Clarissa was imagining things and that if she did not have a care, she would soon find herself confined to an asylum."

Pausing for breath, he considered his companion. Elizabeth was fidgeting with the edge of the tablecloth.

"Why did her husband not believe her?" she murmured, as though wrestling with an abstruse mathematical problem.

Dickens gave a shrug of the shoulders. "At all events, the next morning saw a further development. While the Major and the housemaid were out of the house, she found a crudely scrawled note tucked under the door of the house. It read simply: *Please meet at nine o'clock behind the Lord Eldon*. And it was signed '*Datchery*'. A name unknown to Clarissa. Having lived in the town all her life, she is certain that no local resident is so called. Frightened by the message, she showed it to her husband to see if he was familiar with Datchery, or could otherwise make any sense of the message. Her candour proved unwise. The Major flew into a fury and accused her of indulging in an unseemly association with another man and concocting a tale about a mysterious tramp to conceal her illicit relations with a lover. With no one else to turn to, Clarissa wrote in haste to seek the wise counsel of her old friend and confidante Elizabeth Gaskell."

"You have seen the letter. The trembling script indicates that Clarissa's nerves are in tatters. She says she fears for her sanity and I can believe it." Elizabeth took a deep breath. "This is what marrying the Major has done to her."

Dickens said grimly, "I look forward to making the acquaintance of the unhappy couple. You have explained that I shall be accompanying you on your visit?"

Elizabeth nodded. "Even though she begged me to come and see her, you will recall that she implored me to say nothing in reply that might antagonize her husband, as he always insisted upon reading correspondence that she received, and she had concealed from him the very fact that she had written to me. I composed my response in terms of the utmost diplomacy, saying merely that I would call upon them while taking you around the sights of Cranford. She has always loved your writing, Charles, and I doubt whether even a bully such as the Major could easily object to our visiting them."

Dickens beamed. "An enthusiast for my work? That settles it, Scheherezade. Poor Mrs Pettigrew is most certainly not in danger of losing her mind."

The two of them strolled the short distance from King Street to Canute Villa by way of the Lord Eldon, an old coaching inn close to the livestock market at Heathside. Dickens insisted upon inspecting the alleyway where, he presumed, the meeting with the ruffian who called himself Datchery was supposed to have taken place.

"Hmmm." He tapped a walking stick on the cobbles. "An interesting spot for a rendezvous. Quiet and not overlooked. Convenient for the Pettigrews' house, so it would be easy to slip away and meet someone here covertly before returning home. There is a good chance that a brief absence would not be noticed."

"Why would this man want to meet Clarissa?"

"My dear woman, the first question is whether it was Clarissa whom he wanted to meet."

"You think the note might have been intended for the Major?"

"Or even the housemaid."

Elizabeth said thoughtfully, "I had not contemplated the thought, but now that you mention it . . . Alice is as obliging as she is pretty. She has been with Clarissa since Mr Drinkwater was alive."

"Are there other servants?"

"At the wedding she mentioned a manservant called Bowden, who was rather sweet on Alice. However, in her last but one letter to me, a fortnight ago, she said that the Major had given him notice and not appointed anyone to take his place."

Dickens wagged a finger playfully. "Ah, elegant economy is practised in Cranford after all!"

"I gained the impression that the expenses of the household were mounting. She said that the Major found it most satisfactory to have a home overlooking a racecourse. No doubt he likes to make a wager from time to time."

"Let us speak plainly. If the craze for gambling has seized him, then the assets of the late Mr Drinkwater risk being squandered in all too short a time." Dickens shook his head. "Come, let us make our visit."

As they followed a path across the Heath, Elizabeth pointed out the site of a grandstand that a new company proposed to erect to accommodate spectators at the races.

"This afternoon the place may be deserted, but they say that with the coming of the railway, the races will attract thousands."

He rubbed his chin. "The world is changing, Scheherezade. Yet people, at heart, do not change."

"I'm not much of a man for reading," Major Pettigrew harrumphed.

Dickens favoured his host with a smile so cordial that it bordered on the oleaginous. "You are a man of action, sir. A pair of humble scribblers such as Mrs Gaskell and myself can do nothing but look with awe upon a soldier who has seen service in far-flung and dangerous corners of the world."

Pettigrew eyed his guest suspiciously but, unable to find obvious fault with the compliment, nodded towards the door leading back into the house and muttered, "We must return to the ladies. As I sought to make clear when you were introduced, my wife is a sick woman. It is most important that she should not over-excite herself."

They were standing in the garden to the rear of Canute Villa. A square lawn was fringed by rhododendron bushes, climbing roses and ancient copper beeches. After the demure housemaid had admitted the visitors to the presence of the Pettigrews, conversation was stilted. It was plain from the Major's brusqueness that he did not welcome guests in his home. However, he could hardly expel such illustrious visitors without observing the common courtesies.

Dickens had convinced himself that, if they were to help Clarissa at all, it would be essential for Elizabeth to speak to her in private. Thus, from the moment they were led into the large and immaculate drawing room, Dickens had chattered without drawing breath before glancing through the bay window looking out on to the lawn and expressing his admiration for the garden in fulsome terms before begging to be allowed to inspect it at close quarters. Elizabeth managed to suppress her amusement at his effrontery and Pettigrew had, albeit with a show of reluctance, consented to show Dickens around the grounds. Once outside, Dickens had talked endlessly about the privations of life as a writer while his host shifted impatiently from foot to foot.

Obediently, Dickens trotted after his host as they returned to the drawing room. Pettigrew was tall and erect in bearing and boasted a splendid dark moustache. Dickens could imagine him charming an older woman, if he put his mind to it, but his chin was weak, and a petulant note was apt to enter his voice when he made even the most commonplace remark.

On entering the presence of the ladies, Dickens caught Elizabeth's eye. She frowned and gave an almost imperceptible shake of the head as he spoke.

"Mrs Pettigrew, may I compliment you? Your garden is as delightful as your charming home."

Clarissa's lips twitched; it seemed to be as close as she could come to offering a smile. Her face was deathly pale and her frail body trembled in the brocaded armchair.

"You are – very kind," she said in a voice so faint that it was barely audible. "To think that we should entertain a guest as distinguished as . . ."

"Yes, yes," her husband interrupted. "Dickens, it is good of you and Mrs Gaskell to have stopped off from your travels to call at our humble abode, but as you can see, my wife is dreadfully fatigued. I do believe, Clarissa, that it would be best for you to go to bed. Come, my dearest, remember what the doctor said this morning. You must not tax yourself. It could be dangerous."

"'*Come, my dearest*'," Elizabeth quoted scornfully when they had repaired to the sitting room at the Royal George. "The man is a hypocrite. He does not care for her one jot."

To see her old friend in such a sorry state had hit her hard. Dickens was tempted to clasp her hand and murmur words of consolation, but a moment's reflection persuaded him of the unwisdom of such a course. He would not wish his good intentions to be misinterpreted. Women could be such fearful creatures.

"What did she tell you?"

"Nothing of value. She insisted that she had been mistaken. Her husband was right and the mysterious stranger was indeed a figment of her imagination."

"What?"

"She apologized profusely for having allowed a momentary nervous turn to summon us on a fool's errand. However much I pressed her, she remained adamant. As for the note from Datchery, she had dreamed it. Stuff and nonsense! I know Clarissa too well. Something quite dreadful must have happened in order to reduce her to such a pitiable state, to cause her to lie to one of her oldest friends."

"You are convinced that she did receive the note she described?"

"Most certainly. The question is – what has happened in between her writing to me and this afternoon to prompt such a crisis of confidence that, even when free of her husband's malign presence, she would not admit the truth even to me?"

"I suspect that . . ." Dickens began.

"Surely the answer is obvious? Pettigrew has intimidated her into denying the truth. For some reason, he is anxious that nobody should know of the tramp, or of Datchery – although I believe that they are one and the same."

"There is an alternative hypothesis, Scheherezade. If the tramp does exist, what is his purpose? Could it be that the Major has instructed him to haunt Canute Villa?"

"To what end?"

"So that his wife comes to believe that she is indeed mad?"

Elizabeth passed a slim hand across her face. "Oh, Charles, what are we to do?"

That question remained unanswered as Elizabeth and Dickens drank coffee after dinner that evening. The venison had been excellent, but their appreciation of a fine meal had been dulled by concern for the woman trapped in such unhappiness behind the bleak facade of Canute Villa. Each time Dickens came up with a fresh notion for confronting Pettigrew, Elizabeth dismissed it, pointing out the difficulties of coming between man and wife. They risked making matters even worse for Clarissa, she warned. But when Dickens demanded to know what she proposed to do to assist her friend, she confessed to being at an utter loss.

"Only one course remains open," Dickens said at length. "We must track down the tramp and press him for the truth."

"But where might he be?"

"This is your home ground, Elizabeth. Where do you suggest a man might seek to hide, or make a temporary home?"

She frowned. "The woodland bordering the Heath is quite dense. And there is the Moor, of course."

"The Moor?"

Elizabeth nodded. "It is the marshy valley below King Street. Tatton Mere peters out into tall reed beds and folk call it the Moor. It has a special place in my affections, since I used to play there for hours on end as a child. Certainly that area is as wild as anywhere in the neighbourhood. I remember when we were young . . . my goodness, Mr Tompkins, what is the matter?"

The proprietor of the inn, a ruddy-faced man of equable temperament, had burst into the room. The colour had drained from his face and he was gasping for breath.

"Mr Dickens! Mrs Gaskell! We spoke earlier about your friend Mrs Pettigrew and her husband the Major!"

"What is it?" Elizabeth asked in a tremulous voice. "Has something – happened to Clarissa?"

Tompkins stared at her. "Oh, no, Mrs Gaskell. At least . . . ."

"Come on, man!" Dickens was shouting. "Tell us what brings you rushing in here as though you have seen a ghost."

"I have – I have seen no ghost," Tompkins stuttered. "But I have seen the body of a man. It is Major Pettigrew, and his eyes were almost popping out of his head. He has been most foully murdered."

Not until the next afternoon did Dickens manage to secure an interview with Sergeant Rowley, the detective charged with investigating the most sensational crime to have been associated with Knutsford since the hanging of Highwayman Higgins, whose exploits had inspired Elizabeth to pen a story for *Household Words*. To his dismay, Rowley was scarcely an Inspector Field or a Sergeant Whicher. Broad-shouldered, ruddy-faced and short of breath, he made it clear that he was not to be impressed either by the fame of his visitor or a close acquaintance with London's principal detectives.

"You will forgive me for keeping you waiting, sir," Rowley said, without a hint of apology in his demeanour, "but the murder of Major Pettigrew is a most serious business and I have been fully occupied in seeking to ensure that the malefactor is brought swiftly to justice."

"I wish you every success," Dickens said. "I thought it might help if . . ."

"Bless you, sir," Rowley said, failing to conceal smug satisfaction, "it is generous of you to offer assistance, but we have already apprehended the culprit. The constabulary of Knutsford may not be as eminent as its counterpart in the metropolis, but I can assure you that our dedication to our work is second to none, the length and breadth of the British Isles."

"There is talk in the town that you have arrested someone already."

"Indeed, Mr Dickens. A fellow by the name of Bowden. He used to work at Canute Villa, but the Major gave him notice two weeks ago."

"You think that Bowden would have waited so long before taking revenge for his dismissal?"

Rowley shrugged. "There is more to it than that. Young Bowden was hoping to marry the girl who works for the Pettigrews."

"Did she throw him over?"

"Not exactly, as I understand it. But the Major was a ladies' man, God rest his soul. There is talk that he had taken a shine to young Alice."

"But she had worked for Clarissa for years!"

"Even so, sir. The Major's a fine figure of a man and it doesn't take much sweet talk to turn a pretty young woman's head."

"So Bowden killed him to make sure he didn't lay his hands on Alice?"

"You're a man of the world, sir, so you won't mind my saying that I'd wager he's already laid his hands on that young lady a time or two. Of course, she won't admit it, any more than Bowden will confess his guilt. But that's where the truth lies, sir, you mark my words. The fellow is a hot head, this would not be the first time he has been involved in a brawl."

"A crime of passion?"

"Indeed."

"Mr Tompkins tells me that Pettigrew had been strangled."

Rowley frowned. "Extraordinary how fast news travels in this town! And how exactly did he know that?"

"He has a friendly rivalry with the landlord of the Lord Eldon and had called upon the fellow to discuss a business proposition." While they were talking, a lad started shouting outside. They went to see the cause of the commotion to find him standing over Pettigrew's body.

"Have you traced the ligature?"

"Not yet. We believe that the crime was committed with a thick cord or rope of some kind. It was pulled viciously around the Major's neck, cutting into the flesh so much that it bled."

"Did you find such a cord on Bowden?"

"No, but he'll have disposed of it somewhere."

"So you are adamant that the man is your murderer?"

"Oh, he reckons to have an alibi. Claims he was drinking at the Angel, and has half a dozen witnesses to prove it, but the Angel is only five minutes from the Lord Eldon. It's my belief that he slipped out while no one was looking."

"And do you suppose the Major would have agreed to make an appointment with the man whom he had given notice?"

Rowley drew himself up to his considerable height. "Rest assured, it is only a matter of time before the details emerge. It is my belief that Bowden lured the Major out there on a pretext, perhaps under a false name."

Dickens looked at him sharply. "Do you have any evidence of that?"

"As yet, sir, none. But we'll find it, you mark my words."

"The fellow is an ignoramus," Dickens said to Elizabeth an hour later.

"I take it that he has never read one of your books?" she replied demurely.

Dickens snorted. "He has a single idea in his head and is determined to stick to it. I have been speaking to Tompkins and he tells me that young Bowden is well-liked in the town. Sergeant Rowley may find it more troublesome than he would wish to break that alibi."

"I have been talking to the staff here during your absence." Elizabeth nodded. "They describe the young man as a hot-head. His temper has got the better of him more than once and he has given one or two other fellows in town a bloody nose. But nobody believes there is real harm in him. So you think that he is innocent?"

"I can accept that Pettigrew wished to seduce the house-maid, and thought the task easier to accomplish with her young man banished from the house. And I can imagine that Bowden might resort to violence. But would he commit murder by strangulation? I would have thought a blow to the head was more likely. Besides, if Bowden is guilty – what of Datchery?"

"Perhaps Datchery is a *nom de plume*?"

"No doubt. The name is uncommon, though frankly appealing – I may steal it for a character one day. There is much here that makes little sense. Suppose the message which Clarissa told you about was intended for her husband, not for her. Why should the Major fulfil the rendezvous twenty-four hours late? Why, indeed, should he wish to meet the mysterious Datchery at all? These are real puzzles. Was Clarissa able to cast any light upon them when you called on her?"

"Naturally, she is deeply shocked by her husband's death and I did not think it right to interrogate her. Do you have a theory that will explain the mysteries?"

Dickens leaned closer to her and whispered. "Certainly."

"Tell me."

He chose his words carefully. "Consider this. What if Datchery were the pawn in a wicked plot on the part of the Major to drive your friend insane? But something went awry with the scheme. Before the day is done, I shall endeavour to discover the truth of the matter."

"Charles, please. The Major was murdered in a most terrible fashion. Promise me that you will have a care."

He beamed, relishing the tremor in her voice and the hint of admiration it conveyed. "Never fear, Scheherezade. If I succeed in identifying the Major's nemesis, think what a story we will have to tell!"

It was easier said than done. Dickens scouted around the Heath methodically for an hour or more, but could find no trace of the mysterious stranger whose appearance had so distressed Clarissa. None of the people he spoke to had seen a man answering Datchery's description and, as the minutes ticked by, Dickens began to lose heart. The theory he had formed – and which he had taken good care not to share with Elizabeth – was outlandish and he could find no evidence to support it. Reluctantly, he found himself wondering if the tramp had any existence outside Clarissa's imagination.

As night fell, a chill settled on the town. Even wrapped in a heavy coat, he could not help shivering as he strode towards the Moor. For all its proximity to the bustle of King Street, it struck him as an uncommonly lonely place. Squelching along the soft, muddy track that people had trodden between the tall reeds, he could hear the rustle of wind in the trees and the scuttling of a fox. Otherwise the Moor was graveyard-quiet.

He regretted his lack of candour when speaking to Elizabeth, but he felt he had no choice. Her sole concern was for her friend's well-being and it would never do to voice his suspicion that Clarissa might have played a part, however unwitting, in the death of her husband. Besides, even if he was right, the chances of learning the precise truth were slim. Tomorrow, he must return to the capital, and make arrangements to spend a few days with Ellen. If he failed to find Datchery tonight, he would have no choice but to leave the Mystery of Canute Villa – as his good friend Collins might like to term it – to be solved by others.

It was slow going with the pathways – such as they were – so treacherous underfoot and visibility fading. Much as he enjoyed walking in the darkness, the terrain was unfamiliar and he needed to take care to avoid slipping into a ditch or streamlet. Every now and then a branch would graze his cheek. It would be so easy for one of them to put an eye out. He found himself yearning for the lights of London at night-time and the warm, reassuring consciousness that, even though invisible, teeming humanity was always close at hand. The countryside was so isolated. Who knew how much wickedness lurked here?

Suddenly, as he trudged towards a small copse, he thought he heard something. A cracking of twigs, succeeded by a cough. Dickens froze, straining his ears. Within a few moments came another sound. A low, painful groan.

Was this a trap? Did someone intend him to suffer the same fate as the Major? He peered through the gloom and thought he could make out the faintest shape amongst the trees. Perhaps it was wishful thinking; too often his imagination mastered him.

Another groan, louder this time, and then another, quite prolonged. He did not believe this was a hoax. Nobody, surely, could counterfeit such a noise of pain and despair.

"Who is there?" he hissed.

No answer. He advanced to the edge of the copse. The darkness was quite impenetrable and a branch grazed his cheek, making his eyes water.

"Datchery?"

This time he heard another sound. Was it a man, dragging himself through the undergrowth? Dickens took a stride forward.

"Datchery! I am a friend of Clarissa. We must speak."

Suddenly, he felt an arm wrap itself around his neck. The shock of the attack knocked the breath out of him for an instant, but there was no strength in the attack. After a brief struggle

Dickens thrust his elbow into the midriff of his assailant. Winded, the fellow lost his footing and Dickens seized his chance. Before the man could right himself, Dickens knelt upon his chest, and gripped his captive's wrists as though his life depended on it.

"Listen! I do not want to arrest you. I just want to talk."

The man said nothing; although strongly built, there was no fight left in him. He was wearing a ragged coat and had a beard and, although in the darkness it was difficult to make out his features, his breath smelled foul. This was the tramp Clarissa had described in her letter to Elizabeth, of that Dickens had no doubt.

"I am Charles Dickens. Do you know my name?"

"Dickens?" the tramp gasped. "What – what are you doing here?"

"I am helping my friend Mrs Gaskell to . . ."

"Mrs . . . Gaskell?" The tramp's shock was palpable.

"Yes." Dickens leaned over the man's face. "You know of her? She is a well-known author from these parts and her friend is Mrs Clarissa Pettigrew of Canute Villa."

"Not Pettigrew!" the man hissed. "Do not call her that!"

"Ah!" A thrill of triumph coursed through Dickens. His guesswork – no, his deduction! – must be correct. "You know Clarissa?"

"I . . . I knew her. Long ago."

"And you ventured to renew the acquaintance?"

"No – I wanted to save her from that beast Pettigrew. That is all."

"Did she recognize your name, Datchery?"

"Of course not. She knew me as someone else."

A shiver of excitement ran through Dickens' body.

"You dared not tell her your real name. What is it?"

The man groaned. "Mr Dickens, I am dying. Let me leave this world in peace."

Dickens frowned in the darkness. It took no more than an instant for him to make up his mind.

"I believe I may hazard a guess at your true identity."

A soft gasp. "You cannot!"

"You are John Stevenson, are you not? Elizabeth's brother."

A long silence. "How . . . how did you know?"

Dickens could not resist a smile of triumph. "Murder by strangulation is a crime often associated with the sub-continent. I wondered if the murderer had learned his craft there. He might have been a past associate of Pettigrew's, but I also remembered that Elizabeth's lost brother spent time in India. And if John had by some miracle remained alive – that might explain Datchery's apparent familiarity with the town and his interest in Pettigrew's wife. As well as explaining why Clarissa, having met him secretly, tried to throw us off his scent."

"Dear Clarissa," the man whispered.

"As for your sister . . ."

Stevenson raised a trembling hand. "She must never know."

Within a few minutes Dickens had teased out the whole story. John had been a free mariner on the private vessels working the Indian Ocean, but one terrible day in the winter of 1828, shortly after arriving at the port of Bombay, he had been attacked by the bosun, who had conceived a deep dislike for him following an argument over a game of cards and had started drinking heavily the moment they reached dry land. A brawl ensued and, in falling to the ground, the man had cracked open his skull and died. Two of the bosun's cronies had accused John of starting the fight and, terrified that he might fall victim to summary justice, the young man fled into the back streets of the city. There he quickly discovered that, in order to survive, he had little choice but to become much more ruthless and dangerous than the cheerful, God-fearing young fellow that Elizabeth, twelve years his junior, had so admired. He became a creature of the shadows, coining the name Datchery as a mark of his decision to become a different man.

Stevenson said little of what he had done over the years, but gave Dickens to understand that the bosun was not the only man who had died at his hands. He had learned the technique of strangulation favoured by the murderous Thugs prior to their suppression. Twelve months earlier, he had finally worked his passage back to London. Whatever crimes he had committed, they were too serious for it to be possible for him, even after such a lapse of time, to dare to assert his true identity. When he learned, with much astonishment, of his sister's celebrity, it made him all the more determined not to bring dishonour upon her by revealing that he was still alive. Although Dickens protested fiercely, the old man was adamant. Elizabeth might have been heartbroken by his supposed demise, but at least she entertained nothing but good thoughts of him. He could not contemplate shattering her faith in his decency.

The privations of a misspent life meant that he fell sick with increasing frequency. On one occasion he collapsed in Covent Garden and a nurse had assisted him. He gathered from her that his heart was fading. A relapse might occur at any time, with fatal consequences.

Thus he had decided to make one last journey to the North. Not to see his sister, that was impossible, but someone whose memory he had cherished for more than thirty years. He had always worshipped Clarissa, but had been too shy to make his admiration known to her. Now it became a matter of obsession for him to look upon her one last time before he died.

After journeying north to Knutsford, he quickly discovered that the woman he had for so long adored was kept virtually as a prisoner in her own home by an avaricious and violent husband. A husband, moreover, of whom he had heard tell during his years in India. Pettigrew had, after a drinking bout, raped a servant girl. Although his superiors did their utmost to hush up the scandal, the story became well-known and Pettigrew was forced not only to leave the sub-continent but also to resign his commission. Stevenson resolved that he would at least do one last good thing in his life. He would free her from the brute.

It took a little while to pluck up the courage to talk to her. He kept watch on the house and eventually hit upon the idea of asking her to meet him. She had not kept the assignation behind the Lord Eldon on the day he sent her the message, but the next evening, terrified lest her absence be discovered by her husband, she dared to venture out. His faith in her innate bravery had been vindicated. Stevenson said that, once she had recovered from the shock of meeting a man she had believed was long dead, she had begged him not to do anything rash. But his mind was made up.

He had lured Pettigrew out of Canute Villa the previous evening by the simple expedient of a scrawled note saying *I know the truth about your time in India.* The stratagem succeeded. Stevenson had confronted his enemy, but on his account the Major lashed out at him. Illness had ravaged Stevenson's body, but the urge to save Clarissa had given him the strength to overcome Pettigew and slowly squeeze the life out of him.

"You must come forward," Dickens insisted. "An innocent man is under arrest for the crime. Besides that, your sister and Clarissa must know the truth!"

The ailing tramp shook his head. He had lost all his strength now and Dickens had to bend forward to catch what he said.

"No. You swore you would keep the secret, Mr Dickens. And you must."

"But . . ."

The old man raised a knobbly hand. "No. I shall not leave Knutsford, Mr Dickens, never fear. Soon they will find me here, dead, and in my coat they will discover . . . this."

He withdrew from inside his coat a thick, knotted cord.

"You see that stain? It is Pettigrew's blood, Mr Dickens, from when I pulled it so tightly around his throat . . ."

Suddenly he made a strange rasping noise and slumped to the ground, still clutching, at the moment of his death, the means of murder.

Dickens insisted that Elizabeth accompany him to Canute Villa the next morning. It was his impression that there was a faint touch of colour in the widow's cheeks. Her voice sounded stronger and her carriage seemed more erect.

"I hear that Bowden has been released from custody," she said. "I have already said to Alice that I am willing to take him back in service. I was distraught when my . . . my late husband gave him notice."

Elizabeth shook her head. "Is there any doubt that this tramp whose body was found on the Moor is the murderer?"

"None." Dickens held Clarissa's gaze. "It has been a dreadful business. And yet – perhaps some good has come of it."

Clarissa gave the slightest nod. There was a distant look in her eyes and Dickens was sure that she was thinking about the man who had loved her without acknowledgment, let alone hope, for so many years, and how he given her the most precious gift of all. Her freedom.

"How sad," Elizabeth said, "that a man should become so depraved that he should commit a mortal crime for no rational cause."

"Who knows what his reasons may have been, my dear Scheherezade?" Dickens said. "Clarissa has given him her forgiveness and so must we."

Elizabeth nodded. "Poor man. To die, unloved."

Dickens cast a glance at Clarissa and said, so softly that only she could hear, "Perhaps not unloved at the very end."

ROSEHIP SUMMER

Roz Southey

It was thirty years and more ago. I remember it as the hottest of years. The valley was ripe with summer; rowan berries flamed in the hedges, heather set fire to the mountain-sides. In the overgrown hedges on either side of the lanes, rosehips flared, inviting the children to go picking. Six pence a pound you could earn from the firm that made rosehip syrup and there was eager competition to collect the most.

All the children picked rosehips except me. I stayed in, because mam told me it would do me good to get out, and because Janey was so good at picking. From my room upstairs, illicitly using our dead father's binoculars, I could watch her striding across the fields, milk cans swinging; in front of her rabbits stiffened, then went bounding away.

Janey and me competed for who could annoy mam the most. We infuriated her by thwarting her prejudices; girls should look good, boys should be stoical. Janey hunted out odd socks and holed cardigans; I moaned and said the sun made me ill, or that my tummy felt queasy. Mam shouted, and the more she shouted, the more we taunted her. Janey was best and usually won, to my annoyance and her triumph. I felt she somehow had an unfair advantage, that she knew things I didn't, and wasn't letting on. I tried to get them out of her but couldn't. Janey never told me anything she didn't have to – we hated each other. But we hated mam more.

That was all right, because she hated us too. We reminded her too much of dad.

As Janey crossed the fields, she carried a huge walking stick. Fred Hudson, who saw her pass, said later he'd had a laugh –

she was so small that when she went behind the hedge, all he could see was the top of the walking stick, bobbing up and down. Only when she reached the gap in the hedge could he see her properly – a skinny child, over-burdened with the stick and with milk cans heavy with rosehips.

Annie Graham saw her maybe half an hour later; Janey was scrambling across a wall, sending a scatter of stones down to the ground. Annie came straight down to mam's to complain. "Bloody kids, breaking down the wall like that. What if the sheep get out? No sense, kids these days." Mam set her lips hard and waited till Annie was gone before screaming at me and sending me to my room. I went, both exultant and angry. Exultant because we'd infuriated mam again, annoyed because it was Janey who'd done it not me.

Halfway through the afternoon, the vicar spotted Janey crossing the field at the foot of the long fell. He was using his binoculars because he thought he'd spotted a hawk and when he swung the glasses round, he caught Janey jumping from tuft to tuft over the boggy ground.

"Aye," mam said. "And we all know what he was looking at, don't we?"

I was only hazily aware of what was so important about Janey's brown legs and the rucking up of her old skirt, but I knew mam was sneering at the vicar and I didn't like that. He was a nice man, full of sweets and titbits of information. And I never believed anything mam said about people anyway, not after the fibs she'd told about dad. And when he wasn't there to answer back too.

After the vicar saw Janey, she must have walked along the edge of the fell, working her way up the line of hedges near the old ruined farmhouse. Joe Edwards spotted her as he brought his sheep down from the fell; she was waiting to cross the track he was using. Both cans were full of rosehips by then; they looked heavy to Joe. "Need a cart to carry that lot," he joked. Janey stared at him blankly, he said afterwards.

At teatime, mam looked out of the back door of the farm-house, saw no sign of Janey, and swore. She slammed the teapot down on the table and starting buttering her bread with one of the ivory-handled knife-set that had been a wedding present.

The two of us sat silently over bread and jam. I'd been asking the vicar about dad's accident, but he wouldn't say anything except it was "very sad". Funny how everyone thinks that if they say nothing, children'll think there's nothing to say. I looked at mam, as her jaw worked over the bread. In a way I didn't want to know what had happened to dad; imagining was better. And imagining how to get back at mam for the accident was even better.

Alice Robinson, driving carefully around the lanes on her way home, saw Janey just after teatime. Janey was hesitating by a milk stand, staring at the solitary battered milk churn on it. Alice stopped to have a word. "Been lucky, have you?" she asked, nodding at the two heavy cans Janey had set by the roadside while she rested. Janey nodded indifferently.

"Bring you in a tidy sum of pocket money," Alice said.

Another nod. Alice waited a moment, could think of nothing more to say except to be careful Janey didn't get run over, and drove on home.

I saw Alice ten minutes later as she drove into her garage; she called out to say how well Janey was doing. I went down to the milk churn and peered into it. The cans were sitting inside, brim-full of rosehips; Janey must have left them there for safe keeping so no other kid could pinch them. I wanted to tip out all the hips onto the ground and trample on them, because otherwise Janey would get loads of money for them, and I'd have none. But then she was going to really annoy mam if she didn't come home before dark, so it was only fair she got some reward. Anyway I couldn't reach far enough inside the churn to get the cans.

Janey didn't come home. I kept making dark hints, like – she'd fallen down a rabbit hole, or twisted an ankle, or run away. All the worst things I knew how to imagine at the time. At midnight, Mam sent me to bed and called the police.

They found the rosehips in the milk churn – Alice told them about those – and pieced together Janey's trip from the witnesses, then they sent out the dogs. The farmers turned out and stomped the fields in stolid silence, and police cars were parked at every farm-track. I stayed at home and asked innocent questions. Did they think Janey was hurt? Did they think she had run away because of that argument with mam? The policemen exchanged glances, took me into the kitchen and offered me chocolate cake to tell them all about it. I told them every story I could think of, all the times mam had slapped Janey or me, or shouted at us. All true, all innocuous – and all capable of misinterpretation.

They found nothing. The dogs were called off and the police moved away to talk to people at railway stations and motorway cafes. I waited until they were all gone then, on the fourth day after Janey disappeared, I took an old milk can from the pantry, broke a stick off a tree and went out.

I'd heard enough of the talking to be able to reconstruct Janey's route and I walked it, throwing scarlet rosehips into my can as an excuse and looking for her body. I knew she must be dead. Janey would never have run away – not when she could spite mam more by staying at home. But I wanted to see her body, to be certain. After all, if Janey was dead, baiting mam was all up to me, wasn't it?

I found the body after a few hours. She'd gone into a wood, probably to get at a particularly heavily-laden rosebush; she must have tried to snag it with the hook of her stick then overbalanced. What she didn't know was that the bush over-hung an old quarry, used hundreds of years ago to build that ruined farmhouse. I spotted a broken branch, or thought I did, and parted the foliage to see the crumpled body below. God knows why the police dogs hadn't found her.

I looked long and hard so I'd not forget any detail of it, then I went home.

The police came back, to question mam again, and I told them she'd been so annoyed by their last visit she'd hit me and knocked me over. I had a scrape on my knee to prove it. I don't know whether they believed me, but they kept coming back.

They never found Janey, and after a while the whole thing was dropped. Except for the neighbours. Neighbours don't allow anything to drop. They kept nipping in to "make sure I was all right"; they'd murmur careless questions about Janey and mam, and I'd tell innocent stories which made them look significantly at each other. Mam got madder and madder, and I made her worse by musing aloud on what had happened to Janey. I've often wondered why she didn't hit me, but I suppose she didn't dare – the neighbours would have called the police at the first sign of bruises. Then she said she couldn't stand it any more so we went off to a town half a country away, where I got laughed at in school for my accent and added that to the list of things I hated mam for. That, and the day I came home and found she'd skipped out.

I had to go and live with a friend, which was all right, but I made sure they all knew how mam hated me. I said I looked just like my dad and hinted that there was something odd about his accident which there was. If only the vicar had told me, if only I'd had real evidence.

I hunted her down and bombarded her with pitiful letters pleading for her to come home. She kept moving. I kept finding her.

Then someone called to say that she was in hospital with cancer. I went to see her and found her surrounded by business-like nurses. I let drop the fact that my dad had been killed in a freak accident when I was two years old and told them that Janey had disappeared under mysterious circumstances, that she and mam had "never got on". On her last day, Mam tried to win the day by confiding her fear that one of the knives had gone missing the day Janey had disappeared. The nurse soothed her and murmured the word "delirious" but I was left with an odd sense of anti-climax. She even contrived to die when I was out of the room.

I've never really recovered from that feeling of dissatisfaction. Now mam's dead, I can't quite get interested in anything any more. I feel aimless. I wanted another glimpse of the old excitement Janey and I felt when we taunted mam. So I came back, thirty years to the day Janey died. I climbed the fell again, on a chill day that seemed to mock that long hot summer and found the wood, though the quarry was harder to discover. The trees had spread and covered the ruined farmhouse, clawing at its walls with thick roots; branches trailed across old paths. In the end, I stumbled into the quarry from below and crashed through shrubs and bushes to where I thought Janey must have fallen. A tangle of wild roses, just going over, marked the place; they must have sprung from the hips in her can when she fell.

The first thing I found was the can, crushed and half-buried in humus. Then a hint of bone – I drew my fingers through the soil and found the long outline of it. Then—

My fingers brushed something metal.

I dug into the chill soil, heart beating faster, wondering suddenly what I'd missed, all those years ago. Having a pre-monition of what it must be, knowing that I ought to have come down here to Janey's body, thirty years ago. I would have seen it then, sticking from her back, maybe.

A knife. An old, ivory-handled knife.

I remembered tea that day. Mam spreading blackcurrant jam on white bread with one of a set of knives. Wedding presents cast haphazardly into a drawer in a whole range of different sizes and shapes. One would not have been missed.

Sitting back on my haunches, I tried to reconstruct that afternoon. I'd been in my room doing homework and stopped to watch Janey from my window with dad's binoculars. I'd heard mam below in the kitchen. Hadn't I?

If only I'd kept watching Janey, instead of going back to my homework. If I'd watched all the time I might have seen mam. I might have seen her kill Janey. All those years, I'd been satisfied with hints and innuendos. And she must have been laughing all the time, knowing I could have had evidence, but didn't.

Crouching there, holding the dirt-encrusted knife in my hand, fuming at my impotence, I knew one thing.

Mam had won and there was nothing I could do about it.

ENTANGLEMENT

H. P. Tinker

. . . A series of unexplained deaths rippling across a city paralysed by overly-ambitious copycat serial killers, bi-curious junkies, homeless Santas . . . 197 exchange students killed in simultaneous unrelated coffee table incidents . . . a travelling salesman mutilated in his bed surrounded by obscene cuddly toys . . . art critics butchered amidst some of the countries most innovative new buildings . . . a motivational dog-trainer garrotted in her car by a 5-inch child's lariat . . . several hundred random business journalists killed by lethal injection . . . the city a vast amoral jungle of blue-haired gamblers and punk rock scholars . . . out on the Sheik-infested streets a thousand tragically sassy beauticians, Rembrandt scholars who don't like Rembrandt, religious activists sexually haranguing timid agnostics . . . the atmosphere of each day eerily in keeping with the vapid production values of the entire *Sussudio* period . . . Q surrounded by photographs, articles, graphs detailing these sly, wittily constructed deaths: dismembered ex-girlfriends, decapitated nuns, disembowelled cardiologists, violently violated violinists . . . Q pondering the dark methodologies at work, regularly raising both eyebrows simultaneously . . .

. . . unshaven in blue underpants, organic cotton, knitted stripes – no logo of any description – Q squinting at cold black newsprint, reading about the death of a former chess champion. Several witnesses saw him fall "almost cheerfully" – after straightening his bowtie, tossing himself from the roof of the building . . . an ever-increasing grin widening across his face . . . on impact he was "practically having sex up against a tree for five to ten seconds."

Q circles the paragraph in bright red ink.

In some advanced technological epoch – Q thinks to himself – perhaps people will wonder why we bothered to circle such articles in bright red ink. Q filing away the latest of the latest unexpected demises . . . *a light-bulb salesman ripped apart by a gaggle of lions . . . renegade schoolgirls exploding into young pieces, their charred remains evenly distributed across the piazza . . .*

". . . my files cannot possibly take the strain of this increasingly worrying information," realizes Q. "Soon I'll be requiring an all-new filing system . . ."

. . . cryptic messages arriving – from disparate loners: infertile child psychologists, lunatic travel agents, broken down house-wives, fairly lethal sounding Hispanic 52-year olds . . . the latest: Mrs A, a glamorous cripple in a dark suit, pale tie, gold shoes, legs splayed about a mile wide: "I must interject into your investigation in my customized wheelchair," she states earnestly, like Kate Bush. "My husband is listed as missing in the places where they list such things – and that's a distressing state for any husband to be in . . ."

". . . regarding your husband—"

A: "I fear he's gone, forever into the overbearing darkness, more overbearing darkness than I had personally bargained for. Having dreamed all my life of romantic trajectories, I now find myself in a full-length narrative of angry policemen, would-be assassins, pre-teen suicide bombers, nothing remotely romantic about it—"

Q: "The rediscovery of a missing husband rarely represents an enormous cause for celebration . . . but if you have any supplementary information that might shed light on your husband's disappearance . . ."

A: "Well, there is one thing – probably not important . . ."

Q: "No, please tell me. Even the smallest grain might prove central . . ."

A: "Well, people do say he bears an unnatural resemblance to Kris Kristofferson . . ."

*   *   *

. . . into his Dictaphone: "– as events turn ever more torrid, I am proud that I have not betrayed myself, not once – well, maybe once – but never twice and, in a corrupt and immoral age where inconsequential dialogue has become the order of the day, that seems important . . ."

. . . Q waking, the smell of maple syrup thick in both nostrils. In a city of foetid fragrances, the mysteriously saccharine odour rapidly hits local radio. One listener describes the smell as "oddly flavoured coffee", another: "rather like maple syrup". A well-spoken spokesperson from the Office of Emergency Aromas asserts: "We are fairly confident that the odour is no way dangerous and that citizens of the city can continue with their usual patterns of early morning business and communication . . ."

Stepping outside, a gigantic billboard overhead reads: ". . . *THERE ARE SOME PEOPLE WHO WILL NOT FULLY COOPERATE HERE* . . ."

. . . an unexpected sight greeting Q along the angular carpeting scheme of Mrs A's apartment: an arm reaching outwards, two fingers raised like a gesture, or sign – or salute; or symbol. Mrs A impaled on the far wall by several metal hooks. Dark scuffs on the linoleum resembling less of a struggle, more a dance of death, possibly the Foxtrot. *Why were murdered women often tortured and mutilated horribly in this fashion?* asks Q. *As if simple murder wasn't enough for them? Was the secret cousin of some rich and powerful people involved? Who else would be up to the task of nailing somebody's wife to a wall with so much obvious enthusiasm?* Recent events unusually frozen on the face of Mrs A in the form of a happy expression . . . *but* – given the circumstances – *was there really anything to be quite so happy about?* Q taking samples of her nightwear away – for special analysis – under his jacket . . .

". . . even previously thick-skinned police sniffer dogs have taken to contemplating their own mortality," Q notes, alone in his office with cheap bourbon, sour conclusions, false assumptions, vague deductions, a Dictaphone, some even cheaper bourbon . . . the telephone spluttering in the ever-dimming dimness. Q picking up, as is his custom. A voice answering like a deceased banker dredged hissing from a lake, some time last May. "When an unhappily married woman is unexpectedly crucified," advises the voice, "her husband is generally called in for questioning . . ."

. . . on a hunch, Q tracing the husband of Mrs A to the Northern fringes of the Latino-Disco Crossover Quarter, where he is rumoured to be professionally dancing the *paso doble* under an assumed initial: "O". A largely colourful room crowded with the contours of humans; in the centre about thirty middle-aged bisexuals thrashing out symbolic acts of dance. Dubious dress codes at work: purple sequinned shirts, casual khaki slacks, Manhattan sandals . . . an unusual man bearing a passing resemblance to Kris Kristofferson in a lime-green rental tuxedo . . . a slim white cane sweeping in front of him, left to right, right to left, like the feelers of an insect socialite.

Q doubts the veracity of this disability, almost immediately . . .

". . . did you ever dance the *paso doble* with Mrs A?"
Silence.
"Did you ever dance the *paso doble* with Mrs A and then not contact Mrs A for some time afterwards?"
Silence.
"Do you still dance the *paso doble* nowadays . . . *with other people?*"
"O" smiles diffidently, the expression of idyllic contentment written across his face: "Sometimes," "O" admits, "I feel like a dead man. But I've made my choice. I have a certain life and I like my new way of thinking. I'm happier where I am today. I remain fairly confident of that . . ."

. . . unperturbed, Q puts on his hat . . . only when he looks down the hat isn't there anymore. Instead, in the place where the hat should be: no hat, a reduction in hat-based circumstance. Out in the street, noticing almost everybody seems to be wearing hats, wide-brimmed fedoras mostly, noting how hats are central to maintaining confidence during daytime detective work in the street.

As a consequence, Q feels hatless and alone . . .

. . . the corridor adjacent to his office: an incredibly angry looking young woman in a rhinestone kilt leaning heavily against an instant coke machine. Q wondering: *what is the source of the young woman's incredible anger? Were her parents incredibly angry throughout her formative youth? Does she have an incredibly angry young husband at home? Are her clothes incredibly angry clothes? What is the significance of the incredible anger of the incredibly angry looking young woman? What is the incredibly angry looking young woman* <u>*really*</u> *so incredibly angry about?*

"You are investigating these crimes not from compassion but from intellectual avarice," she tells him – incredibly angrily. "That may sound totally asinine – but that's never stopped me before . . ."

The incredibly angry looking young woman then invites Q to supper at her brownstone townhouse. Having already slept with more than five hundred young women during his investigations, Q welcomes this latest development . . .

". . . you can disappear in this city," explains Q. "Its belly is death . . . you can become entangled in the everyday nuisances here, ensnaring you like a pop career you never even wanted."

"That's why this city needs you," she snaps. "Some people don't realize it yet. Others, however, are only too keenly aware . . ."

". . . but" – Q flounders – "my masculinity appears to have become badly eroded, over time, to the point where I am starting to feel like I'm trapped inside a bad Phil Collins song . . ."

"How can you say that!?" she shrieks. "That implies there are *good* Phil Collins songs, which, as we both know, there are not . . ."

. . . down in the square, a travelling carnival in residence: a procession of bearded ladies, Siamese triplets, marching penguins, fire eating gypsies, alcoholic strong men belittled by self-

doubt . . . under the shadow of the big wheel, two men appearing like plain-clothed policemen, lingering across the street like
plain-clothed policemen, blending in with their environment
like plain-clothed policemen, smartly dressed in homburgs like
plain-clothed policemen – Q suddenly suspecting that these
men . . . *might* . . . *actually* . . . *be* . . . *plain-clothed* . . . *policemen* . . . as if to confirm the hypothesis, grabbed from behind by
thick-set arms – thrust into a wall, gun pushed into the nape of
the back.

"We have certain questions," they say together, nonchalantly
waggling a subpoena. "Questions of a certain nature. Concerning a certain matter. Although we are not authorized to release
any further information at the present time."

There is no struggle. Q not being guilty of anything, – other
than a cheap haircut and a sexual trajectory that had roused
latent curiosities, perhaps – no need for a struggle. "I am not the
person who crucified Mrs A," Q informs them, forearms
wrapped around his head . . .

. . . beneath the ethereal lighting of the interrogation room, Q
continues: "People are happily killing each other, cheerfully
maiming themselves. And I am genuinely fearful for this city
and any future implications for its general populous. Death
is being interwoven, intimately connected on some level I
don't understand. My findings have surprised me on many
levels. I never knew there were so many deaths of a suspiciously
transvestite-based nature, for instance . . ."

Chief Inspector S bends forward, removes the gilt-edged
silver coffee spoon from his mouth with a confounded sigh and
guffaws through a quick-fire series of shuddering jowls and
crumpled face-skin: "So what is it you are trying to tell me
exactly?" he says, voice incredibly loud, expression extremely
close up.

"People are dying," Q tells him. "Some are vanishing.
Others are being co-opted by the ghosts of the formerly
living."

"Who are these people exactly?"

"I don't know."

"Where are these people now?"

"I don't know that either . . . but their lives form part of the wider investigation."

"And how wide has this investigation got?"

"At least twice as wide as it is long."

Droopy-eyed and sanguine, Chief Inspector S appears to be wearing a white turtleneck pullover and gold chinos, a prize Smith & Wesson half-cocked down the front of his pants like an utterly meaningful trophy. On his feet: a pair of tartan espadrilles tapping enigmatically to a soundtrack of smoothly-syncopated swing standards recreated by an authentic orchestra of recognized legal experts . . .

"Have you managed to reach any firm conclusions yet?" Chief Inspector S asks.

"Absolutely none," Q confesses, "of any firmness whatsoever . . ."

. . . more deaths . . .

Frozen motorcylists. Electrocuted clergymen. Castrated hoteliers. Barbecued spouses. Casually skinned multi-storey car park attendants . . . Q occupying chairs, manipulating desktop toys, looking at women adjust themselves through digital binoculars – from high vantage points . . . slouching in gay revue bars, starting to feel like James Stewart at the end of *Harvey* . . . encountering an unusually tall man in heavy-rimmed sunglasses and yellow rubber gloves – in a gay revue bar – who tells him: "Come with me and you will find the answers you seek . . ." before sprinting unhelpfully in the opposite direction. Following a high-speed jog through the futuristic ruins of the city, Q tails the unusually tall man in heavy-rimmed sunglasses and yellow rubber gloves to a back street, down a side alley, through a sliding door, up dark creaking steps, into the grubby hallway of a communal spa which – Q guesses – is probably funded by an anonymous pervert millionaire for his own private purposes: the enjoyment of watching strangers conduct themselves nakedly, in private, via a two-way mirror system . . .

. . . behind the reception desk: a young Asian woman with the high-browed demeanour of Virginia Woolf, wearing a tartan turban.

"*Who are you?*" she demands in a refined voice, rich and plummy with strong overtones of Merlot. "You don't belong here. *What could you possibly want?*"

"Well," Q explains, "entanglement is weaving a path through time, very strongly, rather like an incendiary device . . . I do have some graphs and charts and other illustrative material to demonstrate this point . . . but outside of the investigation, my life is an empty canvas minus myself and prior to this I was desperate, down-on-my-luck, back against the wall, hand to mouth, mouth to hand, always questioning myself: *what am I saying? who am I? what is my destiny? why won't she answer my calls? has she rekindled her relationship with a former saxophonist?* because in essence, you see, I have been sucked into a vortex by all the beautiful absences in my own life, so many beautiful absences I couldn't possibly list them all, well, maybe I could, but it would take a very long time . . ."

– only partway into one of the longest sentences he had ever attempted, Q notices the young Asian woman striking her turban violently against the hard, glossy edges of the reception desk. She pauses momentarily, gazes around, forehead glistening purple. Realizing she is still conscious, she repeats the action until almost completely concussed . . .

. . . in the steam of the communal spa, the unusually tall man in heavy-rimmed sunglasses and yellow rubber gloves reclines on a long pinewood bench: naked except for a trilby hat now, his body improbably misshapen. The man signals with expansive homosexual mannerisms towards a half-raised portcullis framed by two portable cannons. Inside the gates: a stone-cold cold stone room, malevolent scarlet wallpaper, the smell of tepid piss, the ambience carcinogenic. Volumes of unread books line every wall, a dark archive of unremittingly obscure easy reading tomes. Over a grand piano, the vast imprint of a swastika, surrounded by a series of portraits, minor Scottish poets lounging indignantly in the semi-nude . . .

. . . suddenly: the fearful drone of traditional bagpipe music . . . 12 figures dressed as Judas Iscariot expressing a slight feeling of bewilderment via a Highland jig . . . behind them, a gnomic man in sparkling jackboots and the habit of a nun. From inside his habit an epic pause ensues. Lowering the hood he reveals: the over-sized head of Princess Margaret. On her face a severe expression. Q having seen a similar expression on the faces of several other people lately. Friends. Family. Lovers. Lawyers. Paramedics. Magistrates.

There's another pause, not quite as epic as the last . . .

"*My name is Herr Schmaltz!*" cries Herr Schmaltz, visibly demented. "*I have recently undergone a complete face transplant and – during the same procedure – had my colon medically revised. However, originally I came from Newark, New Jersey, where I trained to be a violist. But when I moved to Leipzig and became the world's smallest basketball player, they accused me of decapitating my nephew during a violent sex call . . . then proceeded to arrest me for something I didn't do . . . then questioned me about my relationship with a comatose futures trader . . . then offered me cocaine, an incredible pay rise, and a part-time shot at redemption in the Scottish hills . . . I quickly became very Scottish and having a head for business I quickly became a millionaire too . . . now, having returned in partial disguise, I shall awaken dormant memories of love and crime and death . . . and nobody shall penetrate the heart of my dark secret . . .*"

. . . dialing the emergency services at the bottom of the fire escape, Q briefly ponders the significance of the incident . . .

. . . that evening, staring down at his manual typewriter, drinking camomile tea. In front of Q: a blank page. Six months later, the same blank page still in front of him, an empty teacup in his hand . . . the telephone spluttering in the ever-dimming dimness. Q picking up, as is his custom. A voice answering like a diseased hooker from a recent weekend in Amsterdam. "If it looks like a duck and talks like a duck and walks like a duck," the voice advises. "Then, in all honesty: it probably is a duck . . ."

Q considers the words carefully, one by one, their residual meaning lingering in the upper reaches of the ceiling for several minutes afterwards . . .

THE MUMMY

Peter Turnbull

Wednesday

The body was found in the shrubs, next to the towpath, beside the York to Hull canal, out in the country, beyond the suburbs where the landscape is flat, and that year, courtesy of a rainy summer, the foliage was lush, lush enough to partially conceal a human corpse. The body in question was wrapped in a heavy-duty plastic sheeting like a rolled-up carpet and had been laid by the canal side, in long grass. It was found by a jogger. He had noticed it rather than found it. It had first caught his eye on the Saturday as he ran past. It was still there on the Sunday, when families walked the towpath. It was there on the Monday and still there on the Tuesday morning. But on the Tuesday evening the man, the jogger, found his thoughts turning on the length of rubber sheeting. It nagged him with a growing realization that the item in question was just the right length and width to be the grossest form of fly-tipping. The realization stayed with him, hovering in his mind like an annoying fly which by its noise took up a disproportionate amount of space. So that on the Wednesday he set out on his normal morning run taking with him a pair of gloves and ran until he reached the spot where the roll of plastic lay, slowed to a walk, and finally stood over it, and waited until another jogger going in the opposite direction had passed by. It had not been moved or disturbed in any way since he had first seen it: It was clearly his fate to find out if it contained what he feared it contained. The plastic was old, stiff, fragile to the touch. He took the edge of the roll and peeled it back.

He saw a hand. Human. Male, he thought.

He replaced the plastic, slowly, reverentially, and carried on jogging. There was a phone box on his route, and it was the closest phone to that stretch of the canal that he knew. He ran at a steady pace, until he reached the phone box. The box was occupied by a middle-aged lady, chatting excitedly, and the jogger sat on a dry stone wall until the occupant had finished talking, whereupon she replaced the phone and exited the box, holding the door open for him, saying she was sorry and hoped his call wasn't urgent.

"No urgency at all," replied the jogger. "No urgency at all."

But he made it a three nines call nonetheless.

The towpath was cordoned off with blue-and-white tape, white-shirted constables politely but firmly turned back the joggers, the strolling, the anglers, and the just plain curious. The plastic, once unravelled, revealed the body of a small, finely made middle-aged man, the sort of man who in life would attract nicknames such as Shorty or Half-pint. He was dressed in a heavy winter jacket, heavy woollen trousers, and winter shoes. Yet he looked as though he had died only recently.

Detective Inspector Hennessey stood over the body, pondering it with a police officer's eye for detail. Doctor Louise D'Acre knelt by the body, pondering it with a pathologist's eye, but also searching for detail. Detail of a different sort. Hennessey sought details to answer his question "Who?" Dr D'Acre sought details to answer her questions "Why?" and "What cause?"

"It's the first time I've ever seen it." Dr D'Acre stood. She was a slender woman in her late forties, short cropped hair, just a trace of lipstick, a woman who was growing old gracefully. She turned to Hennessey. Their eyes met, briefly, knowingly, then she turned her head away.

"It?" There was a note of warmth in his voice.

"Mummification." D'Acre looked down at the body. "I've read about it, of course. I'm familiar with it, theoretically speaking, but I've never come across it . . ."

"In the flesh?"

"I was trying to avoid using that phrase. But yes, this is the first time I have met mummification. But now I can cross it off my 'things to do' list. Explaining the warm clothing . . . the height of summer. He could have been dead for years."

"Years?"

"Mummification. No decomposition of the flesh or the features, but inside he'll be hollow. He'll be very light to carry. It means that immediately upon death he was placed in an airtight place. No insects to eat up the lovely juicy flesh. The flesh itself became as parchment and as such was of little interest to present-day – this time, this day – insects. But decomposition is beginning, a much slower rate than if he was fresh, but the sooner we get him to York City, the better."

"So he was placed in an airtight room . . ."

"Or container."

"Or container, possibly for years, and then for some reason removed a few days ago and left in a very exposed place. Why?"

"Well that, Inspector, is definitely your department. I, for my part, have to address the question of how? How did he meet his end, before his time?"

"Amstrad" was a Persian. His true given name was obscure even in his native land, which he claimed was and always would be Persia – he having left before, and distancing himself from, the Ayatollah's rule. In the United Kingdom, the closest his British colleagues came to the accurate pronunciation of his name was that of a British electronics company. So Amstrad he was, though he occasionally remarked that no one, not even his darling English rose of a wife, could pronounce his name like his dear mother had once pronounced it; but he bore the mispronunciation with patience, tolerance, and good humour. He was a diligent man and was so on the day he carefully extracted the garments from their sealed cellophane wrapper, and laid them one by one, side by side, on the surface of the bench, his bench, in Her Majesty's Forensic Science Laboratory, Wetherby, West Yorkshire. There were undergarments, of the thermal variety, so-called "long johns", two pairs of socks, a pair of heavy walking shoes, thick woollen trousers, a thick shirt, a pullover, a heavy jacket, fleece lined, all of the size that would fit a small man, or a growing boy. Amstrad Baft was a small man too, but larger than had been the owner of these garments. Bespectacled and white-coated, he began a minute square-inch by square-inch survey, trawling for clues, anything, anything at all which would indicate the recent history of the clothing, or perhaps the cause of death of the wearer.

Finding nothing of note from the normal-vision examination, he made a search of the pockets. All were empty, except the right-hand pocket of the jacket. It contained a till receipt from the Co-op supermarket in the centre of York, timed at 18:06 hours on the 15th day of January – eight years earlier. A man would not keep a till receipt in his jacket pocket for eight years, but it would, reasoned Amstrad Baft, be the sort of thing that wouldn't be noticed if someone else was rifling through the pockets. He placed the receipt in a cellophane sachet and then began to examine the fibres of the clothes under the electron microscope.

Thursday

On the Thursday morning, Chief Inspector Hennessey took two telephone calls which were relevant to the inquiry into the death of "the mummy", as he had privately come to think of the man found by the canal. The first was from Dr A. Baft of the Forensic Science Laboratory at Wetherby, who gave his first name as something which to Hennessey's ears sounded like "Amstrad", but he was unsure and so addressed the caller as "Dr Baft", as indeed he would have done anyway. Dr Baft informed him that the clothing was clean and of high quality, indicating a man of substance, though perhaps short of stature. The clothing seemed old, of earlier fashion, but had not deteriorated, and Dr Baft advanced that it had been preserved in some way.

"Dr D'Acre, the forensic pathologist, believes the corpse to have been mummified in some way." Hennessey glanced at the word "substance" on his notepad, circled it, and wrote "money motive?" beside it.

"That would explain the preserved clothing," Dr Baft said. "I also came across a till receipt."

"Oh?"

"Yes, in the pocket of the jacket, just where a fella would put a receipt at eighteen-oh-six hours on the fifteenth of January eight years ago. He went to the Co-op in York and bought foodstuffs. He paid with a ten-pound note and got two pounds, fifty-three pence in change. He bought vegetables, some tinned stuff, four pints of milk, and a pizza, a frozen pizza . . . and a packet of tea bags."

"A bachelor?"

"You think so?"

"Living alone, anyway, one frozen pizza is a single person's purchase."

"I suppose it is, come to think of it. That's a police officer's brain working, I would never have thought of that."

"If indeed the receipt is his, but who carries other folks' till receipts around in their pockets? It was probably the last purchase of his life. Four pints of milk, a large packet of tea bags, he was stocking up. He didn't expect to die."

"Again, a police officer's brain."

"Too long in the job, Dr Baft."

And the two men smiled at each other down the phone. It was the first time they had spoken to each other, and a mutual liking grew rapidly.

"The year," Dr Baft said "that was the year my daughter was born, she was born in May, but I remember taking my wife to antenatal clinics in dreadful weather. That was the year of that bad winter. I despaired of it going, I thought the next ice age had arrived, didn't let up until mid April."

"I remember, who could forget? My dog loved it, though. Like all dogs he suffers in the heat."

"There was nothing else in the pockets. No wallet, no loose change, no letters, no utility bill, nothing, as if someone had rifled his pockets, but hadn't found or hadn't bothered with the till receipt."

"Which, in the end, told us much."

"It appears. I've had a glance at the plastic sheeting, found nothing, but I'll give it a closer examination this P.M."

"Appreciated."

The second phone call in respect of "the mummy" came from Dr Louise D'Acre.

"A single massive blow to the skull." Louise D'Acre spoke matter-of-factly. "No other injuries, no trace of poison. He once wore a wedding ring, but had taken it off. Its 'shadow' was on his ring finger."

"Ah . . ."

"Is that significant?"

"Answers a question. We found a till receipt in his pocket; the indication of the purchases was that he was a bachelor. It now seems he may be a divorce. But a man who lived alone anyway."

"He was a man in his mid forties. Forty-four, -five, or -six. I took a tooth from the upper set of teeth, cut it in half. Gave me an age of forty-five, and that test asks that a margin of twelve months on either side be allowed."

Hennessey wrote "45 ± 12/12" on his pad. "He took good care of his teeth, British dentistry, so there'll be dental records to check once you have a possible name for him."

"Always useful to confirm on ID."

"Returning to the injury. It's a concentrated impact point, from which the skull fractures radiate outwards, like spokes from a hub. A hammer blow, or a brick . . . something like that. But not a long object, like a golf club, that would have caused a linear fracture."

Hennessey replaced the phone. He glanced out his office window at tourists walking the medieval walls beneath the vast blue sky. He glanced at the clock on the wall, above the police mutual calendar. Midday. Time for lunch. Like the citizens of York, Hennessey knew the quickest way to walk the city is to walk the walls, rather than the street-level pavements, and so he signed out and walked the wall from Micklegate Bar to Lendal Bridge, and thence to Lendal, and the fish restaurant.

The file on "the mummy" case grew. Hennessey now knew the man to have been murdered by being struck with a hammer, or similar object or instrument. He knew that in life the deceased had been wealthy, for he wore not the clothing of a poor man. He knew that the deceased probably lived alone, and most significantly he knew the deceased had been murdered shortly after six P.M. on the 15th day of January, eight years earlier. The man was clean-shaven and very short of stature. And his dentistry work was British. All added together, Hennessey knew it would be enough for the missing persons bureau to suggest a name. He picked up the phone on his desk, pressed a four-figure internal number, and when his call was answered he said, "Collator?"

"Yes, sir."

"Hennessey here."

"Sir."

Then Hennessey gave all the details he had on the deceased, adding, "not necessarily local."

"I see, sir." The collator was eager, anxious to please. "I'll come back asap," which the collator pronounced "aysap," to Hennessey's irritation, but the world was changing, he was closing down fast upon his retirement, and it was the small things which crept up on him from time to time, and reminded him he wasn't changing with the world. In his day, he would have returned "a.s.a.p." or "as soon as." But "aysap" . . . he sighed as he put the phone down. He cared not for "aysap", no matter how efficient was the youthful collator. He rose and went to the corner of his office and switched on the electric kettle and observed Micklegate Bar as he waited for the kettle to boil, the open-topped double-deckers, the people of the town hurrying, the tourists ambling. He returned to his desk carrying a mug of coffee.

The collator was efficient, so efficient that he returned "aysap" before Hennessey's mug of coffee had cooled sufficiently to allow it to be consumed. Tony Watch, the collator informed him, had been reported missing by his sister on the 16th of January eight years earlier. Physical description matched; he was wealthy because of an information technology company he had formed, and was recently separated at the time he went missing. His home address was out near Selby; his sister, the reportee, lived "on the other side of the planet", in Holgate. Hennessey thanked the collator and replaced the phone. He left his office and walked down the corridor to the office of the younger, life-all-ahead-of-him Sergeant Yellich, and tapped on the doorframe of his office doorway. "Grab your sun hat, Yellich, we're off to sunny Holgate."

"We are, sir?" Yellich stood.
"We are, sir."

Holgate is that part of the Faymous and Faire Citie of Yorke ye tourists never see. It is black-terraced houses in rows, beyond the railway line, where washing hangs from lines suspended across the street. Hennessey and Yellich went to St Pancras' Wynd, to number 57, being the given address of Mrs Torr, who eight years earlier had reported her brother to the police as a missing person.

"Never did like her." Mrs Torr was a frail woman who looked older than her sixty-three years, as if stricken by an internal growth. "I grew up in these streets, so did Tony, well, he would – he was my little brother. Our dad worked on the railway in the steam days, you could smell the smoke from the railway station in these streets. I'd lay awake at night and listen to the chuff and clank of the steam trains. Now they whirr past on continuous rails with hardly a sound by comparison. Such a safe, solid sound the old steam trains used to make, I really miss the sound, but then I'm a lass, I never had to get up at three A.M. and fire one so it would be ready for eight A.M. That's how long it took to fire one from cold, and that was a small one."

"Your brother . . .?" Hennessey saw the old lady's need to reminisce, especially because of her apparent medical conditions, but he had a job to do.

"Aye, Tony. He did well for himself. Those machines, I never understood them, but they came in so quickly. Ten years between me and Tony, just ten years, but I was too old for them, he was just right. Got himself out of Holgate all right. Me, I married a lad from the next street who worked on buses, and didn't get out. But Jack was a good man. I had two children and I've got six grandchildren. So I had my wealth in other ways. So Tony's body has been found, you say?"

"We think it is his body. The description fits. There's indications that fit with the time you reported him missing."

"I reported him murdered. Missing! I reported him murdered. But would they listen? I had to make a 'misper' report. That's what they called my little brother, a 'misper' report, not even a 'missing person', but a 'misper'."

"Why did you believe him to have been murdered, Mrs Torr?"

"Well, that cow, that calculating cow he married of course. She was one scheming female. Still is. Still in that house, Tony's lovely old house he worked so hard to pay for, now she's got it. He's dead and she's got it. He took her off the streets, gave her a house. He was forty-four, she was twenty-five. I warned him. I could see her for what she was, a woman can see another woman for what she is, a man can't, not always, anyway. My waters told she was bad for Tony. But would he listen? He was in his forties, born premature, and was small, never a success with the girls. He was known as Pocket Watch at school, Tony Watch the Pocket Watch . . . but he became a computer geek and made a fortune . . . and then the blond bombshell who's young enough to be his daughter drops in his lap . . . he couldn't believe his luck. 'Worth waiting for' was his attitude. Then just six weeks, I mean six weeks into the marriage, he came round here, devastated. Heard her on the phone . . . talking to a girlfriend. . . . She said, 'I've only got to stick it for six months, then I get half the house.' What she was saying was that if she separates after six months, she'll get half the house as part of the divorce settlement. Tony would have to sell it, give her half the proceeds."

"It's not that simple."

"She didn't know that. But the point was, Tony knew why she had married him. If it was a marriage." Mrs Torr looked at the summer-empty hearth and then the mantelpiece on which stood a framed photograph of a young couple, arms round each other. "Not like my marriage. I had a marriage. A proper marriage. But Tony was clever, wouldn't agree to a divorce, wouldn't give her grounds. By then she'd seen a lawyer, I think, and the lawyer told her it doesn't matter what her mates tell her, she wouldn't get her hands on half the property quite so easily. It was then that she moved out, left him. But they were still married. Tony got frightened then. Feared she would 'do something'."

"Do something?"

"He feared for his life. Took to phoning me each day, then one day he became a 'misper', except I knew my little brother was dead. After two years he was presumed dead, so she, as his wife, got everything. She didn't get half the house, she found a way of getting it all. Each Christmas she sends me a card with a smiley face on the inside."

Hennessey and Yellich both thought Mrs Torr's description of her late brother's house as being "lovely, old" was apt. It was eighteenth century, graceful, balanced lines, the type of house which had given way to the Victorian Gothic style. It stood in landscaped grounds and was ivy-clad. A rabbit hopped across the lawn, doves cooed in a dovecote beside the house, a black-bird sang.

Mrs Watch, when she was met, was a woman with cold eyes. Tall, slender, all in proportion, but moved like a woman with considerable physical strength. A rapid piece of mental arith-metic by both officers put her age at thirty-three. She did indeed look about that age, having reached that age with a life blessedly free of arthritis-inducing drudgery or figure-ruining multiple pregnancies. Her clothes were sombre in a tasteful and expensive sort of way, but by far the most striking feature of her appearance was her jewellery, not her taste but her love, nay need of it: earrings; long necklaces; heavy, multiple bracelets; also heavy, multiple rings, too many to count; ankle chains on both ankles. She "received" the officers in the drawing room, after they'd been shown in by the muscular youth with timid eyes who had answered the door.

"My husband?" She had a hard voice. "He disappeared. He disappeared eight years ago. Presumed dead six years ago."

"Well, he's now reappeared. At least, his corpse has."

The woman threw an angry glance at the youth who looked sheepishly away despite his well-toned bulk, hidden only by T-shirt and shorts and training shoes.

Hennessey saw the glance, as did Yellich. No police officer would have missed it. Both officers knew that this case was about to crack wide open.

"You may have seen the TV reports . . . the body on the canal towpath?"

A second angry glance at the youth, who was, it appeared, no more than eighteen or nineteen years of age. Hennessey wondered if he called Mrs Watch "Mummy." It seemed that sort of relationship.

"When did you last see your husband, Mrs Watch?"

"When I walked out on him. We had a row. I left him. He lived here in this huge house all by his little self for a while. Then he disappeared one night. During the bad winter."

"What did you row about?"

"Can't remember."

"You can't? Your last row and you can't remember what it was about?" Hennessey had been married. His wife had died young of natural causes, so natural not even the medics knew what had caused it and offered only "sudden death syndrome", which seemed embarrassingly inadequate to explain why a twenty-three-year-old woman of perfect health could suddenly collapse in the street as if in a faint, but in fact in death, probably before her head met the pavement. George and Jennifer Hennessey had had one row, it had taken place thirty years earlier, and he could recall it word for word. It had been about whether to have a pond in the garden or not. He had capitulated but wasn't able to dig the pond until two years after he had scattered her ashes in the garden, where he still went to talk to her each day, rain or shine.

"I can't. Something silly, like all rows, but it was the end. I left him then."

"No matter. The body on the towpath. It had mummified. It had been kept in airless conditions for eight years. Where? Would you know?"

"No."

Hennessey turned to the youth. "Do you know?"

"No . . ." He glanced at the woman and shook his head vigorously. He looked nervous. He had something to hide.

"Eight years ago, you were how old, son?"

"Eleven."

"Got your life ahead of you, haven't you? Pity to throw it away on a murder charge."

"I didn't murder him."

"I'm sure you didn't, but if you had anything to do with the remains, the body, and placing it on the towpath, you can be charged with conspiracy to murder. Even eight years after the event, when at the time you were in short trousers learning algebra."

"And it could carry a life sentence," Yellich added.

The youth paled.

"Got a name, lad?"

"Kevin."

"Kevin what?"

"O'Reilly."

"All right Kevin, you're coming with us." Hennessey saw that there'd be no confession from Mrs Watch. After eight years, forensic evidence would be difficult to prove.

"Is he under arrest?" Mrs Watch flushed with anger.

"No, he's coming of his own volition, aren't you, Kevin?"

Kevin O'Reilly pulled nervously on the cigarette.

"Didn't think we'd get much out of you with madam the queen there." Hennessey smiled as he handed O'Reilly a white plastic beaker full of piping-hot coffee. "Believe me, you've got more to fear from her than you do from us. We, Sergeant Yellich here and me, we've been doing this for a long time. You've got guilt written all over your face, you're shaking like a leaf. You're in over your head, aren't you?"

Kevin O'Reilly nodded.

"Known her long?"

"About six months. We met at the gym."

"The gym?"

"She works out, desperate to keep her figure. She invited me home. It went from there. She made all the running . . . I was . . . I mean, I'd never . . ."

"All right, Kevin."

"Do I need a lawyer?"

"If you want one. But this is still off the record."

"Did you mean what you said about a life sentence?" O'Reilly looked at Yellich.

"Oh, yes. Technically it's possible. Unlikely, but possible. But you'll collect a good seven or eight years, minimum."

"I couldn't handle prison."

"I know you can't, Kevin. Big strong lad, but you're a little boy inside. I can see that."

"There's only one way you can avoid the gaol, Kevin."

"There is, isn't there?" He looked round the interview room, dark, spartan. "I moved the body, I left it where it was found."

"Alone?"

"She drove the car. I told her I'd put it in the canal and it had sunk. She told me to do that, but I panicked. Just dropped it on the canal side."

"Where was the body kept?"

"In the cellar. There's a little alcove. She put the body in there, and then bricked it up. She has to sell the house, you see. She sold his business, lived off the proceeds for six years – holidays, clothes, jewellery. Mainly jewellery. You'll need a van to shift all her jewellery, she's got a room put aside just for the jewels. But the money's dried up so she's got to sell to raise money to live, move to a smaller house. 'Trading down,' she said. Anyway, couldn't sell the house with a body in the cellar. Now I think she picked me up in the gym for that job and that job alone. But she could have done it herself, there was no weight in him at all."

"Did she tell you she had killed him?"

"Not in so many words, but it all points that way."

"Does, doesn't it?"

"I've helped myself?"

"Hugely. You may even escape prosecution for this information." Hennessey smiled reassuringly. "All right, let's get this down in the form of a statement, then we'll get back and have a chat with Mrs Watch."

NORA B.

Ken Bruen

She had a mouth on her.
  Jesus, like a fishwife.
And mean with it?
You fooking kiddin?
She'd slice your skin off with three words.
I was a cop, out of the Three Seven in those days.
Man, we'd do the night shift
Give me
Your scumbags
Your dopers
Your skels
Your preds
The zombies
Had 'em all and twice over.
  They came out of the fucking sewers, menacing, feral and lethal
  And lemme tell you, we were ready for em
. . . . no fucking innocents there.
  We had a stone simple rule.
  Fuck 'em first.
  We did.
  Always.
  Our Sarge, half wop, half Mick and deadly, he'd go,
  "Bring em down, fast, don't let em ever . . . .
and I mean fucking ever, get up, got that?"
  We did.
  Did we fucking ever.
  My wife had run off with some carpet salesman and if I'd had
the energy, I might have cared.

Got a free carpet though.

Nice Persian job, I piss on it every chance I get, which is most mornings after the usual boilermakers with the guys.

First though, we clocked off, we went over to May's, diner Eighth and 28th.

There is no May, it was owned by a Polack hardass who wouldn't give you the time of day if you paid him.

Our kind of guy, he never charged us neither and we kept an eye on the joint. He was the cook too, did hash browns, eggs over easy and bacon like your mother might have, if she'd ever been sober.

How I met Nora, the guys had been yapping about this Irish broad who'd been working there a time, I missed her first two weeks as I caught a knife in the gut from a domestic. The guy, he caught the fucking hiding of his life, you gut a cop, better have more than a small blade.

But it put me in the hospital for four days and then I had some time coming so I went fishing.

Like fuck.

I went to the OTB and the track.

Lost me whatever savings I might have had.

You might say, I came back on the job, a wiser, more cautious guy.

You might say shite.

I was meaner, more violent, more intent than before and lemme tell you, I was no Mr Nice to start.

So, me and Richy, we're heading for the diner and Richy says, "Wait till you get a load of Nora."

"The fuck is Nora?"

Like I gave a flying fuck.

Richy, he was a small guy, but he had my back and he was real good in the close-up stuff, a guy got in his face, he lost his face.

Think I'm kidding?

But here he was, sounding kinda . . . . goddamit . . . . shy?

He said, "Jeez, Joe, she's like . . . . I dunno, special, I'm thinking of you . . . . know, mebbe asking her out, a drink or something?"

I gave him the look, but the poor bastard, he was . . . . . what's the word . . . . smitten . . . . or better, fucked.

I cuffed his ear and he didn't even notice.

We went into the place, got our usual booth at the back, watch the exits, yeah, cop stuff.

And there she was.

I felt something move in my heart, like a melting. Ah Jesus, I'm not that kind of guy, but a jolt and I hadn't even had me my caffeine yet.

She was small, red hair, green eyes, nice, nice figure, real built but not showy with it, she knew what she had, didn't need to push, pretty face, not spectacular but there was an energy there, you found it hard to look away. She had her pad out, and of course, the coffee pot and without asking, filled our coffee mugs, cops, you gotta ask? She smiled at Richy, said,

"Tis himself."

He smiled like a love-struck teenager, I wanted to throw up, then she leveled those eyes on me and here was the goddamn jolt again, asked.

"And who is Mr Silent here?"

Richy blurted out about me being his partner, how I'd been in the hospital and she cut him off, asked me,

"Cat got your tongue, fellah?"

Something had, I had a million put-downs, couldn't bring one to mind, I put out my hand.

Jesus.

She looked at my hand, laughed, said,

"Tis shaking hands now is it, my my, aren't you the polite devil."

Fucking with me.

She said to Richy,

"Usual?"

He nodded like an idiot and to me,

"What about you, gorgeous, you able to eat?"

I mumbled something about having the same as Richy.

She gave that smile again, said,

"Christ, what a surprise."

And took off.

Richy was almost panting and I swear, he had a line of sweat above his eyes. He asked,

"Isn't she something?"

I wanted to bitch slap him, but I went with,

"Got a mouth on her, I'll give her that."

He had his Luckies out, lit one with a shaking hand, hard to believe that back then you could smoke anywhere, he persisted,

"But you like her, don't you, I mean, she's hot, isn't she?"

Fuck yes, I felt the heat offa her the moment she rolled up to us and I knew I was in some sort of serious bind, had to bite down, keep my cool, said,

"Whatever . . . . so you going to the ball game Sunday?"

She was back, balancing the plates with easy grace, put them down, gave me a look, asked,

"You have a touch of Irish in yah, haven't yah?"

I wanted to put more than a touch of Irish in her, right there, right over the mess of eggs, bacon and linked sausages. I said,

"Second generation."

She blew that off like it was horseshit, said,

"And a house full of harps and Irish music, fecking sad."

Left us to our food.

Her voice, the real deal, the soft lilt, those gentle vowels, you could have her cuss at you all day and still want more of that sound.

I gulped some coffee, it was bitter, black burned my tongue, just the way I liked it, like my fucking life.

We don't get a bill, we leave a fat tip on the table, that's how it works, Richy left a twenty and seeing my look, he pleaded,

"I'm gonna ask her out, can you give me a minute?"

When he went to ask her, I switched the twenty for a five . . . . no point in madness.

*   *   *

I waited in the prowl car, the radio squawking and my head full of her, she was dancing across my heart . . . . fuck and fuck.

I lit a Lucky, tried to figure out what the hell had just happened to me.

Richy came back, shit-eating grin all over his dumb face, said, "She said yes, can you believe that?"

I said, as I put the car in drive,

"Guess the twenty did the trick."

I didn't have to look to see the disappointment on his face, like his school project had been trampled on.

Tough.

The next couple of weeks, Richy was gone, signed sealed and fucked. He was taking Nora to fancy restaurants, clubs, buying her shitloads of jewelry, clothes, and crackin on about her, till I went,

"Shaddthefuckup."

He didn't.

He couldn't.

Where was the money coming from and it took a lot of moola.

Richy had grown up with wiseguys and now he was on the pad. He'd hinted I might like me some of the action till he saw my face and I could tell, deeper and deeper in the hole to these scum, he was going.

He was my partner, what could I do, watch the disaster take shape and get ready to annihilate him.

I watched.

One evening, I was sitting in the Mick bar, down a block from the precinct, fuming, the constant simmering rage in barely reined leash. I had me a Jameson rocks, Guinness back, and it wasn't my first. Someone slipped onto the stool beside me and I got the whiff of that perfume, swoon stuff.

Heard,

"Tis himself."

I turned to face her and my damn treacherous heart skipped some beats, those eyes and that Irish colouring and she had lips, you wanted to run your finger, gently across them and kiss them till they bled. She was wearing a tight dress that had to be against some law, least one that protected fools like me. She asked,

"So will himself buy a girl a jar or have I to beg?"

She had a double Old Grandad, Bud back. I asked,

"You're not gonna drink an Irish brand?"

She gave me a look, her eyes half lidded, said,

"Sure I'm in America, I can have the other stuff at home, wouldn't I be stone mad not to try yer drink?"

She put a cigarette between those gorgeous lips, waited and said,

"So Mr Grumpy, are yah going to light me up?"

Jesus.

I did and she held my hand as I did so, I swear, I had a tremor in me fingers and she said,

"Christ fellah, calm down, I'm not going to bite yah . . . . yet."

An hour later, I was buried to the hilt in her, sweating and groaning and howling like a lunatic and she goaded,

"Ride me like yah loved me."

After, her head on my chest, I asked,

"What about Richy?"

She was pulling at the hairs on my chest, said,

"Tis a bit late to remember him now."

I sat up, that hair-pulling, the sucker hurt, said,

"So you'll finish with him?"

She laughed, asked,

"Are ye mad entirely, he's loaded and I love money."

I tried for some decency, not that I know much about it, said,

"He's my buddy."

She began to massage my dick, asked,

"And how do you treat yer enemies?"

Another month of me fucking her twice a week, Richy buying her more and more shit, getting deeper in the hole and one evening, over a few brews, his face a riot of agony, he said,

"Joe, I'm in trouble."
I thought,
"You've no fucking idea, pal."
I said,
"Spill."
Deep, huh?
He drained his fourth bottle, now, he hit the Jameson, hard, said,
"I owe some guys and I can't meet the vig, never mind the freaking principal and Nora B, she's wanting more and more."
I echoed,
"Nora B . . . . what's with the B?"
He was puzzled, said,
"Jeez, I never asked . . . . beautiful, I guess."
Bitch, I thought
I said I'd see if I could maybe help him out.
Right.

The following Monday, Richy had his kids, and against my better judgment, I went back to Nora's place, always, we'd used my pad, we were deep in it when the door opened and there was Richy, his face a mask of stunned bewilderment. Nora, cool as an Irish breeze, slipped out of bed, naked, said,
"How 'as your day dear?"
He was reaching for his piece when she shot him in the head, twice, said,
"I just wouldn't have been able for all that whining he'd have done . . . . you?"
I was too shocked to speak and she said,
"Let's make it look like his shady friends got fed up with him, you can fix it to look like that, can you sweetheart?"
I could and I did.
And worse, I was part of the team that went after the wiseguys.
Nora disappeared, taking every cent Richy had stashed under the bed, she left me a note,

> *Joe a gra*
> *I'm tired of policeman, ye are too serious.*
> *I was thinking of getting some sunshine,*
> *so if you're ever in Florida, look me up.*
> *Tons of kisses,*
> *Nora B.*

'Course, she wasn't in Florida or anywhere else I could find her. She just seemed to vanish.

The years went by, and I managed to retire with most of my pension, and a cloud over my whole career.

Most nights, I sit and listen to that Irish wailing music, they give free razor blades with it, and I see Richy in my dreams, always with that lost look.

A few days ago, I heard from an old cop buddy, there was a hot joint up on the west side, run by a hot Irish broad, she had the most stunning red hair he said . . . . and get this, green eyes.

I got the knife from a guy in a bar, and soon as I finish the next Jameson, I'm gonna take a stroll up there, after I chop off that red hair, and before I sever the jugular, she's gonna tell me what the fucking B stands for

It's like, been . . . . bugging me.

THE END OF LITTLE NELL

Robert Barnard

They were all poor country people in the church, for the castle in which the old family had died, was an empty ruin, and there were none but humble folks for seven miles around. They would gather round her in the porch, before and after the service; young children would cluster at her skirts; and aged men and women forsake their gossips, to give her a kindly greeting. None of them, young or old, thought of passing the child without a friendly word; the humblest and rudest had good wishes to bestow.

Right! That's enough of that garbage. Though I've a lot more of it up my sleeve before "Little Nell" can be allowed to die. The great British public can't get enough of such sentimental twaddle, and they shall get it a-plenty. When the book is finished I shall offer it to Mrs Norton, or Mrs Gore, and if it's not in their line I'll load it off on to Charles Dickens, who is certainly a low fellow, but he does a nice line in weepies himself. He'll take it on, put his name to it, earn a tidy sum.

I have to say I sometimes enjoy writing about Nell myself, but that's probably because I enjoy re-creating myself in a totally false image. I think the image assumed its final perfect form for the pervy schoolmaster we met early in our travels – though I'd done the sweet *ingénue* quite often while serving in the Shop. Oh! that schoolmaster! What a twerp! All one ever got out of him was solicitude, tears and references to his favourite pupil who died back in the old village. You'd think people would have got suspicious of a schoolteacher who built his emotional life around a bright pupil who was dead. Particularly a bright *boy* pupil. But not everyone has my sophistication in these matters.

My re-creation of myself in the syrupy-sweet image of "Little Nell" began when the gaming houses and casinos of London started to get wise to grandad's and my little scam. That scam involving my taking three or four years off my age and being always taken to gambling dens by Kit Nubble – a dim spark if ever I saw one. Grandfather always went on his own, so no one ever associated us, and I could wander round the tables where he was playing and then sign him the details of what was in their hands. When they did get wise to us every establishment in London was circularized with our details, which was mighty unfair, and meant we had to take to the road and find out-of-town establishments where we could ply our trade without detection. We kept moving, because if one person keeps winning the big boys soon get suspicious. Sometimes we tried a bit of begging, but that was mainly for laughs. My grandfather has a great sense of humour.

Mind you, I don't like the road, not as I like London, where I always feel at home. You see some really odd types on the road. Take Mrs (a courtesy title, I wouldn't mind betting) Jarley, her of the waxworks – musty mummies trailed around the country in a procession of carts and caravans, and presenting a very cut-price version of Mme Tussaud's classy show in Baker Street. Mrs Jarley really took a shine to me, and it didn't take me long to guess that she was of the Sapphic persuasion.

"Such a sweet child," she would say, patting me on the thighs, the arms, and any joint that took her fancy. "She reminds me of the dear young queen."

The dear young queen strikes me as having a mental age of about twelve, and looks like the chinless wonders who inflict their feebleness on the Household Cavalry and any regiment with colourful gear to camp around in. I did not take kindly to the comparison.

"Her Majesty seems very neglectful of her duties as head of the Church of England," I said. "Sad that one so young shuns the proper Sunday observance."

"I had no idea," said Mrs Jarley, stopping her patting.

"Ah – London knows," I said. "And London keeps it to itself."

There's nothing like a bit of Metropolitan insider knowledge to make provincials feel inferior. And if you haven't got any insider knowledge, make it up.

I enjoyed my time with the waxworks display. I enjoyed presenting myself as a child barely into double figures. I enjoyed luring people into the tatty display by highly inflated claims of what it contained. I enjoyed most of all slipping off in the night to various rustic gambling hells to ply our trade and hone our skills. The Jarley routine of moving from one place to another made this last pleasure easier to procure. One or two visits to the local low place and we were on the road to another source of income. Grandfather was over the moon, and kept his winnings about his person. He never knew exactly how much he had won, so when I was putting him to bed drunk in the early hours I could abstract a bit for my own use.

Needless to say I put a rather different gloss on these activities in the manuscript I was preparing to hawk to Mrs Norton or that vulgar, jumped-up newspaper reporter Mr Dickens.

This pleasant life changed when we met up again with Codlin and Short. We had made their acquaintance a few months earlier, somewhere near Birmingham. You won't be surprised to hear they were an odd couple. I had no problem with them because I was used to the phenomenon from our London circles: the pair of men, usually middle-aged, who squabbled and competed and bad-mouthed each other to outsiders but who really were as close-knit as a nut and a bolt. And Codlin was definitely the nut. He was always insisting that *he* was my real friend, not Short, and I never quite realized what his motives in doing this were – whether he had plans for some scam or other that required a young, virginal, stupendously innocent creature. Or was he hoping to get tips on my grandfather's unrivalled techniques in card-play, the tables, horse-racing and cock-fighting?

We were on the way to Stratford-on-Avon, and Mrs Jarley was stroking my hair and telling me what a wonderful Shakespearean actress I would make in a few years – instancing Cordelia, Miranda and Celia, and I guessed these were innocent, slightly wet creatures, without an ounce of spunk.

"You have an aura," she was saying, "a heavenly atmosphere that envelopes you, so that you would be an ideal embodiment—"

My mind strayed from this fulsome garbage and I saw, further along up the main street of the small town we were passing through, two peak-capped figures gazing into a shop window. Peelers. Members of that elite body of men recruited by Sir Robert Peel when he was Home Secretary, to reduce crime in the cities by their unique combination of brains and brawn. I *don't* think! Just look at how much, or little, they get paid and guess how likely it is that the job will attract the elite.

I was just thinking the set of the two backs bending forward to survey the wares exhibited in the window reminded me of people I knew when they turned round as they heard the approach of hoofs and wheels.

Codlin and Short!

As we passed them by I raised my hand, and was rewarded by a double wave, very enthusiastic, in return. They began walking vigorously along beside us, only slowly getting left behind.

Fortunately we stopped at a public house on the edge of the town. Well, not fortunately – inevitably. We stop in nearly every town, so that Mrs Jarley can lubricate her coster-woman's voice and her travelling hands. When she had steamed off to get her gin and water, grandfather brought me my shrub, with double rum to taste, and he went to mingle with the local mugs while I waited for the precious pair to catch us up.

"Well, you have landed on your feet!" came a voice from the caravan doorway. Actually I was still recumbent on Mrs Jarley's well-padded couch, but I knew what he meant.

"We'd heard about the two new members of the company, and we guessed it had to be you and grandad. Mrs Jarley taken a fancy to you, has she?" asked Short.

"Actually I am extremely useful to the Museum management," I said demurely. "I've brought hundreds through the door."

"Didn't answer my question, did she, Codlin?" said Short, grinning.

"Don't be so personal, Short. A girl's got a right to her secrets, hasn't she, my darling?"

"And does Grandad get hundreds through the door too?" asked Short. "Or does he suggest a quick game of vingt-et-un, and line his pockets that way? His sort of swindle is not so different from Jarley's kind, when you come down to it."

Codlin nodded.

"Morally speaking I think you've hit the nail on the head, Short."

"I'm not used to hearing you moralize," I said. "I suppose it's the new job, is it?"

"Oh, the new job! No, my darling, Sir Robert's successor doesn't pay us to moralize. He pays us to catch criminals. Or failing that to keep track of them." Short paused. "It's a real police state he's created, but we're the *last* people who can talk about that. We get messages and send messages, and that means some little placeman in Westminster can put pins in his wall-map of England and show where all the big criminals and most of the small ones as well are at any moment."

"Which is why we're happy to have caught up with you again," said Codlin.

"But why? We're not big criminals."

"You're middle-ranking. And the gambling industry has a lot of good friends in this government, thanks to their readiness to grease the right palms. So we're just telling you: there are stories going round linking a widespread gambling scam to a certain travelling display of ageing wax-works. Get me? And if you or your revered grandfather slips us a ten quid note and renews it every time our paths cross, we'll keep you informed and tip you the wink when it's time to move on."

"Wouldn't Sir Robert, or his successor, be angry if he found out?"

"Livid – if he found out. But if he wants to stamp out corruption in the nation's police force he'd better start paying us what we're worth." He wagged a finger in my face. "Until then he'll find that the work never gets done."

"We're public guardians bold and daring," sang Short, in a quavering baritone: "When danger looms we're never there."

"But if we see a helpless woman, or little boys who do no harm," took up Codlin, "we run 'em in, we run 'em in – I say, is that your revered Grandaddy I see coming towards us?"

It was, and when he heard what the pair were offering he stumped up. Always good to have friends in high places. We decamped quietly from the waxworks display that evening, taking a quite different route from them, and leaving Mrs Jarley with nowhere to put her hands.

The places we stopped at, on all of which we left our mark, I will not mention in detail, but we rarely stopped long enough to need a warning from Codlin and Short. We were on to a very good thing. Our lives changed, however, when we happened on the village to which the schoolmaster whom we had encountered early on in our travels had moved. Here he was, large as life and just as dispiriting. He was still mourning the bright young pupil he had had years before, and still polishing the young hypocrite's halo every day of his life. A right little teacher's pet that limb of Satan must have been! It occurred to us that this was the sort of place we could well settle down in.

Well, as soon as the idea occurred to us, we wrote to Codlin and Short. We explained that there were several towns within walking distance, as well as several lucrative hell-holes. We had made a series of nocturnal excursions after the village was asleep (at about 8.30, in order to save candles), and we really felt the place would answer, at least for a year or two. We heard back from them that they could think of no reason why it shouldn't, and they would keep us informed as to anything they heard of that could be construed as a threat. And so things went on for three or four months.

Then I got bored.

I suppose we should have expected that. The night excursions still held a charm, but the daytime was terrible – catching up on sleep and enduring shiver-making visits from the schoolteacher or from his equally unappetizing friend The Bachelor – a local notable of similar habits and notions (my impersonation of infantile goodness and sweetness confirmed all his preconceptions about the non-carnal nature of the English female). I was tired of them all. I wanted London, I wanted stir, glamour, rich pickings. I was even nostalgic about Dan Quilp, one of our London friends, who had managed to evict grandfather from the Old Curiosity Shop: beneath his ugly, dwarfish exterior there lurked a diabolical energy, both criminal and sexual. He radiated an indiscriminate hunger and love of wreaking havoc. I understood why women were both repelled and thrilled by him. I wanted to get a share in that electricity, match myself with him. I hadn't been so excited since those lovely years when I was the only girl member of Fagin's gang.

I always remember the ending of Codlin and Short's letter, when we had written to them to broach the problem. It read: "Why doesn't she die?"

When we wrote asking them to elaborate on the question, they sketched in the plan which eventually with slight changes we adopted.

"Have dear little Eleanor sicken, slowly, inexorably. Orchestrate a chorus of village concern as she sinks, passing into a better world. Resist the temptation to open the deathbed scene to the general public at a shilling a time. Do it all tastefully. Have her practise short breathing – getting tiny gulps in in a way that hardly moves the lungs. When she is 'dead' have a simple funeral, though one marked by inconsolable local grief. Take the coffin to the local church and have grandpa mount guard over her all night. Keep a supply of sand in the vestry (NOT rubble, it tends to rattle). Fill (or half fill) the coffin with it. In the morning have the ceremony, bury the sand, and get Nell off to London suitably disguised – as her real self, we would suggest. Hey presto! In the future she can come back to visit her grandad if she wants to – posing as a long-lost cousin."

It was a wonderful idea! It left grandad free to use his great gifts in the country gaming holes, and it left me in London sampling the high life of Mayfair and the low life of Dan Quilp and his haunts. I liked the idea so much that I fell ill the very day we got the letter.

I didn't overdo it, of course. I am nothing if not tasteful. At first I was very brave, denying that I was ill at all. When they commented on my pallid complexion (flea powder) I shook my head bravely, then said there was nothing wrong. Then I thought it must be something I had eaten. Then I lost the use of my legs (they all shook their heads gravely at that). Before ten days were out I was permanently confined to bed, offering my visitors sickening platitudes, and sweetly prophesying I would soon be up again and as busy as ever. Tears flowed like

cataracts. Behind their hands everyone started making suggestions for the gravestone.

The end was unutterably poignant. We made it semi-public.
The schoolmaster and The Bachelor were there, and a couple of
rustics who could be relied on to get everything wrong and then
rehash their account to the whole village, over and over again. I
was visibly failing, and much whiter than the sheets on my bed.
When the little knot of witnesses was assembled I began the
tearful climax to my short life.

"Grandad," I said (he was sitting on my bed, and now
clutched my hand in his horny one), "I think a change is
coming. I think I am getting better. Is the sun shining? How
I would love to see the sun again. It is getting light. The whole
world is becoming brighter. I feel I am in a new place – better
and more lovely than anything I have known before—"

And so on. And on. I managed about ten minutes of this, and
then my voice started to fade. Words could be heard – "world",
"bright", "sun" and others, but nothing together that made
sense until I suddenly said "Grandad, give me the sun" and my
head fell back on the pillow, and my grandfather let out an
anguished howl.

Artistic, I'm sure you'll agree.

The witnesses clustered round, observing the lifeless corpse
and the sobbing frame of that old fraud my grandfather. Then
he stood up, still wracked with sobs, and ushered them out of
the door.

He drew the heavy curtains, locked the door, and then the
pair of us had a good if quiet laugh. After a while grandad
slipped out to order a coffin from the village carpenter. He
found it was almost ready, as the carpenter with his practised
eye had made a note of the likely size and had done most of the
work a couple of weeks earlier. We, or he, took delivery that
evening.

We made a slight change of plan. The nights were drawing in
and the days were nippy. I didn't fancy (as we had planned) a
long day in the staircase leading up the church tower while the
funeral went ahead and night fell. We agreed to do the sub-
stitution in the cottage. We had a showing of me in the coffin
next day, when the whole village and rustic dolts from miles

around filed past uttering idiocies like "She do seem at peace" and "Oh what a 'eavenly hexpression she do 'ave". When that collection of human rubble had passed through I jumped out of the coffin. Grandfather and I heaved the sack of sand (purloined by him from a building site) into the coffin and he nailed it down extremely tightly. We heaved it on to a trestle and went to bed in Grandad's bed. It will not have passed my sharper readers by that, whatever else he was, Grandad was certainly not my grandfather.

I have, writing now from the Old Curiosity Shop and awaiting another visit from dear, excitable Mr Quilp, who is finding me a bit of a handful, only one or two details to add. The next day, the funeral, was a big laugh. It was the last day of Little Nell, that brilliant creation the world had come to love. The vicar was in church, and the schoolmaster, the Old Bachelor, the gravedigger and Grandad assembled in our cottage to carry the coffin to the churchyard. As they were heaving it up on to their shoulders the schoolmaster said, in his typically spiritless tone of voice:

"I'm sure Little Nell is already there, at home in Paradise, chanting with the heavenly choir."

"I'd lay you ten pounds at whatever odds you choose to name that she's up there now, singing along with them other angels, lungs fit to bust," said Grandad, winking towards the bedroom door, where I was surveying the delicious scene through the keyhole and barely suppressing my roars of laughter.

I laugh when I think of that now. We made such fools of them all, Grandad and I. Putty in our hands, that's what they were. I long to have Mr Quilp helpless like the yokels, also putty in my hands. Already he is mad with jealousy every time I look at a London swell, which is fairly often, because they're on every street corner. But I must go very slowly. I have so much to learn from Mr Quilp about crime, about gaining the upper hand over the fools around me. I learned a lot from Fagin, but I could not use my sex with him, for obvious reasons. With Quilp I can use my sex to get from him every jot and tittle he knows. I said to him two evenings ago I needed above all to learn, and he was my chosen master, the one who would lead me up the path to my being Europe's Queen of Crime. "Wait till I see you next time," said my dear Quilp. "I'll give you a lesson as'll last you a lifetime."

I think that's him. Those are his uneven steps on the stairs. I can't wait to see his delicious deformed body. His hands are on the doorkn—

Here the creator of Little Nell fell silent for ever.

JOHNNY SEVEN

David Bowker

His name was Johnny Seven.

You think the name is weird, you should have seen his eyes. They were real blue and bright, like the eyes on some kind of light-up action figure. First time I saw him, there was this silence, like that part in a western when the stranger walks into the saloon. The new kid was thin and not very tall, with longish fair hair. He had a tiny rip in the left elbow of his jacket, like his folks were on welfare or something. Pretty neat jacket, all the same. He sure didn't carry himself like he was on welfare.

We were all sitting down, waiting for the teacher to show. For a few moments, Johnny boy hung around in the doorway of the classroom like he'd rather be somewhere else. But then Griff came up behind him, put his hand on Johnny's shoulder and steered him right in. "This is Jonathan Severn and I'm sure you'd all like to welcome him."

Griff wasn't even our real teacher. He was some fucked up old man who they brought in when the real teachers were sick. He probably should have been in an old people's home. He was always telling us things that weren't suitable for middle school kids to know, like what the Germans did to the Jews in the war. Once he gave us all paper and crayons and asked us to draw a Martian pancake. The point was that no one knew what a Martian pancake looked like, so everybody had to use their imaginations. I drew a car crash with bodies on the road and blood everywhere. Griff said to me: "That isn't a Martian pancake." I said: "How the fuck do you know?" so he sent me to the Vice Principal.

It was unlucky for Johnny Seven that the first teacher he met was this senile old guy who wasn't even his real teacher. When Griff asked us all to welcome Johnny, no one did. So Johnny just stood there, hanging his head like he found the whole situation humiliating. He walked over to the only free desk, some of the girls smiling at him, then he sat down, not really looking at anyone, eyes straight ahead. Griff launched straight into his dull old routine. "Johnny, maybe you have an opinion about what took place today?"

"Took place where?" said Johnny. No sir, no nothing.

I laughed. Griff shot me a look that said shut the fuck up.

"You're from New Jersey and you really don't know what happened?" Griff just wasn't buying this.

Johnny shook his head, real steady and slow. The way he did it, you could tell he knew exactly what had happened that day. Griff knew it too. Suddenly there was this electric feeling in the air. Something different was happening. Everyone could feel it. Griff was doing what teachers always do. He was holding up a hoop for good little boys and girls to jump through. But the new kid just wasn't playing.

Griff looked around the class. "Anyone?"

Bugaski put up his hand. Bugaski always put up his hand whether he knew the answer or not, just so it looked like he was making an effort. Bugaski's report card probably says "This kid has got a name like one guy sticking it to another guy, he's practically a vegetable, but he sure as hell can wave his arm in the air."

"Sir!" said Bugaski.

At first, Griffiths ignored him.

"Sir, sir!" said Bugaski, wriggling and pleading like he was about to hatch a monster turd. "Sir, was it Bob Hope?"

"No," said Griff. "Come on. The news today. Someone must know. Anyone?"

Blank fuckin' faces.

"Come on. Something happened to someone associated with this state."

Anne Marie held her hand in the air. I like her, she's so nice you hardly even notice she's a whale. "Somebody Davies," she said.

"Hallelujah," said Griff. Real sarcastic. "That's close enough. *Jack David*. He was executed this morning. Anyone know why?"

"Was he a poor black guy that never did anyone any harm?" I said.

"Be quiet, Newton," said Griff. He turned back to Anne Marie. "Maybe you could tell us?"

"He blew up a library."

"Blew up a library?" said Warren Sherman, real shocked. "Really? They executed a guy just for blowing up a library?"

Griff sneered. "It had people in it, Sherman."

Even so . . .

This is how fucked up Griff was. I complained to the Vice Principal about him but she never listened. He should have been teaching us about algebra or some shit. Instead, he asked us whether we thought the US government having the power to kill one of its own citizens was good or bad. Bugaski put up his hand as usual and said, "Sir, sir, is it a good thing, sir?"

Griffiths kind of sighed. "Bugaski, this is not a quiz."

I said: "If you ask me, it's a terrible example to set to children."

"But no one's asking you, Newton," said Griffiths.

As well as being senile, Griff was a Christian. He was one of those weird Christians who hates the whole human race. He once told us wars were terrible things, but they were useful for keeping down the excess population. Guy like that, would he count murderers as excess population? I guess he would.

Kirsten Wells, dumb but gorgeous, held up her hand. "If Jack David didn't want to die for his crime, he shouldn't have planted the bomb in the first place."

Wow. Great fuckin point, Kirsten. A real sizzler.

Griff gave a nod, just to humour her. He was probably thinking he had to stay on the right side of her, in case the bomb went off and him and Kirsten were the last two people left alive. Dumb or not, a girl who looked like Kirsten could be pretty useful in a post-nuclear situation.

My dad already explained why Jack David did it but I wasn't really listening. It was something to do with protesting about the government. All I know is the whole senate ganged up on this guy. It wasn't just a state crime, it was something called a federal crime, which means you've insulted the whole of America. Like saying, "Fuck off America."

And now I was feeling sorry for Griffiths. All he wanted was for the new kid to throw him a bone but Johnny was sitting there like Whistler's mother. Griff tried again. "Five years ago in this very city, the Melton Library was blown apart by a bomb that David left in an elevator. Over two hundred people died."

Big silence. Suddenly the new kid sighed, like he wanted to get something out but didn't know how. "Okay," he said. "Okay."

"Yes?"

"I don't like talking about it, sir, but actually, yeah," said Johnny, all solemn and still. "I remember that day very well."

"Hmm?"

"I didn't want to say, sir. My mom worked in the City Library. We lost her that day."

Shit. The whole room was in shock. Griff's face turned purple nearly, and his mouth dropped wide open. Teachers aren't meant to have feelings, but now he looked like he was about to cry. "Oh. Oh." That's all he said. It's like he couldn't move, he was paralysed.

"I didn't want to say," said Johnny like he was about to cry. "You forced it out of me."

"I'm extremely sorry, boy," said Griff. He said it like he meant it.

"Wasn't just mom. We lost my dad that day," said Johnny. "And my big sister. They were only returning their books, too."

Griffiths stared, open-mouthed.

"Yes sir, Mr Griffiths, sir. My uncles and aunts all got killed, too," said Johnny. "Along with the little dog who lived down the fucking lane."

Griff kind of rocked on his heels and his face went all pink. Then Griffiths dragged that kid out of his chair and damn near threw him halfway across the room. "How dare you! Get out!" Griffiths was screaming.

Johnny left like he was told. He looked real happy to be going.

"You shouldn't have done that," I told Griffiths. "Throwing kids is against the law."

That's all I said, but the way Griff turned on me, you'd have thought it was me who blew up the fucking library. "You too, Newton."

"Sir?"

"I said get out!" I get a real big blast of his breath. It smelled like he'd been eating dogshit with a mayonnaise dressing.

"Hey!"

"Don't 'hey' me, boy! Out!"

I looked at my friend KC, hoping he'd put in a good word for me; tell Griffiths I didn't mean to cause offence. KC kind of shrugged with his eyes like it wasn't really any of his business.

"What did I do?" I said.

"You're an idiot. Get the hell out of my classroom!"

In the corridor, Johnny Seven was smoking a cigarette. I couldn't believe it. "What is wrong with you, man? You're gonna get yourself expelled on your first day," I said.

He smiled at me and blew smoke in my face. "Let's hope so."

At lunch, Johnny wandered through the yard on his own, kids giving him a wide berth in case getting hurled across a classroom was contagious. Me and KC were smoking behind the wall. KC was a year older than me. His real name was Kevin Chester, but he called himself KC because he thought his real name sounded gay. He was fucking right.

Wasn't just his name, either. When he got drunk, KC was always dancing and taking his clothes off, even when there weren't any girls around. But if you reminded him of it when he was sober, he punched you on the fucking arm. KC switched schools and had to start the eighth grade all over because he wasn't achieving his full potential. His grades were so bad his parents were afraid he'd grow up to be President of the USA.

"Maybe we should talk to the new kid," said KC.

"And say what?"

"I dunno. Anything. Tell him you're sorry about his family blowing up."

"You fuckin' idiot. He was making all that shit up about his family. That's why Griff threw him out."

"Oh. Really? I thought he was just lying about the dog."

Kevin's dad drove a limo, and I don't mean he was no chauffeur. He worked for some big chemical corporation and smoked cigars and wore a smoking jacket in the home. When I first saw this smoking jacket I thought it was some kind of comedy robe. If I visited Kevin's house, his dad always shook me by the hand like I was an old friend and asked about my parents. Kevin's dad wouldn't have known my mom and dad if he'd driven over them in his fucking limo.

"You don't know what it's like," says Kevin. "Switching to a new school is the worst fuckin' feelin."

"Worse than what? Worse than having boiling oil poured in your ears?"

"Fuck you."

"Anyway, you did know somebody. You already knew me when you came to this school."

"Exactly, Newton."

"What's that supposed to mean?"

"Whatever the fuck you want it to mean."

"You already done the eighth grade once. You're familiar with all the fuckin' subjects. You said so yourself. What's so tough about that?"

Kevin punched me on the shoulder.

The last school KC went to was this Catholic place run by a bunch of real monks. Except instead of being all peaceful and holy, these were the kind of monks that stank of sweat and twisted guy's nipples when they stepped out of line. I told KC that twisting nipples was illegal. KC said that if it was in the Bible, it's okay for monks to do it.

Kevin got a lot of shit from his mom and dad, about how he had to work real hard to fulfill his dream. What dream? Far as I know, he didn't have a dream, apart from wanting to own a Harley someday. Kevin was a big tough kid with real muscles but when his dad told him he was letting down his family, he cried like a baby. I saw him do it once.

"You comin' round Maya's house tonight?"

Maya was allegedly Kevin's girlfriend. She was twelve years old, with no tits whatsoever. That kind of thing might go down well in Mississippi, but it looks pretty sick in New Jersey.

"Yeah. Okay."

"Her cousin's comin round. Mirabeth. Did you ever hear such a stupid name?"

"How old is she? Seven?"

This time, he tried to kick me. It was a pretty half-assed attempt, though. For an athlete, Kevin was getting a little porky. Every day, his lunchbox has about two million cookies in it. Kevin says this is because his mom used to be trailer trash and never had enough to eat as a kid. But her dad, KC's grandpa, worked real hard until one day, he became the trailer trash that owned the trailer park. Suddenly Kevin's mom found she could eat all the cookies she wanted. And now she made sure her little boy always had his fill of cookies too, so he wouldn't stand out in a crowd of Americans.

"You scared?" said KC.

"What of?"

"I dunno," said KC. "I just feel something bad is going to happen."

"That's right," I said. "It's called the rest of your fucking life."

That night, KC called for me. We were going to hang out at the mall, spitting off of the balcony before going over to Maya's. On the way, we saw old Johnny Seven sitting on his bike outside a house with paint peeling off the front door. There was an old fucked-up pickup truck parked in the drive.

"Yo," I said. "What're you doing here?"

"I live here," he said.

A big freight train rattled by. The railroad ran past the back of Johnny's house. We had to wait until the train had passed before we could hear ourselves talk.

"Your name's really Johnny Seven?" said Kevin, with a big smile. "That's one cool fuckin' name."

"But it's not seven like the number," said Johnny. "It's got an 'r' in it." He spelled it out for us. "S-e-v-e-r-n."

"Oh. I prefer Seven," said Kevin.

"My uncle says Johnny Seven was the name of a toy you could buy when he was a kid. It was a plastic rifle with toy grenades that you could actually fire."

"Yeah?" I said.

"So your mom and dad named you after a toy? That's cool," said Kevin, who never listens.

"I ain't got a mom," said Johnny. "My dad raised me by himself."

We didn't know what the fuck to say to that. Then Johnny said: "That Griffiths is a real grade-A cunt, don't you think?"

"Yeah," I said.

"One of these days someone's going to shoot that guy in the head while he's begging for mercy," said Johnny.

It was a weird thing to say, all right. Kevin kind of stared. "Yeah. Like you'd fuckin' do it."

"I fuckin' would," said Johnny. "I'd do it just like that."

"You'd shoot a teacher? Yeah. Fuckin' right."

"Certainly wouldn't shoot a kid," said Johnny Seven.

"You're full of shit," said Kevin.

"The rights of children are sacred," said Johnny, not like a preacher would say it, but in the voice of a real person. "Any adult who violates those rights shall die."

We didn't know what to say to that neither.

So me and Kevin said goodbye to the new kid and cycled away real fast so it looked like we were on some kind of secret mission for the government. On the corner of Chatsworth, we spotted Wheelchair outside his house. It was like he was lying in wait. Except he was sitting, not lying.

"Oh, fuck, no," said KC.

We were so depressed we almost turned right round and went home again. Wheelchair was the same age as me. Shelton's his real name, but one day my mom accidentally renamed him by telling me I should see the person, not the wheelchair. I took a real good look at the person and guess what? I preferred the wheelchair.

All year long, Wheelchair sits at the end of his drive and accuses kids of all kinds of crazy crimes he's imagined. My mom says it's not Wheelchair's fault, the poor bastard can't tell the difference between dreams and reality. She may be right, I don't give a fuck. It's upsetting to be heckled by a cripple.

Tonight, Wheelchair gave us one of his old favorites.

"You're the kid who stole my boomerang!" he shouted, pointing right at me.

We stopped to look at him. Wheelchair wore glasses that magnified his eyes, so he always looked angry and sad. Maybe he was. Guess he had every fuckin' right to be. Thing is, some people in wheelchairs wish they could walk. I swear this kid wished everyone else was in wheelchairs.

"He never touched your stupid boomerang," said KC.

"I saw the bastard do it!" yelled Wheelchair.

"I think you're mistaken, pal," said KC in a reasonable kind of voice.

"Liar!"

"Anyway, when'd you ever even have a boomerang?" I said. "Bet you never even seen a boomerang."

I felt bad as soon as I've said it. Not as bad as Wheelchair, though. His bottom lip trembled and he glared at me like he wanted to kill me. Then he started to cry. Right away, I knew I'd committed a major sin. I'd made a kid in a wheelchair cry. KC stared at Wheelchair, dead serious. When we rode away, he said: "What the fuck did you have to go and say a thing like that for?"

"You were the one who said his boomerang was stupid," I said.

"Sometimes you're a real prick, Garrett. You know that?" said KC.

In my defence, Wheelchair isn't the easiest cripple to get along with. My kid brother Monkey, who writes compositions about what a swell guy Jesus is, went up to Wheelchair once and tried to make friends with him. Wheelchair was real grateful, so grateful he tried to pull Monkey's pants down. That's the trouble with the less fortunate. One minute you're trying to do them a good turn. The next minute they're pulling your pants down.

When we turned up at Maya's house, she was with her cousin Mirabeth. Name like that, I thought Mirabeth would be terrifyingly ugly. Mister, she was not. She was the same age as her cousin. Long dark curly hair and no tits, also like her cousin. A pretty face, though. I really liked her. Right away, I wanted to impress her so I pretended to fall off my bike. Mirabeth laughed a lot, so did Maya. I felt I was off to a great start.

Maya's mom and dad were out at the store with her kid sister, so we all went inside to listen to music. Except Maya didn't have any music, all she had was her mom's fuckin' Neil Diamond CDs. Me and KC were supposed to listen to this shit and act like we enjoyed it, just for the privilege of sitting in the same room as two girls. Except I didn't pretend, I said right away that in my opinion, Neil Diamond didn't deserve to live.

Mirabeth and Maya went off to fetch us some cokes from the kitchen. Then Maya came back to say that in *their opinion*, I was very immature and didn't deserve to be in their grown-up company.

"What?" I said to Maya. "You're kicking me out?"

Maya nodded. Mirabeth passed me my coke and shrugged, like it wasn't up to her.

"Seriously? You are seriously asking me to leave? What about Kevin?"

"Kevin stays," said Maya.

"What about my coke?" I said.

Maya told me to drink it outside. I waited for Kevin to take my side and say that no buddy of his took orders from a flat-chested moron but he just sat there same as fucking usual, sipping his coke like enamel wouldn't melt in his mouth.

I told Maya I admired Neil Diamond really, really admired his wig and the way he pretended he had a deep voice. But it was too late. The bitch said no, I was leaving anyway. She kept saying I was immature. I got my revenge by farting real loud outside the window.

By the time I'd finished my coke it was getting dark. I was sulking on the porch when Johnny Seven rode by on his bike. He saw me and right away slammed on his brakes *eek-eek-eeeek*.

"Hey," he said.

"How's it goin'?" I said. Feeling awkward because I hardly knew anything about the kid, apart from the fact that he was a little insane.

"What did you say to Shelton, man?"

"You mean Wheelchair."

"No. I fucking don't. I mean Shelton."

"Shelton Wheelchair. What about him?"

"What did you do?" said Johnny. "I just seen the kid, he was almost hysterical."

I told him everything about the conversation. Johnny leaned over and spit on Maya's drive. "He's a kid, Newton. One of our own. We've got to look after our own."

"Yeah. But he's crazy. He scares me."

"He's scared too, man," said Johnny patiently. "Shelton can't tell dreams from reality."

"How the fuck would you know?"

"Because I talked to him."

I doubted this. Far as I knew, Shelton's only topic of conversation was boomerangs. Johnny gave me a stick of gum. "Thing is, I don't want kids ripping on other kids. I don't like it."

"You don't like it? What the fuck's it got to do with you?"

"Just go easy on him," said Johnny. "I'm asking you as a favour."

"Hey, you're not the boss of the neighborhood. You only just moved in. You don't ask me a fucking thing."

Johnny just looked at me, like he thought I was better than this. I kept looking at him like I fucking wasn't. After ages had passed and we'd both turned into old men with grey beards and crap in our pants he said: "Listen, my dad's out looking for me. If he comes by, you guys haven't seen me? Okay?"

"Okay," I said.

"I appreciate it," said Johnny. Then he did a wheelie for about half a fucking mile.

A minute later, Maya threw Kevin out. They were getting a divorce. She'd asked him to kiss her, so he did. Then she accused him of kissing her with his eyes open and asked him to leave.

"Oh, that is fucked up," I said. "How was you supposed to find her mouth if you didn't have your eyes open?"

"Exactly," said Kevin. "Exactly."

"I mean a guy wants to know what he's kissing, doesn't he?"

We were standing in the road, debating about why girls are so full of shit. Then we heard a voice shouting: "Johnny? Johnny!"

I remembered what the new kid had said about his dad looking for him and told Kevin. We figured the guy calling out was Johnny's old man. He sure as fuck didn't sound friendly. I was still pissed at Johnny for lecturing me about Wheelchair so I yelled: "Fuck you, dad!"

I nearly cried with laughing at how Johnny's dad would think it was Johnny who said it. Johnny's dad made this big roaring sound like an animal in pain. Then KC joined in. "Dad, fuck off! You big ugly cunt!"

Now we were both creased up, cackling so hard we were nearly in tears. Then the guy started running and we could see right away that he was fast and didn't move like no daddy we'd ever met. We got scared and pedalled off. The wind was in our faces and we thought we were safe when we heard this big bastard's feet pounding the road behind us. Man, that spurred us on. Our hearts and legs didn't stop racing until we reached my house. When we looked behind us and saw he wasn't there we started laughing again, this time with sweet relief.

"Fuck you, dad," I said.

KC howled and so did I. Then I had an idea. "Let's go over to his house, maybe we'll see what happens when Johnny's old man catches up with him."

So what we did was climb the railway bridge and walk down the tracks in the moonlight. We were still pissing ourselves. KC or me only had to say "Fuck you, dad" and we'd crack up. Then we had to stop, bending over and holding our ribs, laughing 'til we cried. Finally we were looking down at Johnny Seven's house. It was as shittily painted at the back as it was at the front. We sat on the verge under the railroad track, staring straight across into the bedroom windows. All the lights in the house were shining.

Out of nowhere, I got this scared feeling. Coming here was beginning to seem like a mistake. "What if his dad looks out and sees us?"

"So what?" said KC. "This isn't his property. Right now we're sitting on railroad property."

To lighten the mood, I said "fuck you, dad" again but the joke had worn kinda thin. I told KC that maybe we should go, but he said we should linger for a few more minutes; see if anything "transpired". KC had a bit of weed and he knew how to make roll-ups, so we inhaled real fucking deep to give

ourselves breathing problems in later life. I hoped it'd give me a
real buzz for once but it didn't so I had to fake it. "Man," I said,
pretending to lose my balance. "I am so high you wouldn't
believe it."

"Damn right I wouldn't," said KC.

We were on the point of leaving when we saw Johnny Seven
walk into one of the bedrooms. Johnny was yelling his head off
at someone out of sight. Then a big guy in a vest walked over to
Johnny and hit him in the face. Wham!

Not a slap but a real, grown up punch, like a boxer whacking
another boxer. KC and me were so shocked that we started
laughing. Johnny Seven dropped like a brick. Then Johnny's
dad picked him up and hit him again. Hit him three times,
holding him steady so he could get a real good aim. Now it
wasn't funny anymore.

"Jesus, I don't believe this," said KC. "Do you believe it?"

"No way."

That kid must have got punched and thrown and kicked
around that room a hundred times. KC got upset. I knew he
would.

"Hey! Fuckin' cut that out!" he shouted. He picked up a
stone and threw it at Johnny's window. I threw another. We
both missed.

We kept on tossing those damn stones but missed every time.
Johnny's dad didn't hear us yelling. He was enjoying himself
too much. He just carried on beating up his boy. KC and me
had to go home, we couldn't watch it anymore.

We started walking. "That's bad," said KC. His voice
sounded strange. "That fuckin' sucks."

"Shit, you see the way his dad laid into him?" I said.

"I saw," said KC. "That is so wrong, man. My dad may have
smacked me round once or twice, he never hurt me. That
bastard was using his *fists*. Goddamn."

There was a train coming. Me and KC slid down the slope to
get out of its way. The train whooshed past. It was a cold lonely
feeling, seeing all the passengers through the windows and
knowing not one of those motherfuckers knew about me or
KC or Johnny Seven or would have given a shit if they had. To
them, we were just a bunch of kids.

We watched the train until its tail lights snaked out of sight. As we headed for the bridge I said: "So what're we gonna do?"

"About *what*?"

"Someone getting half-killed, that's what! Do we call the fuckin' cops or not?"

"Are you joking?" said KC. "What good would that do?"

"We witnessed a violent assault."

"We witnessed shit. We were spying, for fuck's sake. Things you see when you spy don't count."

"Hey, I'm shaking," I said. "Look at me. I'm shaking all over."

KC sniffed. Might have been snot, might have been tears. I didn't ask. "I hope that kid's all right," he said. "Because, God help me, if he dies, it's your fucking fault."

But Johnny Seven lived. A week later, he was back at school. His mouth was all swollen and his left eye was so bruised he could hardly see out of it. No one asked him how it had happened, not even the teachers. By now, both me and KC felt we owed Johnny something so in recess we went over to be nice to the kid. At first, he ignored us but we wouldn't let up. It became like a fucking mission with us.

We asked him to play catch. But he was so sore he couldn't raise the mitt properly. So instead we sat on the wall and talked. We didn't say anything about the terrible way Johnny looked and you could tell Johnny was real relieved that we didn't mention it. And we certainly had no intention of telling him it was our fucking fault he looked that way.

"I was thinking of going shooting after school," said Johnny Seven. "Wanna come?"

"Shooting who?" I said. "Griff?" The idea kind of appealed to me.

"M-h." Johnny shook his head. "Just trees and stuff. My old man collects handguns. He wouldn't miss one."

We were impressed but trying not to show it.

"What happened to your mom?" said KC. "She die?"

"No sir. She just walked out, man. My dad never wanted to go anywhere or have friends over so she kept getting depressed and finally she just left."

"Where'd she go?" said KC.

Johnny shrugged.

"What's it feel like, not knowing if you're ever gonna see her again?" I asked him.

KC acted all shocked. "Fuck, Garrett, what kind of asshole question is that?"

"S'okay," said Johnny. "Way it is, when you got a mom, you sometimes think you'd be better off without her. But when you don't even know where she is, it feels like you wanna hurl all day long."

KC nodded respectfully. "I bet it does. I bet it really does feel that way."

We met in the woods near the lake. There was a fucked-up old ruined house near the lake. It was called the Retreat, because that was its name when people lived there. The walls were half down and it didn't have any windows because so many kids had thrown rocks at them. KC told Johnny "The Retreat" was an unlucky name to give a house, because retreating was what cowards did in a battle. Johnny looked at me and smiled. He could see that KC was pretty dumb but would never have said it out loud. That wasn't Johnny's style.

So Johnny took this gun, this police special with six chambers and he let me and KC hold it and said we could have two shots each. We got a rock and scratched the shape of a naked lady on the side of the wall, then we each took a couple of shots at her. When the gun went off, it was real loud, like thunder, so loud that we were sure someone would come running, but no one did. Johnny walked half a mile away. He fired twice and got the woman smack in the nipples. It was like he was Clint Eastwood or somebody.

"Where'd you learn to shoot like that?"

"We had a ranch in Oklahoma," said Johnny. "That's where my folks come from. We used to shoot at things all the time. I can drive a car, too."

"No fucking way," said KC.

Then it was my turn to shoot. The gun went off before I was ready and I didn't hit a fucking thing. KC laughed but he didn't do any better. I had one more shot and I fired it straight into the ground because I felt like it. Johnny said what I'd done was a waste of ammunition. "What?" I said. "But it ain't a waste to shoot at a picture of some tits?"

Later we went back to Johnny's house and he let us in, said his dad was out and wouldn't be back until late.

"Like how late?" I said.

"Who knows?" said Johnny.

"Wow," I said. "You could stay out until midnight if you wanted."

I could see KC looking pretty surprised. Me and him usually had to be home by ten, on the fucking dot, or we got grounded. And there's Johnny coming home to an empty house. The place was a fucking mess, though. There was this thick layer of dust on the TV and the kitchen looked like someone had been throwing soup at the walls.

Johnny took the gun back to his dad's room then got us some cold beer from the icebox. We couldn't believe it. It was real German beer. He got out a CD, someone called Martha somebody. "Listen to this, she swears her head off in it." It was a boring song, except at the end when this woman calls someone a mother fucking asshole. She sang it about six or seven times. Man, we rolled about laughing. When the song was over, we played it again just to see if we'd heard it right the first time. After one can of beer each we were all pretty drunk.

Johnny got us another beer, even though he'd said we could only have one each. Then he put on another song we hadn't heard. It was some really old party record called The Monster Mash. On account of the song being about monsters, KC had the bright idea that we should listen to it in the dark. I knew what he was planning. I fucking knew. Sure enough, next thing he was asking Johnny if he had a flashlight. Johnny said sure. So KC asked Johnny to aim the flashlight at him while he did a dance to the record. In no time at all, Johnny was pointing the spotlight at KC while he flashed his big white ass in the dark. Jesus, it was funny. Johnny was laughing so much he was crying. KC wasn't laughing, though. His face was all serious, like he was concentrating on giving an artistic performance.

Then the light turned on and Johnny's dad was standing there. From a distance, he'd looked like the main villain in a gangster movie. Close up, he was just a normal looking guy, average size, ordinary hair and clothes and his belly starting to bulge, like any dad from anywhere in the world. He just looked at us. No expression on his face or nothing.

KC tried to pull up his pants, his belt buckle rattling. Johnny's dad walked over to him and pushed him. KC did this sort of hopping dance, still holding onto his pants. Then he fell over. Johnny tried to get up off the sofa, but his dad got to him first and held him down with one hand over his throat. I thought he was going to hit Johnny, but no. He just kept on squeezing his throat like he wanted to strangle him. I said: "Stop." That's all I said. Johnny's dad turned and slapped me on the ear so hard I could hear humming.

Now Johnny was turning red, trying to knock his dad's arm away. But he was too little and weak. He was making clucking noises in his throat. And what was really scary was that his fucking father still hadn't said a goddamn word. Both me and KC felt sure he was going to kill his own kid. We kept yelling at him to stop but he was like a maniac. The guy was so mad his forehead was throbbing.

KC was crying his eyes out. He picked up the shitty dusty old TV and used it like a battering ram, slamming Johnny's dad in the side of the head. Johnny's dad looked confused and blew out air like he'd just done ten push-ups. Then he fell over. KC smacked the TV down on top of the guy's skull. The TV didn't break. The guy's head did. When he was lying down, all three of us started kicking his head and stamping on it. There wasn't nothing mean about it. We were just scared shitless of what the bastard might do if he ever stood up again.

When we'd finished stomping, it was pretty fucking obvious the guy wasn't much of a threat to anyone no more. He wasn't moving, his eyes were wide open and his tongue was hanging out. He looked like a dog I saw once that had been hit by a car.

"He fucking deserved it," said Johnny.

"He really fucking did," I said. Even my voice was shaking.

KC hadn't stopped crying the entire time. "You dumb fucking bastards," he kept saying. "Now we're all going to get lethally injected, just like that guy Griff told us about."

I was scared and trying not to show it. "They won't kill us. We're minors."

"They wait until you're eighteen and then they fucking do it," said KC.

"They won't do nothing," said Johnny. "Because they ain't gonna find out. My dad had no friends. He never spoke to nobody. Who's gonna know?"

"The body's gonna stink," said KC. "It fucking stinks already."

"There's a big old freezer in the garage," said Johnny. "We can put him in there."

"I ain't gonna cut anyone up," I said.

"We don't need to," said Johnny. "We just take the frozen stuff out and lift him in."

"Someone's gonna know," I said. I was shivering just like Scott of the Antarctic. "You can't live here on your own without someone knowing."

"This is America," said Johnny. This kid was calm as anything. I think he was even relieved. "Long as you keep paying bills, no one cares about you. I lived in lots of places, that's how it works. People only knock on the door if you owe them money or they want you to join their church. I'll keep going to school, just like normal. I'll pay the bills and sign checks while the money lasts out."

The more we thought about it, the more it seemed like the ideal solution. Even KC could see the sense of it. We wouldn't admit to killing Johnny's dad, we'd just pretend he was alive. It wasn't such a big lie, anyway. Most kids spend their entire childhoods pretending their parents are alive.

BUMPING UGLIES

Donna Moore

"Hey! That's *my* fucking bag, you fat junkie bitch." Nice mouth on her, for all her expensive gear and fancy-looking Prada handbag. The handbag that was now in *my* possession as I legged it across the concourse of Central Station. Serves her right for putting it down on the seat beside her. Everyone knows that Central is like a well-stocked buffet of Glasgow's junkies, pickpockets and lowlifes. I considered it teaching her a lesson.

I could hear her stilettos pecking away like a crow on steroids as she tried to run after me. I wasn't worried that she would catch me – the shoes were too high and her skirt too tight. As I dodged startled passengers hurrying for their trains, I heard a shriek followed by the thwack of a bony Versace-clad arse hitting concrete. Excellent. Now I just had to avoid the cops. Half of Strathclyde's finest hang around Central Station. It's an easy way of meeting their arrest targets for the month. Just nip into Central and huckle a few likely characters – the nylon shell suits and Burberry baseball caps are a dead giveaway.

There are plenty of exits out of the station and, within seconds, I was down the stairs and out onto Union Street.

"Fuck's sake, hen . . ." The Big Issue seller I slammed into spun like a bearded prima ballerina.

I raised my hand in apology but didn't turn. "Sorry pal." I didn't stop until I got to the Clyde where I stood puffing and wheezing for a while, wondering if I was going to throw up. Running is not my forte. My chest is too big and my lungs are too wee. It was quiet by the river at this time of day and I sat on a bench and emptied the contents of the handbag out beside me, giving each item the once over before laying it down on the flaking blue paint of the bench.

First out was a wallet containing five crisp twenties, some loose change, gold credit cards and a handful of store cards – Frasers, John Lewis, Debenhams. Mrs Gillian McGuigan – according to the cards – certainly treated herself well. Then there was a top-of-the-range mobile phone with a diamante-studded G hanging from it. Tacky. Enough MAC cosmetics to stock a stall at The Barras, an appointment card for hair, nails and sunbed at The Rainbow Room and a couple of letters. She lived in Bothwell, and she would certainly fit in there amongst the footballers wives and ladies who lunch. High maintenance and flashy.

I opened the mobile phone and thumbed through the messages from oldest to newest. There were a couple from female friends and one or two from someone called Stewart. Since they were of the "Need loo rolls" and "working late, c u at 9" type, I assumed that Stewart was the poor, long-suffering Mr McGuigan. Probably had to work late to keep his wife in bling.

Most of the texts were from Tom. "Wear the red basque on Friday," "Kate at sister's this weekend. Can u get away?" "Can't live without u. We need to do something about K and S" and "Seeing lawyer Thurs." It looked as though poor Kate and Stewart were in for a shock.

There were a couple of texts from someone called Billy. The most recent read, "One hit £10k, cd do both for £15K." Billy might be the solution to the problem, but if he was a lawyer, he was pricing himself out of the market. I checked the rest of Gillian's received texts and moved on to the sent box. They told quite a story. It would appear that the shock for Kate and Stewart was of the "shot in the head and dumped in the Clyde" sort rather than the "I now pronounce you ex-husband and wife" sort. Still, it was nice to know that "buy one, get one half price" extended as far as contract killings. I assumed that even taking into account the cost of the hitman, Gillian stood to make more as a widow than she would as a divorcee.

As I sat with the phone in my hand, pondering the best course of action, it rang. I might have guessed. The woman *had* to be my age at least. Nearly forty and she had a Justin Timberlake ring tone. The screen said "Home" so I flipped it up and answered.

"Gillian McGuigan's secretary. How may I help you?"

"You can fucking *help* me you cheeky fucking skanky whore by letting me rip that greasy ponytail out by the fucking roots you bitch. I want my bag back."

"Ouch. I'm hurt. Not all of us can afford to go to the Rainbow Room you know. I wonder what it is that Tom sees in you . . . your bleached blonde hair? Your orange sunbed tan? Your hatchet face? Your shrill voice with its extensive vocabulary?"

The sharp intake of breath practically sucked my ear off. "You've read my text messages you nosy bitch. I'll fucking *kill* you."

"Well, why not? That seems to be your answer to everything. Hopefully you'll get a bulk discount from your friend Billy."

"I . . . shit . . . I . . . You're fucking dead. Fuck . . . you've got to let me have the bag back. Please . . ." In the space of one sentence her voice changed from harridan to whiny six year old.

"No. Actually, doll, I don't have to let you have the bag back. I don't have to do heehaw." I shut the phone when the shrill voice started up again. I wondered whether Stewart was deaf. I'd been speaking to her for two minutes and that voice was really starting to grate on me. Some women give the rest of us a bad name.

I hugged my jacket closer to me and stared at the muddy Clyde as I thought about what I should do next. When I stole the bag it was a spur-of-the-moment thing. I'd been watching the woman for a while and when she put the bag down I just acted on impulse. Things had taken a surprising turn, but I was sure I could turn the situation to my advantage. I just needed to work out how.

The phone rang.

"Listen you fu . . ."

It rang again.

"Don't hang up."

"Then do try not to insult me. All that swearing is getting on my tits." I was enjoying this. It would seem though that poor Gillian would not recognize irony if it jumped up and bit her on the arse.

"Insult you? Where do *you* get off being so high and mighty? You're the fucking junkie, bag stealing bitch . . ."

She may well have been right, but I cut her off anyway. Besides, if we were talking about taking the elevator to the moral high ground, at least *I* was getting on it about halfway up. I think adulterous, hitman-hiring shrews were roughly three floors below the basement.

"Please don't hang up."

"Better. Now, give me a good reason why I shouldn't."

"A hundred pounds."

"What is?"

"I'll give you a hundred pounds if you give me my handbag back."

I laughed. "Is that supposed to be a tempting offer?"

"Aye. Fuck . . . I don't know. It might save you sucking some guy's dick up an alley. What's the going rate for smack these days you . . ."

"Now now, Gillian. You know what happens when you start hurting my feelings. And if I hang up this time I'm going to take a wee wander up to Pitt Street and visit Strathclyde polis. I have an idea they might be interested in the contents of your phone."

"Oh, aye. That'll be right. I can just see you walking in there and saying 'Officers, here's a bag I mugged off of some wee wifey at Central Station.'"

"Maybe not, but I might just take one of these crisp twenties in your lovely flash handbag and buy some stamps. If I send it registered post it might even actually get there."

"Shite. How much do you want?"

I thought for a moment. I didn't want to come across as too cheap, but on the other hand, I didn't want to name a price that was so high that she would take the chance on me not going to the police. "Two thousand pounds."

"Two grand? You're kidding me, right?"

"Nope. I'm not smiling here. Two thousand. I think that's very fair. Tell me . . . just out of curiosity . . . does Tom know about your little plan to off your respective spouses?"

"Tom . . .?"

"Yeah, you know, the poor misguided fool you're bumping uglies with."

"Of course he knows. It was him who gave me the idea."

"Really? Sounds like you're a match made in heaven."

Again, the irony was lost on her. "We are. We love each other. Can't keep our hands off each other. His wife is apparently a fat, frumpy bore, and my husband can't get it up any more."

"No wonder. You've probably sucked the life right out of him. And not in a good way."

"Oh shut the fuck up, you blackmailing bitch. When do I get my bag back?"

"Well, let's see. When can you get the £2,000?"

"Tomorrow."

Obviously I should have asked for more. "Do you know the Necropolis?"

"The big cemetery? I know of it, yeah."

"OK. Egyptian Vaults. Eight p.m. tomorrow night. You can get a map off the internet. Oh, and bring your bit on the side. I'd quite like to see what all the fuss is about."

I shut the phone off before she could whine. I could tell from the noises on the other end of the phone that she was winding herself up to go off on one and, quite frankly, I'd had enough of her. She was mouthy, self-centered, trashy and shallow. Her plans proved that she was also dangerous and I didn't trust her one little bit. If I was going to meet her and Tom I needed some insurance. I opened the phone again and went to her contacts list. The phone was answered after one ring.

"Aye?"

"Billy? I want to buy a gun."

The Necropolis was locked up at dusk, but it's easy to get in, and so huge that it's impossible to ensure that no one does. I'd arrived at seven p.m., crossed the Bridge of Sighs, and made my way to the Egyptian Vaults via a circuitous route, just in case Gillian and Tom had planned a wee surprise for me. The place was not exactly welcoming during the day, but it was even less so after dark. Dilapidated and overgrown, it was a haven for junkies, wee neds drinking Buckfast and taking illegal substances, the homeless and the hopeless. Between some of the gravestones and in the sheltered spots beside the vaults were sleeping bags – as yet unoccupied – their owners perhaps at the soup kitchen on East Campbell Street, getting a little warmth and light before returning to this creepy place to sleep.

I wasn't worried about the dead. It was the living that concerned me, and I gripped the gun tighter. Billy had put me in touch with an acquaintance, who knew a guy, who had a friend who could possibly lay his hands on a gun. All very cagey, lots of ifs and buts, but I think Billy thought I was Gillian, since I was ringing from her phone, so he opened a few doors for me. I guessed that the fifteen grand she had paid him would help. I assured him – as Gillian, of course – that I wasn't going to do a DIY job and cut him out. I just said I needed the gun for protection.

I met Billy's contact behind a pub in Possilpark. Just to be on the safe side I wore a blonde wig and sunglasses. I felt like Dolly Parton in a bad spy movie. The transaction had been quick and easy. The guy had turned out to be a man who could have been anywhere between forty and sixty. His cheekbones were prominent and angular and when he sucked at his cigarette his face turned into a skull.

"Do ye ken how tae use it?" Spittle came out of his mouth with every word. He had a set of false top teeth that he appeared to be breaking in for someone with a much bigger mouth, and no bottom teeth at all, which caused his face to cave in when his mouth was closed.

I nodded. I had grown up on a farm. "Aye." I held out the money we had agreed on and he passed over the padded envelope containing the gun.

He took one more drag of his cigarette. "Good luck, hen."

"Cheers, pal." And that was that. I don't know what I'd expected, but it was like going into the newsagents and buying the *Evening Times*.

I reached the Egyptian Vaults and chose a vantage point where I could see but not be seen. Just before eight o'clock I heard footsteps coming up the path.

"This woman's a weirdo. Why the hell did she want to meet us in this godforsaken place?" I recognized that shrill, whiny voice.

"Don't worry babe. We'll get the bag back and that will be that. These scumbags are only out for a quick score. I hope she's on time. Kate's expecting me home by nine."

I recognized *that* voice too. Cheating, murderous bastard. I stepped out of the shadows. "Don't worry, Tom. When you're not home by nine, I'll assume you have a good excuse."

"Kate?" Tom said.

"Kate?" Gillian repeated, looking at Tom and then at me. "You mean this fat junkie bitch is your *wife*?"

"Well, Tom? What do you say to that?"

"I . . . She . . . I . . ."

"Apparently Tom is lost for words Gillian. So, yes, I am the fat, frumpy bore married to your boyfriend. Not, however, a junkie. That was an assumption *you* jumped to. Understandable given the circumstances, I'll grant you that."

"How did you . . .? What are you . . .?"

"How did I know about your sleazy little affair, Tom? Well, let's face it, you're not exactly Mr Discreet. And you look so guilty when caught answering text messages that are supposedly from your mates. So I followed you one day. And, well, not to get all Hercule Poirot about it, here we are."

Tom started towards me with his hands outstretched. "I'm sorry you had to find out like this, but let's just go somewhere and talk."

I raised the gun. "Just stop right there."

"A gun?"

"Ooooh, well *done*. That's exactly what it is."

"She's a fucking lunatic Tom. I told you what she was like on the phone. She . . ."

"Tom, tell her to shut the fuck up. This is between you and me right now."

"Don't you talk to me . . ."

"Gillian, just do as she says and shut the fuck up."

Gillian subsided into whimpering silence. It still sounded like fingernails scraping down a blackboard, but as long as there weren't any actual words, I could tune her out.

"So, did you go and see that divorce lawyer?"

"I . . . well . . . I . . ."

"No. The answer you're groping for is 'no' Tom. Because you chose a slightly more dramatic way out."

"It was Gillian's idea." His voice had turned from pompous to bleating and I could see him starting to sweat now.

Gillian's eyes opened wide. "You were all for it."

Tom ignored her. "It was easier for her because of the money. She would lose out on a fortune if she divorced Stewart. But I didn't want anything to do with it." A wavering smile appeared briefly as he tried to look sincere and honest. He looked about as sincere and honest as a politician caught with his trousers down in a brothel.

"You said it would be the best way. You lying bastard!"

We both ignored her. "I was caught up in it all, Kate. I wouldn't have hurt you. You've got to believe me."

This time it was my turn. "You lying bastard."

"Honest, Kate . . . I . . ."

"Tom, you wouldn't recognize honesty if it gave you a hug and called you mother." I could feel tears pricking behind my eyes. "Get your clothes off, both of you."

"What?"

"Clothes off." I gestured with the gun. "Now. And fold them up neatly in a pile."

"Look, okay, you want to humiliate us, I understand." Tom hopped on one leg as he struggled to remove his jeans.

"Nah. I don't want to humiliate you. Now, lie down on the grass."

"I'm not doing—"

"Gillian, just shut it and do what I say. Lie down on the grass and put your arms around each other. Tom, you're looking decidedly unaroused. I've never seen it quite so shriveled and tiny. What's wrong? Lost your desire?" It was a cheap shot, but I couldn't resist.

They were on the ground, naked and shivering.

"Look Kate, this is just ridiculous. Let's go and talk somewhere like civilized . . ."

The shots were louder than I'd expected. And there was more blood. I pulled Tom's wallet out of his jeans and picked up Gillian's handbag. I would throw them in the Clyde on my way home, along with the gun. I wiped my prints off Gillian's phone and left it under the pile of clothes. If the police didn't think this was a mugging gone badly wrong, then maybe the text messages would lead them in Billy's direction. As far as he knew, Gillian had bought the gun. There was nothing to lead the police to me, and plenty to lead them away.

As I made my way out of the Necropolis and back to my car, it struck me that Gillian's handbag was another Prada. If nothing else, I'd saved Tom a small fortune in accessories.

EPIPHANY

Margaret Murphy

"You've got to hold my hand!" Trina's got her cross face on, because we're late and it's my fault, 'cos I didn't get ready fast enough. Her eyebrows are all bunched up and her eyes are squinty.

"No! You squeeze too hard!" I hide my hand behind my back, but she's ten and big and I'm only seven and little, so she wins.

"I don't want you – I want my mummy!"

"Well your mummy doesn't want you."

This is so horrible, I gasp. "You're a big fat liar!"

Trina really is fat, so she gets even crosser. "Am not! Your mummy's a wacko."

"She is NOT." I try to hit her, but I've got my school bag in the other hand and it's too heavy, so I don't get a good swing.

Trina gives me a big tug and starts to sing, "Loony-bin, loony-toon, she's so mad she bays at the moon!"

"Stop it!" I shout. "It's not true. She's just op*pressed*."

Trina laughs – it's that loud hard laugh – when you know it means she doesn't think it's funny at all. "It's not *o*-ppressed it's *de*pressed – muppet." She squeezes and squeezes until I cry.

"I'm in charge. And your mummy says you've got to hold my hand to cross the road." she says.

I don't see why, 'cos there's Pelican lights and everyone knows you just have to wait for the green man, but no matter how hard I wriggle, I can't make her let go. If you looked at her face you'd think she was smiling, but she isn't, she's showing her teeth, like Uncle Pete's dog does when he doesn't want you to stroke him.

A mummy comes up with her kids while we're waiting, so I cry harder and shout, "You're hurting my HAND!" The mummy looks at Trina, and she lets go, but only a bit, so it doesn't hurt so much.

She smiles and pretends to be nice. "Don't be silly. You wouldn't want to get squished, now, would you?" Explaining like I'm a baby. She wipes my nose with her tissue, when I didn't even need her to and it's probably full of bogies, anyway.

She has to keep pretending, because the mummy walks behind us. They're late, too, but the mummy is kind to her children and tells them not to worry, to just tell the teacher the car wouldn't start. I look over my shoulder because I can't hear them talking any more, and she's at the gate of the county primary, which isn't the same as our school.

The mummy waves bye-bye and smiles, so they don't worry. When she looks at me I can tell she's thinking if I was her little girl she would walk me to school and she wouldn't squeeze my hand too hard.

"Come *on.*" Trina pulls, so I nearly fall over and she has to squeeze my hand hard again or I'll fall. "Saved your life!" she says. "Now you owe me forever."

This makes me afraid, in case she makes me eat worms to pay her back, but something makes me say, "You nearly killed me, now you owe *me* forever."

She lets go of my hand 'cos we're on the field, now, and the school is at the top of the hill, up the grey path. My fingers have gone white and stiff, so I tuck my hand under my arm.

"Baby." Trina walks fast deliberately so I have to run to keep up.

My fingers are so cold. Trina walks faster and faster so I'm afraid I'll get left behind and I won't know what to say to Miss Irvine. "My fingers hurt!" She pays no attention, but she's almost catched up to a lady with a dog, and I think about how she felt guilty in front of the mummy, and I shout, "You BROKE MY FINGERS!"

She stops, like a soldier when the sergeant calls halt. Then she turns and marches up to me and bends down, so her face is right in front of mine. Her cheeks are red, but everything else is white, 'cept her nose. "You're such a brat!" Her eyes are big and angry.

"I'm not! I'm not a brat, it's just my hand hurts and my fingers are cold."

"I told you. You should've worn your gloves," she says, and grabs my hand. I try to escape, but I'm too slow 'cos I'm upset. "Hm," she says, examining it like a doctor. "I see . . . Stone cold. That's frostbite, that is. I'm afraid those fingers'll drop off by playtime."

I snatch my hand back, pushing it into my coat pocket.

"One by one," Trina says. "Snap! Snap! Snap! Till all you've got is stumps and you won't be able to write or eat or dress or anything and they'll put you in a home."

I start to cry again and she gets behind me and gives me a big shove. "Cry baby! Get a move on, or I'll snap one off right this minute!"

I feel all fluttery, like when Mummy and Daddy used to argue. "Please don't!"

Trina makes another grab for my hand, but I run onto the grass.

"Snap! Snap! Snap!" she says. I back away and she hunches over like a big bear that would eat you. "Snap! Snap! Snap!"

I turn and run. I run and run and Trina can't catch me, because she might be able to walk fast, but she's too fat to run.

"You can't go off on your own!" she shouts. "You're not a-*loud*!" I run until I can't even hear her shouting any more. When I turn around, I can't see Trina. My footsteps have made a track – pale green shoeprints on the white frosty grass. I run around in circles for a bit, in case she tries to follow me, and I end up in the trees. *Can't go in there on your own, you're not aloud.*

I'm not aloud 'cos there might be Bad Men, waiting to pounce. But I can be quiet as a whisper. I've had lots of practice, 'cos Mummy needs me to be quiet when she has a headache. My mummy is sick and she gets headaches a lot.

Like a steel band around my head! Like someone's hammering nails in my skull!

Steel bands make a lot of noise – I know 'cos they had one at the harvest festival and they're VERY aloud, so no wonder they give you a headache.

The path is glittery and some of the twigs and stones are white, like a tiny bit of snow is on them. I hear a noise. It might be a lion or a wolf or a Bad Man. But if I tiptoe very softly and don't look, it'll be okay. Only I don't feel okay, cos my heart feels very big and it's bashing my chest so hard I can see it through my jacket. I'm wearing my new one that I got for Christmas, with the fur trim, so I really hope it isn't a wolf, in case he thinks I'm a nice juicy deer to eat.

I look in front and behind and on the left and on the right, but there's nobody, 'cos me and Trina was already late and all the kids are in school and all the mummies and daddies are at home or in work. I cross my fingers and hold my breath and walk very quiet and pray to God that the wolf won't eat me.

The sound comes again, and I jump. It doesn't sound like a wolf, it sounds like a cat's miaow. What if a kitten has got lost and can't find her mummy? I take a big deep breath and hold it again, only this time, it's so I can listen. There it is!

The miaow is coming from under a bush, which is quite near the end of the path, where there's a gate onto the street, so maybe the kitten just wandered off.

"Here, kitty, kitty, kitty." The kitten doesn't come out, so I kneel next to the bush. It isn't very muddy and I don't get dirty at all, because anyway it's all frozen. "*Here,* kitty."

It's all wrapped up in a yellow blanket. The blanket moves and I'm a bit scared in case the kitten scratches me. But there's nobody else to rescue it, so I take one corner, where the silky bit is, and lift it very carefully.

"Oh!" It isn't a kitten at all – it's a baby. I look around, but there's no mummies about who might have dropped it – and anyway, you don't just drop a baby and not know about it. Then I remember Mummy said when you have a baby you have to go out and find him. And the most popular place is under a bush.

It's *my* baby . . . For a minute, I just kneel there, smiling because I'm so happy. Its cheeks are pink, but its lips are a funny colour. It isn't miaowing, it's crying, but very softly. Maybe that's 'cos it's not aloud, like I'm not aloud when Mummy's feeling Bad, *Or you'll get a SMACK and locked in your room, my girl!*

"*Miaow,*" it goes.

I pick it up. It's bigger than my Baby Suzy doll, and much heavier. Heavy and squirmy, but I'm quite strong for my age, and once you get the hang of it, babies are easy. I go the back way, so nobody sees me. The baby gets warmer from the exercise and doesn't look so funny any more. Its lips are normal lip-colour, and it just stares at me, like it knows I'm its mummy.

I take it to the shed and cuddle it for a bit. If Mummy looks out, she won't see me, 'cos I'm too far away at the bottom of the garden and Trina won't tell them I ran away, 'cos if she does I'll tell them she was going to snap my fingers off and she'll be in Big Trouble.

There's three reasons why a baby cries: if it's hungry, if it's sick, or if it's nappy needs changing. Oh, and if it's tired, but mostly they just go to sleep if they're tired.

My baby needed its nappy changing. I have to find a clean nappy, which is easy, 'cos my mummy put all the baby things in the shed after she lost her baby. I don't mind changing its nappy, 'cos I can hold my breath for ages and anyway, Mummy showed me how to change Joseph's nappy, before he got lost. My baby's a boy as well – I would have liked a girl, better, but a boy is almost as good.

The nappy's cold and the baby cries a bit until I put a vest on him, and a fluffy suit that has feet in it like little booties, and a hood so he's warm and toasty.

"Hush little baby, don't say a word, Papa's gonna buy you a mock-in bird."

My daddy used to sing that to me when he lived with us. He doesn't live in my house any more – he lives in an apartment, because Mummy and Daddy need some time apart. When Daddy comes, they don't look at each other, like they're not friends any more. Mummy always cries when he's gone, though, so I know she wants to be friends again.

And now the baby's crying again – not miaowing any more – he goes "Wah!" quite loud. I think he must be hungry. Babies drink special milk, only out of a tin, instead of a bottle. You've got to mix it up with hot water and put it in a bottle with a teat on it. I tried it once, before Joseph got lost, and it's disgusting, but babies like it. There's some in the baby box, only I'm frightened of going inside the house for the hot water, 'cos Mummy's having a Bad Day, and I'm not supposed to be home yet.

"Sush, Baby. You'll just have to wait." But he won't wait. He goes "WAH!" even louder.

If my baby was like the Baby Jesus, he wouldn't cry. For a minute, I think what if it *is* the Baby Jesus, 'cos it's Christmas, and the Wise Men are supposed to come today, and I found him all on his own, like a miracle.

But Mummy says all babies are miracles, and anyway, there wasn't any Star of Bethlehem, with it being in the daytime and there wasn't any shepherds as well. Also, the Baby Jesus was born in a manger, which is like a stable, only with cows and sheep, and my baby was under a bush, like a normal baby.

"Wa-aah!" And Baby Jesus was a good baby.

"Now, you're just being naughty!"

It makes no difference, he goes, "Wah! Wa-aah!" until I'm fed up of it and take the milk stuff and close the shed door, so no one will hear. The kids next door have got a swing, but there's nobody on it, so it mustn't be lunchtime, yet. They always come home for lunch and they always get to play on the swing. It isn't fair. But today it's covered in frost, so they mustn't be home, yet, and I look up into the sky, and cross my fingers and make a prayer there's enough in the clouds to make it snow.

The back door is open, so Mummy must be in. I leave the door wide, so I can sneak out if I hear her coming downstairs. The tin is open from last time Joseph had some. I put the bottle on the table and take off the lid. You have to put the powder in with a special spoon called a scoop. Then you add boiled water. Mummy won't let me use the kettle, so I use hot water from the tap, instead. Then I put the lid on and shake and shake and SHAKE!

Mummy must be asleep, 'cos she doesn't hear me. Sometimes, she sleeps all day when she's Bad. Being Bad isn't the same as being naughty. Being Bad is when your sick and it makes you cry all the time and you don't want to make a costume for the school play about Baby Jesus. And *This isn't all about you, you know! This whole bloody world doesn't revolve around you!* Miss Irvine said it didn't matter and gave me an old one from the box under the stage but it smelt of cobwebs and Trina said she didn't know angels were stinky. Trina's horrible.

I'm *starving* because I didn't have time for breakfast, and anyway there wasn't any milk. There's peanut butter in the cupboard so I push the dirty dishes out of the way and make two sandwiches, with peanut butter on both of them. Then I stick my finger in the jar and have a bit extra, 'cos nobody's looking.

There's nothing on TV, so I put a DVD on instead and watch *Shrek* for a bit. I have to cover my mouth so I didn't laugh too loud and wake Mummy up. Daddy says Mummy's like an ogre when she's got her angry head on. Only she isn't funny, like Shrek, and she isn't green. I don't like Mummy's angry head.

I hear a *flump*. It's coming from upstairs, and I think it might be Mummy. I switch off the TV and run to the door. If you open it a tiny tiny bit, you can see out with one eye. The toilet flushes, but Mummy doesn't come downstairs.

I know where the floor creaks, so I can get down the hall quieter than a mouse with slippers on. The baby's bottle isn't hot any more, but maybe it won't mind. Because it's my baby, I'm the only one that can give it a name, but the only name that keeps coming into my head is Joseph. I frown and frown like Mummy, to stop it coming back. Maybe that's why Mummy frowns – to keep her baby's name out of her head?

I have to run to the shed and hope Mummy isn't watching. She isn't, because I count to fifty and she still doesn't come. The baby is very, very quiet.

"Good boy!" Look what Mummy's brought you. I cuddle it, while I give it the bottle. It sucks and sucks and sucks until all the milk is gone, then suddenly, *Bleurgh*! It's sick everywhere.

"Naughty boy!" I have to get a wet wipe and clean his face and his fluffy suit, but it still smells of sick and he starts to cry.

"Wah! Wah!" Looking after babies is HARD.

Mummy should be glad she doesn't have to look after Joseph. It's his own fault if he got lost, 'cos you should always hold your mummy's hand if you don't know how to get back.

"I'm going to count to five. If you don't stop crying I'll give you a SMACK!" Mummy says smacking is a – *something* – of failure. I forget what. But she hasn't got Joseph going, "Wah! Wa-aah! Wah!" And he won't stop.

"Laura?"

My heart stops. Then is starts again, really fast, like it's trying to catch up. I cover the baby's mouth but it's all wet and snotty and anyway it doesn't stop.

"*Laura!*"

I come out of the shed and close the door. The baby goes "Wa-aah!" So I run halfway across the lawn. Maybe she won't hear.

"Are you home already?" she says.

"You forgot my dinner money." This is true, but Mummy looks at me like I'm trying to hide something behind my back. "I had to come home," I say, which is also true, but not in the same way.

She blinks, like she's just woken up. "Come in, you'll catch your death of cold."

"Can't I play out?" I can hear the baby "*Wah! Wa-aah!*" but it sounds far away.

"You haven't even got your gloves on! Can't you do the simplest thing?"

I don't say anything, 'cos it just makes her more cross.

"Did Trina walk you home?"

I nod, because I always give myself away if I tell a fib.

She doesn't say anything for a while, and I'm afraid she's listening for the baby. But then she turns away from me. "Inside," she says.

I want a cup of cocoa with marshmallows, but Mummy goes straight back upstairs. Maybe I can make some using hot water out of the tap. But I can't find a clean cup and the cocoa is in one of the wall cupboards, but I push a stool over and climb up.

BANG!

At first I think Mummy's fallen over, but then I hear her running down the stairs. Really running. Thud, thud, thud, thud! She pushes the kitchen door so hard it crashes against the wall and the door wobbles and the wall gets a dent in it. I'm so frightened, I just stand on the stool and I can't move.

"You bloody little liar!"

"Mummy . . ."

"It's eleven o'clock in the morning. What the *hell* are you doing home?"

My mouth is dry and my legs are so shaky I can't even jump down off the stool. "Your clock must've stopped," I say. "It really is—"

Suddenly, my face is burning. I lose my balance, but she grabs me by the arm and pulls me down. "Ow! Ow, it hurts! Mummy, please, it hurts!"

"How dare you lie to me – I just heard it on the radio, you wicked, wicked girl!" Whack! Whack! She smacks me as hard as she can on my bum and my legs and my back.

"Mummy, *please!*"

Then she pulls me upstairs and it hurts so much 'cos she's twisting my arm, but when I try to tell her she whacks me again.

"Bloody liar!"

She throws me onto my bed. There's toys on it, because I was playing with them before school. I land on them and they dig into my back. "Ow! Mummy!"

"Look at this pig sty! How can you find anything in this pile of filth! You dirty, dirty girl. No wonder you've no friends – you make me ashamed!"

"Mummy! I'm sorry!" I can hardly talk because I'm crying so hard. "I – Trina hurt my hand. I had to run away 'cos she was going to break my fingers off!"

"Stop lying! I've had ENOUGH!" She's screaming so loud I cover my ears, but I can still hear her. "Enough of you. Enough of your lies and your whining, your complaints and demands. You're never satisfied, are you? ARE you?"

"Yes, Mummy."

She slaps my legs. "Don't be insolent! What am I going to say to Miss Irvine? That you lied? That you ran away?"

"Please, Mummy, don't. Don't tell Miss Irvine!" I'm sobbing, and Mummy hates that, but I can't stop. It's like somebody poured all the sadness in the world into my heart, and my heart is so full it's spilled into my tummy, and I have to cry or I'll burst.

Mummy comes up close. Her eyes aren't like my mummy's eyes. They're hard and glittery and I'm afraid to look. "SHUT UP!" she screams and slaps me across the face again.

I close my eyes and hold my breath. I hold it and hold it to stop myself from crying, and after a long time, she goes away. *Mission.* Mummy says smacking is *a mission* of failure.

When she's gone I cry for a long time, but very, very quietly – 'cos crying's not aloud. I crawl under the duvet and curl up and pretend I'm a dormouse and I'm going asleep till the winter's over. I'm awfully tired . . .

"Sweetie?"

I lie still under the duvet. Maybe she won't notice me. Then I feel her hand on my shoulder, and I make a little sound, which I didn't mean to make, but I couldn't help it. "Laura – sweetie – it's all right. Mummy isn't cross any more." I don't say anything, in case it's a trick.

"Mummy's very sorry." I still don't say anything. "Look, I've brought you a surprise." She lifts the duvet a tiny bit to let the smell in. Scrambled eggs on toast. My favourite.

I slide out from under the covers, but I don't sit close to her. I go and sit on my pillows, instead, so I can look at her. She hasn't got her angry head on any more. She looks sad and her eyes are red, like *she's* been crying.

"Oh, sweetie!" she leans over and at first I'm afraid, and I duck.

"Shhh . . ." she says. She was only going to stroke my head this time. I'm all sweaty, 'cos I've still got my coat on, but Mummy doesn't shout or be mad at me. "Mummy doesn't mean to be cross," she says. And now she's definitely crying, which makes me want to start all over again.

"Won't you have something to eat?" she says. It does smell lovely. She's brought it up on a tray, like when I'm sick. I feel like telling her no, but I'm *so* hungry. It's already night-time, so I must have fallen asleep.

I nod, to show I'll try. It hurts my face, but you don't have to chew scrambled eggs, and the toast is soggy – the way I like it – so it's not too bad. She helps me to take my coat off, and looks at my arms and cries again. Then she sits next to me, and I can see that she really isn't cross any more and she really is sorry.

"You can have hot chocolate with extra marshmallows and two chocolate biscuits after," she says, and kisses me very soft on the forehead, and I love her more than the whole wide world. "I'm sorry, Mummy," I say, and I can't help crying. My lips wobble and I feel like I've got something stuck in my throat, but I haven't. "I didn't mean to upset you."

"It's not your fault," she says. "I shouldn't have – oh, *darling*, I didn't mean it, you know that, don't you? It's just, since Joseph . . ." She never says the next bit. *Since Joseph got lost. Since I lost Joseph*. Maybe she blames herself for losing him. 'Cos Uncle Pete says you've got to watch kids like a hawk.

Mummy's fast asleep. It's still night time, but my watch says it's only eight o'clock, which isn't even my bedtime. I tiptoe down the stairs to the kitchen. I have to go out to the shed, so I'll need a torch – there's one under the kitchen sink. I've got an idea – see, the baby is mine, 'cos I found him fair and square. He *is* big though. And heavy. And *smelly*. And he cries all the time. I can hear him, "(Wah! Wah!)" very faintly, as I walk across the grass. And Mummy really likes changing nappies and bath-time and all that stuff. I could share him a bit – Mummy says nice little girls share their things – and I wouldn't mind, so long as I get to cuddle him and dress him sometimes. And maybe take him for walks. I haven't even given him a proper name, yet – just "Baby", so I could call him whatever I like. It's a good idea, and I giggle when I think what a surprise Mummy will get.

I open the door and: "WAH! WAH!" Baby will have to stop crying, or he'll spoil everything.

"Baby, you HAVE to stop!" I say. But of course he doesn't. I find a dummy in the baby box, but he spits it out. He smells of sick and dirty nappies. "Baby, *please*." But that does no good. I take his dirty clothes off and give him a new nappy and everything, but he STILL won't stop.

"Now just you stop it! You wicked, selfish boy! You're never satisfied – you always want more more more! Stop it. Stop it RIGHT NOW!"

But he screams even louder.

"I've had ENOUGH!"

Mummy's still asleep, when I go back to my room.

"Look, Mummy, I brought you a surprise." She stretches and sighs and but she doesn't open her eyes. Joseph looks lovely in his clean rompers and booties. He seems heavier than before. Maybe I'll just put him next to Mummy so she can see him when she wakes up properly. He's nice and quiet now. And with all that crying, he could do with the rest.

CALL ME, I'M DYING

Allan Guthrie

7:15 p.m.
Every year on the fifth of June we pretend we're married. This year is no different.

I look across at him, try to mould my face into the right expression.

"I'll get the soup," he says, getting to his feet.

Same menu as last year, I expect. And the year before.

I don't know, I'm guessing. I don't cook. I don't want to cook. I'm not paid to cook.

James likes to cook but he likes to play safe, too. Goes with the tried and tested.

Doesn't bother me.

I'm easy, so they say.

The food is a bonus.

Makes the sex easier.

7:16 p.m.
"You need a hand?" I ask him, knowing how he'll reply.

I'm dandy.

Sure enough. From the kitchen: "I'm dandy."

He's not that.

Supposed to be our tenth wedding anniversary and he's wearing a tatty checked shirt and jeans.

Could have made an effort.

We'll shower later.

I always insist on that.

7:17 p.m.

He carries the soup pan through. If it was me, I'd ladle it out in the kitchen.

It's not me.

If it was me, I'd have passed on the appetizer, gone straight for the main course. Takeaway pizza. Pepperoni and pineapple.

Each to his own, okay?

He places the pot on the table, takes off the oven gloves, removes the lid with a dramatic gesture and says, "*Voila!* French onion."

Now there's a surprise.

"Smells good," I say. And I shouldn't be harsh on him. It does smell good.

7:18 p.m.

"There we are," he says. "Shall we say Grace?"

I nod.

Then he hits me with this *you* or *me* thing, where he's just being polite 'cause we both know it's not going to be me. I grew up with it, and look how I've turned out.

"On you go," I say.

He nods, clears his throat, closes his eyes, adopts a tone somewhere between respectful and agonized. "For what we are about to receive," he says, "may the Lord make us truly thankful."

That's it. Good.

I blink. Pretending I've had my eyes closed too.

He's not fooled, but he joins in the game anyway.

It's all a game.

I always win.

I don't think he understands the rules. I'd ask him but I can't be bothered. I just want to get this over with.

I have things I'd rather be doing.

I'm liable to yawn and I don't want to upset him.

7:19 p.m.

"Nice?" he asks.

I pause, spoon halfway to my mouth. "Lovely."

"The key is to use plenty of butter."

That's it.

I lower the spoon, let it rest in the bowl. I'm not taking another sip. Butter. Plenty of it.

Is he trying to kill me?

I smile.

He smiles back. His hand edges across towards me

"You don't mind?" he says.

Intimacy. Yes, I do mind. But I let him hold my hand anyway.

7:20 p.m.

"Your soup's getting cold," he says.

Fine by me.

"Not having any more?"

"Saving myself for the main course," I tell him.

"Oh," he says, disappointed but understanding.

Makes me want to smack a frying pan off his jaw.

At least he's let go of my hand.

I get a flash of him panting. In my ear. Sticky breath, getting faster and faster. I'm moaning, telling him he's the best, oh, yeah, the fucking best.

He likes it when I swear.

He comes and then he cries.

Wets my hair.

Every time.

Every year.

After dessert.

7:21 p.m.

He's talking. He's bought a boat. Not a fancy yacht, oh no. He laughs. Tells me about his boat.

I nod and smile, tuned out, wondering what I'm missing on TV.

White noise, his voice.

I smile from the heart, 'cause that rhymes.

Get a smile back, bless him.

I wonder if he'll be hard or if I'm going to have to play with him first.

7:22 p.m.
So excited babbling about his new boat, he spills soup on himself.

I grab a napkin, dab at his chin.

He likes that.

I wonder what precedent I've just set.

He excuses himself, says he has to change his shirt.

At least he doesn't ask me to do it for him.

I offer to clear the plates away.

He won't let me.

Always the gentleman.

7:25 p.m.
Back again wearing an almost identical shirt.

Took him long enough.

I heard the toilet flush, though. All that soup. Runs right through you.

Voila!

Must be the onions.

"You had enough?" he asks.

"Plenty," I say, only just managing to keep my hand from patting my stomach. A false gesture if ever there was one and I'm a better actress than that.

"Sure you don't want a hand?" I ask as he starts clearing away the plates.

"Just stay where you are," he says. "Keep looking beautiful."

7:27 p.m.
Still smarting from that comment.

Beautiful.

Bastard.

7:28 p.m.
The casserole dish is on the table, steaming.

Beef stew. Yep, same as last year.

Predictable, is our James the Sarcastic.

Smells good, though. I'm going to have to eat.

I don't want to. I want to punish him.

He might like that.

"Shall I be mother?" he says.

We know he's going to be mother. I don't know why he asks. "Yeah," I say. It's a role that suits him.

He slops some of the stew onto my plate. "More?" he says. I nod. I hate myself.

7:29 p.m.

The beef's tender, melting into soft strings in my mouth. The sauce is sharp, peppery.

I swallow. Lick my teeth.

"Good, darling?"

Darling.

Have to play along. "Yes, *dear*," I say.

He puts his hand on mine again.

"This is nice, isn't it?" he says.

"Lovely," I tell him. Fuckwit.

7:30 p.m.

The phone rings. It's persistent.

He doesn't move.

"Answer it," I say.

"Not tonight," he says. "This is a special night. We don't want any interruptions."

So maybe you should have turned off the ringer.

"It's annoying," I say. And it is. Least he could have done was set up his answer machine to take it. At home, four rings is all you get. If I don't pick up by then, you're on to the machine.

Still ringing.

"You don't have an answerphone?"

"Yeah," he says.

"So how come it hasn't kicked in?"

"Dunno," he says. "Takes a while."

I lay down my knife and fork. "Go sort it," I say. "Turn it off."

He looks sheepish as he gets out of his seat. "May as well answer it, then," he says.

Course, by the time he gets there, it'll have stopped. I'd bet on it.

The phone's at the other end of the room. Amazingly it's still ringing when he picks it up.

"Hello," he says. Then gives his number.

Doesn't say anything else.

Just listens.

Then puts the phone down gently, like it's hurting.

7:31 p.m.

"Wrong number?" I ask.

He shakes his head, still standing there, hand on the receiver, receiver in its cradle.

"Not much of a conversationalist, then?" I say. "What did they say?"

He makes his way back to the table, silent.

"Well?" I say.

"You won't believe me," he says. He looks bemused, like a stranger just hit him with a fish.

"You'd be surprised," I tell him.

"It was a man," he says. "I didn't recognize his voice."

He stops. Bites his bottom lip.

"I don't have all night," I say. More to the point, *he* doesn't have all night. He isn't paying for that. Just till midnight.

"He said my name." He looks at me. Looks away.

"And?" I make a circular motion with my fingers to try to speed him up.

"He told me I had thirty minutes to live."

7:32 p.m.

That's weird, I have to admit.

"Why would anyone say that to you?" I ask him.

He doesn't answer, just sits at the table staring into his plate. He picks up his fork, holds it for a second, drops it. It clatters against the plate.

"Maybe it was a wrong number," I say.

He says, "He said my name."

"Maybe it was another James Twist," I say.

He doesn't bother to answer. We both know that's unlikely.

"It's a joke, then," I say.

That piques his interest. "You think?"

"Sure," I say. "A friend, a colleague."

"I don't think so," he says.

I spread my fingers, palms up. *Why?*

"I don't have any friends," he says. "And I haven't worked in ten years."

7:33 p.m.

Well, well.

"You're not an architect?" I ask him.

He shakes his head.

"Were you ever an architect?"

He shakes his head again.

"What did you do? What was your last job?"

"Postman," he says.

I can't believe I'm angry at him, but I am.

"You've been lying to me for years," I say.

"Sorry," he tells me.

"How can you afford to buy a new boat?"

He doesn't answer.

"That was a lie too?"

"Yes," he says.

"What about this place?"

"My mum pays for it."

"Oh," I say. "She didn't die when you were four?"

7:34 p.m.

It can't be helped, I suppose. The guy I didn't like wasn't the guy I thought he was.

Interesting.

"If it's not a friend or colleague," I say, "then maybe it's a member of your family."

"Just me and Mum," he says.

"And it wasn't her?"

"It was a man," he says.

"What happened to your dad?"

He pulls a face.

For a second, I don't know what he's doing, or why. Then I realize it's involuntary. A spasm. I've never seen him do that before.

He does it again, his eyes screwing up tight, lips curling.

Like he just sucked a grapefruit.

And then it's gone.

"Your dad?" I remind him.

"He's dead," he says. Looks at me. "Honest."

"I'm sorry." I reach over and place my hand on his.

7:35 p.m.

He moves his hand so it's on top of mine. He squeezes.

We stare at our hands, don't look at each other.

Time drags past.

He strokes my hand. Over and over and over again.

I'm intrigued by the phone call. And by what I'm finding out about James.

"Your mum have a boyfriend, maybe?" I say, at last.

He tears his hand away from mine, swipes his plate onto the floor.

Don't fucking hit me. Don't you fucking dare.

He doesn't, although he looks at me like he wants to.

7:38 p.m.

He picks up shards of broken plate, lays the pieces on the table.

"I don't know why—" he says.

"I should leave."

"Please don't," he says. He sits, wipes his fingers on his napkin. "That call, it's thrown me."

I shrug. "Not surprising," I say.

"I'd like you to stay," he says. "I don't want to be alone."

"All right," I tell him. "But don't get violent."

"I won't."

"If you do," I say, "I'll kick the shit out of you."

He grins. Doesn't believe me.

He's never been aggressive before. I try to avoid men who are. But I've learned to deal with them just in case.

I can look after myself.

I teach self-defense classes when I'm not working.

I'm not scared of James.

7:39 p.m.

"We should clear up that mess," I say. "The carpet's a state."

"Just leave it," he says.

"It'll stink."

"That's okay."

"It'll stain."

He's quiet.

"You don't care if it stains?"

He shakes his head.

"Your Mum's carpet anyway," I say. "Her problem. That what you're thinking?"

"No," he says. "I have other things to think about."

"Then let me do it," I say.

"It's our anniversary, Tina," he says. "You can't clean the floor tonight."

I sigh. If I can't clean the carpet, I might as well eat. "What's for pudding?" I ask.

7:40 p.m.

He thinks I'm joking.

I don't push.

He already looks like he might cry and I don't want to send him over the edge.

"Why did you stop working?" I ask him.

He looks at me, eyes dark and uncomprehending.

"You said you used to be a postman."

He nods. That's it, though.

I have to help him.

"Were you a postman for long?"

He plays with his fork again.

I anticipate another clatter.

"Five years," he says.

"Did you enjoy it?"

"Yeah."

"So what happened?"

"They let me go."

Another topic I shouldn't have introduced. I'm on a roll.

"I'm sorry to hear that," I say.

"Me too," he says.

And as I'm watching, he slams the fork into his hand.

Screams.

I scream too.

He wrenches the fork back out.

Blood's leaking out of the four holes he's made, running together, tracking down the back of his wrist.

"What the fuck?" I say. "What the fuck are you doing?"

His mouth's open and he's panting.

"He's after me," he says. "Don't look at me like that. He is."

"That's maybe so, James," I say. "But put the fork down and let's see what you've done to your hand."

"It's okay," he says. "I feel better."

"It doesn't hurt?"

"It does," he says. "But it takes a little pain to let the evil out."

7:42 p.m.

Holy shit.

I'm torn between legging it out of here and making sure James is okay. He needs to go to the hospital. Leave him here on his own and God knows what he'll do to himself.

Between last year and now, hc's turned into a headcase.

Presumably there was nobody on the phone. He made all that up about somebody telling him he only had thirty minutes to live.

This guy who was after him was a figment of James's fucked-up brain.

But the phone had rung. Someone had called.

I get to my feet.

7:43 p.m.

"Where are you going?" he says. "Don't leave me."

He's cradling his hand now.

"I'm going to check something out," I tell him. "I'll be right back."

I walk over to the phone. Punch in the code to find out who just called.

And hear: *You were called today at 7:30 p.m. The caller withheld their number.*

So much for that theory.

7:44 p.m.
"Let me take you to get your hand fixed," I say.
　"No." He shakes his head hard.
　"Then let me look at it."
　He thinks about it. Then relaxes. Holds his hand out to me.
　It's a bloody mess. The puncture wounds have coagulated,
though. The blood's stopped flowing.
　Not that deep.
　Good.
　He'll be okay.
　"You got a first-aid kit?" I ask him.
　"No," he says.
　"Antiseptic wipes? Plasters?"
　He looks vague.
　"A clean cloth? Water?"
　He grins. "Of course."

7:46 p.m.
So I've got the stuff and I'm cleaning his hand.
　He winces like I'm scraping my nails on his heart.
　"How come you had to do that?" I ask him.
　For a moment he forgets to act pained. "Huh?" he says.
　"Stabbing yourself. Seems . . . extreme."
　He shrugs.
　"You do that often?" I've never noticed any scars.
　"My feet," he says. "The soles of my feet."
　Ow.
　"To let the evil out?"
　"I wouldn't expect you to understand," he says.
　Thing is, I do.
　I do.
　Me and razor blades, we go way back. Not that I'm going to
tell James, though. None of his business.
　He's my business, not the other way round.
　I opt for, "You'd be surprised."
　He gives me a look, winces again.
　"You said he was after you," I say, dropping the cloth in the
bowl of water.
　"This is going to bruise." He flexes his fingers.

"I expect so. Who's after you?"

"I can't say."

"Maybe I can help," I tell him.

7:47 p.m.

His words come out slow and staggered. I'll summarize.

Started about a year ago when James began to feel he was being followed every time he walked home. Never spotted anyone, but just had the sense someone was watching him. Heard footsteps but couldn't swear they weren't echoes of his own.

And then he felt he was being followed whenever he left the house, too.

He started taking the car.

A vehicle always followed him. Not always the same vehicle, though. So it was sometimes hard to spot.

I wanted to ask him if he had surveillance cameras under his fingernails, and transmitters implanted in his brain.

I held my tongue.

He carried on. Told me how he was being watched all the time now. His stalker was close. Maybe watching him now. Him and me.

I say, "But if this is true, why does injuring yourself help?"

A textbook case of paranoia.

"Because of what I've done," he says.

Do I want to know?

"If you tell me," I say, "will you have to kill me afterwards?"

7:50 p.m.

"My uncle came back," he says.

He has an uncle?

"I thought you had no family," I say.

He says, "He's not really an uncle. He . . . went out with my mum for a while."

"Came back from where?" I ask.

"Disappeared a long time ago," he says. "Went off to Brazil. Never heard from him again. You assume the worst after a while."

"So you thought he was dead?"

He nods.

"And he's not?"

He nods again.

"And you stabbed yourself in the hand because of that?"

"No, no," he says. "It's a lot more complicated."

I expected so. I look at my watch.

"Maybe you better keep it simple," I say. "According to your uncle, you only have ten minutes to live."

A cheap shot, I know.

So I'm a bitch. What can you expect from a whore?

7:51 p.m.

"It wasn't him," James says. "I'd have recognized his voice."

"But you do think he's behind it?"

"Yes," he says. "No question. He's made my life hell since he's been back."

He flexes his fingers, a pained expression scrawled across his face.

"He must have hired somebody to make the call," he says.

"And why would he do that?"

"To scare me," he says.

"You think the threat's serious?"

"Definitely."

"James," I say. "What did you do to him?"

7:52 p.m.

He tells me.

"It's not that bad. Not the sort of thing you'd kill somebody for.

Listen:

"I torched his car."

See?

"His dog was in it."

Oh.

"But I didn't know that."

Still.

"And he said he'd have to leave the country or he'd kill me."

"Why?" I ask.

"Because of the dog."

ALLAN GUTHRIE

"No," I say. "Why did you torch his car?"
"Because," he says, and swallows. "He raped my mum."

7:53 p.m.
There's not much more to it.
Uncle goes out with Mum. Mum calls it off after a few weeks. Uncle returns and rapes mum. She won't go to the police, and who can blame her, the way we're all made to feel like it's our fucking fault. *What were you wearing?* As if that makes any fucking difference. Anyway, James torches dog and car. Uncle leaves country. Uncle returns several years later. Uncle's still angry.
But there's no way he's still going to be murderously angry. Not after all that time.
I say, "He's messing with you."
James says, "No."
"How can you be sure?"
"Cause I know him. I know what he's capable of."
"Well," I say, and I can't think of anything to add, so I say, "well," again and leave it at that. There's only one way to prove to James that it's all a hoax and that's to sit it out with him. I owe him that.
After all, he's paying for my time.
"I like dogs," James says. "Honest."
"I believe you," I say.

7:54 p.m.
Back in the sitting room, James keeps glancing towards the door.
He's shaking all over, poor soul.
No, I do feel sorry for him. I do.
He did something he shouldn't have. But he did it out of love. The dog was an accident.
But when I think about it, I can't imagine a dog not barking. They're territorial. A stranger approaches the car, close enough to set it alight, the dog would let him know it was there.
Wouldn't it?
James is lying.
But why?

Is he lying about the whole event? Or is he just lying about the dog?

7:55 p.m.
"You did it deliberately, right?"
"What?"
He knows what I mean.
I stare at him till he looks away.
He doesn't deny it.
But I have to say it: "You killed the dog."
He says, quietly, "It was an accident."
"So why do you cut yourself? What evil is it you're letting out?"
He makes that face again.
"Jesus," I say. "How long ago was this?"
"I was seventeen."
"Then it's about time you forgave yourself," I tell him.
"I can't," he says. "I can't, Tina."
"Well," I say. "I don't blame you, really."
"You don't?"
He starts to cry. Before long these horrible wracking sobs are jerking his shoulders up and down.
I put my arms round him, let him rest his head against my neck. His tears drip onto my neck, but what the fuck. I'm used to that.
"Thank you," he squeezes out between sobs.
"Shhh," I say, like he's a baby.

7:56 p.m.
He stops as suddenly as he started.
"How long?" he asks, wiping his eyes.
I tell him.
"I have to lock the door," he says.
He jumps to his feet, runs through to the hall where I can't see him any longer.
I hear him scrabbling about.
Then I don't hear anything.
For a while.
For too long.
I get worried.

7:58 p.m.

There's no sign of him anywhere.

He's not in the hall.

Not in any of the bedrooms.

Not in the bathroom.

He's gone.

Did he leave of his own accord?

If so, why didn't he tell me he was leaving?

Did his uncle sneak in, grab him, steal him away?

Sounds dramatic, and I don't believe a word of it.

I check the front door. It's locked. There we go.

It's crazy, I know, but I go back through all the bedrooms, look in the wardrobes, under the beds. I check everywhere, but he's definitely not here.

I'm feeling uncomfortable.

I get my things together.

I'm not hanging around here.

I'm going home.

8:00 p.m.

Outside, the traffic's busy.

Across the road, I see a face I recognize.

James.

He's wearing that screwed-up expression, the one I'd never seen until I mentioned his father.

He's standing by the curb, an older man in a long raincoat by his side.

I raise my hand, wave.

James stares right through me.

I shout to him.

The man in the raincoat thinks I'm shouting at him.

I can't say whether James is pushed in front of the bus, or whether he steps in front of it.

The impact is swift and brutal.

He never had a chance.

I wet myself.

After the shock passes, I remember the man in the raincoat.

But he's gone.

The bus has stopped.

The street is silent.

Nobody moves.

We're frozen like this, like a painting, and I wonder if James still has that expression on his face.

HEROES

Anne Perry

Nights were always the worst, and in winter they lasted from dusk at about four o'clock until dawn again towards eight the following morning. Sometimes star shells lit the sky, showing the black zigzags of the trenches stretching as far as the eye could see to left and right. Apparently now they went right across France and Belgium all the way from the Alps to the Channel. But Joseph was only concerned with this short stretch of the Ypres Salient.

In the gloom near him someone coughed, a deep, hacking sound coming from down in the chest. They were in the support line, farthest from the front, the most complex of the three rows of trenches. Here were the kitchens, the latrines and the stores and mortar positions. Fifteen-foot shafts led to caves which were about five paces wide, and high enough for most men to stand upright. Joseph made his way in the half-dark now, the slippery wood under his boots and his hands feeling the mud walls, held up by timber and wire. There was an awful lot of water. One of the sumps must be blocked.

There was a glow of light ahead and a moment later he was in the comparative warmth of the dugout. There were two candles burning and the brazier gave off heat, and a sharp smell of soot. The air was blue with tobacco smoke and a pile of boots and great coats steamed a little. Two officers sat on canvas chairs talking together. One of them recited a joke – gallows humour, and they both laughed. A gramophone sat silent on a camp table, and a small pile of records of the latest music hall songs was carefully protected in a tin box.

"Hello, Chaplain," one of them said cheerfully. "How's God these days?"

"Gone home on sick leave," the other answered quickly, before Joseph could reply. There was disgust in his voice, but no intended irreverence. Death was too close here for men to mock faith.

"Have a seat," the first offered, waving towards a third chair. "Morris got it today. Killed outright. That bloody sniper again."

"He's somewhere out there, just about opposite us," the second said grimly. "One of those blighters the other day claimed he'd got forty-three for sure."

"I can believe it," Joseph answered, accepting the seat. He knew better than most what the casualties were. It was his job to comfort the terrified, the dying, to carry stretchers, often to write letters to the bereaved. Sometimes he thought it was harder than actually fighting, but he refused to stay back in the comparative safety of the field hospitals and depots. This was where he was most needed.

"Thought about setting up a trench raid," the major said slowly, weighing his words and looking at Joseph. "Good for morale. Make it seem as if we were actually doing something. But our chances of getting the blighter are pretty small. Only lose a lot of men for nothing. Feel even worse afterwards."

The captain did not add anything. They all knew morale was sinking. Losses were high, the news bad. Word of terrible slaughter seeped through from the Somme and Verdun and all along the line right to the sea. Physical hardship took its toll, the dirt, the cold, and the alternation between boredom and terror. The winter of 1916 lay ahead.

"Cigarette?" the major held out his pack to Joseph.

"No thanks," Joseph declined with a smile. "Got any tea going?"

They poured him a mugful, strong and bitter, but hot. He drank it, and half an hour later made his way forward to the open air again and the travel trench. A star shell exploded high and bright. Automatically he ducked, keeping his head below the rim. They were about four feet deep, and in order not to provide a target, a man had to move in a half-crouch. There was a rattle of machine gun fire out ahead, and closer to, a thud as a rat was dislodged and fell into the mud beside the duckboards.

Other men were moving about close to him. The normal order of things was reversed here. Nothing much happened during the day. Trench repair work was done, munitions shifted, weapons cleaned, a little rest taken. Most of the activity was at night, most of the death.

" 'Lo Chaplain," a voice whispered in the dark. "Say a prayer we get that bloody sniper, will you?"

"Maybe God's a Jerry?" someone suggested in the dark.

"Don't be stupid!" a third retorted derisively. "Everyone knows God's an Englishman! Didn't they teach you nothing at school?"

There was a burst of laughter. Joseph joined in. He promised to offer up the appropriate prayers and moved on forward. He had known many of the men all his life. They came from the same Northumbrian town as he did, or the surrounding villages. They had gone to school together, scrumped apples from the same trees, fished in the same rivers and walked the same lanes.

It was a little after six when he reached the firing trench beyond whose sandbag parapet lay no-man's land with its four or five hundred yards of mud, barbed wire and shell holes. Half a dozen burnt tree stumps looked in the sudden flares like men. Those grey wraiths could be fog, or gas.

Funny that in summer this blood and horror-soaked soil could still bloom with honeysuckle, forget-me-nots and wild larkspur, and most of all with poppies. You would think nothing would ever grow there again.

More star shells went up, lighting the ground, the jagged scars of the trenches black, the men on the fire steps with rifles on their shoulders illuminated for a few, blinding moments. Sniper shots rang out.

Joseph stood still. He knew the terror of the night-watch out beyond the parapet, crawling around in the mud. Some of them would be at the head of saps out from the trench, most would be in shell holes, surrounded by heavy barricades of wire. Their purpose was to check enemy patrols for unusual movement, any signs of increased activity, as if there might be an attack planned.

More star shells lit the sky. It was beginning to rain. A crackle of machine-gun fire, and heavier artillery somewhere over to the left. Then the sharp whine of sniper fire, again and again.

Joseph shuddered. He thought of the men out there, beyond his vision, and prayed for strength to endure with them in their pain, not to try to deaden himself to it.

There were shouts somewhere ahead, heavy shells now, shrapnel bursting. There was a flurry of movement, flares, and a man came sliding over the parapet, shouting for help.

Joseph plunged forward, sliding in the mud, grabbing for the wooden props to hold himself up. Another flare of light. He saw quite clearly Captain Holt lurching towards him, another man over his shoulder, dead weight.

"He's hurt!" Holt gasped. "Pretty badly. One of the night patrol. Panicked. Just about got us all killed." He eased the man down into Joseph's arms and let his rifle slide forward, bayonet covered in an old sock to hide its gleam. His face was grotesque in the lantern light, smeared with mud and a wide streak of blood over the burnt cork which blackened it, as all night patrol had.

Others were coming to help. There was still a terrible noise of fire going on and the occasional flare.

The man in Joseph's arms did not stir. His body was limp and it was difficult to support him. Joseph felt the wetness and the smell of blood. Wordlessly others materialized out of the gloom and took the weight.

"Is he alive?" Holt said urgently. "There was a hell of a lot of shot up there." His voice was shaking, almost on the edge of control.

"Don't know," Joseph answered. "We'll get him back to the bunker and see. You've done all you can." He knew how desperate men felt when they risked their lives to save another man, and did not succeed. A kind of despair set in, a sense of very personal failure, almost a guilt for having survived themselves. "Are you hurt?"

"Not much," Holt answered. "Couple of grazes."

"Better have them dressed, before they get poisoned," Joseph advised, his feet slipping on the wet boards and banging his shoulder against a jutting post. The whole trench wall was crooked, giving way under the weight of mud. The founds had eroded.

The man helping him swore.

Awkwardly carrying the wounded man, they staggered back through the travel line to the support trench and into the light and shelter of a bunker.

Holt looked dreadful. Beneath the cork and blood his face was ashen. He was soaked with rain and mud and there were dark patches of blood across his back and shoulders.

Someone gave him a cigarette. Back here it was safe to strike a match. He drew in smoke deeply. "Thanks," he murmured, still staring at the wounded man.

Joseph looked down at him now. It was young Ashton. He knew him quite well. He had been at school with his older brother.

The soldier who had helped carry him in let out a cry of dismay, strangled in his throat. It was Mordaff, Ashton's closest friend, and he could see what Joseph now also could. Ashton was dead, his chest torn open, the blood no longer pumping, and a bullet hole through his head.

"I'm sorry," Holt said quietly. "I did what I could. I can't have got to him in time. He panicked."

Mordaff jerked his head up. "He never would!" The cry was desperate, a shout of denial against a shame too great to be borne. "Not Will!"

Holt stiffened. "I'm sorry," he said hoarsely. "It happens."

"Not with Will Ashton, it don't!" Mordaff retorted, his eyes blazing, pupils circled with white in the candlelight, his face grey. He had been in the front line two weeks now, a long stretch without a break from the ceaseless tension, filth, cold and intermittent silence and noise. He was nineteen.

"You'd better go and get that arm dressed, and your side," Joseph said to Holt. He made his voice firm, as to a child.

Holt glanced again at the body of Ashton, then up at Joseph.

"Don't stand there bleeding," Joseph ordered. "You did all you could. There's nothing else. I'll look after Mordaff."

"I tried!" Holt repeated. "There's nothing but mud and darkness and wire, and bullets coming in all directions." There was a sharp thread of terror under his shell-thin veneer of control. He had seen too many men die. "It's enough to make any man lose his nerve."

"Not Will!" Mordaff said again, his voice choking off in a sob.

Holt looked at Joseph again, then staggered out.

Joseph turned to Mordaff. He had done this before, too many times, tried to comfort men who had just seen childhood friends blown to pieces, or killed by a sniper's bullet, looking as if they should still be alive, perfect except for the small, blue hole through the brain. There was little to say. Most men found talk of God meaningless at that moment. They were shocked, fighting against belief and yet seeing all the terrible waste and loss of the truth in front of them. Usually it was best just to stay with them, let them speak about the past, what the friend had been like, times they had shared, just as if he were only wounded and would be back, at the end of the war, in some world one could only imagine, in England, perhaps in a summer day with sunlight on the grass, birds singing, a quiet riverbank somewhere, the sound of laughter, and women's voices.

Mordaff refused to be comforted. He accepted Ashton's death, the physical reality of that was too clear to deny and he had seen too many other men he knew killed in the year and a half he had been in Belgium. But he could not, would not accept that Ashton had panicked. He knew what panic out there cost, how many other lives it jeopardized. It was the ultimate failure.

"How am I going to tell his Mam?" he begged Joseph. "It'll be all I can do to tell her he's dead! His Pa'll never get over it. That proud of him, they were. He's the only boy. Three sisters he had, Mary, Lizzie and Alice. Thought he was the greatest lad in the world. I can't tell 'em he panicked! He couldn't have, Chaplain! He just wouldn't!"

Joseph did not know what to say. How could people at home in England even begin to imagine what it was like in the mud and noise out here? But he knew how deep shame burned. A lifetime could be consumed by it.

"Maybe he just lost sense of direction," he said gently. "He wouldn't be the first." War changed men. People did panic. Mordaff knew that, and half his horror was because it could be true. But Joseph did not say so. "I'll write to his family," he went on. "There's a lot of good to say about him. I could send pages. I'll not need to tell them much about tonight."

"Will you?" Mordaff was eager. "Thanks . . . thanks, Chaplain. Can I stay with him . . . until they come for him?"

"Yes, of course," Joseph agreed. "I'm going forward anyway. Get yourself a hot cup of tea. See you in an hour or so."

He left Mordaff squatting on the earth floor beside Ashton's body, and fumbled his way back over the slimy duckboards towards the travel line, then forward again to the front and the crack of gunfire and the occasional high flare of a star shell.

He did not see Mordaff again, but he thought nothing of it. He could have passed twenty men he knew and not recognized them, muffled in greatcoats, heads bent as they moved, rattling along the duckboards, or stood on the firesteps, rifles to shoulder, trying to see in the gloom for something to aim at.

Now and again he heard a cough, or the scamper of rats' feet and the splash of rain and mud. He spent a little time with two men swapping jokes, joining in their laughter. It was black humour, self-mocking, but he did not miss the courage in it, or the fellowship, the need to release emotion in some sane and human way.

About midnight the rain stopped.

A little after five the night patrol came scrambling through the wire, whispered passwords to the sentries, then came tumbling over the parapet of sandbags down into the trench, shivering with cold, and relief. One of them had caught a shot in the arm.

Joseph went back with them to the support line. In one of the dugouts a gramophone was playing a music hall song. A couple of men sang along with it, one of them had a beautiful voice, a soft, lyric tenor. It was a silly song, trivial, but it sounded almost like a hymn out here, a praise of life.

A couple of hours and the day would begin, endless, methodical duties of housekeeping, mindless routine, but it was better than doing nothing.

There was still a sporadic crackle of machine-gun fire, and whine of sniper bullets.

An hour till dawn.

Joseph was sitting on an upturned ration case when Sergeant Renshaw came into the bunker, pulling the gas curtain aside to peer in.

"Chaplain?"

Joseph looked up. He could see bad news in the man's face.

"I'm afraid Mordaff got it tonight," he said, coming in and letting the curtain fall again. "Sorry. Don't really know what happened. Ashton's death seems to have . . . well, he lost his nerve. More or less went over the top all by himself. Suppose he was determined to go and give Fritz a bloody nose, on Ashton's account. Stupid bastard! Sorry, Chaplain."

He did not need to explain himself, or to apologise. Joseph knew exactly the fury and the grief he felt at such a futile waste. To this was added a sense of guilt that he had not stopped it. He should have realized Mordaff was so close to breaking. He should have seen it. That was his job.

He stood up slowly. "Thanks for telling me, Sergeant. Where is he?"

"He's gone, Chaplain." Renshaw remained near the doorway. "You can't help 'im now."

"I know that. I just want to . . . I don't know . . . apologise to him. I let him down. I didn't understand he was . . . so . . . ."

"You can't be everybody's keeper," Renshaw said gently. "Too many of us. It's not been a bad night otherwise. Got a trench raid coming off soon. Just wish we could get that damn sniper across the way there." He scraped a match and lit his cigarette. "But morale's good. That was a brave thing Captain Holt did out there. Pity about Ashton, but that doesn't alter Holt's courage. Could see him, you know, by the star shells. Right out there beyond the last wire, bent double, carrying Ashton on his back. Poor devil went crazy. Running around like a fool. Have got the whole patrol killed if Holt hadn't gone after him. Hell of a job getting him back. Fell a couple of times. Reckon that's worth a mention in dispatches, at least. Heartens the men, knowing our officers have got that kind of spirit."

"Yes . . . I'm sure," Joseph agreed. He could only think of Ashton's white face, and Mordaff's desperate denial, and how Ashton's mother would feel, and the rest of his family. "I think I'll go and see Mordaff just the same."

"Right you are," Renshaw conceded reluctantly, standing aside for Joseph to pass.

Mordaff lay in the support trench just outside the bunker two hundred yards to the west. He looked even younger than he had in life, as if he were asleep. His face was oddly calm, even though it was smeared with mud. Someone had tried to clean most of it off in a kind of dignity, so that at least he was recognizable. There was a large wound in the left side of his forehead. It was bigger than most sniper wounds. He must have been a lot closer.

Joseph stood in the first paling of the darkness and looked at him by candlelight from the open bunker curtain. He had been so alive only a few hours ago, so full of anger and loyalty and dismay. What had made him throw his life away in a useless gesture? Joseph racked his mind for some sign that should have warned him Mordaff was so close to breaking, but he could not see it even now.

There was a cough a few feet away, and the tramp of boots on duckboards. The men were stood down, just one sentry per platoon left. They had returned for breakfast. He realized he could smell cooking.

Now would be the time to ask around and find out what had happened to Mordaff.

He made his way to the field kitchen. It was packed with men, some standing to be close to the stoves and catch a bit of their warmth, others choosing to sit, albeit further away. They had survived the night. They were laughing and telling stories, most of them unfit for delicate ears, but Joseph was too used to it to take any offence. Now and then someone new would apologise for such language in front of a chaplain, but most knew he understood too well.

"Yeah," one answered his question through a mouthful of bread and jam. "He came and asked me if I saw what happened to Ashton. Very cut up, he was."

"And what did you tell him?" Joseph asked.

The man swallowed. "Told him Ashton seemed fine to me when he went over. Just like anyone else, nervous . . . but then only a fool isn't scared to go over the top!"

Joseph thanked him and moved on. He needed to know who else was on the patrol.

"Captain Holt," the next man told him, a ring of pride in his voice. Word had got around about Holt's courage. Everyone stood a little taller because of it, felt a little braver, more confident. "We'll pay Fritz back for that," he added. "Next raid – you'll see."

There was a chorus of agreement.

"Who else?" Joseph pressed.

"Seagrove, Noakes, Willis," a thin man replied, standing up. "Want some breakfast, Chaplain? Anything you like, on the house – as long as it's bread and jam and half a cup of tea. But you're not particular, are you? Not one of those fussy eaters who'll only take kippers and toast?"

"What I wouldn't give for a fresh Craster kipper," another sighed, a faraway look in his eyes. "I can smell them in my dreams."

Someone told him good-naturedly to shut up.

"Went over the top beside me," Willis said when Joseph found him quarter of an hour later. "All blacked up like the rest of us. Seemed okay to me then. Lost him in no-man's-land. Had a hell of a job with the wire. As bloody usual, it wasn't where we'd been told. Got through all right, then Fritz opened up on us. Star shells all over the sky." He sniffed and then coughed violently. When he had control of himself again he continued. "Then I saw someone outlined against the flares, arms high, like a wild man, running around. He was going towards the German lines, shouting something. Couldn't hear what in the noise."

Joseph did not interrupt. It was now broad daylight and beginning to drizzle again. Around them men were starting the duties of the day: digging, filling sandbags, carrying ammunition, strengthening the wire, re-setting duckboards. Men took an hour's work, an hour's sentry duty, and an hour's rest.

Near them somebody was expending his entire vocabulary of curses against lice. Two more were planning elaborate schemes to hold the water at bay.

"Of course that lit us up like a target, didn't it!" Willis went on. "Sniper fire and machine guns all over the place. Even a couple of shells. How none of us got hit I'll never know. Perhaps the row woke God up, and he came back on duty!" He laughed hollowly. "Sorry, Chaplain. Didn't mean it. I'm just so damn sorry poor Ashton got it. Holt just came out of nowhere and ran after him, floundering through the mud. If Ashton hadn't got caught in the wire he'd never have got him."

"Caught in the wire?" Joseph asked, memory pricking at him.

"Yeah. Ashton must have ran right into the wire, because he stopped sudden, teetering, like, and fell over. Probably saved his life, because there was a hell of a barrage came over just after that. We all threw ourselves down."

"What happened then?" Joseph said urgently, a slow, sick thought taking shape in his mind.

"When it died down I looked up again, and there was Holt staggering back with poor Ashton across his shoulders. Hell of a job he had carrying him, even though he's bigger than Ashton . . . well taller, anyway. Up to his knees in mud, he was, shot and shell all over, sky lit up like a Christmas tree. Of course we gave him what covering fire we could. Maybe it helped." He coughed again. "Reckon he'll be mentioned in dispatches, Chaplain? He deserves it." There was admiration in his voice, a lift of hope.

Joseph forced himself to answer. "I should think so." The words were stiff.

"Well, if he isn't, the men'll want to know why!" Willis said fiercely. "Bloody hero, he is."

Joseph thanked him and went to find Seagrove and Noakes. They told him pretty much the same story.

"You going to have him recommended?" Noakes asked. "Mordaff came and we said just the same to him. Reckon he wanted the Captain given a medal. He made us say it over and over again, exactly what happened."

"That's right," Seagrove nodded, leaning on a sandbag.

"You told him the same?" Joseph asked. "About the wire, and Ashton getting caught in it?"

"Yes, of course. If he hadn't got caught by the legs he'd have gone straight on and landed up in Fritz's lap, poor devil."

"Thank you."

"Welcome, Chaplain. You going to write up Captain Holt?"

Joseph did not answer, but turned away, sick at heart.

He did not need to look again, but he trudged all the way back to the field hospital anyway. It would be his job to say the services for both Ashton and Mordaff. The graves would be already dug.

He looked at Ashton's body again, looked carefully at his trousers. They were stained with mud, but there were no tears in them, no marks of wire. The fabric was perfect.

He straightened up.

"I'm sorry," he said quietly to the dead man. "Rest in peace." And he turned and walked away.

He went back to where he had left Mordaff's body, but it had been removed. Half an hour more took him to where it also was laid out. He touched the cold hand, and looked at the brow. He would ask. He would be sure. But in his mind he already was. He needed time to know what he must do about it. The men would be going over the top on another trench raid soon. Today morale was high. They had a hero in their number, a man who would risk his own life to bring back a soldier who had lost his nerve and panicked. Led by someone like that, they were equal to Fritz any day. Was one pistol bullet, one family's shame, worth all that?

What were they fighting for anyway? The issues were so very big, and at the same time so very small and immediate.

He found Captain Holt alone just after dusk, standing on the duckboards below the parapet, near one of the firing steps.

"Oh, it's you, Chaplain. Ready for another night?"

"It'll come, whether I am or not," Joseph replied.

Holt gave a short bark of laughter. "That doesn't sound like you. Tired of the firing line, are you? You've been up here a couple of weeks, you should be in turn for a step back any day. Me too, thank God."

Joseph faced forward, peering through the gloom towards no-man's-land and the German lines beyond. He was shaking. He must control himself. This must be done in the silence, before the shooting started up again. Then he might not get away with it.

"Pity about that sniper over there," he remarked. "He's taken out a lot of our men."

"Damnable," Holt agreed. "Can't get a line on him, though. Keeps his own head well down."

"Oh, yes," Joseph nodded. "We'd never get him from here. It needs a man to go over in the dark and find him."

"Not a good idea, Chaplain. He'd not come back. Not advocating suicide, are you?"

Joseph chose his words very carefully and kept his voice as unemotional as he could.

"I wouldn't have put it like that," he answered. "But he has cost us a lot of men. Mordaff today, you know?"

"Yes . . . I heard. Pity."

"Except that wasn't the sniper, of course. But the men think it was, so it comes to the same thing, as far as morale is concerned."

"Don't know what you mean, Chaplain." There was a slight hesitation in Holt's voice in the darkness.

"Wasn't a rifle wound, it was a pistol," Joseph replied. "You can tell the difference, if you're actually looking for it."

"Then he was a fool to be that close to German lines," Holt said, facing forward over the parapet and the mud. "Lost his nerve, I'm afraid."

"Like Ashton," Joseph said. "Can understand that, up there in no-man's-land, mud everywhere, wire catching hold of you, tearing at you, stopping you from moving. Terrible thing to be caught in the wire with the star shells lighting up the night. Makes you a sitting target. Takes an exceptional man not to panic, in those circumstances . . . a hero."

Holt did not answer.

There was silence ahead of them, only the dull thump of feet and a squelch of duckboards in mud behind, and the trickle of water along the bottom of the trench.

"I expect you know what it feels like," Joseph went on. "I notice you have some pretty bad tears in your trousers, even one in your blouse. Haven't had time to mend them yet."

"I dare say I got caught in a bit of wire out there last night," Holt said stiffly. He shifted his weight from one foot to the other.

"I'm sure you did," Joseph agreed with him. "Ashton didn't. His clothes were muddy, but no wire tears."

There were several minutes of silence. A group of men passed by behind them, muttering words of greeting. When they were gone the darkness closed in again. Someone threw up a star shell and there was a crackle of machine gun fire.

"I wouldn't repeat that, if I were you, Chaplain," Holt said at last. "You might make people think unpleasant things, doubts. And right at the moment morale is high. We need that. We've had a hard time recently. We're going over the top in a trench raid soon. Morale is important . . . trust. I'm sure you know that, maybe even better than I do. That's your job, isn't it? Morale, spiritual welfare of the men?"

"Yes . . . spiritual welfare is a good way of putting it. Remember what it is we are fighting for, and that it is worth all that it costs . . . even this." Joseph gestured in the dark to all that surrounded them.

More star shells went up, illuminating the night for a few, garish moments, then a greater darkness closed in.

"We need our heroes," Holt said very clearly. "Any man who would tear them down would be very unpopular, even if he said he was doing it in the name of truth, or justice, or whatever it was he believed in. He would do a lot of harm, Chaplain. I expect you can see that . . ."

"Oh yes," Joseph agreed. "To have their hero shown to be a coward who laid the blame for his panic on another man, and let him be buried in shame, and then committed murder to hide that, would devastate men who are already wretched and exhausted by war."

"You are perfectly right." Holt sounded as if he were smiling. "A very wise man, Chaplain. Good of the regiment first. The right sort of loyalty."

"I could prove it," Joseph said very carefully.

"But you won't. Think what it would do to the men."

Joseph turned a little to face the parapet. He stood up onto the firestep and looked over the dark expanse of mud and wire.

"We should take that sniper out. That would be a very heroic thing to do. Good thing to try, even if you didn't succeed. You'd deserve a mention in dispatches for that, possibly a medal."

"It would be posthumous!" Holt said bitterly.

"Possibly. But you might succeed, and come back. It would be so daring, Fritz would never expect it," Joseph pointed out.

"Then you do it, Chaplain!" Holt said sarcastically.

"It wouldn't help you, Captain. Even if I die, I have written a full account of what I have learned today, to be opened should anything happen to me. On the other hand, if you were to mount such a raid, whether you returned or not, I should destroy it."

There was silence again, except for the distant crack of sniper fire a thousand yards away, and the drip of mud.

"Do you understand me, Captain Holt?"

Holt turned slowly. A star shell lit his face for an instant. His voice was hoarse.

"You're sending me to my death!"

"I'm letting you be the hero you're pretending to be, and Ashton really was," Joseph answered. "The hero the men need. Thousands of us have died out here, no one knows how many more there will be. Others will be maimed or blinded. It isn't whether you die or not, it's how well."

A shell exploded a dozen yards from them. Both men ducked, crouching automatically.

Silence again.

Slowly Joseph unbent.

Holt lifted his head. "You're a hard man, Chaplain. I misjudged you."

"Spiritual care, Captain," Joseph said quietly. "You wanted the men to think you a hero. Now you're going to justify that, and become one."

Holt stood still, looking towards him in the gloom, then slowly he turned and began to walk away, his feet sliding on the wet duckboards. Then he climbed up the next firestep, and up over the parapet.

Joseph stood still and prayed.

MOTHER'S MILK

Chris Simms

Just a glimpse across the graveyard at a hundred yards and he knew that milking her dry would pose no problem at all.

To an ordinary person she was a sad-looking woman in her forties, fat thighs bulging as she bent forward to replace the dying flowers before the gravestone with a fresh bouquet.

But to Daniel Norris she stank of need. The need for company. The need for human warmth. The need for someone to lavish kindness upon. So acute was his ability to sniff out and exploit vulnerability, she may as well have held a loudhailer to her lips and announced to the cemetery, "In sickness and in health, please, God, give me someone to care for."

He slid into the shadow of a moss-furred crypt and waited for her to pass. As he stood there out of the weak October sun, a breeze whispered between the graves and a shiver ran through him. The ugly clacking of two crows squabbling in a nearby yew tree masked the sound of her approaching steps, but he soon heard the crunch of gravel as her stout legs took her back towards the gates, hair dull and brown, head held up in an attempt to bravely face the grey afternoon.

As soon as she was out of sight he hurried over to the grave she had just left. The headstone was new. He sneered at her tacky taste. Shiny black marble topped by two maudlin cherubs trumpeting a silent lament to an unhearing God. His eyes scanned quickly over the inscription, letters chiselled out then painted with a layer of fake gold. Something about her babies now being with the angels. His eyebrows raised in slight surprise: he had assumed it was a husband and not young ones she'd lost. Not that it mattered to him. He knew she was alone in the world.

424   CHRIS SIMMS

He studied the large and expensive bouquet. If this was the weekly ritual he suspected, she had plenty of cash to spare. He rubbed his hands together in the chill autumnal air. Wealthy widows were particularly easy to fleece.

Several days dragged by as he eked out an existence between dimly lit boozers and dingy bookies, their floors littered with torn paper slips. A win on the dogs on Friday provided some much-needed cash for the weekend. He combed his grey-flecked hair and put his blazer on over his only decent shirt. Then he treated himself to twenty Bensons, leaving the dented tin of rolling tobacco in his hostel room before heading to the Tap and Spile.

During a visit earlier in the week he'd read the small sign above the door and noted the licensee was a single woman. Jan Griffiths. He'd watched her from a shadowy corner, noticing the lack of wedding ring as she pulled the pints while keeping up an easy flow of conversation with her regulars. He'd liked her dyed blond hair, throaty laugh, and sparkling blue eyes.

Now he walked into the pub with an easy roll in his step, one hand in his pocket. Confident and at ease with his place in the world. He slid his thin frame onto a barstool, nodded at her with a wolfish half-smile, then watched as she registered the expression. He knew it never failed to pique the interest of her type.

"You look like the cat who's got the cream," she stated, a wary curiosity in her voice.

"Do I?" he said, taking the twenties from his pocket. "Just got some good news on a business deal I'm in town for. A bottle of your best champagne, please." Nothing ventured, nothing gained.

She smiled, pleased to be filling the till so early in the evening. "I'll need to get it from upstairs. How many glasses would you like?" she replied, eyes moving to the empty seats behind him.

"Well, I'm hoping you won't make me drink it alone. So, two, please."

She smiled again, turning on her heel and looking back at him over her shoulder. "Never can say no to a bit of bubbly," she said archly, hips swinging slightly as she headed for the stairs.

Peeling the cellophane from his cigarettes, he looked around the cosy pub at the scattering of drinkers quietly sipping their pints. A warm glow spread across his chest. "Nice place," he said to himself, thinking he could get used to it.

She reappeared a minute later, bottle of Moet standing upright in the ice bucket in her hands. "One bottle of bubbly."

He watched as she took the foil off and then expertly prised the cork loose with a soft pop. A small gush of foam emerged and his eyes wandered to her generous cleavage.

"So what's the business deal?"

He glanced up, realizing she'd seen where his eyes had strayed. She didn't seem bothered. "Oh, a new retail development in the town centre," he replied. During his first recce round town he'd spotted a large commercial property for sale. "The one next to that big Barclays.

"On Prince's Street?" She sounded impressed. "That's massive. Have you bought it?"

"I wish," he said with a smile. "I'm just the middleman between the vendor and the buyers. Venture capitalists from the Middle East. Still, I get my commission as a result."

She placed two glasses on the bar and he nodded at them. "Will you be mum?"

She poured them both a drink and handed a glass to him. "Well, here's to your deal."

"Thanks."

They clinked glasses and he took a large sip, briefly savouring the sensation of bubbles popping against the roof of his mouth before swallowing it down. "Delicious," he sighed, offering her a cigarette out of the new pack.

"So where are you from?" she asked, taking one and leaning against the bar.

He reached for the cheap disposable lighter in his pocket, but changed his mind. "Have you any matches?"

She flicked him a book and he lit their cigarettes. "Wherever business takes me," he replied. "I'll be in town for a while yet, tying up loose ends of this deal, sorting out planning permission for the shops."

"It's going to be a shopping centre, then?"

"That's the intention. My clients want retail units put in, then they'll offer out the space to the usual suspects. Boots, Topshop, WH Smith, and the like."

He took another sip, aware of her eyes assessing him, and he realized she'd have heard countless tales of bullshit across the bar.

"So how long have you been in the pub game?" he asked casually.

"Donkey's years." She laughed. "It's all I know."

"You run a nice place here," he said, glancing round.

She gave a small smile. "It's not bad. Business-wise, I mean. The big pubs they've opened in the centre have taken away a few customers, but mainly the younger ones. I prefer a quieter crowd."

He refilled their glasses. "Absolutely. Not enough places like this left."

She moved away to serve another customer and he almost drained his glass, wondering how quickly she'd come back to him. To his satisfaction, it was almost straightaway.

The allure of strangers. Deciding not to push things too early, he finished his drink and patted the tops of his thighs. "Well, I'd better be off. My clients are taking me to dinner at seven o'clock."

Her eyes went to the unfinished bottle. "What about your champagne?"

"If it would keep, I'd say put it behind the bar for tomorrow," he replied, hinting at his return. "You have it. My treat."

"Well . . . thanks," she answered uncertainly, wrong-footed by his sudden departure.

"See you again," he smiled, heading for the door.

He returned to the cemetery exactly a week after he first saw her. Earlier in the morning he'd picked up a drab suit in a charity shop, pairing it with his oldest shirt and tie. Finally he'd put on a pair of battered leather shoes, pleased with the look of someone down on his luck but determined to keep up appearances nonetheless.

She appeared at eleven o'clock, making her way straight to the grave, another large bouquet in her arms. He made a rip in the paper that wrapped his bunch of cheap chrysanthemums, watching as she plucked a couple of weeds from the bed of marble chippings in front of the headstone before exchanging fresh flowers for the wilted. After standing in sad contemplation for a good five minutes, she started to turn around.

He stood up, walking over a couple of graves to make the path that would intersect their routes. Two lost souls, drifting alone in the world. As he walked with head bowed, he tried to drag up any memories that might bring tears to his eyes. God knew he'd been witness to enough pain. But the anguished weeping of so many women had all been his doing, and the images of their distraught faces did nothing to stir his heart.

Now she was less than twenty feet from his side. He caught his foot in a nonexistent crack and stumbled forward, flowers cascading to the ground as the wrapping tore completely. Regaining his balance, he stooped forward as if to start picking them up. But then he placed his hands on his knees and let out an anguished sob. He heard her footsteps stop beside him and, knowing that it would clinch his act, the tears he'd been failing to summon suddenly appeared.

A hand was placed on his shoulder and he looked up at her face as it wavered and shifted through the liquid filling his eyes.

"There, there," she murmured, pressing his head to her bosom.

Within four days he had packed his few possessions, moved out of the hostel, and was sleeping in her spare room. She'd lapped up his story of a childhood spent in care homes, adult years wasted in a directionless drift, not anchored by family to any area. Then his long search for his real mother – a search that had finally ended in the town's cemetery, at a grave that had only been dug the year before.

She brought her blubbering under control by clucking and fussing around him. Bustling around in the kitchen, carrying through dinner on a tray as he sat dejected on her sofa, his eyes furtively searching the room while she'd cooked his food.

Every night she'd conclude her nursing routine by bringing him a mug of Ovaltine. Creamy, smooth, and comforting, it was a taste he quickly came to look forward to. "That's because I make it with milk, the proper way," she'd say and smile, her look of pleasure increasing with his every sip.

But the need to get to a pub and enjoy a cigarette in a comfortable seat rather than standing out on her bloody patio was steadily growing. So he began to recover from his feigned despondency, apparently revived by the succession of meals she so lovingly prepared. One day he announced that it was time he sorted himself out. Found a job and place of his own.

Her eyes had widened in alarm at his mention of moving out. "Stay as long as you like. The house is too big for just me. I like you being here. Please." The desperation in her voice surprised him. It was going to be so easy cleaning her out of everything.

He pondered her words, thinking of the three bedrooms upstairs. The spare room he slept in, her pink nightmare, and the locked door with the nursery placard on it. He'd peeped through the keyhole at the first opportunity and was just able to make out babyish wallpaper and some cuddly toys on a chest of drawers. Three bedrooms and a decent garden. Worth what? Two hundred grand at least.

"What happened to your family, Marjorie? What happened to your babies?" he whispered, curious that, apart from her creepy shrine, all traces of them had been removed from the house.

The question obviously distressed her and she waved it away with an agitated flutter of her hands. "I really can't speak about it. Not yet. I'm sorry, it's still all too . . . raw," she said, fingers grasping at the crucifix around her neck.

He nodded. "I understand, Marjorie, I understand. But I must repay your kindness somehow. Let me pay you some rent at least."

She shook her head. "Really, I don't need it."

He paused, always amazed at his ability to bring out the maternal instincts of women. "Think of it for me. For my self-respect if nothing else. There's a job I spotted when I first arrived here. A salesman for those industrial vacuums they use in pubs and restaurants. It's something I've done before. They'd take me on, I just need to brush up a bit . . ." His words died away and his eyes dropped to his scuffed old shoes.

She sprang to her feet. "You need proper work clothes." She

crossed to the dresser in the corner, took out a file from the top drawer, and extracted several twenty-pound notes from inside. "Here, take this. Buy yourself a nice new suit."

"No, Marjorie, I couldn't," he protested, holding up his hands while making a mental note of the file's whereabouts.

"Then take it as a loan," she insisted.

"Okay," he agreed reluctantly. "And I'm paying you back every penny, understand?" he added, knowing she'd never ask for it back.

He scoured the shops for a sale. After finding one and then mercilessly bargaining down the young assistant, he picked up a suit, three shirts, and a pair of shoes for a steal. The deal left him with over eighty pounds in change. He headed straight for the nearest pub with a copy of the *Racing Post*, where he picked his runners over a couple of pints and several cigarettes.

When he set off back to Marjorie's at five o'clock that afternoon he was fifty quid and several more pints up. As he ambled happily along he wondered how to explain the state he was in. She opened the door to find him swaying on her doorstep, shopping bag hanging from one arm.

"I rang them. I've got an interview tomorrow," he sighed.

"Well, that's good news, isn't it?" she said, confused by the look of sadness on his face.

"But then I went back to my mother's grave. Oh, Marjorie, if I hadn't dithered for so long before tracing her, I might have spoken to her before she died. I'm afraid I've had a few drinks."

"Come here," she said, arms outstretched.

He slipped inside and endured a crushing hug.

"You mustn't punish yourself. Now take that jacket off and sit down." She led him to the sofa in the immaculate front room. "I'm making tea. Is beef casserole all right?"

"Great, thanks," he replied with a weak smile.

She sniffed at his jacket. "This reeks of cigarettes. You really shouldn't smoke."

"I know. It's only when I'm stressed."

She nodded. "Well, I'll give it a good airing on the washing line."

"Thank you," he said, reaching for the TV's remote control as soon as she was out of the room.

He woke with a sore throat and cursed himself for smoking so heavily the day before. She'd washed and ironed his shirts the previous evening and he walked down the stairs straightening his tie.

"Oh, Daniel. You look the perfect gentleman." She moved across the kitchen, encroaching on his personal space. "Stand still, you've got a stray strand of hair."

He fought the urge to slap her hand away, instead gratefully smiling as she smoothed it into place.

"Perfect," she said, standing back. "I've ordered you a cab. We don't want you going by bus and getting there late."

He sat down and waited for her to cook him breakfast.

"Just here's fine, mate." He leaned over from the rear of the cab.

"The betting office?" the driver replied, confused after hearing the pudgy woman wish the passenger good luck in his job interview.

"Yeah, here will do."

"That's four eighty then, please."

He counted out the exact money, then climbed out, the cabbie not bothering to thank him as he drove off. A bout of coughing caught him by surprise as he walked towards the bookie's and he lit a cigarette to quell the itch in his throat.

The morning was spent working out his bets. He rang Marjorie at midday. "I've got the job. Can you believe it?!"

"Daniel, that's brilliant. I'll cook something special for tea."

"They want me to start straightaway. I've got a sales patch right in the centre of town. Mainly pubs, so I'll probably end up smelling of cigarettes each day."

"Never mind. Did they say what they'll pay you?"

"It's commission only, but the vacuum is a great product. I'm sure I'll sell loads. I've got to demo it to prospective customers. They're dropping me off and have given me a special trolley to wheel it around on."

"They're making you carry one around town?"

"Yes. And I have to drop it back off at the factory at the end of each day."

"That's ridiculous. You need a car."

He smiled to himself. "I'll manage somehow. Now I've got to go. See you later."

He hung up and then walked over to the Tap and Spile. "Hello there," he said, taking the same stool at the bar, straightening a pristine shirt cuff.

She looked up, a tea towel in her hand, eyes passing briefly over his suit. "Hello again. Thanks for the champagne the other night."

"My pleasure," he replied.

"How's business going?"

"Okay," he said. "There's a few question marks over the rates the council wants to charge. I'm arguing it's a multi-let property, so not subject to the standard commercial tariffs they'd levy if . . ." He paused. "Sorry, that's probably more of an answer than you were expecting. How about you?"

She looked round the deserted pub. "Lunches tend to be quiet. But I'm not giving up the bar meals. Every decent pub should offer them."

He picked up a menu. "What do you recommend, then?"

"I don't know," she said, polishing another glass. "The chicken pie is good."

"Homemade, too, I see."

"Of course."

"Is it breast or leg?" he asked provocatively.

"You'll have to see," she replied, one eyebrow arching upwards.

"Fine with me. I love both," he said, placing an elbow on the bar.

He walked back to the bookie's a couple of hours later, stopping at a newsagent's to buy some Rennie for the burning ache at the back of his throat. Things were looking good. Marjorie was proving as easy as he knew she would be and it was going better than he dared hope with Jan. So good, in fact, he'd asked her out to dinner on Sunday night. He pictured her face, her cleavage, and realized she was really growing on him.

If his plans for Marjorie worked out, he and Jan could look forward to some fun times together.

The next morning he woke with a headache and a metallic taste in his mouth. He struggled out of bed, a bout of coughs wracking his chest. God, he felt awful. He counted back the number of drinks he'd got through in the pub. Not enough to warrant a hangover like this. He'd have to have a word with Jan about how often she cleaned the pipes in her pub.

In the bathroom he stared in the mirror. His skin looked grey and a latticework of tiny veins marred the whites of his eyes.

"'Morning," he said dully, shuffling into the kitchen in a bathrobe and slippers.

"Daniel, are you all right?" Marjorie said, lines of concern across her forehead.

"Not so good, actually. I'm glad it's Saturday. I don't think I could have faced working today. Have you got any aspirin?"

"Yes," she said, immediately opening a cupboard and reaching up to the top shelf. He watched the flesh wobbling under her thick upper arms with disgust.

"Here we are. Now you go and sit on the sofa. Can you manage some tea and toast? I'll bring everything through."

She bustled in with a blanket shortly after, tucking it around him before carrying through a tray piled with toast, a pot of tea, a glass of milk, and two aspirin in a little pot.

"Thanks, could you pass me the remote?"

She appeared again a couple of hours later, hovering by the sofa and aggravating him with her presence. "I'm going to the cemetery today. I always take flowers for my babies on a Saturday. Do you feel up to coming? We could take some for your mother, too."

Her and those bloody babies, he thought, dragging his eyes from the TV screen. Normally a lie would appear instantly on his lips, but his mind seemed to be working sluggishly. "Erm, no. No, thanks."

"No to coming with me?"

"Yes, I still feel terrible."

"How about I take some flowers for your mother? You'll need to tell me exactly where her grave is."

He raised his fingers to his temples and shut his eyes. "No, don't worry. I'd feel guilty if you took flowers for me. It's something I'd prefer to do myself."

"Okay, then. Would you like more tea? Or an Ovaltine, perhaps?"

He looked at the huge pot, still half full. "Yes, an Ovaltine sounds good. And a couple more aspirin, please."

Once she'd gone he sat sipping his drink, swallowing down the aspirin with the last gulp. Then he kicked off the blanket, walked over to the front window, lifted the net curtain, and peered down the street. No sign of her. His temples were thudding and he realized his heart was racing uncomfortably fast as he turned to the top drawer of the dresser and took the file out.

Everything was there. Details of several savings accounts, bank cards, cheque books, even the deeds to the house. He flicked through to the back of the file, grunting incredulously when he found the sheet of paper with all the passwords for her savings accounts neatly written out. Stupid, stupid bitch. He thought forward to his meal with Jan the following evening. If everything went smoothly, he'd start draining Marjorie's accounts dry the next day. Then he could invite Jan on a luxury cruise and be out of this horrible house within a week.

He turned to the envelope at the front and counted the cash inside. Almost four hundred quid. Taking the phone and a copy of the Yellow Pages back to the sofa, he found the number for the bookie's he'd become a regular in. "Hi, George, it's Dan Norris here. Can I place a few phone bets?"

The keys clicked in the front door after lunch and she walked into the front room, a rosy flush on her chubby cheeks. "How are you feeling?"

"Rotten," he said, shifting on the sofa. "This headache seems to be getting worse."

"Poor baby," she said, shrugging off her coat and pressing her fingertips to his brow. "Perhaps I should take your temperature. You could be coming down with the flu. It's that time of year."

"You might be right. My joints are starting to ache, too."

She brought the thermometer through from the kitchen, perched on the edge of the sofa, and popped it in his mouth. As they waited he was aware of her large buttocks pressing against his legs. After three minutes she took it out and tilted it towards the window. "It's a bit up."

"Maybe I just need some fresh air," he said, wanting to get away from her cloying company. But when he tried to stand, the blood surged in his head and red clouds filled the room.

When he came to he was stretched back out on the sofa, the blanket now tucked up to his chin. She was sitting on the arm, looking down at him, her fat face filling his vision.

"You fainted, you poor dear. It's lucky you hadn't got to your feet."

Feeling weak as a child, he shut his eyes again. "My head's pounding. I need more aspirin."

She instantly stood. "Of course. I think you're dehydrated, I'll get you a drink, too."

When she returned a minute later he saw she was carrying a steaming mug and a small bottle. "I've made you some more Ovaltine. I'm afraid you've had all the aspirin. But I've got some Calpol."

"Calpol? Isn't that for kids?"

"Yes. It was for . . ." Tears brimmed in her eyes. "We'll give you an extra big dose."

Too exhausted to protest, he watched as she poured out a tablespoon of the red liquid. Once he'd swallowed it, she placed the mug of Ovaltine in his hands. "Now drink up. We can't have you like this, can we?"

He spent the rest of the evening lying on the sofa, listlessly watching the telly as his pulse rose and fell again and again. At eleven o'clock she came over and stood in front of the sofa. "I think it's beddy-bed time. Shall I help you up?"

Irritated by her patronizing choice of words, he waved her away. "I'm fine here. I'll head up later."

"Head still bad?"

He nodded once. "If there's no improvement by tomorrow I think we'd better call for a doctor."

*   *   *

She found him there the next morning. He was lying on his back, a shallow pant coming from his mouth.

"Oh dear, still feeling poorly?"

His eyelids fluttered open and he looked at her from the corner of his eye. "I'm more than poorly. I need a doctor," he croaked, gesturing weakly to the phone which lay just out of his reach. "Can you pass it to me? I can hardly move. And bring me the copy of the Yellow Pages, too," he added, thinking he needed to call Jan to cancel their dinner date.

"Let me get you a drink, your throat sounds awfully dry."

"Okay. Yes, a drink would be good."

She returned a minute later with a mug in her hands. Kneeling in front of the sofa, she reached an arm round his neck and lifted his head off the cushions.

"What's this? More bloody Ovaltine? I just want water."

"Now, now," she clucked. "I've made it with milk, just how you like it. Take a sip, it's not too hot."

With a reluctant sigh, he did as he was told. Once it was finished she laid his head back down.

"Now can you please call me a doctor? I'm seriously ill here."

She picked up the phone and placed it further out of his reach. "We don't need a doctor. I'm here to take care of you."

A surge of self-pitying anger made the dull thump in his head more pronounced. "Listen, I need more than cups of bloody Ovaltine. I need medical help. Now call me a bloody doctor."

She held a finger up. "Any more language like that and I'll wash your mouth out with soap. Now let's get you upstairs, you need to be in bed."

He tried to shrug off her arm as it slid back round his neck. "Give me the phone," he gasped, thinking of Jan, the only person in the world he could turn to for help. Not caring if it meant revealing the truth about himself to her.

Ignoring his demand, she pulled him into a sitting position, then draped one of his arms round her shoulders.

"Get your hands off me," he protested feebly.

"Okay," she said brusquely. "One, two, three, up!" She hoisted him to his feet and his vision swirled and faded.

"What are you doing?" he mumbled helplessly, unsure if

they were actually moving until he felt the edges of the stairs banging against his shins. "I need the toilet."

"There, there. Everything will be okay," she grunted, getting him onto the landing.

His vision cleared a little and he realized they'd stopped outside the door marked Nursery. She took a key from her pocket. His head lolled forward as she unlocked the door. The room had the letters of the alphabet running below the picture rail. The jungle-animal blind was drawn and a mobile of toy animals hung over an enormous cot in the corner.

"What . . . what is this?" he said, trying to focus.

"Don't you worry, I'm here to take care of you," she replied, lowering the bars of the cot and laying him down.

"I need the toilet. I have to go to the toilet." He started to cry.

"That's fine," she said, stripping off his pajamas and taking a pair of incontinence pants from a drawer.

He felt her slipping them on and he looked at the photos lined up on the shelf to his side. Framed photos of gaunt-faced men, all lying in the cot he now found himself in.

"Who are they?" he whispered.

"My babies, of course," she answered brightly, picking up each picture in turn. "All dead now. All dead." She looked down at him, a smile on her face. "All my babies die. It's what God wants."

He stared up at her, remembering the inscription in the cemetery about her babies being with angels, realizing there were no actual names listed on the gravestone.

"Now, it's time for your feed. Mummy will get it." She raised the bars back up and he heard her go downstairs. While she was gone he tried desperately to summon the strength to move. Sobbing with exertion, he was only able to lift a hand just clear of the blanket.

She returned with a large baby bottle, dripping a bit from the teat onto her upturned wrist. "Just right."

He tried to shy away from her as she bent over him. But she cupped his cheek and turned his face towards her.

"What's in that? What is it?" he said through gritted teeth as the teat was forced between his lips.

"Mother's milk, my sweet one. Mother's milk."

THE SHAKESPEARE EXPRESS

Edward Marston

1938

"Have you travelled on the Shakespeare Express before?" she asked.

"No," he answered. "This is our first visit to England. Mary Anne and I are still trying to find our feet."

"It's a wonderful train. In the old days, you could only get to Stratford by changing at Leamington Spa – a dreadful nuisance. Ten years ago, they introduced the Shakespeare Express so that we could go direct from Paddington to Stratford-upon-Avon."

"That will suit us fine."

Cyrus and Mary Anne Hillier had been standing on the railway platform that morning when they fell into conversation with the attractive young woman in a tailored suit that somehow managed to look both smart and casual. Dipping down towards one eye, her hat concealed much of her close-cropped fair hair. Since their arrival in the country, they had found English people rather reserved but here was the exception to the general rule. Tall, shapely and impeccably well bred, she described herself as an unrepentant worshipper at the altar of the Bard.

"Then you and Cyrus are two of a kind," said Mary Anne, looking fondly at her husband. "He's written books on Shakespeare."

"Really?" said the other woman. "How marvellous!"

"Cyrus is Professor of Drama at Penn State University. In fact, he's the chairman of the department."

"That means nothing over here, honey," he said modestly.

"Well, it should do."

"I'm just an anonymous member of the audience today."

"You're an expert," his wife insisted.

"I agree," said the younger woman. "If you've written books on a subject, you must be an authority." She offered her hand. "It's an honour to meet you, Professor." They shook hands. "My name is Rosalind Walker, by the way. I'm not an authority on anything."

"Except the Shakespeare Express," noted Cyrus.

They shared a laugh. The three of them were soon on first-name terms. Rosalind learned that they had saved up for years in order to make the pilgrimage to Stratford-upon-Avon. She warmed to them. They were a delightful middle-aged couple who seemed to complement each other perfectly. Cyrus was a short, stout man with a bushy black beard flecked with silver. He was shrewd, watchful and bristling with quiet intelligence. Mary Anne, by contrast, a trim, angular woman, was spirited and voluble. It was left to her to boast about her husband's academic career, to talk about their two children and to recount the pleasures of their Atlantic crossing.

"How long are you staying in Stratford?" asked Rosalind.

"Three nights," replied Mary Anne. "At the Shakespeare Hotel."

"Very appropriate."

"That's what we thought."

"Tony and I usually stay at the Billesley Manor."

"Tony?"

"My brother. He's as mad about Shakespeare as I am." Rosalind glanced at her watch. "He should be here by now. Tony had better get a move on. The train leaves at nine twenty-five on the dot."

"What time does it reach Stratford?" asked Cyrus.

"At eleven thirty-three precisely."

"You certainly know your schedule."

"On the Great Western Railway, punctuality is a watch-word."

"Do we stop on the way?"

"Yes – at High Wycombe, Leamington Spa and Warwick. There'll be something of an exodus at Leamington Spa."

"Will there?" asked Mary Anne in surprise. "Why catch a through train to Stratford then get off before we reach it?"

"The passengers will reach it in time," explained Rosalind. "Their trip includes a coach trip, you see. They visit Guy's Cliffe and Kenilworth before having lunch at Warwick Castle. The coach then brings them on to Stratford so that they can see all the sights before catching the train back to London."

"I bet you can tell us the exact time that it leaves," said Cyrus.

"Five-thirty."

He grinned. "Are you employed by the railway company?"

"No – I'm a regular passenger, that's all."

"So I gather."

"Matinee performances start early so that people will have a chance to get back to the station in time to catch the train home. The Memorial Theatre prefers to give a full text."

"I'm all in favour of that, Rosalind. I want my money's worth."

"It does mean that performances can be very long. The last *Hamlet* went on for well over four hours."

"Cyrus could sit and watch all day," said Mary Anne, beaming with approval. "He relishes every single word."

"So do I, as a rule," said Rosalind, "but I doubt if I'll do that this afternoon. *Troilus and Cressida* is not my favourite play – too dark and brutal for my taste. But it's so rarely performed that I felt I had to catch it."

"I love the play," admitted Cyrus. "I did a production of it with my students last year. In my view, *Troilus and Cressida* is a neglected masterpiece. And, as it happens," he went on, "its themes have taken on an unfortunate topicality."

"In what way?"

"Look at the newspapers, Rosalind. The situation is increasingly grim. War clouds seem to be gathering all over Europe."

"Too true!" she sighed, pulling a face.

"The play is essentially about war and its implications. It's a pity you can't invite Adolf Hitler over to see it. He'd learn how futile war really is. One of the papers reckoned that, if things go on as they are doing, Britain might be dragged into the conflict."

"Oh, I hope not. Tony would rush to enlist."

"A good patriot, obviously."

"My brother just likes adventure, that's all."

As they were talking, the platform had been slowly filling up and the noise level had risen markedly. There was a tangible air of anticipation. When the train came into the station, everyone surged towards the cream and brown carriages. Rosalind stood on tiptoe to look around her.

"Where on earth can he be?" she said anxiously.

"You'll have to go without him," suggested Mary Anne.

"Impossible – Tony has our tickets!"

"Oh dear!"

"Ah, there he is," declared Rosalind, looking back towards the barrier. "Do excuse me, I'll have to go." She moved away and tossed a farewell comment over her shoulder. "I'll see you at the theatre."

"What a charming young woman!" said Mary Anne.

"Yes," agreed Cyrus, helping her into the carriage.

Lifting up his suitcase, he paused long enough to watch Rosalind Walker greet a tall young man near the rear of the train. After exchanging a few words, the two of them got into a carriage. Mary Anne put her head out of the open door.

"Come on, Cyrus," she cajoled. "What are you waiting for?"

The locomotive was an elegant green monster of gleaming metal. It left on time in an explosion of steam and sustained clamour. When it hit its cruising speed, the train took on a steady rhythmical beat. Mary Anne was soon asleep. Travel of any kind invariably made her eyelids droop and her husband was grateful. It meant that he was spared any conversation and could concentrate on going through the text of *Troilus and Cressida* once more, savouring its multiple pleasures without having to persuade his wife that they actually existed. Mary Anne had many virtues and he loved her for them. She was not, however, an academic. Plays only existed at a surface level for her. She missed their deeper subtleties.

After stopping at High Wycombe, the train steamed on through the Oxfordshire countryside, rattling amiably and leaving a thick, grey cloud of smoke in its wake. When it eventually slowed again, Cyrus looked up, expecting to see the name of Leamington Spa on the station. Instead, he discovered that they were making a brief stoppage at Banbury. Back in motion once more, the Shakespeare Express gathered speed, its insistent chuffing like an endless stream of iambic pentameters.

It was not until they reached their destination that Cyrus nudged his wife awake. Mary Anne blinked her eyes and sat up abruptly. She peered through the window.

"Where are we?" she asked.

"Stratford-upon-Avon."

"Already?"

"You've been asleep for two hours."

"Never!"

"As long as you don't do it during the matinee."

"I won't, Cyrus, I promise. I'd never let you down."

"William Shakespeare is the person you'd be letting down."

Mary Anne was alarmed. "I'd never dare to do that – it would be a form of sacrilege."

The jewellery shop was a double-fronted establishment in the High Street. It had a wide selection of rings, brooches, necklaces, watches and clocks on display. Inside the shop, it also had a range of silver cups that could be engraved on the premises. Albert Ives was a slight individual of middle years who prided himself on his ability to sum up a customer instantly. When the young man came into the shop, Ives needed only a glance to tell him that his customer had serious intentions. The man was there to buy rather than browse.

"Good morning," said the newcomer affably. "I'm looking for an engagement ring."

"What did you have in mind, sir?" asked Ives.

"Well, you have a tray in the middle of the window that rather caught my eye. One, in particular, looked promising. Solid gold, twenty-two carat, with a cluster of five diamonds."

"Would you like to take a closer look?"

"Yes, please."

"One moment."

Albert Ives unlocked the glass doors and reached into one of the front windows. The customer, meanwhile, glanced idly around the shop. When the tray was placed in front of him, he took out a monocle and slipped it into his eye, examining the array of rings with care. Ives took the opportunity to study the man. Tall, well-dressed and well-groomed, he wore an expensive suit and a trilby that sat at a rakish angle on his head. A neat brown mustache acted as a focal point in a face that was pleasant rather than handsome. Ives noticed the costly gold cufflinks.

The customer was intrigued. "This is the one that I liked," he said, indicating the diamond ring, "yet this solitaire is almost twice as much. Why is that?"

"The stone is of a far higher quality, sir."

"But it's smaller than the cluster."

"Size is not everything," explained Ives. "If the solitaire were identical to the one that first caught your eye, then the price would be considerably higher."

"Really?"

Customers did not often show such a genuine interest in the trade so Ives made the most of his captive audience. He talked at length about the virtues of the respective diamonds and drew the attention of the young man to the way that they were cut.

"Fascinating!" said the other.

"All that glisters is not gold, sir," said Ives complacently.

"I'll remember that, old chap. Well, it looks as if you've saved me from buying the wrong one." He indicated the most expensive solitaire. "Is this the best one you have in the shop or do you have any others?"

"We do keep a small selection in the safe."

"That's alright," said the customer airily as the other man raised a questioning eyebrow. "Money is no object. There's beggary in the love that can be reckoned." He laughed. "Heavens above, one only gets engaged once in a lifetime! Why spoil the ship for a ha'p'orth of tar?"

Ives ventured a smile. "I think you'll find it will be rather more than ha'p'orth, sir. But, as you say, it's a unique occasion."

"Let me see what you have."

"I will, sir."

Albert Ives moved to the back of the shop and drew back a small curtain that hung at waist height. A large safe came into view. After using a key to begin the opening process, he then twiddled the tumblers until he found the correct combination. The heavy door swung silently open. Ives was about to reach into the safe when he realized that his customer was now standing directly behind him. Before he could turn, he was knocked unconscious with a vicious swing of a cosh. The safe was ransacked within seconds.

After checking into their hotel, the Hilliers had a light lunch before sauntering along to the theatre in the bright sunshine. The river swarmed with activity. Young men in baggy trousers, white shirts and boaters were showing off their punting skills to decorous sweethearts who lounged on leather cushions under their parasols. An occasional rowing boat went by. Gaudily painted barges were moored along the towpath and swans glided effortlessly past, viewing the invasion of their territory with utter disdain. Crowds milled on both banks. Invisible to the eye, Shakespeare was nevertheless a discernible presence.

The Memorial Theatre commanded a fine view of the river. Opened six years earlier, it was a big, solid, unimposing structure. The Americans were very disappointed. Having walked along streets that were filled with half-timbered Tudor houses and dripping with character, they found the stark modernity of the theatre rather incongruous. Mary Anne turned to her husband.

"Why didn't they build it like an Elizabethan theatre?"

"I guess they had their reasons, honey," said Cyrus.

"It's such a let-down. The architect missed a golden opportunity. He should have designed it like the Globe playhouse."

"The architect was a woman – Elizabeth Scott."

"Then she should have known better," said Mary Anne.

"Let's not condemn it on its exterior," he suggested. "That would be unfair. The only way to judge a theatre properly is to watch a play being performed there. Come on."

They joined the throng that was converging on the building. The Memorial Theatre could accommodate thirteen hundred people and it seemed as if every one of them was in the lobby. It was so congested that Cyrus and his wife had difficulty getting in. Over the heads of the crowd, he saw a counter where programmes were being sold.

"Stay here, honey," he advised. "I won't be long."

"I'm not going anywhere," she said. "I can't move."

Cyrus forced a way through the press with polite firmness and joined the queue at the counter. A familiar face materialized beside him. Rosalind Walker gave him a warm smile.

"How nice to see you again!" she said.

"Hello, Rosalind. Is it always as crowded as this?"

"One gets used to it."

"The lobby should have been bigger."

"That's only one of its defects. The seats could be more comfortable, the upper balcony is too far from the stage and – forgive my being indelicate – the ladies' cloakroom is woefully inadequate for this number of people."

"It's the stage that worries me. Proscenium arch, I'm told. Poor old Will wouldn't even know what that was. Why not try to recreate the performance conditions of his time?"

"A good question." After chatting for a couple of minutes, they got to the counter and bought their programmes. Rosalind looked around. "Where's your wife?"

"Over by the door," said Cyrus. "If I can get back to her."

"Tony is out on the terrace, enjoying a cigarette."

"Wise man. Best place to be."

"I'm sure that he'd like to meet you. In the interval, perhaps."

"Yes. That would be nice."

"Where are you sitting?"

"Front stalls."

"We're at the back," she said easily. "And don't worry about the hordes. A lot of these people have actually got tickets to the balcony so they won't be down here in the interval. People in the stalls usually make a beeline for the bar." She moved away. "Enjoy the play."

"Oh, I will," he promised her. "Every moment of it."

Mildred Conroy was a full-bodied woman in her early sixties with a romantic streak. She always took a particular pleasure in selling engagement and wedding rings. When the couple entered her jewellery shop that afternoon, she sensed the distinct possibility of a sale. The young man was clearly a person of means and the two of them were evidently in love. The woman was darting affectionate glances at him and he kept his arm around her waist.

"Can I help you?" asked Mildred with professional sweetness.

"We'd like to look at some engagement rings," said the man.

"Of course, sir. Does the young lady have any preference?"

"Well, I rather hope it's for me, actually."

"Oh, David!" scolded his companion as he burst out laughing at his own joke. "That's not what we were being asked and you know it." She turned an apologetic smile on Mildred. "Do excuse him. Perhaps we could look at some of those in the window?"

"Of course."

Mildred unlocked the glass doors and lifted out a display unit that held a dozen diamond engagement rings. The woman gazed at them with fascination and began to examine each in turn. When she asked for the respective prices, the man did not blanch at the high cost. Mildred was encouraged. She was both furthering their romance and doing good business at the same time. While the woman was full of questions about the various stones, the man simply looked on. He was there to pay. All that he wanted was for her to be happy.

"While we're here," said the woman, "we may as well see them all. Could I trouble you to get the others out of the window as well?"

"Of course," replied Mildred. "Look at the full range."

"They're so beautiful!"

"Just like you," said the man into her ear.

Mildred heard the surreptitious whisper and smiled. They seemed such a happy couple. There were three more trays of rings in the window and she had to stretch in order to retrieve them. It took her a little while before all four displays were side by side on the counter. Some of them could be discounted immediately but the woman did pick out a sapphire ring to try on. After flexing her hand, she showed the ring to the man.

"Is that the one, darling?" he asked.

"I'm not sure." She selected a ring from the first display. "The diamond was my favourite at first but the sapphire is so gorgeous." She smiled at Mildred. "Might I ask how much it is?"

"Money doesn't come into this, Venetia," he said.

"I'm interested to know."

"They're virtually the same price," said Mildred. "They're also two of the best rings in the shop. I congratulate you on your taste."

"Venetia has excellent taste," boasted the man. "That's why she chose me – isn't it, darling?"

But the young woman was too preoccupied with comparing the rings, holding them side by side, then removing one so that she could try on the other. She slipped it off her finger and gave it to Mildred.

"It's between these two," she decided.

"Toss a coin," suggested the man blithely.

"David!"

"Well, we can't take all day."

"I'd like to think it over. What time do you close?"

"Not until five-thirty, madam," said Mildred.

"Oh, we'll be back long before then. David and I will pop into that Tea Shoppe just up the street. By the time we come out, I'll have decided between diamond and sapphire." She became anxious. "You won't sell either of the rings while we're away, will you?"

Mildred shook her head. "No, madam. I'll put them aside."

"Thank you."

After a last look at both rings, they gave her a nod of farewell and left the shop. Mildred put the rings into a small box and unlocked a drawer under the counter. When the box was out of the way, she began to replace the trays in the front window, taking care not to nudge any of the other items on display. The last tray was the one that she had first taken out. As she picked it up, Mildred glanced at it. Her blood froze. Shorn of its most expensive ring, it still contained eleven others but it was not the number that startled her.

It was the fact that several of the rings were not the ones that had been there earlier. They had been replaced with rings that were similar in appearance but of a much lower value. Mildred had been tricked. While she was reaching into the window, the switch had been made. Her romantic streak had been a fatal distraction. She had just been robbed in broad daylight.

Cyrus Hillier had been enraptured by the performance of *Troilus and Cressida* and Mary Anne had been overwhelmed by the quality of the acting. When the interval came, they were in something of a daze as they made their way up the aisle towards the lobby.

"It's wonderful!" said Cyrus. "A definitive production."

"But not as good as yours," countered Mary Anne loyally.

"I only had amateur actors. These are real professionals."

"I still preferred your version, Cyrus."

"Thanks, honey."

As they came into the lobby, a young man bore down on them.

"Professor and Mrs Hillier?" he asked.

"That's us," admitted Cyrus.

"Anthony Walker," said the other, offering his hand. "I believe that you've met my sister, Rosalind."

"We have indeed, young sir."

Handshakes were exchanged then they moved to a corner where they could discuss the play. Anthony explained that his sister had rushed off to the ladies' cloakroom before the general invasion. He shared their enthusiasm for the production though he had severe doubts about the play itself.

"Not the jolliest piece that Shakespeare wrote, is it?"

"It does have its comic moments," argued Cyrus. "There was a lot of humour in that scene with Ajax and Thersites."

"But it's still a rather pessimistic play."

"Pessimistic or realistic?"

"Ah, well," said Tony with a grin. "That's a matter of opinion."

"Wait until you've seen the whole play."

"I will, Professor."

Rosalind soon joined them and they had an amicable debate about the theatre itself, all agreeing that it had its shortcomings. It seemed only minutes before the warning bell sounded to mark the end of the interval. Rosalind was saddened.

"We'll have to say goodbye now," she said, "because Tony and I have to dash off the moment the performance is over."

"I thought you were staying at a hotel," said Mary Anne.

"We usually do and we'd loved to have stayed on so that we could watch *The Merchant of Venice* this evening. But we have to be on the Shakespeare Express at five-thirty."

"What a pity!"

"Needs must when the devil drives," said Tony, shaking their hands in turn once more. "But it was a delight to meet you both and I hope that you enjoy the rest of your stay in England."

"Thank you," said Mary Anne. "And goodbye."

After a flurry of farewells, they went into the auditorium. Cyrus and Mary Anne took their seats in the front stalls. Her mind was still on the two friends they had made.

"It's such a shame they have to leave when the play is over," she said. "It would have been nice to have a drink with them afterwards."

"Perhaps," he said quietly. "Perhaps not."

They were soon lost in the second half of the production. It was an exhilarating experience and gave them plenty to discuss when they returned to their hotel afterwards. The evening performance of *The Merchant of Venice* was equally satisfying though Cyrus felt that the play was inferior to the one they had watched that afternoon. On the stroll back to the Shakespeare Hotel, he explained why. Mary Anne was, as ever, an attentive listener. Cyrus had hoped to continue the conversation over supper but, as soon as they entered the hotel, they were intercepted. A stocky man in his forties introduced himself as Detective-Sergeant Cyril Rushton and, after showing them his warrant card, asked if he might have a word with them. Mary Anne was patently discomfited.

"We haven't done anything wrong, have we?" she asked.

"Not at all, Mrs Hillier," said Rushton. "I just need your help." He glanced around. "Is there somewhere private where we can speak?"

"Our room might be the best place," said Cyrus.

"Lead the way, sir."

Mary Anne was upset at being accosted by a detective but Cyrus seemed to be completely unperturbed. It was almost as if he had been expecting it. When they got to the room, he sat on the edge of the bed while the others occupied the two chairs. Rushton produced a notebook from the inside pocket of his jacket and flicked through the pages until he found the one he wanted.

"I believe that you know a Miss Rosalind Walker," he began. "It was she who told me where I could find you both. I understand that you met the lady this morning."

"Yes," said Mary Anne. "It was at Paddington Station."

"And you travelled on the train to Stratford with her?"

"We did, Sergeant Rushton. The Shakespeare Express."

"Did you share the same carriage?"

"No, she was in another carriage with her brother, Anthony."

"That's what she claims."

"It's exactly what happened, Sergeant."

"Not necessarily," said Cyrus.

"What do you mean?"

"Let the Sergeant finish, Mary Anne."

"But you were *there*, Cyrus. You saw them get on the train."

"Miss Walker also claims that she and her brother attended a matinee performance of *Troilus and Cressida*," said Rushton, referring to his notebook. "Can you confirm that?"

"Yes," said Mary Anne.

"No," added her husband.

"Cyrus, don't be silly," she chided. "We met them."

"We talked to them in the lobby, maybe. But that doesn't mean they actually watched the performance."

"Of course they did. They came into the auditorium with us."

"But did they stay – that's the question?"

"Ignore my husband," she said with a touch of irritation. "He's had a lapse of memory. I can vouch for them. Rosalind and Anthony Walker saw that play this afternoon." She looked at Cyrus. "How can you possibly deny it?"

"Because I don't like being *used*, Mary Anne."

"What are you talking about?"

"The Sergeant will explain."

Rushton took his cue. "At approximately eleven o'clock this morning," he told them, "a jewellery shop in Banbury was robbed. The manager was injured in the process. The thief – a young man answering the description of Anthony Walker – got away with a substantial amount of jewellery."

"It couldn't possibly have been him, Sergeant," said Mary Anne defensively. "He was on the train and it doesn't even stop at Banbury."

"Yes, it does," observed Cyrus.

"It's not a proper scheduled stop," continued the Detective. "They slip a carriage at the station, that's all. No passengers are allowed to join the train."

"But they could leave it."

"They could indeed, Professor Hillier. You stopped at Banbury at ten forty-one. That fits in with the timing of the robbery."

"Did anyone see Anthony Walker leaving the train?" asked Mary Anne, refusing to believe that he could be implicated in a crime. "Well, did they?"

"No, Mrs Hillier."

"There you are, then."

"You don't understand, Mary Anne," said her husband gently. "Rosalind's brother could not leave the train because he was never on it in the first place."

"Yes, he was. You saw them get on together."

"I saw her get into the train with a young man but there's no guarantee that it was Anthony. Apart from anything else, he lifted his hat to her when they met. Is that the kind of greeting you'd expect from a brother?" He looked at Rushton. "My guess is that it was Rosalind who got off at Banbury."

"Quite right, sir," said Rushton. "The stationmaster confirms it."

"I begin to see why she never mentioned that stop to us. She told us everything else about the Shakespeare Express."

Mary Anne was baffled. "What's going on?" she wondered.

"We were tricked into providing an alibi."

"I don't understand. All that we did was to talk to her. In any case," she went on, "how can Rosalind possibly be involved in the crime? The Sergeant said that it was committed by a young man."

"We've reason to believe that she was at the wheel of the car that was waiting outside the jewellery shop," said Rushton seriously. "We have a number of witnesses who saw it being driven away at speed by a woman."

"Oh!" Mary Anne was deeply shocked. "Are you saying that her brother was the thief?"

"I doubt very much if he was her brother, honey," said Cyrus.

"Right again, sir," said Rushton. "The second crime took place around two-thirty this afternoon – another jewellery shop, right here in Stratford. This time, both of them were involved. While the manageress of the shop was distracted, they switched expensive rings for cheap ones."

"Two-thirty, did you say?" Mary Anne shook her head. "It wasn't them, Sergeant. They were watching the matinee."

"That's what they wanted us to think," said Cyrus. "And they were very convincing. I daresay they've done this before."

"More than once, Professor," said the Detective. "The first time, their target was a jewellery shop in High Wycombe. The Shakespeare Express stops there. My belief is that Miss Walker left the train there and was picked up by her accomplice in a car. On the second occasion, a jewellery shop in Warwick was robbed. Weeks later, they followed the same routine in Leamington Spa and got away with thousands of pounds worth of diamond rings. Today, however," he concluded, "was the only time they committed two major crimes on the same day."

"Overreachers," mused Cyrus.

"What's that, sir?"

"People whose greed and ambition drives them too far. It's a concept with which Shakespeare was very familiar though it's another playwright who gave it real definition. Does the name of Philip Massinger mean anything to you, Sergeant?"

"Afraid not, Professor," confessed the other. "I've lived in Stratford all my life but – I'm ashamed to say – I've never once been to a play here. Mind you," he added by way of mitigation, "I was on duty the night the Memorial Theatre burned down in 1926. Who was this Philip Messenger?"

"Massinger – a Jacobean dramatist who wrote *A New Way To Pay Old Debts*. One of its main characters was a ruthless extortionist called Sir Giles Overreach. Like the two people we met earlier, he was brought down when trying to extend his grasping hand too far."

"I still can't accept that they were criminals," said Mary Anne. "They were too nice, too thoroughly decent."

"And we were too thoroughly American, honey."

"What do you mean?"

"That's why we were singled out at Paddington. We looked like a pair of innocent, defenceless, trusting American tourists. Think back. Who initiated the conversation?"

"She did, Cyrus."

"Exactly. She befriended us to secure an alibi and she no doubt chose other unsuspecting Americans on the previous occasions."

"In those cases," said Rushton, "they were never called upon as witnesses because there was no arrest. This time, it was different."

"Where did you catch them?"

"In their room at the Billesley Manor Hotel. They'd driven there to count their takings. It wasn't just the jewellery shops that suffered, you see. The pair of them are accomplished pickpockets as well. They mingled with the crowd at the theatre in search of victims. People are off-guard in that sort of situation. After the matinee, the manager had a number of complaints from people who'd been robbed."

"They seem to have followed a pattern," said Cyrus.

"That was their mistake, sir. It all started with the Shakespeare Express. They hit a different town each time but always pretended to go to a matinee here."

"And they were arrested in a hotel?"

"In bed together, as it happens."

Mary Anne was scandalized. "A brother and sister?"

"Incest is the one thing we can't charge them with, Mrs Hillier. In reality, they're not related and their real names are nothing like the ones they gave to you." He got to his feet. "Well, I'll detain you no longer. Now that I know you won't speak up on their behalf, I'll be on my way. Thank you for your help."

"She picked the wrong dupes this time," said Cyrus, crossing to open the door for him. "I began to suspect that something about Rosalind Walker was not quite right when she pumped us for information. She wanted to know exactly where we could be found. What clinched it for me was her little ambush at the theatre."

"Ambush?"

"The lobby was packed to the rafters, Sergeant. She'd never have found me in that crowd. Knowing that I was bound to buy a programme, Rosalind lurked by the counter where they were being sold. When she pounced on me, I knew something fishy was going on."

"You're something of a detective yourself, sir."

"I take no credit. Shakespeare must do that."

"Why?"

"When I watched the second half of the play this afternoon, something suddenly clicked at the back of my mind. It was a speech of Ulysses about Cressida."

Rushton was mystified. "Who are they?"

"Characters in the play. Cressida has just greeted a succession of strangers with a familiarity that appalls Ulysses. I was reminded of the way that Rosalind – or whatever her name is – fell on us at Paddington station. She was altogether too open and friendly."

"That's what I liked about her," said Mary Anne.

"I was taken in myself at first. Then Ulysses spoke up."

"What did he say?" asked the detective.

O these encounterers, so glib of tongue,
That give accosting welcome ere it comes,
And wide unclasp the tables of their thoughts
To every ticklish reader.

"That sounds like her, Professor. She could talk the hind leg off a donkey. Glib of tongue sums her up perfectly."

"In short, she was thoroughly un-English. A clear danger sign."

"I didn't see it," said Mary Anne, shaken by the turn of events. "Both of them fooled me. I feel such an idiot."

Cyrus chuckled. "I don't," he said. "It was rather exciting to be caught up in this crime spree and to play a small part in convicting the villains. Their problem was that they chose the wrong profession."

"Did they?"

"Yes, honey. They were both such accomplished actors that they could easily have made a living on the stage. Instead of using the Shakespeare Express as a base for their crimes," he pointed out, "they could have caught it to come to work here in Stratford."

THE OTHER HALF

Colin Dexter

Recently retired, aged fifty, from Thames Valley Police, with the rank of Detective Chief Inspector, I now styled myself a freelance investigator – and business was bad. The previous week my sole assignment had been to examine the dubious legality of a Bulgarian immigrant keeping a boa constrictor in his council-house bath. I was therefore hopeful of better prospects when the phone rang early on Monday morning.

Mrs Isobel Rodgers introduced herself with a pleasing, slightly husky voice and I guessed the state of play immediately – husband trouble. As I was listening to myself telling her that ninety-five per cent of wives underwent the same affliction, she interrupted me, saying, "Is it my turn to speak now?"

She was, she claimed, almost completely certain of her husband's infidelity, and was determined to get rid of that "almost". When I asked if she wanted anything else, she replied simply, "Divorce." Before I could comment further, she terminated the interview by saying, "It will be worth your while. Come round and see me. You have your diary handy?"

I was in due course ushered into a detached house in North Oxford by this peremptory lady, who was younger than I'd imagined and considerably more attractive, with brown hair framing a pair of startling eyes. Green eyes.

"Drink?"

I shook my head, congratulating myself on not trotting out the policeman's cliché, whilst she leaned back in a black leather armchair, fondling a tumbler of what looked like water, but most probably wasn't.

"Cigarette?"

I stoically shook my head once more.

"I'm glad you don't smoke. My husband Denis is a very heavy smoker."

"But that's not what you—"

"What I want to talk to you about, no." Her eyes arrested mine, and in an unemotional voice she began to recount her suspicions about Denis' recent philandering. First indictment – those phone calls. "Can I speak to Mr Rodgers, please?" "Who shall I say is speaking?" Line suddenly dead. "Hello, yes?" Line suddenly dead. If Denis answered, only the briefest *sotto voce* exchanges, "wrong number" being his only reply to subsequent queries.

"And you think—" I began.

"You know very well what I think!"

Second indictment. Denis ran a small publishing business called The Cavalier Press in North Parade in Summertown. A fortnight previously he had thrown an office party to celebrate the awarding of the prestigious Georgette Heyer Prize to one of his authors. A three-book deal was in the offing, soon to be signed by the winner, and Denis was predicting a further upturn in his company's already flourishing fortunes. It was way after midnight when he had finally come home. He had admitted to being half-seas over and in need of a shower, and had gone to sleep things off in the spare room instead of clambering into the conjugal bed.

"I'm afraid we all occasionally—" I started, but she ignored my interruption.

In the morning she had found two long curly blonde hairs across his jacket. She had reason to believe that they had fallen from the head of Jade, Denis' newly appointed PA, who preferred to be known as "Blondie", it seemed – a young woman whom Isobel had not yet met, and most decidedly did not wish to meet.

"Pity you didn't keep—"

"What makes you think I didn't?"

Third indictment. The previous week, when her customarily immaculately dressed husband had returned from the office, she had observed something unprecedented about his appearance. He was wearing no tie and the buttons of his shirt were crudely out of alignment. Isobel suggested that even the most inveterate liar would have had trouble coming up with a credible explanation for this state of dress.

Fourth indictment. Isobel pointed to a brown envelope on the coffee table between us. "In there, along with one strand of blonde hair, you will find one half of a letter which was torn in two. I found it in Denis' wastepaper basket. Just let me know what you think about all this when you come on Friday."

"But that's only—"

"Yes, but I know that you can manage it. Same time? And you'll want this as well." She handed me a second envelope, a white one, laid a hand on my sleeve, and whispered almost conspiratorially, "Good luck!" Then she showed me to the door.

I called in at The Dew Drop on my way home, and over a couple of pints of Real Ale, I thought of the singular commission given me that morning. And I thought, too, of Isobel Rodgers . . . I suppose I should have opened the brown envelope first, but I didn't.

Inside the white envelope I found a cheque made out to me, and I looked and looked again at the middle handwritten line there.

Five hundred pounds

I decided to put the cheque into my account immediately. Whilst I stood waiting in the queue at Lloyds Bank, I looked yet again at the small neat writing and at the signature there.

Isobel Rodgers

As I look back on the following few days, I feel somewhat guilty about having accepted such a generous fee for my services – which amounted to the following.

First I went to the local British Telecom offices to determine if I could get a lead on Isobel's mysterious phone calls. The patient lady there first explained the various methods for discouraging replacement-window specialists and other persistent unwanted callers. Then she went on to tell me that, unfortunately, the telephone numbers of stalkers and crank callers were generally untraceable, as those callers usually took precautions to make sure that they were. I already knew all this, and I suddenly wondered if Isobel Rodgers knew it all, too. But I figured it had been worth a try.

I spent the whole of the lunch hour on Wednesday in North Parade Avenue, a very narrow thoroughfare off the Banbury Road. At 12:30 p.m. two bonny-looking blondes left the offices of The Cavalier Press and walked along to The Gardener's Arms. I followed them into that hostelry, then stood behind them as each ordered a spritzer and a packet of plain crisps. A few moments later I took a seat opposite them in one of the spacious alcoves and introduced myself with a carefully rehearsed spiel, telling them I was a reporter from *The Oxford Times* writing an article on the local literary scene.

Both Jade and Sadie (as they introduced themselves) appeared quite happy to answer my questions. The Cavalier Press was doing fine – yeah! – especially after the recent big thrill of having the Heyer prize awarded to one of its authors. And Mr Rodgers had thrown a party to celebrate. "Great wasn't it, Sadie?" And there'd been a super article in *The Bookseller* on Eddie Young, the prize-winner, who wrote under the *nom de plume* Virginia Stirling.

"A lot of these women are men, you know!" Jade giggled. "And Eddie's going to sign an exclusive three-book deal with us. Great! Mr Rodgers is over the moon, isn't he, Sadie?"

My eyes shifted to the slimly curvaceous Sadie, the quieter of the two, who nodded slowly, then finished her spritzer. I got to my feet and insisted on ordering further spritzers for my blonde informants. Jade's pin-straight hair was cut quite short, while Sadie's wonderfully curly locks were shoulder length. Sadie's hair was a better match for the strand Isobel had found. If this race turned out to be of the two-horse variety, it would appear that Isobel had placed her bet on the wrong filly.

On Thursday morning I called in at A Cut Above for a long overdue haircut, then, following my usual custom, I went home immediately afterwards to shake out the hairs from inside my shirt and rub my back with a towel. As I fastened my shirt buttons, something clicked in my sluggish brain about Isobel's wayward husband and his mismatched buttons. But what of the letter? Each evening I had pondered on that handwritten piece of paper, torn vertically down the middle.

il our weekend meeting
citing thing that's ever
fe, and the thought of
ours being spent with
ed makes me the most
ver,
die
rling)

Certainly there were plenty of suggestive possibilities down the torn edge of the note: "exciting", "life", "hours", "bed", "lover", "Sadie", "darling". But the more I studied things, the more I convinced myself that this could just as easily be interpreted as a wholly innocent missive. In the end, I typed out both versions, the innocent and the not-so-innocent, aligning the joins as neatly as my primitive keyboard skills would permit.

I was determined to be fairly honest with Isobel the following morning, but there were three matters on which I determined to remain silent. First, I would not mention the fact that on Wednesday night I had experienced a mildly erotic dream about her. Second, I wouldn't tell her that I had composed another possible – no, quite probable – left-hand half of the letter, written this time by Sadie. Third, I would not confess that fairly early on I'd had strong suspicions that the hand-writing on the letter was extremely similar to that on the cheque Isobel had given me, especially those 'd's and 'r's, and that I now felt certain that Isobel, for some strange reason, had written the letter herself.

She smiled at me winsomely that Friday morning when I asked if a drink was still on offer, and if she'd mind if I smoked whilst I recounted my findings.

She said nothing when I told her of my unproductive trip to the British Telecom offices. And when I gave her a truncated account of my encounter with the two blondes, she ventured just a single comment: "So you're saying the hair wasn't Jade's?" When I nodded (hallelujah!) she did betray some surprise for once.

My proffered explanation of the shirt re-buttoning incident occasioned little reaction, and in reply to my question she admitted that Denis had been for a haircut about that time, yes.

There remained the final hurdle, though. The letter. I could, of course, have shown her my alternate version, in which "Sadie darling" figured as the happy valediction. But I instead handed Isobel my original reconstruction, then watched her closely as she read it.

Hardly can I wait unt **il our weekend meeting.**
Writing is the most ex **citing thing that's ever**
happened to me in li **fe, and the thought of**
so very many further h **ours being spent with**
my PC going full spe **ed makes me the most**
happy fellow alive.

                    As e **ver,**
                    Ed **die**
            (Virginia Sti **rling)**

"This is the best you could come up with?" she said dismissively.

"Yes," I said, somewhat defensively. "It would have been another matter if you'd managed to find the other half."

"And what makes you think I haven't?" she said as she dipped one elegant hand into her Louis Vuitton handbag. "I found the left-hand half only yesterday – very careless of Denis!" Here she passed me two halves of a typewritten letter cellotaped together.

"But . . . but those are typed—" I began.

"Yes, they are. And they are the originals. I made a handwritten copy of the half I had found because I am not a computer person, I have no access to a photocopier, and I wanted to keep the original safe. Do you understand?

"Yes, I understand."

"I'm a little surprised and, to be honest with you, just a little disappointed that you hadn't noticed the similarities between the writing on the cheque and that on the letter. I'm also surprised that you put your money on Denis' prize author. But go on! Read it!"

Dearest,
I count the hours un   **til our weekend meeting.**
You are the most ex   **citing thing that's ever**
happened to me in li   **fe, and the thought of**
endlessly sensuous h   **ours being spent with**
you in a four-poster b   **ed makes me the most**
happy woman alive.

Your lo   **ver**
Blon   **die**
(1000 x's, da   **rling)**

As I read the letter, I was conscious of Isobel's green, green eyes upon me, and perhaps I succeeded in showing a wholly bogus surprise – bogus, that is, until I read the office nickname at the bottom: Blondie, aka Jade. Isobel had been right all along then, and I had been wrong. She had correctly guessed the winner of a two-horse race, while I had backed an outsider and lost. As we walked to the front door, I resisted the temptation to defend my ratiocinative powers (after all, the hair couldn't have been Jade's). Looking at Isobel for the last time, I wished that . . . well, that things had turned out differently.

Three weeks later I received a handwritten letter with no salutation and no valediction. It was no matter, though. I recognized the writing instantly. It read:

> "Denis and I have agreed upon an amicable separation, so divorce is no longer my dearest wish. I would like you to come and have dinner with me this coming Friday – just the two of us."

Oh dear! I had already been invited out to dinner at The Randolph on Friday evening by an attractive Anglo-Indian lady with deep dark-brown eyes. She had asked me to mediate in a squabble with her neighbours over her chatterbox of a parakeet from Paraguay, which she had somehow imported into the UK during the bird flu crisis.

In any case, I've always preferred dark-brown to startling green.

Well, that's what I told myself.

THREAT MANAGEMENT

Martyn Waites

I could see her from where I was crouching, behind the bushes. She was walking along the pavement, getting bigger as she came towards me, like all I could see was her. Only her. Wearing her usual stuff, business suit with a kind of belted mac thing over it, a short, beige one. Looked good in it, an' all, her long black hair loose down the back. Umbrella up. Her heels made that crunchy, clacking noise on the tarmac – kind you only hear in films and think it must be made up till you hear it in real life. There were probably other people around, but I didn't see them. Cars going past made a wet whoosh in the drizzle but I hardly heard them. Saw only her. Heard only her heels clack-clacking. Sounded louder than bombs.

I have to be honest, I wanted her then. Any man would.

By the way, this is a true story. I'm not making any of it up. I don't do that any more. Which is something, which is progress. No, this is exactly how it happened. Exactly.

I've watched her every day this week. Know her routine better than mine. What time she gets up, what time she leaves the flat. Which bus she catches, tube station she gets off at, train she gets on. Which branch of Costa she gets her regular cappuccino, skimmed milk, at. What time she gets in to the office. In the city. Nice place. All steel and glass. Huge. Know what she does in there. Yeah, I've been in. Seen her.

She didn't see me, though.

A solicitor, she is. A legal mouthpiece.

Then lunch breaks, usually a Marks and Sparks sandwich at her desk, sometimes a trip down to one of those flash new places off Spitalfields Market with a couple of the girls from the office.

Sometimes with Tony. Another solicitor. Met at some party. Her boyfriend, so she claims. They're an item. Not so sure he'd say the same thing.

And then coffee breaks – sometimes she'll come down to the Costa again, just for a walk, stretch her legs. But no fag breaks. Doesn't smoke. Too healthy. Know which branch of Holmes Place she goes to, after work sometimes. And what times. Watched her work out.

Well, apart from that time when she had a broken arm. Just straight to work and back home, then. Alone.

That Tony, he's a cunt. Really, he is. He doesn't appreciate her, not nearly enough. Not an item. Cunt.

Then all again in reverse: tube, bus, home again. Unless she's been going out. Cinema, theatre, dinner. A bar. Usually up in town, nothing round here. Well not much. A couple of times she's been in my local. Once with a mate of hers. And once on her own. Sampling the local atmosphere, I heard her say to Mike behind the bar. But Mike behind the bar wasn't impressed. If he can't shag it or make money out of it, he doesn't want to know. And she wasn't about to become a regular. And she was way out of his league. So really, she knows no one round here.

Except me.

I unscrewed the small bottle, took a big swallow of whisky. Smacked my lips, savouring the aftertaste, feeling the burn. Good. Kept me warm. Helped me concentrate.

The rest of the pubs on the high road and the estate, she's too good for them. Wouldn't want her going in them again, I told her that. The men in there, they're animals. They'd tear her apart. And I might not be there to protect her. I mean, I try my best, but I can't be with her all the time.

I told her that the first time she came in the pub. She laughed then, asked what I did. I told her. Showed her the card. She said nothing.

The second time she came in the pub she said plenty, though. It was accidental, really. I just bumped into her in the street. Like I said, accidental. I hadn't been following her or anything like that.

Honest.

I asked her if she'd like to come for a drink with me. Couldn't believe it when she accepted. Took her to the pub, squired her round. All the other old bastards in there couldn't believe it. She was with me. Me.

We had a great time. Talked all night. She really listened, you know? To everything I had to say, no matter how stupid it sounded. She made me feel like the most important person alive. To have a pretty girl listen to you, and talk to you, it's the most beautiful thing in the world.

She made me feel special.

When she left, Mike from behind the bar said I should forget it. Get her out of my mind, she was too good for me. Whatever she had to say, she was just using me, stringing me along. I got angry with him. Told him just because she didn't like him or want to talk to him he was jealous. He just shook his head, walked off to restock his bottles.

I wasn't falling in love with her then. Honest.

It was dark now and cold. The fog made big patches of blackness between the street lights. You could see your breath in front of you. I breathed out into my hand, up my sleeve. I didn't want her seeing mine. I watched.

She turned off the pavement like she usually did, made her way to the front of her block of flats. 1930s I think, lots of that type in this part of South London. Old, but still going strong. And worth more than where I lived.

I guessed what she would do next: put her head down, start rummaging through her handbag for her keys. I was right.

I'd been in that flat. Told them all in the pub that she'd invited me in. They didn't believe me. They never do. But she had done. Made me a cup of coffee, even. So yeah, I was really there, true. Let the others in the pub think what they like. Say what they like. I was there.

Honest.

It was comfortable. Really comfortable. That's the best way to describe it. The sofa looked like the kind you'd want to sink into after a hard day's work. The TV looked like the kind you would want to watch. On the shelves were books that looked interesting if you liked that kind of thing and CDs that I'm sure would have been good to listen to. There were other things around too, like candles and little ornaments and small lamps that gave off soft, warm glows. Rugs that reminded you of the expensive foreign holidays that you'd never be able to afford to take.

Not a bare bulb in the place. Not one piece of never-never furniture from Crazy George's that'd given up on you before you'd finished paying for it. No mismatching knock-off carpet remnants, donated tables and chairs. Not like my place at all.

I told you I was there.

And in the middle was her. Sitting on the sofa, sipping some real coffee, not the instant shite I was brought up with. She was like the flat. Nice. Dark hair that was long and well cared for. Green eyes that made you want to smile just to look at them. And she had dress sense and style.

She was so sweet, so honest. So loveable.

Then she told me her troubles. Her problem. I listened, all sympathetic like. And when she'd finished, I knew. Knew I could help her. And I wanted to help her. Protect her. Because she was lovely. Really beautiful. And there's a lot of bad things, bad people, out there, just waiting to snatch that beauty away. Because they're cruel. It's what they do. She might live in this area of South London but she's not of it, if you know what I mean. So she needed me to look after her. Like her own guardian angel.

Of course, I didn't say any of this. Just drank my coffee, said I'd help her. But I think she knew. I could tell the way she was looking at me. Could tell what I was thinking.

She touched my hand. Told me how much it would mean to her if I would help. And I got that feeling, that little zing of electricity going up my arm like I'd just stuck my finger in a live socket. And I looked at her. Her eyes. Big enough to fall in to.

I swallowed hard. Said I would do what I could. She could rely on me.

She smiled. And I felt my heart lift. Really lift. Like getting a blessing from an angel.

I smiled back. She just jumped like I'd hit her. I saw myself in the mirror over the fireplace when I did it. Don't blame her for jumping. Not a smile but a grimace. A blood lust one like apes do when they've just arse-fucked an outsider to the tribe and killed him by pulling his arms off. Once a squaddie always a fucking squaddie.

I stopped smiling. I was angry with myself, ashamed. She kept her hand there. Gave me another smile.

And that told me everything between us was still OK.

Now like I said, I wasn't falling in love. That would have been fucking stupid.

The hand in the bag was my cue. I'd planned the shortest route to her while I'd been waiting. I hadn't forgotten. The best view, the most camouflage, the quickest escape route. The bushes in the grounds of the flat. Obviously. Away from the road, the street light. Other people. Sarge would have been proud of me. Vicious old cunt.

I stood up, still hidden, breathing heavy, hand in front of my mouth, getting psyched, ready to run forward, ready for what was about to happen.

I thought about her all day long. All night. Even when I slept. Beautiful but vulnerable. I began to think things I'd never have considered a couple of months ago. Make little plans in my head. For the future. Thinking of her smile, the way she'd looked at me.

The future.

She stood on the front step, rummaging.

I waited.

But not for long.

They said at this charity that I go to that my problems go further back than just the shellshock. Go way, way back. Before the army. When I was a kid. To stuff that happened to me then. Bad stuff.

But I don't think about that now.

They said I needed an outlet. So I got one. When I told them in the pub what I was doing, when I showed them the cards, they just laughed. As usual. They never take anything I say or do seriously. Think I'm some mentalist, some nutter, spend all day at the library reading private eye novels. Thinking, like the counsellor at the charity said, like I'm the hero of my own fantasy. They think I'm away with the fairies. Delusional, they say.

Well, we'll see.

They say the drinking doesn't help either. I should stop it. Just feeds it.

We'll see.

They say that if I could just stop living out this fantasy life and get on with the real one then that would be something. That would be progress.

We'll see.

She got her key out, tried to put it in the lock, dropped it. She bent down.

And then he was on the doorstep with her. Tony. The cunt. Mouth open, hands going, talking to her, explaining something. Couldn't hear what, didn't matter. Didn't want to know.

And then his hands were on her. Grabbing her shoulders, his voice raised.

The cards I had printed. Threat Management. That's what they said. Got them done at a machine at Elephant and Castle shopping centre. Threat Management, that's what they say. Then my name. And a contact phone number. The pub's. Haven't got one of my own.

He grabbed her, pushed her up against the door. Her bag dropped on the ground. His arms were on her shoulders, holding hard. A blur of something dark and shiny flashed between them. Tony looked down, found the blade in his fist. Her body went towards his, his mouth was up against her ear. Saying something to her. Something unpleasant. They struggled, like two reluctant dancers. Locked together, they moved towards the side of the block of flats, like he was dragging her off.

That second night in the pub. On her own. Said she needed someone to take care of something for her. Someone she could trust.

Threat management.

Tony. The one who gave her the broken arm. Who thought women were there to do what he wanted. Who couldn't take no for an answer. Who claimed they were never an item in the first place but couldn't accept it when she dumped him. Who threatened to hurt her even more.

Hurt her bad.

Wanted someone to do that to him.

And once he was gone she would be grateful. Very grateful.

I was out of the bushes, adrenalin pumping the stiffness out of my legs, straight on him. My arm round his neck, his head in a tight lock, I pulled hard as I could, cutting off his air supply. He choked and gurgled. I pulled harder. Got my mouth close to his ear, said something unpleasant of my own.

He kept struggling.

With my other hand I grabbed for the knife, twisted him round. Saw fear in his eyes. Knew that feeling well. Had enough of that in the army. When you're up against something you don't know, something that could kill you. For me it was in Basra in Iraq. It was shellshock. It was anger. It was things I did there that I know will haunt me till I die. What I got thrown out of the army for. For him it was someone bigger and harder than him when he was only used to hurting girls.

He let her go. Now it was just him and me.

I heard her voice.

Take him . . . do it . . .

I twisted his hand, felt something snap. He dropped the knife. Gave a strangled gasp. I still had him round the throat, didn't want to let him get away. I pulled harder. Even in the darkness I could see him start to change colour.

I started to pull him away. Just like we planned. Into the bushes round the back of the flats, give him a talking to, get a bit heavy, teach him a lesson. Threat management. Dead easy. I started to drag him away.

Didn't get very far.

Because she was there, in front of him, on his chest. Calling him stuff that I would never have imagined she would ever say, stuff even I wouldn't say out loud.

Hissing at him, her voice low, like liquid hate pouring out of her mouth. I was stunned, she was like a whole different person. An angry, nasty, venomous one. I didn't know her.

The gurgling sound in his throat changed tone. I looked down. She had the knife in both hands and it was buried in his chest, right up to the hilt. Blood pooling round it, running down, staining through his clothes.

She stepped back, stared. Smiled. It wasn't pretty.

I didn't know what to do, I was too stunned to react. I left go of him, let him drop. He crumpled to the ground.

Ambulance . . . I said. Oh, Jesus Christ, call a fucking ambulance . . .

She gave me a look, shook her head with a look on her face like she was laughing at sadness, then ran inside the block of flats.

I looked at him. Felt helpless. No phone, like I said. Just stood there, with this bloke I didn't know but was supposed to hate because she had said so, watching the life drain out of him, his face wet with tears and rain.

He flopped and squirmed, like a fish hooked out of water and gasping, trying to get its gills to work properly and failing.

I don't know how long I stood there. But it didn't seem long before the sirens arrived. Police and ambulance. The works. Suppose I should have felt important.

She came out of the flat then. In tears. Looked like her old self, the one I had enjoyed being with so much. The pretty one, beautiful and vulnerable.

The one I absolutely, honestly, hadn't fallen in love with.

I heard her talking to the police. Picked out words.

Delusional.

Alcoholic.

Dangerous. Anger management issues.

Mental problems.

I said nothing. Just stared at her. Stood there in the rain with my parka hood up, face in shadow like some horror movie monk.

Threat management. I could have laughed.

She was a solicitor. A legal mouthpiece.

I forgot that.

She was clever.

They put me in the car. I let them. No sense in arguing. Drove me to the station, processed me, stuck me in an interview room. I told them everything. Everything I've said here.

Well, they listened, I'll give them that.

Then they went out. Left me.

And here I am. I don't know when they'll be back, but it doesn't matter. Because I know what they'll do with me. I know what's going to happen. And it's nothing like the future I was planning a few days ago.

The fantasy future. If anything was delusional, that was.

So what can I do now? Nothing.

But at least I've told the truth. I didn't make it up. Honest.

I've told it exactly how it happened. Exactly.

So I suppose that's something. I suppose that's progress.

FINGERS TO THE BONE

Andrew Taylor

1: The Arteries of Wealth

Robbie Trevine saw Mary Linnet before she saw him. She was standing under the archway, tucked in the angle between the wall and a trolley laden with corded boxes. She wore a dark cloak that belonged to her mother, and she had drawn up the hood, holding it across her face with her hand. Her fingers were white and thin, like bones.

Two trains had recently come in, one of them Robbie's, and people hurried through the archway to the city of Bristol beyond. He wriggled through a group of soldiers, arrogant in scarlet and gold, and touched her on the arm. She flinched and pulled away, jarring her shoulder on the wall. She glared at him as if he were a stranger.

"Mary, what is it? It's me."

"Creeping up like that! You scared the life out of me!"

"What are you doing? Collecting?"

"No." She looked away. "Not today."

Sometimes Mary collected money for the Rodney Place Missionary Society, though usually she took her box up the hill to Clifton or, down to Queen's Square, where the pickings were better because the people were rich enough to afford to be generous. Sometimes she was sent further afield, to Bath or Chippenham or Swindon. The railways had made the world smaller, more manageable.

"So why are you here?" Robbie asked.

"Taking the air."

"Here? At Temple Meads?"

"Why not? The doctor brought a nurse, Mrs Allardyce. She's sitting with Ma."

"How is she?"

"No better. Worse, if anything. And what are you doing here?"

"Tried for a job. Just digging, that was all. Foundations for a signal box. But they'd already—"

"Robbie," she cut in. "Go now, please. Go."

He gawped at her. "But why?"

A door had opened on the other side of the porter's trolley. A man laughed. A cloud of cigar smoke wafted through the air.

Mary gripped his arm. "Too late. Look at that notice. You don't know me."

"You've lost your wits."

"Just do as I say."

He turned away and pretended to study a notice concerning the transport of livestock on the Great Western Railway. The fact that he could read it all was due to Mary's mother. Several gentlemen emerged through the doorway. They exchanged farewells and most of them strolled through the archway to waiting carriages.

But two of the gentlemen lingered. Side by side, cigars in hand, they surveyed the seething crowds. Porters shouted and cursed. Trains murmured and hissed and rattled. The sounds rose to the high vault of the roof.

"Ten years ago this wasn't here, Sir John," said the younger and smaller of the two. "Twenty years ago it was barely conceivable. Thirty years ago it would have been beyond the wildest dreams of an opium eater."

"Impressive, I grant you," answered his companion, a white-haired gentleman of perhaps sixty years of age. "But the noise is intolerable."

"Noise? Yes, indeed. It's the sound that money makes. The Great Western Railway has restored prosperity to the towns it touches. Railways are the arteries of wealth. As you yourself will discover, I trust, when the Lydmouth and Borders Railway is built."

"You go too fast for me, sir."

"Because there is no time to waste!" cried the younger man, waving his cigar. "The fruit hangs ripening on the tree. If we do not pluck it, then someone else will. Which is why my directors and I are so desirous of your joining us on the board. Where Sir John Ruispidge leads, other men will follow. Your position in the county, sir, your influence with the administration, your friends in Parliament – you have it in your power to smooth our way considerably and, I may add, to reap a just reward for doing so. Once the line is built, you may transport your coal at a fraction of the price you now pay, and at many times the speed. The general prosperity the railways bring – the freer movement of people and capital – cannot but have a benevolent effect on the fortunes of all those concerned."

"Ah, but the investment must be considerable. Nothing will come of nothing, as the Bard tells us."

"I speak from experience. You must allow me to show you the figures from South Devon." There was another wave of the cigar. "And consider the convenience of it. You will be able to travel from your country seat to your house in town within a day, and in the utmost comfort. If Lady Ruispidge desires quails in aspic from Fortnum's, they could be on her table within a few hours."

"You are a persuasive advocate." Sir John took out his watch. "Alas, I must leave you until tomorrow."

"Good God! Is that a Breguet watch?"

"It is indeed. You have sharp eyes, Mr Brunel."

Robbie's eyes swung towards the little man. The great Brunel himself!

"I trust I have a sharp eye for any piece of machinery so elegantly conceived and finely constructed as one of Monsieur Breguet's watches. But in this case I have a personal interest. My father sent me as a very young man to work for Monsieur Breguet in Paris. He told me there was no better person from whom I might learn what I needed."

Watch in hand, Ruispidge bowed. "Your father was indeed a man of perspicacity."

The watch was dangling on its chain from the old man's hand, swinging to and fro like a pendulum, coming perilously close to the wall. Mr Brunel, Robbie thought, was growing agitated for the watch's safety.

At that moment, the world tilted on its axis and became an entirely different place. Mary came to life. His friend Mary, whom Robbie had known since he was a child in short-coats; who had played the part of sister to him for most of his life; who went to church at least once, usually twice, on Sundays – his friend Mary, with whom he was more than half in love – well, she picked up her cloak and skirt with her left hand and ran forward, keening like a madwoman.

She snatched the old man's watch from his hand. Sir John and Mr Brunel froze, both with their cigars moving towards their open mouths. Mary dived into the crowded station yard, dodging among the carriages and horses and wagons until she was lost in the seething mass of humanity.

2: A Gown of Yellow Silk

Robbie Trevine lodged above a cobbler's near the market, where they let him sleep under the rafters in return for sweeping floors and running errands. By the time he had finished his jobs for the evening, the sky was darkening. He slipped out of the house and made his way to Hotwells, to the damp and crowded house by the river where Mary and her mother lodged in a tiny room up four pairs of stairs.

Mary opened the door. When she saw him, she stepped back to allow him into the room. He glanced towards the curtained alcove beside the empty fireplace.

"She's asleep," Mary whispered. "The doctor gave her something."

"Give my love when she wakes."

Robbie reckoned that Mrs Linnet had given him more love than his own mother, though that wasn't hard because, when he was three years old, his mother had gone off for a few days' holiday with a Liverpool publican and never come back.

Mary's face was impossible to read in that shadowy room. "I was afraid you'd come."

"Why did you do it? Why did you steal the gent's watch at the station?"

"I had to do something. The doctor don't come cheap, and Ma needs medicines, and proper food. The nurse is coming back later this evening. It all costs money."

"But if they catch you—"

"They won't."

"But selling something stolen is almost as risky as taking it in the first place."

She shrugged and turned her head away from him. "There's someone I know."

"This isn't the first time, is it?"

Mary said nothing. They listened to the breathing of the sick woman.

Robbie said: "I'd do anything to help. You know that."

"Go now," she said. "Just go. I don't want you here."

Robbie stumbled out of the room. He crossed the street and took shelter in the mouth of the alley on the other side. There was a tavern on the corner, and the constant bustle of the place made him almost invisible.

A distant church clock chimed the quarters and the hours. He calculated that he waited nearly an hour and a half before Mary appeared in the doorway of her house. She was hooded and cloaked as before, but he would have known her anywhere. She set off up the street, her wooden pattens clacking on the cobbles. He followed her, holding well back, keeping to patches of shadow and varying his pace. Soon they began to climb towards the dark mass of Clifton Wood.

Mary followed the rising ground towards the Downs in the northwest. They were not far from the tower of Brunel's unfinished suspension bridge, looming over the Gorge and the river Avon. Before she reached the Downs, however, Mary turned into a terrace of great stone-faced houses set back from the road. Only one of the houses had shuttered windows, and this was the one she approached. Robbie, watching from across the street, saw her dark figure descending into the basement area in front of the house.

He crossed the road. A plate had been screwed to one of the gateposts. It was too dark to decipher the words engraved upon it. He ran his fingertips over the brass, tracing the cold metallic channels of each letter.

THE RODNEY PLACE MISSIONARY SOCIETY

Mary knocked on the basement door. A candle flame flickered in the black glass of a nearby window. Bolts scraped back. The door opened.

"Child," said Mr Fanmole in his soft voice. "You are long past your time."

"I beg pardon, sir. The nurse was late and I couldn't leave my mother."

When she was inside, Mr Fanmole closed and bolted the door. He wore a long grey dressing gown of a silken material that gleamed in the candlelight; his little head was perched on a broad neck that rose from narrow shoulders.

"Come, child." He led the way along a whitewashed passage vaulted with brick, his shadow cavorting behind him on the wall. "You saw him?"

"Yes, sir. He came out with the other gents, and then he stopped for a while and talked with one of them. Mr Brunel himself."

She followed Mr Fanmole into a room at the back of the house. A coal fire burned in the grate and there were shutters across the two windows. He sat down at a mahogany table laden with papers and angled his chair to face the fire. He beckoned her to stand before him.

"Well, child? What did you learn?"

"He's interested in a new railway, but he hasn't made up his mind. He's lodging at the Great Western Hotel. And . . . and I took his watch."

Mr Fanmole slapped the palm of his hand on the table, and his pen fell unnoticed to the carpet. "I told you to be discreet, you little fool. This was not an occasion for thieving."

"But he was playing with it, sir, just asking for it to be prigged. And my ma, she's took bad again, and she needs a nurse as well as a doctor – and it's a good watch, too, sir. You give me a sovereign for the last one, and I'm sure—"

"Hold your prattle."

"Sir, he didn't see my face, I swear it. And I was away through the crowd before he knew the watch was gone."

"Give it me," he commanded.

Mr Fanmole held out his hand and she dropped the watch onto his palm. To her surprise he smiled. "Ah! He will be enraged. He's deeply attached to his Breguet timepiece."

"Sir," she asked timidly, "how much will I have when you sell it? My mother—"

"It's too precious to sell, child. Far too precious."

"But, sir, I don't understand."

He gazed at her, whistling tunelessly, and put down the watch, very gently, on the table. "You don't have to understand."

"I – I thought you'd be pleased, sir."

Suddenly he was on his feet and looming over her. His hand shot out and seized her by the hair. He dragged her to a tall cupboard built into the wall on the right of the fireplace. He opened the door. Hanging inside was a yellow silk gown.

"This is how to please me, child."

3: Not Quite the Gentleman

In the opinion of Sir John Ruispidge, Mr Brunel was not quite the gentleman. But it would be churlish to deny that he had been kindness itself after the distressing theft of the Breguet watch at Temple Meads Station. He had summoned police officers and urged them to prosecute their enquiries with the utmost vigour. He had ordered advertisements to be placed in the Bristol papers, offering a reward of twenty guineas for the watch's safe return.

"Not for the world, my dear sir," he had said, "would I have had such an incident occur."

Sir John could well believe it. The long and the short of it was that Brunel had every reason to keep him sweet.

That evening he dined in Queen Square with two men who might become fellow directors if he decided to accept Brunel's overtures. Still shaken by his experience, he drank deep and left early. The loss of his watch had been a double blow – first the watch itself, which he cherished, and second the circumstances of its theft. As an old soldier, Sir John prided himself on being a man of action, always prepared for the unexpected. But he had not even tried to apprehend the young person. He had behaved, in short, like a milksop.

But he would not be caught unprepared again. As the carriage whirled him back to his hotel near the Cathedral, Sir John patted the pocket of his overcoat and felt the reassuring outline of his Adams revolver. Only recently patented, it was a double-action model enabling rapid fire; according to his gunsmith, its bullet would stop a charging tiger.

The carriage drew up outside the hotel. A servant let down the steps and opened the door. As he climbed down, Sir John stumbled, and would have fallen if the man had not steadied him. He was perhaps a trifle bosky, but he prided himself on being a man who could hold his liquor. There might even be a case for a little brandy to aid digestion before he retired.

His apartments were on the first floor. He opened the sitting-room door and discovered that the people of the house had forgotten to bring lights and make up the fire. He marched towards the fireplace, intending to ring for a servant.

But something stopped him in his tracks, something amiss. There was a perfume in the air, clearly identifiable despite the underlying smell of his cigars. He acted without conscious thought. He pulled the heavy revolver from his pocket. Simultaneously he glimpsed a shadow shifting on the far side of the room.

The revolver went off with a crash that stunned him, the echoes almost masking the sound of scuffling and a cry and the closing of the door to the bedroom next to the sitting room. He was so surprised he nearly dropped the gun. He had not intended to shoot; he had forgotten that the Adams revolver was self-cocking and lacked a safety catch.

"Stop, thief!" Sir John cried, and the words came out little better than a whimper.

He moved unsteadily to the connecting door and flung it open. The bedroom appeared to be empty. A second door, leading directly to the corridor, stood open; the corridor was empty, too.

Trembling, Sir John returned to the bedroom and tugged the bell rope so hard it came away in his hand. As he looked about him for the brandy decanter, a piece of material on the carpet caught his eye. He picked it up and examined it under the light.

It was a scrap of yellow silk.

*   *   *

During the following day, Robbie earned a few coppers helping a stall holder at the market. Everyone was talking about the burglar at the Great Western Hotel, and how an old gent had put a bullet in him. When Robbie got back to his lodgings, the cobbler called out to him from his workshop.

"There's a woman asking after you. That nurse, Mrs Allardyce. She said you was to go over to Mrs Linnet's. But first things first. I need a dozen tallow candles from Hornby's. If you look sharp you'll catch them before they close."

Robbie ignored the order, just as he ignored the shout that pursued him up the street. He ran all the way to Hotwells. The house where the Linnets lodged was full of lights and noise but their window was dark. He climbed the stairs and tapped on the door. There was no answer. He turned the handle and went inside the room. The air made him gag.

"Mrs Linnet? Mary?"

"Robbie?" Mary's mother whispered from the alcove near the fireplace. "Is that you?"

"Yes. Shall I light the lamp?"

He blundered through the darkness and found the oil lamp and a box of matches on the mantel. Mrs Linnet's face appeared in the wavering light. She was lying on her pallet, huddled under a mound of blankets.

"What's happened? Where's Mary?"

"She didn't come back last night. Mrs Allardyce stayed till morning but then she had to go."

"Is she coming to sit with you tonight?"

The head rolled on the pillow. "No. I can't pay her. Mary said she'd bring some money. Where is she, Robbie? I'm worried."

"I'll find her. Did she go out again last night?"

"Again? What do you mean? She went out once, and she never came back."

Mary Linnet was on fire. Her lips were chapped and she felt as though her skin was flaking away. Her tongue lay huge and dry in her mouth. She was aware of the pain in her left shoulder. There was moisture, too, dark and thick and tasting of iron.

She did not know how long she had lain in this dark place, drifting in and out of consciousness. Once, in the glow of a candle, the Reverend Mr Fanmole loomed over her like a great grey slug in a dressing gown. She remembered Mr Fanmole waiting for her with a closed carriage when she had stumbled through the side door of the hotel. She remembered his hot breath on her cheek, and how he had made her lie on the carriage floor as they jolted up the hill to Clifton.

"Don't sit on the seat, you stupid child, you'll bleed on the leather."

Now Mary was lying on a thin layer of straw spread over a flagged floor with a mound of logs in the corner. A barred window was set high in a wall. Sometimes there was natural light on the other side of it – not much, but enough to see the outlines of her prison.

But perhaps that was a hallucination, too. She could no longer distinguish between what was inside her mind and what was without. Once she saw the Breguet watch swinging like a pendulum before her eyes, measuring away her life.

Another time she saw as clear as day Robbie's face framed by the little window. He tapped on the glass with fingers that were pale as bones, and she opened her mouth to call him, but she could no more speak than she could move.

4: A Tribe of One

On the second evening of his visit, Sir John Ruispidge dined at the Great Western Hotel. After his adventure the previous evening, he was pleased to discover that he was regarded as something of a hero. The story had already reached the newspapers – how a distinguished visitor to Bristol had surprised a burglar in his room and coolly put a bullet through the scoundrel. The villain had not yet been apprehended, but traces of blood had been found.

Returning to his rooms after dinner, Sir John passed through the lobby of the hotel. A young man was engaged in an altercation with two of the hotel servants.

"I'm not going," the man was saying in a strong Bristol accent. "Not till I've seen him."

"You'll be pitched out on your ear. I'll summon a constable."

To judge by his clothes, the young man belonged to the labouring class, but he looked clean and respectable. He had a pleasant, manly face, Sir John considered, and he appeared sober. To the baronet's surprise, the fellow pointed at him.

"Why, there he is! Sir John, sir, let me speak to you."

"What is it, my man? Who are you?"

The man pulled off his cap. "Robbie Trevine, sir, at your service. It's – it's about your watch. And what happened last night."

Sir John frowned. "The burglar? What had he to do with my watch? It was stolen hours earlier."

"I know, sir. If you'd let me explain?"

"Come over here."

Sir John led the way to a sofa near the fire. He sat down and the man stood cap in hand before him. The servants hovered but kept their distance.

"The watch was stolen by a young woman I know," Trevine said.

Sir John's eyebrows rose. It had not been given out that the thief was a woman. "Go on."

"She's not a thief, sir, I swear it, not by nature. Her mother's ill, and she can't pay for the doctor."

Sir John waved a hand. "Right is right, Trevine, and wrong is wrong. Nothing can alter that."

Trevine's lips tightened. "Yes, sir."

"Do you know where she is now?"

Trevine nodded.

"Then I'm obliged to you. If this results in an arrest and the recovery of my watch, I shall see that you receive the reward. Tell me where to find her and leave your direction with—"

"I don't want your reward."

"What?"

Trevine lowered his voice. "She's wounded, sir. I saw her through a window not an hour ago, lying in a yellow dress like a street-walker's. There's blood on her, all over the place. Maybe someone shot her."

"Stuff and nonsense."

"Yes, sir."

Sir John glanced at the servants, making sure they were still out of earshot. He remembered the scrap of yellow silk he had found on his bedroom floor. "And – and where precisely is she?"

"If I tell you, you'll help her, sir?"

"I make no promises." Sir John wished he had not described his burglar to the authorities as "a hulking great brute". "But I'm not a vengeful man. If this young woman can procure the return of my watch, I shall be content to let sleeping dogs lie. But first things first. Where is she?"

"In Clifton, sir – up near the Downs where they're building the new bridge. Rodney Place."

"What number?"

"I don't know, sir. But it's where the Missionary Society is. Mr Fanmole's house."

Sir John slumped back in his chair as though flicked by an invisible finger. The air rushed from his lungs. "Fanmole?"

Trevine looked at him in astonishment. "Yes, sir. A reverend gentleman."

"Little fellow with a fat neck? Slimy voice and a laugh like a hacksaw?"

"That's him to the life, sir."

Sir John stood up. "Damme, I see it all now." He waved to the nearest servant. "You there! Whistle up a hackney carriage." He turned back to Robbie Trevine. "Wait – I must fetch something. Then we'll see what Mr Fanmole has to say."

When he came back to the lobby, he was wearing a hat and a big overcoat and swinging what looked like a weighted walking stick. He swept Robbie into the hackney carriage at the hotel door and they rattled up the hill to Clifton. Sir John talked as they drove – he would have talked to anyone; he was as full of pressure as a GWR Northern Star locomotive.

"That damned rogue Fanmole! My brother gave him one of our livings just before he died. But it didn't take long for the rumours to start. Tittle-tattle about the village girls. Then the mother of one of my tenants died, turned out she'd just altered her will in Fanmole's favour. Next thing I knew, he'd invested some money on behalf of his curate, and the money was lost; and the poor fellow blew out his brains; and guess who owned the company? Fanmole's aunt, or some such. I could have taken him to court, but the scandal would have looked bad. So I made him resign the living, and I had a quiet word with the bishop, too."

"Mary says it's his aunt's house in Rodney Place," Robbie said.

"And what does the aunt say about her precious nephew, eh?"

"If she does any talking, sir, no one's taking much notice. She's in a private asylum in Totterdown. But he runs his Missionary Society from her house."

"For the benefit of the heathen, eh? A tribe of one, I'll be bound, and its name is Fanmole. Any servants?"

"None that live in, I believe."

The hackney carriage drew up in Rodney Place. Sir John told the driver to wait, stormed up the steps, and hammered on the door. A moment later, bolts scraped from their sockets, and the door opened.

Fanmole blinked up at them. "Why such unseemly noise, my dear sir? In any case, the Society is closed until the morning."

Sir John thrust his stick into the doorway. "You black-guard."

He shouldered his way into the house with Robbie at his heels. Fanmole gave ground before them, retreating up the dimly lit hallway.

"Where's my watch? Where's that unfortunate girl?"

"The girl you shot, Sir John?" Fanmole said. "Who now lies at death's door? She came to me for help, and I gave her shelter. She is a common prostitute by the look of her, but no doubt that was part of her charm for you. I wonder what Lady Ruispidge will say when she hears that you consort with common sluts and then murder them."

5: Nothing Begets Nothing

In the hall of the house in Rodney Place, Robbie said quietly, "You lie. Mary's no slut."

Fanmole's eyes flicked towards him and then returned to Sir John. "I assure you, sir, the girl is a prostitute, and a thief besides. I found a watch in her pocket when I was tending her, and I cannot believe she came by it honestly. I have prayed for her. *Joy shall be in heaven over one sinner that repenteth, more than over ninety and nine just persons, which need no repentance.* Luke, chapter fifteen."

"If she's a thief," Robbie said, "it is because you made her steal."

"Take us to her," Sir John demanded. "Let the girl put her side of the matter."

"You are not master here," Fanmole said with his harsh laugh.

Sir John pulled a revolver from his pocket. "I've not come here to argue with you."

Fanmole shrugged. He picked up a candlestick from the hall table and led the way through a green baize door. With their shadows dancing beside them on the whitewashed wall, they descended a flight of stairs and reached a passage running from front to back of the house.

"She's in a wood store," Robbie said. "Lying on the floor without even a blanket."

"She was feverish," Fanmole said over his shoulder. "She could not abide to be covered. The wood store was convenient since it is near the office where I conduct the business of the Missionary Society. Ah – here we are."

At that moment the candle went out, and total darkness enveloped them. There was the sound of a blow. Sir John cried out. Hobnails scraped on stone. Something clattered to the floor. Robbie blundered into a wall.

A match scraped; a flame flared. Mr Fanmole had the pistol in his hand. Keeping his eyes on Robbie, he lit the candle, which was now standing on a narrow shelf near a door at the back of the house. Sir John lay motionless on the floor, and there were streaks of blood in his silver hair.

"You've killed him."

"I doubt it," Fanmole said. "I hit him with the candlestick but I used no more than reasonable force. You are my witness. He threatened me in my own house with a stick and a pistol. But let us be charitable. Age has infirmities of the mind as well as those of the body." The barrel of the gun swung from Sir John to Robbie himself. "And what would a court make of your role in this, young man? Much depends on how you act now. Our first step must be to restrain this poor gentleman before he does any more damage. Open the back door. You will find the wood store beyond. He might as well cool his heels in there, along with his young woman. And you shall keep him company."

A revolver is a powerful argument. Robbie did as Fanmole had told him. The back door led to a basement area containing the wood store. Robbie unbolted the door, conscious all the while of Fanmole behind him. Light from the candle spilled across the floor. There was no sign of Mary near the heap of logs.

"Take Sir John's legs," Fanmole said.

Robbie turned back. At that instant he saw Mary, standing by the doorway in her bloodstained yellow dress, her face as pale as wax. She held a finger to her lips. In her other hand was a hatchet.

"Hurry, damn you," Fanmole urged.

Robbie bent down and took the old man by the ankles. He dragged him slowly into the wood store. Fanmole advanced slowly, the revolver in his right hand. He reached the doorway and gripped the jamb with his free hand.

"Where's the slut gone?" he cried.

Robbie felt the air shift by his ear. There was a thud. Fanmole screamed. The revolver fell to the floor. Robbie saw the muzzle flash before he heard the crash of the shot. Mary fell backwards on to the logs. Fanmole danced with pain, blood spurting from his left hand, flashes of bone where the tips of two of his fingers had been.

As the echoes of the shot subsided, another sound forced its way down from the house above them: the pounding of the knocker on the front door.

Fanmole raised his head. His nostrils flared.

"The police," Robbie said. "They've come for you."

Fanmole ran up the steps to the garden at the back of the house. Robbie snatched up Sir John's weighted stick and set off after him. With surprising agility, the little clergyman darted down the garden. The distant hammering continued. Fanmole unbolted a gate and slipped into the cobbled alley beyond. Robbie followed the running footsteps. Once, when they passed the lighted windows of a tavern, Fanmole looked back. His pale features were contorted with pain and effort, the face reduced to something slimy and inhuman, a creature of nightmare.

They ran through Sion Place and burst into the open. On the crest of the Downs, the Observatory was a black stump against the paler darkness of the night sky. Fanmole veered to the left, towards the edge of the Avon Gorge.

"Stop!" Robbie cried, but the wind snatched away his words.

The clergyman ran towards Brunel's unbuilt bridge. Within a stone's throw of the Clifton tower, he stopped. His breath came in ragged gasps.

"Leave me." He fumbled in his waistcoat pocket and pulled out something that glittered faintly. "Take this, Sir John's Breguet watch. Sell it or claim the reward. Just go. Say I gave you the slip in the dark."

Robbie did not reply. The memory of Mary filled his mind, and the bloody stain spreading over the yellow silk dress. He moved slowly towards the clergyman. Fanmole clambered on the low wall around the abutment on which the tower stood, intending to drop down to the little footpath beneath. But Robbie's advance made him change his mind and retreat along the parapet of the wall.

"No," he said, flapping his hand as though waving Robbie away. "Pray leave me. I have valuables concealed in a place nearby. I shall tell you where to find them."

He held out the watch. Robbie stepped forward and snatched it. But Fanmole jerked backwards immediately afterwards. By now he was on the corner of the wall, where it swung through ninety degrees to run parallel with the river more than 200 feet below.

"Watch out," Robbie shouted.

But the clergyman's hunched figure was still moving backwards. His left leg stepped into nothing.

Nothing begets nothing, as my mother used to say, Robbie thought.

Fanmole toppled out of sight. Branches snapped and crackled as he tumbled down the steep slope. He cried out only once. Then came a moment's utter silence.

At last there was a thud: and another, longer silence, this time as long as the century.

6: Postscriptum

Clearland Court
Lydmouth
23rd January

My Dear Brunel,

You will have heard from my solicitor that I have decided to accede to your request: I hope it will not be too many years before the Great Western Railway will bring you to Lydmouth.

As to that other business, I cannot tell you how glad I am that the girl, Mary Linnet, is no longer at death's door. Without her intervention in Rodney Place, I might not have survived to write this letter. Both she and her mother are now on the road to recovery and I shall find them respectable employment when their health is restored.

It was fortunate that, with the obstinacy of his breed, my hackney driver chose to pound on the door to demand his fare. Trevine tells me that Fanmole believed the knocking heralded the arrival of the constabulary, and that this precipitated his fatal decision to flee.

I am informed that goods worth several thousand pounds were found in the shed which Fanmole rented by the Gorge. It appears that the work of his so-called Missionary Society among the poor allowed him to recruit weak-minded young people, such as Mary Linnet, and set them to thieving and other mischief on his behalf in Bristol and neighbouring towns. (So you see, my dear sir, the railway is not an unmitigated blessing!)

But Fanmole's desire to have revenge on me proved his undoing. When he saw my arrival in Bristol announced in the newspapers, he sent the girl to discover where I was staying; she was then to take hold of me when I returned to the room, ring the bell, and complain vigorously that I had assaulted her! His design was to destroy my reputation as, he believed, I had destroyed his.

As you know, the matter turned out very differently: and this was in great part due to the young man Robert Trevine, who returned my late brother's watch to me. He appears honest; he can even read and write. I offered to find him a situation on one of my estates – but no! the fellow wants nothing better than to stay in Bristol or its environs and work for you in some capacity on the Great Western Railway! It is true he shows some mechanical aptitude, but I fancy that the presence in the city of a certain young woman may have something to do with it. In any event, I should be very grateful if you could find him a position.

I am, sir, yours very truly,

J. Ruispidge

THE PRICE CONFEDERATE

Andrew Martin

Peter the librarian held up a thin file of papers. He didn't need to say anything, just grinned, and Anthony recognized the handwriting immediately.

"Where d'you turn these up?" he said.

"They were mis-filed," said Peter. "They weren't under "Price" but "Prince" – not that there's any signature here."

Anthony nodded.

"Price went through phases of wanting to be known as 'Prince'," he said.

"Why?" asked Peter.

"To ally himself with the Prince of Darkness," said Anthony.

"Oh," said Peter in his camp way. "Sorry I asked."

". . . So really it's his own fault that his books and papers have been wrongly catalogued ever since," said Anthony. "He has nobody but himself to blame."

Peter the librarian passed over the papers and adjusted his tie as if to say "Anything else I can do for you?" He was a good librarian. He also dressed very well indeed. Anthony admired the way he could wear, say, a yellow and brown silk tie with a blue and white checked shirt, but he was at the same time aggrieved that a librarian should be better dressed than he himself.

"I haven't a clue what it is," said Peter, nodding again at the manuscript.

This might well have been a lie, but the librarians at the Mayfair Institute would not be so crass as to spoil your day by flagging up the contents of a book or document in advance. The readers were there to read, after all.

". . . I mean, it's not topped and tailed," Peter continued. "It's a fragment."

He was coming dangerously near to admitting that he'd read it, and Anthony always wanted Price to himself, so he said:

"I shall enjoy this Peter, thanks very much," and turned away.

Anthony took the file and pushed open the door of the Main Reading Room. He was hoping that one of the four red leather armchairs arranged before the fireplace would be free. In fact, all four were, and he didn't know which one to choose. There was only one other man in the reading room, at a far desk. He seemed very magnanimous, spurning the fireplace, and what was more, he didn't sniff or cough as he worked.

The fire of course was unlit. Books and real fires didn't go together. It *was* lit once a year, on Christmas Eve, when the Trustees of the Institute gave a sherry party. Anthony wasn't eminent enough to have been asked, but that would come. Price would see to that. Anyhow, it was a fine Spring afternoon with no need of a fire. White blossom floated about above the trees of the Square beyond the windows, unwinding out from them like a benign, slow explosion. Mayfair was a good mix of old buildings and trees. It was like an American's dream of London: the red buses were redder in Mayfair, the black taxis blacker, and you felt that a bowler-hatted man might be just around the next corner.

Anthony selected an armchair, guiltily aware that he much preferred the Institute to his own home, and that he over-used the place. The librarians ought not really to know his name, or that he was fixated on Arthur Price. He ought to use the Institute in the correct, gentlemanly way: as a respite from the serious literature; to kill a couple of hours before attending a social function; to wait for sunset and the Mayfair cocktail hour while reading a story by Oliver Onions or V.L. Whitechurch.

From the outside the place resembled a giant carriage clock, and the reading rooms were like a series of drawing rooms, with only about as many books on the wall as you'd expect to *see* in a drawing room. The collections were mainly stored in the three levels of basement, where a different order of librarian roved – ones not as confident or well-dressed as those in the building proper, and sometimes the readers would hear the rumble of the primitive trolleys being pushed along the subterranean walk-ways. It was a confirmation of your status to know that this work – a species of academic mining – was going on for your benefit.

The subscription was a thousand pounds a year – not cheap – and you'd only pay it if you were interested in the books and manuscripts of a particular kind of author. The type had never been officially defined, but everyone knew it: the under-regarded marginals, the writers of ghost stories, mysteries, crime, the better class of pornographer, and if you asked for something wholesome like a copy of *Pride and Prejudice* (which only an outsider or a new member would ever do) the librarians would disapprovingly respond, 'I'm afraid we don't stock books like that." The Institute had been built and was funded by grants from the more successful genre writers, and its grandeur was a kind of reproof to the critics, who ignored their works.

Anthony looked at the topmost page of the file. It was thin – poor quality paper presumably. The handwriting was elegant by modern standards but Price's full stops were never quite conclusive; they were elongated, more like dashes, with the result that anything he wrote never seemed to stop, but became a steady stream of bile.

"I did Wilson's, the one in Chelsea," Anthony read, "by putting my arm through the letterbox hole in the outer shutter and unscrewing the bolt, this being wrongly placed (why put it so close to the letterbox aperture?). With me were some good fellows whose names I wouldn't mention for fortunes. It was no trouble at all then to roll up the shutter. The glass of course I just smashed – took my Malacca cane to it. I enjoyed that."

His tone was all there in those few sentences: a combination of the literary and the streetwise, and the shrill arrogance was betrayed by that parenthesized question: "Why put it so close to the letterbox aperture?" as if he knew how to design protective shutters for jewellers' shops better than the men who did that for a living. Well, he probably did. Arthur Price had written crime stories, but he'd gone one better in that he had actually been a criminal as well. He made his living by "doing" jew-ellers' shops together with a little band of followers, the Price

Confederates. He was often interrupted in his round of thefts by arrest and imprisonment (hence the books – he wrote while inside) but it was a relentless cycle that had continued, Anthony presumed, until his death.

Anthony had first come across him in *Pelham's Guide to Interesting Out-of-Print Authors*, which was written in telegraphese, as though the title was a bluff, and the authors didn't even justify full sentences. Of Price, Pelham had written: "Roguish character. At once hated and aspired to join literary establishment. Author of crime stories, habitual theme a criminal's bloodthirsty revenge. Repellent style oscillates between coarse and grandiose. Definitive collection: *Tales of the London Night* (1904). Arthur Price disappeared in about 1910."

Anthony had appreciated the languor of that one proper, concluding sentence. It had got him hooked, and he had immediately read such Price stories as survive. They were all more or less the same. A decent, honest, brave criminal is minding his own business robbing or assaulting people when a policeman presumes to arrest him, or an associate betrays him. The criminal then murders the policeman or the associate, sometimes summoning in aid mysterious dark forces raised by rituals and incantations described at great length.

But Anthony was more interested in the writer than the writing. Price's first publishers had to take out an injunction to keep him away from their offices. A reviewer who had written that *Tales of the London Night* was "too lurid for the common taste, but undoubtedly vigorous" – which was just about the best thing that any contemporary said of Price – was sent a loaded revolver in the post with no address to which it might be promptly returned, but instead an order to meet Price at dawn in St James' Park in order to fight a duel.

Price had turned up for the occasion accompanied by Paul Mayer, who proposed doing duty as his second. Mayer was an educated man, and yet, as one assize court judge had observed, he was "practically enslaved" to Price. He'd been a Price Confederate, but he'd also been a journalist on the *Times*, and at one point had been committed to a mental hospital in South London. He believed not only that Price was the Prince of Darkness, but also that he – Mayer – had lived in the future;

that he had, in the past, lived in the future, and would be liable to go back there again. Mayer's problem, among others, was that he found it hard to stay put in any given century. He had often complained about it in writing.

"Wilson's shop was preferred to Maxwell's," Anthony read, "only on account of the dairy across the road from the latter, which never closed but ran right round the clock, seven days a b——— week. Maxwell thought his place safe as a bank. I know because I called in masquerading as a customer looking for a new watch (silk waistcoat and Malacca cane well to the fore) and he said so. What f——— rot. The man's protected only by the little doxies put to slaving around through the night over opposite . . . and what honour is there in that?"

Anthony quickly read the whole six pages and then stood up and walked towards the window. The manuscript had been an account of a series of jewellery shop break-ins, probably written to impress an associate. Anthony doubted that it was a confession. Names had been kept back, and Price wasn't the confessional type. He'd made no mention of his writings, and there had been no mention of his cohort Mayer, who particularly intrigued Anthony, perhaps more so than Price himself.

But what mattered now was not what Price wrote about himself but what *Anthony* wrote about *him*.

The man at the far desk had gone. From the Square came the sound of heavy rain – and a helicopter. The rain was coming down so heavily that Anthony had the idea of a sort of crisis going on, with the helicopter as part of an evacuation. It might have been a different day entirely from the last time Anthony had looked.

The relationship between Arthur Price and Paul Mayer – the autodidact force-of-nature and his educated, middle-class disciple . . . This would be the theme of the book that would make Anthony Latimer's name. He would write it in the Institute, and on publication he would buy a new flat that would enable him to establish a continuum between his home life and his working life. The flat would have thick red carpets and tall sash windows like the Institute, and he would find out whether a yellow and brown silk tie against a blue and white checked shirt worked for him, too.

The book would be a novel, but based on the real characters of Price and Mayer. He was sure it would do better than his own series of crime novels with Edwardian settings, and the critics might take an interest for once, because Price was under-chronicled. There had been no biography. (There wasn't enough material to generate one – just a few letters threatening his various literary mentors, the couple of dozen stories, and now this document unearthed by Peter. No photograph of Price had survived.) The core of reality would give legitimacy to Anthony's novel. People generally couldn't be persuaded to take an interest in the imaginings of an obscure individual like himself. Pure fiction by the non-famous was regarded as whimsy and that was that.

Anthony looked at his watch: five o'clock. Not late enough, on the whole, to justify the darkness of the sky. He wanted a pint but he stayed on by the window, watching the rain. He saw now that it fell on a policeman on a horse. The copper wore one of those big capes that covered not only his own body, but much of the horse's. They were both in it together, stoically receiving the rain at the corner of the Square.

Anthony turned back towards the chair and picked up the manuscript. He had been thinking he might write his book from the point of view of Mayer. He imagined that Mayer had originally regarded Price in the same way that he himself did: with appalled fascination. But the trouble with this plan was that Mayer had been found battered to death in the West End (just on the borders of Mayfair, in fact) in 1907, three years before the end of the story of Price. Obviously, Price had done it. Anthony was sure of that, and he would make the case in his novel.

He walked through the empty Reading Room, and through the double doors, where he saw Peter at the book desk. He found that he was *relieved* to see him.

"Thanks for that, Peter," he said, handing back the docu-ment.

"What was it?" asked Peter.

"Oh, just . . . Descriptions of how he broke into various jewellery shops."

"Charming," Peter said, and he laughed.

Collecting his coat, which was the last one left in the cloak-room, Anthony thought: he wouldn't laugh if he knew anything about Price. There was nothing funny about him. He was no gentleman thief, and the robberies had sometimes lead to violence. Newspaper cuttings mentioned one associate of Price's who had been found murdered – a known receiver of stolen goods. Price had missed a court appearance to attend the man's funeral, which was ironic in several ways. For a start, he'd killed the man. Anthony was certain of that, and the killing would make a scene for his novel.

Anthony walked out into the Square. The policeman had gone, and the place was deserted, the rain coming down on the trees alone. They were – what? – twenty times taller than a man. Seemed unreasonable somehow. They were rocking in the warm wind that was blowing through the rain, looking restless.

Anthony left the Square by the first available street, but that was all right because it led to one of the best pubs in Mayfair. He walked quickly along the street of distinguished, reserved buildings, moving in the opposite direction to the water flowing along the gutter. All other pedestrians seemed to have retreated in the face of his advance. Anthony took his mobile phone out of his pocket. He pressed the "on" switch and white light seeped between the number keys, but there was a worrying, restless little display on the screen: dots in a line groping after something, like an ellipsis. It was a new phone and he'd not seen this before. Then the display went all still and sullen, and the message read: "No signal." Was it to do with the rain?

The pub, The Unicorn, glowed in the rain like a little blue lantern, cosily framed by antiquarian bookshops. With the bulge at the front, and the flagpole that came out over the doorway, it looked sea-going somehow. Opposite was a block of flats: Horace Mansions. Anthony had earmarked Horace Mansions for when he became successful. It was Edwardian, which was his period.

A century away was a perfect distance of time: distant enough to be strange, near enough to be comprehensible. Anthony had set all of his thrillers in that period, and this was why he would be able to do justice to an Edwardian maverick like Price. Also he spoke the lingo: Anthony knew that the Edwardians called a jacket a coat (a coat in the modern sense was a "top-coat"); a weekend, to the Edwardians, was a "week-end"; and when they were tired they were "all-in". Anthony aimed always to wear a suit like Edwardian men; he wore boots rather than shoes, wrote with a fountain pen. He would in time become a full, flamboyant Edwardian dandy rather than the muted dandy he was at present.

There were three or four people inside the pub, all turned away from him. A clock ticked. Anthony liked the fact that there was no piped music in The Unicorn, but that clock was *loud* and couldn't be turned down. And there was no barman to be seen. Anthony was joined at the bar by one of the silent customers. The pub was all buckled wood, as though the ceiling was too heavy, pressing down. There didn't seem to be much air.

The man next to him wore a black suit, and it was muddy – mud splashes up the trouser legs. Mud in Mayfair. Anthony nodded at him nonetheless, and he didn't nod back. His eyes were a very pale blue in the thin red face; his hair was black and pulled back with grease or oil that smelled like lemon, but another smell came off him at the same time: a bitter smell of a small room in which a dozen people have been smoking cigars around the clock. But the man now took *cigarettes* out of his pocket. He kept them in a tin. Anthony had once thought of doing that, but he'd stopped smoking a year ago. The Unicorn, actually, was a non-smoking pub. The man opened his mouth to put in the cigarette, and it went into a mass of blackness – no teeth.

Anthony didn't have to put up with this; there were plenty of other pubs in Mayfair. He walked through the open door of The Unicorn, and straight into a new noise: spattering rain in the gathering darkness, and a metallic rumbling and grating. He noticed a countrified smell, which was almost pleasant, until he looked down and saw that he was standing in horse manure. Had the police horse been this way? He looked over the road, and the block of flats was being dismantled. They had started dismantling the block of flats within the past five minutes. No, on the contrary: scaffolding, a tarpaulin sheet, lanterns, a wheelbarrow dangling from a pulley . . . the block of flats was being *built*. Anthony both knew, and didn't know, what was happening, He felt that he was about throw up. He looked up at the sky, searching for an aeroplane – there were always jets above Mayfair – or the helicopter growling away. But the sky was clear, apart from the falling rain, and the drifting smoke. Who was having a fire? On the rooftops all around, chimneys were smoking. Hundreds of chimneys were smoking.

The man from the pub was behind him, and there were two others with him. The man from the pub was talking fast, the blackness coming and going as he opened and closed his mouth. Anthony couldn't make out the words. Was it English? Anthony thought to himself: I have been caught in a landslide, and removed to another place. The rain fell more softly now, but it seemed to be the same rain; it made him wet in much the same way as before, and even though he knew he was in terrible trouble, Anthony was trying to take comfort from this as one of the men – not Price – approached him and spoke out in a voice of the kind you didn't hear much any more. He was unquestionably addressing Anthony. "Paul," he said, ". . . come here Paul. The governor wants a word."

POPPING ROUND TO THE POST

Peter Lovesey

Nathan was the one I liked interviewing best. You wanted to believe him, his stories were so engaging. He had this persuasive, upbeat manner, sitting forward and fixing me with his soft blue eyes. Nothing about him suggested violence. "I don't know why you keep asking me about a murder. I don't know anything about a murder. I was just popping round to the post. It's no distance. Ten minutes, maybe. Up Steven Street and then right into Melrose Avenue."

"Popping round to the post?"

"Listen up, doc. I just told you."

"Did you have any letters with you at the time?"

"Can't remember."

"The reason I ask," I said, "is that when people go to the post they generally want to post something."

He smiled. "Good one. Like it." These memory lapses are a feature of the condition. Nathan didn't appreciate that if a letter had been posted and delivered it would help corroborate his version of events.

Then he went into what I think of as his storyteller mode, one hand cupping his chin while the other unfolded between us as if he were a conjurer producing a coin. "Do you want to hear what happened?"

I nodded.

"There was I," he said, "walking up the street."

"Steven Street?"

"Yes."

"On the right side or the left?"

"What difference does that make?"

According to Morgan, the detective inspector, number twenty-nine, the murder house, was on the left about a third of the way along. "I'm asking, that's all."

"Well, I wouldn't need to cross, would I?" Nathan said. "So I was on the left, and when I got to Melrose—"

"Hold on," I said. "We haven't left Steven Street yet."

"I have," he said. "I'm telling you what happened in Melrose."

"Did you notice anything in Steven Street?"

"No. Why should I?"

"Somebody told me about an incident there."

"You're on about that again, are you? I keep telling you I know nothing about a murder."

"Go on, then."

"You'll never guess what I saw when I got to Melrose."

That was guaranteed. His trips to the post were always impossible to predict. "Tell me, Nathan."

"Three elephants."

"In *Melrose*?" Melrose Avenue is a small suburban back street. "What were they doing?"

He grinned. "Swinging their trunks. Flapping their ears."

"I mean, what were they doing in Melrose Avenue?"

He had me on a string now and he was enjoying himself. "What do you think?"

"I'm stumped. Why don't you tell me?"

"They were walking in a line."

"What, on their own?"

He gave me a look that suggested I was the one in need of psychotherapy. "They had a keeper with them, obviously."

"Trained elephants?"

Now he sighed at my ignorance. "Melrose Avenue isn't the African bush. Some little travelling circus was performing in the park and they were part of the procession."

"But if it was a circus procession, Nathan, it would go up the High Street where all the shoppers could see it."

"You're right about that."

"Then what were the elephants doing in Melrose?"

"Subsidence."

I waited for more.

"You know where they laid the cable for the television in the High Street? They didn't fill it in properly. A crack appeared right across the middle. They didn't want the elephants making it worse, so they diverted them around Melrose. The rest of the procession wasn't so heavy – the marching band and the clowns and the bareback rider. They were allowed up the High Street."

The story had a disarming logic, like so many of Nathan's. On a previous trip to the post he'd spotted Johnny Depp trimming a privet hedge in somebody's front garden. Johnny Depp as a jobbing gardener. Nathan had asked some questions and some joker had told him they were rehearsing a scene for a film about English suburban life. He'd suggested I go round there myself and try to get in the film as an extra. I had to tell him I'm content with my career.

"It was a diversion, you see. Road closed to heavy vehicles and elephants."

Talk about diversions. We'd already diverted some way from the double murder in Steven Street. "What I'd really like to know from you, Nathan, is why you came home that afternoon wearing a suit that didn't fit you."

This prompted a chuckle. "That's a longer story."

"I thought it might be. I need to hear it, please."

He spread his hands as if he was addressing a larger audience. "There were these three elephants."

"You told me about them already."

"Ah, but I was anticipating. When I first spotted the elephants I didn't know what they were doing in Melrose. I thought about asking the keeper. I'm not afraid of speaking to strangers. On the whole, people like it when you approach them. But the keeper was in charge of the animals, so I didn't distract him. I could hear the sound of the band coming from the High Street and I guessed there was a connection. I stepped out to the end of Melrose."

"Where the postbox is."

"What's that got to do with it?"

"When you started out, you were popping round to the post."

"Now you've interrupted my train of thought. You know what my memory is like."

"You were going towards the sound of the band."

He smiled. "And I looked up, and I saw balloons in the sky. Lots of colours, all floating upwards. They fill them with some sort of gas."

"Helium."

"Thank you. They must have been advertising the circus. Once I got to the end of Melrose Avenue I saw a woman with two children and each of them had a balloon and there was writing on them – the balloons, I mean, not the children. I couldn't see the wording exactly, but I guessed it must have been about the circus."

"Very likely." In my job, patience isn't just a virtue, it's a necessity.

"You may think so," Nathan said, and he held up his forefinger to emphasize the point. "But this is the strange thing. I was almost at the end of Melrose and I looked up again to see if the balloons in the sky were still in sight and quite by chance I noticed that a yellow one was caught in the branches of a willow tree. Perhaps you know that tree. It isn't in the street. It's actually in someone's garden overhanging the street. Well, I decided to try and set this balloon free. It was just out of reach, but by climbing on the wall I could get to it easily. That's what I did. And when I got my hands on the balloon and got it down I saw that the writing on the side had nothing to do with the circus. It said *Happy Birthday, Susie.*"

Inwardly, I was squirming. I know how these stories progress. Nathan once found a brooch on his way to the post and took it to the police station and was invited to put on a Mickey Mouse mask and join an identity parade and say "Empty the drawer and hand it across or I'll blow your brains out." And that led on to a whole different adventure. "Did you do anything about it?"

"About what?"

"The happy-birthday balloon."

"I had to, now I had it in my hands. I thought perhaps it belonged to the people in the house, so I knocked on the door. They said it wasn't theirs, but they'd noticed some yellow balloons a couple of days ago tied to the gatepost of a house in Steven Street."

"Steven Street?" My interest quickened. "What number?"

"Can't remember. These people – the people in Melrose with the willow tree – were a bit surprised because they thought the house belonged to an elderly couple. Old people don't have balloons on their birthdays, do they?"

"So you tried the house in Steven Street," I said, giving the narrative a strong shove.

"I did, and they were at home and really appreciated my thoughtfulness. All their other balloons had got loose and were blown away, so this was the only one left. I asked if the old lady was called Susie, thinking I'd wish her a happy birthday. She was not. She was called something totally unlike Susie. I think it was Agatha or Augusta. Or it may have been Antonia."

"Doesn't matter, Nathan. Go on."

"They invited me in to meet Susie. They said she'd just had her seventh birthday and – would you believe it? – she was a dog. One of the smallest I've ever seen, with large ears and big, bulgy eyes."

"Chihuahua."

"No, Susie. Definitely Susie. The surprising thing was that this tiny pooch had a room to herself, with scatter cushions and squeaky toys and a little television that was playing *Lassie Come Home*. But the minute she set eyes on me she started barking. Then she ran out, straight past me, fast as anything. The back door of the house was open and she got out. The old man panicked a bit and said Susie wasn't allowed in the garden without her lead. She was so small that they were afraid of losing her through a gap in the fence. I felt responsible for frightening her, so I ran into the garden after her, trying to keep her in sight. I watched her dash away across the lawn. Unfortunately, I didn't notice there was a goldfish pond in my way. I stepped into it, slipped, and landed facedown in the water."

"Things certainly happen to you, Nathan."

He took this as a compliment and grinned. "The good thing was that Susie came running back to see what had happened and the old lady picked her up. I was soaking and covered in slime and duckweed, so they told me I couldn't possibly walk through the streets like that. The old man found me a suit to wear. He said it didn't fit him anymore and I could keep it."

"All right," I said, seizing an opportunity to interrupt the flow. "You've answered my question. Now I know why you were wearing a suit the wrong size."

He shrugged again. He seemed to have forgotten where this had started.

It was a good moment to stop the video and take a break.

Morgan, the detective, watched the interview on the screen in my office, making sounds of dissent at regular intervals. When it was over, he asked, "Did you believe a word of that? The guy's a fantasist. He should be a writer."

"Some of it fits the facts," I pointed out. "I believe there was a circus here last weekend. And I know for certain that the cable-laying in the High Street caused some problems after it was done."

"The fact I'm concerned about is the killing of the old couple at twenty-nine, Steven Street, at the approximate time this Nathan was supposed to be on his way to the post."

"You made that clear to me yesterday," I said. "I put it to him today and he denies all knowledge of it."

"He's lying. His story's full of holes. You notice he ducked your question about having a letter in his hand?"

"Popping round to the post is only a form of words."

"Meaning what?"

"Meaning he's going out. He needs space. He doesn't mean it literally."

"I'd put a different interpretation on it. It's his way of glossing over a double murder."

"That's a big assumption, isn't it?"

"He admitted walking up the left side of Steven Street."

"Well, he would. It's on his way to the High Street."

"You seem to be taking his side."

"I'm trying to hold on to the truth. In my work as a therapist, that's essential." I resisted the urge to point out that policemen should have a care for the truth as well.

"Are those his case notes on your desk?" Morgan said.

"Yes."

"Any record of violence?"

"You heard him. He's a softie."

"Soft in the head. The murders seem to have been random and without motive. A sweet old couple who never caused anyone any grief. In a case like this, we examine all the options, but I'd stake my reputation this was done by a nutter."

"That's not a term I use, Inspector."

"Call him what you like, we both know what I mean. A sane man doesn't go round cutting people's throats for no obvious reason. Nothing was taken. They had valuable antiques in the house and over two hundred pounds in cash."

"Would that have made it more acceptable in your eyes, murder in the course of theft?"

"I'd know where he was coming from, wouldn't I?"

"What about the crime scene? Doesn't that give you any information?"

"It's a bloody mess, that's for sure. All the forensic tests are being carried out. The best hope is that the killer picked up some blood that matches the old couple's DNA. He couldn't avoid getting some on him. If we had the clothes Nathan was wearing that afternoon, we'd know for sure. He seems to have destroyed everything. He's not so daft as he makes out."

"The suit he borrowed?"

"Went out with the rubbish collection, he says. It didn't fit, so it was useless to him, and the old man didn't want it back."

"Makes sense."

"Certainly does. We're assuming the killer stripped and took a shower at the house after the murders and then bundled his own clothes into a plastic sack and put on a suit from the old man's wardrobe. Very likely helped himself to some clean shoes as well."

"I'm no forensic expert, but if he did all that, surely he must have left some DNA traces about the house?"

"We hope so. Then we'll have him, and I look forward to telling you about it."

"What about the other suspect?"

There was a stunned silence. Morgan folded his arms and glared at me as if I was deliberately provoking him.

"Just in case," I said, "you may find it helpful to watch the video of an interview I did later this morning with a man called Jon."

★   ★   ★

I knew Jon from many hours of psychotherapy. He sat hunched, as always, hands clasped, eyes downturned, a deeply repressed, passive personality.

"Jon," my unseen voice said, "how long have you lived in that flat at the end of Steven Street?"

He sighed. "Three years. Maybe longer."

"That must be about right. I've been seeing you for more than two years. And you still live alone?"

A nod.

"You manage pretty well, shopping and cooking, and so on. It's an achievement just surviving in this modern world. But I expect there's some time left over. What do you enjoy doing most?"

"Don't know."

"Watching television?"

"Not really."

"You don't have a computer?"

He shook his head.

"Do you get out of the house, apart from shopping and coming here?"

"I suppose."

"You go for walks?"

He frowned as if straining to hear some distant sound.

"Just to get fresh air and exercise," I said. "You live in a nice area. The gardens are full of flowers in Spring and Summer. I think you do get out quite a bit."

"If you say so."

"Then I dare say you've met some of your neighbours, the people along Steven Street, when they're outside cleaning their cars, doing gardening, or walking the dog. Did you ever speak to the old couple at number twenty-nine?"

He started swaying back and forth in the chair. "I might have."

"They have a little toy dog, a Chihuahua. They're very attached to it, I understand."

"Don't like them," Jon said, still swaying.

"Why's that? Something they did?"

"Don't know."

"I think you do. Maybe they remind you of some people you knew once."

He was silent, but the rocking became more agitated. Momentarily his chin lifted from his chest and his face was visible. Fear was written large there.

"Could this old couple have brought to mind those foster parents you told me about in a previous session, when we discussed your childhood, the people who locked you in the cupboard under the stairs?"

He moaned a little.

"They had a small dog, didn't they?"

He covered his eyes and said, "Don't."

"All right," I said. "We'll talk about something else."

"You'll get thrown out of the union, showing me that," Morgan said. "Isn't there such a thing as patient confidentiality?"

"In the first place, I don't belong to a union," I said, "and in the second, I'm trying to act in the best interests of all concerned."

"Thinking he could kill again, are you?"

"Who are we talking about here?" I asked.

"The second man. Jon. He seems to have a thing about old people. He's obviously very depressed."

"That's his usual state. It doesn't make him a killer. I wanted you to look at the interview before you jump to a conclusion about Nathan, the other man."

"Nathan isn't depressed, that's for sure."

"Agreed. He has a more buoyant personality than Jon. Did you notice the body language? Nathan sits forward, makes eye contact, while Jon looks down all the time. You don't see much of his face."

"That stuff about the foster parents locking him in the cupboard. Is that true?"

"Oh, yes, I'm sure of it. I'd be confident of anything Jon tells me. He doesn't give out much, but you can rely on him. With Nathan I'm never sure. He has a fertile imagination and he wants to communicate. He's trying all the time to make his experiences interesting."

"Falling into the pond, you mean? Did you believe that?"

"It's not impossible. It would explain the change of clothes."

"I was sure he was talking bollocks, but now that you've shown me this other man I'm less confident. I'd like to question Jon myself."

"That won't be possible," I said.

He reddened. "It's a bit bloody late to put up the shutters. I've got my job to do and no one's going to stand in my way."

"Before you get heavy with me, Inspector, let me run a section of the second interview again. I'm going to turn off the sound and I want you to look closely at Jon. There's a moment when he sways back and the light catches his face."

I rewound the tape and let it play again, fast-forwarding until I found the piece I wanted, the moment I'd mentioned the old couple and Jon had started his swaying, a sure indicator of stress. "There." I used the freeze-frame function.

Jon's face was not quite in focus, but there was enough to make him recognisable.

"Christ Almighty," Morgan said. "It's the same guy. It's Nathan."

I let the discovery sink in.

"Am I right?" he asked.

I nodded.

"Then what the hell is going on?"

"This may be hard for you to accept. Nathan and Jon are two distinct identities contained in the same individual, a condition we know as Dissociative Identity Disorder. It used to be known as Multiple Personality Disorder, but we've moved on in our understanding. These so-called personalities are fragments of the same identity rather than self-contained characters. Jon is the primary identity, passive and repressed. Nathan is an alter ego, extrovert, cheerful and inventive."

"I've heard of this," Morgan said. "It's like being possessed by different people. I saw a film once."

"Exactly. Fertile material for Hollywood, but no entertainment at all if you happen to suffer with it. The disturbance is real and frightening. A subject can take on any number of personality states, each with its own self-image and identity. The identities act as if they have no connection with each other. My job is to deconstruct them and ultimately unite them into one individual. Jon and Nathan will become Jonathan."

"Neat."

"It may sound neat, but it's a long process."

"It's neat for me," he said. "I wasn't sure which of the two guys is the killer. Now I know there's only one of them, I've got him, whatever he calls himself."

"I wouldn't count on it," I said.

He shot me a foul look.

"The therapy requires me to find points of contact between the alter-personalities. When you came to me with this double murder, I could see how disturbing it would be for Jon. He carries most of the guilt. But this investigation of yours could be a helpful disturbance. It goes right back to the trauma that I think was the trigger for this condition, his ill-treatment at the hands of foster parents who happened to own a dog they pampered and preferred to the child."

"My heart bleeds," Morgan said, "but I have a job to do and two people are dead."

"So you tell me. Jon thinks he may have murdered them, but he didn't."

"Come off it," he said.

"Listen, please. Nathan's story was true. He really did have that experience with the balloon and the little dog and falling in the pond. For him – as the more positive of the identities – it was one more entertaining experience to relate. But for Jon, who experienced it also, it was disturbing, raising memories of the couple who fostered him and abused him. He felt quite differently, murderous even."

"Hold on," Morgan said. "Are you trying to tell me the murders never happened?"

"They happened in the mind of Jon, and they are as real to him as if he cut those old people's throats himself. But I promise you the old couple are alive and well. I went to Steven Street at lunchtime and spoke to them. They confirmed what Nathan told me."

"I don't get this. I'm thinking you're nuts as well."

"But it's important that you do get it," I told him. "There's a third identity at work here. It acts as a kind of conscience, vengeful, controlling, and ready to condemn. It, too, is convinced the murders took place and have to be investigated.

Recognizing this is the first step towards integration. Do me a favour and have another look at Jon's face. It's still on the screen."

He gave an impatient sigh and glanced at the image.

"Now look at this, Inspector."

I handed him a mirror.

THE UNINVITED

Christopher Fowler

The elaborate silvered gates stood wide apart, ready to accept guests. You couldn't arrive on foot, of course; there was nowhere to walk, except in the drive or through the sprinkler-wet grass, and it would have looked foolish climbing towards the house in the headlights of arriving cars.

Inside, the first thing I saw was an avenue of rustling palms, their slender trunks wound with twinkling blue and white lights, like giant candy sticks. Two robotically handsome valets in gold and crimson jackets were parking the cars, mostly sparkling black Mercedes, Daimlers, Volvos. The staircase was flanked by six teenaged waitresses in tiny red Santa outfits tentatively dispensing delicate flutes of champagne. A floodlit house, oblong, low and very white, was arranged on two levels between banked bottle-green lawns. I could hear muted laughter, murmuring, a delicate presence of guests. I saw silhouettes passing before the rippled phosphorescence of a pool with translucent globes pacing its perimeter. There was no sign of our host, but on the patio a butler, chef, bartenders and waiters were arranged behind banks of lurid, fleshy lobster tails and carrot batons.

There was a muffled beat in the air, the music designed to create ambience without being recognizable, Beatles' songs rescored for a jazz trio. It was the end of the sixties, the age of Aquarius. Smokey Robinson and Dionne Warwick were in the charts, but there were no black people there that night except me.

In Los Angeles, parties aren't about letting your hair down and having fun. They're for networking, appraising, bargaining, being seen and ticked from a list. There were two kinds of guest roaming the house that night, ones who would have been noticed by their absence, and others who had been invited merely to fill up dead space. It goes without saying that I was in the latter group. Only Sidney Poitier would have made it into the former.

It was the home of Cary Dell, a slow-witted middleweight studio executive at MGM, and I remember seeing plenty of almost-familiar faces; Jacqueline Bisset, Victoria Vetri, Ralph Meeker, a couple of casting directors, some black-suited agents lurking together in a corner, fish-eyeing everyone else. The important people were seated in a semi-circular sunken lounge, lost among oversized purple cushions. The area was so exclusive that it might as well have had velvet ropes around it. Everyone else worked hard at keeping the conversation balloon-light and airborne, but couldn't resist glancing over to the pit to see what was going on at the real centre of the party.

There was another kind of guest there that night. Dell had invited some beautiful young girls. No one unsavoury, they weren't call-girls, just absurdly perfect, with slender waists and basalt eyes. They stood together tapping frosted pink nails on the sides of their martini glasses, flicking their hair, looking about, waiting for someone to talk to them.

Parties like this took place all over the Hollywood hills; the old school still arrived in tuxedos and floor-length gowns, but studios had lately rediscovered the youth movie, and were shamelessly courting the same anti-establishment students they had ridiculed five years earlier. I had made a couple of very bad exploitation flicks, usually cast as the kind of comic sidekick whose only purpose was his amusing blackness. Back in those days I believed in visibility at any cost, and always took the work.

I had a feeling I'd been added to the guest list by Dell's secretary in order to make up numbers and provide him with a sheen of coolness, because I wore fringed brown leather trousers and had my hair in an Afro, and hadn't entirely lost my Harlem jive. He sure hadn't invited me for my conversation; we'd barely spoken more than two words to each other. If we had, Dell would have realized I came from a middle-class family in New Jersey, and I might not have got the work.

I remember it was a cool night toward the end of November. The wind had dropped, and there were scents of patchouli and hashish in the air. The party was loosening up a little, the music rising in volume and tempo. Some of the beautiful girls were desultorily dancing together on a circular white rug in the lounge. I had been to a few of these parties and they always followed the same form, peaking at ten-thirty, with the guests calling for their cars soon after. People drank and drove more in those days, of course, but nobody of any importance stayed late because the studios began work at 4 a.m.

I was starting to think about leaving before undergoing the embarrassment of waiting for my battered Mustang to be brought around front, when there was a commotion of raised voices out on the patio, and I saw someone – a gaunt middle-aged man in a black suit – go into the pool fully dressed. It was difficult to find out what had happened, because everyone was crowding around the water's edge. All I know is, when they pulled him out of the chlorine a minute later, he was dead. I read in the *LA Times* next day that he'd twisted his neck hitting the concrete lip as he went in, and had died within seconds. He was granted a brief obituary in *Variety* because he'd featured in a lame Disney film called *Monkeys, Go Home.* I remember thinking that the press reports were being uncharacteristically cautious about the death. I guess nobody wanted to risk implying that Dell had been keeping a disorderly house, and there was no suggestion of it being anything other than an unfortunate accident. Dell was a big player in a union town.

As I drove back to the valley that night, passing above the crystalline grid of the city, I passed one of the beautiful girls walking alone along the side of the road with her shoes in her hand, thumbing a ride, and knew she'd come here from the Midwest, leaving all her friends and family behind just so she could be hired as eye-candy to stand around at parties. I remember thinking how nobody would miss her if she disappeared. I felt sad about it, but I didn't stop for her. Black men didn't stop to pick up white girls back then; you didn't want a situation to develop.

The work dried up for a couple of months, but on a storm-heavy night in February I was invited to another studio party, this time at a more low-key affair in Silverlake, where single palms crested the orange sky on the brows of hills, and Hispanic families sat in their doorways watching their kids play ball. You can tell poorer neighbourhoods by the amount of cabling they carry above their houses, and this area had plenty. I pulled over by an empty lot and was still map-reading under the street lamp when I heard the dull thump of music start up behind me, and realized the party was being held in a converted brownstone loft – they were pretty much a novelty back then – so I parked and made my way to the top floor of the party.

The building's exterior may have been shabby, but the inside was Cartier class. The whole top floor had been stripped back to brickwork and turned into one big space, because the owner was a photographer who used it as his studio. He handled on-set shoots for Paramount, and had coincidentally taken my head-shots a couple of years earlier. It was good to think he hadn't forgotten me, and this event was a lot friendlier than the last. I recognized a couple of girls I'd auditioned with the month before, and we got to talking, then sharing a joint. The music was Hendrix – *Electric Ladyland*, I think. Pulmonary gel-colours spun out across the walls, and the conversation was louder, edgier, but it was still a pretty high-end layout.

It was the photographer's thirtieth birthday and he'd invited some pretty big names, but it was getting harder to tell the old money from the new, because everyone was dressed down in beads and kaftans. The new producers and actors were sprawled across canary-yellow beanbags in a narcoleptic fug, while the industry seniors stuck to martinis at the bar. I was having a pretty good time with my lady-friends when I saw them again.

Perhaps because nobody had noticed me at Dell's house, I noticed everything, and now I recognized the new arrivals as they came in. There were four of them, two girls and two men, all in late-teens to mid-twenties, and I distinctly recalled them from Dell's Christmas party because they'd stood together in a tight group, as though they didn't know anyone else. They were laughing together and watching everyone, as though they were in on a private joke no one else could share.

I admit I was a little stoned and feeling kind of tripped out, but there was something about them I found unsettling. I got the feeling they hadn't been invited, and were there for some other purpose. They stayed in the corner, watching and whispering, and I wanted to go up to them, to ask what they were doing, but the girls were distracting me and – you know how that goes.

I left a few minutes after midnight, just as things were starting to heat up. I went with the girls back to their hotel. They needed a ride, and I needed the company. When I woke up the next morning, they had already vacated the room. There was only a lipstick-scrawled message from them on the bathroom mirror, plenty of kisses but no contact numbers. I picked up the industry dailies in the IHOP on Santa Monica, and there on page five found a report of the party I'd attended the night before. Some high-society singer I'd vaguely recalled seeing drunkenly arguing with his girlfriend had fallen down the stairs as he left the party, gone all the way from the apartment door to the landing below. He was expected to recover but might have sustained brain damage. Fans were waiting outside his hospital room with flowers.

Two parties, two accidents – it happens. There were studio parties all over town every night of the week, but it felt weird that I'd been at both of them. You had to be invited, of course, but there wasn't the strict door policy that there is now, no security guards with headsets, sometimes not even a checklist. People came and went, and it was hard to tell if anyone was gatecrashing; the hosts generally assumed you wouldn't dare. They were insulated from the world. I remember attending a shindig in Brentwood where the toilet overflowed through the dining room, and everyone acted like there was nothing wrong because they assumed the maids would clear it up. Hollywood's like that.

Maybe you can see a pattern emerging in this story, but at the time I failed to spot it. I was too preoccupied; with auditions, with my career, with having a good time. The town felt different then, footloose and slightly lost, caught between classic old-time movie-making and the rising counterculture. They needed to cater to the new generation of rootless teens who were growing impatient with the world they'd been handed. The producers wanted to make renegade art statements but didn't know how, and they couldn't entirely surrender the movies of the past. People forget that *Hello Dolly!* came out the same year as *Easy Rider*.

Strange times. In Vietnam, Lt William Calley's platoon of US soldiers slaughtered 500 unarmed Vietnamese, mainly women and children, at My Lai. Many of us had buddies over there, and heard stories of old women thrown down wells with grenades tossed in after them. Those who were left behind felt powerless, but there was an anger growing that seeped between the cracks in our daily lives, upsetting the rhythm of the city, the state, and eventually the whole nation. I'd never seen demonstrations on the streets of LA before now, and I'd heard the same thing was happening in Washington, Chicago, even in Denver.

But nothing affected the Hollywood elite; they hung on, flirting with subversion when really, what they wanted to make was musicals. They still threw parties, though, and the next one was a killer.

This was the real deal, a ritzy Beverly Hills bash with a sizeable chunk of the A-list present, thrown in order to promote yet another *Planet Of The Apes* movie. The sequels were losing audiences, so one of the executive producers pulled out the stops and opened up his mansion – I say his, but I think it had been built for Louise Brooks – to Hollywood royalty. This time there were security guards manning the door, checking names against clipboards, questioning everyone except the people who expected to be recognized. Certainly I remember seeing Chuck Heston there, although he didn't look very happy about it, didn't drink and didn't stay long. The beautiful girls had turned out in force, clad in brilliantly jewelled mini-dresses and skimpy tops, slyly scoping the room for producers, directors, anyone who could move them up a career notch. A bunch of heavy-weight studio boys were playing pool in the smoke-blue den while their women sat sipping daiquiris and dishing dirt. The talent agents never brought their wives along for fear of becoming exposed. I'd been invited by a hot little lady called Cheyenne who had landed a part in the movie purely because she could ride a horse, although I figured she'd probably ridden the producer.

So there we were, stranded in this icing-pink stucco villa with matching crescent staircases, dingy brown wall tapestries and wrought-iron chandeliers. I took Cheyenne's arm and we headed for the garden, where we chugged sea breezes on a lawn like a carpet of emerald needles. Nearby, a fake-British band playing soft rock in a striped marquee filled with bronze statues and Santa Fe rugs. I was looking for a place to put down my drink when I saw the same uninvited group coming down from the house, and immediately a warning bell started to ring in my head.

It was a warm night in March, and most people were in the torch-lit garden. The Uninvited – that's how I had come to think of them – helped themselves to cocktails and headed to the crowded lawn, and we followed.

"See those people over there?" I said to Cheyenne. "You ever see them before?"

She had to find her glasses and sneak them on, then shook her glossy black hair at me. "The square-jawed guy on the left looks like an actor. I think I've seen him in something. The girls don't seem like they belong here."

"What it is, I'm beginning to think there's some really harmful karma around them." I told her about the two earlier parties.

"That's nuts," she laughed. "You think they could just go around picking fights and nobody would notice?"

"People here don't notice much, they're too busy promoting themselves. Besides, I don't think it's about picking fights, more like bringing down a bad atmosphere. I don't know. Let's get a little closer."

We sidled alongside one of the men, who was whispering something to the shorter, younger of the two girls. He was handsome in a dissipated way, she had small feral features, and I tried figuring them first as a couple, then part of a group, but couldn't get a handle on it. The actor guy was dressed in an expensive blue Rodeo Drive suit, the other was an urban cowboy. The short girl was wearing the kind of cheap cotton sunflower shift they marked down at FedCo, but her taller girlfriend had gold medallions around her throat that must have cost plenty.

Now that I noticed, they were all wearing chains or medallions. The cowboy guy had a ponytail folded neatly beneath his shirt collar, like he was hiding it. Something about them had really begun to bother me, and I couldn't place the problem until I noticed their eyes. It was the one thing they all had in common, a shared stillness. Their unreflecting pupils watched without moving, and stayed cold as space even when they laughed. Everyone else was milling slowly around, working the party, except these four, who were watching and waiting for something to happen.

"You're telling me you really don't see anything strange about them?" I asked.

"Why, what do you think you see?"

"I don't know. I think maybe they come to these parties late, uninvited. I think they hate the people here."

"Well, I'm not that crazy about our hosts, either," she said. "We're here because we have to be."

"But they're not. They just stand around, and cause bad things to happen before moving on," I told Cheyenne. "I don't know how or why, they just do."

"Do you know how stoned that sounds?" she hissed back at me. "If they weren't invited, how did they get through security?" She reached on tiptoe and looked into my eyes. "Just as I thought, black baseballs. Smoking dope is making you paranoid. Couldn't you just try to enjoy yourself?"

So that's what I did, but I couldn't stop thinking about the guest dying in the pool, and the guy who had fallen down the stairs. We stayed around for a couple more hours, and were thinking about going when we found ourselves back with the Uninvited. A crowd had gathered on the deck and were dancing wildly, but there they were, the four of them, dressed so differently I couldn't imagine they were friends, still sizing things up, still whispering to each other.

"Just indulge me this one time, okay?" I told Cheyenne. "Check them out, see if you can see anything weird about them."

She sighed and turned me around so that she could peer over my shoulder. "Well, the square-jawed guy is wearing something around his neck. Actually, they all are. I've seen his medallion before, kind of a double-headed axe? It means *God Have Mercy*. There are silver beads on either side of it, take a look. Can you see how many there are?"

I checked him out. The dude was so deep in conversation with the short girl that he didn't notice me. "There are six on each side. No, wait – seven and six. Does that mean something?"

"Sure, coupled with the double axe, it represents rebellion via the thirteen steps of depravity, ultimately leading to the new world order, the *Novus Ordor Seclorum*. It's a satanic symbol. My brother told me all about this stuff. He read a lot about witchcraft for a while, thought he could influence the outcome of events, but then my mother made him get a job." She pointed discreetly. "The girl he's talking to is wearing an *ankh*, the silver cross with the loop on top? It's the Egyptian symbol for sexual union. They're pretty common, you get them in most head shops. Oh, wait a minute." She craned over my shoulder, trying to see. "The other couple? She's wearing a gold squiggle, like a sideways eight with three lines above it. That's something to do with alchemy, the sign for black mercury maybe. But the guy, the cowboy, he's wearing the most potent icon. Check it out."

I looked, and saw a small golden five lying on his bare tanned chest. Except it wasn't a five; there was a crossed line above it. "What is that?"

"The *Cross of Confusion*, the symbol of Saturn. Also known as the *Greater Malefic, the Bringer of Sorrows*. Saturn takes twenty-nine years to orbit the sun, and as a human life can be measured as just two or three orbits, it's mostly associated with the grim reaper's collection of the human soul, the acknowledgment that we have a fixed time before we die, the orbit of life. However, we can alter that orbit, cut a life short in other words. It's a satanic death symbol, very powerful."

I got a weird feeling then, a prickle that started on the back of my neck and crept down my arms. I was still staring at the cowboy when he looked up and locked eyes with me, and I saw the roaring, infinite emptiness inside him. I never thought I was susceptible to this kind of stuff, but suddenly, in that one look, I was converted.

We were still locked into each other when Cheyenne nudged me hard. "Quit staring at him, do you want to cause trouble?"

"No," I told her, "but there's something going down here, can't you feel it? Something really scary."

"Maybe they just don't like black dudes, Julius. Or maybe they're aliens. I really think we should go."

Just then, the Uninvited turned as one and walked slowly to the other side of the dancing crowd until I could no longer see them properly. A few moments later I heard the fight start, two raised male voices. I'd been half-expecting it to happen, but when it did the shock still caught me.

He was in his late fifties, balding but shaggy-haired, dressed in a yellow *Keep On Truckin'* T-shirt designed for someone a third his age. I saw him throw a drink and swing a fat arm, fist clenched, missing by a mile. Maybe he was pushed, maybe not, but I saw him lose his balance and go over onto the table as if the whole things was being filmed in slow motion. The kidney-shaped sheet of glass that exploded and split into three sections beneath him sliced through his T-shirt as neatly as a scalpel, and everyone jumped back. God forbid the guests might ruin their shoes on shards of glass.

He was lying as helpless as a baby, unable to rise. A couple of girls squealed in revulsion. When he tried to lift himself onto his elbows, a wide, dark line blossomed through the cut T-shirt. He flopped and squirmed, calling for help as petals of blood spread across his shirt. The music died and I heard his boot heels hammering on the floor, then the retreating crowd obscured my view. Nobody had rushed to his aid; they looked like they were waiting for the Mexican maids to appear and draw a discreet cloth over the scene so that they could return to partying.

Why didn't I help? I have no answer to that question. Maybe I was more like the others back then, afraid of being the first to break out of the line. I feel differently now.

Cheyenne was pulling at my sleeve, trying to get me to leave, but I was looking for the Uninvited. If they were still there, I couldn't see them. They'd brought misfortune to the gathering once more and disappeared into the despairing confusion of the Los Angeles night.

As I had twice before, I found myself searching the papers next morning for mention of the drama, but any potential scandal had been hastily hushed up. I lost touch with Cheyenne for a while, even began to think I'd imagined the whole thing, because the next month my career took off and I stopped smoking dope. I'd landed the lead role in a new movie about a street-smart black P.I. called Dynamite Jones, and I needed to keep my head straight, because the night schedule was punishing and I couldn't afford to screw up.

We wrapped the picture in record time, without any serious hitches, although my white love interest was replaced with a black girl two days in, and our big love scene was cut to make sure we didn't upset the heartland audiences. Perry Sapirstein held the wrap party at his house on Mulholland because they were striking the set and we could keep the studio space. I figured it was a good time to hook up with Cheyenne again – she'd been in Chicago appearing in an anti-war show that had tanked, and wanted to get a little more serious with me while she was waiting for another break out West.

I thought I'd know everyone there, but there were still some unfamiliar faces, and of course, the Beautiful Girls were out in full force, hoping to get picked for something, anything before their innocence faded and their faces hardened. The Hollywood parties were losing their appeal as I got used to them. I could see the establishment would never be unseated from their grand haciendas. They flirted with rebellion but would revert to type at the first opportunity, and everyone knew it.

I'd forgotten all about the Uninvited. People were caught up in the events unfolding in Vietnam, and fresh stories of atrocities on both sides were being substantiated by shocking press footage that brought the war to everyone's doorstep. I didn't meet anyone, ever, who thought we should be there, but I was in liberal California, and it would take some time yet for the mood to sink in across the nation. The sense of confusion was palpable; hippies were hated and feared wherever they went, and the young were viewed with such suspicion beyond the Democrat enclaves that it felt dangerous to step over state lines. Folks are frightened of difference and change, always were, always will be, but back then there were no guidelines, no safety barriers. There was no one to tell us what was right, beyond what we felt in our hearts.

We couldn't see how far we were blundering into darkness.

Even in the strangest times, somebody will always continue to throw a party and act like there's nothing wrong. So it was on Mulholland, where the gold tequila fountains filled pyramids of sparkling salt-rimmed glasses, and invisible waiters slipped between the guests with shrimps arranged on pearlized clamshells.

Everything was strange that last night I saw them. I remember being freaked by shrieks of hysteria that turned into bubbles of laughter, coming from the darkened upstairs floor of the house. I remember the hate-filled glare of a saturnine man leaning in the corridor by the bathroom. I remember going to the kitchen to rummage for some ice and seeing something written in maple syrup on the bone-white door of the fridge, the letters running like thick dark blood. I peered closer, trying to read what it said, expecting something shocking and sinister, only to feel a sense of anticlimax when I deciphered the dripping, sticky word:

HEALTH

So much for Lucifer appearing uninvited at Hollywood parties.

But the second I dismissed the idea as dumb, a scampering, shadowy imp of fear started scratching about inside my mind again. The more I thought about it, the more the room, the house and everyone in it felt unsafe, and the sense kept expanding, engulfing me. Suddenly I caught sight of myself reflected in the floor-to-ceiling glass that separated the kitchen from the unlit rear garden, and saw how alone I was in that bright bare room. There was no one to care if I lived or died in this damned city. Without me even realizing it, everything in my world had begun to slip and slide into a howling, emptying abyss. There were no friends, no loyalties, no good intentions, only the prey and the preyed upon.

No haven, no shelter, just endless night, unforgiving and infinite.

If this was the effect of giving up marijuana, I thought, I really needed to start smoking again.

But the line of safety was thinner then. We felt much closer to destruction. These days we live with the danger while cheerfully ignoring the data.

I once attended a class on the structure of myths at UCLA where we discussed the theme of the uninvited guest, the phantom at the feast, the unclean in the temple, the witch at the christening, the vampire at the threshold, the doomsayer at the wedding, and all these myths shared one element in common; someone had to invite them in to begin with. I wondered who had provided an unwitting invitation here in California.

I remember that night there was a very pretty blonde woman in the lounge – although I only saw her from the back – whom everyone wanted to talk to. One of her friends was drunkenly doing a trick with a lethal-looking table knife, and I thought *what if he slips?* And just as I was thinking that, I became aware of them, standing right alongside me. I turned and found myself beside the square-jawed one who looked like an actor. His grey deep-set eyes stared out at me very steadily, holding the moment. The light was low in the main hall, which was lit only by amber flames from an enormous carved fireplace. I saw the Satan sign glittering at his neck, and he smiled knowingly as I flinched.

"Who the hell are you?" I half-whispered, finally regaining my composure.

"Bobby." He held out his hand. "You're Julius."

"How do you know who I am?"

"I have friends in the business. We know a lot of people."

I didn't like the way he said that. "I've seen you before," I told him. "Seen your friends, too."

"Yeah, they're all here. We hang out together." He pointed. "That's Abby, Susan, Steve."

They all looked over at me as if they'd picked up on their names being spoken. The effect of them moving with one shared mind was unnerving. I meant to say "Who do you know here?" but instead I asked "What are you here for?"

Bobby was silent for a moment, then smiled more broadly. "I think you know the answer to that. We're here to taste death."

"What do you mean?"

He looked away at the fire. "You have to know what dying is before you can know life, Julius."

"I don't understand you."

"I mean," Bobby leaned in close and still, his eyes filling with morbid compassion as they stared deep into mine, "we're leading the rise to power. We've already started the killing, and this city will become an inferno of revenge. The streets will run with blood. There will be a new holocaust, revolution in the streets, and the world will belong to the Fifth Angel."

"Man, you're crazy." I shook my head suddenly tired of this white supremacy crap. I'd just spent two months mofo-ing around in some Stepin Fetchit role given to me by rich white boys, and I guess I'd just had enough. "Bullshit," I told him, "if the best thing you can do to start a revolution is shove a few drunks around at parties, you're in trouble. I saw you at Dell's place. I know you pushed that guy into the pool and broke his neck. I saw you in Silverlake, and at the house on Canon Drive where that guy was cut on the table. I know you don't belong here, except to bring down chaos."

"You're right, we don't belong here any more than you do," he said, distracted now by something or someone moving past my left shoulder. "There's no difference between us, brother. The rest of them are just little pigs." He exchanged glances with the others, and the two girls turned to go, slipping out through the crowd. He pushed back to take his leave with them.

"Wait," I called after him, anxious to keep him there. "How did you get in through security?"

Bobby looked over his shoulder, quiet and serious. "We have friends in all the places we're not invited."

"Nothing's going to happen tonight, right? You've got to promise me that."

"Nothing will happen tonight, Julius. We're leaving."

"I don't get it." I was calling so loud that people were turning to stare at me. "Why not tonight? You made this stuff happen before, why not now, right in front of me? Let me see, Bobby, I want to understand. You think you can summon up the devil?"

His eyes were still focused over my left shoulder. "The devil is already here, my friend."

I twisted around to see who he was looking at, but when I looked back he had gone. They had all gone. And the tumble of the party rushed into my ears once more. I heard the blonde girl laughing as the man fumbled his knife trick, and the point of the blade fell harmlessly to the floor, where it stuck in the wood.

When the girl turned around, I saw that she was heavily pregnant, and heard someone say, "Come on Sharon, I'm going to drive you home, it's late. What if Roman calls tonight?"

She lived on 10050 Cielo Drive, I heard her say. And she had to get back, because the next night she was expecting her friends Abby and Jay, and they'd probably want to stay late drinking wine. She wasn't drinking because of the baby. She didn't want anything to happen to the baby.

The next day was August 9th, 1969.

It was the day our bright world began its long eclipse.

They caught up with Charlie and his gang at the Spahn ranch, out near Chatsworth, but by then it was too late to stop the closing light. There were others, rootless and elusive, who would never be caught.

I remembered those parties in the Hollywood hills, and realized I had always known about the rise of the Uninvited. Much later, I read about Manson's children writing *Helter Skelter* on their victims' refrigerator door, only they had misspelled the first word, writing it as *Healther*.

I saw how close I had come to touching evil.

The world is different now. It's sectioned off by high walls, no-go zones, clearance status, security fences, X-ray machines. The gates remain shut to outsiders unless you have a pass to enter. The important parties and the good living can only continue behind sealed doors. At least, that's what those who throw them desperately need to believe. That's what *I* need to believe.

I married Cheyenne. We have two daughters and a son. Against all reason, we stayed on in California.

And we no longer know how to protect ourselves from those who are already inside the gates. I guess we lost that right when we first built walls around our enclaves, and printed out our invitations.